9⁹⁵

SONGS IN
ORDINARY TIME

SONGS IN

ORDINARY TIME

MARY McGARRY MORRIS

VIKING

VIKING
Published by the Penguin Group
Penguin Books USA Inc., 375 Hudson Street,
New York, New York 10014, U.S.A.
Penguin Books Ltd, 27 Wrights Lane, London W8 5TZ, England
Penguin Books Australia Ltd, Ringwood, Victoria, Australia
Penguin Books Canada Ltd, 10 Alcorn Avenue,
Toronto, Ontario, Canada M4V 3B2
Penguin Books (N.Z.) Ltd, 182–190 Wairau Road,
Auckland 10, New Zealand

Penguin Books Ltd, Registered Offices:
Harmondsworth, Middlesex, England

First published in 1995 by Viking Penguin,
a division of Penguin Books USA Inc.

PUBLISHER'S NOTE
This is a work of fiction. Names, characters, places, and incidents either are
the product of the author's imagination or are used fictitiously, and any
resemblance to actual persons, living or dead, events, or locales is entirely
coincidental.

ISBN 0-670-86014-X

Printed in the United States of America
Set in Sabon
Designed by Ann Gold

TO MICHAEL WITH LOVE,
AS WELL AS
VINCENT, JOHN, BILL, AND DAVID
WITH LAUGHTER, THE SONG.

SONGS IN
ORDINARY TIME

On the day that Duvall came Benjamin Fermoyle was twelve. In a year he had not grown an inch or gained a pound, and no one had noticed. He was not sick, but fixed, immured in the vastness time becomes when you are twelve, when a month's events can flash by in a day, when certain days, certain hours, even moments can seem to last, to go on and on and on for weeks, indeed forever.

Untouched, and for days on end, ignored, he was not a child and not a man. His only friend was six-year-old Louis, who lived next door. At home he had the television with its tears and love and death, lives he could turn on and off at will, much in the way he mastered his own existence, perceiving himself as a kind of image lodged in the airwaves of visible space somewhere between stars and rooftops, a voiceless speck that by the touch of a button or a word might be summoned, briefly, safely. It was in his dreams that he felt most threatened, so often lately pursued by the relentless drumbeat of dark footsteps and the warmth that oozed sticky and shameful and nameless, and always so unexpectedly, that he did not dare sleep in pajama bottoms, but in a towel, the same towel by morning hidden damp and wadded behind the bureau, then taken out again at night and wrapped stiffly coarse around his hairless groin and thighs.

It was late May on the day that Duvall came. It had been a raw, rainy spring in those mountains, where spring was never a season proper, so much as a narrow passage, a blink of the eye, a flicker of light from ice to green, where even in the valleys every bud, sprout, and shoot held so tight and fast that it seemed certain nothing more could ever bloom or thrive again. Nothing.

Omar Duvall had been in Woodstock the night before he came down over the mountain into Atkinson. He had sat in his car that last cold night, sleepless and shivering as he waited across the street from the little jailhouse, its white paint shimmering in the moonlight. How many times had he turned the key, countless, countless times, ready to flee, but then stayed instead, went on sitting, shivering, waiting, and did not know why. Later, he would tell how he had heard summer's first cricket. In here, he would say, striking his breast. It was a stirring, he said, feeling it before he heard it, and then had not really heard it at all, he would insist, but had felt it; no, not even felt it, for it was like a heartbeat, and who ever hears the beat of one's own heart, much less the beat of another's, he would say, his piercing eyes on the boy's mother. But Duvall said he had, and Benjamin would believe him, because through that same rawness had come the midnight dream of his father's drunken fists demanding entrance at every door and window, while inside the house, the boy dared not breathe or move on his scratchy towel, but lay listening to his mother's dead voice at the door, "Go home, Sam. Leave us alone." And then his sixteen-year-old brother, Norm, the man of the house for ten years then, his voice cold and menacing: "Get the hell outta here before I call the cops!" And then his seventeen-year-old sister Alice's quick gasp down the stairs: "No! Oh please, Norm, no!" her small voice quick like the sputter and hiss of a brief wick doused as the glass shattered inward onto the cellar floor. The shards would fall, they fall, they fell, piece by piece, all night long like the faucet's steady plink, plink, plink.

Benjamin lay awake listening to the floors creak and the strapping ping, and he began to hear from outside the faint sigh of warming sap race through the trees, from root to root, as the earth buckled with sudden shoots that tore through the ground all night long as that plink, plink grew nearer with dawn, and louder. *Plink plink plink* as the grass greened and thickened overnight with the same suddenness of the new leaves that had not been at his window the night before, but were there then, that morning of the day that Duvall would come.

So of course the boy would believe Duvall when he described the stirring in his heart that night. There seemed no mystery in any of it, for he had always known that Duvall was on his way, his coming as inevitable as the summer's fiery sun, and as unstoppable.

It was early morning on Main Street. In the second-floor window of the big brown boardinghouse sat Judge Henry Clay. From here could be seen the roofs of the stores downtown on Merchants Row, and distant church spires, and farther on, the woolly green mountaintops hugging the valley. The Judge's right eye was closed, his left eye fixed blankly on the park across the street with its graceful elm trees and the pagoda-roofed bandstand built thirty years before, when he was mayor of Atkinson.

On the corner of the park, in his leased stand, was Joey Seldon, the blind man who sold popcorn and soda. On the opposite corner a dusty station wagon idled noisily at the red light. Inside the car were three dark men and a tall man in a white suit and straw hat. Suddenly the tall man threw open the back door and ran down the street. The car screeched around the corner after him in a burst of fumes and querulous voices. Joey Seldon cocked his head curiously.

Up in the window, the curtain fluttered, then blew across the Judge's face. A moment later, a tiny woman with bluish-white hair backed into the room with two stemmed glasses of orange juice on a mahogany tray. This was May Mayo, who with her younger sister, Claire, ran the boardinghouse. May quickly set down the tray on the table by the bed, then hurried to lock the door. "Oh dear," she gasped, seeing the Judge's head swathed in curtain gauze. She unwound the curtain, then wet her fingers and patted his mussed gray hair. She sat in the floral chintz chair next to his and drank her juice. When it was gone she picked up the Judge's glass and sipped daintily as she stared out at the empty park.

The Judge had been one of the town's most respected and influential citizens. But now only a handful of his old clients ever called him and even fewer came here. In this last year the Judge had failed rapidly; his legs buckled easily, and his mind grew keener with the past than the present as he fell in love over and over with every sweetheart, wife, and mistress he'd ever had, never noticing how each one spoke in May's shy giggly voice.

One evening as she was straightening his room, the Judge had seized her hand. "Lie down," he had whispered from the bed. "Lie down with me." And so she had, that night and every night until the last. In the morning she would steal down the hall in time to be roused by Claire's demanding knock on her own door.

She reached over now and touched his cold rigid hand. From time to time voices and footsteps moved along the corridor past the locked door, and in a light gay tone, she would address the Judge. "Such a day! At last! Summer's finally here. Really? I didn't know that. Well, what can one—"

Her voice broke off, and her hands cupped her ears. From the Judge's innards, there seeped another eerie hiss and with it, now, this first foul smell. Locking the door behind her, she hurried down the dim corridor to her own room, then tiptoed back with her cut-glass atomizer of Sweet Lily. First she sprayed the rose-papered walls, the stained Persian carpet, the Judge's soft bed, his wardrobe of limp dark suits, his oak filing cabinets inurned with a half century's pledges and breaches and secrets, and now, finally, she sprayed the good Judge himself, now entering his thirtieth hour of death.

T hrough the dawn and the pale empty streets, their voices rose and fell like squabbling birds.

"Slow down!" he said.

"Mass starts in five minutes and we're late," she said, hurrying on.

"Late 'cause of you," he called ahead. "Settin' pin curls jest to clean house and wash winders for a dollar an hour," he scoffed.

"Windues, not winders," she said.

"Windues, winders, you still gotta wash 'em," he muttered.

These were the Menka twins, Howard and Jozia. Howard was the Monsignor's handyman at Saint Mary's. Jozia worked across the street from the church for the Fermoyle family, whose housekeeper she had been for thirty years.

They began to climb West Street hill, Jozia's long legs carrying her yards ahead of her shorter brother. Every now and again he trotted to catch up. This morning she walked even faster. Today was trash day, and she wanted to finish her work early so she could go down and visit with Grondine Carson, the muscular garbage man. This time she'd make sure it was all done so Mrs. LaChance wouldn't get mad like last week when she came out on the porch and yelled down to Grondine, didn't he know a standing swill truck drew flies and oughtn't he hurry it up and move on, instead of bothering people that had plenty of work to do?

"Slow down!" Howard ran up to her. "What's your big rush?" He glanced away sadly when she did not answer. He knew what her big rush was, just as he knew the reason for the pin curls under her yellow kerchief and the blue perfume bottle in her pocketbook. He had seen her gooney-eyeing that old pigman Carson over the Fermoyles' barrels enough times now to know what was happening. Last Friday Carson had given her the blue perfume bottle. All week-end long, it sat on the kitchen table staring at him like a cold watery eye. He shivered.

"Lookit them geraniums," he chattered now in a high-pitched nervous voice. "Not half's big as the ones I did." He trotted up to her again. "I put manure on mine. Miz Arkaday said not to, but I did." He giggled into his palm. "I did anyways."

Jozia glanced down at him. "You oughter do like you're told," she said. "Specially to Miz Arkaday."

"She ain't my boss," said Howard. "The Monsignor's *my* boss. Not her!"

"Miz Arkaday runs the reckery," Jozia said. "So she's your boss to the Monsignor. Jest like Miz LaChance's my boss to her mother. It's called a . . . a change of demand, Miz LaChance says." She flicked him a haughty smile, then strode briskly on.

Howard paused, fists clenched, mouth trembling. He ran up to her. "You think you're so smart. You think you know everythin', don't ya?"

"Shet your mouth," Jozia snapped. "Or I'll shet it for ya." She did not break stride.

Hurt swamped his sluggish face. "Least on my job I ain't got four bosses!" he yelled after her.

She turned. "Who's four?"

"The two ya got and Sam and Mr. LaChance," Howard said, pleased that she was waiting.

"Sam Fermoyle ain't my boss. You know that! And Mr. LaChance, he don't count. He ain't nobody's boss," she huffed, and started walking again. Secretly she considered herself Mr. LaChance's boss. She liked to think that Mr. LaChance was as scared of her as he was of his wife, Helen. "And pretty soon," she called back to Howard, "you're gonna have three bosses. Monsignor's getting a new priest."

"I know that!" Howard said. "I knew before you did!"

"You did not!"

"I did too!"

"Did not!"

"Did too!" he shouted, running up to her.

They were in front of the armory. Across the street on the corner of the park, Joey Seldon was stocking his red cooler with cans of soda. Like the milk truck rattling by and his radio songs, their voices were such a part of the blind man's morning that he did not raise his head as they passed.

"Then how come you never said nothin'?" Jozia demanded.

" 'Cause!" Howard's chin went out. "Monsignor said I'm not sposta say what I hear. What I hear's God's business and nobody else." He looked up slyly. "And I hear all kindsa good stuff."

Jozia rolled her eyes. "You're jest full of it. Fack, you're so full of it, I got to laugh. Ha ha!"

With Jozia in the lead, they continued across Main Street.

"There's the Judge," Howard said as they approached the Mayo sisters' boardinghouse, where the familiar figure in the upper window stared past them.

"Finer man ever live," Jozia sighed in the same tone Mrs. LaChance always used. As they passed the gabled and turreted house with its weedy front lawn and its striped awnings faded and torn, Jozia's eyes blurred and her mouth sagged in a wet smile.

Her faraway look frightened Howard; she was thinking about that pigman again. He nudged her. "I know somethin' else too. Somethin' about Miz LaChance," he said loudly.

She blinked. "You don't know nothin' I don't know," she sniffed. She held up two knobby crossed fingers. "'Cause Miz LaChance and me're jest like that. Jest like sisters almost."

A little smile perked Howard's face. "I know that house ain't hers. Not really."

"'Course it's hers," Jozia said. Now that they were a block from church she pulled off the kerchief and slipped the bobby pins from her hair. The little curls clung to her head like shiny round worms. "Hers and old Miz Fermoyle's, and someday, *all* hers."

"Oh no, it ain't," Howard whispered. "Nossir!"

"Oh you're jest so full of it, you make me wanna puke sometimes."

Howard shuddered. Jozia knew he hated that word, *puke*. Just the sound of it turned his stomach.

"Whose house is it then if it ain't hers?" Jozia smirked.

"Never mine," he said, lagging behind.

"Never mine 'never-mine'!" Jozia snapped. "'Cause you don't know, that's how come 'never mine.'"

"I do so know! I know better'n you!"

"You don't know nothin' better'n me! Fack, you don't know nothin' better'n anybody. Fack, you're 'bout the dumbest person I ever knowed!"

"Oh yah?"

"Yah!"

"Okay! Okay! Then I'm not tellin'! And next time you wanna know who was that comin' outta the reckery crying, go and ask . . . somebody else." Howard blinked. He had almost said, *Go and ask Grondine Carson.*

"See! You're jest making things up again to get my goat."

"Okay, then. It's Sam's house, that's whose house!" he blurted.

"Is not!" Jozia said bitterly.

"Is so!" His chin went way out this time. "And Miz LaChance's scareda him finding out. She told Monsignor, she said it's all a trust. That only the Judge knows. And her." There were a lot of things only Mrs. LaChance knew, like poisoning her husband's nice dog Riddles and making Howard bury him out in the backyard before Mr. LaChance got home from work. After that he'd quit working for

Mrs. LaChance. A lady that could do that to such a nice dog could do anything to anyone.

Jozia shook her head so violently that her lips trembled. "You're crazy. You got it all messed up. It's old Miz Fermoyle's house. Then when she dies, it's gonna be all Miz LaChance's house. Jest yesterday Miz LaChance, she said to Sam, 'This is my house,' she said. "And I don't hafta put up with no crazy drunks.' " Jozie nodded vehemently. "That's what she said and everybody knows what a holy woman Miz LaChance is."

"She ain't holy," Howard muttered. "Jest cheap."

"Cheap!" Jozia laughed that shrieky superior laugh of hers that so rankled her twin. "Cheap don't go buying two new doors for the church!"

"That's when I heard her!" Howard said. "After the man from the paper took the picture of her and Monsignor with the doors, and Monsignor said thanks, and Miz LaChance said it was least she could do. 'Beside,' she said, 'better the money be going to the church than the barroom.' And Monsignor said, 'Acourse not,' she could trust him. And Miz LaChance said she knew that, and Monsignor said how the church needs a new roof and the convent boiler's not gonna make winter and the Bishop's all outta money to help, so's the only way to do all them repairs is bake sales and bingo, only he don't have a church hall. And then he said how she and her mother's house being right across the street'd be perfeck and would she ever thinka selling to the parish. Acourse he shouldna even ask, 'cause he could never pay the whole price it would cost. And Miz LaChance said she was awful shamed to say it, and how nobody knew but the Judge and now him. She said the house was her brother's and her mother's, and after her mother dies, it's all Sam's house, and not one bit hers, after all her work, all her slaving. And Monsignor said how that ain't fair, and Miz LaChance said her mother spoiled Sam rotten, and how he was always the favorite and she was always the one to pick up the pieces, and Monsignor started saying he thought the phone was ringing, so he'd better go get it, like he does when he's sicka talking. And Miz LaChance started crying and saying how all she ever got was leftovers her whole life, nothing but everbody's leftovers, and if anything ever happened to her mother, she'd be out in a street. And

Monsignor said, 'Well, probably you'll be getting your mother's three tenement houses, Helen.' And Miz LaChance really started bawling then, and she said no, she wouldn't even get them. She said they's going to Sam's kids. Each kid'd get one."

Jozia blew her red nose into her kerchief. Tears streamed down her face. "Poor Miz LaChance," she sniffed.

"How 'bout poor you?" Howard said. "Soon's old Missus Fermoyle's dead, they ain't gonna be no more job left. And then watcha gonna do?"

"I dunno and I don't care!"

"You gotta care!"

"You shut up, Howard! You jest shet your mouth!" she said, speeding ahead. "I'm so sicka you and your mean mouth!"

"Wait fer me!" Howard cried as she hurried down the walk to the white marble church.

Jozia paused and shouted, "You jest go by yourself. And you jest sit by yourself, too. I'm sicka you!"

Howard bounded up the steps and reached past her for the door, just as she reared back at him with her purse, and the perfume bottle inside met his cheekbone with a stinging jolt. She ran into the church. Touching the welt, Howard tried to blink back tears before going inside. He staggered down the aisle to the front pew, their favorite one, but Jozia knelt steadfastly at the entrance and would not let him in.

At eleven o'clock the Judge's telephone rang.

"I'm sorry," May said softly, "but the Judge can't come to the phone just now." She glanced at the back of his head and lowered her voice. "Could I take a message?"

"If you would," replied a woman's stern voice. "This is Helen LaChance calling. Helen Fermoyle LaChance. The Judge will know. . . . Would you tell him I'm having a . . . a bit of a problem here."

"Of course," May said. In the background she heard a man's drunken bellow.

"Get back in your room," Helen LaChance hissed away from the phone.

"This is my house just as much as yours," Sam Fermoyle cried. "And if I say she's fired, she's fired." His voice grew louder. "You hear me, Jozia, you're done! You're fired! Now get the hell outta my sight, you stupid, no good . . ."

"Excuse me," Helen LaChance said into the phone, then with her hand over the mouthpiece, her muffled voice warned the obstreperous man, "I've got the Judge on the line. . . ."

"Lemme talk . . . Judge!"

"Get away from me!"

"Give me the goddamn . . ."

With the dark struggle thrashing at the end of the line, May's eyes held on the Judge as if to keep him from being toppled in the scuffle.

"Get back . . ."

"We'll see who's . . ."

"Don't you touch me. . . . Judge! Judge! I want those committal papers signed. . . ."

"Hey." The drunken voice laughed, receding into the distance. "I was only kidding. You know what a kidder I am, Jozia. Jozia!"

"Get back in your room!"

A door slammed.

"I'm sorry," Helen LaChance said breathlessly. "It's my brother. He's trying to fire my housekeeper. . . . Wait! You just wait! Where do you think you're going?" Mrs. LaChance demanded suddenly. "Excuse me," she said desperately. "But my brother just stormed out of here. Tell the Judge I don't want Sam to see Mother's papers. Tell the Judge . . . oh . . . oh, I'm sorry."

The sun rose higher and higher and higher still, straight, straight up, until all at once, in a dizzying moment, there was heat. And from the percussion of glare and shadow, there erupted a blaze of bees on petals, a dazzling blur of colored balls, spinning spokes and racing bikes, a motionless whir of skipping ropes and

schoolyard screams, and the thump and clatter of quick dark bur-
rowings, and scamperings, and the cicadas' hard dusty hum, and
the close ear-buzz of bugs and the tender flesh-bite of gnats, and the
bone-clang of shovels sparking stone beneath the giddy, bright-
flapping, tattered frenzy of birdflight, spinning faster and faster,
nearer and nearer the sun. All over town winter-grimed windows rattled up, and front doors creaked open.

Omar Duvall crept from yard to yard, his white suit streaked
with dirt, his straw hat shapeless in his sweaty clutch. They
were still looking for him. He had spotted them twice since morning,
cruising the streets slowly, slowly, with all the time and patience in
the world to search until they found him.

The early-afternoon sun poured in on the Judge, who had shifted
in the chair. His chin hung farther down on his chest as his
shoulders hunched closer together.

The phone began to ring. It was Joey Seldon. From the window
May could see the blind man down in the telephone booth that was
across the street from his popcorn stand. He shouted to be heard
over passing traffic.

"I'm sorry," May said. "But the Judge can't come to the phone
just now."

"Tell him it's Joey," he hollered. "He'll come."

"I'm sorry, but he's not feeling very well."

"He's not sick, is he?" Joey's voice tightened.

"A little." May closed her eyes.

"Oh no!" Joey groaned. "He won't miss the council meeting, will
he? It's tomorrow night."

"Um . . . I really don't know," May said, her eyes burning. There
was no air to breathe.

"Look, tell him he's got to make it. Tell him Greene just stopped by, and tomorrow night's the vote. Tell him Greene says he's got enough votes this year to turn down my lease for the stand."

"Yes," May muttered as if scribbling this all down. "Of course . . . enough votes . . . to turn down lease. . . ."

"Tell him Greene's on the warpath again. . . ."

". . . on warpath . . ."

"And tell him this—he'll like this. Tell him Greene says it's the end of an era. . . ."

"End of an era . . . ," May repeated dully, her gaze settling on the Judge's contorted hands, the fingertips just beginning to blacken.

"Tell him it's a matter of life and death," Joey shouted over the rumble of Grondine Carson's garbage truck as it accelerated up West Street.

"A matter of life and death," came May's vaporous whisper. There was a click, but she stood listening to the dial tone, steadied by its urgent drone.

A few blocks away in the School of Holy Innocents, Benjy Fermoyle glanced out the window to see his father staggering through the schoolyard below. In the front of the room Sister Martin snapped her pointer against the green continent on the canvas map. They were supposed to know this for tomorrow's exam; the major exports and imports of each country as well as their capitals. What she wanted them to learn was not just miles and oceans away, but worlds, lifetimes removed from Benjy, when all he could perceive of distance and other lives was the father who came looking for his younger son only when he was drunk, the father who at any moment might come bursting through that doorway.

"The capital of Venezuela is . . ." Sister Martin nodded at Linda Braller's waving hand.

"Caracas," Linda answered.

"The capital of Uruguay is . . ." Sister Martin looked at him. Just then the bell rang, and all heads bowed with the departure prayer. Benjy stared in horror as Mr. Lee, the school's janitor and crossing guard, came out of the building and hurried after his father. Mr. Lee grabbed his father by the arm and managed to steer him back onto the sidewalk. Just as his father stepped into the road, a car turned the corner. Benjy looked up to see Sister Martin's lips moving with the class prayer as she stared out at the schoolyard. Her eyes widened with the squeal of brakes. A man was shouting. Benjy lowered his head.

"Please, dear God," he prayed, "it's okay if he's dead. But not here. Anyplace but here."

The second bell rang, and Benjy rose slowly as his classmates jostled up the aisles for the door.

"Benjamin! Wait!" called Sister Martin with a glance toward the window.

"Look at that guy out there," Jack Flaherty called, pausing at the window. He pointed. "Mr. Lee's helping him up. Look, he's so drunk he can't even stand up. Let's go see!" Flaherty cried, his newly deep voice cracking with delight.

When they were gone Sister Martin closed the door. He squirmed as she came down the aisle. The long black beads at her waist rattled against the desk as she sat in the chair next to his. She was a young nun with a deeply pocked face and bushy eyebrows that massed over the bridge of her large nose. He'd known from the first day of school that she didn't like him. She was always singling him out, calling on him when he didn't even have his hand raised. Try, she would urge, at least just try. Most of the time he knew the answers, but hated the silence in that terrible moment of everyone staring at him. She had finally given up. She wet her finger now and rubbed at an ink smudge on the desktop. He tried to remember if he'd done anything wrong today, but he knew he hadn't. He never did. The classroom smelled of chalk dust and the heat of her black wool, warm brown apple cores, the limp remnants of bologna crescents and peanut butter and jelly crusts and lead pencil shavings that filled the black metal wastebasket.

"Benjamin," she said, then paused, her coarse face reddening. Sweat leaked from under her stiff white wimple as she stared at him. "I just want you to know . . . I . . . I want you to know that I . . . I understand. I know how hard it can be to have someone . . . to have such a situation going on in your life. But you're not the only one,

Benjamin." She tried to smile. "Believe me when I tell you that. We all have these, these crosses to bear. Do you know what I'm saying?"

He both nodded and shrugged, which seemed to irritate her. The shouting grew louder in the schoolyard. A horn tooted. He glanced down, relieved not to see his father.

"Look at me! Don't look away. Look at my eyes. See my face. Do you see? Do you know what I'm saying? I'm homely."

He was shocked. He stared at her.

"It's a fact of life. I'm a homely person, aren't I?"

"No," he said, and she smiled.

"It's my affliction, my cross to bear, just as your father's condition is his affliction, his cross to bear. Benjamin, I said, look at me."

He tried to keep his gaze on the solid furry line of her eyebrows.

"I want to help you, that's all. But you have to let me help you. Please, Benjamin," she said softly. She leaned closer. "Now, I know your father has a drinking problem, and when I saw him out there . . ."

"That wasn't my father."

". . . and how you seemed to shrink up . . ."

"That wasn't him."

She sighed, blinking. "Yes, it was. I know that was your father."

He shook his head. "No, it wasn't."

She bit her lip and sniffed, and he was afraid she was going to cry. She reached across the aisle and put her hand over his.

"It's all right, Benjamin," she said softly. "Whatever he is has nothing to do with what kind of person you are. Do you know what I'm saying?"

"But that wasn't him," he said, grateful when her hand slipped away.

Benjy came up the street from school, walking close to the dusty hedges. In their yards, dogs lazed in pools of sunlight, panting under their wintery coats. Cars full of teenagers cruised the streets, windows down, convertible tops peeled back, radios blasting, voices shrill and heedless. From everywhere came music and motion and young mothers wielding squeaky baby buggies past porch rails bannered with bright scatter rugs, beaten and airing now in the first lilac's welling sweetness.

He stopped dead. Ahead on the corner was Jack Flaherty with his hands cupped to his mouth. Flaherty stood in a circle of older boys, one of whom was Bobby Busco, sixteen years old, the same age as Norm, Benjy's older brother, but twice Norm's size. Busco was lighting Jack's cigarette. "Suck it," Busco kept saying. "That's it, deep! Deeper!" The younger boy's face purpled until he spit the cigarette onto the ground in a spasm of choking and coughing. The older boys roared, laughing as Busco thumped Jack's back so viciously that he dropped to his knees, gasping for breath.

Benjy started to walk fast. Just a few more yards and he would be around the corner.

"Lemme try it again," Jack begged. "I took too much!"

"Yah . . . Sure, Flaherty . . . Go buy your own. . . ."

"C'mon! That ain't fair. Gimme one!"

"So long, creep," one of them called as they turned to go.

"Wait! Hey, wait, you said you'd. . . . Hey, see that guy?"

Benjy's father was coming toward him.

"That's Norm Fermoyle's father."

"Yah, I know, and look, that's his brother."

Benjy froze.

"Benjy!" his father called. "Jesus Christ, Benjy," his father cried, throwing his arms around him. He reeked of liquor and sweat. His eyes were raw and his cheeks were dark with stubble. "You gotta help me. I gotta go see the fucking Judge, and I don't feel so good right now."

The boys watched from across the street. Someone was laughing.

"I can't," Benjy said. He pulled away and his father grabbed his arm, twisting it as he jerked him back. "I can't," he said again, and his father slapped the side of his head.

"What do you mean you can't," his father bellowed and hit him again. "I'm your father, and I need your fucking help, you fucking little weasel you . . ."

But now he pulled back with all his strength and was running as fast as he could from the shameful reach of that bawling howl and the boys' stunned laughter.

lice Fermoyle, Benjy's sister, had gone straight from school to Cushing's Department Store. She sat there now in the personnel office, picking the cuticle on her thumb as she watched Miss Curtis glance at the application she had just filled out. Alice smiled her nervous, gulping smile while Miss Curtis explained that the only summer opening left was in Cosmetics. "What we need is a girl with, well . . . you know, to demonstrate the makeup . . . we need someone who's a little more . . . a little older."

"Alice's thumb began to bleed. She sucked at it, then reached quickly for her books, which fell onto the floor as she stood up to go.

"Have you tried the Taylor Shop? They always seem to need . . ."

Alice nodded and backed toward the door.

"Well then, what about Birdsee's Sweets. . . . You did? . . . What about the library? That might be more . . . Oh. Well, what can I say? Better luck next time," she called after Alice, then closed the door and sighed. "But I doubt it."

The white-haired receptionist rolled her eyes and whispered, "I didn't want to say anything, but that was Alice Fermoyle, you know, Sam Fermoyle's daughter?"

"Oh!" said Miss Curtis, looking toward the door. "And Marie, the secretary from Briscoe's Sporting Goods, that's her mother, right?"

"I didn't want to say anything," the receptionist said, "but Lord knows, the last thing you'd want is him in here drunk, trying to see the daughter, the way he does his wife over at Briscoe's."

"Or the mother on my back," Miss Curtis added. "I see her in church, and she's always got this look, like she's just waiting for somebody to cross her."

"Well," the receptionist said, "poor thing's had a time of it, I guess. But then again, she asked for it, running around with a thirty-year-old man when she was still in high school."

"You're kidding!" Miss Curtis said.

"That's the truth," the receptionist said. "I remember. Everybody does. 'Course, no one ever says much, we all felt so bad for Mr.

Cushing and our poor Nora. It was one week before the big wedding, and Sam Fermoyle runs off and marries a teenage girl."

Lester Stoner was waiting for Alice in front of the store. "Well?" He grinned hopefully. "Did you get it?" he asked, falling in step beside her.

Eyes wide, she shook her head no. Her face still burned.

"My father knows the Cushings," Less was saying. "Maybe he could put in a word."

She wished he'd shut up, always acting so superior to everyone else, when he could be such a creep sometimes, always hanging around the nuns. He could make her feel so inadequate. That was it, if he said one more word she'd break up with him.

"Come on, Alice, don't feel bad. There's a lot of jobs in town. You'll see."

She walked faster. It wasn't his fault. She couldn't believe she'd just done that, gone in there for a job, into Cushing's, where of course they'd all known. She could tell, especially that old lady with her patronizing smile: *I used to play bridge with your grandmother Fermoyle.* Say it! Say, *You're Sam's daughter.* Damn! Why had she done that? Why couldn't she ever stand up to her mother? "Cushing's!" she'd almost shrieked this morning, standing over her mother as she swept up the broken glass. He got drunk. He kicked in the cellar window and put his fist through the back door pane, so now she'd pay. Her, the one whose fault it all was, would always be. "Cushing's," her mother's dead voice repeated, not even looking up, daring her to argue, daring her to be ashamed, daring her to be afraid, for fear was the worst offense. Cowards were afraid, and damn it, Marie Fermoyle wasn't working her ass off to raise cowards, so if her younger son Benjy was afraid of water, then he'd damn well spend every day this summer at the public pool, and if her daughter was afraid of what people might think, then she'd march straight into Cushing's to offer herself, Alice Fermoyle, Sam's daughter; Sam and Marie; the worm in her mother's unwed belly, the reason for it all—her, the shameful, sinful, lustful reason. Her brother Norm was lucky. He wasn't afraid of anything. She envied him his good looks, his strength, his confidence, his quick brutality, his rawness that was so much like hers, their mother's.

"How about Birdsee's?" Lester was saying as they waited for the light to change.

She shook her head.

"The luncheonette!" he said as they passed Eunice Bonifante's restaurant on the corner. Eunice was his aunt. She was a widow now, and, so the rumor went, having an affair with Lester's father, her dear sister-in-law's husband.

"I'd hate that," she said. "All those people at the counter staring at you."

"They don't stare *at* anyone," he said. "They just stare. Like my father does. He chews and he stares." He looked at her and seemed to realize for the first time how upset she was. "What's wrong, Al?"

"I hate this town!" she said, walking faster now, because her eyes were filling with tears. "I hate these dinky stores and these crummy streets and people watching you every minute; like right now, every place we go by, somebody's looking out, saying, 'There's that Fermoyle girl, what's her name, she never says two words, and that's Lester with her, his father's Sonny Stoner, the chief of police, and Lester is valedictorian of his class, such a smart boy, wonder what he sees in her!' "

Lester laughed. "They don't say that!"

She looked at him. "Did you ever wonder what it would be like to be invisible? You could do anything you wanted and go anyplace and no one'd know."

Lester stepped in front of her now and whispered, "Yah, and you could see what everyone else was doing. Can you imagine, being invisible up at the Flatts, looking in all the windows at the parkers." He grinned, his small bright eyes glowing the way they had in his darkened kitchen when he had her listen to the calls coming over his father's police radio. "It's better than TV," he had whispered above the static. "It's almost like being God," he'd said, laughing.

A garbage truck rumbled down the hill, leaking rancid juices from its seams, its stench everywhere.

"I could get a job at the lake!" she said suddenly. "Mary Agnes said there's a couple of waitressing jobs at the hotel. She said I could. . . ."

"No!" Lester said, stopping in the middle of the sidewalk. "I'll never see you!" His voice quivered, reminding her of a chemistry class last year when some kids switched beakers on Les, and when he put his on the Bunsen burner, the smoky explosion of ashes blackened his face.

She didn't know what to say. They'd only been going out for a month and Lester was her first boyfriend. He looked the way he had in chemistry that time, mad enough to cry.

"They all stay in this dumpy cabin behind the hotel," he said, his eyes blazing with indignation. Spittle frothed the corners of his mouth. "And there's no adult supervision and there's drinking every night and parties! And I know for a fact Mary Agnes had Tony spend at least one night there last summer, because his mother's call came into the station, and I heard my father on the radio send Victor out in the cruiser, and sure enough, that's where they found him. With her, Mary Agnes, that tramp!"

"Les! She's not a tramp." Mary Agnes had been her friend since second grade. But in the last few years Mary Agnes's best friend had been Tony.

He glared at her, his mouth puckered sourly. "Take my word for it! She's a tramp and I know!" He always seemed to know all that was bad or tainted in town. Alice wondered how many calls he'd heard concerning her father. Thank God, Norm hadn't called the police last night.

Lester walked alongside her in rigid silence. Pale-eyed and pink-skinned, he was always too serious, too smart, too polite, too good. Tall and slim, he moved with this ramrod intensity that adults valued as ambition, high-mindedness, an intensity his classmates had always mocked.

The closer they got to Lester's house, the more distant her troubles became. Here, the air was sweet and green and still. Lester's shoulder brushed hers and her eyes blurred and her legs felt weak. Her insides burned. Yesterday he had touched her breasts for the first time. Neither one spoke now as they came up the brick walk toward the trim white Cape.

Inside, her eyes raced hungrily over the living room, with its gold plaid sofa and matching club chairs, its rust-and-green braided rug. The lampshades were patterned with eagles, as was the pale green wallpaper, its gold eagles perched atop crossed fifes and drums. She'd give anything to live in a house like this, where the slightest drip of a faucet or squeal of a door would not be allowed. She wished they could sit up here, but Lester always hurried her downstairs to the paneled rec room.

She waited down here now while he ran up to relieve his mother's day nurse. Lester's mother had been sick in bed since Easter. Though no one would speak the word, they all knew it was cancer. Alice put on her glasses and spread her books and notes over the coffee table. Finals started tomorrow, but it was no big deal for seniors. Most either had their jobs lined up or knew what colleges they were going to, so these final grades wouldn't even really matter.

Alice had been accepted at the state university, but after her mother's initial thrill had come days of depression about where the money would come from. It came up daily now, in every conversation. Lester had also been accepted at UVM, but his father wanted him to go to Castleton State so he could be near his mother these last few months. According to her doctors, Mrs. Stoner wouldn't live to see Christmas. Alice had heard that from her brother Norm, whose best friend Weeb's mother was Mrs. Miller, the nurse Les was showing out the front door now.

"The pills were by the bed again," Mrs. Miller was saying. She sounded irritated.

"I had to leave early. I had my first final," Les said. Alice glanced toward the stairs. Lester had left early to walk her to school. He hadn't had a final.

"I told you yesterday, Les. They're awful strong."

"I know. I forgot."

"And she's in so much pain now, sometimes she can't think straight. She's liable—"

"I'll go put them on the dresser," Les said.

"In the bathroom's best," Mrs. Miller was saying. Her voice seemed to be out front now. "Then when she needs one, somebody'll have to get it."

"I'll go right up and move them now." As soon as the front door closed, Lester bounded down the stairs and onto the couch.

"Your mother's pills!" she said.

"She's sound asleep," Les said, leaning against her as he reached up to turn out the light.

She took off her glasses, surprised; usually there was the pretense of homework for at least fifteen or twenty minutes. He fell against her, clenching her arms so tightly that they hurt.

"Don't go," he begged, kissing her eyes, her cheeks, her neck. "Please don't go to the lake," he whispered against her lips. "Don't leave me alone here, please." His mouth was open, his tongue shoving against her tongue until she finally opened her mouth. It was strange the way he could be so irritating, such a sissy, until he was down here in the dark, pressed against her, kissing her so frantically, running his hand so hard up and down her thigh that she couldn't think straight, couldn't even picture what he looked like, and for a moment as he pushed her bra up over her breasts, she wasn't even sure who he was. This was a different Lester. She had this power over him. She could make him do bad things. A sharp ache filled her chest and she was afraid she was going to cry.

Downstairs, the doorbell rang. The boardinghouse shook with Claire Mayo's heavy footsteps. Claire was the younger sister, square-jawed and stocky, the one with the head for business. It was Claire who berated the grocer's delivery boy for worms in the lettuce or the linen service for stained sheets.

"You will not!" she barked from the front parlor. "You most certainly will not! This is a—"

A man's heedless voice engulfed hers.

Upstairs, May drew the afghan over the Judge's lap. Her wrinkled fingers lingered on the swollen crotch. Her breath grew short and her ears began to ring and her heart began to pound until the whole house throbbed with its blind ruckus.

When the door flew open, she did not clearly see or hear them, though she knew they moved about the room in a commotion of heat and anger.

"He's dead!" her sister, Claire, wailed, falling back against the bedpost. "The Judge is dead, sister. He's dead!"

"Don't look at me," Sam Fermoyle cried, lurching back out the door. "I didn't lay a hand on him. As God is my witness," he sobbed drunkenly as he tripped and staggered down the stairs and onto the street and through the horn-blowing traffic with dogs snapping at his heels and little boys stumbling and laughing after him, teetering on curbstones, bouncing off telephone poles.

May opened her eyes and watched curiously as they careened through the park, where Joey Seldon cocked his doughy head to hear the little boys parrot Sam, "The Judge is dead! Jesus Christ, the Judge is dead!"

Joey Seldon spun dizzily in his ramshackle stand. "Wait!" he called. "Tell me what happened!" he shouted, pawing the air with enormous hands. He groped for the door, then made his way to the sidewalk and waited, listening up and down the street for someone to tell him what had happened.

To make sure he wouldn't run into his father again, Benjy came through the woods that horseshoed the eastern edge of town and sloped from the wild flatlands that were the foothills of Killington Mountain. He had been in here before with his brother, Norm. But now, as he ran alongside Moon Brook, he realized that this was the first time he had ever been in these woods alone. If he stayed with the brook, at some point soon it should curve around a huge boulder, which would put him almost directly behind his street.

In here the heat was thinner, the trees pale with new growth and far enough apart so that sunlight slanted down in wide silvery bars. He stopped running now and began to walk. His eyes flickered warily to the left, toward that menacing ridge of pine woods beyond which lay the Flatts, where people lived in tin-roofed shacks and trailers. They were all blonds and redheads with strange first names like Bonaparte and Fantasia and Benito and Hemingway and Coolidge and Blue. Their last names might be Carper or Mansaw or Hunsen or Kluggs or Wallace, but they shared the same flattened brows and close-set, palely lit eyes, and ghostly pallor that seemed to devolve, not only whiter with each brood, but thinner; so that there glowed in their flesh now that cold depthless translucence of blue ice, like wintry mountain runoff, that marked them as offspring of cousins, so that husband and wife often looked enough alike to be brother and sister.

Though she wasn't related to any of those people, Benjy's own mother had lived for a time in the Flatts, in a small house her father had rented from Grondine Carson, the pigman, whose hog farm was next to the town dump. His feet were wet, his shoes heavy with the ooze of the spring forest. The usually narrow cut of the brook had swamped in every direction through the wild laurel and the white cedar and stunted pines, and nowhere could he see the boulder.

He had come too near the Flatts. Here, the trees grew closer, and he thought he could hear the eerie squeal of pigs in the distance. He went on a few feet more, heading for a rocky incline; then he stopped and listened, certain he had just heard a voice. No, he kept telling himself as he climbed, it's the pigs. It's got to be the pigs. It couldn't be his father.

Suddenly, when he had reached the top of the hill, he darted back and fell to one knee, crouching in the tangled sweep of a willow tree. Below, in the clearing, stood two men, a young black man and a tall, barrel-chested white man in a white suit and a straw hat, which he pressed to his chest. The young man was shorter and wiry, and now as he moved catlike toward the white man, Benjy thought he saw the sharp glint of metal in his right hand.

"Don't!" the white man said. "Please! I been your friend."

"Which is why you took out your knife, right?"

"I was only tryna make you listen to reason," the white man said in a Southern accent, a drawl much like the young man's.

"Well I got the knife now, so it's your turn to listen, Omar," said the young man.

"First put that down!" the white man said, waving the hat. "You hear me, boy. Down, I said!"

"I don' wanna hurt you," the young man warned. "Just give it over, so's we can get on home."

"Now, Earlie." The white man laughed weakly. "You and your grandpa been paid, and Luther, too. Fair and square, what more do you want?"

"You know what I want," the young man growled.

"You got the car and everything I own in it!" the white man whined, wagging his head. His slick black hair gleamed in the sun. "I gotta have a few dollars. I deserve th—"

"Just give it over," said the young man, taking another step. "Give me the money!"

"I been good to you!" the white man cried, then whipped his hat at the stealthily approaching young man. "I put shoes on that old man's feet, and I put food in your bellies, and you know, every time you asked, Earlie, a woman in your bed, and—"

"Give it!" the man named Earlie snarled.

"And back there I could've run off when they started waving that woman's check around, but I didn't, did I? Not only that, but I went and paid bail. I sat outside all night. All night long, waiting for the courthouse to open. I could've run, but I didn't! I could've told them it was Luther that changed them figures, but—"

"No, you couldn't!" Earlie cried, and stamped his foot in outrage. " 'Cause Luther don't read and Luther don't write!" He gestured angrily and his palm flashed white in the sun. "You was the one that changed them checks and the old man damn knows it now. Just like he knows they ain't no black old folks' home, and they ain't no Stankey Magazine Company, Incorporated. They's all lies you made up, just like them Bibles we been giving, half the pages empty and no damn good, like you, Duvall!" The young man moved closer. "And I bet none of them subscriptions ever once came to them people. 'Cause you kept all that money, didn't you? And no five dollars neither. Ever' check for five we brung back you changed to fifty, didn't you? Didn't you?" he snarled, hunching closer.

"Now you just settle down," the white man sputtered. "You're makin' a mighty big commotion outta one desperate little incident," he said, sidestepping; and so did the young man, in a rippling crouch, shoulder muscles taut beneath his bright red-and-yellow diamond-patterned shirt, every step pacing the white man's, another step, and another, until they were directly below the boy, whose gaze fixed in horror on the blade in the young man's hand. Just then, there came the high-pitched squeal of a rooting sow. The young man's head jerked up and his yellow-shot eye snagged on the boy's thin face peering down through the pale willow leaves. And in that instant of hesitation, the white man, seeing his chance, pivoted, then sprang toward the pine woods, toward the pig farm. The young man wheeled after him, and then they were both gone. And so was the boy, back down the hill, and through the woods, his heart pumping his heavy wet feet until they met pavement, one street over from his own.

B enjy sat on his sagging back steps with six-year-old Louis Klubock, who lived next door. It had been a terrible day, but he felt safe now in this naked heat with chubby Louie beside him and the Klubocks' old black Lab dozing at their feet. Delicate music drifted across the driveway from the open windows of the newly painted yellow house as Mrs. Klubock played the piano and sang in a high sweet voice. Sometimes when Mr. Klubock joined in, Benjy's heart would almost split in two with joy and longing. Mr. Klubock was at work now in the butcher shop. Louie was lucky. He had everything.

"My uncle Renie used to have a dog," Benjy said, reaching down to pet Klubocks' dog. "His name was Riddles. My mother said my aunt poisoned him. But Uncle Renie said he just took off. He's got a cat now in his store. But it's a secret cat. Nobody knows about him."

Benjy knelt down and scratched the white ruff on the dog's chest. The dog rolled onto its side.

"I like cats," Louie said.

"We had one once, a kitten, a little white one."

"Yah, I remember that," Louie said. "Your mother brought him home and then she took him away. How come she did that?"

"I don't know." *Careful.* With so much not to tell, so many feints and dodges, and all the bobbing and weaving, he could feel his brain become this fluid, slippery, shimmying mass behind his eyes. "She says cats are the worst pets of all." He continued scratching the dog's chest. "She says they're just like people. All they care about's themselves. She says boy cats are the worst, 'cause they're just like men, staying out all night and getting into fights and dragging home in the morning just to have a place to sleep."

Klubocks' dog got up then and lifted a leg and wet on the foundation. Its yellow stream trickled down the newspaper that was stuffed into the broken cellar window.

"Your father broke that," Louie said.

"I know," Benjy said, watching the dog cross the driveway, then disappear into the coolness of the lilac bushes that bloomed at the edge of Klubocks' yard.

"He was drunk," Louie said.

"I know." Some things just couldn't be bluffed.

"Your father's always drunk," Louie said, watching him.

"Not all the time."

"Do you hate your father?" Louie asked suddenly.

"Why, do you hate yours?"

"Yes!" Louie said, and Benjy laughed. "He makes my mother cry. Sometimes the phone rings and she picks it up, but nobody's there. Just some breathing. My father said she likes the calls. He said she likes men to look at her and call her up, and she always cries when he says that."

Louie's small round face moved in close to Benjy, who stiffened back. The dog was growling in the lilac bushes. Now Mrs. Klubock's music sounded heavy and sad. He thought he heard squealing tires.

Louie was telling him how they might have to move to Arizona because of his father's swollen hands and knees. His mother had cried because all her life she was scared of snakes. She said a lady in Arizona was going to the bathroom once and she heard this splashing noise in the toilet and she jumped off the seat and this ten-foot rattlesnake was swimming in the pee water. "You think that's true?" Louie asked, his eyes suddenly raw and watery. "You think a snake can come up the toilet like that?"

Benjy leaned forward, looking toward the white blur turning

the corner of the driveway. It was the same man he had seen in the woods. His chest was heaving, and his face was fiery red, and the cuffs of his pants flopped with mud.

"Is that your father?" Louie asked as the man stumbled down on one knee, then scrambled frantically to his feet with a backward glance.

"No!" Benjy said, his eyes wide with fright.

The lilac bushes quaked with the dog's barking. A horn sounded on the next block, a long steady blare.

"Don't tell them niggers I'm here, boys," the man panted as he ran behind the house.

"What're niggers?" whispered Louie.

"A Negro," Benjy hissed, eyes shifting between the road and the back of the house. "A black man and he's got a knife!" he whispered.

"He's got a knife!" Louie wailed, bolting off the steps into his house.

The music wrenched to a stop. Moments later, Mrs. Klubock held up Louie to her kitchen window. "See," she said loudly. "It's only Benjy!"

"A nigger's gonna come," Louie wailed. "The man said so, and he's got a knife!"

"No, no. It's only Benjy," she soothed, putting the boy down, then coming back to the window. "I'm surprised at you, Benjy. Scaring Louis like that! I think Mr. Klubock's right. I think it's about time you hung around with boys your own age and left Louis alone!" She slammed the window shut on Louie's screams. The dog's barking had subsided into a low steady growl.

Benjy sat frozen on the step. He sat for a long time, staring up at the Klubocks' kitchen window. In its reflection was the crooked chimney of his own house. He scratched a bite on his arm and the little hairs bristled. He slid to the end of the step and glanced around the corner of the house, relieved to see no one there. He ran inside and locked the door. He turned on the television and sat on the couch, his knees drawn to his chin. The house filled with strange crackling, scratching, moaning voices. He turned the volume up as loud as it would go and stared at the familiar faces on the screen. As the scratching grew louder, he felt himself grow smaller and tighter.

Once, a few years ago, his father had broken into the house and crawled into his bed. All night long, his father held him in his arms, until morning, when his mother threw his father out of the house. She yelled at Benjy for not waking her up and telling her he was there. He couldn't explain how scared he'd been. How tightly coiled he'd lain all night, smothered by his father's arms and breath. Now, as then, the trick was to almost stop breathing, to not even be here, and then the scratching would go away.

With his eye at the crack in the garage door, Duvall could see down the driveway to the street. He crouched in a cold sweat as the black Lab scratched at the door, growling. Duvall ducked back as the dog snuffled its muzzle along the crack and then began to bark. A car was coming down the street, now slowing, now rumbling into the driveway, its brakes grinding metal against metal. The dog's barking grew frantic. Duvall closed his eyes. The car door creaked open, slammed shut, and then footsteps raced toward the garage. He buried his face in his sweaty hands, whispering, "Deliver me, Lord. Deliver me, and I will never, ever . . ."

"Get out of here!" a woman hissed. "Goddamn dog . . . go on!"

He watched through the crack as she went to the lilac bush and snapped off a switch of new blooms and swatted the fleeing dog's rump. "Get over in your own yard and stay there!" she called, throwing the branch after him.

The dog ran onto the back steps of the yellow house, still barking. With her arms folded, the woman stood on the edge of the driveway, staring back at the dog. Something in her stance and the sag of her shapeless skirt reminded Duvall of a child, willful and hard-edged where softness had probably never been allowed, who would, if she had to, stand out there all night, facing that ugly animal down.

The screen door of the yellow house opened and a slender woman with soft blond curls leaned out and caught the dog by its collar. "Marie, I'm sorry. Really I am. Louis keeps letting him off the rope," she called, and when she got no response, pulled the struggling dog inside the house.

"Yah, you're sorry," Marie muttered as she came around the front of her dented old car. "Sorry he didn't take my arm off." She sighed then and hurried into her own house.

A few minutes later a girl with limp brown hair dragged down the driveway with an armload of books pressed to her chest. The seat of her navy blue school uniform was shiny and wrinkled. She hesitated on the back steps a minute, then squared her shoulders and went inside. Next to arrive was a stocky boy, his baseball cap rimming a practiced scowl. When he turned at the door, Duvall saw that his shirt was ripped halfway up his back.

After another hour had passed and no one else had come, Duvall closed his eyes and sank back against a stack of newspapers that were bundled and tied with string. He hadn't slept in twenty-four hours and wasn't sure when he last had eaten. His exhaustion and hunger had rendered him numb. As soon as it was dark he would be on his way. By tomorrow's sunset he would be rolling again. Many's the time he had been down before. "Many's the time," he whispered into the gloaming silence of the cluttered garage. But never down for long, he reminded himself. "Never for long," he groaned softly, drifting into sleep.

A little while later, his eyes shot open with the smell of frying meat. His stomach growled, and for a split second his eyes washed with tears, for it seemed he was a young man again, awaking for the first time in a cell.

From the house now, their voices rent the stillness like stabbing thrusts.

"Did you see about the job?" the woman asked.

"I had a game," her son said.

"Who ripped your shirt? You know what Mr. Graber said, if you were in one more fight."

"We were just fooling around. Some of the guys—"

"Just fooling around, huh? Doesn't matter! Brand-new shirt, what do you care?"

"Mom!"

"Did you see Jarden Greene about the job? Uncle Renie said—"

"I had a game! I told you!"

"Uncle Renie said not to wait, to be the first one to apply. . . ."

"Mom! I told you! I had a game!" the boy shouted.

"And I told you to get this job! That nothing else matters! Nothing's more important, you hear me, than this goddamn job! No game! No practice! No goddamn fooling around! Nothing on this earth is more important right now than that! Just like your sister in there!" And then her voice changed, mimicking a young girl's sing-songing whine. " 'Cushing's won't hire me. Nobody in this stupid town will hire me. So I think I'll just go to the goddamn lake for the—' "

"Mom! I'll get the job!" he interrupted. "I said I'd get it!"

"When?"

"As soon as I can. . . ."

"When? When you feel like it? Next week? Next month? When?"

"Tomorrow! I'll go tomorrow! Just leave me alone, will you?"

"I'll leave you alone!" she shouted back. "I'll leave you all the hell alone and then see what happens. See who pays the bills or does a goddamn single thing for any one of you. Nobody will! Nobody on this earth but me. I'm the only one! The only one!"

Doors banged. Pans rattled; then all at once there was quiet, that uneasy, bated, writhing, staticky quiet.

He stared into the garage rafters, his eye fixed on the narrow strip of coppery sky where a roof board had rotted inward. He was remembering the quick wordless scuffle amid the sour rise of pig muck and Earlie's astonishment at seeing the blade in his own hand and Duvall's suddenly turn and then, with one quick thrust, slice through flesh and sinew; and then the long, long fall, through days, weeks, seasons, in segments of buckling knees and hip joints folding; and then the odd little thud his head made as it met the ground. He had blinked—that was all, the one little blink like a word in the air between them—and then he lay with his eyes wide, as a fat bee buzzed from clover to clover around his head.

I'll get help, Duvall had whimpered, then added, begged, *Don't move. Please don't move,* certain that Earlie would never move again, but by saying it, by stumbling off only a few yards more before calling back again, *Don't move,* had absolved himself, had given just cause to his flight, had left the faithless Earlie with the will to move, and had pronounced him alive and well enough so that he could be certain by now Luther and the old man had not only found Earlie, but had gotten him to a hospital where the doctor would assure them it was only a flesh wound, which was why the blood had gushed and run so. Just a nick, really, the blade kind of slid in sideways, the doctor, by this time, would have already explained, illustrating with a quick pass of his hand under Luther's cold dumb eyes. "Thank the Lord," the old man would sigh of his grandson, Earlie, his only living relative.

Outside, the crickets' song quickened with deepening shadows, and he assured himself that they were probably on their way home this very minute. Probably drive all night with Luther smoking his dope in the oncoming rush of the bug-pocked headlamps, while in the back seat, the old man's husky gibberish would soon have Earlie snapping at him to shut up and go to sleep. Duvall's eyes widened with their voices: *Just saying my prayers,* the old man sighs. *When you gonna be done?* Earlie asks. *When you done sinnin',* the old man replies, and Luther laughs, his head swaying dreamily over the wheel, laughs and says what he always says, *Then you gonna be prayin' a long time, old man. Maybe forever.*

Duvall sat up dizzily, his stomach still churning on those bald tires and all those endless miles of bad food as he willed them farther and farther away, absconding with his car, his clothes, all that he had ever possessed, until like a dissolving comet they had shrunk to a speck of dusty taillights, and now with the blink of an eye were gone. Gone.

He looked around and saw the dusky shadows rush to take the shapes of a wheelless bike upside down on its seat, a large steam presser, a lawn mower, its rust-frozen blades laced to the wall with spiderwebs, a mud-encrusted shovel; and he felt the passage of days into weeks, into months, until whole years seemed awash in the smell of sizzling pork fat and the rustle of walled voices that had stirred in him this abject and limitless hunger. Suddenly he was on his feet and opening the garage door. And as he made his way to the lilac shrub and broke off the thickest blooms, he knew, not with his brain, but

from deep in his belly, what he would do next, and where he would
go, and what he would say to her. For with a glance he had already
appraised the peeling clapboards and buckled roofing tiles and knew
not just by the seam of ragged lawn where the boundaries lay, but
knew by instinct. Just as he already knew that woman in there, knew
that she waited. Marie, whose high-boned cheeks and weary eyes he
had met a thousand times before. For such things, his heart was as
keen as the musician's ear or the artist's eye, his mastery, as theirs, a
born gift, but his, having been so rawly honed by desolation, would
always be the more skillful and tenacious.

Approaching, he noted well the paper-plugged cellar window, the
creaking inner door and its cardboard-taped pane where a man's fist,
in a last howling plunge, had demanded entrance. And as he went to
remove his straw hat, his eyes shot into hers with the awful certainty
of where the missing hat must at this very moment lie. She seemed to
smile, and he noted the awkwardness with which her hands met the
lilacs, and then the hands themselves, ringless and broken-nailed
and, like the daughter's beyond her at the table, nervous and
self-inflicting.

The boy at the table was younger, the staring child Duvall had
seen on the steps. She would refer uneasily to the older boy, and
Duvall, eyeing the untouched setting, the cracked green plate, the
bent-tined fork on its blue paper napkin, would understand. The
older boy had been sent to his room in this neglected little house,
where she was ever more master than the brief mistress who had
bothered to fold the paper napkins into ship sails; next week it would
be back to white again, and some weeks there would be toilet paper
squares beneath the forks.

The lilacs would stand in a milk bottle. Of course there was no
vase, for who here had ever received flowers? Not *her*, certainly, who
in a self-conscious gesture set them in the middle of the table, then
kept glancing at them. Later, when they were all in bed, she would remove them to pare the woody stems to symmetry, then return them
to the table, thinking no one would notice, but they would. They
would all notice, just as now they saw her hands flutter to her throat
and the softening of her mouth. "They're lovely," she said, and with
the curious tilt of their heads, Duvall knew the rarity here of such a
word. Lovely. Yes, they were lovely.

First it was only a crust of bread and a glass of water for which he would beg. And then as he picked crumbs from his soiled lapel and laid them on his tongue and saw her quick eyes flinch between his and that last chop, the son's, on the split platter, he quickly thanked her for her goodness and edged toward the door, knowing as he moved how soon that bone would be gnawed clean of its meat and fat and gristle; and then as he placed two grateful quarters on the table and saw her long neck stiffen with the refusal of stubborn pride, he saw how easy the next request would be, the ride to the bus depot; and then the ride back here after his mock shame at the ticket window to find his pockets empty; and the next, even easier, not even voiced, as he fluffed and set the pillow on the pallet of blankets she carried to the garage, passing them through, her eyes averted as shyly as if she stood outside his bedroom door.

Then, as he settled himself with a weary sigh, on the edge of sleep, he remembered how queerly her younger son had watched him, his grave eyes alert, until he had laid aside the gleaned bone and begun his tale, and then the relief easing the boy's frown. It was as if the boy needed the tale told and needed it told right; as if he knew it all as well as any rhyme, and in the telling would have every word and rhythm right. Had the boy's lips actually moved with his? Duvall wondered. Or had his rapt gaze only made it seem so?

"I am Omar Duvall, this morning a peddler through these emerald mountains. And tonight a helpless beggar, first disgraced and then plundered by a sorry band of black-hearted strangers who, out of the kindness of my Christian soul, I took on board and tried to help with their magazine selling while I did mine. . . ." His eyes scanned the messy countertops. "Household utensils!" he cried, seizing a wire whisk clotted with butterscotch pudding. "Eggbeaters and spatulas and can openers and these." He smiled, reverently touching a slotted spoon. "These humble kitchen tools, these nuts and bolts of the family, of the heart, in a manner of speaking."

And as he spoke, it had come to him, as it did now and would later with the day's first light sifting through the rotting roof, that here he might finally be safe.

The older boy might be a problem. He had come from his bedroom into the kitchen, and when he saw his dinner eaten, and in his place at the table, at the head of the table opposite his mother, a stranger, a male stranger, his lip had curled and instinctively his fists had clenched. "What the . . ."

"Norm, this is Mr. Duvall," Marie said, her cheeks bright.

"Omar," Duvall corrected, extending his hand; but the boy turned to his mother, demanding to know what was left for him to eat.

"Cereal," she said. "Or some toast," she added absently, looking back to Duvall. "Where are you from?" she asked.

"From everywhere," he said. "But lately," and he spoke sadly for it had become the truth, "from nowhere."

The fragrance of lilacs filled the kitchen. Benjy stared at the cornflakes box as he chewed.

"Good morning, sunshine!" the radio announcer called and Benjy winced. He dreaded going to school today and facing the boys who'd seen his father hit him yesterday.

"It's now eight-oh-five in the valley. Outside our studio on State Street, the temperature is sixty degrees and rising by the minute! It looks like the coldest, wettest spring on record is finally over, thanks to the high pressure that's moving rapidly up from the south. It looks like summer's finally on her way!"

The little house began to tremble with vibrating pipes and an outburst of cranky voices. Norm had to get into the bathroom to brush his teeth, but Alice was still in there. His mother hollered from the top of the stairs for Alice to give Norm his toothbrush. She slid it under the door.

"Now there's crud all over my toothbrush!" Norm complained.

"Better than crud all over your teeth," Alice yelled from the bathroom.

The telephone was ringing.

"I got it!" Norm hollered.

"If it's your father, I'm not here," Marie yelled down.

Benjy's eyes never left the box as he chewed. He hadn't told his mother about meeting his father. He never told her bad things. The news was on the radio. "Woodstock police warn that a group of door-to-door con artists were last seen . . ." The radio sputtered with static. Behind Benjy, the washing machine gurgled as it changed cycles. Now it began to suck and pump out its wash water. The floor vibrated and the lilacs trembled on the table and the cereal box teetered back and forth, so that Benjy had to hold on to it as he ate. The shaking stopped as the machine began to fill with water.

"Benjy, pour the bleach in," his mother yelled on her way downstairs.

He got up and added the bleach, then slammed the lid down when he saw his sister's bloodstained underpants. He sat back down and blinked at the cornflakes box, waiting for his mother's attack.

"And this just in," the radio announcer said excitedly. "Last night the newly planted grass in the town park was torn to shreds by a pack of unidentified hoodlums who drove their cars and motorcycles up and down the paths. Department of Public Works head, Alderman Jarden Greene, assures us that most of the damage will be repaired in time for the season's first band concert. Greene also says that as bandmaster he will not tolerate any of the hooliganism that spoiled last year's . . ."

From the other room came a tattoo of hollow thumps as his mother banged on the bathroom door. "What the hell are you doing in there?" she demanded. "I can't be late again." At the sound of her footsteps, Benjy closed his eyes, but she ran back upstairs.

"Out of respect for one of its oldest members, tonight's town council meeting has been postponed. Funeral services for Judge Clay . . ."

Benjy looked up as Norm ran into the kitchen with his toothbrush clenched between his teeth. "Guess what!" He grinned, tucking his shirt into his pants. "Craig's got a busted ankle. Last night a bunch of seniors went drinking up to the Flatts and they started pegging rocks off the pigman's roof and then he started chasing them and Craig fell in the brook and ca-rack!" Norm chuckled. "No catcher for tomorrow's game but me! Tell me there's no God." Norm laughed. He flipped his tie over his shoulder, then took the toothpaste from his pocket and started to brush his teeth over the kitchen sink.

Behind the cornflakes box Benjy sighed, relieved that it hadn't been his father calling.

"Tell me there's no such thing as Fate." Norm glanced back with a foaming smile. "For every calamity there's a great man! For the Civil War there was Lincoln!" After each declaration he spat into the sink, then brushed furiously. "For the Depression there was FDR! And now for the Atkinson–Saint Mary's game, there's Norman Fermoyle!" He looked back. "Weeb said they got no choice. They gotta play me!" He held his tie to his chest and bent to drink from the faucet. "Damn ants," he muttered, splashing them down the drain. "I was at Weeb's house one time and Mrs. Miller saw an ant on the windowsill, one little ant, and she went nuts. Meanwhile this dump's headquarters for every ant in the state."

At this, Benjy's tension erupted in a burst of laughter. Norm looked at him. "Jeez, you're just like Weeb. You'll laugh at anything!"

Swallowing hard, Benjy blinked himself into somberness. Norm sat down and drummed his fingertips on the table. The washing machine gently swished and splashed. From the radio Johnny Mathis was singing "The Twelfth of Never." A faraway look came over Norm's face. "The minute I woke up I knew something was going to happen today. Something special, something . . ." He looked at Benjy. "Something that'd make a real difference. You know what I mean? You know how sometimes you just know? I mean, nobody's gotta tell you. The minute the phone rang, I knew it was gonna be Weeb, and before he even said it, I knew he was gonna tell me I'd be playing tomorrow." Norm sighed and shook his head in amazement.

"But how does Weeb know for sure?" Benjy asked. Because of a fight in the first game, Coach Graber hadn't let Norm in a game all season.

"Where've you been?" Norm groaned in disgust. "He's the manager!" He stood up and opened the back door. " 'Course, if you'd play a little ball yourself instead of hiding in the house, watching TV all the time . . . Hey! Where the hell's my glove?" He pointed up at the empty nail in the back hall. "I put it right there!"

Benjy shrugged. "Maybe you left it at practice."

Norm's eyes narrowed on him. "You didn't take it, did you?"

"No!" Benjy said.

The rinse water drained out of the machine with a sucking groan. Paul Anka was singing "Lonely Boy."

"You did, didn't you, you little thief." Norm pounded the table. "You took my glove!"

"No! Honest, Norm!"

From the other room a door slammed, and then came his sister's shrill cry as she ran upstairs in her robe. "I don't see why we can't have a shower like normal people!"

"Because we're not normal people!" their mother shouted from the bathroom. Upstairs, another door slammed.

Norm leaned over the table. "I can tell you're lying. You took it! Jesus Christ, Benjy," he pleaded. "I gotta go! Tell me where it is!"

"I didn't take it!"

Now Norm's square jaw quivered and his handsome face twisted as he sprang at Benjy and, grabbing him by the collar, yanked him half out of the chair. "Today's my big chance!" he panted. "I gotta have my glove!"

"I don't know where it is," Benjy insisted. "Honest, Norm!"

The washing machine clanged to a stop. Paul Anka's voice wailed into the sudden silence. Outside, Klubocks' dog began to bark.

"Please, Benjy," Norm begged. "You don't know what this means to me."

"Maybe that guy last night took it," he said, remembering Duvall's hungry eyes coveting every object in the room.

"What guy?" Norm asked.

"The one in the garage."

"What do you mean?" Norm went to the back door and looked out at the garage. "I thought she took him to the depot."

"She did and then she took him back here."

"Why?" Norm asked, and Benjy shrugged. "You mean, he's out there? That creep's out in the garage?" Norm said in a high voice.

Now the machine began to spin, its insides grinding, turning faster and faster and faster with the deafening, grating screech of metal on metal.

His mother raced into the kitchen in her slip. At the corner of her mouth was a jagged red smear where the lipstick had jerked when the machine went berserk. "Damn that Renie!" she cried, trying to push in the dial that would turn off the washer, but it wouldn't budge. The machine continued its spin cycle with such force now that it shimmied out from the wall toward the table. "Bastard," she groaned, pushing every button. With an angry clang the machine lurched and rocked out even more. There was no stopping it. She began to beat it. She pounded the quaking lid with her fists. Her hair hung in her face. Feet braced, back arched, she put both hands on the machine, trying to wrest it back. It was all Renie's fault, she groaned, her ex–brother-in-law who had sold her this piece of shit, secondhand because she couldn't afford new, never could, nothing but junk that never worked and a car that was on its last legs and "bills, nothing but god-damn bills and nobody cares! Nobody in the whole goddamn world cares!"

Alice came to the doorway pulling curlers from her hair. Norm yelled at his mother to stop it. With the machine still advancing, Benjy slid out of its way, out of everyone's way, to put his bowl in the sink, where a clot of ants massed over the gravy on last night's supper plates. He lifted the curtain from the window over the sink and saw Mr. Klubock in his white butcher's coveralls pause on his back steps and glance warily across at the Fermoyle house. Down in the drive-way sat Klubocks' dog, its head cocked curiously up at Benjy.

"Get out of the way!" Norm bellowed, then reached behind the machine and yanked the cord from the outlet. Benjy turned off the radio and for a moment the only sound was Mr. Klubock's car cruis-ing down the street.

"What's the matter with you?" Norm cried. "Are you crazy?"

His mother sagged against the refrigerator with her face in her hands, her shoulders heaving.

Norm threw down the cord. "That's all you had to do! That's all!"

At this her head whipped up. "That's all? That's all, huh?" She laughed a bitter teary laugh. "You think it's so easy. You think every-thing's so damn easy!"

Benjy looked away from his brother's familiar sneer.

"Are you kidding?" Norm laughed. "In this nuthouse! With some bum sleeping in the garage! How the hell could anything be easy here?"

Her eyes flashed. "Nuthouse? Is that what it is?" Pointing, she came toward Norm, teeth clenched. He stared down at her hand jabbing his chest. "Then get the hell out, if it's such a nuthouse. Go live with your father! See how you like it in that nuthouse with your god-damn vicious aunt . . ."

"Mom!" Alice kept saying. "Mom!"

Sometimes Norm and their mother almost seemed to enjoy these battles, as if vying to see who could be sharper, more clever, more cruel.

". . . and her creep of a husband, and your crazy senile grand-mother singing nursery rhymes all night long in her crib, and your no-good, spineless, drunken father not giving a damn if his own kids live or die," she hissed with one last strike at Norm's chest.

He took her hand away and dropped it. "I'll get out!" he said.

"Gladly, but first you tell that little creep I want my glove!"

She spun around to Benjy.

"I don't have his glove!" he said.

She laughed, but there were tears in her eyes. "A dollar a week I'm paying for that glove. A dollar a week Mr. Briscoe takes out of my measly paycheck and you lost it?" she sobbed, shaking her head at Norm. "You're so damn careless! Nothing means anything to you, does it? All you care about is you!"

"It's up there!" Alice cried, pointing to the top of the refrigerator. "Where you put it, Norm!"

Norm started to say something. Instead he grabbed his glove and books and ran down the driveway.

Marie Fermoyle's jaw trembled, then set like a closing fist.

From next door Jessie Klubock's voice pealed like a glass bell through the warm spring morning. "Louis! Louis! You forgot to kiss Mommy goodbye!"

Coach Graber's whistle blew. Practice was over, and Norm's heart leaped. It was official. Tomorrow he would catch in the biggest game of the year.

"Wait up!" Weeb called. He was picking up the bases. Usually Norm helped, but today he followed his teammates off the field. He was the only sophomore on varsity. Weeb had been cut the first day, but he kept on showing up at all the tryouts and then the practices, so Coach Graber let him run for water and shag balls, and then he made him assistant manager.

In Norm's first game he had struck out with such force in his last swing that the bat had flown down the baseline as he spiraled into a foolish heap over the plate.

"Asshole," someone had muttered, and the next thing Norm knew, Graber was peeling him off the moaning bloody-nosed catcher by the seat of his pants. Ever since, Graber had hated his guts. He told everyone Norm was a hothead, a poor sport, a disgrace as a Catholic, and a lousy catcher. But that was all right, the rest of the guys liked him. And more important, they respected him. They never gave him the shit jobs like they did poor Weeb, he thought as he trailed the older players back to the locker room, his gait the same rolling heel-to-toe strut as theirs, his shirttail out, his cap low to his eyes and mean, his square younger face aglow in the lowering sun and the warmth of their camaraderie. And now as they trooped into the dark locker room he shivered with pleasure in the musky commingling of their hard-earned sweat and their rude talk as they lingered over the long, gouged benches.

Weeb rushed in and stacked the bases in the corner. Always out of breath and erratic with energy, he ran up to Norm and squealed, "Jesus Christ, Norm, you did every fucking thing fucking perfect." He pummeled Norm's arm with a flurry of harmless jabs.

"Hey Miller," Billy Hendricks, the tall senior first baseman, came in and called out to Weeb. "Graber says you forgot the fucking first-aid kit."

"Shit. Shit," Weeb muttered as he ran off.

Norm looked around at his teammates' grimy faces limned with sweat and their sun-reddened eyes, and a jolt went through him. Suddenly he understood why wars were fought and how it was with buddies willing to heave themselves onto bouncing hand grenades. In here it was Audie Murphy and John Wayne and Knute Rockne. In here was the most he'd ever seen of truth and goodness and fair play. In here boys were men and the Gipper was all there was of sorrow and courage and nobody gave a fuck if his father'd been drunk for the last two weeks and out of work for years. In here there was only unity and heroes, and the weak were never trampled, but goaded gently to strength.

Weeb ran back inside with the first-aid kit and the canvas bat bag, which he dumped under the stairs. Talking all the way, he followed Norm to the toilet stalls, entering the one beside him. "Great practice, Norm! You're really firing the ball to second! You must've blocked five pitches in the dirt! Jesus Christ, Norm, I never saw you do so good. I mean it!"

In the privacy of the stall, Norm shook his head and grinned at the machine-gun rattle of the sudden laughter from the shower room, laughter he had practiced so often that now it was his laugh, too.

Billy Hendricks's voice rose over the laughter. "Hey Brady," Hendricks hollered and then snapped his towel.

"Cut it out!" Brady yelped.

Norm smiled, knowing that Brady's ass had just been stung by Billy's wet towel. The towel snapped again.

"You fucker, Hendricks!" Bobby Busco bellowed.

In the next stall Weeb's foot arched. Last week, when Hendricks snapped his towel at Weeb, he had burst into tears with the pain.

"Hey Busco," Hendricks shouted. "Tell 'em about Fermoyle's old man hitting his little brother."

"Oh yah, I couldn't believe it," Busco yelled back. "The guy was so drunk."

"Shut up!" Brady hollered. "Norm's—"

"He's gone," Hendricks shouted. "And even if he wasn't, he's such an asshole. Tell 'em!"

"I never saw anybody so far gone," Busco shouted for everyone to hear. "The guy can barely stand up, and then Fermoyle's kid brother comes along, and he's smacking him and the kid's crying, and then he takes off, so then we go over and we start shoving the asshole and saying, How come you did that. . . ."

Norm bit the inside of his cheek until it bled and then he flushed the toilet and held the handle down so Weeb wouldn't hear him gag. As the last of the water swirled down the slimy bowl, he opened the door and he heard Weeb call weakly, "Don't, Norm . . ."

He wanted Busco, but all he could see through the steam was

Billy Hendricks's dripping-wet face and the meaty splat of his lips under his fist, but then Hendricks fell and for a minute he couldn't find him in the sudden writhing steamy contortion of hairy legs and shriveled peckers, but now he had found him, was on him again, this time with both fists. He couldn't breathe. Someone was choking him, pulling him by the throat over the slimy floor.

It was Graber, Coach Graber dragging him, then dumping him against the bench where Weeb stood now, whimpering as he dabbed at his face with a towel, then jumped back with a gasp when Graber returned screaming, screaming at Norm like a woman. He grabbed his shirt, yanked him to his feet, then shoved him through the door on his hands and knees out into the dust. Graber opened the door once more to let a stricken-faced Weeb out to his friend. The door opened again and he threw out Norm's glove. As the door closed, Weeb hollered, "It wasn't Norm's fault."

The door opened again and Graber's mouth opened, but before he could say a word Norm had picked up his beloved glove and flung it square and hard in the coach's ashen face. Graber picked up the glove and ran to the railing and whipped it at Norm's feet. "You're done! You're dead! You hear me?" Graber's voice trembled down.

Norm kicked aside the glove. "Fuck you, Graber," he roared as Weeb grabbed the glove and tried to hustle him away.

H e was in the backyard hanging the dripping wash on the sagging clothesline. His mother had called from work with a list of chores to do before she got home. This was his last task. Now as he stuck clothespins on the corners of the towel, he glanced toward the large wooden box where Louie and his dog crouched so Mrs. Klubock wouldn't see them over here. Louie was telling him about a second-grade girl who'd wet her pants in school today. This was a great fear of Louie's. He was always talking about someone who'd wet their pants in front of everyone.

"Where's that guy?" Louie asked. "The one yesterday." He looked toward the garage.

"I don't know," Benjy said. "Took off, I guess."

"My mother saw him go in your house. She said nobody goes in your house," Louie said.

"Sure they do. Lots of people do."

"I never do," Louie said.

"You're too young." Benjy reached into the basket for Norm's undershirt.

"How old do I have to be?" Louie asked.

"Ten."

"I can go in when I'm ten?" Louie looked pleased.

"Yup," Benjy said. He had run out of clothespins. He looked on the ground for some. Whatever fell in this yard stayed there. Next to the wooden box that the washing machine had come in three years ago was a bent aluminum lawn chair, its torn webbing shredded and embedded in the tall grass. A thin waxy slip of poison ivy was entwined around one of the legs.

Along the dark eastern side of the house, where once there had been a split-rail fence, now two bleached posts were all that stood. The rest, poles and rails, were rotting somewhere beneath the bramble of honeysuckle and wild juniper of the advancing woods from which had already crept, dark and unnoticed, a fibrous vine thick as a rope, up the rusted drainspout, then up along the roof, its hairy tentacles rooted in the curled brittle shingles that flashed the crooked chimney. Next to the chimney, dangling from Benjy's bedroom window with the tenuity of a tree's last leaf, was a black shutter, the only one left on the house, its last touch of ornament.

Benjy returned to the clothesline with three spongy, muddy clothespins. With one he pinned five washcloths, and with another a bunch of cleaning rags, and with the third, he hung his mother's two white blouses together by the collars. The clothesline creaked, then sagged closer to the ground. He caught the pole just in time. He looked up to see Norm coming down the driveway. His eyes were red and puffy, and one side of his face was streaked with dirt.

"You little faggot!" Norm growled. "C'mere! You get in here!"

"Norm! I can't! The—" Benjy was trying to explain as he braced up the clothesline, but Norm flung his glove at him and growled, "I want to talk to you! Now!" He stormed inside and slammed the door.

"He's mad at you!" Louie whispered from the box. Just then the dog darted out and snagged Norm's big webbed, deeply oiled glove, then rolled on its back, whipping the glove from side to side.

"Louie!" Benjy called. With both hands supporting the line there was nothing he could do. "Get the glove!"

But the dog was already on its feet and trotting toward the woods with Louie scrambling after him. At the edge of the yard Louie froze.

"Get him!" Benjy called, but Louie wasn't allowed to leave the yard, so Benjy let go of the sopping-wet line, and before it had even hit the ground, he was running after the dog, calling to it, panting, begging it to stop, come back, drop the glove. "Please! Please! Please!" he cried as he ran. But the dog was gone. He had lost him.

The dog, ears perked back, head slung low, ran with a mighty speed, disappearing into the woods, galloping some distance until it came to the rich ooze of the lower banks of Moon Brook, foul with runoff from the pig farm and the dump. Suddenly the dog stopped. It sniffed the air, then turned and crept deep into a viny thicket. Here in the dark earthen coolness, it lay down panting, its drooling muzzle on the soft glove while it watched the man's quiet quiet body.

Benjy was confused. Norm acted as if the drunken scene outside school yesterday had been all Benjy's fault. Norm said he should have gone the other way the minute he saw him. Benjy said that he had tried to. Then he shouldn't have talked to the asshole. Benjy said that he hadn't really. "But you were there," Norm exploded. "Don't you see? Don't you get it?"

He didn't, and yet he did. Somehow he was culpable. Everyone was. Everyone but his father, whose condition, whose very nature absolved him of responsibility.

They were eating dinner now and every time Norm looked at him, he felt sick inside. He'd really hate him when he found out about his glove, Benjy thought. Alice asked where the salesman had gone, but their mother interrupted to ask Norm about the street department job interview with Jarden Greene. Norm said he hadn't made it to town hall today. She put down her fork and for a moment seemed to be smiling. Relieved, Benjy smiled too. "What, what do you mean, you didn't make it? You didn't feel like it? You didn't have time?" She kept hitting the table. "Or maybe you've got something better, is that it?"

"I got held up," Norm said. "But I'm going tomorrow, I promise."

"Right after school!" she said, seeming disarmed by his earnest gaze.

"Right after school," Norm said.

"You damn well better," she warned.

"I said I would," Norm said softly. He smiled. "And I will."

"Make sure you do," she said, her chin out.

Benjy was shocked. The big game was tomorrow, but he didn't dare remind Norm for fear he'd ask about the glove.

"Where's that Mr. Duvall?" Alice asked again, her cheeks red and irritated-looking. Her lips were chapped and her eyes were bright and her blouse was inside out.

"I have no idea," their mother sighed, looking toward the back door. "Probably got his car back and now he's on his way."

"Weird guy." Alice sighed with a distant little smile as she pushed food around her plate. "A traveling salesman! Can you imagine!"

Marie looked quickly at Alice, her eyes narrowing. "Where'd you go after school?"

"Oh"—Alice shrugged—"around. You know . . . stopped in to see Mrs. Stoner, and I was looking for a job, of course. Before I saw Mrs. Stoner. . . ."

"Where'd you go? What places?" Marie interrupted.

Benjy and Norm watched their mother lay the trap. They watched Alice stumble toward it.

"Some stores."

"What stores?"

"The Taylor Shop and then Pilgrim's." She shrugged.

"With your blouse inside out?" Marie said, the words forced through lips of wire.

Alice's hand flew across her chest. "Oh no!" she said, her face reddening as she looked up at them. "It must've been like this all day. Ever since this morning."

Marie got up and picked up her plate. "No, it hasn't," she said, staring down at Alice. "When you left, it was on right."

After dinner, Norm said he'd be in his room studying for the two finals he had tomorrow. And then he'd be going to bed. The radio played loudly in his room and Marie called up twice for him to turn it down.

Alice was taking a bath. The sweet steam of soap, shampoo, and talcum powder seeped under the bathroom door. Benjy didn't know why wearing a shirt inside out was so bad, but Alice and his mother still weren't speaking.

His mother had set up the ironing board in the kitchen doorway so she could see the television. Benjy watched from the couch. Milton Berle was under a sheet on an operating table. Every time the doctors and nurses touched him, he giggled. His mother laughed and Benjy smiled. Though he didn't think Milton Berle was very funny, he loved watching this show with his mother because it made her so happy. She held up Norm's ironed shirt and put it on a hanger. She paused now as Milton Berle ran around the operating room in his hospital johnny with the doctors and nurses chasing him. Suddenly Norm's radio blared so loudly that they couldn't hear the show. Marie sent Benjy upstairs to tell Norm to turn it down. When he opened the door the lights were on, and the bed was covered with textbooks and folders and papers, but Norm was gone. The window was open. Benjy turned down the radio and hurried back downstairs.

"Is he still studying?" his mother asked.

"I guess so."

"I don't know how he can think with all that racket," she said as she unrolled a wet towel on the arm of the couch. She shook out another damp starched shirt. The iron hissed as she pressed it into the collar. Benjy squirmed, wishing he'd turned the radio off. What if it got loud again and she went up herself?

"God, he's funny!" she said, shaking her head, as a new skit began. Milton Berle wore a wig and a dress as he battered a policeman with a purse. The audience screeched with laughter. Leaning over the ironing board, Benjy's mother hugged herself and laughed until there were tears in her eyes.

He smiled uneasily. *Be careful,* he was thinking. *Be careful.*

"He's so funny!" she gasped.

Outside, a car had just pulled into the driveway. Klubocks' dog was barking. The rap on the door was hard and curt. His mother opened the front door, which was beside the television, so in an odd way it seemed to Benjy that he was watching two screens, two shows. There was a Pepsodent ad now on one screen with a toothbrush dancing around a tube of toothpaste, while in the other stood Billy Hendricks with head bowed and a swollen lip he kept touching. Beside him was Mr. Hendricks, who still wore his mailman's uniform.

"Oh," Marie said, stepping directly in front of them, making it clear they couldn't come in. "It's you, Eddy. The light's broken. . . ."

"We just came from the dentist, Marie. Billy here's got to have a new cap made and I know times are tough right now, but it seems to me fair's fair, which is how I brung my boys up, so your Norm's the one ought to be responsible now, Marie, because a lesson lived is a lesson learned, I always say. And believe me, I know how hard it is for—"

"Eddy! What're you talking about?" she finally broke in.

"His cap," Mr. Hendricks said, nudging his son. He was nervous. "Show her . . . show her!" Mr. Hendricks ordered until Billy opened his mouth, revealing the black gap of a missing front tooth.

Just then, Alice came out of the bathroom in her old red chenille bathrobe with its raised white roses on the pockets. Her wet hair dripped onto her shoulders. "Oh!" she said when she saw Billy, his lip being stretched up now by his father, who was pointing at the damage and explaining that Dr. Yale had promised a rush job so it would look all right for graduation. "Agh . . . agh," Billy groaned, pushing away his father's hand.

"Oh, hi," Alice muttered, turning her head. Looking just as miserable, Billy muttered "Hi." She ran so fast up the stairs that she tripped on her bathrobe and fell forward. Benjy stared down at the floor.

"Norm!" Marie called. "Get Norm," she said through clenched teeth.

He closed his eyes on his way upstairs, praying, hoping that Norm had climbed back in through the window.

"Bastard," his mother groaned, flying past him into the room. "Where is he? Where the hell is he?" she cried, turning in a bewildered little circle. She ran to the window and looked out, and then she locked it. "He'll pay," she cried, kneeling by Norm's bed and reaching under the mattress. "Damn right he'll pay," she said, pulling out Norm's thirty-one dollars. Benjy couldn't believe she'd do that. That money was for the used car Norm wanted. For the past year he had saved every penny that came his way.

At ten o'clock, Norm still wasn't home. Marie sat on the couch staring at the door, waiting.

Alice lay in bed. She saw the lights go out in the Klubocks' upstairs windows and she stroked her thigh, imagining Mrs. Klubock in a sheer nylon gown opening her soft arms to Mr. Klubock.

In his room Benjy heard the first clink. Clink clink clink from the backyard. Then louder and more insistent. *Clink! Clink clink!* He crept to the foot of his bed and with his cheek against the cool wood of the window frame, he could see the tall white-suited form of Omar Duvall, bracing the clothesline while he pounded the metal pole into the wet night earth with a rock, down deeper and deeper.

At ten o'clock, Weeb Miller peeled his father's white-and-coral Pontiac out of the weedy gully where they'd spent the last hour drinking and waiting for parkers. They threw their empty cans out the window, and Norm unwrapped three sticks of gum for himself, Weeb, and Tommy Mullins, who sat in back, his huge arms hanging over the front seat between Weeb and Norm.

"Sit back!" Weeb hollered. "For chrissakes all I can see in the mirror's your fat face, Mullins!"

Tommy laughed. Instead of sitting back he lowered his head, digging his chin into the top of the seat.

"That's no good!" Weeb groaned, and so Tommy laid the side of his head on the back of the seat. Norm laughed. Mullins was a hopeless creep, but his father owned the bakery and he always had money. When they couldn't get beer out of Weeb's father's refrigerator in the garage, they always picked up Mullins to buy it for them from Mrs. Carper up in the Flatts.

"So what do you think, Norm?" Weeb said, once again bringing up tomorrow's game. "It's worth a try anyway." All night long, Weeb had been after him to have his mother's boss, Ferdinand Briscoe, call Coach Graber like he had the last time Norm got in trouble for fighting. "At least ask him," Weeb said, his voice getting whiny. "Graber'd eat shit if Briscoe said to." Mr. Briscoe supplied Saint Mary's with free baseball uniforms.

"Hey"—Norm laughed—"I just don't give a shit." And right now he didn't. Not after six beers. Plus he'd rather miss the game than have his mother find out he'd been kicked off the team again.

"You give a shit," Tommy Mullins said. " 'Course you give a shit."

They both looked back at him. This was none of Mullins's business. Mullins shook a cigarette from his pack and offered it to Norm, who was about to say he was in training. Instead he lit it with a deep satisfying drag. Norm turned up the radio. Ricky Nelson was singing "It's Late." Weeb reached under the seat for his drumsticks, which he beat on the wheel, dashboard, and windshield as he drove. Tommy sang loudly. He knew the words to every song, and he had a loud catchy voice Norm envied. Norm put his head back with his eyes closed while he smoked. He was thinking of Alice with her blouse inside out and the horrible look on her face as their mother bore down on her. Jesus Christ, sometimes he thought they were all nuts. Sometimes all he wanted was to get as far away as he could from this whole fucking disaster his life was turning into. He thought of Billy Hendricks's startled, flattened face, and he turned toward the open window and couldn't help smiling.

When they got to the 4-Clover Bowling Lanes, Weeb's father's team was still bowling, so they headed in to watch. Norm caught their reflection in the plate-glass window. Their walk was the same, thumbs tucked into their side pockets and on their faces a scowl that was supposed to be menacing, but instead came off looking peevish.

He saw his uncle Renie bowling inside. He was afraid his uncle might say something about the job interview at town hall. If he did get the job, he didn't want everyone knowing it had been with the help of a creep like Renie LaChance. He hung back in the doorway and watched Uncle Renie's short thick body approach the lane. Nervously, Renie kept wiping his hand on the sides of his pants. Then he wiped his brow and, taking the ball, went into a frantic running delivery that wobbled the ball along the edge of the lane, missing every pin. Someone laughed. Asshole, Norm thought as his uncle tried again, rolling the ball into an erratic spin that sank into the gutter halfway down the lane. Renie wiped his hands on his pants as he hurried back to his seat. When he sat down, none of the men spoke to him. Renie smiled happily, watching each man get up, and when his team did well, he shook his fist in the air and hollered to no one in particular.

While Weeb and Tommy stood behind Mr. Miller's team, Norm waited by the desk, watching Bernadette Mansaw up on her platform, where she gave out shoes and, when they were returned, sterilized and buffed them.

Bernadette was the same age as Alice, but here under the fluorescent lights she looked older, her flesh faintly lined in purple creases. Her eyelids were painted deep blue and her full mouth was a slick red. She sat on a stool smoking. She yawned and smiled at Norm, then watched the shoes pass slowly by on the conveyor belt that fed them through the sterilizing ultraviolet rays of the glass box. Every time the light in the box flashed on, it outlined the long sling of her heavy breasts in her thin white sweater that was buttoned down the back.

"League night sucks," she said, yawning again.

Norm glanced back, then realized she was talking to him. To him! The ball rolled down the alley. The pins rattled and fell with a roar from the crowd.

Bernadette sighed. "I'm glad someone's happy. I missed my ride and now I gotta walk home and I got my groceries." She nodded at the two full bags on the floor. She looked at Norm. "You waiting for somebody?"

He nodded, still chewing his gum.

"Who you waiting for?"

"My friend Weeb. Well, his father . . . Weeb's waiting, too."

"Oh." She looked disappointed. Her gaze fell dully back to the glass box. She passed another pair of shoes through, then with a chamois dipped in cream buffed their heels and toes. "The thought of walking all that way kills me," she sighed.

Norm looked back at the lanes. With all the beer and now this glare and racket, his head was starting to spin.

"They're almost done," she said, picking up another pair of shoes. "Hey, what's your name?"

"Oh yah!" she said when he told her. "You're Alice Fermoyle's brother." She ground out her cigarette in a large ashtray loaded with red-ringed butts. "I was in school with Alice. All the way to freshman year. After that I kinda quit on school. Couldn't take the nuns." She lit another cigarette. "I never could figure them out. I mean never getting married or having kids or having a good time, but Jesus Christ, lemme tell you, they got the life!" She laughed. "The voice of experience, that's two kids later talking!"

The men were coming out of the alleys, jabbing each other's arms and wiping their faces with towels. After them came Tommy and Weeb, who carried his father's duffel bag. Mr. Miller was a serious red-faced man who always looked worried. He had a government job, the nature of which Weeb had only recently confided to Norm. Mr. Miller was a venereal disease specialist with the State Health Department. Weeb said his father was afraid people might take it the wrong way. Weeb said it was mostly the kidding his father couldn't take. He said his father hated kidding, hated fooling around, especially about sex.

"See you next week, doll. . . . Take it easy, sweet lips. . . . Don't do anything I wouldn't do, unless I'm there," the men called out to Bernadette in spite of the fact that most of them had children her age.

"Yah . . . Hey . . . sure . . . you can bet on it. . . . Hey, Harry, up yours." She laughed, then whooped as Harry Temple vaulted the counter and bent her back in a swooning embrace. As she giggled and struggled to get free, Norm watched those thick fleshy breasts drag over Mr. Temple's arm. He followed Mr. Miller, Weeb, and Tommy outside. "Hey!" he heard his uncle call. "Norm! Hey, that's my nephew there! Quite a baseball player, that one . . ."

"Norm!" Mr. Miller said, getting into the car. Norm was already in back with Tommy. "That's your uncle calling." Norm waved as Weeb pulled out. "Renie's an alternate," Mr. Miller said. "Somebody couldn't come."

They drove with all the windows open to flush out the smell of beer. Weeb told his father they were going back to Norm's house and try to cram one more history chapter in before tomorrow's final.

"Good luck, men," Mr. Miller said, giving them the thumbs-up sign as he got out of the car. With his long, straight stride up the moonlit path to his front door, he looked like the officer he'd been in the war. Weeb said his father had a scar from his groin to his neck that was purple and lumpy and throbbed in cold weather. Norm had told Weeb that his father had been wounded in the war too, but then when Weeb didn't ask him about it, he felt like an asshole for lying.

As soon as Mr. Miller was in the house, they burst out laughing and turned on the radio as loud as it would go. Fats Domino was singing "Blueberry Hill," and with Weeb rapping his sticks all over the inside of the car and Mullins singing, they headed back toward West Street along the route Norm said Bernadette Mansaw would be taking.

"What'd she say?" Mullins asked.

"It's not what she said," Norm said, his heart a strange pinching beat in his chest. "It's what she wants." He scanned the sidewalks ahead.

"What's she want?" Weeb asked, his voice pitching recklessly high the way it did whenever girls or sex was the subject.

"Me," Norm laughed. "She fucking wants me!"

"She's fucking married!" Mullins gasped.

"She's not fucking married," Weeb said.

"Well, she's got two fucking kids," Mullins said.

"So?" Norm laughed.

"And her boyfriend's a fucking convict. He's in fucking jail!" Mullins said. "And his fucking brother's Blue fucking Mooney!"

"Holy shit, that's right," Weeb said, turning down the radio. "Norm, I don't want to—"

"There she is!" Norm yelled. "There she fucking is!"

Ahead, teetering along the dark sidewalk on stiletto heels, her beehive hair swaying, her small round hips churning, her arms hugging two grocery bags, was Bernadette Mansaw, seventeen-year-old legend.

"Slow down . . . slow down!" Norm cried with a jab in Weeb's ribs that made him yelp. "Want a ride?" he called out the window.

"Oh shit, do I ever! Am I happy to see you!" Bernadette groaned.

Norm made a squealing noise, and in the back seat, Tommy Mullins giggled as Bernadette climbed eagerly into the front between Norm and Weeb. She smelled of leather and shoe polish. Norm put his arm over the back of the seat, his fist nudging Weeb, who stared over the wheel, his mouth fixed in a foolish smile as they cruised along.

Bernadette lived across from the post office, above a fruit and vegetable store. To get to her apartment she had to go down the alley and then climb an exterior flight of wooden stairs.

"I can get 'em . . . I got 'em," she said, backing out of the car with her groceries.

"No sir," Norm insisted. "Those're too heavy. You'll hurt yourself."

"You might get a hernia," Weeb called out the window. "Let Norm carry them."

"Yah," Mullins chimed in. "Old Norm'll be glad to."

Her apartment was at the end of a damp black corridor lined with boxes and fruity-smelling crates.

"So you got kids," Norm said as she unlocked the door. She turned on the light. Her apartment was small and surprisingly neat. The stove and refrigerator were on the wall opposite a red couch that was already pulled out and made up into a bed with sheets and a spread.

"Yah, I got kids all right," she sighed. "Two, Merry and Noelle.

They're both Christmas babies." She took the bags from him and set them on the table.

He wasn't sure what to do next. "Well," he said somberly. "It was nice uh, carrying your bags. . . . Unh, I guess I better go."

She was taking cans and boxes out of the bags. "Hey, want a drink or something?" She looked in one of the bags. "This week I got root beer. It was on special." She dropped ice cubes into a glass and poured in root beer. After she gave it to him, she kicked off her shoes and reached back to undo the top two buttons of her sweater, then continued to unload her groceries.

"Good root beer," he said, wiping froth from his mouth. She was so short he looked down on the crown of her head.

"If you want some more, help yourself."

With trembling hands he poured more into the glass. He went to drink and his teeth clinked against the rim. He wondered if she'd charge him anything. He'd heard the guys she liked were free. He stayed close by the table, where she was checking the register slip against the items she'd unpacked. He thought of his thirty-one dollars. No. No, he wanted his car too much. Maybe she'd let him pay a little at a time.

"Hey, Norm." She looked up from the slip.

"Yah!" He winced, knowing he'd sounded too eager.

"What's three for eighty-nine if you only get one?"

"One what?" His voice cracked in his dry tight throat.

"Tomato juice."

"Thirty," he said, his heart thudding with her approach.

She handed him the register slip. "What's that one, two for sixty-nine if I only got one?"

"Twenty. I mean, thirty-five!" he said, staring down at the beads of sweat on the back of her neck.

"Well, thanks," she said, looking up. "Thanks a hell of a lot." She patted her hair and groaned. "I was beat, lemme tell you. Lately, I been working my tail off and I'm just beat all the time." She grinned. "You waiting for something? A tip or something?" she said, giggling.

"Oh no! I'm just leaving," he said, his tongue growing heavy. "I'm just going."

"You're cute," she said, pulling his head down as her mouth covered his. "Okay?" she murmured, holding his face in her hands, and he nodded, but it wasn't okay. He wanted more. This time he kissed her, running his hands up and down her back, squirming against her, moaning, his eyes closed so that he never saw the door swing open.

Blue Mooney stood in the unlit doorway in his black pants, black T-shirt, black boots. Only his yellow hair and pale flesh gave any light through the darkness. In each arm he carried a sleepy-eyed child. The older girl, a redhead with pale blue eyes, leaned forward with her arms outstretched, crying, "Mommy, Mommy!"

"Your ma said their pants're . . ." Mooney said, then peered closely. "What the . . . Who the hell's . . . Bernie!" he bellowed as she shoved Norm away.

Just then, from the hallway came a roar as a stack of empty orange crates crashed to the floor. In one motion, Mooney set both children down and darted into the hallway, then returned a second later clutching Weeb and Mullins. He shoved them at Norm and they staggered into one another.

"Son of a bitch!" Mooney snarled, his square jaw set, his sharp lower teeth exposed. "You ever come up here again, I'll break your fucking legs and then I'll break your fucking arms . . ."

They were running out the door and down the creaking wooden stairs, and they could still hear his voice: ". . . and then I'll break your fucking back and then I'll break your . . ."

Benjy dreamed. He dreamed clear dreams of such detail that they seemed more real than life itself. He dreamed that the man in the white suit was still outside, hammering and sawing, raising the rotted fence posts and laying on the rails, and tearing out the rooted vines and weedy trees with his bare hands, and every now and then his sighs stirred the night like a breeze through the leaves and curtains. He did not stop. In the cool night dirt, he dug and he raked and he dug and he raked, his soft leather shoe working the shovel like a spotless gloved hand, digging and raking, all night long, smoothing, sculpting the yard to the symmetry of a garden in bloom, fragrant and densely green with broad dark leaves that curled and swayed like fans, and tiny white blossoms and blue bell-like flowers that bobbed, and through the tender white roots worms burrowed, and a hard cold snail inched its way up each stem and down each leaf. Its shell was white in the moonlight and its probing eyes at the end of the soft gray feelers were as blue as the morning sky.

Benjy's eyes opened wide. Doors were slamming. Windows were closing. Norm was home.

"That's my money!" Norm bellowed. "You can't do that! You can't just take my money!"

"No! Not me, but you and your godddamn bullheaded temper, that's what took your money! And for sneaking out of the house you can't go out for two weeks."

"Two weeks!" Norm cried.

"Two weeks, mister, and I don't want to hear another word," she shouted.

When she had gone to bed, he could hear Norm sobbing in his room, and Benjy realized that it wasn't just the money, but his glove. That must be where he'd gone tonight. Benjy felt terrible. Norm had been out all this time trying to find his glove for tomorrow's game.

No one was speaking. Benjy and Norm were eating breakfast when the back door creaked open. "Good morning, folks!" Omar Duvall called heartily. "And oh what a beautiful morning it is!" He had a stubble of whiskers and his suit was soiled and frayed. In the true north light he seemed much older. Wrinkles outlined his eyes, and his hair looked white at the roots, silvery white as if in a night he had lived twenty years.

"I got just so far," Omar was telling Benjy's mother, who had hurried into the kitchen at the sound of his voice, "and it was dark and this terrible feeling came over me. . . ." His voice lowered. "I felt like I couldn't breathe, like if I took one more step"—he sighed—"one more, and I would surely die."

"You were probably exhausted," she said nervously. "All the commotion you've been through."

"I have passed through a torrent, through a water unsupportable," Duvall drawled in a strange monotone. He stared at her. "And the snare, the snare is broken."

The two brothers looked at each other. "Holy shit," Norm said under his breath. Benjy couldn't tell if his mother was clearing her throat or laughing nervously, or both.

"There's more toast," she said. "And there's coffee. Would you like some?"

"Oh this is wonderful!" Duvall cried, already chewing. "This is truly wonderful!"

"It's just regular bread," she said.

"I mean just being alive!" With his rising voice the very air seemed to darken and swell, the way air does before a storm. "And being here with all of you!"

The woman lived in her dining room in an enormous crib with hinged, slatted sides. This was Bridget Fermoyle. At the foot of the crib there was a massive buffet that had once contained platters and linens and silver, and now was stocked with huge diapers, baby oil, cotton balls, and her pastel bed jackets. A large mahogany mirror hung over the buffet.

Once again Bridget had no choice but to watch the old woman in that mirror. So homely, she thought. The old woman in the mirror had no teeth and her skin creped in dry folds over sharp bones and blue veins. Bridget watched her daughter, Helen, feeding the old woman mush on a spoon. Helen patted the dribbles that leaked down the woman's chin. Helen and the housegirl, Jozia Menka, used to set the old woman on a bedpan. But a few years ago they had fractured her shoulder lifting her, so now they pinned big diapers around her skeletal hips. Since then Bridget had been spared the horrible sight of the old woman perched atop the bedpan, blinking and grunting, her wizened face reddening like a child's as she strained.

Today was a better day. Today she could see better. The vapors were gone. Today the voices were clear, not staticky and run-together. But the words still confused her. She recognized them, but could not always recall their meanings. It was the same with faces: like this grim-eyed daughter spooning mush into the mirror. What was her name? Bridget watched the old woman clamp her mouth shut to the raised spoon.

"Open," her daughter said wearily.

The old woman in the mirror pointed at Bridget's daughter. "Sam?" the old woman said, then gulped as the spoon spilled into her mouth.

No, Bridget thought. *Not Sam. Not Sam. Don't say that! She gets mad.* And sure enough, her daughter's head drew back with a sigh of disgust.

"Helen, Mother. It's Helen, your daughter, who feeds you and washes you and changes your diapers." As she spoke, she shaved mush from the old woman's chin with the edge of the spoon. "It's Helen, who cooks and slaves for a husband who brings home a handful of change from his store and dares tell me they're the week's receipts. It's Helen, who hides her drunken brother's bottles and cleans up his vomit and can't hold her head up in public and—"

"Sammy?" the old woman in the mirror said hopefully, raising a hand to the daughter's.

Helen's eyes closed. "Oh Mother," she sighed. "Why did you do this to me? I'm so sick of it. And now with the Judge dead it's all up to me."

Bridget watched her daughter take the old woman's bony hand and hold it against her cheek.

"All I'm trying to do is what you wanted, Mother. But I'm so tired," she whispered.

Bridget picked up her sock doll and hummed softly. She was tired of the old woman and her bitter daughter, whose voice grew garbled and staticky. She hugged her doll and looked out the window at the locust tree. When Sam was little he used to climb to the top of that tree. Sometimes when everything was just exactly right, she could see him there still.

W ell, here it was noon with the gentlest of June breezes like fingers up and down his shirt back. Noon, and for twenty-four hours Omar Duvall had been free of them. Free! He felt so free he actually had to take deep breaths just to weight his feet to the pavement; so free, he was thinking now, he probably shouldn't have told that woman and her children his name. He should've taken a new one, a name like Bart Truedell. Truedell had been his mother's name, a good honest American name, the kind of name for the kind of man who'd make this country great.

Ahead on the sidewalk was a young red-haired woman in a peach dress. She swung a bowling bag as she walked toward him. He smiled and she smiled back. He winked and saw the blood rise in her freckled cheeks. Yes, he thought, continuing along, he was that kind of man, the kind who could sell toothpicks one day and combustion engines the next, the kind of man for whom the marketplace was America's last frontier, a virgin vastness of such hope and possibility that for a moment now his eyes blurred with tears as he stared at the street sign. Now, that meant something. Main Street, the very heart of America. He looked at the park across the street with its tall elms and its white globe gas lamps and its lovely round bandstand. What he did not notice were the rutted tracks scarred through the grass, because he turned suddenly when he saw the hand-lettered cardboard sign tacked to the porch rail of the old brown house.

ROOM TO LET.

He hurried across the street. He didn't even see May Mayo, still as a bird in the dusty porch shadows, until he was on the top step.

"Hello," she whispered, the blue wash of her hair pale as her eyes. She twisted a hankie in her lap, weaving it tightly between her fingers. "I thought we had another hour," she said, mistaking him for one of the Mounts from the funeral home. She started to get up. "I'll get Claire."

"How much is the room?" he asked, motioning her back into the rocker.

"Ten a week," she said so softly he could barely hear her. "Fifteen with board."

"I'm a clean-living man," he said, squatting next to her, and tall as he was, she had to look down into his eyes. "A man of religion," and seeing the flinch in her gaze, he explained, "that is to say, of faith, of faith in my fellow man. Because of my lifetime of diplomatic assignments, I have been everywhere, lived everywhere, seen so much hoopla and exotica that all I want now's a quiet little room on a quiet street in a quiet town, far, far from the dangers of communism," he said, laying the ten-dollar bill in her hand. "I have family in town. Distant family that's begging me to move in, and so as not to affront their generosity completely, I will be taking meals at their table. Thank you," he said, rising now and taking her hand in his. "Thank you, kind lady."

After school Benjy headed down the hill on the way to the store where his mother worked. She had errands for him to run. Like the streets downtown, Briscoe's Sporting Goods was empty. Benjy came through the vacant aisles, his footsteps the only sounds in the store. With his hands jammed into his pockets he glanced up at the second level to the glassed-in walls of Mr. Briscoe's office. He was surprised to see mirrors in place of the glass. Now it would be so much easier, he thought. Before when he had taken things, it had always been from the warehouse, never from the store. Ahead on the right aisle was the baseball display. If no one was around he could get a glove for Norm. But he didn't dare. Mr. Briscoe might be down any one of these aisles, and besides, taking something from the store really would be stealing. Tennis balls and badminton birdies and fishing flies from the boxes out back were one thing, but a catcher's mitt right off the counter, with a price tag—no, that was too expensive, too planned. He put it back on the counter.

He continued to the back of the store, through the warehouse, toward his mother's office, a windowless cubicle she shared with Astrid, the part-time bookkeeper. Astrid's slurpy voice and the steady tap of a typewriter filled the dim warehouse like gray rain. Directly under Mr. Briscoe's office, he paused. The windows on this side had also been replaced with mirrors. He looked around at all the cartons and wooden crates. One entire wall was lined with bicycle boxes. He proceeded slowly, hands clenched in his pockets, eyes scanning labels on the stacked boxes. His last time in here, he'd gotten Norm a jar of cream to rub on his glove. While Norm professed dismay with his thievery, he always kept what Benjy brought him. It had come to be their punishment for Briscoe's underpaying their mother. Whenever there were loose tennis balls he always took a couple for Klubocks' dog.

"It was just three couples," Astrid was saying. His mother's office had no ceiling, only walls, and a frosted-glass door. He knew his mother must be glad Mr. Briscoe couldn't look down into the office anymore. As much as she admired Mr. Briscoe's keen business sense, she thought he was too nosy. "Some people from the wire plant," Astrid continued. His mother's typewriter never stopped. "Well to hear him, you'd think I'd invited the whole town."

The phone rang once. The typing stopped and his mother's musical store-voice answered, "Briscoe's Sporting Goods. Yes, we carry them, but Jake's not on the floor right now. . . . That's right. . . . He's at the Judge's funeral. . . . Call back around four." His mother resumed typing.

"I think we drank maybe three six-packs total." Astrid sighed. "The thing is, because he's older, he thinks I'm always comparing him to younger guys." There was a pause and then she giggled. "And I keep telling him, 'No, Bobby, it's you I want, you and all your money.' "

The typing continued. His mother never said a word. Astrid better watch it, he thought as he opened the door.

Astrid grinned at him. "Hey! Look who's here!" she laughed. "My favorite boyfriend!" She winked, snapping her gum as her fingers darted over the adding-machine buttons. A long roll of paper unfurled to the floor. Astrid was small; a woman's body at child's height. Her harlequin glasses flashed with rhinestone chips. Her teased and sprayed hair seemed an aureole of spun glass. Her skin was lovely, so clear, so moist it glistened. He loved looking at her.

Certainly she was the most exotic woman he had ever known. She had started working here last fall. His mother said she wouldn't last very long, that she was out of her element in this dull little town, a Las Vegas showgirl married to a homely insurance man old enough to be her father.

"Just a minute, Benjy," his mother said. Here, she acted different; she never swore or banged things in anger. Like the pleasant voice that had just answered the phone, this smile was seen only here, set with a calmness that looked almost painful. Only her eyes betrayed her; boiling and quick, they probed him like fingers. Compared with Astrid, his mother looked tired and plain. He waited by the desk while she finished typing a letter. "She'll be right with you, honey. Your mom's a champ, a real champ. 'Course what she needs is a little fun." Astrid gave a rueful laugh. "Don't we all. I mean, you'd think three couples was a mob or something."

It was a moment before he realized she was talking to his mother again. After each phrase she slurped saliva in through her teeth. In a picture she'd shown his mother she was dressed in a skimpy black costume, spike heels, and a little white apron. It had been a year ago in Las Vegas that she met Bob Haddad one night and married him the next. Benjy had seen them together recently and he'd been shocked at how homely Haddad seemed, how dark and loutish next to Astrid's clear pink skin and silvery hair. She had a brand-new convertible and she wore outrageously glamorous clothes for a place like Atkinson. People said Bob Haddad was going crazy trying to please her. He'd bought her a new house and new furniture. Astrid claimed she did part-time bookkeeping here and at the wire plant just to keep busy and meet people, but his mother said the word around town was that Bob Haddad was deeply in debt. Benjy knew a lot of odd facts like that about adults in town. Alice said it was because their mother had no friends, no one else to talk to but her children.

"So now he says no more parties. He says we got to get more serious about life. More serious! If he gets any more serious, I tell him, he'll be dead. You can't get much more serious than dead, huh, kid?" She winked. Her fingers tapped, the rings sparkling as they flew. "Everything's such a goddamn calamity, you know . . ."

When Marie finished typing she opened her desk drawer and took out a paper bag. The broken washing machine dial was in it.

". . . like this thing up in the park," Astrid continued, "the blind man's popcorn stand. So what if it looks shitty. So what if it's gonna fall down! Who cares! Who the hell cares!"

"Bring it to Uncle Renie," his mother was saying, so inured to Astrid's monologues that she hadn't bothered to apologize. "Tell him if it's not one thing wrong, it's another, and I'm sick of it!"

Astrid glanced their way. "Yah! And that goes ditto for me, too!"

"Remind him this is the eighth time in two years that washing machine's broken down on me!"

"Yah! And don't take any crap from him, either, kid!" Astrid grinned.

"Astrid!" his mother said, her voice tight. "Would you please shut up!"

He cringed, afraid his mother would start screaming the way she did at home.

"I was tryna help!" Astrid said. "That's all. . . ."

"Well I wouldn't do this to you if you were in the middle of a conversation," his mother said.

"Well I wouldn't care if you did," Astrid said, pouting. "I wouldn't get all worked up!" Her voice grew whiny and small. "I wouldn't say anything to hurt your feelings. You think you're the only one with problems. Well you're not!" She stood up so suddenly that her chair flew back. "Other people have problems too, you know!" she shouted, slamming the door behind her. The cubicle's walls shook.

His mother had been staring down at the desk. She took a deep breath, then looked up, her eyes as flat as her voice. For a moment he had a sense that, like him, she had another life and this other life was a terrible burden sometimes. "You tell Uncle Renie he either fixes the timer or gives me a new washing machine, okay?"

"Okay," he said, knowing he could never say any of it.

"Benjy!" she called when he was at the door.

"Yah?" He started back. His toes curled in his shoes. Was it the lost glove?

"Oh, nothing," she said, gesturing him off. "Just . . . just . . . if Mr. Duvall comes to the house, would you call me?" she said thinly, breathlessly, hopefully. "I want to be sure I have food . . . if he comes, that is. I asked him, but he never really said."

He hurried through the warehouse to avoid Astrid, who must have run into the bathroom. The toilet kept flushing. He squinted now as he entered the store, blindingly bright with its fluorescent lights and shelves of colored boxes and glass cases of hunting knives and pistols. In the middle of the store, dangling by nylon wires from the ceiling, was an orange rubber life raft. As he passed underneath, it rocked gently as if on invisible waves. At the baseball display he stopped. There, heaped on the counter, were baseball gloves of every size and shape, and right on the very edge was a soft lustrous catcher's mitt exactly like Norm's. Opening his bookbag he tapped the glove into it, then ran to the front of the store. He grinned as his hand closed on the cold brass handle.

"Hold it!" a voice boomed from above, from everywhere. "Hold it! Hold it right there!"

He turned. Overhead a mirror slid open. Mr. Briscoe leaned out from the waist and pointed down at him. "You wait right there, young man! Don't you dare move!"

It took Mr. Briscoe a few minutes to get down into the store. He was a portly man, red-faced and always panting. By the time Mr. Briscoe reached him, Benjy realized he should have put the glove back on the counter, but now it was too late. Mr. Briscoe had just retrieved it from his bag. He held it up and rocked back on his heels.

"You didn't have to do this, son. No boy ever has to steal from Briscoe's. Especially you, Benjy. Why'd you do this?"

His eyes fixed in terror on the door into the warehouse. He expected to see his mother charge through it, her face white, eyes wide, her fists swinging.

"You want this glove?" Mr. Briscoe asked, holding it out to him.

He shook his head no. He could not speak. He could barely breathe.

"Take it," Mr. Briscoe said, jabbing the glove into his chest. "It's yours. You can have it!"

He shook his head, his hands heavy at his sides.

"Here!" Mr. Briscoe insisted. "Take it!" His face was getting redder. "Don't you want it?"

All he wanted was to get out of here before his mother saw him. "I'm sorry," he tried to say, but it wrung out of him like a whimper.

Mr. Briscoe tossed the glove onto the counter and sighed. "I know what it's like growing up in a house without a father. Things get all out of whack, don't they?" He touched his breast pocket. "You get this empty feeling. You want something, but you never know what." His cheeks blistered with a fine sweat as he bent closer. Benjy could almost taste the sweet cologne seeping from his pores. "Isn't that right?"

He shrugged and nodded. He was losing track of Mr. Briscoe's meaning.

"You thought you wanted a baseball glove; well, you didn't really, did you? You just wanted something. You weren't sure what, so you picked up the first thing you saw. And the whole time, all you really wanted was a friend, Benjy. That's all!" Mr. Briscoe said, his voice rising. He clapped his hands together and grinned. "And by golly willikers, young man, you've got one now!" He extended his hand, and Benjy was surprised at how hard and rough it was. "Ferdinand T. Briscoe at your disposal!" he said with a vigorous shake. "Just name your pleasure, son." Briscoe's gleaming gaze swept over the shelves and counters of merchandise. "Baseball, badminton, golf, swimming or camping, or backpacking, or fishing. Fishing!" Briscoe cried. "We'll go out in the boat."

Benjy's eyes widened in horror on the swaying orange raft.

"That's what we'll do! The perfect sport. Oh Benjy, you'll love it. We'll go fishing. Just the two of us. There's something about fishing, Benjy, a man and a boy in the middle of a great body of water . . ."

"But I can't!"

"Of course you can! I'll speak to your mother. We'll go as soon as school's out."

"No, I don't like boats."

"Don't like boats!" Briscoe cried. "What kind of a boy doesn't like boats!"

"I can't swim." To be in water over his head terrified him.

"Can't swim!" Briscoe reached down to muss his hair. "Well, you'll just have to learn how, then."

"No, I can't," he said, shaking his head. "I don't want to."

Briscoe looked at him. "I'll tell you what, you learn how to swim and I won't tell your mother about you taking the glove." He smiled and held out his hand. "How's that for a deal? Then, when you can swim, we'll go out in the boat."

As they shook hands Benjy felt sick to his stomach.

Benjy stood in front of Uncle Renie's appliance store. A billhead was taped to the door. It said:

Closed for funeral.
Please come back at 5.
I will be open an extra hour tonight to make up for any inconvenyunce.

Sorry and thank you
Yours truely,
Renie LaChance

With his cheek against the glass door, he peered into the long, narrow store. Uncle Renie's big yellow cat was asleep on top of a washing machine. He banged on the door, but the cat did not look up. "Here, kitty, kitty, kitty," he called, and still the cat did not stir. From the corner of his eye he saw the dark uniforms of two girls in his class crossing the street at the corner. He headed in the opposite direction. The minute he was out of their sight, he began to run up the hill. As he neared the park he could hear the tinny music from Joey Seldon's radio. Joey was all dressed up. He wore a gray suitcoat, pale blue pants, a white shirt, and a gold string tie. He sat on his stool, his hands in his aproned lap, his big fleshy head swaying to the music. Benjy crossed the street, passing onto the grass so he wouldn't be heard as he came by the dilapidated popcorn stand. He looked up to see Joey's head cock back, and then his hands reached out and gripped the sagging boards of his serving counter. He faced Main Street, where a black hearse turned the corner. As it approached the stand, the hearse tapped its horn lightly and Joey's hand shot to his temple in a stiff salute. His cheeks shone with tears.

Next round the corner chugged the Mayo sisters' ancient Ford, with its running boards and rumble seat. High at the wheel sat Claire Mayo, her square jaw chomping up and down, while beside her, tiny and black-veiled, was May. Her gaze never left the hearse. In the second car came all the boarders, little ladies with pastel waves and bright anxious eyes. A parade of cars followed, all flying small blue flags on their hoods. Twenty-eight, twenty-nine, Benjy counted and then in the thirty-fourth, the last car, he saw Uncle Renie, waving proudly from his old green Nash. Beside him Aunt Helen's profile was as sharp as cut stone under her black velvet cloche. She stared straight ahead.

Benjy continued through the park, where the sight of the trampled shrubs and torn-up grass shocked him. In the distance was Saint Mary's Church, its white marble spire gleaming oddly cold in the afternoon sun. Behind the church was the rectory. It was a trim white house with a ladder leaning against it. Balanced on the top rung was Howard Menka. He was brushing dirt from the black shutters. When Howard worked for Benjy's grandmother he used to give Benjy sour balls. Always soft and fuzzed with pocket lint, they would sit on his tongue like dry bitter cotton. Now that Howard worked for the Monsignor he and Benjy pretended they did not know each other. In a way being rid of Howard's awkward attention was a relief, and yet he never passed by without feeling bad about his silence. He did not turn the corner. This was his father's street and he would not walk here when his father was drinking.

The church bells rang four times and he started to run, spurred on by the sudden hope that Klubocks' dog might have retrieved the glove. Maybe it was beside him in the driveway right now or in the lilac bush, and if he ran really fast, he could get it down to the baseball field. . . .

"What's your big rush?" someone hollered. He glanced back to see Norm, his hands in his pockets as he kicked a stone along the sidewalk. His chest ached. Norm hadn't even gone to the game. Of course not. Without his glove he couldn't play. Benjy waited for the thump on the back he deserved.

"Guess who I just saw?" Norm said, catching up with him. He gave the stone a final kick into the gutter. "That peddler Duvall, walking along with a big loaf of bread under his arm."

The minute his mother got home from work Benjy told her about Uncle Renie's store being closed. "I'll bring the dial tomorrow," he promised.

She nodded absently and began peeling vegetables and chopping them into a stew that she put in the pressure cooker. Next, she made five bowls of chocolate pudding. He slipped into the front room and turned the television on low.

"Benjy!" she called from the kitchen. He took a deep breath before going in. So this was it. Mr. Briscoe must have told her. She glanced into the front room. Norm was upstairs and Alice wasn't home yet. She bent close, and his head ran with sweat. "Did Mr. Duvall call or come by?"

When he said no, she turned down the burner on the stove. She got out the stubby broom and swept the kitchen floor, and then she opened the front door and swept out dirt from the rug. She tried to straighten the lampshade but it was still crooked. She went into the bathroom, where she stayed for a long time. When she came out, her thick dark hair had been brushed flat and her lips were red with lipstick and she smelled of a heavy perfume he would always associate with the sadness of his mother's waiting. Norm had come down from his room and was sitting on the couch with Benjy.

"Did you go see about that job today?" his mother asked. She and Norm were barely speaking.

"I did," Norm said, his eyes on the television. "But town hall was closed. The Judge's funeral."

"You'll go tomorrow then?"

"Yah, I'll go tomorrow," Norm sighed.

"You damn well better," she said.

"I said I would!"

"Mr. Hendricks called me at work. He said the dentist's going to charge fifty-six dollars." She pointed at him. "That's fifty-six you pay. Not me."

"I know that!"

"Don't be so damn smart!"

"I'm not! But how come you just take Hendricks's side? How come you never asked me what happened? What am I? What do you think, I'm some jerk that goes around beating people up for no reason?" His face was red.

"I think you're a hothead!" she said, her chin out like his, her face as red in their strange commingling of pleasure and rage. "A bullhead who doesn't think, who just starts swinging!"

"Yah?" he answered with every charge. "Yah? I just walked up to Hendricks and for no reason I hit him, huh? Is that what you think?" He kept glancing at Benjy.

"That's what I think!" his mother said.

"Well then you're st . . . wrong!" Norm caught himself.

"Then tell me!"

"He said something about Dad. They were all laughing about him being drunk."

"Oh God," she sighed. "Oh God, God, God."

Out on the street, car doors began to open and bang shut. The Klubocks were having a party. It was Mr. Klubock's fortieth birthday. Mrs. Klubock was twenty-eight. Louie had told Benjy that his mother had been planning this party for a long time.

Marie stood behind the curtain with the light off, watching the cars arrive. "Some nerve," she muttered as two cars pulled in front of their house, their wheels up on the grass. "Don't give a damn about anybody else. . . ." She leaned closer to the window and quickly ran her fingers through her hair, and then he was at the door with a stick of Italian bread wrapped in white paper, still knocking as she opened the door. Sighing at the wonderful smells from her kitchen, he apologized for being late, but the most wonderful thing had happened. He'd found a room in a boardinghouse run by two old women.

"The Mayo sisters," she said, taking the bread.

"Why, yes," Omar said. "And they're letting me stay a night or two until I find work." He sighed. "Or run out of money."

"Work?" she said. "Are you looking for a job? Here? In Atkinson?"

Norm looked toward the kitchen.

"A man's got to work," Duvall sighed as he sat down at the table. "Isn't that what life's all about?"

"Asshole," Norm muttered, nudging Benjy.

"The wire plant's always hiring," she said in a rush of activity between the refrigerator, sink, and stove. "The girl I work with says they're on two shifts now. You should try there! I can tell you right where it is!" Her voice had a quick brittle ring. She had been slicing bread and putting it on a plate and now she laid a stick of butter on a chipped gold-rimmed saucer. She set them in the middle of the table.

"Well now, that's good news on a lovely night with such wondrous vapors in the air." He looked toward the stove and sniffed. "Beef Bourguignon?"

"Stew," she said with a weak shrug.

"Thank the Lord," Duvall said.

The back door squealed open and Alice came into the kitchen. His mother's head jerked around and she stared. Alice's cheeks were red and her mouth was red and sore-looking. Alice said a quick hello and tried to hurry into the front room, but Duvall called her back. She stood in the doorway, her fingers grazing her blouse front, checking each button.

"Ah," he said, smiling. "The maiden's cheeks so rouged with love that her eyes, her eyes . . ." He peered at her. "Her eyes burn holes in the blackest night."

"That's beautiful," his mother said, looking at Duvall. "Who wrote that? No, Alice, you tell us. Alice is good in English."

"I never heard it before," Alice said, and his mother looked disappointed.

"Of course not," Duvall said, buttering a slice of bread with graceful, almost loving strokes. "That is from a 'Sonnet to Love.'" He looked up at Marie and lowered his voice. "By Omar Duvall, a little-known sonnet by a littler-known poet." Still staring, he bit into the bread.

In the other room, Norm howled. "Unbelievable!" he cried. "This is the funniest show I've ever seen!"

"Who's the lucky young man?" Duvall asked over Norm's high-pitched laughter.

"Lester Stoner," Alice said, blushing.

Norm had come into the doorway. "You probably know his father," he said. "He's the police chief."

"Can't say that I've ever had the pleasure, son," Duvall said, swallowing, licking his lips, then with two fingers crimping crumbs from the corners of his mouth.

"My name's Norm," he said, frowning.

Duvall nodded. "I know that, son." He squinted, then flashed a quick smile. "Norman. Not unlike Omar. Norman . . . Omar without the *n*'s."

"Surprise!" From next door came the shout of many voices with noisemakers and clapping. "Surprise!"

Across the driveway, they all began to sing "Happy Birthday" to Harvey Klubock, who had just arrived. He stood on his back steps in his stained butcher's overalls dazedly looking into his own house at all those people, neighbors and friends of his wife, all of them dressed up, younger than he and wonderfully happy that he was another year older.

Omar Duvall had gone to the window over the sink and parted the water-stained curtain. With a quick push he lifted the window that was never opened, the window that looked directly into the Klubocks' kitchen. "Happy Birthday"—his deep rich baritone joined the singing, funneling across the driveway—"Happy Birthday, dear Harvey . . ."

"Oh don't," his mother said, reaching out with one hand but not touching him. Her face was white. "Oh please don't."

As the hot cooking air was sucked through the window, the little kitchen grew cooler.

Benjy turned off the television and closed his eyes. It sounded as if the party were right in the kitchen, as if the whole street were in there. He wondered what it would be like to have a party in his own house.

The next day after school Benjy headed downtown with the washing-machine dial in his bookbag. When he came to the park he glanced at the Mayo sisters' boardinghouse, expecting it to look different now with Omar living there, the way his own house had seemed to change with the exuberant man's presence. Last night Omar had greased the squealing door hinges and propped up the sagging back step with a brick. "It's so quiet," Benjy's mother had said, opening and closing the door. "I can't believe all it took was a little lard."

"Ingenuity, my dear. It's my stock-in-trade," he had said with a wink.

Maybe Omar was in there now, doing little jobs for the Mayo sisters. It gave him the creeps to think of Omar sleeping in the same room where the Judge had died. He stared at the second-floor window. Maybe even in the same bed! As he crossed the street, he remembered the black man's angry face that day, and a chill went through him. If his mother knew about the fight he'd witnessed, she wouldn't like Duvall, and he wanted very much for her to like him.

He paused on the corner of the park and looked down one of the paths that bisected the broad green square from each of its four corners. Two men pushed lawn mowers in opposite directions. In the damaged quadrant three men raked stones from the freshly rolled loam. In the center of the park a crew of laborers swarmed over the bandstand with paintbrushes and hammers, readying it for the first concert. There was a man in the bucket of a cherry picker feeding electrical lines to two men on the bandstand roof who were hooking up the loudspeakers.

Benjy came down West Street toward Joey Seldon's popcorn stand, where one of the laborers stood drinking a bottle of orange soda.

"I can't," the laborer was saying to the blind man in the stand. The laborer kept looking warily around. "This reseeding shit's set me back days."

Joey's hand groped along the weathered countertop to a hole in one of the boards. "It's rotten right through," he said. "And the corner posts are gone too." He shook a post and the whole stand trembled. He cocked his head expectantly, his eyes rolling in their sockets like milky marbles. "You're the foreman, Kenny. You can do it if you want."

"Look, I told Greenie," the laborer confided. He stepped closer. "I said, 'The whole thing's so much dry rot, one stiff wind'll take her down,' and he says, 'Then let it!' "

At this, Joey sank heavily onto his stool. "He's probably right. Just let it go," he said.

"Aw c'mon, Joey," said the laborer. " 'Course he's not right. I'm just saying my hands are tied. I can't shit on the job without Greenie's say-so. The man's an asshole, a little nothin', but he's got the power."

Joey had been shaking his head. "No," he sighed. "It's not just him. Things're changing. People are getting sick of me." He laughed bitterly. "And I'm getting sick of them."

"C'mon, Joey." The laborer reached in and patted Joey's shoulder. "People want you here! Christ, you're an institution! You'll see. Sonny'll get up at the council meeting just like the Judge used to and he'll talk about your war record and that'll be that. They'll vote your space again, and then I'll be up here first thing the next morning, fixing the old stand all up for another summer."

Joey rubbed his eyes, a dismal gesture.

"It's all the vandalism. Greenie's going off the deep end," the laborer said. " 'Course, your radio blasting last year during his grand finale didn't help much."

Joey smiled. "I wish I could take credit for that." He chuckled. "Damn kids, they really pulled one off that time."

During the last concert of the season someone had rigged Joey's radio up to the loudspeakers. They turned the volume high as it would go and moved the radio off the counter, down behind the stand. By the time Joey located it, Jarden Greene's violin solo had been completely drowned out by Jerry Lee Lewis's "Great Balls of Fire." Benjy hadn't been there, but Norm said kids were dancing and even the grown-ups were laughing and cheering and clapping their hands while Jarden Greene fiddled away.

"The thing is, he thinks the park's his, so he takes everything personal," the laborer said.

As Benjy started past the stand, Joey's head cocked. "Who's that?" he called.

"It's me. Benjy Fermoyle."

"What'll it be, Benjy?" Joey asked, his face brightening. He stood up and wiped his hands eagerly on his white apron.

"Nothing, thanks."

"Need some money? If you haven't got any cans or bottles to return, then you can give me a hand stacking the empties," Joey said of the cases of empty cans and bottles next to his stand. All the kids brought their empties here because Joey didn't give them a hard time the way stores did. And if you needed money and Joey liked you, he'd put you to work.

"They're all stacked, Joey," the laborer said warily as if Benjy were trying to take advantage here.

When Benjy came to the Telephone Building he darted into the doorway as a man lurched across the street. At first he thought it was his father, but it was only Buster Kennedy, a shell-shocked veteran who delivered loud impassioned speeches all day long as he roamed through town. Benjy wondered if Buster's kids had ever ducked into doorways and dived into hedges at the sound of their father's voice. In a way Benjy's father was more a sense of dread than an actual presence. The flesh-and-blood father was never as terrifying as this pervading fear, this long, dark shadow with its staggering footsteps, penitential tears, and vomitous breath always pleading for them to love him, please, please, please; the terrible phone calls, when the only sound on the line was his father's weeping, his breathless gasping, desperate to tell of his love, that raging, hounding, erratic need, a love of such dizzying polarity it could wrench a smile to a sneer, an embrace to a twisted arm. And yet, he could think of no one who had ever spoken to him of love but his father, whom he did not think he loved, this father, this power he respected and feared the way one does as dark and ungovernable a force as a nightmare or hurricane or plummeting comet.

Uncle Renie's appliance store was on a narrow back street between a shoe repair shop that opened only on Saturdays and a card shop that had closed two years ago when Cushing's Department Store had added its own card and wrapping-paper department. Twirled across Uncle Renie's window was a faded streamer of red crepe paper, a courtesy purchase from the card shop's bankruptcy sale.

Across the street were the parking lot and the glass vestibule that was the rear entrance to Cushing's Department Store. Customers streamed in and out of Cushing's, carrying its familiar red bags with the big black C. No one was in the LaChance Appliance Company. Benjy tried the door but it was locked. He peered through the grimy glass, relieved. All the lights were off inside. As he started to turn away, Uncle Renie's balding head shot up from behind the counter.

Smiling eagerly, Uncle Renie unlocked the door. "It's so good to see you!" he cried, locking the door behind them. Something about his uncle always made Benjy uneasy. It was a kind of stale breathlessness, as if the stout little man were always waiting for some wonder or cataclysm to occur, had always been waiting, would wait forever. He gave his uncle the dial and explained that his mother wanted a new one.

The store smelled of fish. Benjy looked around. "Where's the cat?" he asked and just then the door to the basement opened and the enormous cat appeared, strutting to the front of the store, as if he were the boss here and Renie LaChance had better watch his step. He jumped onto the counter, stretching, and arching his back, purring while Benjy stroked his sleek fur.

"See? He heard you," his uncle said. "He likes you. Tommy likes you." Uncle Renie turned the dial over and poked inside with a nutpick.

"Nice kitty, kitty, kitty," Benjy whispered against the cat's neck.

"He don't like too many," his uncle said. "He's a very excriminating cat, that Tommy is."

"He ever run away?" Benjy asked.

"Oh no! Tommy wouldn't do that. He's very homey. And he don't go out ever."

"Where's he sleep?"

"Down the cellar," his uncle said, moving nearer the window for light. He peered into the dial. "He got his own bed and his food and box for bat'room." He looked up and smiled. "You should see how fancy I made it. You should see. It's got two pillows in that there velvet and all his toys, his catnip mouse. There," he grunted, squinting and biting his thick lip as he probed the pick deeper. "Same as last time . . . just a loose setting . . . one more turn . . ." He grinned and held out the dial. "Good as new and no charge, tell your mother."

From out on the street came a screech of brakes followed by a roar of drunken curses. Uncle Renie ran to look through the door. "Quick," he called, gesturing. "Get outta sight. It's your dad again." Uncle Renie ran around the counter, grabbed the cat, and sank onto a wooden box that he used to stand on to adjust the ceiling fan or to sit on back here when he had to hide.

Benjy opened the door at the end of the counter and ran into the bathroom. He could hear the front-door glass rattling as his father shook the knob.

"Open up! I know you're in there," Sam Fermoyle bellowed and pounded on the door. "C'mon, Renie! You son of a bitch, you . . ." he muttered darkly.

There was silence, and it was a few moments before he dared open his eyes. When he did, what he saw on the walls of the sour-smelling little bathroom shocked him. Every inch of space was covered with glossy colored pictures of naked ladies. His face flamed. He felt dizzy. He held his breath against the pissy stink as he turned in dizzy wonderment at all those shiny arms and legs and breasts and nipples writhing out toward him.

His father was still bellowing from the street.

On the floor beside the toilet was the telephone and the phone book. He sat on the closed lid and picked up the phone book to keep his eyes off the walls. Some of the numbers were underlined and some were circled. Turning a few pages he saw that Klubocks' number was underlined and next to it his uncle had written *Jessie.* Next to every underlined number a woman's first name was written. Bonifante: *Eunice,* his uncle had printed.

"If you open the fuckin' door, I'll tell you where your fuckin' dog, whashisname, Riddles is." His father paused and then he laughed. "Yah, dead fuckin' Riddles. Your fuckin' wife, my fuckin', whashername, sister poisoned him. You hear me, Renie? She gave him rat poison and then she took him out back and she had Howard bury him in her garden. You hear me? We got a real problem on our hands. We gotta stick together, boy. 'Cause she's after us next. . . ." The door rattled again. "Okay, you ugly little frog, have it your way. But don't say I din' warn ya. . . ." As after the quick burst of a storm, the dark voice drifted away. ". . . she tries to feed you those fuckin' tomatoes. . . . Hey! . . . Watch where you're . . ."

A horn blasted. Tires squealed. Someone shouted. In the distance a siren wailed.

I hope he's dead, Benjy thought. *I hope he's dead. I hope he's dead.*

When he came out of the bathroom his uncle was still sitting on the box. He had his head in his hands. Benjy stood by the nickel-plated cash register, where his uncle had long ago taped pictures of himself and Norm and Alice. Once when he had brought his mother's shoes into the shop next door, the old cobbler had written LaChance on the ticket. He had thought Benjy was Renie's son.

Uncle Renie looked up and took a deep breath. "Well!" he said. He didn't move.

Benjy leaned in close to the curled and faded photos. He hated his father for saying that about Uncle Renie's dog. But he didn't feel much pity now for his uncle, not with those disgusting pictures plastered on his walls.

Slowly, with a great sigh, Uncle Renie stood up and fumbled under the counter for his CLOSED sign. He put the cat in the cellar. "We'll go have pie. I never do that and today I will," he said, fastening the card on the door. He turned the red plastic hands to 4:30—BE BACK. "C'mon," he said to the boy. "Whoever comes comes, you know? I wait, they don't come. If I leave they come. Maybe," he added, locking the door with three different keys that were attached to a long leather cord snapped to his belt loop. Benjy recognized the cord as Riddles's old leash. When Riddles disappeared, his uncle had shut down the store for three days to search for him.

As they walked around the corner, Benjy was conscious of his uncle's labored breathing, the wheeze of his lungs with every step. They paused in front of the luncheonette and his uncle said, "You know that bat'room's a sight. I'm sorry you seen that. The guy that owns my building put those pictures up and I been after him and after him to take 'em off, but he don't care, I guess. Don't say nothing, okay, Benjy? Your mother'd kill me, huh?" He opened the door. "You like pie?"

Benjy nodded, then passed under the cabbagey smell of his uncle's sweaty arm as he held open the door to the little restaurant. After the glare of the sidewalk it seemed black and white inside with upright gray shadows that materialized into people, all of them men, hunched over the counter and the little white-sparkled Formica tables and booths. Renie paused at every booth to say hello. A few men nodded.

"Here," Renie said, pulling out a chair at a small round table set like an afterthought by the swinging door into the kitchen. Benjy spotted Mr. Briscoe at the counter and he slouched to avoid being seen. Uncle Renie bobbed up and down in his seat trying to catch Eunice Bonifante's eye, but she was at the end of the counter talking over her shoulder to Chief Sonny Stoner, her sister-in-law's husband, while she made a tuna-fish sandwich.

"Guess she don't see me," Uncle Renie said before he finally got up to place his order at the counter, two apple pies, a coffee, and a milk. Without once looking at him, Eunice served him the pies, the drinks, took his money, rang up the sale on the register, and gave him change, while she continued her animated conversation with the Chief. Benjy noticed how the Chief said hello to Uncle Renie and handed him the napkins he dropped, and when he came back for their drinks, Chief Stoner passed him the sugar bowl.

Suddenly the plate-glass window shook with a blast of noise as two motorcycles roared down the street. On one of them was Blue Mooney, his pale blond hair blown against his cheek as he skidded around the corner. The Chief shook his head. Last year Mooney and his older brother broke into Eunice's gas station up on Main Street just a few nights before Blue was supposed to leave for Marine boot camp. His brother, who had actually been inside the station, went back to jail, but Stoner got the D.A. to drop the charges against Blue provided he went straight into the Marines. But now for the last month Mooney had been back in town.

"Summer's here," someone at the counter said. "Just like fleas, Mooney and his nitwits are out."

"Just for a time," the Chief said. "He's home on leave. Some special assignment he's waiting to be called up for."

"Special assignment!" another man scoffed. "He's nothing but trouble waiting to happen, that's all."

"You done?" Eunice snapped, glaring at the man, without its being at all clear whether she meant his sarcasm or his coffee. She laid a top slice of bread on the sandwich.

"Onion on that, Eunice," the Chief said quickly.

"No kisses for you tonight." She laughed and the Chief blushed.

The men at the counter shifted uncomfortably. A couple of them exchanged looks. "What a thing to say to a man whose wife's dying," the man across from Benjy whispered.

"Well," his companion said, his shrug summing up all of Eunice's troubles, excusing her.

Eunice had been married to Al Bonifante, the Chief's brother-in-law. Three years ago Al had committed suicide. He had been a hard-working, quiet man, who'd owned the Mobil station and this luncheonette, which Eunice had always run. After Al died, she just threw herself into both businesses, working night and day, weekends, holidays. That had ended a year ago, when she ended up in the hospital completely broken down. Just when her sister-in-law Carol and Sonny got her back on her feet, Carol found out about the cancer.

"It's for Joey," the Chief was saying.

"You should've said," Eunice said, slapping on a wheel of red onion. She reached for the mayonnaise jar. "Joey's always onion and extra mayo."

At the far end of the counter a stool turned with a squeal. It was Jarden Greene, his thin mustache quivering. He had recently been re-elected head of the town's Public Works Department. He was also the conductor at the Sunday-night band concerts in the park. Greene had come up through department ranks on a street crew, scooping sludge from catch basins and raking leaves from gutters with hands God had created to make music. Now he wore his power as trimly as his pin-striped suits and small lustrous black shoes.

"Did I hear correctly?" Greene said in disbelief, as he tightened the knot of his tie. "Our police chief is now a common errand boy for Joey Seldon?"

Stoner turned, his taut face white. "What's that, Jarden?" he said.

Greene passed a cool smirk to the men beside him. On his right was Thomas Holby, who owned the Holby Coal Company.

Greene spoke loudly and now the entire luncheonette grew silent. "I'll tell you what, Chief. When I ran for Public Works, I ran on a platform of public trust and honesty. I promised if I was elected, I would root out greed and corruption and the god-awful waste of tax-payers' hard-earned money. And I *was* elected and, by Jesus, I won't stand by silent while Joey Seldon's raking in the dough from his popcorn shanty that stands rent-free on town property. And I won't stand silent while our chief of police commandeers a town vehicle and town gas to run sandwiches up to that leech!" Greene pounded his fist on the counter. "I'm too much of an honest man . . . too much of an . . ."

"Asshole," Eunice groaned, rolling her eyes. She came the length of the counter and threw down his check. Greene pushed it away. "I'll pay when I'm through."

"You're through," she said. She picked up his coffee cup and the plate of half-eaten chocolate cake.

"Eunice!" the Chief said, trying to set things straight again. Greene's humiliation embarrassed him. Like his father, who had been chief before him, Sonny Stoner believed himself keeper of the town's virtue, and to this end had kept his heart as accessible and unblemished as his badge.

Greene was demanding his cake back. "This is an outrage!" he cried.

"Get the hell out!" Eunice growled.

"You can't do that," Greene fumed. "This is a public establishment and I'm entitled to that cake."

"That's right," Ferdinand Briscoe called down the counter. "Jard ordered that cake fair and square and you can't take it away just because you don't like what he said."

"Oh yah?" she said, reaching for Briscoe's cherry pie.

"I paid for that!" Briscoe cried.

"Not yet you didn't!" she howled. Her eyes moved menacingly along the counter, threatening Bart Doore's muffins and Holmby's hot dog, which was halfway to his mouth. Holmby glanced from side to side and under Greene's peevish stare laid down the hot dog. He chewed drily and coughed a little before he spoke. "Jard and Ferd have every right to say what's on their mind."

"And I got a perfect right not to listen," Eunice said, snapping up the hot dog plate and throwing it onto the stainless-steel work bench.

Sonny winced. The shattering plate might as well have struck him, for the pain and the misery on his face. A dark murmur rose among the diners. From out on the street came the squeal of brakes and then the blast of Mooney's motorcycle.

"Aw c'mon, Eunice," pleaded Sonny as she moved along the counter with a plastic bin, into which she slid everyone's cups and glasses and plates. "Just settle down now." He looked at the sputtering men. "Everybody just settle down. . . . There's no need to—"

"Shut up," Eunice said.

"No! This is all my fault," Sonny was saying. He leaned over the counter toward her. "Maybe Jard's right. I probably should've used my own car on my own time."

Robert Haddad, Astrid's husband, stood up and tried to mediate. "You gotta understand Jard's position, Eunice. He makes some good points."

"Shut up, Haddad," she said.

"Now that's not fair, Eunice!" Haddad fumed. "We're all tryna make a living and do what's right." He looked around at the nodding men. "Nobody gives us free rent. Nobody sets us up in business. It's like there's two sets of rules. Hell, morality's right out the window."

At that, she spun around, certain he'd meant her as well.

"Get your ass out, Haddad, and get it out now!"

He opened his mouth and she pointed at him. "Don't!" She shook her head. "Don't!"

He eased past the man beside her and left, closing the door without a sound.

Now she moved from booth to booth, clearing each table. Benjy and Renie's half-eaten pies were the last she took. She turned off the fryolaters, the grill, the overhead lights, and the ceiling fan. Its grease-slicked paddles whirred to a sluggish stop. The sudden dim silence was frightening.

"Out!" Eunice ordered, pointing at the door. Like admonished children they hurried to leave.

At the counter Sonny turned on his stool. "This is crazy!" he said. "Eunice, what's got into you?"

"You too!" she said, chest heaving and eyes thick with tears.

He said her name again, but now Benjy and his uncle were out on the sidewalk.

They parted at the appliance store, with Benjy promising to drop in again soon, though he knew he wouldn't. To avoid running into his father he stayed off the streets and came through back alleys. He was behind the luncheonette now. The metal-sheeted back door was open to the narrow white kitchen and inside he saw Chief Stoner and Mrs. Bonifante.

The Chief held her uniform collar down while he kissed her throat and her shoulder. Mrs. Bonifante's head was back, her eyes closed, her hands down the back of the Chief's blue trousers. Just as Benjy stepped back, her eyes opened. She was crying. Biting her lip, she stared back at him while the Chief kept kissing her.

Renie LaChance watched the gold-banded glass doors that led into Cushing's Department Store. Every time the doors opened the sun struck them with a beam of light that bounced off Renie's store window. Most of Cushing's customers were women. He estimated that those leaving with purchases must have spent an average of three dollars each. Here came another now, an older woman with two shopping bags. He glanced down at his tally. Two hundred and twenty-two dollars and that didn't even include the times he'd had to hide today when his brother-in-law, Sam, showed up or the twenty minutes in the luncheonette with Benjy. Twenty minutes wasted, he thought, then corrected himself. No. It had been good seeing the boy. He only wished the other two would come more often. Especially Alice. Just thinking of her pleased him. She was pretty like her mother, but without Marie's sharp tongue and suspicions.

He looked up as another woman left Cushing's, this one also carrying a bag. He opened his ledger and crossed out $222 and wrote $225; and that was just what came through the back door! The day before Christmas, 1959, had been the best ever: 326 people times $3 had come to $978. He wondered if old Mr. Cushing knew how many people came through that back door. Maybe he'd like to see the records, he thought, idly stroking the cat's neck. Maybe they could have lunch together, him and the old man. . . . His heart sank as his fingers snagged in the silky fur. Without an introduction Mr. Cushing wouldn't know who he was. Mr. Cushing might think he had nothing better to do than stare out the window all day counting Cushing's customers.

But it was true; lately business was terrible, his stock outdated, overpriced, and covered with a fine soot he could not muster the energy to wipe away. Ever since the big Montgomery Ward catalog store had opened up on Route 4, his business had nose-dived. A year ago February, in a burst of optimism one morning after Helen had been unusually pleasant at breakfast, he had ordered seventy-five fans and twenty air conditioners from a young Fridge-Kool salesman he'd taken a shine to the minute he came into the store. The young salesman had reminded Renie of himself at that age. As soon as the salesman had removed his gloves, Renie's heart had ached at the sight of the man's wide palms and short thick fingers. Could it be? he had asked himself. Was he the child Renie had never seen? In a cold sweat he had nodded at everything the young man said. "Yes . . . Yes . . . Okay . . . Uh-huh . . ." He had stared at the young man's face, pleased to find him not at all ugly, as he'd dreaded, but appealing, round-faced and blond.

"Supposed to be a scorcher this summer," the salesman had said, scribbling to get his pen working.

"Yup."

"I'd figure a good-size order early. Then when they drag in here boiling hot, you're ready. You're merchandisable!" The young man had smiled and handed him the pen. "Because you've got the goods!"

Renie had signed the order, his swollen heart crowding out every other organ in his body.

"Great!" the young salesman had said, checking the signature.

"How old are you?" Renie had blurted.

"Twenty-three," the salesman had answered.

"You sure?" Renie had cried. "You sure you're not twenty-eight? You were born in New York in 1931. In the fall sometime."

"I'm twenty-three," the salesman had said, hurriedly packing his leather valise. He gave Renie a copy of the order. "I was born in Burlington," he had said, backing out the door. "Delivery'll take three to six weeks, sir."

Of the original order Renie still had sixty-nine fans. All of this year's models looked smaller, and his seemed even bigger than they were last year. Sometimes he thought they had actually grown bigger. Sometimes he thought God hated him. No matter what he did or how hard he tried, God thwarted him. If he weren't a Catholic he might even wonder if there was such a thing as God. Maybe there was only love. Maybe that's how it was two thousand years ago, with people crowded around Jesus to hear him speak of love the way Frank Sinatra sang about it now. Love, that old hot rush rose in his groin. He reversed the OPEN sign on the front door to CLOSED and hurried into his windowless, airless chamber where he sat on the closed toilet lid and began to dial. He knew most of the numbers by heart now. The first one wasn't home. The second one answered on the first ring, her small voice breathless and sweet. "Hello?" she kept saying.

He closed his eyes and pictured that blur of yellow curls and creamy pink skin. "I love you," he whispered.

"Who is this?" Jessie Klubock demanded.

"I love you so much."

"Don't do this," she said. "Please stop . . . please. . . ."

"I love everything about you," he said, eyes closed.

"You've got to stop. My husband . . . he . . . oh, please don't call here anymore. . . ."

"I love your sw—" he said, then, realizing she'd hung up, he dialed the next number.

"Hello," answered a woman who'd bought an electric mixer from him two years ago.

"I love you," he whispered, his thick lips close to the mouthpiece.

"Go to hell!"

He dialed the next number, a young woman who worked at the candy store.

"Hello," a man answered, and Renie hung up quickly, wiping sweat from his upper lip.

His favorite was Eunice Bonifante. Usually he had to wait until late at night to get her home, but now he dialed the luncheonette.

"Hello!" she answered irritably.

He listened a moment.

"Oh shit. It's not you, is it?"

"I love you," he whispered.

"Not today you don't. Today's the worse day I ever had. Jesus, it was bad."

"I love you any day."

"Yah? Well, you must be pretty hard up, then." She sighed and he could tell she was lighting a cigarette. "I'm kinda crazy today. You know what I did? I went and threw all my customers out!"

She laughed bitterly. "Some days I just don't give a damn. Some days all I think about is dying. I don't mean me. I mean everything, all the people I care about, it seems." Her voice broke off.

"That's okay," he said tenderly. "Some days're awful, huh?"

"Some days! Lately, every day."

"Well, I love you . . ." He winced, adding, "Sweetheart."

"Yah?" She laughed. "I'm glad somebody does."

Alice waited in the Stoners' living room while Lester got his instructions from Mrs. Miller before she went off duty. Alice loved this house. Even the television had doors to hide its blank gray screen. Every window was shuttered inside as well as outside. She glanced toward the kitchen, where the only jarring note was the police radio on the white metal utility cart. From the mantel she picked up the brass-hinged framed photographs of the Stoners, one taken on their wedding day and the other when Mr. Stoner had been sworn in as chief of police. With Lester a toddler in her arms, Mrs. Stoner gazed proudly at her handsome young husband, whose one hand was on the family Bible and the other upraised as he was sworn in by his father. Alice looked more closely at the wedding picture. Mrs. Stoner's maid of honor had been Eunice Bonifante, her sister-in-law. Alice had heard the awful rumor about Mrs. Bonifante and Lester's father, but she knew it couldn't be true. Mrs. Bonifante might run around; she certainly looked the part with her big pointy breasts and messy hair and brassy makeup, but not Chief Stoner.

"I had to give her another pill," Mrs. Miller was telling Lester on their way down the stairs. "She was in a bad way and I hated doing it, but I had to. You tell your dad that, now. . . ."

"I will," Lester interrupted with a glance at Alice that was heavy with longing. They came here straight from school every day now. Alice smiled at him.

"The point is, she shouldn't have her regular dose next time. She's all set, but if she wakes up and says it's bad, then you better call Dr. Hess. I wouldn't give—"

"I won't, Mrs. Miller," Lester said, opening the door. "I'll call Dr. Hess first."

"Be sure, now," Mrs. Miller said. "She wants them sooner and sooner these last few days. I know her pain's—"

"Don't worry," Lester said, starting to close the door. "When it gets bad, I just start talking and she can't get a word in edgewise."

"God bless you, Les. You're a good boy," Mrs. Miller sighed before the door closed.

Lester called to Alice that he'd be right back down. He had to check on his mother, he called over his shoulder as he bounded up the stairs. He was back in less than a minute. "She wants to see you," he said, rolling his eyes. "She's funny-acting on these pills, so if she sounds weird, you'll know why," he whispered as she followed him upstairs into a dry redolence of sweet powder and undisturbed dust. He peeked into the bedroom. "Mother! You're crooked," he said, tapping the side of his head.

Mrs. Stoner's honey-blond wig was pushed back, exposing her patchy scalp. She looked old and befuddled. Her eyes were puffy and pinkish and her pallid skin gleamed with sweat.

Alice forced a smile, hoping it looked natural, but she could feel her lips quiver.

Distant and labored, Mrs. Stoner's soft voice seemed more breathing than words. "Would you like lemonade?"

Alice nodded, but Lester fibbed and said they'd just had some downstairs.

"I have these delicious chocolates," Mrs. Stoner said, straining forward. "Over there," she told Lester. "On the dresser. Do you like chocolate?" Mrs. Stoner asked.

"I love chocolate," Alice said.

Lester opened the door. "We have to study, Mother. And I'm working on my graduation speech. Alice has to be my audience." He gestured for Alice to follow him.

"She looked so disappointed," Alice whispered as they hurried down the stairs.

"She was just trying to be polite. She doesn't even like chocolate," he said so sourly that if he had added, "And she doesn't like you either," she wouldn't have been a bit surprised.

It was four-thirty, and they were still downstairs in the dark rec room, the high small basement windows curtained and the door at the top of the stairs latched. They sat on the musty divan with a scratchy wool plaid blanket covering them to their chins. They had been making out for an hour. Alice's mouth was tender and her neck felt stiff. "Oh . . . oh," she gasped, and Lester grunted, as the hand of each worked at the other's crotch.

"Faster," Lester groaned.

Her eyes shot open. She thought she'd heard a noise upstairs. Maybe it was Lester's mother. She was too weak to get out of bed by herself, but she might be calling Lester to help her. Maybe the pain was getting bad again.

"Faster! Faster!" Lester panted. He had taken his hand away from Alice and was covering his face with both hands.

"Sh!" she said, listening. She stopped.

"Please!" he moaned behind his hands.

It was a creaking sound. "Did you hear that? I heard it again!" she said. She pulled her hand away and switched on the table lamp.

"It's the cat," he said, wincing, turning his head from the light. His eyes were thick and inflamed.

"What if it's your mother?" She leaned forward, listening.

"My mother hasn't been out of bed in two weeks!" he said.

"Then maybe it's your father."

"He's on duty," Lester said.

"Maybe he stopped by."

"He'd never do that," Lester said. "Not when he's on duty."

She listened, her eyes moving along the ceiling and up the stairs to the door.

"It's Precious," he hissed. "That's all."

"Are you sure?" She leaned toward the lamp. He closed his eyes. "Please," he said in a small pained voice as he guided her hand under the blanket.

She turned out the light and moved close to be kissed, but he had covered his face again. With her touch he arched his back and made a whimpering sound. Her hand froze. "I'm sorry!" she gasped, thinking she'd hurt him.

"Please," he groaned and she started again. All she knew of sex were the basics she'd read about in the encyclopedia. Certain couples she knew were said to have been going all the way for a long time. Supposedly Marilyn St. Marie and Jimmy Sloane had been doing it ever since eighth grade. Chrissie Barrett had told her that you could tell which girls had done it a lot by the size of their hips. Wide-hipped girls were the most experienced and skinny-hipped girls were usually virgins. Alice had believed her until she finally realized that Bernadette Mansaw, the town slut, had hips as slim as her own.

"Don't stop," Lester grunted. He stretched back, trying to pull down his pants. "Take off yours!" he groaned in that hard thick voice.

"What?" Again she was afraid she had hurt him. Her hand fell away, and she was shocked by the stiffness she felt.

"Take off your underpants," he said.

She sat very still. She could smell her own sweat mingling with the damp sourness of the rug and this musty divan, an odor she'd never noticed before.

"Please," he begged, the desire in his voice more exciting to her than any of his kisses or caresses.

"We love each other," he groaned as she removed her panties. "You know we do. We can't stop now . . . we can't," he groaned, lying on top of her. "We have to . . . oh, my God, we have to. There's nothing we can do . . . spread wide. Oh God," his voice boomed and he drooled in her ear. "Help me," he cried. "Help me, help me, help me," he gasped over and over, his voice growing shrill.

Her eyes were so deeply closed they'd never open again. It was supposed to hurt the first time. But it didn't. She heard a deep animal-like growl, and it was a moment before she realized it had been her own voice. Of all the things she'd ever felt in her whole life, this was the most beautiful, the most wonderful, the deep, deepest . . . God . . . Oh, God . . . It didn't hurt at all. . . .

Lester gasped and his back arched, then suddenly he pulled away.

Blindly, she reached out, grabbing his arm. "Lester!" she cried, trying to pull him back to her.

"I'm sorry!" he cried as he struggled into his pants. "I'm so sorry!"

"Oh Les," she sighed, then, realizing he was crying, she sat up and tried to put her arms around him, but he pulled away, sobbing softly as he tied his shoes. She tried to tell him it was all right. It wasn't his fault. She'd been just as willing. "What's important is that we love each other," she said, swamped with tenderness. In fact, until this moment, she realized, she'd always felt uneasy with Lester. His voice was too high, his hair too thin, his pants too short, his hands too clammy, his eyes too ready to glisten with tears. It amazed her now how completely love could abrade those sharp edges. She felt as if she could take on any burden. Life was changed; she was changed. She felt whole and good and calm. Nothing mattered, not her father, not that weird Omar Duvall her mother had invited to supper two nights in a row. All that mattered was Les. No, she thought. Even Lester didn't matter. All that really mattered was this wonderful peace inside.

"Even if I got . . . you know . . . if that ever happened . . . I mean, we love each other," she said, laying her cheek on his back.

"I pulled out," he said, his voice thin and flat. He stood up quickly and turned on the light. Wincing, she pulled down her skirt, and he turned off the light.

"I thought you were dressed!" he said, sounding shocked. He cleared his throat, then through the darkness said, "I read this article in the *Holy Courier*."

She felt along the floor for her panties. The *Holy Courier* was the diocesan Sunday paper. Aside from nuns and priests, Alice had never heard anyone say they'd actually read it.

"I cut it out," Lester said. "For you to read. But then I thought you'd be mad."

She heard him sit down in a chair on the far side of the room.

"What did it say?" She could smell his Old Spice, though he sounded far, far away.

"It says that girls like you . . . you know how your father's . . . that is, girls from broken homes . . . well, that girls like that are confused . . . you know, kind of mixed up, not just emotionally, but you know—morally. That they're, well . . . always trying to find love."

"What're you talking about? Why're you saying this?" Her face stung as if she'd just been slapped.

He coughed, clearing his throat. "What just happened," he said hoarsely. "I feel so . . . so lousy . . . like I took advantage of you. . . . I mean, I knew all about it, and I went ahead and did it anyway. It's like I knew exactly what was wrong and exactly what'd happen and I went ahead and you know, did it, and now I feel so crummy . . . like dirt. . . . I feel like a piece of crud."

"I don't know what you mean." And the minute she said it, she knew exactly what he meant. He meant that dark part of her, that taint she thought she could hide if she was good enough and kind enough and polite enough and quiet enough and neat enough and clean enough.

Her face burning with shame, she stood up and felt for her schoolbag.

Lester's voice through the darkness was mournfully cloying, as if forgiving her for a sin she had caused them both to commit. "So I thought we should just sit together at lunch and stuff like that," he was saying. "Go downtown and the library. Stuff like that."

He followed her up the stairs. "I wouldn't want anything to happen," he said at the front door. "I'd feel so . . . it's so wrong!" he burst out. "You know what I mean, Alice!" he called as she hurried down the path. "Alice! Alice!"

The lilacs were shriveled now, their faint dry fragrance more memory than scent as the days grew longer, hotter, fuller. There were afternoons when the air swelled in such a tumescence of heat and light that the leaves on the trees hung as limply as if they were dying. Sometimes there would be a dark ripeness, a foulness, a stench that seemed to seep out from the very bowels of the earth. No one was sure where the smell was coming from. But there were a couple of old men in town, whose hands gripped their porch rails as with narrowed eyes they sniffed, then turned away troubled, these few who knew that indescribable odor of decaying human flesh.

Most people blamed it on the pig farm. They complained that the pigman wasn't taking the care he once had. And they were more right than they knew. He wasn't. Turning soil and liming swill were meaningless now to a man who thirty years ago had lost his sense of smell and then in the last few months had lost his heart to Jozia Menka, whose big strong hands weakened him with their touch.

His old black truck shimmied as it backed into the Fermoyles' driveway. The brakes caught with a great sigh. Grondine Carson wiped his hands on his shirtfront. Up on the rear porch the door flew open, and Helen LaChance hollered over the racket of the engine. "It's Thursday," she kept yelling down at him. "Not Tuesday. It's Thursday!"

With a glance in the rearview mirror, he wiped away a smudge under his left eye. Only recently had he realized that he wasn't a homely man at all. Just plain. He was long, bony, and plain as an old tree, and all his life about as unnoticed. The contrast of his short-cropped white hair against his deep clayey tan was his only distinguishing feature. He climbed down from the truck and closed the door.

"It's Thursday!" Helen LaChance called. "It's not my day! I don't need a double pickup, and I won't pay for one!"

He couldn't hear what she was saying. He looked past her to the sagging door screen.

"Jozia here?" he called, his unused icy voice cracking with the pleasure of her name. It had occurred to him as he completed the day's route that he had never eaten a meal with Jozia. He would take her to dinner, maybe to the Palms for pizza or maybe the Kong Chow for egg rolls and spareribs. His stomach and heart churned with hunger. Heat waves dazzled off the chugging hood of the truck and fat black flies clung to its warm, splattered sides. He stepped closer and cupped his hands to his mouth. "Jozia here, Miz LaChance? I come for Jozia Menka."

Her lips twitched as she regarded him with horror.

"She's mine," he thought she answered, until he heard her say, "She's gone. She already left."

He climbed back into his truck and drove off with an iridescent cloud of black crows flapping overhead and dogs chasing his slimy tires. When he came to Jozia's street, he slowed and looked up at the small curtained windows of her apartment over the religious articles store. Because of her brother, she would not let him come here. Howard was very jealous, she'd told him. "He thinks he owns me," she'd said. "He thinks he's the boss." *Oh Jozia,* Grondine thought as he drove around the corner. *Oh how I love you.*

"He wanted to pick up twice," Helen LaChance was complaining. "He thought he could get away with it, that I wouldn't notice. Hah!" she sniffed, stirring the pot of soup Jozia had started. Jozia stood by the back door, looking at Mrs. LaChance's small back and rounded shoulders, her sparse hair set in finger waves. Mrs. LaChance was shrinking. Like her mother she would grow smaller and smaller. Once such a thought would have numbed Jozia with fear. But lately she felt braver and stronger, and smarter. It wasn't that she was changing so much as that there seemed to be a whole new Jozia growing inside the old Jozia.

From here she could see old Mrs. Fermoyle dozing in her huge crib. She was all white: hair, skin, bed jacket, sheets; nothing about her moved or seemed alive. Sometimes she had to press her ear to the old woman's narrow chest and listen for her heartbeat. It seemed to Jozia more and more lately that the old woman actually dwelled in death, that sometimes she was dead and sometimes she was alive. For years she and Mrs. LaChance had struggled to keep the old woman alive; together they had staved off death—and Sam.

"There's something wrong with that old pigman. He's getting pretty odd if you ask me; pretty strange, living all alone out there in that dirty, disgusting, godforsaken pigsty of a house. Lord knows what goes on."

Jozia untied her apron and hung it on the hook by the door. A faint smile eased her heavy mouth. Soon, Grondine's house would be every bit as clean as this one. Room by room she was taking it apart, scrubbing and polishing it back into a real nice place. Every room she did felt like hers somehow. Even Grondine thought so. He wanted to pay her for all her work, but she'd refused.

"Don't look like the same place anymore. Looks like a real house," he'd said last week as he watched her rehang the freshly ironed cotton curtains in the front room. Her cheeks flushed now at the thought of doing the upstairs, even though Grondine said he never went up there anymore. He slept on the couch and kept his clothes in the back hall closet.

"They ought to shut him down," Mrs. LaChance said, shaking salt into the soup.

Mr. LaChance wasn't supposed to have any salt, so Jozia never added it. The one time she'd reminded Mrs. LaChance of this, she'd almost taken her head off.

"If he can't run his business right, then he shouldn't be in business."

"What's that?" Jozia had lost track of the conversation. It always confused her the way Mrs. LaChance got so fired up over things and ranted and raved.

"That awful smell. Even the people in the Flatts are complaining, if you can imagine."

"It's the dump," Jozia said. Sometimes Mrs. LaChance was a real snob, but that was her mother's fault. In front of people old Mrs. Fermoyle had acted like nobody could hold a candle to the Fermoyles. In private she was always worried what people might think. "Grondine says it always smells like that when it's hot."

"Who?" Mrs. LaChance's head whipped around. "Who says?"

"Mr. Carson," Jozia said, her bulging eyes wide, her high round cheeks ablaze.

"What did you call him?" Mrs. LaChance asked, turning.

Jozia shrugged. "Grondine?" she said shyly, softly, as if it were a question.

"Grondine!" Mrs. LaChance cried. "Imagine! Grondine!"

After work Jozia hurried across the street to the rectory, where Howard waited on the side steps. His eyes were bright and he couldn't stop talking. Even seeing the pigman's truck in the Fermoyles' driveway earlier hadn't been enough to quell his excitement. "Well, guess what? The new priest came. His name's Joe, he said. 'Just call me Joe,' he said, so I did, but Monsignor said, 'No, his name's Father,' so I call him Father, and the new priest said, 'Call me Father Joe, then.' So I did, and Monsignor come out, and he said, 'No, his name's Father Gannon,' so I ain't gonna call him nothin', I guess. That way, nobody's mad. But he's real nice. Real nice. Hey!" Howard skipped to catch up with his sister. "Wait up!"

She walked faster, her strong arms swinging her along. Grondine hadn't come for a double pickup, but to see her, probably to ride her home, probably didn't even tell Mrs. LaChance. Grondine could be awful shy. She was smiling.

"Gonna be a busy day tomorrow. Gotta wash the car and get it all waxed. It's graduation tomorrow. Monsignor said, the grass gotta be cut and all the bushes and the flowers gotta be weeded and the marble chips gotta be raked back. . . ." His voice trailed off and he stood a moment, watching sadly as she hurried on without him.

"I heard something," he said. "But I can't tell. Something 'bout the new priest." He fairly ran to get beside her. "Don't say nothin'. But he just come outta a mental place."

Jozia stopped and looked down at him. "You know something, Howard. I think you're the one that's mental. 'Magine!"

"'Strue. I heard the whole thing. I heard Monsignor call the Bishop. 'You can't do this to me, your Lexcency.' That's what he said!"

"Do what?"

"He said, 'You can't send him to me straight outta the funny farm.' He said, 'I need a priest here, your Lexcency. Not a mental patient.' "

"Is he crazy?" Jozia asked, starting to walk again.

"Oh no," Howard said. "He's just like us."

That night while Marie Fermoyle washed the supper dishes, Omar Duvall sat at the table with one of the kitchen chairs upside down on his knees. He had just glued the joints and now was looping twine around the legs.

"You should've pressed for what was due you," he grunted as he tied a tight knot on each leg.

She kept rinsing the same plate. As soon as they were alone after supper, he had asked about her divorce and whether or not she had gotten any support money. She glanced back. This was none of his business. "It's just that I can't bear injustice, particularly when children are the victims." He got up and laid the chair upside down on the table to dry.

"It's all water over the dam now," she sighed, wringing out the dishrag.

He picked up a dish towel and began to dry the frying pan. "Why didn't you do anything, then?" he asked.

Her eyes flashed angrily. "What could I do? I had no more money for a lawyer. A month after the divorce, he'd quit his job. I called the Judge and he said, 'You can't get blood out of a stone, Marie. Some things you just have to accept.' Every time I called Helen she'd hang up on me, and his mother was going senile. So I just kept on working." She took the frying pan from him and jammed it into the cupboard, then closed the door quickly on the falling clatter. *Mind your own business,* she thought, keeping her back to him, trying to hide her irritation. *Leave me alone. Who the hell are you to judge me. I did my best, goddamn it.*

"Oh, I wish I'd known you then, lady. I wish I'd been around." He looked at her so long and hard that she blushed and lifted the curtain over the sink, staring out with burning wet eyes. The Klubocks were playing croquet in their yard with another couple. Jessie Klubock's pale dress swirled around her slender legs as she leaned forward to take her shot. The mallet whacked into the wooden ball, and the women laughed as the men groaned. Marie smiled, sensing herself part of this symmetry, a finely tuned meshing and turning of gears and parts, a harmony she had never known. Just then Jessie looked up and seemed to smile back at her. Marie turned suddenly. *Bastards,* she thought, with each whack of the ball. *They have no troubles. It's too easy for them.* She tried to think back. What had been her first mistake, fear or love? Or were they one and the same for people like her?

"All that support," Omar was saying. "All those years he never paid—that's probably a lot of money by now. Let's see . . . fifty-two weeks times ten dollars times, what, ten years . . ." He looked up. "Why, that's five thousand two hundred dollars you're owed," he said softly, repeating the sum, his tone holding it aloft like some fragile offering.

She laughed. "God! Sam doesn't have two nickels to rub together. Helen's a bitch, but at least she takes care of her brother."

"With such funds to use as she sees fit to insure his good health and well-being," Omar said.

"What's that supposed to mean?" she said quickly.

"You forget whose room I occupy, whose bed I sleep in, whose ancient file cabinets are in every corner."

"Old Judge Clay!"

"Judge Clay, who, as the Fermoyle family lawyer, drew up a trust apparently at the behest of old Bridget Fermoyle. A trust that named Helen LaChance as trustee and Sam as beneficiary. Because of the pending divorce trial and Sam's"—here, Omar cleared his throat—"uh, weakness, the very existence of the trust was to be kept a secret from him." He shook his head ruefully. "And apparently from you, under the heading of 'all others.' "

She was confused, amazed, shocked that Bridget Fermoyle would have done this to her, to her grandchildren. "How much was in the trust?"

Omar had stepped closer to her. "Ten thousand dollars, which in all likelihood has been accruing interest all this time. And if you consider the fact that the man, your former husband, has few if any expenses, certainly no overhead, living as he does in his mother's home, then I think you'll agree that the trust is probably pretty close to being intact." His eyebrows arched with his dazzling smile. "Wouldn't you say?"

From outside came another quick whack of the mallet. Her stomach twisted with sourness.

"It appears, Marie, that you have been the victim of a vast conspiracy here. You've got to do something! For your children!"

He seemed to loom, to be everywhere her eyes darted.

"You just might be able to parlay this debt into something big, into some kind of"—he paused, searching for the words—"some kind of investment—maybe even your own business!"

She felt dizzy. He had folded the thin dish towel over his forearm and stood now with clasped hands. Sweat ran down his face and his eyes glistened. "Think of it!" he whispered, bending as if she were a child. "Independence! Security! A better life for your children!"

He stood so close her legs felt weak, as if she should be kneeling.

"Call Sam," he urged. "Tell him what you know."

"I can't. Not when he's drinking," she whispered, looking toward the other room, where Benjy was watching television.

"Speak to the trustee, to his sister, to her Christianity, and if that tack fails . . ." He snapped his fingers. "Then tell her you'll sue, you'll take her to court."

"I couldn't do that," she said faintly.

"Of course you could! You can do anything, Marie Fermoyle, once you make up your mind."

"But not that . . . not court again," she said, remembering the shame of testifying to Sam's blows with the eyes of everyone in the courtroom turned on her with loathing and condemnation, judging her, their suspicions confirmed: the butcher's daughter had only gotten what she'd asked for; of course he hit her; of course he resented those children who had trapped him; of course he drank; who wouldn't?

So here she was, on her way to 15 Kensington Avenue, to the home she hadn't entered in years. She bit her lip, then turned the bell key and heard its jarring buzz inside. When she was first married and searching for clues to Sam's drinking, she had even seized on the stab of this doorbell's angry ring as a cause.

She glanced up at Sam's darkened window, praying he was either asleep or out. The house was in the worst shape she had ever seen it. The paint was peeling. Some of the porch floorboards had rotted through and the steps sagged back against the house. *This is what they've come to*, she thought, *rot and neglect, wasted lives.*

To her right a curtain fluttered; then Helen's small tight features flicked into the door opening.

"What is it?" her former sister-in-law asked, her eyes filming coldly.

"I have to talk to you," she whispered, her throat constricting. She coughed.

"I was going to get ready for bed," Helen said, her imperious tone chiseling each consonant to a sharp edge.

"It's important, Helen," she whispered. "I tried to call, but it was busy."

There was a creaking from the end of the dark hallway, and Marie stiffened. "Is he here?" she whispered.

"Sam's at the jail," Helen said. "They're keeping him for the night," she said with a long, enduring sigh. "I called Hale Longly. It's not an arrest, so it won't be in the paper."

As the creaking receded into the distance, she realized it had been Renie. "I saw the picture they took of you and the Monsignor and the new church doors," Marie said, following Helen along the hallway with its familiar dank smell of musty horsehair and cedar and mothballs. She would be calm and as coolly duplicitous as Helen. "The new doors are beautiful," she said, when in truth she hadn't been able to look at them without bitterness, without thinking, New doors for the church from the Fermoyle family, when her children were Fermoyles; Fermoyles in old clothes and sometimes just barely enough food for the week; Fermoyles who were better and stronger than any of these.

"Yes," Helen said. That was all. Yes.

They passed the dining room, and glancing in, Marie was sickened by the sight of the once fearsome old woman, now a foolish child with ribboned white braids, high behind the bars of her enormous crib, whispering slyly into the gnawed ear of a dingy cloth doll.

"Bridget," she said, approaching the crib. The old woman's gaze lifted and held blankly while her flat white thumb stroked the doll's frazzled yarn hair. "It's Marie," she said through the bars to the old woman she hadn't seen in almost ten years, and now she remembered her odd affection for Sam's mother, who had only wanted the best for her son, for whom the best was all he feared; and in a smothering alliance of distrust and hope, mother and wife had often conspired to make him whole, to sober him up, to get him working again.

"She doesn't know you now," Helen said.

At the sound of her daughter's voice, old Mrs. Fermoyle looked toward the mirror at the foot of her crib.

"Actually," Helen sighed, "this is one of her better days. Lately, it's become a matter of sustaining her." She reached through the bars to fluff the pillows. "There, now," she murmured, her glasses sliding to the tip of her nose. On the other side of the kitchen door, a cupboard squeaked open. A cup rattled against a saucer. Helen glanced peevishly at the door. "Would you mind?" she called in shrilly.

Marie turned to face her. "Helen . . . I . . . You know I always thought the Judge took care of things," she said, her thoughts rushing in a torrent now. "And so I never asked. You know that, Helen. The support money—I never made a stink out of things, you know that."

"That's between you and my brother. It has nothing to do with me!" Helen drew back from the crib to look at her.

"No—because you run things, Helen. I know that now. . . . I know all about the trust." She stepped closer. "Helen, all I'm asking for is what's mine and the kids'. . . ."

"Nothing is yours!" Helen said, blanching. "Nothing!"

"That's not true, and damn it, Helen, you know it's not!"

"Don't!" Helen warned, drawing back. "Don't raise your voice to me! Not in my house!"

Marie looked at her. Now she understood. "You're the one who set up that trust! You did it, after your mother was senile, when she—"

"Oh no! Oh no!" Helen kept saying, almost laughing. "No! It was all her idea." She gestured to the old woman, who stared at the mirror. "Believe me, this hell on earth was all her doing."

"I've got a lawyer, Helen. A damn good lawyer," she lied, emboldened by Helen's misery. "And if you won't help me, then he will! I'll get that money. I'll fight you every inch of the way for it." Her hands were shaking.

"Maybe there is something," Helen said in a low voice. "Maybe there is a way. The only reason I've kept Sam here all these years is because of Mother. It hasn't been any picnic. You must know that. My life hasn't been my own. But I knew she wanted him sheltered. She wanted a roof over his head and she wanted him with people who cared." She pushed her glasses back into place. The hairs on her upper lip were wet. "But what she wanted most was to see him back with his family . . . where he belongs."

"What are you talking about?"

"Take Sam back and keep him," Helen said. "Stay with him and be a family, and what's left of the money is yours." Her voice rose over Marie's laughter. "I've never seen him this bad. He's in terrible shape. It's probably all he needs. Lord knows"—she sniffed—"things couldn't get much worse for the both of you than they are right now."

"Oh yes they could," Marie roared. "I could get like you, Helen. Married to a man I despise just to have a roof over my head and a ring on my finger! Just so I could kneel down at the Communion rail with all the other phony bastards! No, you keep him, Helen, like you keep her locked up in her cage, like you keep Renie on his leash. . . ."

"Get out!" Helen demanded, jabbing her finger in Marie's face. "And if you ever dare step foot in here again, I'll have you arrested!"

She grabbed Helen's wrist, her fingernails deep in Helen's cold thin flesh. "You bitch!" she gasped. "You selfish, selfish bitch. I'll get that money. You'll see!"

"Call the police!" Helen began to shriek, jerking her head back from Marie's. "Call the police!"

The door to the kitchen opened slowly on Renie's tired, sad face. "You better go," he said. "You better get out, Marie, so there ain't no trouble now."

Bridget's fingers skittered over the doll's body as if they were typing. Fixed in the mirror, her eyes were small bright points and her breath came in eager pants. She started to hum. She remembered that one, remembered how she had knocked on the apartment door and had begged that one to take him back, her mouth at the door crack, the stripe of inner, lighter air cool against her dry lips that could not suck them through, could not set them straight, could not deliver him through love or faith or promises.

"Whatever you want," she had told that one, just as hard and deliberate as ever; not one whom she would have chosen for her son, but in the end she had come to believe that Sam must have somehow known she would be the better mate, young enough to be hopeful, base enough and coarse enough to fight against him and for him, though in the end not strong enough.

"Just open the door," the old woman had hissed, shamed to have her tenants witness this.

"No!"

"I'll help you. . . ."

"Help him!"

"Whatever you want . . ."

"I *want* you to take him away!"

"I'll take care of things. I'll—"

"It's too late. It's him! He doesn't want us."

"Oh I do," Sam had moaned, his brow at the door. "I do, my pet. I do!" His soiled and shapeless clothes, his wet rheumy eyes leaking tears seemed too unjust.

"Here!" the old woman had cried, her heart breaking. "Here!" And she had slid the bankbook under the door. "Ten thousand dollars," she'd said, then listened to the pages being turned.

"What good is this? It's in both your names."

"It'll be yours! Both of yours! Just be a family again!"

The bankbook had skimmed back under the door.

"Tell Sam that, Bridget. Not me!"

The last day of school had just ended. Benjy walked slowly toward his grandmother's house with his mother's note in his bookbag. This morning his mother had still been mad after her fight with Aunt Helen, plus she was nervous about Alice's graduation tonight. She had been running around the house in her slip trying to iron her skirt for work, write a note he was supposed to bring to his father after school, pick up the house, and plan for the special graduation dinner she was cooking tonight. Suddenly, she had been on them for everything, things that had nothing to do with Aunt Helen or graduation. It was always like that before an event or in any crisis: she would bring up the strangest things, complaining about old sins, while on her hands and knees she tried to sweep scarves of matted dust out from under the couch and growled up at Benjy that instead of hanging around the house watching TV all summer, he would walk up to the swimming pool every day for swimming lessons so he could go out in the boat with Mr. Briscoe. And Norm, she had yelled at the bathroom door, had better be at town hall today or not bother coming home. And Alice had better get off her high horse and realize there was more to life than mooning over Lester Stoner.

Benjy rang the doorbell, then held his breath, waiting. He hated these missions to his father. Norm refused to go on them anymore and his mother wouldn't think of asking Alice. Relieved when no one answered, he was tempted to leave the envelope in the mailbox, but his mother had insisted he make sure his father got it, and not Aunt Helen. He knocked on the door. Still no one came. Someone had to be inside with his grandmother, who throughout his memory had been senile and bedridden.

The three of them used to visit here every Sunday after Mass. But that had ended when Aunt Helen accused Norm of stealing her mission box. She said there were five dollars' worth of dimes in it, enough to feed two Chinese babies for one year. His mother went crazy. She told Helen she had a hell of a nerve accusing her son of thievery when she, Helen, was the biggest thief in the whole world. And, Benjy knew, a liar, too; there had been only thirty-one dimes in the box. Visions of those two Chinese babies' shrunken cheeks and bloated, starving bellies so tormented him that he finally slipped the money into Sister Mary Agatha's mission box at school. When the nun discovered the money, she told the class that among them sat a true Catholic, a giver who desired no recognition and no extra recess star on his tally sheet.

He knocked again, then listened. He could hear the drone of a vacuum cleaner. He ran off to the back door, where he knocked even louder. Still no one came. He could see the bars of his grandmother's crib through the window. Growing close to the house was a gnarled locust tree. He climbed onto a lower branch and tried to see in her window, but he was too low. Holding his breath, he climbed higher, then eased along a newly leafed limb until he could lean both hands on the sill.

There behind the bars his grandmother huddled in her pale bedclothes, her face narrow and small, her nose a sharp little beak. Her startled eyes darted toward his and she shivered. The gauzy bed jacket ruffled at her throat and her blue lips moved.

"Samuel!" she said suddenly, pointing at the window. "You get down now!"

"Wha . . . ? What the hell!" came Benjy's father's voice from the rocker at the foot of the crib. He had been sleeping. "Shit," he groaned, bracing his head on his hand.

Benjy drew back from the window so quickly that he almost fell. His father's blood-veined eyes peered blearily past the bars, and the old dread stirred in Benjy's heart of the hot foul breath and the clutch of those long, hard fingers demanding love and loyalty or even the change he always thought he heard jingling in his sons' pockets. Benjy held up the envelope. His father leaned closer, but Benjy had slid down the tree and was already at the back door, laying the envelope on the threshold. He ran down the driveway.

Helen LaChance slipped the envelope into her apron pocket. Just then the inside door opened and her brother sagged against the frame.

"Where'd he go?" he slurred, wincing in the sun.

"Who?"

"Benjy."

"He's not here," she said, heading back to her garden.

"I just saw him." Sam gestured. "Up in the tree there . . ."

She rolled her eyes and sighed.

Stepping past her, Sam bellowed, "Benjy! Benjy! Benjy!"

"Get inside!" she hissed. Across the street the rectory door was opening. Howard Menka looked out.

Sam looked up at the tree, then scratched his head and went back inside.

Helen drove her rusty trowel deep into the warm black soil. In all the yard only this patch of earth was fertile enough to yield. This was all she had saved from the sea of weeds that by summer's end would again be vined in a tumble of jungly growth. It was all Howard Menka's fault. Now he was trying to turn his sister against her. But so far, Jozia was still loyal. "Thank God," she sighed, crossing herself quickly with the trowel. She leaned back and pulled another tomato seedling from the flat. She set the plant in the newly dug hole and scooped soil over its thin white roots. She smiled. The Jet Stars were always the first to bloom and ripen. This year the Monsignor would have her juicy tomatoes before anyone else's.

Last summer Sam had staggered out here and fallen into the garden, crushing all her Jet Stars. Iris McAvoy's Beefsteak tomatoes had gotten to the rectory before hers. So this year, to be on the safe side, she had ordered a roll of chicken wire and metal stakes. Six dollars' worth. Six more dollars added to the tally of her brother's sins.

She sat back on her heels and ripped open her sister-in-law's letter. *Dear Sam,* she read, shaking her head at the profane groveling, the threatening accusations. . . . Her eyes widened. *I am hiring a lawyer to look into that trust fund,* Marie had written. Helen's mind quickly computed each account. In her file box was every receipt, every bill received since her first day as her brother's guardian.

> *That money is yours and therefore also your children's. If you won't help me with Alice's tuition money, Sam, then my lawyer will take you and that sister of yours to court. I have been advised that we will end up with every cent of that ten thousand dollars.*

Let her, Helen thought, as she shredded the letter. With her trowel she dug another hole, into which she pressed the pieces. "Let her hire ten lawyers," she muttered. Everything was perfectly legal and aboveboard. She had followed the old Judge's counsel to a T. Her records were perfect. Every penny had been accounted for. "I am above reproach," she whispered, and as she stood up, that old bile seeped into her throat to think that this house of her childhood would eventually be her brother's and not hers. With her mother's death she would be homeless. *Odd,* she thought, looking toward the buckled roofing shingles, *odd that Marie hadn't said a word about the house and the tenements going to Sam and his children. Maybe Marie didn't know.* She hoped not, because once Sam found out, her life would be a nightmare. Well, he won't get much, she thought, her shrewd eyes scanning the peeling paint and rotting clapboard. Let it fall to pieces. He had never cared, so why should she?

From the back door of the rectory, Howard Menka had watched Benjy Fermoyle run down the driveway and up the street. As the boy ran down Main Street, Howard shambled down the rectory steps with a step stool and a bucket of soapy water in which floated his big yellow sponge. He set everything down next to the Monsignor's car.

The Monsignor wanted his car clean for the high school graduation tonight. Howard dipped the fat sponge in and out of the water bucket until it was squishy with soap bubbles and then he climbed up on the stool and began to scrub the roof of the long, black Oldsmobile. The Monsignor had bought this sponge for him last year in Greece. When he had showed it to Jozia, she said she wouldn't be proud if Mrs. LaChance gave her a mop for a present. In fact, she'd be insulted. Now even his special sponge made him sad. All day long, everything had made him sad. He averted his gaze from the Fermoyle house, where Jozia might be watching him this very moment. He came off the step stool with a groan. Last night's fight with his sister had left him with more of an ache from his heart than from the lump on his head.

The Menka twins had been together all their fifty-one years. They lived in a spotless but gaudy little apartment over the Holy Articles Shoppe, and they were the store's best customers. They now possessed almost every saint's statue the store sold, and in front of each was a red-glassed votive candle that they lit on Sundays and holy days. Jozia's favorite was the Infant Jesus of Prague, because she could dress it in so many different outfits, linen gowns and satin robes with high stiff collars that they bought from their landlady. Howard's favorite was Saint Joseph because people were all the time saying how simple Saint Joseph was. And that's what people said about him, too.

The church bells rang three times and Howard looked around, thinking he'd forgotten to bring something out. For weeks now he'd had this sense of loss. It had started that morning Jozia wouldn't let him sit with her at Mass. Howard had always loved church: it was the only place he felt safe, and church never changed. Now everything seemed to be changing. Sunday Mass used to be his favorite time because they could get all dressed up, and after, they'd buy doughnuts on the way home. But even Sundays had gotten spoiled ever since Jozia had told him to buy doughnuts just for himself because she was watching her weight. Howard asked her who she watching wait. And he stood there in front of the bakery looking up and down the street while Jozia rolled her eyes and said what she meant was, she didn't want to get fat and doughnuts make you fat. So then, of course, he didn't feel like eating doughnuts all by himself, and so Sunday hadn't felt like Sunday. And now he wasn't even going to enjoy washing the Monsignor's car, because he kept thinking what she'd said about the sponge.

He moved the step stool and began to scrub the other side of the car's roof. Soapy bubbles rose from his fingers like glass rings. He smiled. There were still two nice times to look forward to: the Fourth of July band concert in two weeks and then his very favorite, their bus trip. Once a month he and Jozia dressed up in their Sunday clothes and took a bus to the state hospital in Waterbury to see their only living relative, a redheaded cousin named Perda.

Almost as pleasurable as the trip was all the shopping they did beforehand at the dime store for penny candy, brightly colored pinwheels, plastic thimbles, and Howard's favorite, wooden squeeze bars with a little tumbling man inside. These they passed among the patients in the ward, partly because they liked them, but mostly to show off their affluence and independence.

The visits were far more important to the twins than they were to Perda, who would lie curled in her bed, her sour face to the wall. "Like a wilty old carrot," they would giggle on the bus home, laughing, and gossiping about the different patients, so that by the time they stepped back into their apartment, they would be feeling not only good about themselves, but close to each other.

He looked up, suddenly troubled by the memory of Jozia staring out the bus window all the way back last month. When they got home she had gone straight to bed. He stood now with the sponge dripping down his side. So even the trips were changing. It was all the pigman Grondine Carson's fault. If Jozia could only get a job somewhere else, then she wouldn't be so handy to Carson and then she'd be just his twin sister again and things could go back to the way they used to be.

He climbed off the step stool and went to the faucet on the side of the rectory. He unlooped the thick black hose and pulled it down the driveway. As he sprayed the soapy car, he stared up at the Fermoyle house. Last winter the paint had lifted on the gingerbread trim of the roofline. Now the peeling had spread like a blistery rash along the clapboards. He knew that the corner section of the porch floor sagged with dry rot. He looked away miserably.

If he had stayed on as Mrs. LaChance's handyman, maybe Jozia wouldn't have gotten so friendly with Carson. But everything had started changing after Mrs. LaChance made him poison that poor dog. After that he couldn't look Mr. LaChance in the eye, he felt like such a murderer, and he couldn't stand being near Sam, who'd pester him about it every time he got drunk. All his bad dreams had started then, too, and then their rent had gone up and Mrs. LaChance refused to give him a raise. Well, one good thing had happened and that was this job for the Monsignor, who paid better than Mrs. LaChance did. But then everybody paid better than her, he had tried again last night to tell his sister.

Jozia had been cooking while Howard told her how that rich Nora Hinds had been to the rectory for some relic the Monsignor had gotten special for her son, who was in the hospital again in Boston. Howard had explained how he was mulching the geranium bed under the study window when he heard Mrs. Hinds talking about her brother's new business. He had just quit the family department store to open a factory that made—

"Toilet paper," Jozia had said, flipping the sizzling hamburg patties. "Grondine already tole me. He says it's gonna open up the end of summer."

"I'll betcha'd make ten times there what she pays you," Howard said.

"Like I was telling Grondine the other day, Miz LaChance and me been together so long money ain't really the point," she said.

"If money ain't the point with the little we got, I dunno what is," Howard said, determined to ignore all mention of the pigman.

"Feelings, that's what." Jozia sniffed. "And caring 'bout people."

"Well I guess you're just about dumb now as you were then," Howard said.

"Look who's calling dumb; you didn't even pass haitch grade!"

"Mebbe not, but I ain't so dumb to make googly eyes at a pigman!" he said.

"Shut up!"

"You shut up!"

"Stupid ass!"

"Stupid ass yourself! And the next time you get all perfumied up for that Carson, ask him if it ain't true what people say him and his pigs do, one to the other. . . ."

That's when the greasy spatula hit the side of his head, so hard the lump was up before the stars were out of his eyes, and then she took off like a bat out of hell. He had staggered to the window and, to his horror, saw Carson's garbage truck stop in front of the Holy Articles Shoppe downstairs. His chest had tightened with pain as he watched Carson jump down from the truck. Carson tucked his splashy orange shirt into his pants, creased like they'd just come off the ironing board. Never had the old pigman looked so fancy. Carson had opened the truck door and helped Jozia in, and then as he walked around to his side, he had spit on his fingers and smoothed back his white hair. When she had returned at ten o'clock she went straight to her room. Howard had brought her cocoa and kept saying how sorry he was, but she had just laid with her back to him, staring at the wall. After a while he gave up and went to bed and had the worst dream of his life: he was walking up and down the dime-store aisles, trying to pick out presents, but everything he saw was either ugly or broken. Then this terrible pain started in his chest and hadn't let up once all day.

Howard laid down the hose and went to turn off the water. When he came back, he found the new priest rolling up his sleeves.

"Thought I'd give you a hand," the priest said in his funny accent. Mrs. Arkaday said he was from New York. Howard had overheard her telling Monsignor this morning that the new priest didn't act like any priest she'd ever known.

"I love washing cars," Father Gannon said, taking the sponge out of the pail and sloshing suds all over the hood.

Howard watched the priest wash the same places he had just done. New people were hard for Howard. Change confused him. Like now; his head buzzed. The priest didn't like the job he'd done.

"Where I come from, hardly anybody has their own car," the priest called over the rumble of an approaching truck. He lifted the wipers and scrubbed the windshield. "The last car I washed was my old . . . my dad's." Father Gannon wrung out the sponge. "All his life he wanted his own car. So he bought this old Dodge and washed it. . . ."

Howard stared at the garbage truck cruising slowly down the street. He saw Carson peering over the wheel up at the Fermoyle house.

"And the next morning it was gone." The young priest laughed.

Howard closed his eyes, certain the garbage truck was stopping, certain he'd see his sister fly out of the house and into Carson's arms.

"Howard?" the young priest said. He tapped Howard's shoulder.

Howard opened his eyes. The truck was at the corner and Jozia wasn't in it.

"Father Gannon!" barked the Monsignor from an upstairs window. "What do you think you're doing?"

"I'm trying to help Howard," Father Gannon said with a wave of the dripping sponge.

"I told you yesterday! Mrs. Arkaday doesn't need your help. Howard doesn't need your help. But I do!" the Monsignor said.

Father Gannon looked at Howard and shrugged.

"Now!" the Monsignor growled.

The young priest ran into the rectory. Mrs. Arkaday came to the screen door and shook her head in disgust at Howard. He turned on the water, and while he rinsed off the gleaming black car, a terrible pain clutched his heart and he was sure a piece of it had just broken off and was spinning loose in his chest. Now everyone was mad at him.

Sam Fermoyle's head pounded. He sat on the edge of his bed with his head in his hands. What had Benjy wanted? Marie must have sent him. They never came to see him. Three kids, and they never came, unless *she* wanted something: the kids need school clothes; they need shoes, boots, books; they need their teeth fixed. But what about him? Nobody gave a good damn about his needs. She'd probably sent him over here to pick his pockets. Once he'd found the kid going through the box of old pictures he kept under his bed. Little thief, goddamn little thief, always after something, scrounging around. Jesus Christ, he thought, she's ruining those kids, training them to shake down their own father. If he had any gold fillings, he'd probably wake up some morning to find one of his kids sitting on his chest with pliers in his mouth.

He scratched his arms, then his chest and legs. It felt like he was crawling with bugs. What if the DT's were starting; it had been over twenty-four hours since his last drink and if he didn't get one soon, he'd be climbing the walls. Goddamn Hammelwitz calling the cops on him.

"Goddamn Hammelwitz, chickenshitlittlefuckingjewbartender," he muttered, cringing with the blast of sound coming down the hallway. It was Jozia's eternal vacuum sucking the brains right out of his skull. The vacuum banged against the door, then banged again before rolling off, its tanklike drone subsiding in the distance.

He looked wearily around this narrow room he had always lived in, except for the bittersweet eight-year limbo of his marriage. There was a mahogany bed with high carved pineapple posts, an old wooden radio he had once set for a moment on the rosewood chair brought in from the dining room and then never moved, and a tarnished brass floor lamp that didn't work anymore. Three pictures hung on the wall over his bed. One was a photo of his mother smiling from her crib and, next to her, Alice in her First Communion veil; the second, Marie and the children in front of a Christmas tree; and the third, a smeared number painting of the Last Supper that Alice had given him one Christmas.

He groaned. His tongue was furry and dry and his throat was raw. He felt sick to his stomach. It was this constant stink, mothballs and cedar, and in every drawer lilac bars and lavender to mask the smell of his mother's long, diapered dying.

He got up slowly and opened the window, squinting dizzily away from the sun that bobbled atop the cross of the steeple. In the rectory driveway the Monsignor's long black car floated in a sea of soap bubbles. Howard Menka squatted down, scrubbing a whitewall tire.

Sam knelt beside his bed and felt underneath as far as he could reach. Then, cursing, he got up and yanked the bed out from the wall. All that he found was a newspaper fuzzed with dust, a sweat-stiffened sock, and a pair of soiled undershorts. On Helen's orders, Jozia was not to clean his room when he was drinking. "Some goddamn housekeeper. Takes my bottle and leaves the dirt!" he muttered as he lurched from the room toward the howl of her vacuum.

Jozia pushed the big upright past him. He followed her into the crowded front parlor. When the table and chairs had been moved in here years ago to make space in the dining room for his mother's crib, all the other furniture had to be pushed back against the walls, so that now, if you sat on the sofa, you couldn't see over the dining-room table to the Morris chair on the opposite wall. But it had never mattered, because in all these years there had been few guests to sit in the parlor and none to dine at the table.

Jozia was trying to get around the table with the vacuum, but she was running out of cord.

"Better tell me where you put it," he warned over the drone, poking the hump in her back to to get her attention.

Her cord caught; she turned, staring at the door. She would speak to him only in his sister's presence. She knew who the boss was in this house, as well as she knew the fragility of his tenancy here, and this enraged him.

"Where'd you put it, feeb?" he snarled, jerking his fist inches from her face.

She continued to stare past him.

"Shit!" he cried with a savage kick at the vacuum. It fell on its side, whining and whirring, its wheels spinning like a tantrum of angry little feet. Without a word, Jozia reached down and set it upright. He kicked it again, and the bag fell off, spewing dirt onto the rug.

"Crazy man," she muttered as she attempted to reattach the bag. "Goddamn crazy man. I'm getting awful sick of it. . . ."

He stepped back, both indignant and a little sobered by the dark clutch of her voice. Her, the dimwit, calling him crazy.

"Grondine's right," she was muttering, "thirty years is just too long. . . ."

He tiptoed over the worn carpet, wincing as the floorboards creaked. He came into the dining room, where his mother huddled in her crib, her head turned to the window. The room reeked of talcum powder and dry urine. Every morning Helen and Jozia bathed her from pitted metal bowls of tepid water and antiseptic soap, but there was still this smell. He started past her, suddenly feeling as giddy and lightheaded as a thieving boy. She turned with a feathery rustle, and her hands flew toward the wooden slats. "The yoke is broken!" she cried out.

He darted into the kitchen and opened the door next to the stove. He knelt down and felt along the cracked linoleum for the change that sometimes fell from Renie's pants, which hung overhead. This was his brother-in-law's wardrobe, as well as the mop and broom closet. Renie never seemed to mind wearing clothes that reeked of onions, fried fish, boiled cabbage. For several years now Renie had slept in the small windowless room that in Sam's youth had been the pantry. Banishment from Helen's bedroom had been triggered by Riddles, a stray dog Renie had taken in one stormy night and the next morning would not relinquish. "I cannot bear deceit," Helen had sniffed, convinced he had lured the dog home, though brother and sister both knew the most heinous deceit of all had been the vile commingling of her dry chaste flesh with the coarse loins of a man who had proffered love, when her deepest desire had been satisfied with the sacrament of matrimony, that blessed and bewildering ligature to a man who snored and farted between her ironed sheets.

Sam stood up, chuckling at the thought of Renie letting one break, ripe and warm, against Helen's rigid back. He groped along the tacky shelves. Renie had once been easy pickings for Sam until an IRS audit a few years ago had cost him eight hundred dollars in back taxes and penalties. Now Renie distrusted everyone, particularly Helen, his own wife, who he suspected had turned him in for the reward.

Sam stood on a chair and probed the back of the highest shelf. All it held was more of Renie's displaced junk: dusty cigar boxes stuffed with sales slips, a framed bowling certificate for perfect attendance as a substitute, and a Good Citizen citation from the Elks. He was climbing down when his eye caught on a book of rent receipts. Opening it, he smiled at the elegant script, the blank inviting lines. He shoved it into his pocket at the sharp approach of Helen's heels.

She watched from the doorway. She was a small woman, her thin frame curiously contradicted by the large drooping breasts, no more than clumsy hindrances now as she tried to fold her arms.

"Jozia tells me you lost something and you think she stole it," she said slowly as if to a child. "What did you lose, Sam?"

He edged toward the back door. "Nothing," he said. "She's just trying to start trouble." He waved his hand in disgust.

Jozia's face constricted over Helen's head. "Yes he did, Miz LaChance. He said I stoled his bottle and I should tell him where I put it or else he was gonna kick my teeth in. And then he kicked the Hoover and then the bag fell off and I been all this time tryna get it back on right. . . ."

"Turn the feeb off," he moaned and, opening the door, stumbled into the trapped heat of the back porch.

"Crazy man! You crazy man!" Jozia spat over the safety of Helen's shoulder.

"Jozia!" Helen hissed, afraid someone would hear.

"I don't have to take that. I don't have to take his mouth. No sir! I can work a lot of better places. A lot!"

"Oh Jozia, please Jozia, just get back in," Helen said. She leaned over the railing and called down shrilly, "Where are you going?"

"I'm running away from home," he called back and then, seeing Mrs. Clarke, their next-door neighbor, peeking out from her bedroom window, he bellowed, "That's right. At the tender age of forty-eight, Samuel Fermoyle is running away to find fame and fortune and bright lights and horny broads, and anyone who wants to come along is sincerely invited." He staggered down the driveway's incline to the street, his right arm crooked at the end of an imaginary bindle and his other hand tipping an imaginary hat, first to Howard Menka hosing the Monsignor's hubcaps, then to the three little Clarke girls, who cringed with giggles as their black terrier nipped after his frayed cuffs.

"Come with me, Howard," Sam called. "Lay down your hose and follow me. . . . Get out of here, common cur. . . . Put aside those menial tools, Howard, and follow me, you stupid son of a bitch." His heedless voice streamered behind as he crossed Main Street on his way to perform that most guarded of Helen's rituals, her weekly descension into the Gut, where she collected the rents from her mother's decrepit tenements.

In the rectory dining room Monsignor Burke sat at the table, head bowed, hands clasped over his plate. "Amen," he whispered, crossing himself, his eyes on the kitchen door. Because of graduation tonight, he was eating dinner early. His stomach growled at the smell of frying fish. Mrs. Kilpatrick had sent over trout her husband had caught. Well, not caught, really. Mr. Kilpatrick was a fish-and-game warden whose job it was to stock the lake with trout.

The doorbell rang. A woman spoke; then Father Gannon spoke. The Monsignor winced. It was that god-awful pest, Mary Squireman, president of the Sodality. Her husband owned Squireman's Press, which printed the Sunday bulletins free of charge. "It's just been too hot for a bake sale," Mrs. Squireman was saying. "I just told Ann Brody we should wait for fall, but now that she's treasurer all she cares about is being the best—"

"Hey now, no back-stabbing!" Father Gannon cut her off. "Maybe we should get Ann Brody in here, too. That way it'd be an honest, face-to-face—"

The office door banged shut and the Monsignor groaned. A cat-fight in the rectory, that's all he needed. This new priest had no polish. His table manners were vile. Even freshly shaved, he had a coarse, swarthy look that embarrassed the Monsignor. As far as he could see, Gannon was a thug whose erratic personality veered between frantic intensity and cold distraction.

The Monsignor tensed with the sound of flatware clanking and tinkling in the kitchen. Now came the scrape of metal as Mrs. Arkaday shook the sputtering fry pan back and forth over the burner. His mouth watered with the hot buttery smell. He was tired of late dinners, and sick calls in the middle of the night, and six a. m. Mass every single day. The Bishop had promised that this new curate would be as young and energetic and ambitious as his last curate, who was pastor now in Glens Falls. A young man could go places from here. Saint Mary's could be a real springboard for a curate willing to pay his dues and learn the ropes.

Mrs. Arkaday backed through the swinging door with the golden trout still sizzling on its bed of buttery rice. The glazed baby beets glistened like jewels.

"Beautiful," the Monsignor sighed. Mrs. Arkaday thanked him, then returned to the kitchen. At least he had an excellent house-keeper. He had eaten in other rectories and had seen how deeply the poorer quality of meals could affect morale. After he had eaten only a few forkfuls, he felt calmer and stronger. He picked the tender flesh carefully from the bones. He would be patient with this young priest. He would guide him. Management, he would tell him. That's what it took. And a good ear. Nodding, he chewed thoughtfully, his rapturous gaze on the plate. He would explain that it takes more than prayer. Today's clerics needed a pious heart and an astute mind. He had petitioned the Bishop for "a modern man, one burning with the zeal of reality." There were roofs to repair, a parish hall to acquire, and he needed a practical man. He rolled his eyes at the thought of that ascetic he'd had six years ago, Father Kaminski, who yearned for sainthood. Almost starved himself to death. Wore long woolen underwear in the summer and wept shamelessly in the confessional.

Mrs. Arkaday returned now with the second trout on a blue platter. It took only a gesture of his fork for her to slide the fish onto his plate. Still chewing, he lifted his napkin to his mouth and delicately extricated two sharp bones. Just then there was a loud bang outside the kitchen door that startled them both.

"Howard," he said, shaking his head. There was another bang. Now, suddenly, the rectory, indeed the entire street, quaked with racket.

The Monsignor blinked with wide wet eyes as Mrs. Arkaday rushed into the kitchen. He clutched his throat, gagging on the bone embedded in his gullet. As the commotion intensified, Mrs. Arkaday's voice rose angrily from the kitchen.

I am dying, the Monsignor thought, staring up at the dolorous face that stared back from the crucifix. *Your faithful servant chokes to death, and you do nothing! Damn you! Help me!* Just then he felt the bone pop, then slide painfully free, and he was not grateful but angry now. Indignant.

"What is it?" he panted as Mrs. Arkaday hurried back into the dining room.

"It's just Grondine Carson's truck. He's stopped in front of the Fermolyles'." She peered out the window. "But that banging noise," she said, pointing toward the driveway. "It's Howard. From the way the garage door's shaking, I think he's inside kicking it."

Norman Fermoyle ran into town hall and up the marble steps to the second floor, where a janitor dozed in a chair. Norm nudged him and asked where Mr. Greene's office was. "I have to see him about a job," he added nervously. He had left the car double-parked, with Donna Creller inside waiting for him.

"Street Department's there," the janitor said, pointing across the hall at one door. "But Greene's in there with the Recreation Department." He pointed to the adjacent door, and Norm hesitated between them. "Better wait in there, though," the janitor said, nodding at the first door. "All hell's gonna break loose."

Once inside, Norm sat in the chair by the door. From the next office came a buzz of voices. He picked lint from his pants, rolled it into a ball, and flicked it across the room. Then he retied both shoes. He cracked his knuckles. After five minutes had passed, he got up to examine the map on the wall. Red and yellow pins had been stuck into various streets on the map. He smiled, imagining the chaos of fleets of trucks rumbling into the wrong neighborhoods, their crews leaping out, jackhammers biting huge chunks from all the wrong roads and sidewalks. Idly, he ran his finger down the map to the lot that his grandmother's house stood on and, there, stuck a large red pin.

The voices grew louder in the next office. He stepped quickly from the map and turned to the pictures hanging on the wall behind Mr. Greene's desk. The subject in all these photographs was Mr. Greene, leading his band. From the next office now came Mr. Greene's irritated voice. "Every year for sixty-two years, the conductors have been able to pick out their own music. I'm sorry, but I don't understand why this year has to be any different."

"We just told you!" someone said. "Because we don't want any more fiascoes like last year."

"Then close down that popcorn shack and you won't!" Mr. Greene said. "The problem isn't my music, and we all damn well know it! The problem's Joey Seldon!"

"No, Jard, it's the kids. They're getting restless!" someone replied.

"It's the thugs that're restless!" Greene declared. "So is that what we've come to? You want me to pander to thugs?"

"Jard's right," came another voice. "What we need are more cops patrolling the concerts. That'll put an end—"

A gavel was rapping.

"That's not the issue here!" piped a woman's high, firm voice. "Here, these are some of the songs the committee's chosen."

Norm could hear papers being passed around. He looked at the clock. He'd been here twenty minutes. He went to the window and looked down at the dented, dusty roof of his mother's car. Jesus, Donna Creller was waving and hollering out the car window to a group of girls walking along with ice cream cones. He cringed as one of the girls came up to the car and gave Donna a lick of her cone. Damn it, he knew those girls. He should have parked in the lot behind town hall. Not only was Donna Creller a flaming beast; she was only fourteen years old. Weeb knew her from mowing her family's lawn. He said the trick was to close your eyes the whole time and just keep thinking it was Sandra Dee. But Weeb had made the mistake of telling everyone and now he'd been lost in the shuffle. Every day at three, Holy Innocents was crawling with high school guys all wanting a crack at the fabled Donna. Norm had thought he had everything planned perfectly, but now Greene's being this late was fouling him up. Donna's mother worked at the library until five, so now he only had an hour left. Plus, he had to get ready for Alice's graduation tonight.

The voices next door rose heatedly.

"I won't do it!" insisted Jarden Greene. "A conductor needs license. He needs artistic freedom!"

"Cripe," groaned a deep voice that Norm recognized as the mayor's. "All we're asking is for you to pep it up a little, Jard. You know, change with the times."

"You're asking me to pander!" cried Greene.

"No, goddamn it!" the mayor roared. "I'm telling you to quit playing the same boring crap you been playing for the last six years!"

A door slammed, then voices rose as the gavel banged.

"Way to go, Greenie!" the janitor called after the hard little footsteps clicking down the marble hall. The door flew open and in stormed Jarden Greene, hands clenched tightly at his sides, his thin mustache quivering over his lip. Norm had never realized how tiny Greene was, until now.

Greene's eyes narrowed on him. "What do you want?"

"I'm supposed to see you about a laborer's job, Mr. Greene? For the summer?"

Greene kept staring as if to place him. "You ever work on a town crew before?"

"No sir."

"How old are you?"

"Sixteen, sir."

"Who sent you up here?"

"The town clerk, sir. Mr. Sheets. My uncle, Renie LaChance, asked him if I could have a summer job, and he said you'd—"

"Oh yes," Green interrupted. "Sam Fermoyle's boy."

"Yes sir," Norm said, determined not to take his eyes off Greene.

"Your father was on one of my crews for a time," said Greene. "For a very brief time."

"Oh, I didn't know that, sir," Norm lied.

Greene sighed. "I'm going to put it to you straight, Fermoyle. It shouldn't be this way, but in the end it all comes down to politics. I pretty much have to hire whatever walks through that door if the town clerk sends him up. Which is how your father got hired."

Norm did not even blink.

"The thing is," Greene continued, "Sheets can get you on, but once you're on, I'm the boss, and I run a tight ship in this department, young man."

"I'm sure you do, sir,"

"No six-man crews in my department to do the job of one man."

"No sir," Norm said, rubbing his nose to hide the smirk.

"Like I said, I'm putting it to you straight, now, Fermoyle, because I shoot straight, and I shoot from the hip." He looked at Norm, hard. "Your father screwed me bad once. Took off with one of my trucks up to Burlington, and when he came back three days later, he couldn't remember where he'd left it. You're not like him, you don't drink, do you?"

Norm's mouth fell open. *The little prick* . . . for a moment he thought he'd said it aloud.

"I'm sorry it had to be said, but I'm that kind. I lay my cards right out."

"Yes sir, you sure do."

Greene smiled. "I like your spunk, young man. You got a straightforward way and I like that." He held out his hand. "This Monday, then! Eight sharp at the town barns."

Norm looked down at the extended hand and put his own in his pocket. He smiled. "I'll tell you what, Mr. Greene. I'm going to think it over, and if nothing better comes along, maybe I'll be there Monday."

Greene's pinched expression might have been satisfaction enough, but not for Norman Fermoyle. Jarden Greene would pay for this. Norm left the office and ran down the hallway, taking the steps two at a time. Greene could shove it! Uncle Renie could shove it! And if his mother didn't like it, she could shove it too. The whole goddamn friggin' world could shove it. He ran along the sidewalk and jumped into the car, where the beastly Donna Creller opened her mouth, glinting with braces, and started whining about how hot she was and how she was so thirsty she could die. He leaped out, opened her door, and pulled her onto the sidewalk, and then he reached onto the seat for her lunchbox, which he threw at her, then jumped back inside the car and peeled into traffic, all without a word, because in his skull there was this scream, this piercing scream.

Sam Fermoyle came along West Street. At five o'clock the day was hot and still sunny, though everything seemed smeared with a watery blur. He kept blinking to clear his eyes and now he rubbed his nose. It was in the air, all right, a stink that turned his stomach. He stopped in front of the post office to uncap the half pint of gin he'd bought three blocks back. One more long swallow and the bottle was empty. "Shit," he muttered, holding it up to be sure. "Shit."

A woman in a yellow sundress came toward him, then veered quickly off the sidewalk. She walked in the street.

"Sealed with a kiss," he muttered, opening the mailbox. The bottle fell inside with a hollow clunk. He patted his pockets, which bulged with the week's rents from ten of the twelve apartments his mother owned . . . or Helen owned . . . he didn't know who owned what anymore . . . it was confusing. He had collected one hundred fifty-one dollars. Most of the tenants hadn't wanted to pay him; they were afraid of Helen. But in the end, to get rid of him, they had all paid as long as they got receipts. "Poor bastards," he muttered, sniffing his armpit, thinking that must be the stink: the squalor had soiled him. He squinted ahead, suddenly indignant. Those apartments were nothing more than hovels: broken railings on the stairs, no window screens, toilets that had to be plunged with each crap. Helen didn't put a penny back into the properties. One older woman had told him that his mother had been kind, but his sister, Helen, was a viper. He had marked the old woman's rent receipt paid up through the summer, and he had promised to get her stove working again. And he meant it. He did. Somehow. Someday. One way or another. A stab of fear lodged between his shoulder blades. The last time he'd screwed around with Helen's rents she'd had him carted off to dry out in Waterbury, the state hospital. But this time he was going to give her the money. Most of it, anyway. All he'd wanted was a few bucks, he'd tell her. If she'd just give him a few bucks when he needed it, if she'd just let him run his own life . . . He'd only done this to prove a point, that was all. That was the main reason. Principle. Sometimes it was just a fucking matter of fucking principle. The important thing was to believe in yourself . . . to believe yourself . . . or something like that. He took a deep breath, straightened his shoulders, then crossed Merchants Row, placing one foot directly in front of the other in a rigid gait that by the opposite curbside had deteriorated into a dizzy reel. Heading straight for the signpost, he caught himself, then took a cautious step onto the curb. By the time he got to Hammie's Bar and Grill, his eyes were sun-blind and raw, his head boiled with heat, and his thirst had become a need so palpable, so beyond his will, it seemed to emerge from his throat of its own accord, unslakable and pulsating, sucking him into this soothing darkness of beer-slicked wood and men's smoky voices.

"Jesus Christ," someone groaned as the door closed.

All he could see were the amber lights around the cut-glass mirror that glinted with bottles. He raised a hand in blind greeting.

"No trouble, now you got that, Sam?"

"No trouble," he said. "Honest, Hammie. No more fuckin' trouble."

He could barely make them out. Their backs were turned. Their indifference angered him. He knew just about every single man here, had bought them drinks, had poured out his heart to them. "Son of

a bitch," he muttered, feeling his way through the tables to the bar.
All the stools were taken, so he stood at the end. "Shot and a beer,"
he told Hammie with a nod.

Hammie held out his hand; Sam put a dollar in it. Hammie put
that into his pocket and held out his hand again. "And twenty more
for the plumber."

"The plumber?" Sam peered up at Hammie's sagging jowls.

"For the toilet you broke."

"Oh my God," Sam said, laying two wrinkled tens in the soft
padding of Hammie's palm. "Don't tell me I ripped the fuckin'
hopper off the floor." He turned and looked at the other men. "My
brute strength. Can you believe it?" He grinned, but no one looked
at him.

"You plugged it up with toilet paper," Hammie said, laying
the shot glass and the beer mug on the counter. "And then you
flushed it."

"Asshole," someone muttered.

"I'm sorry," he said, turning now with his beer. He'd already
downed the shot. There was no place to sit.

"This time you wanna piss, you leave," Hammie warned. "Next
time it's not no lockup. Next time I press charges!"

Sam just stood there. *Fuckingsonofachickenshit,* he thought, his
eyes and mouth heavy with insult, his head bobbing slightly. As a kid
he had felt sorry for Abraham Hammelwitz's son, covered with
chicken crud, delivering the family eggs from store to store, house to
house.

"Got a job, Fermoyle?" asked the dark man hunched next to
him. He gestured at Sam's wadded bills and said his name was
Haddad.

Squinting through the haze, Sam tried to place him. Plastic
pocket liner stuffed with pens. Renie wore one, too. Some kind of
salesman . . . some kind of poor sniveling, pestering bastard no one
likes.

"Beer, buddy?" Sam asked, nudging his arm. Sam's beer sloshed
from the mug and ran down the counter.

"For chrissakes!" Haddad exploded, jerking his arm from Sam,
who tightened his grip as he tried to apologize. "Look what the hell

you did!" The thick dark hairs on Haddad's hands and arms glistened with beer.

"Jesus Christ," another man said as Sam lost his balance and collapsed against his back. His money fell to the floor.

"Get out!" Hammie ordered.

"Now look," Sam began, but Hammie's dense flesh was already at his elbow, nudging him along. "Now look . . . that's my . . ." he kept saying and trying to turn back. He wanted to tell Hammie his money was back there on the floor, but Hammie had butted him to the door. "Stay outta here!" Hammie growled, opening the door. "Go someplace else to die!"

"My rents!" Sam cried, clutching his wrist. His voice broke. "Oh shit, Hammie. My sister'll kill me. All the rents're in there. I dropped the fuckin' rents!"

Hammie turned toward the bar. "See any dough on the floor?"

Some of the men glanced down and shook their heads. Hammie took a step inside. "You see his dough, Haddad? Maybe you got it for him?"

"Oh yes!" Haddad said, jumping off the stool and making his way toward them. "I didn't think he should . . . you know," he said, gesturing, his mouth at Hammie's ear. "I was gonna have you hold it . . . you know, after." He gestured at Sam.

"Really? Is that what you were gonna do?" Hammie sneered. He snatched the bills from Haddad and stuffed them into Sam's shirt pocket. The men at the bar laughed.

"C'mon," Haddad grunted with a tug at Sam's elbow. "C'mon, old buddy. Let's get a move on," he said, steering him onto the sidewalk. "I'll give him a hand," Haddad called.

"Yah, I'll bet you will," Hammie called back sourly, and the men laughed even louder.

Haddad's office was a dingy haze of dented file cabinets and dust. There were three different calendars on the wall, each showing a different month. In the corner on the floor was a large black typewriter. Sam sat at Haddad's desk, which was strewn with papers and with an ashtray overflowing with butts. From here, Sam could see the blue tubing that said HAMMIE'S BAR AND GRILL.

"I'm Bob Haddad." He held out his hand to Sam. "Haddad Realty Insurance and Finance Company. Haddad RIFCO." He cleared his throat and drew back his hand. "My wife, Astrid, works with your uh . . . with Marie."

"Marie," Sam repeated numbly, nodding again. The steel wall rose in his brain, blocking thought and memory.

"I see your daughter around with Les Stoner, the Chief's kid. Boy, that's a tough one. Stoner's one of my policyholders. His wife. She's kind of had the course. Won't see Christmas, last I heard." Haddad's face darkened and he shook his head. "My luck, let me tell you. Twenty-five thousand and the week after he signs the policy they find out she's gonzo!" Haddad wiped his sweaty brow.

"Gotta butt?" Sam asked thickly. His tongue swelled in his mouth. His jaw hung open. He had to keep refocusing to see Haddad, who shook a cigarette from his pack and gave it to him. Sam let Haddad light it, but it kept sliding from his lips. It fell onto the papers, and when he didn't pick it up, Haddad placed it in the ashtray.

"What time is it?" Sam asked. "I gotta go."

"You going to the graduation? You got plenty of time."

Sam stared at the smoking cigarette. The graduation. Alice. Had it come so soon? She was just a baby. They were all babies, and he was a young man again. He felt in his pockets for her baby picture to show Haddad. He pulled the crumpled bills from his shirt pocket and dropped them on the desk. No pictures. Fucking Helen. She took everything. Everything! He picked up the cigarette and took a long, deep drag. "I gotta go," he sighed.

"You got her graduation present?"

Sam shook his head.

"You got the dough for one."

Sam looked down at the money.

" 'Course all the stores are closed now. I know! How about that typewriter?" Haddad said. "I'm selling it. It's used, but all the keys work." He pushed aside the money, papers, and ashtray and set the typewriter in front of Sam. He rolled in a sheet of paper and standing next to Sam began to type: *My name is Sam Fermoyle. This typewriter is a gift for my lovely daughter, Alice.*

Sam smiled. Now that was nice. That was a really nice thing to do. "How much?" he asked.

Haddad's eyes fixed on the money. "Fifty dollars'll do it." He spit into his handkerchief and began to rub the grime coating the keys. "Belis is a really good name. Kinda like Mercedes. You only ever see a few."

Sam hunched over his money, peering as he unwrinkled five tens.

"You got any life insurance?" Haddad asked, quickly slipping the money into his pocket.

Sam shook his head.

"You should, you know, for the kids and all." Haddad squeezed his shoulder. "Those are great kids you got, but *pow!* What're they ever going to have, Fermoyle, if anything should happen to you, God forbid." He shook his head sadly. "Without you, Sam, they got nothing but nothing. Plenty of nothing."

Sam's eyes blurred. He wiped his dripping nose with the back of his hand. He clutched Haddad's wrist and with his free hand groped in the air for the words. "I love those kids!" He burst into tears. "I'd do anything for my kids." He buried his head in his arms. "Anything," his muffled voice bawled. He kept seeing Benjy's fearful eyes staring at him through the leafy bars of his mother's crib.

". . . to assure them a secure financial future," Haddad was droning. "So many men like you, Sam, are so busy, so caught up with the todays, that they think they can put off the tomorrows." Haddad leaned down, whispering hoarsely. "But all the tomorrows are gone, Sam. Today, right now, that's all that's left."

"Huh?" Sam said, his weighted eyelids sagging.

"Here," Haddad said, moving the typewriter, handing him a pen, blowing ashes off a paper before he smoothed it out on the desk.

Sam couldn't get his fingers around the pen. It fell to the floor. A trickle of sweat coursed the ridge of Haddad's nose as he picked up the pen. He wrapped Sam's fingers around it. "Where it's underlined . . . right there . . . what do I have to do, fucking sign it for you?"

Sam scrawled an *S*. He couldn't remember how to start the *a*. He looked up sheepishly. He had forgotten why he was here.

"Honest to God . . . you said you wanted the policy!" Haddad said as he pressed Sam's fingers around the pen and, gripping them, completed his signature.

"Very good. Very, very good, Sam," Haddad said, examining the signature under the hanging bulb that lit his office.

Sam smiled at him.

"This," Haddad said, slapping the paper, "is your new lease on life. You just bought a whole lot of tomorrows for everyone." Haddad's brain reeled with anticipation. It was his only sale after weeks of febrile nights with Astrid's back turned to him. She had come to loathe his promises and his coarse hairy body almost as much as he did.

He was getting better every day, so much better, and yet business got worse and worse. For the last couple of months he'd had to live off the few premiums that came in. Like Stoner's policy, many had been canceled now for lack of payment. That's what he'd use this money for, to see if the main office would reinstate Stoner's. At least that one. Oh Jesus, why now, just when he was getting better, when all he needed was a break. The main office hounding him, his wife belittling him with her two jobs; they wouldn't be patient: graphs and figures were all that mattered to any of them. He was getting so desperate. They kept pushing. He was holding on by his fingertips and they just kept pushing, when all he needed was time to set this juggling act straight. All his life he'd had nothing but bad luck. Jesus Christ, there were so many unpaid policies out now, he could barely keep track. Life, auto, homeowners, it was all catch-up, like Stoner's nonexistent policy. Jesus Christ, the chief of police. When he thought of it, the shit ran down his leg. He'd cover it somehow. This would help. He'd steal the rest, then beg if he had to, crawl into the main office on his hands and knees. Somehow he'd get it all straight. With this money. With time. Yes. Yes, with just the right break and just the right timing, all the pieces would fall into place.

He counted out the bills for Fermoyle to see. ". . . seventy, eighty, ninety. That's three months' premiums. Now you can pay me ninety quarterly like tonight, or thirty a month; whichever's easier on the budget. . . ."

Sam sagged forward onto the desk.

"Shit," Haddad muttered and set him upright before he called a cab.

After he and the cabdriver got Sam into the car with the typewriter beside him on the seat, he turned off the light in his office and stood by the window, looking out. This was good, he told himself. He had done a good thing.

In the distance he saw a woman with a blond ponytail coming down the street, her white shorts gleaming through the shade. His eyes narrowed on Astrid. A car drove by her and honked. She waved. Next came a motorcycle driven by that thug Blue Mooney. The cycle slowed down with Mooney's black boots tapping the road alongside her. She said something and then he roared off.

Haddad's breast fired with rage. He grabbed the doorknob. *Slut,* his brain cried. *Slut!* "Get home!" he was screaming. "Get off the streets! How can you do this to me?" It wasn't Astrid. The young woman looked at him and hurried across the street. He ducked back into the shadows, his face pressed to the door. The worse things got for him, the more moral he felt, the more indignant, the more outraged at women who flaunted themselves, women like that, women like Astrid, women he loved, women who thought him vile and repulsive, making him love them all the more. It was the same with his business: the more money he took from it, the more thievery sickened him.

His indignation and outrage cleansed him, comforting him with the knowledge that things weren't as bad as they seemed. They couldn't be, not when a man cared so much. Such caring would make up for everything; that, and a few more premiums, just to keep the bank and the main office and his landlord off his back.

Marie Fermoyle turned the sputtering steak, then wiped her eyes with the dish towel. All day long her insides had been this fierce jumble of dread and rage. She jammed the dish towel over her mouth to muffle the sob that surged in her chest. "No, not tonight," she whispered into the towel. "I want them to remember tonight." She took a deep breath now as Omar came into the kitchen and stood behind her at the stove. He touched her arm, and she cringed.

"Marie? Marie! You're crying! What's wrong?"

She shook her head.

"Tell me," he said, trying to lift her chin.

She drew back stiffly.

"It's my fault, isn't it? I shouldn't have told you about the trust. I shouldn't have interfered."

"No, it's not that. I appreciate your trying to help me. I do." She tried to smile, but was crying again. "Oh God," she moaned, shaking her head. It was finally here, the most important night of her daughter's life, and she was falling apart, going to pieces. She felt as limp and helpless as a child in the jaws of some rabid beast.

"What, then? Is it the graduation? Are you nervous about tonight? You are, aren't you?"

She nodded. It was that. It was everything. "I never go anywhere," she whispered, grateful for the anger steadying her voice. "Except to work and church, and this is the way I feel when I go there, only worse."

"Why?"

"I don't know. I go, but I don't want to go! People look at me. I hate it! I hate the way they look at me!" she whispered, then bit her lip hard and stared at him as if looking away now might affirm the very worthlessness she felt.

"Of course they look at you!" Omar laughed. "Every man there looks at you and thinks, 'Now there's one handsome woman.' And all the women think, 'There's a woman who's done what I could never do: she's raised a good family—alone. She's bought her own home—when every bank turned her down! She's held the same fine job for eight years! Bought her own car! Her own clothes! Fed and clothed her children—alone! Without any man to hold her up!' "

Now when he lifted her chin, she let him. "Because that's what I thought the first moment I laid eyes on you. Your strength was a magnet, Marie." Sweat bathed his face and his voice trembled. "I wake up in the middle of the night filled with despair at ever getting back on my feet, and I hear this sound, like a drum through the darkness, and it's the beat of your heart, dear lady, your strong, strong heart." He put his hands on her shoulders. "I do mean that." He squeezed, working his fingers deep into her muscles. "I do!"

Her insides weak, her brain not thought but colors, blinding ribbons of color, and all she was doing was turning off the burner—*click*—spearing the steak onto the dish as the grease sizzled in the pan on the chipped enamel stove, that was all. Supper was cooked. They would sit down and eat the way they had thousands of other nights. "Milk," she whispered, taking it from the refrigerator. "Butter." And salt. The shaker was empty. She threw open the cupboard. Where was the salt box? Oh God, what if there wasn't any?

"Now," he was saying, rubbing his hands eagerly, "let's get this kingly feast moving, strong heart, or I shall be forced to scratch on your neighbor's window screens, begging a cheese sandwich."

They took their places at the table with an awkward, almost shy silence. They were already dressed for graduation, except for Norm, who had just come from his meeting with Jarden Greene. She could tell he was itching for a fight. Not tonight, she vowed, filling the shaker. Tonight was special. When Norm saw Omar take her chair at the head of the table, he gave a snide snort and sprawled in his seat.

"Just so you'll know, I'm not working for any creep this summer," he said, looking up as she tied her apron around Benjy's neck. His white collar was yellowed and frayed, and obviously too big. "Damn," she muttered, then caught herself as Benjy glanced up at her. *Be calm. Tonight is special.*

"Well, I'm not," Norm said, then winced. "Ow!" he cried, grabbing his leg where Alice had kicked it. "Do it again!" he warned raising his hand. "Go ahead!"

"Grow up!" Alice hissed.

"Let us now give thanks," Omar Duvall said, bowing his head. "Dear Lord," he began, his prayerful ebullience clearly intended to drown Norm's anger.

Marie stood by her chair and surveyed the table nervously.

"Amen!" Omar concluded brightly, shaking out his paper napkin as daintily as if it were linen.

"Amen," Alice and Benjy echoed softly.

"Praise the Lord!" Norm called loudly, and Marie stared at him.

"And pass the blessed butter!" Omar called even louder.

Alice and Benjy looked around, then laughed.

"And send down them holy rolls!" Norm shouted.

Now they were all laughing. Marie pulled out her chair, then turned abruptly to the closed curtains above the sink and with a defiant sweep pushed them open. Next door, on their back porch, Harvey and Jessie Klubock's heads flicked in surprise at the naked window. Jessie's hand lifted in an uncertain wave. Marie turned away quickly. Tonight the nosy Klubocks could look all they wanted. Tonight her oldest child graduated from high school. Tonight was special. She even had a cake from the bakery that said *Best Wishes, Alice* in blue icing.

"Well! What're you waiting for?" She laughed self-consciously when she realized Omar and the children were looking at her. They had been waiting for her to sit down. "Go ahead! Start eating!" She waved for them to start and felt her face flush as she sat down and lit the candle. The wick flickered hesitantly, then licked upward into a bright yellow tongue. Too happy to even lift her fork, she watched them eat, her temple moistening with this sudden warmth that bled through her like the bursting of some feverish organ. She loved them.

I love you all, she thought. And it had been so long since she had felt or even thought of love that now the sense of it so startled her with its purity, with its ferocity, that her hand flew to her throat with giddiness and she wanted to pound her fist on the table and bellow, *My God, how I love you all!* Somber Alice, who could not bear to be touched, who even as a child would not be held; Alice inside Alice inside Alice inside Alice, who smiled and told her nothing. And strong handsome Norman, whose soul was stalked by the same angry cunning tiger that stalked hers, fierce son, fierce, fierce son. And Benjamin, in whose eyes the flame was now a dazzling orange iris, this sweet and gentle son who hid from all things cruel and hard. *And you,* she thought, lowering her eyes from Omar's.

She could not say it. They know, she told herself. They must know. She slumped in her chair, hands limp in her lap; feeling drained, diminished now by the passing of peas and butter and the clatter of a fork and the pouring of milk into cups and their one unbroken glass. The candle flame bent and glinted on the chipped rim of Omar's plate, and she was alarmed that she had not given him a better one, but looking around, saw that they were all like that, the five she owned, grained with hairline splits, one so cracked—this one, hers—that now, as she began to cut her steak, her elbows stiffened, and she dared not press too firmly on the knife for fear the plate might break in two, spilling the meat's juice like blood onto this cloth cut from an old sheet, the stain seeping through the threads, spreading red, red like some terrible wakening evidence of her shame, of her failure. No, no, she thought, getting up quickly to open the window, for suddenly there was no air to breathe. *This is a special night,* she kept telling herself as she watched the Klubocks down in their yard now, side by side, shoulders touching as they broke dead blossoms from the lilac bushes. Louis Klubock worked behind them, gathering the pinchings and stems in a peach basket.

But look at my children, she thought, turning back to the table, *their shabby clothes, their thin nervous faces. I am a terrible mother. He doesn't know that. He doesn't know this rage.*

"Lovely, lovely," Omar said when she sat down. "Heavenly."

But she was looking at Alice's plain, ten-dollar dress, wishing it had come from Cushing's instead of the Bee-Mart Outlet, where the farmers' wives shopped when they came to town.

"What's Mary Agnes's dress like?" she asked, moving her food on her plate.

"I don't know," Alice shrugged. "Her aunt took her to Albany."

"Naturally," Marie said so bitterly they all looked at her.

"Who's her aunt?" asked Omar, chewing as he speared his second helping of steak.

Norm looked at her. It had been the last piece.

"One of our local phonies, that's who," she said, staring Norm down, her tone all the warning he would get.

Alice laid down her fork. "Mom! Why do you say things like that? You don't even know Mrs. Mangini."

Her eyes blazed at her daughter. Mrs. Mangini was a widow. *I'll tell you why,* she wanted to say, the words bile on her tongue. *Because her husband is dead, she has everything she wants. She doesn't have to work a day or a minute for the rest of her life. She can go to a movie with a man on a Saturday night, and the next day in church no one looks at her and thinks, Harlot, sinner, as she marches up to the Communion rail, while I kneel alone, surrounded by empty pews, judged and condemned for a sin that is not mine, but your father's.*

"Cooked to perfection," Omar sighed, his round smooth cheeks swelling with the meat, mashed potatoes, and peas he had stuffed in his mouth.

She took a deep breath. She would start over again. Calmly. She would be happy and strong, and then so would they. She would make them happy. She sensed that this might be an art, a weaving in and out of who they were and what they knew about each other, the light and breezy way people talked in movies. "Lester's giving the valedictory speech tonight," she told Omar.

"An ordeal I well remember," Omar replied.

Relieved, she turned to Alice. "Is Lester's mother going to be there tonight?" she asked, pouring more milk into Benjy's cup. She would try. For them she would try. For them she would do anything.

"I don't know." Alice shrugged.

"That poor woman," she said. Actually she'd never liked Carol Stoner. But now with her illness and her husband's betrayal, she felt a kinship: Carol Stoner had slipped into the ranks of wounded women. She glanced at Alice, puzzled by her expression. "Well, Sonny will be there, I'm sure."

"I don't know. He's been out almost every night on some big investigation," Alice added quickly.

Omar's eyes darted from the bread he was buttering to Alice.

"What's he investigating?" Norm asked eagerly, but Alice didn't answer.

"I can just imagine," Marie blurted.

"Maybe it's those men," Benjy said softly, glancing at Omar.

"What're you talking about?" Alice asked Benjy.

"Pass the potatoes, please," Omar said, loosening his tie. He dabbed his temples with his napkin.

"That poor thing suffering all alone," Marie mused, sad now for Carol Stoner. "And you watch, when she's gone he'll be tearing his hair out, but it'll be too late then."

"Maybe he saw them," Benjy said, gripping his fork at the edge of the table.

"What's he talking about?" Norm asked Alice. "What the hell men're you talking about?" he asked Benjy.

"Dad," Benjy said. "I meant Dad."

"Where there is no wife, he mourneth that is in want," Omar said quickly, his watery eyes fast upon the untouched meat on Marie's plate.

"That's beautiful," she sighed.

Omar steepled his fingertips over his empty plate and smiled at her. "He that possesseth a good wife hath all possessions. She is a help, a pillar of rest and trust to him who hath no rest and must lodge wheresoever the night taketh him." He lowered his eyes. "As a wanderer that roameth from city to city," he whispered.

Now her heart swelled again. She blushed and had to look away from this good and gentle man who was so much alone, who seemed at moments like this almost priestly, beyond love, beyond understanding. And yet she felt she had known him forever. Had he come only weeks ago? The lilacs had been blooming.

Alice was staring at Benjy. They had been whispering. "Who told you that?" she asked again.

"Mom," he answered.

She looked at her mother. Her whole body had slackened. "Dad was in jail?" She threw down her napkin.

"Here," Marie said, pushing her plate over to Omar. "Finish this while I get the dessert. Wait now, Alice, this is special." Why had Benjy told her that? They had been talking about the Stoners. She hadn't been listening, hadn't been alert, in charge.

"Oh that's nice. That's really nice," Norm said. He started to get up.

"You stay right there," Marie ordered. "I have a special dessert. In Alice's honor. Sit down, Norm, and tell us what happened with Jarden Greene while I get it." She felt short of breath. She tried to smile. Damn it, this was all her fault. Damn it, damn it, why couldn't things ever go right?

Norm slouched in his chair. "Nothing happened. Can I go get dressed?"

"Nothing?" she said, her voice rising. "What do you mean, nothing? Did you see him? Did you talk to him? What did he say?"

"I saw him, and he didn't say much."

"Well, do you have the job or not?"

Norm stared at her. "I don't want the job. But I'm not going to talk about it now." He glanced at Alice. "Not now. I'm tired, and I want to get dressed."

"Tired!" She laughed. She couldn't help it. "You're tired?" She thumped her chest with her fist. She couldn't help it. He had pushed her. He had gone too far. And look at her, that one, sitting there, sulking as if it were Marie's fault her father had been put in jail. Why did they do this to her? "I'm the one that's tired from working my fingers to the bone for lazy kids who don't give a damn!"

Norm stood then and stalked from the table.

She grabbed his arm and spun him around to face her. "You'll take that job. You'll take it, you hear me?"

"Don't," he warned, pulling from the bite of her grip.

"Mom!" Alice pleaded.

"You'll take it, and you'll pay me ten a week room and board, and the rest you'll put in the bank so you don't end up like Miss High and Mighty over there, looking down her nose at everyone, Miss Lazy Ass who's supposed to go to college in three months, three god-damn short months and not one red cent to pay for it."

Alice ran out of the kitchen.

"Look what you did!" Norm cried. "What the hell did you do that for?"

"What I did? What I did? No! What you did, damn you!" she roared, bringing her hand across his face in a stinging slap.

"You go to hell!" he snarled.

She slapped him again, this time with such force he stumbled against the wall. His mouth was thin, his eyes cold and dark. Instinctively, his hands had closed into fists. Now they fell limply to his sides, as had hers. They couldn't look at each other.

". . . see here," Omar was saying, ". . . way to speak to your mother . . . down on your knees . . . thank God . . . such a wonderful mother . . ."

They did not listen, did not speak, instead turned from each other. "Sit down," she told them, calling Benjy back from the living room, where he had turned on the television, and Alice back from the bathroom. Her hands shook as she opened the cake box. The glazed blue letters had begun to run in the heat. Under the window, Klubocks' dog was barking. Omar belched softly into his napkin;

then Norm burped loudly, imitating him, she knew. She couldn't get the cake out of the box. A car was coming down the street. A huge ant walked across the windowsill. She had smeared frosting on her blouse. Klubocks' dog snarled frantically. "Damn dog," she muttered as she lifted the cake onto a cookie sheet, then turned with a forced smile and placed it in front of Alice.

"Oh," Omar sighed. "What do you think of that, now, Alice?"

"It's nice," Alice said quietly.

Nice? she wanted to scream, wanted to grab those scrawny arms in that cheap white dress and demand, Nice? Five ninety-five and all she could say was nice when her mother didn't even own a dress, would sit there tonight with all those dressed-up people looking at her in the same skirt and blouse she wore to work. No. Not tonight. Tonight was special. "Here. You cut it," she said, giving the knife to Alice. She couldn't breathe. Her hands still trembled. Someone was out in the back hall. Not those nosy Klubocks, she thought, turning to see the back door fly open. It was Sam. He leaned in the doorway, his shirttail hanging, his hair strung thinly over his forehead, his nose red, his bleary eyes adjusting to the light.

"Alice?" He held up a dented old typewriter, its keys sprung. "Look what I got for my little girl." He lurched into the kitchen, then stopped short, pointing at Omar. "Who the hell's that?"

"Sam!" she gasped. Please . . ."

"Who the fuck is he?" he asked, squinting at Omar.

"A family friend." Omar rose from the chair. "Merely a family friend," he said, edging sideward like an enormous crab into the living room. The front door slammed, and Sam started to laugh as he staggered toward Marie with his arms out. "Daddy's home," he laughed.

"Get out!" she warned. "Get out now!"

"Baby. My pretty baby," Sam said. He put his arms around her and buried his face in her neck.

"Get away from me!" she said and pulled away, sending him reeling toward the table. His hand shot out for balance and rammed down into the cake. He wiggled his frosting-coated fingers, and he chuckled. "Alice, did your mother throw this cake at me?"

"Bastard!" Marie screamed as she lunged, trying to drag him to the door. As if with a sudden unmanacled strength, he reared back, shoving her away. She grabbed the knife from the table and held it out in front of her. "You ruin everything. You ruin every goddamn thing I've ever had!"

Sam teetered, blinking curiously at her.

"Mom!" Alice screamed.

"Don't!" Norm was shouting. "I'll get him out! I'll get the bastard out," Norm called as he swooped his father through the open door. Outside, there was Norm's angry voice and then the car started with a roar.

"He's gone," Benjy kept saying. "He's gone, Mom!" He took the knife and threw it into the sink.

She sagged into Alice's arms. "I'm sorry. I'm sorry," she moaned as Alice helped her into a chair.

"It's okay, Mom," Alice kept saying as she patted down her mother's hair.

"No, it's not," she wept. "Nothing's ever right! Nothing! Ever!" she sobbed into her hands. "Not even for your graduation."

"You don't have to go," Alice was saying. "You just rest. You stay here."

She lifted her head. Of course she'd go. She'd face them all, goddamn it.

Norm knocked on the door, at the same time trying to support his limp father against his shoulder. Above them a window opened and Aunt Helen's narrow face pressed against the screen. "Take him to your mother, or to jail, or dump him somewhere like the trash he is! He stole my rents and I wash my hands of him!" she called down.

"*Her* rents!" his father muttered.

"Aunt Helen, open the door or I'm going to kick it in!" Norm threatened.

"Don't you be fresh, Norman, or I'll come down there and slap your face!" she hissed.

He let his father sink to a mumbling heap on the porch floor while he beat on the door with his fists. When she still didn't come, he rammed into it with his shoulder.

"Tha's-a-boy," his father said. "Give it to the old bag, Normy! She can't push us around."

He reared back and hit the door, this time so hard the frame cracked. As the door opened slowly, Uncle Renie's pale face appeared over the chain. "Just take him away, Norm," he whispered. "Bring him back at eleven. She'll be asleep then, and I'll let him in."

"Uncle Renie, I can't!" Norm begged. "Please open the door!"

"Renie!" warned his aunt's shrill voice. "Don't you dare let that trash in my house!"

Sam raised his fist and shook it at his sister. "Get the hell out of my room, you skinny bitch!"

"Your room!" she shrieked down. "Not anymore, mister!"

"Uncle Renie!" he pleaded.

"Here," his uncle whispered. A five-dollar bill fluttered out through the closing door.

He had driven all over town, and he still didn't know what to do with his father, who alternated between incoherence and vile threats at passing motorists. A few minutes ago, Norm had almost given him Uncle Renie's five and let him off in front of Hammie's. Now he was driving past the park. The church bells were ringing. Seven o'clock. Graduation started in a half hour. He jammed on the brakes. "C'mon!" he said, hauling his father onto the sidewalk. He looked around. Except for Joey in his popcorn stand, the park was empty.

"I wanna go home," his father whimpered as Norm maneuvered him through the shadowy park and up the steep bandstand steps.

"Just sit here," Norm grunted, easing him onto the concrete floor of the bandstand.

"Don't leave me," his father begged, throwing his arms around his waist. "Please, Normy . . ."

"C'mon, Dad," he said, prying away his hands. "I'll be right back!"

"Promise?"

"I promise," Norm said.

"I love you, Normy," his father choked.

"Okay, Dad," he said, turning quickly from this helpless man who hadn't been sober in weeks, this father who had lost control of his own life, yet still, bewilderingly, remained so fast at the helm of everyone else's.

The hot gymnasium was jammed with families. Benjy sat between his mother and Norm. Up on the stage, Lester Stoner stood at the podium reading his valedictory address. Benjy looked up at the clock. So far, the speech had lasted fifteen minutes. People were coughing, fanning themselves with programs as their feet shuffled under the creaking metal chairs. Lester's father leaned against the side wall with his arms folded. Even he looked bored, Benjy thought as Lester's voice pitched higher. "And into this new world, walk bravely with Christ always on your right and the most blessed Virgin on your left. And when temptation and adversity cross your path, you will find strength in your most holy guides and salvation at the end of this long, arduous journey we call life."

The audience burst into grateful applause. Lester bowed his head humbly, then with the back of his hand wiped his eyes. The audience clapped louder as he returned to his seat.

"Poor thing," Marie Fermoyle whispered on one side of Benjy, clapping furiously.

"Jeez, what a creep," Norm groaned and slid down in his chair. His mother reached across Benjy and pinched the soft underflesh of Norm's arm. "Sit up!" she said through clenched teeth.

"Cut it out!" Norm whispered loudly.

Between them Benjy froze, fully expecting a flurry of punches to pass before him. There was an uneasy wait now, because Monsignor Burke had fallen asleep in his chair behind the podium. His young curate, Father Gannon, was trying to wake him up. During the lull the graduates on the stage smirked and elbowed one another, causing fat Jim Cox to slide from his end seat onto the floor. From the front row Lester Stoner turned and shook his head disapprovingly at his classmates. Sister Jean Andrew, the principal, stormed out of the wings and faced the class with her hands on her hips.

Roused, the Monsignor hiked the skirt of his voluminous cassock and lumbered up to the podium. Sister Andrew returned to her post. The Monsignor adjusted his thick black–rimmed glasses, then took a deep breath into the microphone. "Well," he began in that faint brogue with which he delivered all sermons and speeches. "I suppose you're all saying to yourselves now, 'Look at the old duffer. Time, maybe, we put him out to pasture; can't even keep his eyes open.' " The Monsignor shook his head ruefully, and the audience roared with laughter. "But as dear old Da used to say to me mother after Mass, 'Sure'n it wasn't napping you caught me at, Meg, but meditating.' " He folded his arms high on his paunch in hearty laughter with the audience. After a moment he raised his hands for silence and said solemnly, "And that's just what I was doing, ladies and gentlemen. Meditating! Marveling at the uniqueness of this singular group of young men and women, these fine young graduates of Saint Mary's High School."

Moments later as the Monsignor began to pass out the diplomas, flashbulbs popped and a few home movie cameras whirred. The Monsignor patted his sweaty forehead. In the twenty-one years he had presided over these graduation ceremonies, nothing had changed; not the faces or the names, he thought. In a few months, a year or two, they would be trooping their troubles into his rectory, their babies into his baptistry. He looked up and forced a smile.

"Alice Fermoyle," he called, peering over his glasses as she came unsteadily across the stage on her new white heels. Like the mother, he thought irritably: skinny, suspicious, vaguely menacing, Marie Fermoyle was one of the parish's few divorcées and the only one still brazen enough to attend Sunday Mass. Sometimes at the beginning of Communion, he had seen a look come over her, a flash of hunger, of a desperation so intense that he would find himself rushing through the distribution of Hosts, fearful that the next quivering tongue above the rail would be Marie Fermoyle's. And then what would he do? Denounce her? Ignore her? Sometimes he imagined himself slapping her. She would shout some profanity. He would slap her again and again. . . .

"Thank you, Monsignor," Alice Fermoyle was saying, as she accepted her diploma. She blushed and quickly switched the tassle on her cap and had just started back to her seat when a slurred voice rose from the back of the gym.

"That's beautiful . . . tha's really, really beautiful," Sam Fermoyle cried.

With their car blocked they were stuck in the parking lot. Benjy sat in back, his mother and Alice rigid in the front seat. The minute the ceremony ended, Norm had left to find his father.

"I hate him," Alice groaned. She took a deep breath, fighting tears as her classmates milled around outside having their pictures taken.

"It's all right," Marie said, staring over the wheel as two squealing girls ran by the car.

"I'm not going to the dance. I just want to go home."

"No, that only makes it worse," Marie said. "Believe me."

"I'm not going!"

"Yes you are!"

Lester was making his way through the cars, looking for Alice.

"Oh God," Alice groaned with his approach. He tapped on her window.

"I don't feel well," Alice told him, barely opening the window. "I'm just going to go home."

"No, you promised me, Alice," Lester begged. "I don't want to go alone. It'll be all right, Alice. Please! You have to! You said you would!"

"Get out of this car!" Marie ordered in a low voice. "Right now!"

"No!" Alice shook her head. "I can't."

"Please, Alice! This is such a special night!" Lester said, his mouth at the narrow opening.

"He's right," Marie said, turning now, glaring. "Alice, if you don't open that door and get out of this car, I'll open it and I'll drag you out in front of everyone, damn it, and you know I will."

"Please? Please, Alice?" Lester begged.

"Just open the door. Open the goddamn door and everything will be all right," Marie said, her low voice steady and sure like a dark path they were compelled to follow.

Benjy stared down at the floor. The door opened. When it closed he heard a sob catch in his mother's throat.

"Help me, sweet Jesus, please help me!" she gasped, watching Alice follow Lester, her shoulders slumped, head down.

What about Alice, Benjy thought. How could his mother do that? How could she make Alice go out there in front of all those people? Sometimes he thought his mother just didn't care. She just didn't love them enough.

When the fire whistle blew the ten-of-nine curfew, Norm had looked everywhere for his father, even Hammie's Bar and Grill. Now he climbed West Street toward the park lights and the tinny music of Joey's radio at the top of the hill.

"Here, have a bag, Norm," Joey said, holding out a grease-streaked bag of popcorn.

"No thanks, Joey," Norm said, still out of breath as he scanned the shadows of the trees and the bandstand in the middle of the park. Before the night was over he was going to beat the shit out of that no-good, fucking drunk. Poor Alice, humiliated like that in front of all her classmates and their families and every fucking teacher in the fucking school. His fists rapped a marching beat on the countertop. "My father been around?"

"He's long gone now, kid. Probably sleeping it off somewhere. Here," Joey said, gesturing with the popcorn. "On the house." He smiled and his eyes rolled to whites.

As Norm took the popcorn Joey's hand groped up his arm to his shoulder. "You don't want to find him now, Norm. What good's it going to do?"

"I gotta go now, Joey. Thanks," Norm said, easing from the em-barrassingly urgent grip.

Joey's hand tapped along the countertop for his rag. "Be seeing you, kid," Joey called out.

"Yah, Joey, be seeing ya." Norm tried to laugh. It was expected.

He walked through the park eating the popcorn. Joey was right. He didn't want to find him. If he did he might kill him. He took off his tie and stuffed it into his pocket. To hell with his father. To hell with all of them, he thought as he turned up the path toward Main Street. It wasn't his fault his father had showed up at the house tonight. It wasn't his fault his father had gone to the graduation. He was sick of being blamed; sick of his mother slamming doors and banging windows shut so the neighbors couldn't hear, when, of course, the crashing-down windows were their signal to listen. He was sick of her pulling that crummy bathrobe tight as a noose around her neck as she turned those dark-circled eyes on him, those eyes that accused and at the same time expected something, needed everything from him, but nothing from the others, because they were the victims while he was supposed to be her one great hope in life or something. . . .

Suddenly he stopped. At the corner on the hood of his car sat Blue Mooney, his hair slicked back hard as a helmet, his sullen profile asharp under the streetlamp. Mooney was talking to three punks who lounged on the hood of the souped-up gray Chevy. His heart stirring with fear, Norm stepped behind a tree and felt on the ground for a rock. Then he slipped back into the shadows and threw the rock as hard and as high as he could, over the treetops; it was sailing, whizzing, then coming down, still coming while he ran across the street. Just as he darted onto the narrow strip of darkness between two houses, he heard the rock's *thunk* on metal and an outrage of curses, then the slamming of car doors as an engine started, and he ran, ran panting through backyards and over a picket fence, through bushes, past trees and frantic dogs.

When he finally emerged from the branch-battering leafy darkness he was beside the library. His chest pounded and his eyes burned as a car came down the street, then slowed behind him. He kept walking, his fists sweating in his pockets.

"Hey, Normy-baby!" Weeb called, grinning.

Norm jumped into Weeb's father's car. "Hey, you dirty bastard," he said with a poke at Weeb's ribs.

"How'd you do with Creller? Was she as good as I said?"

"Better," Norm sighed, watching for Mooney or the gray Chevy.

"Yah?" Weeb was breathless.

Norm turned on the radio. Fats Domino was singing "I'm Walkin'." Norm played the dashboard like a piano and sang loudly, shaking his head from side to side.

"What happened?" Weeb called over the music, barely able to keep his eyes on the road. Norm sang louder. Weeb switched off the radio.

"Turn it back on!" Norm snapped. His mother's car had no radio. He loved music in cars.

"C'mon, tell me what happened," Weeb begged. "Quick, before I pick my sister up at the armory."

Norm sat forward and looked at Weeb. "The armory?"

"Yah, the bus is letting her off there," Weeb said. "What'd Creller do?"

"The bus from where?"

"From college, stupid. C'mon, tell me quick!" Weeb slowed the car to ten miles an hour. "Get much?"

"Enough," said Norm as he looked up the street for Janice Miller.

"How much?" Weeb demanded, and then he groaned. "Aw shit, there's the ball-breaker."

In front of the armory, Janice Miller was sitting on her suitcases with her long legs crossed over the curb.

"How much, for chrissakes!" Weeb squealed.

"Everything," Norm said, pulling the wrinkled tie from his pocket and slipping it under his collar.

Weeb was too overwrought to notice. "All the way? You did the deed?" he screamed.

"Shut up! Your sister!" Norm tightened the knot, and as the car approached, Janice got up and stepped down into the street.

"Jesus!" Weeb groaned. "I can't take this—was it all the way or wasn't it?"

Janice leaned down to the window on Norm's side. "Running out of gas or just this anxious to have me home, little brother?" she asked, laughing.

Norm jumped out and put her luggage in the trunk.

"Have you grown!" Janice said as he got back into the car. She sat between them. "You must be almost six feet!" she said to Norm, then turned to her brother. "How tall are you?"

"Five-six," Weeb mumbled, straining his head over the wheel.

Janice laughed and began chattering on and on about her sorority sisters' farewell party and the jugs of Mateus rosé they had smuggled into the house and how sick she'd been all morning. "That's why I called Mother to say I couldn't get a bus out until tonight. I barfed all morning long! At one point there were six of us barfing into the same hopper. It was too much!" She lit a cigarette and the smoke curled in tendrils around her face. Her shoulder was touching Norm's. Her perfume with its faint tinge of stale wine made him dizzy. "Oh God, look at those creeps," she said as they turned the corner at the park.

Driving slowly along one of the paths was the gray Chevy with its high beams on, and sitting on the hood of the Chevy turning a flashlight from side to side was one of the creeps he'd thrown the rock at. Norm slid low in the seat.

"I don't know how I'll ever get through the summer here," Janice said, gesturing contemptuously at passing streets. "After Boston, this will be death, I know. And Russ can't come up," she sighed.

"Who's Russ?" Norm asked and sucked in his breath until his chest ached.

"Russ is a Delt Psi. We're lavaliered," she said as if he must have known.

"Oh," he said weakly.

"And what the hell is lavaliered?" Weeb sneered.

She laid her head back on the seat and ran her fingers through her wavy blond hair, which undulated with the lights of a passing car. "That, dull boy, is the first step before getting pinned." She handed Norm her cigarette to throw out the window.

He held it a moment, wanting to put it in his mouth and taste the sweetness of her wet pink lips.

"Big thrill," Weeb said and turned on the radio.

"Oh look!" she cried, leaning forward and pointing. "Who's that? Look! Oh my God, will you look at that man peeing on the Monsignor's geraniums. I don't believe it!" She roared, laughing, and lit another cigarette. Her leg brushed Norm's, and she glanced at him, at her cigarette butt that was burning down to his fingertips.

His insides shriveled. That man peeing on the Monsignor's flowers was his father. Weeb accelerated and never said a word.

Blue Mooney sprawled on his mother's new red couch. So his cousin Anthology had been right. Here it was only nine-thirty and already five different cars had come creaking down the dirt road. Each one had parked close by the mailbox, engine idling, waiting for the porch light to come on, which was the same signal their grandmother had used to show she was open for business. When the light didn't come on, the cars had peeled out bitterly down the road.

The television flickered over the dark room. A pillow half covered Mooney's face. His two younger brothers lay on the floor watching *77 Sunset Strip* on the television his mother had finally bought. She sat stiffly on a ladder-back chair in the kitchen doorway. A tiny woman with thin brown hair and a spray of freckles across her nose, she kept straining to see out the window. She fidgeted and bit her lip. She was dying for him to leave so she could get on with business. Anthology figured she was selling a good three cases a night, weekends twice that; and tonight being graduation and the party at the lake, there was no telling how much she'd sell. The minute that bug light came on, they'd start trooping up here, some so young they'd only have enough money for a couple of cans.

When Mooney's grandmother had sold beer out of her trailer he hadn't cared at all. In fact it had been a kind of honor growing up as Hermione's grandson. After his grandmother's death he just never expected his mother to take over the selling. He watched her from under the pillow as another car came up the road now. This time the car stopped and a door banged shut.

She looked right at him. "I got something to do here, Travis," she said, starting for the door.

"What's that?" he asked, his sails for a moment sagging, for she was the only one who ever called him that weak-kneed, lily-livered, country-twanging name of Travis. Travis Ted Mooney. No sir, he was Blue Mooney, and that was all there was to it. Blue Mooney, a living legend in his own time.

Heavy footsteps crossed the porch, bringing a hard knock on the door.

"You just mind your business!" she hissed, switching on the porch light. All the windows glowed yellow.

"Miz Carper!" called a voice outside.

"Don't, Ma," he said, gesturing at his brothers. "Not in front of them."

"Miz Carper!" Now the knocking grew as insistent as the voices. "You got customers, Miz Carper." With the light on, more cars were pulling in.

"You don't live here. I don't see you helping out any, so you can just shut the hell up." She put her mouth to the door. "How much?" she called.

"Two six-packs," came a shout.

"Peter, go down get me four sixies," she said to her son, who drew himself to his knees, his eyes lingering on the last few seconds of screen action before he ran down cellar.

No, Mooney thought. No, no, no, no, no, no! Things were a mess. Not only had he been kicked out of the Corps, but he had no money, no job, and his mother wouldn't let him move back in because of all his trouble. He jumped off the couch and reached past his mother. Out on the porch, jostling for position at the opening door, were five guys in suits and ties with carnations pinned to their lapels, all Saint Mary's seniors with their crew cuts, and their wiseass grins dying on their faces.

"Get the hell outta here!" he snarled, and they backed down the steps.

"But we got . . ."

"All we need's . . ."

"*You* get out of here! *You!*" his mother cried, pushing him with both hands out onto the porch. "And don't come back!" She slammed the door in his face.

He turned and caught them snickering. "I said get the hell outta here!" he bellowed, stalking them as they ran toward their cars.

The Lake Hotel by night put Mooney in mind of an ocean liner, the way its bright windows shimmered and seemed to sway on the pitch-black water. There was dance music playing inside, and out here the parking lot was filled with their daddys' cars, all washed and waxed for the big night. It was Saint Mary's graduation dance.

Blue Mooney squatted next to a pink-and-white Pontiac as he stabbed the ice pick into the fourth tire. Air hissed out of all the tires. He ran in a low crouch and started on the next row of cars. Jimmy and Al Bibeau were working so fast that the hissing was almost as loud now as the music. All around them cars sank slowly on their flattening tires.

The main door to the hotel flared open, and Mooney ducked behind a car as a girl in a white dress rushed onto the veranda followed by a thin boy in a pale blue suit. The girl hurried down the steps and her date ran after her. "Wait!" he kept calling. "Will you just wait!" At the edge of the parking lot, he grabbed her wrist and tried to pull her back.

"I can't stand it! You're making such a fool of yourself!" she said, yanking free.

"I'm just having fun. I'm just dancing!" he pleaded in a high tremulous voice.

"They're all laughing at you. That's why they're all standing around clapping. Can't you even tell when people are making fun of you, Les?"

"Oh I guess I'm not as . . . as astute as you!" And with that he stormed toward the hotel, then suddenly turned and raced back after her.

Mooney peered over the fender. For a second he thought sure the guy was going to hit her.

"I can't go back in there alone and you know it!" he said.

"I just want to go home, that's all," she said.

"That's all, yah, sure! Go ahead and wreck the biggest night of my life, what do you care?"

"Please, Les. I just want to go home," she said, rubbing her arms as if she were cold.

"This is all because of your father tonight, isn't it? Well, did it ever occur to you that you're not the only one in the world with problems?"

At that she turned and headed into the parking lot, and he grabbed her again.

"Well, I'm not leaving, so you'd better get back inside," he said, trying to pull her toward the hotel. "You're just trying to make a fool out of me, aren't you? Aren't you?" he demanded.

"Lester!" she cried, struggling. "You let me go!"

"No! I'm not going back in there alone. You're . . ."

Mooney inched up behind the car. The creep was hurting her. Every time he shoved her back toward the hotel, she tripped on her high heels. The creep was making her cry.

"Please . . . oh please," she begged.

Mooney glanced back as Al Bibeau crept up to him. Al gestured, whispering. "We better split, man. His old man's . . ."

"You son of a bitch," Mooney moaned, leaping now when he saw him grab the girl again. He was shaking her and screaming, his words lost in the louder dance music.

"Blue!" Bibeau called after him.

The creep hadn't even seem him coming. Mooney shoved him aside, and the girl sagged forward, her face in her hands, with muffled sounds, her shoulders trembling as she grew smaller and smaller in her white dress, which suddenly seemed to be all there was of her, just that thin white dress and air.

The creep started toward her, his long face a mask of shock. "Alice!" he gasped, extending his hand as if over a stream he would guide her across. But she did not even look up.

Mooney glared at Stoner, who suddenly turned and ran for the safety of the bright hotel. In the cavernous night he felt strong and hard, insuperable, with his arms around her like this. "Don't cry. Please don't cry," he crooned over her head. She smelled of trees and grass and warm night air, light in his arms, and he could hear lake water lapping the shoreline in and out to the pulsating mud song of frogs, and then the band played louder. She stiffened and jerked away.

"Wait!" he called as she ran back inside the hotel. He took a step, then stopped, conscious now of Jimmy and Al Bibeau watching him. "Little cunt," he growled, and they laughed.

"Monsignor, wake up! It's Sam Fermoyle," whispered Mrs. Arkaday, the rectory housekeeper. She glanced anxiously at the vestibule.

The Monsignor had fallen asleep over his chessboard. With a fitful snore he snuggled his face into the dark wing of the chair.

"You in there, Bubbles?" came Fermoyle's voice from the other side of the door.

The Monsignor's eyes flew open. He blinked and gripped the chair's velvet arms at the hateful nickname of his drooling childhood.

"Come on out, Bubbles."

"I don't understand this, Mrs. Arkaday," the Monsignor said irritably.

Mrs. Arkaday bristled at the sharp tone. "I told him you were asleep, and then he started to go upstairs." She sniffed. "He said he wanted a room with a view."

The Monsignor sighed and hefted himself from the chair. The gleaming parquet floors creaked underfoot. He was tired. Graduation had been too long; endless, like the Mass he said daily. He paused with his hand on the doorknob. "And where's Father Gannon?" he asked wearily. It had been just an hour ago that the president of the Holy Name Society had called, upset because at this morning's breakfast meeting, Father Gannon had suggested that their Spring Dinner Dance profits be used to bring a poor Puerto Rican family from New York City to live in Atkinson. The Monsignor had tried his best not to lose his temper, but he ended up shouting at Father Gannon to "be realistic!" Father Gannon had stalked upstairs in the middle of his tirade.

"He said he was going to bed," Mrs. Arkaday said, then stepped closer to confide, "but his radio's playing and I can see the light on under the door."

"Get him down here!" he ordered before he stepped into the hallway.

Fermoyle leaned against the front door. He grinned when he saw the Monsignor. "Hey, Bubbles, that was a great job you did tonight," he said, holding out his hand to shake the Monsignor's.

"Zip up your pants, for heaven's sake, Sam!" The Monsignor turned away, his face purpling with revulsion, while Fermoyle swore and struggled with his zipper.

"Okay, Bubbles, you can look. The pecker's gone now," Sam laughed.

"What do you want, Sam?"

"I need some help. It's my sister," he said with a sudden sob.

"Sam, look—go home and sleep it off, and then we'll talk tomorrow, when you're feeling better."

"But she won't let me in!"

"She always lets you in, Sam. You know she will."

"Not this time," Sam cried. "She won't!" Tears ran down his cheeks.

"Sam, I'm very busy here tonight," said the Monsignor, turning to his study door. "You go home and go to sleep and then . . ."

"Jesus, Bub, you're not listening!" Sam exploded. "She won't let me the hell in my own house!"

The Monsignor closed his eyes and took a deep breath. "Why not, Sam?"

Sam looked at him. He opened his eyes wide and drew back indignantly. "All I did was use the rents to buy Alice a present. And the reason I did that's because she steals my money, Monsignor." Sam shook his head sadly. "My sister's a thief! She's a common, fucking thief! Now I could report this to the police, but first I wanna give you a chance to talk to her."

"Helen?" he asked softly, stalling for time. He glanced up the stairs. Where was Father Gannon?

Sam nodded. "Yes, Saint Helen with all my money in her underpants. You don't know the shit I have to put up with! Talk about being on the dole, she doles me out haircut money, aspirin money, laxative money, newspaper money. . . ." Sam took a step, teetering close to the Monsignor. "Wanna hear something? If I want some new socks, I gotta show her the old ones with holes before she'll give me fifty fucking cents for some new ones." Sam laughed bitterly. "Almost as bad as being a priest, huh?"

F ather Gannon was coming down the stairs. He kept his hand in the pocket that contained the letter he had been writing to Bishop O'Rourke when Mrs. Arkaday called him down here. At the bottom of the stairs, Sam Fermoyle smiled, then threw his arm around the young priest's shoulder.

"Hey, Bub, I remember when you were a young piss-ant like this guy. Every time you gave a sermon, your face got red and your voice'd get all high and screechy like an old . . ."

"You can take over from here, Father?" the Monsignor said sourly. "Good night, Sam." He slipped into his study.

Fermoyle slumped onto the mahogany bench below the staircase. He folded his arms and crossed his legs, as if settling in for a long stay. Father Gannon leaned against the curved balustrade, his thoughts still jumbled with phrases from his letter. The last sentence bothered him. He had written: "There are too many reasons to write of here." That sounded childish. Now it came to him! He took his pen and paper from his pocket, crossed out the last line and wrote, "The reasons are too many and too compelling to list in a letter."

Just then Fermoyle's broke wind. "You're excused," he said solemnly to the young priest.

Father Gannon folded the letter and returned it to his pocket. "Have you tried AA, Mr. Fermoyle?"

Fermoyle chuckled. His eyes were closed; his chin lay on his chest.

"They've helped thousands of men like you, Mr. Fermoyle."

Sam raised his hand to reply, then shook his head as the hand sank over the arm of the bench.

"I could call them for you right now." Father Gannon sighed. He wasn't up to this, not tonight.

"Bubbles coming back?" Fermoyle muttered.

"I don't think so."

"He's a horse's ass, you know." Fermoyle looked up at him.

"He's very dedicated," Father Gannon said dutifully.

"A dedicated horse's ass, then." Fermoyle shrugged and burped. "But tha's okay. Don't get me wrong; we all got tricks. 'Cept I don't like it when a horse's ass starts believing his own tricks." He looked up expectantly. "I'm a horse's ass, too." He smiled. "But I don't believe my own tricks," he said in a ragged whisper that startled Father Gannon.

Fermoyle was on his feet, moving unsteadily toward the front door. "Thanks for nothing, Father Piss-ant, and tell Bubbles not to worry, I'll be back!"

Father Gannon trudged upstairs and flopped down on his hard bed. Mrs. Arkaday had turned off his radio and the lights. From the bathroom across the hall came the sounds of water splashing into the sink and the Monsignor's explosive gargling. He lay with his arms under his head and stared at the ceiling as the Monsignor grunted and groaned. The toilet flushed. The light switch clicked, and past his door padded the Monsignor's velour slippers.

His eyes widened. He should have gone after Fermoyle. He should get out of bed and write his letter. He should pray. His arms grew so numb he could not move. He would lie forever in austere rooms, listening to the intimate sounds of strangers, all the while waiting for the ring of a phone or a knock at the door. His superiors had cast him aside. They would forget him here. He would grow fat and pale, and every Sunday at noon he would giddily lock the study door, his fingers trembling as they stacked the quarters and lovingly smoothed out the dollar bills.

The night had grown cooler. Still dressed, the young priest was dreaming now, dreaming of blankets, a rainbow of blankets piled to the sky, enough blankets for the hundreds and hundreds of people waiting in line. The line stretched for blocks. They waited quietly and patiently. They were accustomed to waiting.

One young woman in the middle of the line began to cry. She lay down on the sidewalk and wept, her body trembling with the cold. "It's too late," she sobbed. "No, no," he tried to placate her, but she would not stop, and soon the crowd took up her cry. "It's too late!" they chanted and began to step from line, milling into sullen clumps. "It's too late!" she began to scream. "It's too late!" they all screamed.

He sat up and jumped off the bed. They wouldn't stop screaming. Lights flashed around him. Spinning red lights. The room tumbled with lights. "Help me! Help me!" he whimpered as he moved in a crouch along the wall. When he came to the window, he blinked with a sheepish smile. The screams had been sirens and the spinning lights were from the police car and the ambulance that had backed up to the Fermoyle house across the street. He leaned on the windowsill and saw Helen LaChance in her bathrobe on the front porch. "I had to hit him. He wouldn't stop," she called out to the approaching officer. Then, as the attendants emerged from the house with the stretcher, she followed them toward the ambulance, wailing, "Is he dead? Oh God forgive me if he's dead!"

Her husband came out of the house then and attempted to put his arms around her, but she pushed him away. "You let him in!" she moaned, then rushed toward the Monsignor, who hobbled barefoot across the street with a black topcoat thrown over his pajamas.

Father Gannon ran down the stairs and out onto the front lawn, waving his arms frantically as the ambulance tore past him down the street.

Sunday's heat felt like a damp-sheeted dream trapping Alice, her hands weighted at her sides as she came down the marble steps from church through this buzz of parishioners, most of whom she knew and hated because they knew, knew and only pretended not to see her past the clasping hands and cheek-brushed kisses in this welter of perfume and Sunday sanctity, their balm of weekly virtue as they waited in line to greet the Monsignor.

She had been forced to do this, to come to Mass this morning. Her mother had made them, had sent them off, once again had thrown them over the side to teach and inoculate them, to rescue them from fear, and as their heads bobbed up she would push them away, whispering, insisting in that low, unbodied voice, urging, shoving, thrusting, nudging them along, her last words at the door, "You didn't do anything wrong. Remember that. He did. Not you. Not one of you!" While behind her, in the safety of the house, Omar Duvall sat contemplating the perfection of two fried eggs, their round yellow yolks shimmering on the plate.

They had come, but Norm had refused to go inside. She and Benjy had stood at the back of the church, and when she returned from Communion he was gone.

And so now she had to wade through the toothy ardor of these sun-drenched worshippers alone, her straw hat bobbing crookedly with every step, but she would not straighten it, or look right or left. *Hurry. Hurry,* she thought as the crowd stalled on the marble path. Ahead, the Monsignor was shaking hands, grabbing arms, calling out hearty introductions between each parishioner and the new priest beside him. "Jim Brody and Claire, come meet Father Gannon. . . . Estelle McManus! Look at you all decked out. . . . My Lord, and these are the Hannons, all twelve kiddoes, six of each, Father Gannon." Now there were only a few people in her way. *No,* she thought. *No, I won't let it happen. Won't let him say, "And this is Sam Fermoyle's daughter. This is the one, the one."* All voices ceased, drowned, as a small plane flew overhead, low enough that its shadow darkened their faces, and in the droning lull, her eyes locked on the Monsignor's in a quick wordless scuffle. She stepped off to the side, then, turning, cut quickly across the lawn.

She was still on Main Street. Someone was calling her name.

"Alice! Alice Fermoyle!" Father Gannon had been running, and now, as he reached her, he was out of breath. "I'm Father Gannon," he said, panting, his hand at his heaving chest. "I just wanted to say how badly I feel . . . and how . . . how responsible. . . ." He waved his hand. "For what happened . . . your father . . ."

"That's all right," she said, cutting him off quickly, her face so red the flesh stung. No one had ever spoken like this to her. It was an invisible stain, a burden to be borne, not examined in the light and dissected.

"No! No, it's not all right!" He kept waving his hand as if to generate the words. "I could have done something! I should have! And I didn't! And that . . . that was wrong!"

"That's all right." She stepped away. He seemed to radiate heat. "Really."

"No! No, I was too self-centered. I . . . I . . ." His dark eyes were oddly bright. "I didn't have it! I saw a man's hand come up from the depths, and I didn't grab it!" With his New York accent and rapid speech she could barely understand him.

"Well . . . I . . ." Again she stepped back. "Thank you, Father." What else was there to say? He came closer. His agitation confused her. She thanked him again and said she'd better get home, but he kept walking with her, gesturing, his hands flying in a commotion of energy, his sentences unfinished as yet another thought churned out of him. A gust of wind whipped the lacy hem of his alb around his legs, and he tugged it free. She was painfully aware of cars slowing to look at them.

"Would you like to see him at the hospital before he leaves?" He stopped suddenly.

Her father had been in the Atkinson Hospital since Friday night. Today he was being transferred to another hospital near Burlington.

"I'll go up with you!" Father Gannon said, taking her hand. "They said eleven! There might be time!" He had turned and was tugging her back toward the church. "If we hurry . . . Maybe we can get there. . . ."

"No . . . no," she had been saying. "Please," she said, stopping. She pulled away. "I'm going home!"

"It might be just the boost he needs!" Father Gannon said, with his hand on her arm. "Seeing you there would—"

"No, Father!"

"You'll feel bet—"

"Please, Father! You're embarrassing me!" she said, glancing at the line of cars at the red light.

"I'm sorry." He looked shocked. "Oh, I'm so sorry." Head down, he continued walking as he tried to explain. His voice, lower now, was still fueled by an intensity she found draining. "I wasn't thinking of you. . . . I just got so . . . it was just how your father'd feel . . . because, you know, I just . . . I just felt like I'd messed it all up. It was shortsighted of me."

She had come now to the mouth of her driveway. "Well . . . I . . . thank you, Father."

"You're not upset, are you?" he asked. "I mean, I know you're upset, but I mean, you're not still upset with me, are you?"

"No. Oh no, I'm not upset. Thank you, Father," she said, backing down the driveway. Anything to get rid of him. "It was nice talking with you." She waved. "Bye!"

"I'd like to speak to your mother," he said, following her to the door. "Just for a minute . . . and tell her . . . well, to see if there's anything . . . if maybe she'd like to go up and see him."

"No!" she said, shocked. "She can't. I know she won't. She's—"

"Just ask her. I'll wait out here." He was waving his hands again. He scraped his foot back and forth in the hard-baked dirt. "I'll just wait."

The door closed and her mother slapped her forehead with the heel of her hand. "What's wrong with you, bringing him here, this morning of all mornings?"

"I didn't bring him!" Alice whispered. "He just came!"

"That's all I need, a goddamn nosy priest out on the front steps! And you know who's upstairs?" she hissed. "Mr. Duvall, that's who!"

In the kitchen Duvall's suit was draped over the ironing board. Benjy sat at the table brushing polish on Duvall's shoes. Marie flew around the living room, tidying up. Onto the coffee table she piled the Sunday paper sections that had been on the floor. She kicked Norm's bathrobe and dirty socks into the bathroom. Alice moved toward the door. "I told him he couldn't come in. I'll tell him you're asleep, that's all."

Her mother raced over and grabbed her arm. "It's too late now. He'll know something's funny," she moaned as she scooped a fistful of dustballs from the corner next to the sofa. "You should've thought of that before," she cried, shaking her head and stamping the curled edges of the gray rug into place. She leaped onto the couch and wrestled with the pitted mirror until it hung straight. In the mirror's reflection her eyes blazed into Alice's. "Do something, damn it! Help me!" She jumped down, ran into the kitchen and covered the dirty dishes on the counter with a towel, then ran halfway up the stairs to tell Omar to stay up there. A priest was outside.

"What do the police want?" Omar called back.

"A priest, not the police," she said. Facing the door, she wiped her hands on the sides of her skirt and took a deep breath. "Go ahead, let him in," she said wearily, then smiled brightly.

They're crazy, all of them, Alice thought, turning from the opening door, her gaze scanning the holes in the walls and Omar's white pants in the kitchen while in the doorway stood a man in a white dress. Her mother thought Omar Duvall could save them. Father Gannon wanted to save them.

"Won't you come in, Father?" her mother was saying. "Sorry you had to wait so long, but I was getting dressed for the twelve-thirty Mass."

Father Gannon blinked uneasily, then, seeing Alice, he smiled. "I won't hold you up, Mrs. Fermoyle. I just—"

"Come in! This is such a surprise. . . ."

"I just wanted to say, if there's anything I can do to help . . . you"—he gestured to Alice—"or your children . . . you know, feel free to call me."

"Well, thank you, Father. That's nice to know." Marie took a step, as if to close the door.

"I'm driving up to Burlington soon to see the Bishop . . . . just a personal matter." His hands began to fly. "If you'd like, I could bring something up to Mr. Fermoyle, food or clothes . . . or . . . or maybe I could take the children to visit him, or even yourself, Mrs. Fermoyle, if you'd like to go."

"I'm divorced, Father Gannon," her mother said warily.

"Well, then," he said nervously. "I guess you're all set, then. I mean, you don't have to go. Alice . . . I could bring her or the other children. . . ."

The phone rang and Alice answered it. Lester's voice was harsh in her ear.

"I've been trying to get you since Friday night," he said.

"Guess I've been busy," she said, turning her back to her mother and the priest.

"I just want to tell you I'm sorry. I hurt your feelings and then when I saw that hood put his—"

"I've . . . someone's here," she said, lowering her voice.

"I heard about your father," he said quickly.

"I really have to go," she said.

"Will you call me back?"

"Well, I . . ."

"Please, oh please, Alice. My mother's been real bad. I haven't been out of the house once."

"I'd better go."

"You don't even care, do you?" he said, his voice thinning. "You think you're the only one with problems, don't you? Well, *don't* call me back! Don't bother!" The phone slammed in her ear.

Father Gannon was out on the steps now. "So, I can call," he was saying to her mother. "Soon as I know when I'm going up, I'll call, and if Alice wants . . ."

"For God's sake," her mother muttered, at the window watching him go up the street. "Bad enough to have a priest nosing around, but a nervous wreck like him." She went into the kitchen to finish ironing Duvall's suit.

Benjy was still at the table working on the shoes. He daubed more polish onto a dark splatter on the toe. Omar was leaving for Bennington in the morning on some mysterious trip that brought a flush to her mother's cheeks every time it was mentioned. Alice watched her match the trouser creases and set them carefully on the ironing board. Her mother smiled absently as she ran the wrinkles flat with her fingers. Then she wet a dish towel and wrung it out over the sink and spread the towel over the pants.

"I'm not going to Burlington or anywhere with him," Alice said.

"I didn't say you were," her mother said as the iron sizzled against the wet towel. She blew up at the perspiration on her forehead and looked at Alice. "But then again, it might be a good chance to talk to him when he's sober, to see if he'll give you any of the trust money for college."

A knot pulled in Alice's stomach. It was time to tell her. She'd made up her mind Friday night. She had to get away from here, away from everyone. "I'm taking that job at the lake," she said as resolutely as she could under her mother's cold stare.

Her mother moved the towel down to the cuffs. The iron hissed on the wet cloth. "No." She turned over the pants, then wet the towel again and wrung it out over the sink.

"What do you mean, no? They make great tips. It's the best—"

"No." The iron sizzled again.

"Mom!"

"You'll spend as much as you make. They all do."

She stepped closer. "I'll send every penny home, I swear!"

"You think you will, but you won't."

"I will!" Her hands clenched into fists. "I swear I will. I give you my word, Mom!"

Her mother laughed sharply. "Hah! Just like you gave me your word yesterday that you'd go to the A+X and apply."

"I did!"

"And?"

"They said they'd call," she lied. All she'd done was get an application from one of the carhops. She hadn't even filled it out. The A+X was a dump, and every tramp in town worked there.

"Don't wait! Call *them!*"

"Well, the guy said he'd call if anybody quit. Or something like that." She could feel her mother's eyes boring through her skull.

"Is that so?" Her mother lifted the steaming pants and draped them over the back of the chair.

Benjy's rag whipped faster and faster over Duvall's shoe. He looked up with a sad smile. He thought she was beaten, but she *would* go to the lake. For once she would stand up to her mother and do what *she* wanted. Norm always did, and her mother respected him because he had backbone enough to defy her and prove her wrong.

Her mother was ironing the lapel of Duvall's jacket. That bitter smile crimped her mouth again. "Better face the facts, Alice." She looked up and sighed. "You'll work in town, and you'll live here, and you'll save every grubby penny you can get your hands on."

Alice turned and walked out of the kitchen.

"Like I do," her mother called. "Every grubby penny I can get my grubby hands on, every grubby day of my grubby little life . . ."

She was at the top of the stairs when she heard her mother start on Benjy. "Do it again! If you're going to do a job, do it right! That's it . . . rub! That's the way, harder! Harder!"

She went into her mother's room, straight to the closet, and drew the old suitcase down from the top shelf. She'd pack tonight, and in the morning she'd call Mary Agnes at the lake. This would be the best summer she'd ever had. As she turned from the closet, her hand flew to her mouth. There on her mother's unmade bed dozed Omar Duvall, arms spread, legs splayed, both his mouth and the fly of his undershorts wide open. Caught in the shaft of window light was his limp penis. She hurried into her room and packed; then she hid the suitcase under her bed. She spent most of the day in her room, reading and waiting. Lester kept calling, but she told Benjy to say she wasn't home. Omar and her mother sat at the kitchen table talking through the afternoon, talking into the night, talking and talking. Soon she would be free of them.

All that night she slept fitfully, and through the dark heat seethed a ferment of dreams, her father weeping and beating at the door while Lester hissed, "Slut, slut, slut," and her mother shook Benjy's chair chanting, "Harder, harder," while Omar Duvall's soft moonlit penis grew longer and longer slithering down the black corridor to her silent door, then lapping up from the side of her bed like a monstrous viper.

The next morning she woke up to a battle between her mother and Norm. It ended with her mother ordering him down to Jarden Greene's office. She lay in bed waiting for her mother to leave for work. When she still hadn't heard the old car pull out of the driveway, she went downstairs. Benjy was at the kitchen table reading a comic book that was propped against a stack of books.

"Where's Mom?"

"At work," he said.

"I didn't hear her go."

"She walked. She left the car for Omar to take to Bennington," he said.

"You're kidding! Why?"

"I don't know. For some job or something." He looked up at her now. "Mom said for you to wash the dishes and put the garbage cans in the garage after the truck comes."

"And what'd she say for you to do?" she snapped.

He gestured at the books. "She said to sit here and read, and then at noon she said I have to go up to the pool."

"To do what? To swim?"

"No."

"Well, what'll you do if you don't swim?"

"Nothing. Same as last summer. Just sit on the bars and watch kids. And then after, I'll walk through the showers to get wet."

"Isn't that boring, just watching people swim?"

He shrugged. "Sometimes."

"Don't you get tired of yessing people all the time, Benjy?"

He shrugged again. "I don't know."

"Why do you always let people push you around? Don't you ever do what you want to do?"

He thought for a moment, then said softly, "I do what I want."

"No, you don't."

"I do too," he said, his chin jutting out. "I just don't like fights. I don't like people yelling at me."

"Well then, Benjy, I'd say you're in for a pretty sad life. That's what I think," she said smugly, folding the dishrag over the spigot.

After she had rolled the empty barrels back into the garage, she went inside and called the bus terminal. The two lake buses were at noon and at seven tonight. It was ten now, so if she hurried, she'd make the noon bus. Next, she called Mary Agnes at the lake. The phone in the cabin rang a long time before it was answered by a sleepy-voiced girl who said Mary Agnes wasn't back yet. Back from work? Alice asked, and the girl laughed. No, what she meant was, Mary Agnes wasn't back from last night yet. She felt a surge of giddy courage. After all, they were out of high school now and free to make their own decisions. God, look at her own mother, pregnant and married at eighteen. She knew two girls her age who were getting married this summer. And then there was Bernadette Mansaw, who had dropped out of school freshman year, pregnant, and now had two kids.

Alice opened the door and set the suitcase on the front steps. She looked up to see Mrs. Klubock waving from a second-floor window, where she sat backward out on the sill spraying glass cleaner on the

windowpane. She wore a bathing suit and a red bandanna tied behind her head.

"It only looks like work! I'm really working on my tan! Come up
and join me!" Mrs. Klubock called with a wave of her rag.

"I wish I could," Alice called back, emboldened by the warmth
of Mrs. Klubock's easy laughter.

She hurried back into the house. Taking her pocketbook from the
closet, she said goodbye to Benjy and told him she was going downtown. She checked her wallet to be sure she'd have enough for the
ticket. Three dollars was missing. There were only two left. "Who
took my money?" she demanded.

"Mom did," Benjy called out from the kitchen. "She had to give
it to Omar for gas."

"That bastard!"

"I didn't know you swore," Benjy said, hanging on to the door
frame so that he couldn't be accused of leaving the kitchen.

She snapped her wallet into her purse. "There's a goddamn
whole lot about me people don't know yet," she said, opening the
front door. "But they will. And you can tell her that for me! You tell
her I'm sick of being pushed around and I'm sick of being walked all
over and I'm sick of—"

The phone was ringing. Benjy held the receiver out. "It's for you.
It's Uncle Renie."

She waved and shook her head no. Next to Lester, he was the last
person on earth she needed to talk to now. Benjy nodded, listening to
Uncle Renie. "Okay . . . okay . . . yup, I'll tell her when she comes
back." He hung up. "He said he's got good news. He said for you to
call him soon as you get back."

She was about to close the door, when Benjy, heedless of his
mother's edict that he not set one foot in the living room or touch the
television all day, rushed after her.

"Call him, Alice! Maybe it's a graduation present! Or maybe it's
money!" he shouted as she marched down the weedy walk with her
suitcase.

"Or maybe it's shit," she muttered, and then was ashamed
because she had forgotten Mrs. Klubock perched up there like a
bird—her mother was right—*like a goddamn eagle,* she thought,

perched up there so she can keep a better eye on the whole neighborhood.

Her arm ached from the weight of the suitcase as she pushed open the door to the LaChance Appliance Company.

"Be right there," Uncle Renie called anxiously as the cowbells clanged on the door.

She rubbed her nose. Aside from the unpleasant smell, not much had changed. It was just as gloomy and dusty as ever. And she felt just as apprehensive as she always did here. Uncle Renie gave her the creeps.

"Be patient," he grunted.

She picked up a brochure from the counter and fanned herself with it. A toilet flushed, then over the gurgle Uncle Renie called again, "Be right with you."

The bathroom door opened and Renie hurried out, buckling his belt. He grinned and his hands jerked up, tangling with the air as if he wanted to grab her. As he came toward her, a huge cat slid out from between two refrigerators and curled around his ankle. "Alice, you gotta meet Tom here." He laughed, bending to pick it up.

"Benjy said you had something to tell me, Uncle Renie?" She patted the cat's head and looked expectantly at her uncle.

"Tom likes you." He chuckled as the cat's tongue scraped her wrist. "He's usually not this nice when he first meets people." He stroked the cat's chin, and it purred faster and louder and swished its great tail. "But then you're a pretty good judge of people, aren't you, Tom?" He laughed. " 'Course, he sees your face all the time," he said, pointing at the faded pictures on the back of the cash register.

She laid the brochure down, and he picked it up. "See that? That's the Golden Toastee line!" he said, his eyes widening as his voice shaded to a whisper. "And I might get the franchise. Look!" He pointed at the cover. "See where it says SOLD ONLY IN THE FINEST STORES? In gold letters!"

This is ridiculous, she thought. Her eyes flickered over the narrow little store, its high tin ceiling strung with sooty cobwebs. Uncle Renie kept talking.

" 'Course, I'm fixing up before they send the sales rep out to check me over." He reached into his pocket, and she leaned forward, thinking this was the surprise. "I got these today. Paint chips for the walls," he said, spreading the colored disks over the counter. He held one up. "You like this green?"

"It's nice, Uncle Renie." She glanced up at the clock. The bus was leaving in forty-five minutes.

"Too dark?" he asked anxiously.

"No, it's nice. It's just I'm in kind of a hurry."

"Oh jeez, listen to me going on." He dropped the chip onto the pile. "I haven't let you say a word in edgewise yet, I been yammering my head off so much." He gestured ruefully down at the cat. "I get so used to not expecting talk back, I just get awful carried away."

She felt bad now. She picked up one of the disks. "This yellow's nice, Uncle Renie." She handed it to him. "Nice and bright."

"Yah," he said, examining it at arm's length. "That's the one, all right." He put the disk in his shirt pocket, then looked at her and took a deep breath.

"What's wrong, Uncle Renie?"

He shrugged. "What happened was I told your mother what the guy said, and she said you'd already brought the papers in, so I called the guy right up, and I said, 'Jerry, the other day didn't you come in the store and say how you needed girls, and didn't you look at my niece's here picture on the register and say, 'She's hired if she wants'? And he said, 'Yessir, I did.' That's how it all got started, Alice. So I called her back. Your mother." He threw up his hands.

He looked so stricken and confused that she couldn't help laughing. "Uncle Renie, I don't know what you're talking about!"

"The A+X. Your mother called me up and said you filled out the papers, and the guy I know said no, you didn't fill out no papers up to his place. He went and checked."

"Does my mother know that?" she asked weakly, and his mournful nod betrayed the magnitude of her mother's wrath. "Can I borrow three dollars, Uncle Renie?"

He stirred a finger through the paint disks. "She said not to give you any money." He cleared his throat. "And she said to tell you if you went to the lake, she'd come get you and drag you home." He reached out, and she cringed with the touch of his damp hand. "Alice, don't look at me like that! Don't be mad at me. I can't help you run away. I can't do that."

She was crying now. "I'm not running away, Uncle Renie. I just want to go to the lake. I'm just so sick of it here. I'm just so sick of everything."

He threw his arms around her and hugged her tight and made a sound as if he were crying, too. "But you can't just run away," he said. "Things are always running away from me." His head twisted to one side and she felt him jerk as if with an enormous jolt. "Oh . . . oh," he moaned. "And I ran away, too. . . ."

The A+X manager was Mr. Coughlin. His bloodshot eyes narrowed on her chest. "Size six?" he asked, then smiled smugly when she nodded. "Here's one," he said, handing her the uniform: black pants, pink-and-black-checked blouse, black vest, and peaked black cardboard cap. "Nights," he said, sitting down behind a ketchup-splattered table that was his desk. "Four to twelve." He widened his eyes and lowered his voice. "The lunatic shift."

On the table was a bronze plaque with raised letters that said SCREW ME AND YOU'RE HIRED. CHEAT ME AND YOU'RE FIRED. The cluttered back room buzzed with flies. Outside in the lot, a car was honking its horn. The sign over Coughlin's head said YOU DON'T HAVE TO BE CRAZY TO WORK HERE, BUT IT HELPS. Stacked in the corners were cartons of cellophaned hamburg rolls. The tiny office reeked of grease and pickles.

"Gotta boyfriend?"

"No," she said.

"Good. Because I won't stand for the studs hanging out all night tying up the stations. Now, first off, take this menu home and study it. Spills and mistakes come outta your pay. Understand?"

She nodded.

"And second thing is, don't try stealing food out to your buddies. It don't work. We gotta system here of numbered checks. Got that?"

She nodded.

"And third, we got the A+X motto—GOOD FOOD WITH A SMILE."

He drew in his chin and looked around. "I got my own motto, Get 'em in and get 'em out—fast! Capeesh?"

She nodded again.

He screwed up his mouth disgustedly. "Jesus Christ! You some kinda mute?" He held out his hands. "What? What? You shy? You scared? What is it?"

"I was concentrating on what you were saying," she said stiffly.

He looked at her. "Oh I get it." He lit a cigarette and squinted through the smoke. "I shoulda known. You're the type that's too good to work here, right? You think this place sucks." He laughed. "And you think I suck, too."

She had opened the door to go outside. He was a pig and she hated him.

"Well, you're right! I do!" he howled. "But you need a job, doll, now don't you?"

As she came to the front of the building, a buzzer sounded over and over again. Through the service window peered the blocky head of the cook, Anthology Carper, his eyes pink as sores, his blue-tinted flesh seeming to glow. "Ninety-two's up!" he screeched into the microphone. "Seventy-five's up!" His eyes caught hers and he stuck out his tongue and wiggled it at her. "Sixty-nine's up," he giggled, wiggling his tongue again.

With his trousers pressed and his shoes gleaming, Omar Duvall strode briskly down the street under a high blue sky, and he felt so good. He felt better than good. He felt sure. He felt nimble. The old spring was back in his step. He bounced up and down on the curbstone now while he waited for the light to change, then laughed softly as he passed in front of the idling cars. Omar Duvall was stepping out. Yes sir, he was on his way. No matter how low a man fell he could always get back on his feet as long as he had faith, faith in himself, and faith in life's unlimited opportunities. He turned the corner, and as he neared Marie's shabby little house, he smiled, relieved to see her car waiting for him in the driveway, just as she had promised. He had an appointment this afternoon in Bennington with the Northeast distributor of Roy Gold Enterprises. He took the matchbook cover from his pocket and read it again.

PRESTO SOAP

Do you want to be safe all your life,
but stuck in the same old rut?

OR

Are you willing to take that first step
onto the ladder of success?

"Where I belong," he whispered as he stepped into the dim back hall cluttered with winter jackets, muddy boots, mops and brooms and snow shovels. "Right on the very top rung," he sighed, impulsively gathering up the shovels and jackets and boots, which he deposited in the garage. On his way back he spotted Marie's laundry basket protruding from the lilac bush. Typical, he thought. That was so much of her trouble: carelessness, a lack of organizational skills. It was sad the way she let life overtake her, leaving in its wake this yard, the chaotic house, her frantic children. The poor woman had no faith in herself. He grabbed the wicker handle, then jumped back from the dark wet growl of Klubocks' dog crouched in the bushes. His hand shot into his pocket, but of course the knife was gone, for that had been another time, another life. Only this was real, this moment, this pang in his breast. Sweat stung his eyes.

"Good morning!" chirped a voice from the trees.

Wiping his brow, he looked around, then saw Jessie Klubock's round buttocks plumped on the second-floor sill, where she sat washing windows. "And a good morning to you, ma'am," he called and she waved her rag.

"Doesn't this look like fun?" she called back, gesturing so excitedly now with both hands that he was afraid she would fall.

"Oh it certainly does," he said, shading his eyes, dizzied by her smallness against the sunstruck glass.

"Then grab a rag and join me," she called.

"I would, except that I am deathly afraid of heights," he hollered up.

"I don't believe that, a great big thing like you." She laughed and began to scrub the windowpane with such exuberance that for a moment he couldn't move. He gazed up with a throb of the old longing, not so much for flesh or even for his own comfort and solace as for a woman's blind unquestioning trust; a woman in need, a woman who would believe.

The back-hall door swung open. "Mr. Duvall?" Benjy called, and Omar hurried inside with the boy at his heels. "I thought you were gone," Benjy said nervously. "I saw you come in the hall and then you left. I didn't know what you were doing."

"Just trying to help your dear mother." He put his hand on the boy's shoulder and felt him flinch. "Which you should be doing as well, son, helping your mother in every possible way." He squeezed the bony shoulder and saw Benjy's face steel with resolve. "Can you do that?" he asked, and the boy nodded. "Promise me, now," he said. "Promise you'll do whatever it takes to make her happy."

"I promise!" Benjy did not blink. He stared up at Duvall, who for a moment could not move or reply.

"Good enough," he finally said in a hoarse whisper, then looked away, heart racing, cheeks flushed, not with the heat of guileful shame, but with awe at this mastery that sometimes left him weak with the burden of his own powers.

"Here's the keys," Benjy was saying. "And she made you a lunch, too." The boy handed him a limp paper bag that smelled of tuna fish.

She had mentioned gas money. Hoping she had remembered, Omar looked inside. There were three one-dollar bills and a note that said: *Call me as soon as you hear anything. Good luck. Marie.* Noticing a smudge above her name, he held the paper to the window and saw where she had erased *Love*.

He said goodbye to Benjy and was starting the car when he realized the boy was still in the doorway, watching with a troubled expression. He rolled down the window. "What is it?" he called.

Benjy's mouth opened and closed, and then he shrugged. "Nothing," he said through a weak smile.

He was backing down the driveway when he saw a head bob

alongside his window. He hit the brake. "Damn it, boy, what're you doing?"

"I was just wondering," the boy called over the engine's roar. Wincing, he blurted, "Are you coming back?"

"Of course I'm coming back. Of course I am!" Omar said, not only amused and flattered by the boy's apprehension, but drawn to it, energized by that mistrust with its inexpressible longing, by the loneliness, the terrible loneliness of lights burning through the night and telephones seized at the first ping, by that pain seeping sometimes into his own sleep, the pain of all those hearts in time with his own, even though he knew there was little one man could do to set it all right, so very, very little. And so, with a sigh, he pulled out of the driveway, then stared down the narrow one-way street. His grip tightened on the wheel and suddenly he knew exactly what the boy knew, that he was not coming back, not ever. He had a car, money in the pocket of his freshly cleaned and pressed suit, and there on the torn seat beside him, his next meal. He was free as a bird with nothing to hold him, nothing to get in his way. He could just keep on going. Why not? What was stopping him? The boy's eyes still on him? Marie? Well, if anything, it would teach her a damn good lesson. Yes sir, a woman alone like that shouldn't ever let a stranger into her home. Lucky for her it had been him and not some thieving, murdering pervert. Oh it was pathetic, it really was, a woman like that, so wanting, so lonely, so desperate she'd open her door to kindness no matter its guise or form.

With his arm on the window well, he cruised down the street, the breeze flapping his sleeve. One of these days, real soon, as soon as he could, he'd write her a letter telling what a fine woman she was. A woman of strength. A woman of character. Yes sir, first chance he got, first opportunity, he'd write and say, *My dear Marie . . . my dear, dearest sweet Marie, I have roamed this vast country far and wide and I have met many a fine woman, but none as good, as lonely, as . . . as . . . as stimulating as—*

"Oh fucking, fucking Jesus!" he cried. His foot shot to the brake and the car lurched to a stop before he could turn. Parked ahead on the distant corner was his old dusty station wagon. He slumped behind the wheel and watched the driver's door open.

Luther climbed out, then walked around to the other side of the car. He helped Reverend Pease out, then steadied him on his feet. The old man clung to the open door while Luther tugged a flimsy jacket onto his shoulders and centered the familiar porkpie hat on his head. Luther led him shuffling onto the sidewalk.

Luther looked up and seemed now to be pointing toward this very corner where Omar sat, eyes glazed with terror, as his hand slipped slowly, so slowly it would take days to pass from the wheel to the stick to shift the car into reverse. The old man shook his head and stomped his feet in the perverse jig that meant he'd been bullied enough by the sullen Luther and now he'd have his way. He pointed toward the next street, which Omar realized must have been where they last saw Earlie. Yes, that was the very street down which Earlie had chased him. But how much did they really know? Had the old man actually seen his grandson follow Omar into the woods? He couldn't have, Omar reasoned, and yet that was exactly where the old man was heading.

Through the mirror, Omar stared back at those crow-infested tangled trees that loomed as the limping old man's magnetic destination. They were the only ones who could link him to Earlie that day, and so he had no choice, no choice now but to stop them. They had forced him to this. He hunched over the wheel, playing it through with such brutal clarity that only a moment later the act would seem blurred and unreal, its commission more dream than deed: the stuck gas pedal; a dip, then a bump in the road; the huge engine accelerating out of control, hurtling the car onto the sidewalk, crushing them both.

He would stagger out as neighbors ran from their houses. "Duvall!" the old man might moan. There would be sirens. Only his eyes moved. Yes, there would be sirens, distant sirens, questions he could not answer. No, better to drive away. His foot eased to the gas pedal, then froze. If he did leave now, he'd be a hunted man whether they found Earlie in there or not. They'd be right on his tail. It was a small town. As soon as Marie reported her car gone, they would know. They knew all his tricks. No sir, he had to stay calm, cool, collected, and he had to keep thinking like them, every minute; just crawl inside the old man's head to know what he knows and go where he goes, because it wasn't spilled blood the old thief was tracking down, but a hard-beating, hard-pumping heart he knew as well as his own. Better to keep the old man pursuing love, a more alluring quarry than death; love to keep the gears turning, to keep them all moving. The old man had faith enough to search forever for his grandson, so Omar would provide the lure, proof that Earlie was still alive, but far, far from here.

He hurried into the kitchen and the boy's head shot up, his cheek smeared with colored ink. He had fallen asleep, drooling on the open comic book.

"Now listen carefully," he said, dragging a chair close. "Remember every word I tell you, because I am in very, very great danger, and I need your help."

Benjy stared, as if peering up from a watery dream.

"It's not just me," he whispered, gripping the boy's arm, demanding, imploring through flesh and bone, his fingertips pulsing a beat of such urgency that for a long time after there would be bruises on the soft white underflesh. "But all of us. We're all counting on you. So listen to every single word I say. . . ."

It was Luther who first heard Benjy. The old man kept walking, each foot lifting with the heft of stone, then falling onto the sidewalk.

"What you want?" Luther asked with the same resignation of the old man's plodding journey. "You want something?" The whites of his eyes were yellow and hot, and his skin gleamed in the sunshine.

The words died on Benjy's tongue. Now the old man looked at him. His gold front tooth sparkled. Next to the younger man's his dark skin seemed dull and as drab as if coated with dust. "You live around here, boy?" the old man asked.

"Yes sir." His reply seemed more gesture than sound. He had never spoken to a black man before.

"You seen this young man around?" the old man asked, moving toward Benjy with his weighted step. The paler palm of his hand cupped a worn tissuey photograph.

It was the picture of a boy not much older than Benjy. He shook his head, then looked up and nodded. It vaguely resembled the man he had seen in the woods that day with Omar.

"When?" the old man demanded, hobbling closer. He reeked of sweat and still dark ponds.

"A couple of weeks ago," Benjy said, Omar's carefully chosen words bobbing to the surface now. "Right down there." He pointed toward the distant woods. "I was on my way home from school, and he came out of the woods, and he asked did I want to buy any magazines, and I said no, I couldn't, I didn't have any money, and he laughed, and he said, 'Money! You need money?' And he pulled out this big thick thing of money, of dollar bills in this silver thing that had a *D* engraved on it and . . ."

"Duvall's clip!" the young man cried. He looked at the old man and yelped. "That be Duvall's clip!"

"And Duvall's cash!" said the old man, so gleefully clapping his hands that he stumbled. Luther steadied him by the back of his shirt. The old man just kept talking. "What he say then? Earlie—what he say?"

"He . . . he said, 'Here,' and he gave me a dollar, and he told me not to tell the big white man in the white suit I saw him because he was on his way down to see his best girl, Laydee Dwelley, in Hankham, Mississippi."

"Oh my Lord," gasped the grinning old man. He laid his hands on Benjy's shoulders. "Try telling me now, there ain't no divine purpose behind all that we do, Mr. Luther Corbett."

Luther just shook his head, apparently conceding the old man right, for once.

"His best girl, who is Laydee Dwelley in Hankham, Mississippi." The old man closed his eyes and sighed. "God did this. God sent this child. And now we're gonna return the favor, child." His bloodshot eyes widened. "That big white man Earlie told you about, his name is Omar Duvall and you ever see him, you watch out, 'cause he is a bad, bad man. He is what you call a treacherous man. He got knives! He got a switchblade with a snakeskin handle and a blade so sharp it can slice through bone, quick as that!" hissed the old man with such a sudden zigzagging thrust of his fist that Benjy jumped.

"You scarin' him!" Luther said.

"But that's the favor," said the old man, drawing back. "Fear. Might just save your life one day, child."

"What's your name?" Luther asked, reaching into his pocket. He held out a quarter.

"I gotta go now," Benjy said. He ran away, relieved, because that must have been just the way it had happened that day in the woods, just as Omar had told him. Earlie had stolen Omar's money, and now he *was* on his way to Mississippi, and he suddenly realized that the glint he had seen that day, that glint through the leaves had not been a blade at all, but the silver money clip they had both been struggling for.

At five o'clock Renie LaChance locked the door and pulled the shade over the glass. He opened a can of cat food and another can of sardines and poured more milk into Tom's bowl. Then he reached under the counter for his slim green ledgers. In one, he printed: 4.50—Mrs. Ottman's vegetable bins. 2.25—Mrs. Crowley's reflector pans. That was the ledger the IRS could see. He opened the second ledger and turned the pages. In this one he recorded the day's cash sales, 12.00—fan. 5.95—lint filter. On the next line he wrote: *Slow day at Cushing's, only sixty-five customers, approximately $195 by my estimation. Temperature—83 degrees. Sunny, muggy. Terrible smell. A stink. Makes some people sick in their stomach. Friday night, Helen hit Sam over the head with her statue. Police came. Now with Sam gone Helen will get meaner and meaner to me like always.*

Best news! Alice came in store and picked out the color yellow. Just like the sunshine! Golden Toastee rep coming to check store next week. I am nervous. If I get it I will put a sign up that says EXCLUSIVE GOLDEN TOASTEE DEALER *in gold letters and people will come from all over.*

He looked at his watch. Only five-fifteen, the part of the day he least knew what to do with. There was no place for him between five and dinner at six-thirty. In a way it was the loneliest part of the day.

All the ladies would be busy now in their kitchens, their hands too greasy or full to pick up their phones, so their children would answer or their husbands. When he had Riddles, this was the time he used to take him for walks. It hurt to remember what Sam had said about Helen burying Riddles, but he couldn't allow himself such a terrible belief. If it was true, he would have to do something; what, he didn't know, but it would be not only final, but probably the worst act he'd ever committed. It might even be murder, he realized, shuddering. Or love, he thought with sudden terror.

All at once he rushed into the bathroom, sat down, and dialed his own number.

"Hello," came Helen's crisp voice. "Hello? Hello! Who is this?" And then she hung up.

He called her two more times. She answered, then slammed down the phone when she got no response. On the third call he stared up at his pictures, his gaze swimming in glossy blindness.

"What do you want?" gasped Helen's thin frightened voice. "Why do you keep calling?"

He touched himself and moaned softly, thinking of the soft white skin on her shoulder.

"Oh," she said. "You stop! You just leave me alone."

He leaned back, legs apart, one hand on the phone at his ear, the other hand gently stroking as he moaned, his eyes closed with her scared little voice in his ear, in his heart, deep, deep in his groin.

When it was over, he watched himself in the mirror as he washed his sticky hands in the small, stained sink and he saw how his eyes glowed and how his cheeks were flushed, and a great wonder seized him because he had never, ever dared do this with any of the others.

He drove home with an ache burning in his chest and the knowledge that he loved his wife very much. As was Helen's custom when he came through the door, she took his plate from the oven and set it on the table. She never ate, but seemed to live on air, he thought, without need of any bodily functions, not sex, not food, not defecation.

"Sit down," he said quickly, before she could leave the kitchen.

"Why?" she asked, eyes steeled for the bad news her life attracted.

"Well, I got things to tell you," he said. From his pocket he withdrew the yellow disk and held it out to her. "For the store," he said, laying it on the table when she didn't take it. He told her about the Golden Toastee line and the salesman he expected and the gold-lettered sign, and now he was amazed to hear himself telling her about his surplus of fans, confessing how foolish he had felt all this past year with them jam-packing the storeroom, but then he'd sold one last Friday and another today, so this heat might turn out to be a real lifesaver . . . *he loved her, loved her fine thin neck and her slim delicate fingers* . . . people were drooping with the heat. They'd pay any price for cool air . . . *he was a lucky man to have such a fine wife*. . . . "Oh Helen!" he cried when she took a step toward him.

"Put your plate in the sink," she said, opening the door. "I'll be outside weeding."

Before the last car had even left her station, Alice yanked off her shiny black hat and apron and stuffed them in her pocket. Most of the girls were already in the back room smoking with Coughlin. She was relieved and flattered not to have been asked to join them. They knew better, she thought as she waited out at the curb for Norm to pick her up. Her third night here and it had been the worst one yet. Her co-workers were crude and impatient with her, and the customers thought for the price of a root beer they could treat her like dirt. She had mixed up orders again tonight, dropped a full tray, and then at the height of the supper rush the bathroom door had jammed, trapping her inside. "Stupid bitch . . . stupid bitch," Coughlin had ranted as he jimmied free the door to let her out.

It was midnight and only a few cars had been by. She leaned forward with each headlight, hoping it was Norm. She could feel Anthology Carper's lewd bulbous eyes on her. All night long she'd slid her orders through his window, holding her breath with her eyes averted, her stomach weak at such propinquity, such familiarity with a creature so ugly, so foulmouthed and cruel that last night when she cut her thumb on a broken glass he'd laughed to see the blood.

Headlights rose in the distance, and now a low-slung gray Chevy pulled into the lot. Stiffening, she tried to cover the side of her face. It was Blue Mooney here for Carper, who was his cousin. He leaned over to comb his hair in the rearview mirror before he got out of the car. Under the floodlights his full mouth and his eyes seemed to gleam. He glanced back and caught her looking at him. As much as he gave her the creeps, there was also this secret fascination. She would see him strutting downtown with his hoody friends or at the band concerts in the park, and it would be an effort to look away. From the corner of her eye now, she saw him turn quickly. She bit her lip, praying he didn't recognize her from the lake. For the past two nights she had managed to avoid him. He was behind her now at the greasy order window, speaking in a low voice to his cousin. She heard her name and now she cringed as his boots clicked toward her.

"You're new here, huh?" he said, grinning.

She nodded, then stared past him at the dark empty road, hugging herself a little tighter.

"I seen you from somewhere, but I can't place where." He passed back and forth, studying her from different angles. "It'll come to me," he said, snapping his fingers while he peered down at her. "One of these days," he said, grinning again. "How about you? You remember me from someplace? I look familiar to you at all?"

"No!" And she knew by his dying grin that he had indeed recognized her and was irritated by her snub. Now she was afraid. He wasn't just a hood but a thief. Last year he and his older brother, who was on parole, had been caught breaking into Mrs. Bonifante's gas station. He'd be in jail now with his brother if it hadn't been for Chief Stoner getting the Judge to let him go into the Marines. Lester had said people weren't happy he was back in town, even if it was only temporarily. She wondered if Lester had told his father about Mooney threatening him graduation night. Probably.

Behind them rose Coughlin's angry voice, then Carper's shrill retort, and now each man simultaneously telling the other what he could do.

"Fuck yourself!"

"Go fuck yourself," like an ugly echo.

"Jerry's a creep, huh?" Mooney laughed, then hooked his grimy thumbs in his hip pockets and stretched, arching his back. "I'd put up with that shit for about two seconds."

She stepped closer to the curb.

"Hey! Need a ride?" he asked, stepping next to her. He gestured at his car. "She's got glass packs," he bragged. "Brand new."

"My brother's coming," she said, tensing as he seemed to move even closer.

He nodded. "Hey!" he said, as if it were a sudden brainstorm. "Maybe sometime tell him don't come, and I'll give you a ride!"

"Well, he has to. My mother wants him to." She stared miserably up the street. Where was Norm?

"Oh yah, well, what're you gonna do, huh? Mothers are like that." He tapped a cigarette from his pack, then offered her one. She shook her head. "Maybe that's him," he said, striking a match with a flick of his thumb. "Guess so," he sighed as Norm slowed down.

Her mother's loud creaky car ground to a stop and she jumped in.

"See you tomorrow night," Mooney called as they roared off.

She turned now and saw Norm's bruised cheek and swollen bleeding lip. Norm and Weeb and Tommy Mullins had been up on Town Line Road chasing parkers when Billy Hendricks and a car-load of his friends blocked Norm's car. Hendricks and Norm had fought in a long, gasping match that had ended only when they were finally dragged apart.

"Why did you do that?" She stared at him. "Do you know how embarrassed I feel? Those are all kids in my class!"

He hunched over the wheel.

"What's wrong with you? What're you always trying to prove? God, Norm, it's bad enough with Dad and now with that Duvall around. . . . I mean, I mean, I just can't take it. It's so embarrassing!" She turned away, trying not to cry. "I can't wait to get out of here! I can't wait! I hate it here so much!"

The car flew along.

"Norm! Slow down! You're speeding! Norm!" she screamed, then grabbed his arm.

He shoved her away so hard that she fell against the door.

"I'll get you outta here!" he hollered over the roar of the engine.

"Norm, stop it, please!"

"Tell me where you wanna go!" he bellowed. "Wanna go visit Dad?" He was crying, pushing her away as she came toward him again. "I know! We'll go get the fuckin' priest, that's what we'll do!"

She looked over his arm at the trembling speedometer. "You're going eighty-five! Please stop! Don't do this, Norm!" She covered her face with her hands.

"Fucking bastards," he growled. "Goddamn fucking no good . . ."

A police siren screamed after them, its light flashing.

"Norm!"

The car rumbled over the soft shoulder, then finally stopped. Lester's father was getting out of the cruiser behind them. She took a deep breath, then leaned forward as his flashlight shone from Norm's face to hers.

"I thought it was your car, Alice," he said. "What happened?" The light fixed on Norm's face. "Who did that to you, Norm?"

"Nobody," Norm mumbled, eyes downcast. "I fell."

"Where you been, Norm?"

"Home," he said, trying to cover his mouth so the Chief wouldn't smell his breath.

"That happen at home?"

"Yup."

"Wasn't that big guy, was it? That friend of your mom's?"

"No!" Norm looked up angrily, and Alice's stomach weakened with the realization that everyone knew about Duvall, too.

"I said I fell!" Norm was saying. "I fell off a ladder!"

"What's going on here? What's the speeding all about?" Stoner asked. From the way he was staring at Norm, Alice was afraid he might arrest him.

"The pedal stuck," Norm said. "I kept trying to pull it up!"

Stoner leaned in the window. He looked at her. "Pedal got stuck?" he said softly.

She nodded.

"It's okay now?"

"It's okay," she said.

"All right, but why don't you drive the rest of the way home, Alice? Just to be on the safe side, okay, kids?"

They both nodded, and she could tell from his hesitation that he wanted to say something about Les; then, thinking better of it, he patted the window well. He stepped back as Norm got out and walked around the back of the car to the other side. She slid behind the wheel. "Take it easy now," he called as she pulled onto the road.

"Norm?" she said when they were out of Stoner's sight. She thought she'd heard him say something. "What is it?"

"I'm sorry," he sobbed. "I mean it. I really am."

"Where am I?" Sam Fermoyle asked, wincing at the stringy sound of his own voice. His head hurt. He touched his bandaged wound where the shaved hair had started to grow back. His fuzzy scalp was itchy, but too tender to scratch.

"You're in the Green Room, sir," the nurse answered.

"Where is the Green Room?" He would play their deadening game.

"The Green Room is right here, sir, in the Bullfinch Building."

"And where's the Bullfinch Building?" He closed his eyes.

"Oh, I see," said the nurse. "You're not a regular guest, are you? Well, then, the Bullfinch Building is our oldest building here at Applegate. Compared to our newer buildings, it is lacking in some of the more modern facilities. But it more than makes up for that in charm and grace. In fact, many of our guests ask for accommodations here each time they come. This old building has a personality all its—"

"How long have I been here?" He looked over at her.

"Let me see. . . . You're Mr. . . . Mr. . . ." She fumbled through the clipboarded papers hanging by the door. "Of course, Mr. Fermoyle! Up from Detox!" She flipped a page and looked up with a bright smile. "You've been here four and a half days!"

"When do I get out?"

Her smile was as crisp as her pleated cap. "Dr. Litchfield will be in shortly for orientation, and he'll explain all the little details to you, sir." She pushed a cart to the bed and cranked it up over his lap. He stared down at the poached egg quivering on a wet slice of puckered toast.

"In the meantime," she said as she opened a delicately barred window, "eat up and enjoy the country air."

The fresh air felt like barbed thread passing through his nostrils. He closed his eyes until the nurse was gone. Then he poked at the egg for a moment before devouring it. Cold yoke dribbled down his chin. He was picking crumbs from the plate when a diminutive, slope-shouldered man with a fixed, wan smile entered the room. He introduced himself as Dr. Arnold Litchfield, then stood by the door, flipping through the papers on the clipboard. "Your sister called again this morning," the doctor said without looking up. He scribbled on one of the papers before coming to the foot of the bed. "Aren't you interested in your sister's call?" he asked watchfully.

"Not particularly," Sam said.

"Your sister seems to care a great deal about you, Samuel."

"Got a cigarette on you, Doc? I could use a smoke."

Litchfield came to the head of the bed and pushed the red button protruding from the maple headboard. He spoke quickly to the nurse when she came to the door. She was back in a moment with a pack of Kools, gold-tipped matches, and a silver-plated ashtray. Sam chuckled as she arranged them on his tray. "Hey, now this is classy!" He laughed. Litchfield watched him tear open the pack. He inhaled deeply and sank back against the pillows.

"So tell me, Doc, how come I'm here and not at the statehouse, where I usually dry out?"

"The statehouse?" asked Litchfield.

"The state hospital—Waterbury. Or were they booked for the weekend?"

Litchfield gestured to his bandaged head. "Nasty fall you took."

"Nasty fall?"

"Your sister said you passed out and hit your head on her bureau." Litchfield peered at him. "Do you remember any of that?"

"I remember. My sister tried to kill me, Doc. I was trying to wake her up, but she wasn't really asleep. Because all of a sudden her hand came up from under the sheet with her statue of the Blessed Virgin in it, and the next thing I knew, I was on the floor, bleeding like a stuck pig and moaning, 'Helen, I'm dying.' And she answered back, 'I hope so.' And she just laid there, and I begged her, I said, 'Helen, help me. Don't let me die. If I die,' I said, 'they'll put you in jail.' And she laughed, and she said, 'No, they'll give me a medal!' " He looked up at Litchfield. "Nice, huh?"

Litchfield perched atop a stool he had pulled close to the bed. He looked down at Sam. "Do you love your sister?"

He blew a chain of smoke rings into the air. "This place expensive?"

Litchfield squirmed and folded his arms. "Since we offer the most enlightened and comfortable care in this part of the country, I would have to say yes."

"I don't get it," he said, scratching his whiskery cheek. "She could've had me committed to the statehouse for zip." Looking up at Litchfield, he laughed so hard that the stitches in his scalp throbbed. "You better run a Dun and Bradstreet on me fast before I even get an aspirin out of this place!"

Litchfield smiled and patted his arm. "The financial arrangements are all in order, Samuel. Your sister is your guardian and she told me herself that money is not to be a factor in your treatment." He leaned forward. "She cares about you, Samuel. She wants you better; it's that simple."

"Simple as shit," he groaned, stubbing out one cigarette and lighting another.

"Why do you say that, Samuel?" Litchfield asked softly.

Looking up, he caught a familiar flicker in the doctor's eyes. "Are we drifting into analysis now, Doc?" he whispered.

"Only if you'd like to," Litchfield whispered back.

His head sank back into the pillow, and he closed his eyes. "Christ, I've been this route a thousand times. Old docs who fart and fall asleep just when you're telling them how you always wanted to rape your mother. And young docs who refuse to believe you never wanted to rape your mother. Sorry, Doc, but I'm just your average American drunk, and all I want to talk about is when the hell I'm getting out of here!"

"When you're reasonably rehabilitated," said Litchfield as he slid off the stool. He stood by the door.

"And what the hell does that tell me?"

"As much as you want it to tell you," the doctor said softly.

"You got me here for thirty days, Doc! That's all, damn it! I know my rights! Thirty days!" he shouted feebly at the closing door.

No one really knew what Omar Duvall did during the day once he left the Mayo sisters' boardinghouse, but every night at suppertime his airy whistle drifted down the Fermoyles' driveway. His appetite was incredible. At dinner's end he would bow his head, declaring himself a burden, a beggar, all the while casting covetous eyes on the few french fries left or the last three peas. Inevitably with dessert would come his promises.

After one night's supper, he had greased the back-door hinges with lard. After another, he had tightened the wobbly table legs, and after another, had glued the chair legs; and then one night as he rolled his eyes in sated gratitude, he saw the ceiling stains from the leaky roof, and to Marie's horror (Marie who would ask nothing, so that nothing could be asked in return), he went next door to borrow a ladder from the Klubocks. He climbed onto the roof and counted the missing shingles he would replace. He might even have to reflash the chimney. He would spackle the holes in the living-room walls. He would pull out the stump on the front lawn and fill in those dusty trenches Klubocks' dog had dug. And while he was at it, he said, pouring the dregs of Benjy's milk over his fruit cocktail, he might as well plant some grass seed. He would replace the pane of glass Sam Fermoyle had kicked through the cellar window as well as the one in the back door. He would mortar the cracks in the foundation and plug each mouse tunnel so tightly that not even the smallest ant could invade this home. Now that he knew the reason for the drawn curtains over the sink, he suggested arborvitae tall enough to block prying eyes. Whatever needed doing, he would do it. Now take that floor, he said, licking his spoon, then pointing with it. Why, in a day, he could scrape up that split linoleum, then lay down tiles as shiny as glass. Just say the word, put the right tools in his hand, and he could work wonders.

He seemed so vital, so powerful a force that just the possibility of its unharnessing thrilled and dizzied her. As he spoke, her eyes widened, and the years of neglect vanished with the sweep of his promises. Here was a man who would not only set things straight, but who had already made his way straight through to the core of her loneliness. Now, the gouged, hairy plaster and the coppery-ringed stains over the stove seemed such minor matters that she no longer noticed them. Now when she pulled into the driveway bone-tired from work, she did not see the stump black as a rotten tooth, and when she came through the back door that swung on velvet hinges, her eyes lifted past the scarred floor in search of Omar. He was a man of not only great strength, but goodness. He reminded her of her father, broad-backed, simple, kind. And very proud. When she had offered to help Omar with his first week's rent, his eyes had welled with tears, and he had turned away, unable to speak. She had wanted to throw her arms around him and hold him close. What had stopped her then and still did now, each time she desired his touch, had been her children's presence in the next room.

For Norm, his mother's happiness these last few weeks seemed a shimmering fragile bubble. Even the shattering pitch of her laughter sent a shiver up his spine, its sudden rawness so much like crying that he would tense, ready to spring, his hands clutching the arms of the chair. He had never seen her like this before, gullible and giggly, at times even shy and blushing. He sensed in Duvall a strange element, some dark and discernible emanation that both fouled and thinned the air, shrinking the tiny rooms in this box of a house smaller still.

Every night after supper, Duvall and his mother stayed at the kitchen table, where they would talk for hours. Actually, Duvall did most of the talking, while Norm lay in bed, listening. Duvall spoke as ravenously as he ate, mountains of words. When Norm finally fell asleep it was with the drugged consciousness of Duvall's voice in the distance. After midnight, he awakened, gasping as if the breath were being sucked from his lungs. Duvall was still down there, still talking as the room swayed, the dark heat undulating with his drawl until

Norm felt sick to his stomach. He got up and knelt by the window, anchoring his chin over the sill, his brow to the screen, as he took deep breaths of the skunk-filled night. Why doesn't he go home? he wondered. What are they talking about? What does he want? And all at once it occurred to him that Duvall *was* home; more home than he had ever been, and he was waiting for Norm to leave.

In this house where flesh never touched except in anger, Omar Duvall was a toucher and a grasper. It gave Alice the creeps to see his large hands reach across the table to cover Benjy's or his sweaty arm on the back of her mother's chair. Over her own untouched plate, she watched how he ate, the little sweat beads quivering on his temples, his lips trembling with anticipation as the fork rose, the delicate chewing, the soft moan and rolling eyes as he swallowed, and her stomach would turn with his gluttony. From nowhere, the stranger at the door had come to be everywhere. Even when she was in her room with the radio on, his languorous voice, like his sweet cologne, seeped up through the floorboards in a sly caress.

She had also noticed the change in her mother. Even if Duvall was the phony Norm claimed, at least their mother's tearful rages and black moods had subsided. The days of numbing despair had been reduced to quick flashes of temper that Duvall always managed to calm. He had given nothing and somehow worked a miracle.

And for this, no one was more grateful than Benjy, and no one was more mystified, because there were times when Duvall seemed as much that hunted face in the raw sunlight, a quivering white slug that clung to the corner of the house, a sweet-talking cold-eyed voice whispering into the telephone when he thought no one was near, as he was a brave man who was afraid of black men, someone with per-haps as many faces and secrets as the boy himself.

Tonight, Marie was exhausted. All these late nights with Omar were as exhilarating as they were tiring. This morning, Mr. Briscoe had marched back a letter that had three typos in one line, and then after lunch he'd caught her dozing with her head in her arms. With a glance at the clock over the sink, she got up from the table and poured more lemonade into Omar's glass. As she started to turn back to the refrigerator, he caught her hand and smiled broadly.

"Such a wonderful woman," he said, gazing up at her.

Her face flamed, and she drew her cheek shyly across her shoulder and eased away.

"You are," he said as she stood at the open refrigerator, staring at its bright emptiness; just yesterday she had brought home another fifteen dollars' worth of food. "And I want to show my gratitude . . . if you'll allow me. . . ." His voice trailed off.

She was conscious of the crickets near the window as well as the refrigerator's motor chugging in the same rhythmic pattern as Omar's breath.

"Come here," he said softly.

She turned slowly, arms rigid at her sides, her chest sore with unexpellable breath.

He took her hands and said, "I am about to make an offer which you will probably turn down. And if you do, I will understand." He smiled painfully. "After all, why should you accept? You barely know me. In fact, you know nothing about me except what I have told you. For all you know, before you here sits Jack the Ripper." He laughed a little. "But you are a woman of faith, Marie. A believer. One of that rare breed who moves by instinct."

She felt her knees weaken, her head weightless and spinning. Her eyes roved blindly. How could she accept the proposal of a man she had known for only a few weeks. He would have to be patient. He would have to understand how it wasn't just her, but her children. First, they would have to get to know him better. Benjy would be easy. She had seen how his eyes trailed Omar, as if he dared not lose sight of him. Norm's bitterness might take a long time to overcome, but Alice . . .

". . . a partner," Omar was saying, "a risk-taker." He swallowed hard. "A woman like yourself," he said, raising his eyes hopefully to hers.

"It's the kids," she started to say. "They . . ."

He held up his hand. "Hear me out—allow me that." He fiddled with his tie points, then cleared his throat. "The only way to look at this is in dollars and cents, Marie. Don't be swayed by my affections or by any pity you may feel for me. Look at this for what it is—an investment—a chance—an opportunity to knock on Fortune's golden door."

She regarded him curiously. For a moment she wanted to laugh. Such a strange proposal from such a strange man. His eyelids were heavy and wet. Sweat glistened on his chin. He's almost fat, she thought. He is fat. He eats too much. He eats as if he might never eat again. A breeze brushed past her legs.

Next door, Jessie and Harvey Klubock had been having a cookout. Now their friends laughed, hooting loudly at whatever game was being played. The smell of meat that had been sizzling on the charcoal still came through the back door. Harvey was a butcher at the Meatarama and always got the best cuts. Oftentimes Marie had seen him open the toolbox in his trunk and lift out paper-wrapped steaks and roasts she just *knew* he had stolen. And Jessie with her fine blond curls and her eager smile, Jessie was everyone's sweetheart—oh, but Marie knew, wished, had seen, or imagined Jessie playing up to the mailman and the meter reader in her skimpy shorts, swinging her tight little hips up and down the front steps all day when the telephone linemen were putting up a new pole. Yes, she thought, Jessie and Harvey were headed for trouble. She looked back at the window, suddenly alarmed, because she needed them there, with their windows shining, their lawn mowed, their hedges pruned, their lives intact now as her own found form.

Omar unfolded a piece of paper, which he smoothed open on the table. "Listen," he said, reading. "Tired of the eight hours a day, the forty hours a week, the month after month, the year after year after year? Tired of the grind? Tired of the rat race? Tired of taking orders? Tired of never getting anywhere?" He glanced up. "Tired of knowing that no matter how hard you work, nothing will ever get better?"

The flesh on her face seemed to shrink on her skull. From next door, a woman cried a little drunkenly, "You're such a peach, Jessie!"

Omar continued to read. "Then this ad is meant for you. Presto Soap is a nationwide company looking for a few bright people anxious to change their lives around through hard work and diligent investment. Get in on the ground floor. Call 771-4812 and ask for

Bob." He stared at her. "I called," he said. He grabbed her hand and squeezed it while he told her how the state franchiser, Bob, was sick, so they had given him another number to call. The national distributor! The number one man!

Omar fumbled through his pockets, laying lint and pennies and candy wrappers on the table until he came to a scrap of yellow paper, torn from a telephone book, scribbled with a name. "Roy Gold," he read. "*The* Roy Gold of GoldMine Enterprises. He said he liked the timbre of my voice. He said he could feel the vibrations of my enthusiasm over the telephone wires. Marie, he said they'd had thousands of calls, but he could tell I was the one!" He banged his fist on the table and grinned. "I've got a shot at being a franchiser for the whole state." He sighed. "But my problem is collateral." He looked at her. "I need help, Marie. A partner. I need a shrewd investor at my side—a woman like yourself."

From the Klubocks' a surge of laughter broke over the night. Marie laughed, too, but her eyes blurred with tears. "I'll tell you a secret," she said in a low voice. "Last year Benjy brought home a kitten he'd found, and I let him keep it for two days, and then I took it to work with me one morning. I let it out behind the fish market. I couldn't even afford to buy cat food, that's how bad things are." She took Omar's glass and rinsed it out. Klubocks' party was ending. Car doors opened and closed.

"Come again!" Jessie cried. "We had so much fun!"

"Thanks for coming!" Harvey called. "See you guys at camp next week."

"We'll keep an eye on her, Harve," a man called.

"I don't know, Harve," a woman called. "You know that they say: when the cat's away . . ."

Omar stood up, pushed in the chair, then lifted the ad from the table and looked at it a moment. "There's the trust money. You could take them to court for all—"

"I can't do that! I can't fight them. I can't go through that! I just can't."

"I understand," he said softly.

———

Omar did not come the following night, or the night after that. Tonight as Marie absently stirred her creamed corn over her plate, Alice asked what was wrong. She stared at her daughter. "Do you really want to know?" Alice's face looked gray. Norm and Benjy grimaced.

"Well, I'll tell you," she said, arranging her fork and knife and spoon next to her plate with exaggerated care. "I'm tired. I'm tired of working eight hours a day. Forty hours a week, year after year. I'm tired of the rat race. I'm tired of never getting ahead. I'm tired."

They looked at her, their eyes shifting imperceptibly as they aligned their vision in the low yellow quiet that filled the room. They were done eating, but didn't dare leave the table. The phone began to ring, and Marie jumped for it.

"Hello?" she said too anxiously. "Oh! She's right here, Les."

Alice took the phone, then turned her back to them. "Um, we're just eating now. Why don't you call back?"

"You won't, though!" Lester was shouting so loud they all heard him. "You never call me back!"

"I will! In a few minutes," Alice said.

"No you won't! I know you won't!"

Alice pressed the button down, then left the phone off the hook.

"No!" Marie said, pointing. "Hang it up! Don't leave it like that!" Omar might be trying to call her at this very moment.

"But he'll just call back, and I don't want to talk to him," Alice said.

"Well, think about the rest of us. Maybe someone's trying to call one of us right now!"

"No one's trying to call me, I don't care," Norm said.

"Me neither," Benjy said. "I don't care."

"Well, I do!" she cried, slamming the receiver onto the cradle. "I care! Goddamn it, I care very much!" She turned back and caught them looking at one another. The phone rang and she picked it up, forcing herself to speak calmly. "Hello?"

"Don't hang up, please," Lester gasped in her ear. "I can't stand this. You've got to forgive me! I'm so miserable, I miss you so much. I ache all—"

"Alice can't come to the phone right now, Lester; she's busy. She's going to be very busy tonight."

"Good!" Alice said when she hung up. "He's driving me crazy."

"He's such a creep!" Norm said.

"Yah!" Benjy agreed.

"He's lonely!" she said. "It's a terrible feeling to be alone. Don't look at me like that, the three of you! You have each other, so you don't know what that's like. You don't know how frightening that can be! How lost and desperate you can get!"

They stared down at the table.

"Believe me, you have no idea!" she said.

Even at dusk the air was still heavy with the relentless heat. Quick black slashes of fleeing birds darted across the orange sky. Benjy was in the yard, unpinning dry clothes from the line, when Louie crossed the driveway.

"Can I go in the box?" Louie asked.

"If you want," Benjy said, pleased to see Louie again after so many weeks. "Where you been?" he asked, twice folding a stiff towel before dropping it into the basket.

"No place."

"What's up?"

"Nothin'. My father's fishing at camp." Louie sat cross-legged in the box opening.

"Oh yah," he said, the twinge of dread recalling Mr. Briscoe's pledge to take him fishing this summer. He no longer carried on the ruse of going up to the swimming pool every day. Now he just lied and said he did.

"Louis!" Mrs. Klubock called from her back steps. "Benjy, have you seen Louie?"

"He's over here. In the box," he called back.

"Louis, get over here!" Mrs. Klubock demanded with a stamp of her foot when Louie dragged into sight.

"She's scared," Louie said quickly to Benjy. "Some man keeps calling, and he won't stop." He looked frightened.

"What did I tell you?" Mrs. Klubock scolded as Louie climbed the stairs. "You stay in your own yard, where I can see you!" She hustled him inside and locked both doors.

Behind Benjy came a quick rustling through the weeds and wild hedges; then the shiny blunt head of Klubocks' dog broke into sight.

"Hey! Hey, boy!" he whispered. He knelt down and held out his hand, but the dog pulled back, its eyes bright with a wary wildness. Clenched in its mouth was a long strip of brown cloth, cuffed at one end like a pant leg. "C'mere! C'mere!" he coaxed, but the dog sprang then, flying past him, diving into the lilac thicket, and as it went, his stomach turned with the stench. It was the most disgusting thing he had ever smelled.

Chief Stoner's love affair had started a year ago January. It had been his wife's canasta night and Eunice Bonifante's car had run out of gas, even though she owned the busiest gas station in town.

Typical, Sonny had been thinking as he buckled his boots and listened to his sister-in-law's throaty laughter coming from the pantry. Ever since her husband, Al's, suicide, Eunice seemed to be either in the depths of depression or laughing hysterically.

She was a careless woman and carelessness made Sonny nervous. His virtue was as much rooted in superstition as in goodness. There were dark forces in the universe, forces ready to pounce on careless men, forces that demanded appeasement. His talismans against such furies were the insurance policies in his strongbox, the bomb shelter in his backyard, the lightning rods on his roof. To this end, he had taught his deputies that keeping their guns cleaned and oiled meant never having to use them.

When Eunice got into his car that January night, she asked him the time. Ten forty-five, he told her as he pulled onto the dark street, heartened by the clank of the tires' chains over the ice. She asked if he'd mind speeding it up a little so she wouldn't be late. Late for what, he asked irritably. My obscene phone call, she sighed.

"Your what?"

"My obscene phone caller. He calls every night."

"Eunice!" he said, never knowing whether to believe her or not.

"It's a riot, Sonny. He breathes, and I breath back." She lit a cigarette and blew out a smoky laugh. "The creep can't believe his good luck."

He glanced at her. After Al's funeral she had invited everyone back to the house, then got so drunk she passed out. He remembered how disgusted he had been to see Carol, red-eyed from weeping, trying to coax Eunice up to bed. Carol had been devastated enough by her brother's suicide and didn't need any of Eunice's trashy scenes. Leave her on the couch, he'd told Carol, but she'd refused, saying Eunice wouldn't have left her.

"I think I know who it is," Eunice said.

"Who?" he asked, frowning over the wheel.

She touched his arm. "Promise you won't tell Carol?" she whispered solemnly. "Last night I heard church bells in the background. I think it's the Monsignor," she said, bursting into laughter. "I think he's got the hots for me!" Just then a call had come over the radio, reporting a disturbance up at the pig farm. He'd check it out as soon as he made one more stop, he said, looking at Eunice.

"Nosirree!" she roared. "The Monsignor'll just have to wait!"

As they drove along the dark winding road to the pig farm, Eunice lit another cigarette and stared out the window. "God, I haven't been out here in years," she said with a shiver. "Al and I used to park somewhere along here."

As they came over the rise, she pointed to the frozen gully below. "Right there's where we parked!" She laughed. "Al used to break branches off and put them over the windows." She was quiet again.

"Al always covered his bases," Sonny said pointedly. Al had been a judicious man; his only lapse in judgment had been Eunice, though Carol used to say she was the best thing that had ever happened to her morose brother.

"Yup," Eunice sighed. "Our own private fuck blind, he called it."

He couldn't help it, he burst out laughing. Eunice just stared out the window.

When they came to the farm, Grondine Carson ran out of the old gray house in his bathrobe and boots to report that someone had been banging on his windows. Sonny walked around the house, beaming his flashlight on the untracked crusted snow, knowing he would find nothing. The pig man had spent too many years alone. He was so accustomed to his trespassers that when they didn't come he invented them.

"See anything?" Eunice asked when he came back.

"Nothing," Sonny sighed, ducking his long body into the cruiser. "Every now and again he just needs to know someone's around, I guess."

"I know the feeling," Eunice sighed, watching the ice-blasted trees flick past as they started back down the road.

He glanced at her. He was more accustomed to her blowsy humor than this melancholy. "Hey," he chided after a minute. "I'm not used to you being so quiet. Cut it out!"

"I was just thinking. Poor Carson, all he needs is a woman. You know, it's tough being alone. It really is. Being alone can make you crazy."

"Uh-uh, no excuse." He shook his head. "You were always crazy, Eunice!"

She laughed. "And you were always a pain in the ass! Just like Al. The two of you!"

At that, he stopped the car, threw it into reverse, and switched on the flashing lights.

"What the hell're you doing?" she gasped as they headed backward down the road.

"I'm bringing the pigman a woman!" He laughed over his shoulder. "Sure will cut down on these late-night runs."

The car filled with her rocky laughter as she grabbed his arm and jammed her foot down on the brake, spiraling the cruiser over the ice, and as it turned, and turned, and turned, he felt it all getting away from him, all that caution, all that good sense, and he wasn't afraid or angry, but laughing just as much as she was, even as the car slid over the soft shoulder, coming to rest against a snowdrift as gently and silently as a head sinks into a pillow. He closed his eyes and kissed Eunice Bonifante's warm wet mouth while the dome light spun red whorls on the snow.

One month later, Dr. Hess had called him at the station and asked him to stop by the office. Before he had even hung up the phone, Sonny knew that the price he'd pay for his sin would be Carol.

Lately, he understood nothing. Carol was dying, and he cried out in his sleep and sat up trembling with cold sweats in the heat. He couldn't bear to look at his ravaged wife. His son got on his nerves all the time. His men thought him demanding and unreasonable with them and far too easy on the town's transgressors. Their Chief never target-practiced with them anymore. At the station he sat in his closed office and stared out the window over Merchants Row, bewildered to find the bright July world so grimed with gray. His men thought it was his wife he mourned, but it was himself.

Tonight, the council room was stiff with heat and surly voices. Sonny Stoner squirmed in the hard oak chair. He had never liked meetings, and this one was always the most grueling. It was the annual vote on Joey Seldon's popcorn stand, postponed these last few weeks because of Judge Clay's death.

"Nothing but an eyesore," John Creller was saying. "And one of these days, the whole shebang's gonna come down on some innocent passerby and then there'll be hell to pay! The town'll be up to their ears in lawsuits."

Sonny scraped his fingernail along the soft grime on the lip of the oak table. The popcorn stand that Sonny had helped build years ago as a boy was now falling apart. All that was left of the original roof was tar-paper strips that lifted in the slightest breeze. Some of the sideboards had buckled from the studs and the rotten cornerposts had become as precarious as the old man's disposition. For years Joey had refused to repair the stand, claiming its upkeep was the town's responsibility. Recently when people had tried to help by repairing the stand themselves, Joey had alienated them with his demands and criticism. And now neighbors around the park were complaining about his radio, which blared past midnight some nights.

"If he'd just say thanks," Creller was saying. "But every year it's the same thing—gimme, gimme, gimme."

Sonny tilted his wrist to look at his watch. He should have been at Eunice's an hour ago. When he'd left the house tonight, Lester had called him a hypocrite when he said he had to work late. Lester wanted to see Alice tonight. He'd never seen his son so angry, so violent. Lester had raised his fists, and Sonny had all he could do to keep from smacking him.

"I say we do the old man a favor and bulldoze the thing," Creller said with a nod. He sat down, and next to him Jarden Greene grinned.

Sonny's foot began to tap. He could feel Craig Bixby, the town counsel and a friend of both Joey Seldon and old Judge Clay, staring at him. Bixby expected Sonny to stand up now and deliver the Judge's yearly speech on Joey's behalf.

Joey Seldon had been Atkinson's chief of police before Sonny's father. Seldon's brief career as Chief had ended one night years ago up on Humpback Mountain with a violent explosion at Towler's still that killed Ark Towler and left Joey Seldon comatose for weeks, and then blind.

Because Seldon hadn't served long enough to qualify for a pension, the town built the popcorn stand and turned it over to him in a festive hero's ceremony. Everyone was there, even Towler's widow and her three little girls. Through all the speeches and songs, she stood under a tree, her blank expression never changing. When the ribbon was cut and Joey was finally led inside the red-enameled stand to applause and cheers, she smiled, then walked away. Joey had been off duty the night of the explosion, and the rumors had already started that he had been at Towler's that night picking up his fee for silence.

Now Craig Bixby was trying to catch his eye, but Sonny just sat there. Let Bixby stick his neck out for once, he thought as he stared wearily at his folded hands.

Other men were looking down the table at him. They knew it was his turn. Why did they do this every year? he suddenly wondered. Why not vote Joey a ten- or twenty-year lease on the stand? Why had no one ever thought of this before?

The mayor rose now and patted his jacket pockets. He leafed through his papers, then, with a glance at Sonny, raised his eyebrows expectantly.

Sonny would not look up. His toes curled in his shoes.

"Well, here we go again," the mayor began good-naturedly. "Beating the same old dead horse . . ."

His eyes glazed with the memory of Eunice's husky voice describing the smooth satin sheets she'd put on the bed tonight.

"And Sonny'll go up there tonight and tell Joey he can stay, but the condition is, he's got to close at nine sharp. No ifs, ands, or buts. . . ."

"You told him that last year," Creller called out. Jarden Greene nodded furiously. "And his excuse last year was he had to keep the radio loud so's he could hear the time when to close." Greene nudged him then, and Creller added, "And even with the radio loud he still stayed open till all hours."

Greene nodded smugly. Greene and Joey had been going at it for years. Each wanted to be the park maestro.

"Okay," the mayor said, rubbing his chin. "Ten-of-nine curfew, then. Sonny, you tell Joey when he hears the ten-of-nine blow, he'd better blow, too."

The council members chuckled. Some had begun to pack up their papers. Craig Bixby was unwrapping the big green vile-smelling cigar that always signaled the end of a meeting. The mayor looked up to take the vote.

"Bet he don't do it!" Creller called out suddenly, with Greene hunched at his elbow. "And instead of a vote on the popcorn stand, by Jesus, I propose we vote on an investigating committee to find out what Seldon was *really* doing up at the still that night!"

The men groaned. Bixby laid the cigar on the table as the mayor looked entreatingly at Sonny.

Creller was one of those for whom every issue had to be a life-or-death struggle. Last meeting, at Robert Haddad's urging, he had made a motion to ban women in shorts from all public places.

Every year it was the same, the same complaints about Joey's arrogance, his lack of gratitude, the same speeches, the same defenders, but then, at the last moment, the same resounding vote to grant the old man his space on the corner of the park for one more year. Now the mayor had taken up Joey's defense again. Sonny felt the room seethe with heat and the bitter smoke of newly lit cigarettes. The men coughed and squirmed in their seats. It was going badly. Jarden Greene was on his feet, arguing with the mayor.

"No sir!" Greene ranted. "This is a matter for the courts. I move we let Bixby here earn the lawyer money we vote him every year, and let the courts settle this popcorn shit once and for all!"

Attorney Bixby swung his black briefcase onto the table, and as he stood up, he cast a last hopeful look at Sonny. Bixby tugged at his tie knot and sighed. "Fine with me, Jard." He smiled down at Greene's pinched face. "Maybe I'm not too bright, but I really don't see the harm in you sending one of your crews over with a jar of paint and a few shingles and a coupla nails to give that damn stand a quick one-two." Bixby peered over the top of his wire-rimmed glasses. "It'd be a hell of a lot cheaper than a court fight."

"A coupla nails and a jar of paint," Greene scoffed, looking up and down the table. "Next thing, Craig'll be up here asking why don't I run a crew down to the tracks and spruce up Nigger Flood's place."

The council chuckled. Greene's remark had been a dig at Mrs. Bixby's annual chairmanship of the Fresh Air Fund, which delivered a dusty busload of New York street kids to Atkinson's green valley every August. Bixby's face reddened and his shrewd old eyes narrowed, and now, as he spoke, Sonny recognized the old courtroom cadence.

"That's right, Jard. There's a lot wrong in this world. A lot of people born a second too late and a step behind, or maybe even just a little different from you and me. And there's not a lot we can do about it. We meet here every week to talk about wild dogs in Cumsin's, and variances, and which department's going to get a new water bubbler, and, of course, Mr. Creller's indignation over public indecency. But every once in a great while we get to vote on one of those big issues—not from any laws or statute, Jard, but from in here," he said, thumping his chest. "We got important business here, Jard, and you're asking us to tear down a poor harmless blind man's popcorn stand? His only means of support?" He paused. "Why, Jard? Wouldn't have anything to do with that little incident with his radio during your last song, would it?"

"Of course not!" Greene spat.

"Wouldn't have anything to do with his popcorn maybe being a bigger draw than your music, would it?"

"You're demeaning me!" Greene hollered over the hoots of laughter.

Bixby stopped pacing and jabbed his finger at Greene. "You're demeaning *yourself*, damn it! Now why don't you just forget this nonsense and get a crew up there and fix up Seldon's stand and be done with it."

The council broke into scattered applause.

"Nossir!" Greene screamed, pounding his tiny fist on the table. "There's a principle here—the same principle that keeps me from hot-topping council members' driveways on town time and seeding their lawns like's been done by every head of Public Works before me." Greene was on his feet now, his spare body trembling with rage. "You can sure as hell fire me, but you can't buy me, and goddamn it, you won't humiliate me!" With that, he stalked out of the room.

The men blinked as the door slammed; then a few cleared their throats guiltily and dared take a breath. Not a one had had their driveways resurfaced free by town crews since Greene had been appointed. Bixby was still staring at the door. "Phew," he said, turning back to the table. "Almost didn't get his cross through," he muttered. There was laughter, but it came thinly, uneasily.

Robert Haddad seemed screwed into a corner of his chair. For one so often indignant lately over everything, tonight he had said nothing. He was biting his nails. He glanced at his watch and sighed.

Looking up and down the table, Sonny felt not only detached but distant from these men, most of whom he had known all his life. And it came to him now, the reason for the Towler widow's cold smile. It had been a smile of triumph as the blind man entered his stand that day, faltering, then lurching like an animal locked in its cage for the first time.

Creller's words were sobering the council; a few nodded anxiously. ". . . hoodlums tearing up and down the streets on their motorcycles, and their souped-up cars blasting their nigger music! While the young girls walk the streets with next to nothing on! Nothing's sacred anymore. Nothing! Because certain persons in this town, in positions of authority, certain officials are so busy hiding their own sins and transgressions, they got no time to do their job."

Sonny stared at his folded hands. He felt drained. It was getting late. Time, what time was it, and what the hell was Creller talking about? He looked up to see eyes quickly averted. Creller had meant him!

"Now, I'm only telling you what was reported to me. I'm only saying that something's very wrong with a dead man sitting in his chair for two days and nobody says a word! I'm telling you it's all going to pieces! They tear up our public property! There's a stink hanging over this town so bad people can't sleep nights.

"The way I was raised, you got a problem, you root it out!" Creller shook his head bitterly. "But of course the way I was raised don't count no more. Used to be, every kid was in his house *before* the ten-of even blew. But now everything's changed. Nobody listens to good men anymore. Now you break and enter and what do you get? A slap on the wrist, that's all! A ride to the enlistment office, in the Chief's car, if you please! I tell ya, our kids are running wild. You go up to that park right now and you'll find their kinda hero with his radio blasting and kids hanging all over the bandstand, smashing bottles and calling filth out to our women passing by."

"You're kidding," Sonny muttered, but no one heard him. He wondered if this could be true, if in the malaise of the past weeks such events had indeed transpired while he had been too preoccupied to notice.

"He's the seed, the cause," Creller ranted. "You can tell him to go home till you're blue in the face, but he don't give a damn for anyone or anything, and those kids know it. And they won't go home, neither. So go ahead, keep on looking the other way, keep on honoring liars and thieves—"

Sonny Stoner jumped up so fast that the table lifted against his legs. "Honor! You call that honor? Harnessing a proud man like Joey Seldon to that ragtag of a stand? Putting him at the mercy of men like you, Creller? That ain't honor. Nossir! I call that the worst punishment of all. I call that degrading!"

A pulsing had begun in the tall man's head, like red-hot pumping blood that both frightened and cleansed him. They looked up stupidly and a little hurt, and yet he kept on, his gentle voice growing so loud that he was sure someone else was talking. "I was just thinking, listening to all this talk, how this is the one meeting out of the whole year everybody shows up for, and you know why? Because it's a chance to play God for a night. We're not here to vote from our hearts. We're here to pass judgment on Joey Seldon one more time.

So forget it, John, of course we're never gonna vote down his stand, 'cause if we do that, then we can't go home feeling good about ourselves that we saved Joey one more time! That we were good men! Well, that don't make a good man, damn it!" He grabbed his jacket from the back of his chair. "I'll tell Joey he's got to close at ten of nine." He leaned his long body right at Creller, and he smiled. "And I'll tell him tomorrow morning a crew'll be up there to fix the place up, and God help you, Creller, if you vote no."

"Is that a threat?" Creller gasped, his puffy face white with shock.

"Yup," Sonny said as he zipped up his nylon windbreaker. "And carrying it out'll be a real pleasure, too." He grinned.

As Sonny drove toward the park he was struck by the clarity of the stars over the black mountaintops and the sharp dark outlines of roofs, and he could hear warm voices through the lit-up windows, and he felt strong, and he felt clean, and for the first time in weeks he could think, and he knew he could take care of everyone. He would take care of his town again. He had never stopped being a good man. Until now he just hadn't been good enough.

Joey chuckled when Sonny finished talking.

"Cite me the law that says I have to close at ten of nine, Sonny."

"Just do it, Joey. Don't make problems," Sonny said.

Joey tilted his head toward the park and smiled. "Tell you what, Sonny. The minute I hear the curfew blow, I'll start closing up."

Sonny unpeeled a stick of gum. "It's almost ten of now, Joey. Can I give you a lift home?"

"No thanks," Joey said. "I like the walk, and besides, takes me a while to close up."

Even as Alice knocked on the Stoners' door, she knew she shouldn't have come. But Lester had called back to apologize to her mother, who then insisted she take the phone. In a low rambling voice Lester had whispered how lonely he was, how unfair God

was, how it was all his father's fault, that he and his father had just
had a terrible fight, that there was too much pressure on him, that everyone expected too much of him, that he'd be better off dead. Please
come, he'd begged. Please . . .

When he opened the door, she was shocked at how pale and
drawn he was. His skin had erupted in sore red pimples. He needed
a haircut, and his clothes were soiled and wrinkled as if he'd slept in
them. Every time she said anything, he would blink.

They were upstairs watching television with Mrs. Stoner in her
bedroom. Lester had made a large bowl of popcorn. He had arranged two chairs next to his mother's bed, but it was soon apparent
that Mrs. Stoner, in her medicated drift, had already forgotten Alice
was there. At first, Lester did all the talking, his incessant, almost
giddy chatter, gossipy and desperate to amuse her, to hold her interest, to keep her here, as if he feared that in a moment's lull he might
lose her. Everything he knew seemed to have come over the police radio, automobile accidents and domestic violence, and now the details
of a prowler who had been in the alley the other night behind
Hammie's Bar and Grill.

"And Vic Crowley said he heard the guy running down the alley,
but when he got on the street, the guy was gone! There was no one
there!" Lester's eyes shone. "It was just like the night'd swallowed
him up! Vic wanted to pick that creep Mooney up for questioning,
but my father said no. There hadn't been any crime committed. You
know how all the tires were flat out at the lake that night? Well, I
told my father it had to be Mooney. I told him I'd swear to it even in
court, I was so sure. And he said, 'But just because he was there
doesn't mean he did it.' He said, 'Because if that's the way it works,
then you were out there too, don't forget.' Can you believe it?"
Lester said. "Can you believe my own father said that?" He laughed,
shaking his head. "About me! His own son!" He seemed dazed, out
of step, like a first-time traveler to a treacherous land.

She stiffened against the hard-backed chair.

Mrs. Stoner's chalky face turned on the stained pillow. She had
been drooling. "What time is it?"

"Eight forty-five," said Lester.

"Is Daddy home yet?" she asked.

"No, Mother," answered Lester.

Mrs. Stoner's eyes had closed again. "He's so busy," she sighed. "What is it tonight?"

"Council meeting—or so he said," Lester added.

"Poor man." She sighed again, then laughed weakly. "Lord knows there's not much to come to here anymore, is there?"

Alice stared at the television so as not to see the crooked nylon wig. All the patterns had been wrenched: the bright rugs smelled of damp and dust. In the bathroom, mildew had invaded the grout, and red towels hung over orange towels. The plants on the windowsill were spindly and yellowing.

It was hot in the bedroom, and the vase of red gladioli on Mrs. Stoner's nightstand kept making Alice sneeze. She wiped her nose and watched the suntan lotion ad that was on television. It showed a girl strolling down a beach past three guys, who jumped up from their blankets and followed her. She envied Mary Agnes, who must be having so much fun at the lake. She should've gone, should've done what she wanted instead of what everyone else wanted. Good little Alice, who always did what her mother said. Poor little Alice, afraid to say yes, afraid to say no. She felt like everyone's wailing wall. If the Klubocks' dog dumped under the clothesline and her mother stepped in it, it was Alice's fault because if she hadn't been "lazy-assing out in the backyard all the day, the goddamn dog wouldn't have come over in the first place." Even the reasons for Omar Duvall's continued absence had become so convoluted in her mother's reasoning that she was to blame. Because so much money was needed to send Alice to college, her mother was being deprived of the opportunity of a lifetime. She made little sense lately. It was getting so bad that Alice had almost begun to prefer being the butt of Anthology Carper's sick jokes to spending a night at home.

"Want some more?" Lester whispered, passing her the popcorn bowl.

She shook her head and tried to see what time it was. Lester caught her looking at the clock, and he checked his mother to see if she had fallen asleep yet. Her eyes were closed, and her breathing verged on snoring. With a nod toward the door, he started out of the chair. Before Alice could get the tissue to her nose, she sneezed.

Mrs. Stoner's eyes opened wide. "Bless you," came her drugged, gluey voice. "You're catching cold."

Lester made a face as if she'd sneezed on purpose. He stared at the television, annoyed that his mother was awake.

"I think I am," Alice said, getting up. "Maybe I'd better go, Les. I'll call you when—"

"It's these damn flowers!" he said, yanking the vase from the bureau.

"Aunt Eunice brought them over." Mrs. Stoner sighed as Les swept past, taking the flowers downstairs. "Poor Eunice, all she did was cry. Do I look that bad?" Mrs. Stoner laughed. The wig dipped over her left temple like a rakish beret, exposing miserly patches of her own hair, which had once been as soft and wavy as Les's.

"You look fine," Alice said, shredding the tissue in her lap.

The tumor in Mrs. Stoner's belly swelled against the sheets. There was nothing the doctors could do; nothing anyone could do, but wait. Wait. Wait for death. It was coming. Coming. No, it was here. There, rising and falling with her every breath.

Les had come back into the room. He bent over his mother and, all in a motion, plumped her pillows, adjusted her wig, and kissed her dry cheek so tenderly that Alice felt her eyes swell with tears. Poor Les. And now as he scooped the tissue bits from Alice's lap and laid a new one there, his hand lingered on her thigh and she smiled weakly at him.

All the way down to the rec room, she reasoned it out. They were both lonely, so why not see each other once in a while. Only this time, they'd just be friends. This time, she'd be strong.

"See," he was saying as he showed her the cord tacked along the stair molding. "I wired the police radio up to my room. I leave it on all night."

"Doesn't Mrs. Miller come anymore, Les?" she asked. It hurt to think of him in the dark listening to police calls all night long.

"That bitch!" he said. "I fired her. Now I'm the only nurse."

When they got downstairs, he didn't even turn on the light. "Oh Alice," he moaned, lying against her on the couch. "I've missed you so much. . . ." He kissed her frantically, murmuring against her lips, "I've been going crazy here. I'd write you a poem . . . and then you wouldn't call me back and I'd burn it . . . here, here," he moaned, pressing her open hand against his bulging fly. "See? See? See how much I've missed you. . . ."

"No, Les," she whispered, trying to pull away, but he held it there. "Let's just be friends," she whispered as he slid his hand inside her shorts. She moaned and lay back, her eyes wide in the darkness. The couch creaked and Lester was moaning.

"No! No!" she said, pushing him away. "No, Les!" She sat up. "It's the same as before!" she said. "What you said that time . . . I was hurt when you said that, but it's true in a way. Things seem all tangled, you know what I mean? Now you're having problems and we're all mixed up in each other's problems. You see what I mean?" she asked. She turned on the light then and forced a smile. "Do you?" she asked hopefully.

"You've always had a twisted way of looking at things, Alice," he said with a sneer. "If someone's nice to you, you wonder what they want."

"I have to go now," she said, getting up. She would not play this game.

He chuckled. "I remember how all through school, you'd just sit there in the back of the room, hoping nobody'd talk to you. Until I started going out with you, you sat in the lunchroom like such a creep, alone every day for four years!" He laughed. "So now you think you're a big deal? Now you've got Mary Agnes and her shitty friends, so you don't need me, do you? What do you do, go over to the lake all the time. . . . Oh, Alice!" he cried, trying to pull her back down.

"You let me go! You make me sick. You're so damn mean. You're the meanest person I've ever known."

"And you're the coldest person I've ever known!" he growled, clenching her wrist.

"Stop it, Lester! You let me go, damn it, or you'll be sorry!" She couldn't wrench her hand free.

He laughed and she froze. "What're you going to do, Alice? Start screaming, Help! Help! Lester's finally gone off the deep end! He's crazy! Crazy! Crazycrazycrazy crazy . . ." Tears bubbled down his cheeks.

Her hand was numb in his hold. If she moved, something would break, would smash into infinitesimal splinters.

"I'm sorry. I'm so sorry! Please stay! Please!" he panted, nuzzling his wet cheek against hers. He ran his hands up and down her back as if to resuscitate her.

Her eyes were on the stairwell. Someone was walking overhead, and now the door at the top of the stairs creaked open.

"You down there, Les?" Mr. Stoner called. "Les?"

"What is it?" Les called back. His eyes darted between her and the stairs.

"Got a little surprise up here. Alice there, too?" Mr. Stoner said self-consciously, as if he thought he'd caught them making out.

"I'm down here!" she hollered, yanking her wrist from the cuff of Lester's fist. His head trembled and his shoulder twitched as if with a seizure.

"C'mon up, kids!" Mr. Stoner called with forced heartiness. "We'll have a party! I'll go see if your mother's . . ."

She ran up the stairs, where Mr. Stoner stood smiling with two pizza boxes in his arms. "That's what I call hungry . . . Alice!" He took a step as she flew past. "What's wrong? Alice!"

She didn't even close the door behind her.

"Lester! Lester!" Mr. Stoner's voice clung to her all the way home like the mist of the damp night air.

Eunice Bonifante was in the bathroom when the telephone rang. She took another slug of beer and continued rubbing eye shadow from her left eyelid. The phone kept ringing through the empty house. Ten o'clock, too early for the breather, and if it was Sonny, he could wait, just like the shriveled pork in the oven had waited. The ringing stopped, then started again, seconds later. She grabbed her beer can from the toilet tank and scuffed into the living room.

"Mrs. Bonifante! This is Carl at the station! Something just happened!"

"What, Carl?" Eunice groaned. Carl was easily rattled at night.

"Mooney was just here. Blue Mooney, him and his whole gang!"

"Christ! What happened?" Damn Sonny and his soft heart, thinking all Mooney needed was a break for once.

"Well, there was a lot of looking around, you know, checking things out, and—"

"How many were there?" she interrupted.

"Uh, three. Yah, three."

"Three! Three what? Carloads?"

"Three guys."

"What'd they do?"

"They got gas."

"Okay, Carl. Let's see now, it's ten o'clock and you wake me up from a sound sleep to tell me three guys just bought gas." She waited. "Did I get that straight?"

"Well, I just thought you should know," he said sulkily. "In case anything happens."

"Nothing's going to happen." She belched softly. "Believe me."

"I hope you're right."

"I'll tell you what, Carl. Why don't you close up now and . . ."

"Thanks, Mrs. Bonifante!" he said, hanging up while she was still talking.

". . . go home . . . you little asshole."

Damn him, she thought. Damn Al for leaving her alone like this. Damn Sonny. Damn all men. She went to the refrigerator and took out another can of Sonny's favorite beer. She went into the living room and flopped onto the sofa to watch television. Fifteen minutes later she went in for another can. "The hell with it," she muttered as she stretched over the arm of the couch and dialed. Grinning when she heard Sonny's voice, she began to pant into the mouthpiece.

"Hello? Hello? Who's there?" Sonny demanded.

"It's me," she giggled.

"What is it?"

"I need you. I need you so bad."

"I see."

"You can't talk!"

"That's right."

"Oh!" she said, closing her eyes. "You're in Carol's room. Oh God."

"No," Sonny hedged.

"Then Lester's there."

"That's right," he said.

"I miss you, Sonny." She sniffed and her eyes filled with tears. "I had everything ready. I've been waiting. . . ."

"Oh. Well . . . why don't you call me in the morning, then. There's not much I can do right now, not without my folder on the case," he added, clearing his throat.

"I wish you were here, Sonny. I'm so lonesome."

"For police business, you really should call the station, sir."

"It is police business, goddamn it! As a matter of fact, Carl just called here all shook up about a carload of creeps that were just at the station. Mooney and his buddies."

"Mooney? Not him again."

"Yah, him again." She laughed. "Now, maybe you should come up here and get all the details while they're still fresh in my mind."

"Is that so?" Sonny cleared his throat again. "Anything happen?"

"Not yet, baby. But it will when you get here."

"Well," Sonny sighed. "In that case, maybe I better check it out, then."

"Oh yah, you better!"

"Okay. Very good, that's what I'll do."

"Pull in the garage and come up through the cellar."

"Will do," Sonny said.

"Roger!" she laughed and hung up.

Sonny hung up at his end. And then, up in her bedroom, so did Carol Stoner. She slipped her hand under the mattress to check her stockpile. She could hear Sonny at the bottom of the stairs. "Probably nothing," he said to Lester. "But I wouldn't feel right if I didn't check it out." After he left, Lester went into his bedroom, and then for the rest of the night all she could hear was the sputtering static of the police radio. Her husband and her son needed their freedom, but she still didn't have enough pills.

Dressed completely in black, Robert Haddad waited in his unlit office, eyes trained on the window of Hammie's Bar and Grill. At midnight the last patron, an old man with suspenders over his white undershirt, lingered in the doorway talking animatedly as, little by little, Hammie inched the door shut. Haddad stood up now so he could see Hammie, who was behind the bar washing and drying glasses while he smiled up at the television.

With all the lights on, Hammie looked younger and happier in the empty glare, and richer. His unvaried routine never exceeded twenty-three minutes. After he set all the chairs on the tables, he would sweep the floor and then he would remove his register drawer and carry it down to the basement, where he'd sit on a wooden Poland Spring box and count his receipts on a round metal garden table. Some of the cash went into a green night deposit bag, which he dropped off at the bank on his way home, but most of it, Haddad knew, was hidden in a padlocked steel box Hammie kept in the base of an unused, capped chimney. This he had learned after many patient nights crouched in the swelter of the dark alley, observing the cranky barkeeper through the mesh-covered cellar window.

Last Saturday night, Haddad had been ready to execute his plan when Vic Crowley, the cop, hurried into the alley. Haddad had ducked into the wedge of the darkness behind the trash cans. When he heard the zip, then the long, steady drumroll of urine against the cans, he scrambled out and ran, leaving Crowley trapped midstream, calling helplessly over his shoulder, "Halt! I said halt!"

Tonight, Haddad was ready. He watched the last light go out. He watched Hammie back his red Buick carefully out of the alley, then drive off. Still Haddad waited. Tonight, there would be no rush. This was the beginning of a brand-new life. He was going to straighten it all out. And from this night forward there would be no more falling behind. No more foolishness. From now on, if he and Astrid didn't have the money, they'd go without. He'd cover the unpaid premiums and set things straight, tonight, with this one act.

That this might be wrong, criminal, immoral was not a consideration, because it was that first step, that fortuitous foothold all successful businessmen needed. And it would be just this one time. It would be the boost he needed. It was in the nature of things. Often, for shrubbery to thrive, it first had to be hacked to the ground. Besides, the whole system was just too unfair, too lopsided, with him having to be accountable for every penny while Hammie's cash trade was untraceable and virtually tax-free. Life was a network of inequities that had to be realigned, readjusted, made fair for all men, he thought with a surge of conviction.

He crossed the street with his new black sneakers springing into the alley. He knelt down and with only a few jabs of his long screwdriver into the rotted wood, pried loose the cellar window and lifted it on its hinges. The dead cellar air seemed to suck him in, so quickly did he find himself dropping down, then scrambling through the dark to the chimney. He needed to turn on his flashlight only once to find the latch on the pitted metal clean-out door. As soon as he had the strongbox out of the chimney, he clicked off the light and unfolded the large grocery bag he'd carried in his pocket. Into it he poured the dollar bills, then returned the strongbox to the chimney, carefully latching the door closed again. It would be twenty-four hours before Hammie discovered his loss.

Haddad lifted himself easily through the window, closed it, then raced back to his office, where, in the dark, he stuffed the bag of cash into his briefcase. He changed into his suit and tie, then started home. Along open stretches of sidewalk he walked with tight deliberate steps, but whenever he entered the safe shadows of trees, he ran, at times careening into them, throwing his arms around their rough girth, holding himself there, flattened, his cheek to the bark, like a man caught in a windstorm, holding on for dear life, and laughing.

It had been a week. At four o'clock Marie called the house from work. Alice answered and said Benjy had come home from the pool a while ago and was watching a show.

"Were there any calls?" Marie interrupted.

"Just that Father Gannon again. He said he'd call you back."

She cleared her throat. "So it's just the two of you there?" she asked, wincing.

"Just us," Alice answered.

After she hung up she resumed her typing, and the minute Astrid left for the ladies' room with her new movie magazine and her cigarettes, she dialed the Mayo sisters' boardinghouse. "Hello, I'd like to rent a room," she said, pinching her nostrils, her mouth close to the receiver. "Do you have any available?"

"Well, I don't know, that is, oh dear, I'm . . . I'm not sure," sighed May Mayo's sweet flutter. "It depends . . . we might. My sister . . . well, you see, we have to wait until the week is up . . . and then we'll know. I hope."

Marie closed her eyes. "So you do have an empty room."

"Not really. Well, it's empty, you see, but the rent's paid till Sunday."

"Has he moved out? I mean, your tenant."

"Well, that's hard to say, dearie. The poor man's only got the clothes he wears. I offered him some of the—"

"Thank you," Marie said and hung up quickly as Astrid teetered back into the office on her gold spike heels. The two women avoided each other's eyes. Astrid smoothed her skirt over her hips and sat down. Marie's hands trembled as she rolled a sheet of stationery into the typewriter. *He's gone,* she thought. *Omar's gone.* She still had six more letters to do. *Oh God, he's gone.* She buried her face in her hands and took a deep breath. She felt like screaming.

"You okay?" Astrid asked, glancing up from her adding machine.

"Just tired." She started to type quickly, before any conversation could start. This morning she had turned off Astrid's radio and asked her to please be quiet, and Astrid, offended, hadn't spoken since. The icy silence had been a relief. As she typed now she could feel Astrid staring at her.

"I'm sorry," Astrid said finally. "I should've thought. I mean, here you are struggling at this shitty job, and I come in blabbing about Bobby's bonus and my new dryer and my new hi-fi."

"It wasn't that," she said coldly, still typing. "I just need quiet when I work."

Today Astrid wore a white satiny dress with a wide gold cinch belt. Even when she didn't look directly at Astrid, her corner of the cramped little office seemed to glow. *Like she's dressed for a nightclub,* Marie thought irritably. With Omar gone, everything got on her nerves, especially this mindless, brash woman who didn't even have to work, whose husband had his own business. Working was just an extension of Astrid's social life, a chance to show off her new clothes, she thought, banging the carriage so hard on every return that the typewriter jumped and now sat crooked on the table.

"I hate quiet, and you hate noise." Astrid sighed, staring, for a moment awed by another of life's conundrums.

Marie kept typing. Frowning, she bent closer to the letter, as if Astrid's chatter were obscuring her vision.

"Of course, I don't have kids and all that, so I guess I just got used to my own commotion." She paused. "Speaking of which, I hear Sam's locked up."

She looked up, blinking, not certain she'd heard correctly.

Astrid smiled. "Must be so nice now, not having that worry hanging over you, you know, of him barging in here or bothering you at night."

Marie started to say something, then closed her mouth. There was nothing she knew to say; not a word came to mind. These were her troubles, which she had never discussed with anyone, and certainly wasn't about to with this gum-snapping sleazy showgirl who had obviously lived such a low life herself she considered everyone else's misfortunes public property like her own. Marie had never understood how women could bare their souls with such ease, exposing themselves so shamelessly to one another. It was a weakness she had always despised. Sometimes the most unsettling legacy of Sam's failure as a husband, father, provider seemed to be this viraginity, this obdurate male soul in female flesh that set her apart from women as well as men. Well, people might find her abrasive, but she'd choose strength and honesty any day over Astrid's perfumed guile and featherbrained duplicity.

"Do him good," Astrid was saying. "One of these days he might

shock the hell out of you and just never take another drink." She
shook her head and smiled. "They're sweet guys, too, the lushes; you
know they've been there. Hey!" Astrid gave a sly wink of her blue-
lidded eyes. "Who's the dreamboat I saw getting out of your car last
week? Tall guy, dark hair, hanging over your window like he hated
saying goodbye. I saw him, and I said to myself, 'Hey now, Marie
don't fool around.' " She raised her hands over her head and shimmied in her chair. " 'She's got herself a *man,*' you know what I
mean?"

Marie jumped up and started for the door. Around her, everything blurred. Hearing Astrid talk about Omar suddenly confirmed
her loss, her failure to keep him.

"Oh Marie," Astrid called, hurrying after her and throwing her
arms around her. "Oh you poor kid. You poor, poor kid," she
crooned, holding her close, so close that Marie was shocked to feel
Astrid's breasts press against her. "It's not easy, is it?" Astrid said
softly, and Marie shook her head. Astrid patted her back, and she
didn't dare move. "They'll drive you crazy," she whispered. "They
will." She stepped back and held Marie at arm's length, then laughed
that quick hard laugh that set everything back where it had been
before.

Marie hunched over her typewriter as Astrid's adding machine
seemed to keep time to her words.

"Christ, it's hot. You know, I was telling Bobby we should get a
place at the lake. Nothing big, just some shacky little cabin-type
thing. Hey, maybe you and the kids could come out. We could have
a big party! Starting early in the morning—you know, all day long, a
beach party! I could invite all my wire plant friends. . . ." She looked
up and sighed. "Bobby kills me. He's got all this money from this big
bonus and every time I mention . . . Hey, I just thought. You ever
need a loan or anything, kid, you just let me know. I mean that!"

Marie kept her eyes on the letter, her face blank. Hell would
freeze over before she ever begged from someone like Astrid Haddad.

"Shit!" Astrid suddenly cried, sucking the tip of her forefinger,
ragged with a broken nail. "That was my best one!" With the alac-
rity a bleeding wound required, she opened her huge white purse and
from it seized a red leather case containing small glinting scissors,

some curved, some blunt-tipped, and tweezers, and nail files, and tiny bottles of oils and polishes.

Marie shivered. The rough drag of the file back and forth over Astrid's nail gave her goose bumps.

"Damn, damn, damn," Astrid muttered with her furious sanding. "I'm so mad I could scream!"

There grew now in the deeper woodshade of the fully leafed trees, blue gentian, and smelly black snakeroot, upon whose feathery white flowers flies clustered, and vines of young bittersweet that had begun to inch toward him. Around his leg, where the trouser had been torn, the first creeper curled, thin and waxy against his skin. His bloated body strained against his clothes, so dust-darkened now that fabric and flesh seemed one.

The humpbacked old dog came daily, usually in the first pale stillness of morning. Watchful, it lay off a few feet on spread haunches, its wet black nose keen to this creature's foul virility.

Whatever gives form to humanness—its features, eyes, nose, mouth, and ears, every protrusion and concavity of bone that suggest strength, propulsion, and contraction—these had subsided and were sinking deeper into the gaseous chemistry of death. Perhaps it seemed to the patient dog, its own vermiculate belly rumbling, that something grew here, that in the carious mass a new life was forming.

After a while the old dog's square, blunt head sank onto its front paws, and it emitted a low imploring growl.

Tonight's Fourth of July band concert in the park would be the biggest one of the year. Alice had to work, and Norm was going with Weeb Miller. Marie had asked him to take Benjy, but he had refused, and then Benjy looked so hurt that she had told him she'd go with him.

Supper was over and she was pouring hot chocolate pudding into three handleless teacups and two mismatched bowls. The extra serving was for Omar, should he happen to come. More than a week had passed without a word from him, and so she'd made up her mind. The days of Marie Fermoyle crawling after a man, any man, were over. Besides, today there had been a ray of hope. Mr. Briscoe said he had a friend who ran the cafeterias at UVM, and, if Marie wanted, he'd write to him about a job for Alice. If she wanted! She had typed the letter immediately and then had run it upstairs for his signature. Plus, she kept telling herself, there was always Sam's trust money. Just knowing about it had given her a new sense of calm. Talking to Helen was useless. She would have to get at it through Sam, now that he was sober and healthier. She had even considered driving up to Applegate with the kids this weekend, but then she remembered that nosy priest, that Father Gannon, offering to bring one of them up to see Sam. Maybe she'd send Alice. Sam might listen to his daughter.

She glanced at the telephone. Maybe Omar had been in Bennington all this time, looking into that soap business he'd told her about. Maybe he'd lost her telephone number. Or maybe he'd realized the last thing on earth he needed was to be saddled with a desperate woman and her three bickering kids.

Norm was complaining about his job again. Today, all the Street Department laborers had been getting the park ready for the concert.

"So I'm up at Joey's stand getting some popcorn and a Coke and Greene drives up and he leaps out of the car and grabs me by the shirt and he says, 'I'm docking you a half hour for this, Fermoyle!' " Norm looked at her now. "The guy's nuts!"

The phone rang and she jumped so fast to answer it that she was sure they were watching, pitying her for caring so much when Omar Duvall obviously cared so little.

"If it's Lester, I'm not here," Alice called as she tied her A+X apron.

"If he gets on my back one more time, I'm quitting!" Norm was saying. "And if he lays one more hand on me, I swear, I'll deck him!"

"I'm sorry, Les, she's not here," she said tersely, her eyes closed. Alice had told her how Lester had acted the other night, and yet she couldn't help feeling sorry for him.

"Would you have her call me when she gets home tonight, Mrs. Fermoyle? It's important."

"Yes, I'll tell her, Les," she said, forcing control into her voice, when it was all she could do to keep from screaming. When she turned, they were eating pudding. Pudding, she thought. Pudding! she felt like screaming. How could they sit there eating pudding when she was going to pieces right before their very eyes.

"You should see what Greene did to poor Joey's stand," Norm was telling them. "He got two-by-fours and just nailed them on the sides from the ground to the roof. Like a jail. Like bars! Joey's mad as hell."

She was running water to soak the pudding pan. She stared out at the two rakes leaning against the Klubocks' house. She was tired of being alone.

Once, soon after the divorce, she had gone out with a resin sales-man from New York. At the end of the night she had cried all the way home. She had even considered going back to Sam. At least it would be better than being so alone, so desperate, she had reasoned, until the next time Sam had showed up, pounding on the door, de-manding to see the kids he wanted to be with only when he was drunk.

Norm had gotten up from the table to stand next to her. He put his hand on her shoulder. "Mom," he said softly, "don't feel bad about that creep Duvall. Okay? Believe me, the guy's a bum."

She turned stiffly, eyes widening. "Don't you, of all people, call anyone a bum! You, with your fights and all your bellyaching about your job!"

He held up his hands as if in surrender. "I'm sorry. All right? I'm sorry, it's just that he's . . ." He shook his head and turned away.

"What?" She spun around. "He's what?" she demanded.

At the table Benjy groaned and looked at Alice, who quickly gathered up the rest of the dirty dishes and brought them to the counter. Benjy fled into the living room, where he turned on the television.

"You know where he's been all week?" Norm asked, trembling. "Do you really want to know?"

"Yes!"

"No, you don't," Norm said. "Because then you'll really feel bad!"

Her face twisted. "What are you talking about?"

"About Duvall and . . . and Bernadette Mansaw!"

"Oh God," Alice groaned.

"Don't be ridiculous!" Marie said. Muttering savagely, she turned on the water and started tossing the plates and cups into the sink. Had he been in town all week? Living somewhere else? That was worse than if he'd just taken off on her. "That doesn't make any sense! He's in Bennington! People in this town . . . they're all . . ." Something cracked. She turned off the water and from the suds pulled out a broken plate. She held it up. "See! See what you made me do! Now all I have is four!" she said, then started to cry.

"I'll do the dishes," Alice said, taking the dripping piece from her.

"C'mon, Mom," Norm said. He put his arm around her. "Go watch TV with Benjy."

At that, she pulled away and stormed around the corner, where Benjy sat smiling at *Queen for a Day*. She yanked out the plug and sparks flew from the outlet. "You and your goddamn television!" She stood over him. Blood seeped between her fingers. She had cut herself on the plate. Benjy kept looking at her hand with a dazed foolish smile that sickened her. "You're twelve years old, damn it! Don't you have any friends? Why do I have to go to the band concert with you? What's wrong with you?" she demanded, all the while thinking *What's wrong with me? What's wrong with me?*

"Mom!" Alice called from the sink.

"Leave him alone!" Norm moaned from the kitchen. "He didn't do anything!"

She ran back into the kitchen, holding her bleeding hand up by the wrist. "I'll leave him alone!" she screamed. "I'd like to leave you all the hell alone!" She held her throbbing hand under the running water.

"Go ahead!" Norm muttered. "Do us all a favor! Ever since he came you've been running around like a chicken with your head cut off. You're either giggling or you're screaming!"

She looked at them. She held on to the counter to steady herself. "Who the hell—"

"Mom!" Alice interrupted in a cold voice. "Can't you see what a phony he is?"

She glanced frantically between them. Didn't they understand that her every thought, every plan and dream was for them? Even the way she felt about Omar Duvall, it was for them. Her hand bled profusely now. She wrapped it in a towel, certain if she looked she would see a finger nearly severed.

". . . selling things from door to door with a bunch of con artists," Alice was saying. "That's so . . . so . . ."

"No," Marie said. "He did his own selling. Those were people he tried to help . . ."

"Mom, everything he says is a lie!" Norm said. "He's like a . . . a flimflam man . . . like one of those shell-game guys at the fair. He gives you a sob story and the whole time he's with Bernadette Mansaw."

"Doesn't that tell you anything, Mom?" Alice said, her voice dropping. "Bernadette Mansaw, Mom! She's my age!"

"And selling things door-to-door, Mom, doesn't that prove anything?" Norm said.

It was them against her. She rubbed her hand. *Help me. God help me,* she was thinking as they watched. *Please help me.*

The back door opened then and Omar's voice oozed over them like soothing ointment. He stood there with a paper bag under his arm. "Yes, Norm, it does prove something." His eyes gleamed over a bruised smile. "It proves again the frailty, the folly of loving too much, of caring about someone so much that when you try to lead them to higher ground, you are often left with the slop of their sins on your own shoes." He stepped into the kitchen and laid the bag on the table. The smell of his limey hair pomade filled the room. He laughed bitterly. "But when you've spent your whole life believing and hoping and wanting to help, you don't ask for proof of someone's goodness. For affidavits of someone's worth." Leaning closer to her, he whispered, "Do you?" He shook his head. "No! You ask for the only truth you've ever needed or known! The word of your fellowman!" His voice trembled, its wounded eloquence fleshing, clothing the words in such credence, breathing into them such wholeness that this room, the very air, seemed to her filled with an almost holy presence.

Watching him, she hugged her bound hand to her chest. He looked back at Norm and Alice then and said sadly, "You know, they were so simple, I made the mistake of thinking of them as children who could be shown, who could be taught, and the very night before they ran off with my goods and my car, I sat them down and told them there were two things I could not endure." He looked hard at Norm, who was smirking, and Alice, who stared at the floor, and he said, "Dishonesty and sinful lust." He sighed. "And look where that sermon left me. Plundered," he whispered. "Deserted." He looked at Marie. "Alone."

B enjy was glad to see Alice and Norm leave. He sat on the front steps waiting for his mother. It was seven-thirty, and the band concert would be starting soon. He couldn't wait to see the fireworks tonight. His mother's voice sifted through the screens as Omar bandaged her hand. She was happy again, but he knew it wouldn't last. It never did.

Just then, Klubocks' dog came across the driveway. The dog hunched up and defecated on the one scorched patch of grass that was their lawn. The dog sniffed at its mess, then trotted up to the steps. Benjy glanced back at the door. He bent close to the dog and whispered, "Go on home! Go!"

Panting, the dog sat at his feet.

"Go on now before she sees you!" he said with a gentle nudge of his foot.

The dog waddled off and sat between the two driveways, looking forlornly across at him.

"Go on!" He said with a stamp of his foot, and the dog got up and started down the street, then disappeared into the woods. He thought of his grandmother behind the bars of her giant crib. His father was locked up somewhere in a place called Applegate. Somewhere far away, he hoped, hearing his mother's sudden laughter.

He blinked and looked up. Galloping down the street from the woods came the dog now with something brown and leathery dangling from its mouth. "Norm's glove!" he gasped, chasing after the dog. "C'mon! C'mere, boy! C'mon!" he begged, zigzagging from lawn to driveway to lawn after the exhilarated dog. Just ahead, the dog paused, waiting. When he got close enough, he reached for the glove, and the dog, its ears pricked back, shot away from him.

Benjy came down to the road. He could hear the dog trotting at his heels, its nails ticking over the asphalt. Suddenly he whirled around and dove on the dog and, with his arms around its head, managed to twist the catcher's mitt free from its strong wet jaw. He sat back on his heels, sorrowfully examining the ruined glove. It was not only stiff and cracked and stained, but it smelled so bad that he had to hold his breath. With his stomach turning, he picked up a stick, which he jammed into the glove. He carried it like that to the garage and hung it on a nail just inside the door.

In the distance the band was starting to play. He started into the house to tell his mother, but stopped at the screen door when he saw Omar kissing her. She was up on her tiptoes with her arms around his neck. Omar's back was against the refrigerator and his eyes were closed. Both of his big hands were open on her rear end. She was making hungry, slurping, groaning sounds. Benjy just stood there. He had never seen her kiss anyone before.

Omar saw him. He said something, and they pulled apart and both started talking at once. She tugged at her skirt and adjusted her waistband. Her face was red. Benjy opened the door and came in. Omar moved quickly to the table and reached into his bag and pulled out a green-and-pink box. This was the soap America was waiting for, he was intent on telling Benjy. It seemed the most important thing anyone had ever said to him. All at once, unmoored, random facts like familiar distant stars suddenly had names along with the stunning realization that they were not just part of a pattern, of a constellation, but before his very eyes had become this great brilliant meshing of gears, driveshafts, pistons, and pinions that would transport them to happiness. Yes, even Benjy could make money selling it. On his bike, door to door. Did he have a bike? Well, then, with Presto Soap he'd have one in no time. Omar snapped his fingers like the guy who did the vegetable slicer ads on television, so much to tell and sell in thirty seconds. And here—Omar reached into the bag and held up a bottle filled with an orangy-pink liquid—here, this was its liquid counterpart, a concentrate so powerful one teaspoonful could eat through a ton of rust, a mountain of dirt.

His mother stood by the back door with the car keys.

It was the cleanser of the future.

They'd better go, she said.

So versatile it could shampoo your hair or shampoo your carpet.

Benjy! she was saying.

Depending on the dilution, of course.

Benjy smiled and couldn't look away.

This contained more than soap. There was nothing this product could not do.

"Omar!" she said.

As they got out of the car the band was playing "My Grandfather's Clock." The crowd clapped to the tick-tocking beat. Many of them had been camped here since early evening with their picnic hampers and lawn chairs. The sun was just sinking behind the dark mountains. Benjy looked breathlessly at the hundreds of young people walking around and around the bandstand, their feet seeming to move in perfect time to the music. Overhead, a bright pinwheel of paper lanterns had been strung from the trees to the gold-leafed weathervane on the bandstand roof. Balloon vendors worked their way through the sea of blankets. Other vendors sold Uncle Sam dolls on sticks and small American flags. A long line of customers waited in front of Joey's popcorn stand. Amid the swirl of music and lights, the lopsided red stand with its stavelike boards looked like some fantastic, hot-air contraption that had just floated haphazardly down from the skies and landed on the edge of the park. Inside, Joey's arms were a blur of motion, scooping popcorn from his churning glass popper and passing out the boxes with the grim intensity of one bailing out a sinking boat.

Across the street in front of the armory, the fireworks technicians were setting up their equipment under Robert Haddad's watchful eye. Haddad was chairman of the Chamber's Pyrotechnic Committee. He shifted nervously from foot to foot. His heart ached. Astrid had refused to come tonight, instead had gone to a cookout with her girlfriend.

Babies cried while others slept hammocked in their mothers' cross-legged laps. And high in a large elm tree in the farthest corner of the park were Norm and Weeb with an arsenal of cherry bombs. Jarden Greene was going to pay tonight.

Marie slipped Omar a dollar to buy ice cream from a boy with a silver cooler strapped to his chest. The three of them came down the path eating peel-away cones as they looked for space to spread their blanket.

"This," said Omar in his booming voice, "is what life is all about. This is America!"

People nudged one another and nodded at this tall stranger, conspicuous in his limp white suit and dark shirt. Marie's face drained as they passed the Klubocks, who sat in a close circle with three other families, all eating fried chicken and potato salad from red-white-and-blue-striped plates. "Marie!" Jessie Klubock called out and waved for her to join them, but Marie pretended not to have heard. Ahead, Howard and Jozia Menka were sitting on a bright afghan. Clutching the strings of their red balloons, they watched in astonishment as Marie and Benjy passed with Omar.

Marie went on until she came to a section of the park where she recognized no one.

"Lovely night . . . such music . . . excuse me . . . wonderful . . . hello, my dear . . ." Omar greeted those nearby as he spread their blanket with a flourish onto the damp ground.

The band were dressed in their usual white hats and white jackets. But this night was different form the Sunday-night concerts. Tonight they all wore red ties that glistened with silver stars. And tonight their expressions over their instruments were a little less complacent. This was their biggest crowd of the summer. After each number everyone in the park whistled and clapped and cheered, and as the night shrank up in coolness, the crowd moved closer to one another on their blankets and they began to sing along with the music. The young people continued walking in their customary circle around the bandstand, the eager clumps of girls in animated conversation, not hearing a word said as their eyes darted from boy to boy.

Beside Benjy, Omar had begun to sing softly, "Goodnight, Marie, goodnight." Benjy saw his mother blush and turn away with the dazed, startled look of a starving woman suddenly confronted with a feast. Just then the first burst of fireworks sizzled into the sky and three umbrellas of shimmering red, white, and blue lights opened in the night, cascading one after the other as the crowd cheered.

Next to the armory was Marco's Pharmacy, where Robert Haddad had been standing by the delivery door. He watched Marco and his wife hurry outside to watch the fireworks display from the sidewalk. Without a moment's hesitation, Haddad slipped inside the drugstore. He rang open the register, scooped the bills into his pockets, then slid out the side door, his prayerful litany, *God helps those who help themselves, God helps those who help themselves,* pounding in his ears louder than the fusillade of rockets exploding into the night.

Sam Fermoyle sank uneasily into the leather chair beside the mahogany desk.

A few moments later the door opened and Dr. Litchfield hurried into his unlit office. "Sorry for the delay," he said, closing the venetian blinds before he sat down.

"That you, Doc?" he asked, squinting.

"It's me." Dr. Litchfield chuckled and turned on his lamp. He'd taken a special interest in Sam's case and was himself conducting the therapy ordinarily handled by a team of staff psychiatrists. Litchfield seemed convinced he could save him with what he called his "pioneering practice plus treatment" program. Sam had been candid in the first few sessions, but now he knew it was the same old bullshit; and no one was better at bullshit than he was.

Litchfield leaned back now while Sam lit a cigarette. "They're mentholated." Litchfield smiled. "I thought you might like those better."

"Look, Doc, I don't mean to sound ungrateful," he said, shaking out the match. "But I've been here two weeks today and I need to go home."

Litchfield smiled gently. "You think you're ready for that, Sam? For your sister? For your ex-wife, for your children? You think you're ready for all that guilt right now?"

"Ready as I'm ever going to be." He sighed, then leaned over the desk. "My kids need me, Doc. That's the thing. I want to help my kids."

"Hmm. I don't know if you want to help them, Sam, so much as you want them to help you," Litchfield mused, toying with his glass paperweight that had a starfish embedded in it. "There's an enormous amount of work to be done in the area of self-involvement, Sam."

Self-involvement. What the fuck did that mean? He ground his teeth. "Whatever you say, Doc."

"You're a sensitive man, Sam."

"I try."

"But that may be the very root of your crisis. You have borne a lifetime of anxiety and guilt, Sam."

"You can say that again."

"And you have accepted these burdens much too readily and without question."

Sam nodded. "I know." He didn't know how many more of these sessions he could stand. He wanted a drink.

Litchfield's voice buzzed like a persistent fly in the room as he paced back and forth. Sam had stopped listening. Litchfield turned abruptly. "You have to learn how to forget the past and focus on what is real, Sam. On what is real to you!" He pointed. "Even if all the world does think it's a lie. For isn't much of life a lie, Sam?" He cocked his head, waiting for an answer.

Sam gripped the arm of the chair. He'd kill right now for a drink.

Litchfield hurried to his side and bent over him. "What I'm asking is, are you an alcoholic or . . ." He peered into Sam's blinking eyes and whispered, "Is it just that you cannot drink moderately? Which is real, Sam? What others say about you or what you believe about yourself? Sam, you've got to search out your own reality, your very own singular meaning, and that . . . that will be all the peace you'll ever need. That's all the peace any of us need."

Sam glanced at Litchfield's wristwatch. Twenty more minutes of this bullshit. He was tired. "I have no meaning, Doc," he sighed.

"And about all the reality I could handle right now is in a bottle somewhere."

Litchfield clutched his arm. "Don't you see? You sit here before me. I touch you. You feel my touch. Right now that's all you need of reality. It's the beginning. You're not real because I'm telling you I'm touching you. You're real because you can feel my hand on your arm."

Sam's stomach growled with hunger. Lunch was still an hour away. Food had become the most important event here. Last night he had awakened throbbing with desire from a dream of fat pink shrimp stuffed with buttery crumbs. Maybe Litchfield was trying to make him think he was crazy so that when his thirty days were up he'd be begging to stay here forever. Where was the money coming from for this? Why the hell was Helen paying to keep him here when she could have had him admitted to the state hospital for nothing? It made no sense. He had written her three letters asking why. She hadn't answered any of them. Seventy dollars a day times thirty days. Twenty-one hundred dollars. Jesus Christ, what had Litchfield promised her? For that kind of money he must have guaranteed her a cure. No, he thought, for twenty-one hundred dollars he must have promised to remove him from her life forever. He stared at Litchfield, who was pacing between the window and the desk, his arms jabbing the air, his cheeks flushed with heat. His voice sputtered and hissed with such passion that he seemed unaware of the lisp that crept into his speech.

"And so, you must not judge yourself too harshly, Samuel. As these sessions go on, your understanding of the real you will grow and you will cease being Samuel Fermoyle, the chronic alcoholic. You will become Samuel Fermoyle, a man caught in an existential vacuum, a very twentieth-thentury man thruggling from the hell of what other people tell him he ith back into the path of what he knowth he mutht become for hith own thingular being and reality." He lifted Sam's hand, sandwiching it between his own.

"Thit!" Sam said and pulled his hand away.

Litchfield flinched as if an old scab had just been gouged. He busied himself with the papers on his desk. When he looked up his face was drained, his eyes arid and clinical. "Your cruelty, Mr.

Fermoyle, is just like your drinking, another form of self-destruction, that's all." Litchfield's jaw trembled.

Sam looked down at his hands and squirmed, his legs damp against the leather chair. Thirst scorched the inside of his mouth. They wouldn't even let him keep shaving lotion in his room. Marie used to hide the vanilla extract and the cough syrup and the can openers and his money and his car keys and, on Saturday nights, his shoes. She was always trying to stay a step ahead of him, running with the ferocious tenacity of a child racing water buckets between the ocean and the forever-draining hole she had scraped in the sand.

His mother had hidden nothing from him, not love, not money, not sorrow. She had nourished him on the catafalque of her sorrow, her disappointment in his father, in him, absolving him with tears until the morning after Alice's birth, when she had plucked him from her life without so much as a catch in her voice. There would be no more denials, she had told him, no more excuses. And then the key had turned in the lock.

He looked up meekly and cleared his throat. He had nipped at the hands that could release him. He apologized.

Litchfield answered softly, gently. "We will polarize your tension and your distress, Sam. We will teach you that they can be very necessary components in an emotionally healthy life. We will take your sadness and your tears and we will learn to savor them, to find meaning for them. I will give you the will to live again. Look at me, Sam. Do you understand what I'm trying to tell you?"

Sam nodded. Litchfield put a box of tissues in front of him and smiled.

"I'm very tired now, Dr. Litchfield," he said, blowing his nose. He had to get the hell out of here. "I'd like to go back to my room and just lay there and think this all through."

Litchfield squatted down, disappearing behind his desk. Sam waited. He heard a drawer slide open. Litchfield's head popped up level with the desktop. His chin rested on the edge and he smiled across at Sam. "I've got a little surprise here," he teased, then ducked down again. One by one, they appeared on the desk, a cut-glass decanter of shimmering golden whiskey, a pair of shot glasses, small as thimbles. Instinctively Sam's body drew forward. He could taste it. He could smell it. He arched back stiffly in the chair.

Litchfield was looking in his closet now. "Here we go," he said, returning to his chair with a plate of Ritz crackers and a pressurized can of cheese spray.

Pursing his lips as he sprayed a dainty cheddar bud atop each cracker, he told Sam that whiskey was one of the oldest medicines known to man, and, if used properly, it could be an art form, an elegant ritual between two gentlemen. He offered Sam the crackers. "This is a closely guarded secret, my new therapy," Litchfield said between nibbles. "I've applied for a grant. You see, I'm trying to prove beyond a shadow of a doubt to my skeptical peers that some men are not just alcoholics, quote unquote, but victims of opinion, victims of labels, if you will, labels pasted on their foreheads sometimes as early as birth, labels that say such ridiculous things as: 'Your father was an alcoholic, your grandfather was an alcoholic, old Uncle Jim is an alcoholic. It runs in the family. It's in our blood.' " Litchfield wagged his finger and deepened his voice. " 'Therefore, *don't drink*, or you will be an alcoholic, too.' " He laughed lightly and popped another cracker into his mouth. "So what was the first thing you did when you got old enough?"

His eyes bulged toward the decanter. He didn't answer.

Litchfield raised the decanter in both hands. "You sneaked a drink, right?" His grin rippled through the amber liquid. "Out behind the proverbial barn, right, Sam?"

"Behind the furnace in high school after a baseball game." Sam gulped and closed his eyes. "Can I have a drink, Doc?"

Litchfield placed the decanter in front of him. "In just a minute, after you understand what I'm trying to do." He hunched eagerly on his elbows. "I'm going to teach you how to taste. How to swallow. How to drink. And the key here will be control—a little bit at a time. When we're done, Sam, you are going to be able to drink socially, like a gentleman, not guiltily, not furtively. But right out in the open—one drink, maybe two, after a lot of therapy, of course, but never, never more than that. Control, Sam. That's the key here, control."

By the time the glasses were finally filled, Sam was in a cold sweat. His hand jerked across the desk, but Litchfield pushed it back. He shook his head. "No, Sam! Relax. Let it sit there a while. Close your eyes. There's no hurry. We're having a lovely little talk here, just you and me. It's been a long day." Litchfield dimmed the lamp. "Picture it now. We're in a small café outside of town, about to have a leisurely drink before we drive home to the wife and the kiddoes. . . ." Litchfield's fuzzy voice droned at his ears. He ground his teeth until they ached.

"Go ahead, now. Open your eyes. Casually place your hand around the glass, each finger closing, one by one, so you can savor the moment, the anticipation that is probably more pleasurable than the actual act. Now raise it . . . slowly, slowly to your lips. That's it. There's no hurry. No rush. It's only—"

"Tea!" he cried, spitting it out. "Weak tea! Christ!"

Litchfield pounded his fist down on the desk. "I was about to tell you that, but you couldn't wait!"

Stunned, he watched Litchfield refill the glass, then calmly raise his own. He stood up and stalked toward the door. "I'm through playing games, you asshole!" he yelled, suddenly sickened by the desperate pitch of his own shrill voice.

Tonight was Alice's turn in the far end of the A+X lot, which was considered the worst station because it only got busy when the rest of the lot was full. But for Alice, its worst feature was the nearness to the bright kitchen doorway, where Anthology Carper lounged between orders, his short legs dangling from the tall metal stool, a cigarette burning between his gray teeth, his colorless eyes trailing her every move.

It was the Monsignor's long black Oldsmobile with Father Gannon at the wheel, and beside him, Father Krystecki, a pale skinny priest with big ears. Father Krystecki had been at Saint Mary's a few years ago, but Alice had only ever talked to him in the confessional. He had been a popular confessor, his most common penance the exhortation to "Be kind."

"Hello, Alice," Father Gannon said, sticking his hand out the window to shake hers. "This is Father Krystecki."

Father Krystecki reached across Father Gannon and also shook her hand.

"Nice to meet you," she said, her face flaming. Why were they here? What did they want? Had something happened? Norm. He'd been in an accident. Norm with his rage, and lately all his drinking. No. Omar had the car again tonight. Maybe that was it. Maybe Omar Duvall had smashed into a tree and died. God, what a relief that would be.

"Father Krystecki used to be at Saint Mary's. Until he got called up to the majors," Father Gannon added, his sudden pronged laughter jolting up her spine.

She nodded, managing a smile.

"I'd hardly call Saint D's the majors," said Father Krystecki.

"Well, being pastor certainly is!" Again Father Gannon's laugh seemed forced and unnatural.

"Oh well, I don't know about that," Father Krystecki demurred.

"He's very modest, isn't he, for the youngest pastor in the diocese?"

"You're really embarrassing me," Father Krystecki said softly.

Father Gannon smiled up at her, and her face grew redder. "Could I take your order, please?" she asked.

"Two root beer floats," he said, still smiling.

While she was clamping their tray onto the car door, a pickup truck peeled out of the lot. Father Gannon craned his neck to watch it speed up the highway. "This must be a great place to work," he said, rubbing his hands together. "All this action! All this life!"

"A bit too lively for me, I'm afraid," Father Krystecki said between slurps.

Father Gannon had yet to take a sip of his float. "By the way, what are your hours?" he asked.

"Four to twelve," she said, sliding her pencil over her ear. A car was pulling in next to the priests', and now another. The movie must be getting out. The lot was almost full.

"Twelve," Father Gannon said with a glance at his watch. "Long day."

As she walked away she could see his reflection in the tall angled sheets of tinted glass. He was watching her and smiling.

At midnight Blue Mooney was in the kitchen eating hot dogs while his cousin scraped the grills clean and drained the fryolaters. Alice watched for Norm by the side of the road so Mooney wouldn't see that she was still here. He had offered her a ride home again tonight, and Anthology Carper had hissed under his breath, "No thanks, scum, I'd rather crawl than be seen with you."

The office telephone was ringing. Coughlin opened his door and called out that her brother said to start walking, the car still wasn't back. That could only mean Omar Duvall hadn't brought it back yet. Lately he drove it so much that he was picking her mother up in the morning and dropping her off at work. Alice didn't mind as much as Norm, who couldn't believe any of this was happening.

The minute Mooney and Carper came out of the kitchen, she hurried up Main Street. The tips in her sagging pockets jingled and banged against her leg. Behind her the headlights of a slowing car flicked three times from high to low beams, each with a soft tap of the horn. She walked faster. "Alice!" called a voice, and she groaned. After that night at the lake, Mooney was never going to leave her alone. He would hound her forever, because now he knew who she was and what she was, and soon everyone would know. She was almost running when the car pulled alongside.

"Alice! Wait! Want a ride?" It was Father Gannon. He said he'd just dropped off Father Krystecki in Proctor. She accepted gratefully when she saw Blue Mooney's car roar out of the lot.

At home, the driveway was empty. She wanted to get inside before Omar Duvall arrived in her mother's car, before she had to explain or lie or, worse, introduce the two men. Father Gannon kept initiating new conversations that fizzled into throat-clearing and now just the uneasy tap of his nails on the steering wheel.

"Well, thank you for the ride," she said, starting to open the door.

"Alice! There's just one thing!" he said with such startling intensity that his voice trembled and his cheeks flushed. "You know, this wasn't a coincidence, my coming to the A+X tonight." He blinked and clenched his fists. "I didn't want to say anything in front of Father Krystecki, but Saturday, I have to drive up to Burlington to take some papers to the Bishop. Applegate's on the way, and if you felt like it, I could drop you off there to see your father, then pick you up on the way back. So, what do you think?"

"No, I can't," she said quickly. She couldn't recall any nun or priest ever embarrassing her about her father until this insensitive, nosy priest. Her mother would have a fit.

"He'd like to see you," Father Gannon said softly. "You know, this is when he needs his family most."

Two weeks ago she had written her father a letter, which he still hadn't answered. She had been careful to write only of cheerful, funny things: Norm washing the car's engine until it gleamed but then wouldn't start because all the water had flooded it; the afternoon when Benjy fell asleep at the movies until six at night, when they called the theater and an usher found him and woke him up; her job, which she had tried to make sound interesting; the robbery at Marco's Pharmacy. "I miss you," she had written, "and I hope you're feeling much better."

"He never writes unless he wants something," her mother had said yesterday as she came in empty-handed from the mailbox.

"The Monsignor got this letter from your father this morning," Father Gannon said, handing her an envelope. "He says he misses his children dearly. He'd like to see you."

She turned it over, then looked up blankly.

"It's all right. Go ahead and read it. The Monsignor gave it to me. I answered it, and he signed it. That's what's meant by religious hierarchy," he said laughing.

JMJ

Dear Monsignor,

It is difficult for me to write this letter in view of these bleak facts: I am (1) a prisoner here, (2) a mental patient, and thus, (3) not to be taken seriously, and (4) without much hope of a near release from this expensive hell hole unless you intercede on my behalf as I, your faithful parishioner, have implored you to do in my previous, unanswered letters.

I am writing this letter in order to humbly ask your for-

giveness for the events preceding my internment here. If, as I
suspect, I embarrassed or insulted you or yours in any way, I
am sincerely and most soberly contrite.

There are some inevitable events in a man's life over
which he has little or no control. In my own I am all the
"events." Beyond that, I offer no excuses but my own pitiless
state of being (or non-being, whichever your viewpoint).

Again, my plea is the same. Please see my dear sister and
convince her that she must get me out of here. (1) This is a
godless place. They tinker with our minds and care not for
our souls. (2) The rates are exorbitant. $70 a day, special
treatments extra. Where will that money come from? (3) I
cannot exist much longer without seeing my children. They
are all that I live for.

Please speak to Helen. Tell her I wither here without the
solace of my Church and family. I want to receive Communion, but I am denied sacraments. Helen would be much better off giving her money to you than to this bunch of fatcat
Protestants. For what she pays here, the Pope would say a
special Mass for her, I'm sure.

Thank you, Monsignor. Please pray for me if you get the
chance.

Sincerely yours in Christ,
Samuel A. Fermoyle

Postscript—Bubbles, you still have not sent that letter to Dr.
Litchfield attesting to my sanity. Just as surely as you know I
am not insane, know that I will do the same for you if your
Bishop should ever decide to farm you out. S.A.F.

She folded the letter, stunned that he would write to the Monsignor but not to his own daughter.

"I mailed a letter back tonight," Father Gannon was saying. "On
my way up to the A+X as a matter of fact." Pausing, he leaned toward her. "Are you all right? The letter, it didn't upset you, did it?
Oh, listen to me. Of course it did. I mean, this must be all so painful
for you. Believe me, I know it is. And I also know how personal this

is. Alice, believe me, this is so confidential it's sacred. I mean, as far as I'm concerned, this is the same as being in the confessional together."

"What did you say to him? In your letter. What did you write?" she asked, rubbing her eyes. The last thing she wanted to do was cry. She pretended to yawn.

"Oh, let's see. It was a long letter. I told him so many things—to keep the faith and pray, and cooperate with the doctors, that God would help him, that his children stood by him, that . . ." He stopped, shocked by what he had just heard. His face reddened. "What did you say?"

"Nothing." She covered her mouth. She couldn't believe she'd said that. It had slipped out.

"You called me an asshole, didn't you?"

"No!"

"I heard you." He looked every bit as shocked as she was.

"I said the word, but I didn't mean to! It just slipped out."

"I'm such an inspiration!" he said.

"I'm sorry," she said. "I'm so embarrassed."

"Don't be. I've been called worse," he said, trying to laugh.

"I didn't mean you!" she said, desperate for a way out of this mess. "You see, I'd go with you to see my father, but I know it would really make my mother mad. She's—"

"No, no! As a matter of fact, she said she thought it was a good idea. She said you'd be the best one to go."

"You already talked to my mother about this?" she asked, stunned.

"Well, I called her."

"And when did she say I could go?"

"Next weekend? That's when I have to go up."

"What time did she say you should pick me up?"

"Well, she didn't really say. But after I leave the nursing home? Ten?"

"And what time would we get back?"

"She said you have to be at work by four."

"Of course," she said with a bitter sigh. "She wouldn't want me to miss work."

"It'll be just the boost he needs," he said as she got out of the car. "You'll be so glad you did it."

Klubocks' dog was sitting by the back steps with a long rag dangling from its mouth. The dog stood and wiggled its rump, but she opened the back door quickly. "My God, you stink! Go on!" she hissed, stamping her foot. "Get out of here!"

Hoping to shorten his stay, Sam Fermoyle was trying his best to relax and become more a part of the Applegate routine. He made up his mind to participate in the group therapy sessions he had been sitting through mutely. He would become the perfect patient. The nurses noticed the change. They brought him magazines from the staff lounge and extra cigarettes. The maids in their navy-blue uniforms and white ruffled aprons took twice as long to clean his room. One of them, an olive-skinned, stout woman from town, made him guanti and smuggled it into his room. "Men who drink need a lot of sugar," she told him as she watched him eat. The powdered sugar fell like fine snow onto the green bedspread. She brushed it off.

"I'm through with drinking," he said hoarsely.

"You should be," she said, handing him a napkin. "A man with a silver tongue like you should be out making a million dollars for himself, like my son."

Though Litchfield wouldn't tell Sam exactly when he'd be leaving, he had begun to make plans. When he got home he was going to get a job, not just any job this time, but one he could look forward to when he got up in the morning, one he could be proud of. He would move out of Helen's and get his own place.

Yesterday, he had written Helen a letter asking her to send the want ads from the *Atkinson Crier*. He would have to get new clothes. He had made up a list of what he'd need for work: two pairs of shoes, one black, one brown. Three white shirts, three ties (blue, red, and brown), two suits (gray and brown), seven pairs of socks, seven sets of underwear. Handkerchiefs. He had started a grocery list, but only got as far as coffee and sugar. He didn't know if his room would have a refrigerator for the cream, or even a stove, for that matter. And where would this room be? Who would rent him a room if he didn't have a job? And who the hell was going to hire him? And if no one would hire him, how the hell was he going to pay for the new clothes? And if he didn't have at least one good suit and a pair of half-decent shoes, he couldn't even hold his head up during an interview. He would write Helen another letter asking for a loan to get him started.

He stood in front of the mirror combing his hair. He changed his part from right to left, then back again. First day home he would get a haircut and a shave. He would ask the barber which side looked best parted. He leaned close to the mirror. He would have those nostril hairs clipped. He felt better already. He started another list, this one, personal-care items: shaving cream, styptic pencil, razors. *Bay rum,* he wrote, then scratched it out with a chuckle.

Marie whipped the potatoes, then set the table quickly around Omar, who ran his finger down the want ads. "Short-order cook," he murmured. "Stock boy . . . telephone repairs. Oh my Lord, my dear, dearest Lord," and as he sighed, his whole body seemed to deflate.

Poor Omar, how much more rejection could he take? She bit her lip. Never had she seen anyone work so long and hard with so little to show for it. It didn't make sense. In the last few weeks he had been working sixteen- and twenty-hour days. He was always in a hurry. The only time she saw him lately was when he drove her to work in the morning and then picked her up when the store closed. He would come into the house just long enough to wolf down dinner before rushing out again on the trail of new leads. He had lined up dozens of people interested in becoming Presto Soap dealers, but he had yet to sell a single franchise.

He turned the page now and yawned. Poor thing, he could barely keep his eyes open half the time, and now he had this skin condition. She had first noticed the deep purple blotches on his neck Thursday morning on the way to work. Just the heat, he had said, trying to make light of them.

"No," she had said, leaning closer and pulling back his collar. "They almost look like bruises."

"Stress," he had said, removing her hand. "That's all, just a phys-iological manifestation of my frustration. A sign." He had smiled sadly. "Marie, I'm afraid I've become just one more problem in your life."

"No! No, you're not! Of course you're not," she had insisted.

"Well, let's just say I don't make things any easier for you, espe-cially with the children, with Norm. I know how bitter he is about me having the car all the time."

No, the only real problem was Norm's surliness. The minute Omar walked into a room, Norm would leave.

Omar yawned again now, as he began to tell her about the gruel-ing two-day sales meeting in Bennington that had ended with the in-duction of new distributors. He had been there as an observer. The company was extremely careful not to put pressure on new people. "The top brass, they were all there," he was saying. "Distributors from all over the country in their pin-striped suits and solid-gold cuff links."

She slid into the opposite chair, a dazed smile forming. She was dying to hear if he'd gotten to talk with Roy Gold, the president.

"There was this one gentleman from Louisville, Kentucky, whom I met when I went into the . . . the rest room." He cleared his throat and she was sure he was blushing.

"And I could not believe my eyes," he continued. "Because there he was, this particular gentleman from Louisville, with his foot up on the washbasin, buffing his wingtips with dollar bills. 'Excuse me, sir,' I said, 'but I think those are dollar bills with which you are buffing your shoes.' And he says in this honey-thick drawl, which if you think mine is bad you should hear him, he says, 'They sure are, Mr. Duvall. A dollar bill'll put a shine on just about anything.' And then he looked at me, one of those kind of sidelong glances when you can just feel all your bones and the fillings in your teeth being enumer-ated, and he says, 'Or maybe you didn't know that, Mr. Duvall.' And then, just like that, he crumpled those dollar bills up and tossed them in the wastebasket like they were nothing, nothing at all to him, a man of his position. Like it was all so . . . so beneath him, and the door wasn't even closed behind him but what I was pawing through that wastebasket, when all of a sudden it hits me, and I'm thinking, I am not like him. In fact I am not like any of them in there with all their, pardon my French, Marie, but their b.s. No sir." He shook his head. "Am not and never will be."

There was a jolt of pain in her temples. Sam used to talk like this. He wouldn't be a week on a new job before he'd be declaring himself too intelligent, too sensitive, the job too menial. Were all men like this? Was it just women who knew that a job was a job; you did what you had to do, whatever it took, and you were just damn grateful you had one. "What about Roy Gold? Did you meet him?" Her hands were shaking.

"I did, and he said he'd like to get together with me." Omar checked his watch.

"Today?"

"No, no." He laughed. "He said to call him soon as I sell my first franchise." He glanced up at the clock, then, frowning, held the watch to his ear.

"Do you have an appointment or something?" she asked.

"Nothing important," he said with a wave. "Just a few more leads, that's all. Or should I say dead ends." He sighed.

"You'll sell a franchise. I know you will," she said, hearing that old desperation in her voice. *Just try. Keep at it. Don't give up. Please. For me. For us.* "What about that Bernadette Mansaw? Didn't you say she's buying in?"

"Well," Omar said, "we're getting there, getting close, but the problem's precedence, which I totally understand, precedence being such a powerful motivating factor in today's business world."

"What do you mean, precedence?" She hated asking; Omar seemed to think she had such a head for business.

"For instance, how do I convince Miss Mansaw that she's joining a flourishing empire when I have no other investors to show her?" He smiled. "You see, not many people can judge character as well as you, Marie. Most of the ones I run into need facts and figures. I'm trying to help them envision a future, and all they want to see is a warehouse filled with product. They lack magnitude and imagination! It's hard with such little people. You want so much to give them that boost, that head start, but they fight you and doubt you and fight you and doubt you. They all want precedence, which I can neither deliver nor avoid." He closed his eyes with a bitter snort. "And thus the dog is doomed to chase his tail around and around and around."

"But what if you just said you had an investor?" Marie said. "You know, just use my name."

Omar laid down the newspaper and gazed at her. "What a good scout you are!" He shook his head in gratitude. "I appreciate your offer. But without a cash investment Roy Gold would never issue you franchise documentation. That man is scrupulous." He grimaced. "Even the slightest hint of impropriety and I'd be through."

"I didn't mean anything dishonest!" she said quickly.

"Oh I know that," Omar answered as quickly.

"I just want to help, that's all," she tried to explain, her face red. He had misunderstood.

"Help!" he cried, pointing at the stove. "This bounty exceeds help. It's sustenance! It's life-giving!"

She could hear Norm and Alice arguing. Norm needed to use the bathroom. Somewhere in the neighborhood a lawn was being mowed. She pressed against the counter edge as the distant motor hummed closer. Omar started to get up.

"Wait! You know I'd buy one if I could. If I had the money."

"Yes, I know that," he said sadly.

"Mom!" Norm called. "Tell her to get out!"

She raced around the corner and banged on the bathroom door.

"I'm late for work!" Alice called back.

"You've been in there for a half hour!" Norm called over Marie's shoulder.

"You let your brother in there right now!"

"God, I hate it here," Alice said on the other side of the door.

"You hate it here?" she panted, her face at the door.

"Mom," Norm said, touching her arm, cringing as she spun around.

"Listen to her! You hate this house? Nothing's ever good enough, is it? I wish I had a color TV like the Stoners have"—she mimicked Alice with a sickening petulance—"I wish I had nice clothes like Mary Agnes. I wish we had a shower like everybody else does. I wish, I wish, I wish, well damn it, don't you think I wish, too?" She hit the door. "Don't you? Don't you? Don't you?"

"If wishes were riches, then beggars would be kings," Omar whispered as he passed through the living room. The front door closed, and she buried her face in her hands. She had lost control. She had driven him away.

Alice had left for work. Norm and Benjy were on the couch watching television. With Omar gone, the house seemed to coil up in a paroxysm of eerie energy. The spell had been broken, and now Marie knew there would never be happiness. The television tubes sputtered and fizzed. Ghostly double images jerked across the screen. There were ants climbing up the baseboard.

"Now he knows," she muttered as she wielded the bug spray, spraying crumb-filled corners and the dark musty recesses behind the stove and refrigerator. "Knows the trash we are." She coughed with the oily fumes that would probably poison them all—if they were lucky. "Worthless, hopeless trash." She laughed hoarsely. "Let him run. They all run, every one of them, useless, weak cowards, lazy no-good bastards."

And then he was back, his arms cradling a damp toweled bundle as he asked for Alice. Norm told him she was gone.

"This is my belated graduation present for her," he said as he snaked a tangle of rubber hosing and grimy couplings from the towel and now a soap-filmed chrome disk.

"Wow," Norm said, rolling his eyes. "She's really gonna be happy."

Omar buffed the disk on his lapel while he explained that one of the roomers at the boardinghouse was a plumbing wholesaler. He had sold Omar his top model.

"How much?" Marie asked guiltily. Just a few days ago she had lent him another ten dollars for rent.

"Just my word," he said as he examined the polished disk under the lamp. "My only currency in trade for this brand-new portable shower."

"That's brand new?" Norm scoffed.

"Brand new!" Omar said with a sweet smile.

"Funny," Norm said, pointing, "but there's water leaking out the hose on your leg."

"Not so funny," Omar said, passing the towel over his stained pant leg. "Naturally I hooked it up at the boardinghouse first to check it for leaks."

"Naturally," Norm said, and it was all she could do to keep from slapping that fresh mouth of his.

Omar looked at him. "Though it may surprise you, Normy-boy, I am not a fool. But I certainly do seem to suffer more than my share of them," he sighed as he stepped into the bathroom.

"Omar!" she said from the doorway. "He didn't mean it that way!" She glared back at Norm.

"Don't you worry, dear lady," Omar grunted through the rattle of pipes and running water. "Norman and I have a fine understanding of one another. In fact, I'd say we're probably peas from the same pod, wouldn't you say, Normy-boy?" he called out.

"Yessuh! Yessuh! Ah'd say so, suh!" Norm called back. Benjy laughed.

Smiling, she watched Omar press the suction-cupped showerhead to the wall high over the tub.

He glanced back at her. "Life can be good, Marie. Take my word for it. It can!"

The sun was hot, the sky pure blue, and Sam had never felt better. This morning there had been a note in his room from Dr. Litchfield. *Good news, Sam!* it said. *Tell you at our session.* His thirty days were almost up, and so it had to be that Litchfield was going to tell him when he could leave. With his newspaper under his arm he strolled through the gardens. His hair was slicked back from the jaunty wave he had set carefully over his brow, and he wore the dark-blue pants one of the orderlies had pressed for him and the white nylon summer shirt he'd snagged from the laundry cart.

Yes sir, he thought, if you had to dry out, you could do a hell of a lot worse than this place. A little chill went through him, but he shrugged it off. It was that old collision of hope and fear that always came as he neared the end of his thirty days. But this time it had to work. It had to. He was getting too old for this shit.

He hurried through the rose arbor. At ten o'clock he would see Litchfield for an hour and then at eleven-thirty return to his room to rest before lunch. After lunch there would be group therapy for an hour, then tea and cookies on the patio, followed by arts and crafts: leathercraft because he had done that before at Waterbury. Naptime was from four to five, and then he watched the evening news on television in the recreation room. Dinner was served at seven. The dining room with its chandeliers, fresh flowers, and linen-covered tables set for six had the elegance and intimacy of the fine old hotel the Bullfinch Building had once been. In an effort to avoid alliances with any of the drunks or having to babble with any of the loonies, he tried to sit at a different table each night. The mental patients usually wore their tumult in their faces; the ghostly rubble of ashes for eyes as if their very souls had been scorched. For some the madness seemed to bubble with molten brilliance from every fissure. The alcoholics were easy to spot; the red or jaundiced flesh, the spurious smiles, the elusive eyes floundering in the limbo of sobriety, and the fidgeting hands tearing at cuticles or drumming out on tabletops relentless hollow beats.

As he stood outside Litchfield's office now, he glanced down at his own hands, which had pleated the edge of the newspaper. He ran his thumb over his smooth, uncallused palm. Sensitive hands, his mother used to say, at one time declaring the long, tapered fingers like those of an artist or a great pianist, or—he chuckled—a lush who hadn't worked in more years than he could remember.

He was five minutes early, but Litchfield took him right in.

"You got my note?" Litchfield asked, and Sam nodded as he lit his cigarette, trying not to look as eager as he felt. All the way over here he had reminded himself to keep playing the game.

"Your ex-wife called, Sam." Litchfield smiled. "She sounds like a very interesting woman. Down to earth. Frank. I liked what I heard."

He held his breath. Holy shit. Marie knew his thirty days were almost up, and she must have been trying to talk Litchfield into keeping him here.

"Don't be fooled, Doc, she's a very bitter woman, believe me."

"Well, now, I didn't get that impression at all, Sam. Quite the contrary. As a matter of fact, I'd say she's quite concerned about you."

"Concerned," he said, chuckling at his last memory of Marie's hateful face and a knife in her hand, though he wouldn't tell Litchfield this, for fear he might decide Sam would be safer here.

"Yes, she wanted to know about visitors. She seems particularly sensitive to your state of mind right now and your—"

"Sensitive!" he cried. "Let's get one thing straight here, Doc, she is probably the most *in*sensitive woman I've ever known!"

Litchfield leaned back in his chair and folded his arms while Sam tried to explain the vast disparities between them. They had come from two different worlds. The marriage had been doomed from the start, and for that he was certainly more to blame, having been twelve years older and college-educated, while she was just barely out of high school. He had tried to make it work, tried his damnedest, but she had absolutely no sense of taste or refinement. Any wreck of a car was good enough as long as it ran. Dinner was usually fried meat and pasty potatoes thrown on a chipped plate. Clothes didn't matter. Taste, beauty, symmetry were frivolous and without meaning for a woman who never read books, just newspapers, and those only to see if someone she knew had died, who looked at a sunset just to determine the next day's weather, who bought a cheap but pleasant print once at Woolworth's, then hung it in a dark corner to hide a stain on the wallpaper. When it came to his future, she cared more about the paycheck than his sense of self-worth. She had never been able to get beyond the thorns to the bloom. She was without abstraction. She had denied him dignity and support. She had fed on his weakness. Because of her he had nothing.

Now he was telling Litchfield about his last night living with his family. It had been ten years ago on Christmas Eve and he had come home late. "I'll admit, I'd been drinking, but it was Christmas!" he said while Litchfield nodded impassively. "We had a few words. She said some things. I said some things. She hit me. I don't know, maybe I tried to get her out of the way or something, but next thing I know, she's down on the floor. She wasn't hurt or anything, but you see, she always had a knack for pushing me too far. She always knew just how to push me right over the edge. It was like she couldn't ever stand to see me happy. She was always so suspicious, smelling my breath when I'd come in, and calling places to see if I'd really gone in to see about a job.

"But anyway, that night she got up and I'm standing there, thinking, Oh Christ, here we go again, but she didn't say a word. She just went to the phone, called the cops, and when they came she told them they could take me to jail or to my mother's house. The next day she sent the kids over to my mother's with my clothes and all their presents for me in a red wagon they had to pull all the way through the snow." He shook his head. "I've got to hand it to her, for a woman with no imagination whatsoever, it was her most ingenious scenario. There I am with a blinding headache, having to grovel through all my things under the Christmas tree while my mother's crying and my sister just sits there shaking her head and sighing."

"You seem to be building some kind of a case here," Litchfield said softly.

"You're damn right I am!" he said. "This isn't all my fault, you know. I mean, I was headed toward a good life. I was!"

Litchfield looked at him. "And what happened?"

"Her! Marie, my wife, that's what happened." He lit another cigarette.

He started with the night he had first seen her, so young and timid with her fear of the prowler who had run his hand down the screen of her bedroom window in the house she and her father rented next door. Every now and again the old man wouldn't make it home from his rounds as a butcher who traveled the hills from farm to farm. It was on one of those lonely nights that the scratching came on the window screen, and so she ran next door in her nightclothes. Sam had been out with friends and when he came home he found her huddled in the corner of his mother's settee, clutching the afghan to her throat as she waited for her father to return. He sat up talking with her. Her father didn't arrive until dawn, his old eyes reddened, his gray hair tousled, his beery tongue thick with apology, and the awkward tale of a broken-down truck and the loss of an awesome cow for which he had paid his last cent.

The week after her high school graduation they were married. She was eighteen and he was almost thirty. His mother was shocked, grief-stricken. His engagement to Nora Cushing had been the high point of her life. Her humiliation and disappointment were soon abridged by the gentle swelling in his child bride's belly. She would have a grandchild after all, she gloated to Helen, never intending the wound that erupted and festered to this day in her sterile daughter's heart.

During the first few months of marriage, he had been happy enough. They took long walks at night. He brought her books from the library to read. She learned to sew and made maternity smocks he tried to admire. Her pregnancy made her look even younger, more childish. In public he felt foolish beside her. Friends kidded him. He remembered buying her a black picture hat and a pair of dangling gold earrings to make her look more sophisticated. She giggled and looked silly in them. He took her to a play once and she fell asleep. She read his poems and said they were nice, and she saved them in a shoe box she had pasted with colored ribbons and magazine pictures. She tried, but everything she did seemed cheap and childish. He took her to a party, and she was so uncomfortable with people she didn't know, with people who were older, better educated than she was, that she burst into tears and begged him to take her home. Already a little drunk, he told her to leave if she didn't like it. He stayed. The next morning they had their first big fight.

During this time he had been having trouble at work. He hated every job and boss he'd ever had. A good part of the problem was his inertia, he'd admitted. He was sorry, but he just couldn't get fired up over the nickel-dime jobs that were all a town like Atkinson had to offer. One day he ran into some old friends and never made it to work. His boss called and told Marie he was fired. Sam told her not to worry, jobs like that were a dime a dozen. He'd have another one before the week was out. As it happened, he was unemployed for months. His mother tided them over. Marie hated it. She grew querulous and suspicious of his every move. With him home all day, her father had stopped visiting, and she accused him of making the old man feel ill at ease and stupid. "He should be ill at ease, looking down his ignorant nose at me because I can't find a job with any kind of a future." He began to stay out late at night. There was always a party somewhere, and Sam Fermoyle was a riot, the life of every party. She threatened to kill herself because she was convinced he was seeing other women, women in slinky party dresses, women who smoked and drank and read the same books he read, women who lived in nice houses, women who had gone to college like he had, women who thought she was ignorant, which he himself had called her once when he'd been drunk.

With the baby due in a few weeks, his mother had gotten him a job selling real estate for an old friend of the family's. He promised not to drink. He came home every night for dinner. With a paycheck coming in every week, no matter how meager it was, Marie was happy. She painted her nails red, set her hair in bobby pins, cleaned the apartment, spent hours cooking his dinner, and took care to set the table the way he had shown her. She starched his shirts, shined his shoes, and kept lint off his suits. She was sewing little nightgowns for the baby, which she laid out on the bed at night for him to see. He sold a house to a doctor and had his first commission. He left work early to buy flowers for his mother and Marie. His mother wept with pride. She slipped ten dollars into his pocket and told him to hurry straight home to his little wife.

He left his mother's house, his home, and drove slowly toward the cramped apartment that his mother had told him was home, his home on the second floor of a dreary tenement whose halls reeked day and night of soiled diapers and spaghetti sauce. As he drove he imagined Marie's girlish squealing over the flowers as she told him once again how beautiful she was going to make those three narrow rooms for him and the baby, and how they could take the door off their bedroom closet and push one end of the crib into it the way Beryl down the hall had done, and how next week when she had enough saved she would buy some muslin at the dime store and make curtains for the window over the divan. He pictured himself sitting on the musty old sofa from his mother's attic as he waited to eat his wife's insipid dinner while her voice pitched higher and higher with the shrill excitement of a twelve-year-old. And then, after dinner, he would try to read while she listened to the damn radio, sitting in front of it by the hour, her belly bulging with the child that squirmed against his back in bed at night, the child he could not begin to imagine or want, while she stared vapidly at the wooden radio knobs as if this were enough for her, would always be enough.

And so he had parked the car outside a small tavern. He went in for a quick one, and before he knew it, hours had passed, the place was closed, and he was leaning against a trash barrel, fumbling for his car keys, wondering why his new suit pants were wet and clinging to his legs.

When he opened the bedroom door he saw that the bed was empty and hadn't been slept in. She was gone, and he fell asleep, relieved there'd be no scenes. The next morning he woke up coughing and gagging as her father yanked him up by the collar. The old man was bigger than Sam and stood squarely in front of him, his thick arms trembling with rage.

"She's up to the hospital with a baby girl. She was bleeding all night. I sat there all night and watched her almost die with your baby, and then the priest comes and gives her last rites, and then he wants to see the husband, and I says, 'There ain't no husband no more.' " The old man shook him and spat the words into his face. "You hear me, Fermoyle? There ain't gonna be no more husband. You're dead and you'll never hurt her again." The old man's stony fist smashed into Sam's face. He lay on the floor with blood trickling from his mouth and nose, staring dazedly through the open doorway at strangers, his neighbors, who gaped in at him.

He went straight home to his mother's. "Why are you here?" she had said in a voice so distant it seemed to have come from behind a closed door in another room.

"Marie had a baby girl."

"I know," she said. "Mr. Luseau was just here. You have no idea how ashamed I was in front of him."

"He's an ignorant old man, Mother. I'm sorry he upset you."

She stood up then, her unbraided white hair hanging to her waist in thin crimped strands as she leaned on the back of her chair and pointed at him. "You are the ignorant man, Samuel. I don't want to see you again until you've seen your wife and child. Now get out of here!"

"But I don't love her, Mother."

"That doesn't matter now that there's a child. Do you understand?"

Litchfield got up and opened the window to let out some of the smoke. The ashtray was filled with Sam's butts.

"So what're you saying, Sam, you don't want any visitors?"

"Visitors? What do I care about visitors now for? I just don't want her holding things up for me. I just want you to know how much of this is her fault."

"Her fault?" Litchfield cocked his head. "Do you really believe that, Sam?"

"Look, Doc." His fists clenched with Litchfield's condescending expression. "I'm just trying to level with you, that's all, because my thirty days are almost up, and I don't want her or anyone else getting in the way of that."

"Thirty days, Sam!" Litchfield sighed. "Therapy isn't a matter of quantification or fixing blame. It's getting at the whys of your very existence."

"Look, Doc," Sam said, pointing at him. "All I know is, my thirty days are almost up, and I just want to get the hell out of here!"

"Sam, thirty days are nothing. That's our minimum period of observation, unless, of course, a patient has signed himself in with a thirty-day stipulation. I thought you understood. This is a private hospital, not a state institution, and your sister committed you without any stipulations as to time. It takes us thirty days to become familiar with your case. We certainly cannot undo the damage of a lifetime in only thirty days, Sam. There's no Eureka! Now-I-know-what's-wrong-so-I'll-be-on-my-way. This is a very long and delicate process."

The intercom sputtered on. His temples had begun to throb. At Waterbury he had known the rules and what was expected of a drunk. He pressed the heels of his hands against his eyes until the sockets ached. So that's why Helen hadn't sent him to Waterbury, as she had so faithfully done six times in the last ten years. There were walls and guards at Waterbury, but because it was a state hospital there were also rules that unlocked the front gate at the end of thirty days if the doctors thought he had played the game well. Before, no matter how desperate or sick he was, he had always won, once he put his mind to it. But this time they were beating him. His sister, Marie, his children—they had all grown tired of him. Like a scurrilous, untrainable dog, he was being put to sleep. They had slid his noose from their necks and freed themselves of him. They had hidden him here out of mind, out of sight, out of their hearts. He wondered if Helen would spend as much on his funeral as she was willing to pay for his incarceration.

A woman's pleasant voice came over the loudspeaker. Today, she said, was Charlie Skinner's fifty-third birthday, which would be celebrated after dinner with cake and ice cream in the third-floor lounge. Her voice now grew stern. Someone in Bullfinch had removed all the screws from the seats of the scoop chairs in the solarium. Therefore, the solarium and its television would be off limits for all guests until every single screw had been returned.

The announcements over, Litchfield continued. "So, you see, it's not just one thing, one piece of the puzzle. It's the wholeness that matters. It's *all* of the whys."

He drew himself up in the chair. "I'm going to give it to you straight, Litchfield. I have no whys. I live from day to goddamn day, and that's the way it is."

"No man can live that way, Sam. Because to have no *why*, no goal, no meaning, is to cease to be." Litchfield smiled.

"Shit!"

"And once the spirit dies, the body's as good as dead," Litchfield said with a rueful shake of his head.

"Look, Litchfield, go shovel your shit on someone else's grave. I live a very simple life. Two things keep me going. Sometimes it's 'I will not drink.' But most of the time it goes like this, 'I need a drink. I need a drink.' Now, how the hell you expect to find any spiritual truth in that is beyond me. I fall down. I get up. I try again. And each time I try harder than the last time. One of these times I'll make it, but it sure as hell's going to be on my terms, because I made it happen, not because I'm locked up in some nuthouse with a frustrated philosophy professor!" He ground out his cigarette and glared at Litchfield.

Litchfield's eyes gleamed. His nostrils flared with excitement. "Finally, Sam! This is truth!"

"Shit!"

"Yes, for the first time since you've been here, you are trying to elucidate truth."

"Doubleshit!" He threw up his hands and laughed. Litchfield was beaming at him. "Hey! Okay, I'll tell you the honest-to-God truth. You see, a lot of people think I'm a natural-born loser, but actually I can win anytime I want. Okay? You like this, don't you? You see, the trick is I'm a lousy winner, but I'm a hell of a beautiful loser. I am comfortable with defeat. I know it well. I understand pain and anguish. They never pull any punches the way happiness does. You see, when you're happy, you're always looking over your shoulder for the big sucker punch. But hell, when you've been down as low and as long as I've been down, you don't have a worry in the world, because the only way from here is up, right?" He winked. "Not too far, though, because you know the big one's out there just waiting for you to stick your head up out of that hole." He laughed at the brightening in Litchfield's eyes. "Hey, I'm some hot shit all of a sudden, huh? I'm just what the doctor ordered, right, Litchfield? I'll bet you haven't had anyone to play with in a long time. Jesus, are we having fun! Hey, I know! Let's call this game Truth. We can make up a board to play on and print up little cards for each player to pull out of the deck. You know like, uh, 'Anxiety—your boss thinks you're a shithead.' That's minus three points off a hundred, right? And the object of the game, of course, is to get to zero first. After that, you go to the Choice deck and draw another card. Of course in the Choice deck there are only two cards, Overcome or Submit. Right? If you get Overcome you get ten points added onto your starting score of a hundred. If you get the Submit card, then you subtract ten points from your score. In other words, if you win, you lose the game. On the other hand, if you lose, if you get to zero before anybody else does, then you win!

"Jesus, we'll be rich! My wife will love me again. My kids'll stop avoiding me on the street. People from all over the world will be beating down my door, calling me on the phone, screaming from the streets, 'Let us buy Truth, Samuel Fermoyle. Sell it to us!' "

He held out his hand to shake Litchfield's. "And to think I owe it all to you, Arnold. You asked me about truth and I spoke from the bottom of my heart, but did I tell about this terrible boredom? Did I tell you how people bore me, how life bores me, how you bore me, how I bore me, how the only time I'm not bored is when I'm sleeping?" He shook his head, laughing.

"Sleep is just an escape," Litchfield whispered.

"Jesus Christ, my whole life's one big escape, Doc, don't you think I know that?"

"You can change that, Sam."

"Why?" He couldn't help laughing. "For what? For my family? My kids can't stand to be near me more than five minutes at a—"

"That's what I wanted to tell you," Litchfield interrupted. "Your wife said she'd like to bring the children up to see you, but her car is too beat-up to make the trip."

"And of course if I was any kind of a man, she wouldn't be driving around in a junk heap, right?" He smiled and stretched his arms back under his head. "She's quite a woman, isn't she, Doc? She never quits. She has spent her life trying to make me feel guilty. She needs that." He stared out the window at the clear sky. "All right, Dr. Litchfield, you win. How much longer do I have here? Tell me the good news."

"Your daughter, Alice, is coming to visit this Saturday!" Litchfield got up and patted his arm on the way to the closet. He opened the door and removed the decanter and glasses.

"That's the good news?" He felt like crying. "That's what you wanted to tell me?"

"Yes," he said, the decanter clinking against the glasses as he filled them with weak tea. Litchfield raised his glass. "To a very important first step," he toasted. "Come now, Sam," Litchfield chided as he stared up at him.

He picked up his glass and, closing his eyes, took a long sip. If only this were the real thing, then soon nothing would matter, nothing would hurt, certainly not this pounding in his chest, this terrible fear of seeing his own daughter.

B enjy lay on the floor watching television as the shadow of his mother's ironing arm swung back and forth on the opposite wall. Every now and again, he saw her glance toward the bathroom, where Omar was taking a shower. Alice was at work and Norm was out with his friends, so it was a perfect night. Omar was here and his mother was happy. Again, now, Omar burst into the same mighty refrain he had been singing since he turned on the water.

> *"This is the one,*
> *The love I have known.*
> *This is the one,*
> *The love I have sown."*

"Here, Benjy," his mother said, aligning the seams of the ironed pants. She slipped them over the hanger. "Put these in the bathroom for Omar. On the hook," she said, gesturing, then turned modestly away when he opened the door.

Layers of steam floated in the narrow, high-ceilinged bathroom. As he hung the pants, he saw something glisten on top of the sweat-beaded toilet tank. There next to Omar's gold watch was a wad of bills secured by a silver clasp. He stepped closer and saw the ornately engraved *D.*

"And I am a man," boomed Omar's voice from the dripping-wet side of the thin plastic curtain. "With nothing to fear . . ."

He backed out and closed the door.

"Nothing but love!" crooned Omar, holding the last tremulous note.

That was the exact same money clip Omar had him describe to the two black men. But maybe he'd been confused and it was Omar who had the money clip and not the old man's grandson. But it didn't make sense that Omar had all that cash when his constant lament was of a destitution so vast that his mother did Omar's laundry, mending, and ironing, and not only lent him her car and cooked his meals but slipped him change when she thought no one was looking.

Strangely enough, it made him feel better knowing Omar had money, because it meant that Norm was wrong. Omar wasn't after anything after all, not money, anyway. Maybe Omar was afraid that his mother wouldn't feel so sorry for him if she knew he had all that money. That was it! It had to be. The money, the very lie was proof of Omar's veracity.

Omar came out of the bathroom, bearing a bundle of wet towels, his dark hair slicked back, his moist flesh taut and pink. His mother smiled as she absently wrapped the cord around the iron handle. The air stirred and Benjy was conscious of some new presence, an image only they were seeing. She started to fold up the ironing board and Omar reached for it.

"It's the least I can do," he insisted, his hand at his breast. "You have to let me."

"No! You'll just get yourself all mussed up," she protested.

Benjy found this amazing; she was always complaining that no one ever helped her.

"Marie! If I can't help in even these small ways, I mean, think how that makes me feel, how weak, how useless, how . . . how unmanly."

"I'm sorry," she said, tilting the ironing board toward him, letting him fold it and pick it up. "See!" she cried, taking her damp pressing cloth to scrub his lapel, soiled by the black rubber tread of the ironing board. "Benjy," she murmured while Omar stared down at her. "Put the ironing board away." They stood so close their chests touched.

In the back hall he swung the ironing board onto the rusting nails he still remembered her driving, pounding, banging over and over into the wood as she cursed this tiny place, this dump, this cramped and miserable house that had no room for anything but trouble, she had chanted as each blow pulsed through the walls. That's all, just trouble, trouble, trouble, trouble, and more goddamn trouble.

Well, not anymore. Not with Omar here, he thought, looking

outside, giving them enough time for whatever they were doing in there. Klubocks' dog was in the driveway. From its mouth hung a strip of bright cloth. The dog's tail wagged, sweeping a cloud of dust back and forth in the dirt driveway. Klubocks' yard was empty. Louie was playing down the street with the children who were his age. Louie said his father thought Benjy was weird because he liked to talk to him. The Klubocks' back door was open, and Louie's bike lay in the grass. Mr. Klubock must not be home yet. He always made Louie put his toys away. Mrs. Klubock didn't care. She said things always got done. Eventually. Life was too short to worry about every silly little detail. Benjy could see her lighted reflection through her dining-room window and knew she was playing the piano. He opened the door, and the dog lunged in an eager, barking charge. He pulled the door shut. He didn't want his mother to start screaming at the dog in front of Omar. He didn't want Omar to see her upset again. He wanted Omar to love her. He wanted them to be as happy together as they were right now.

The phone rang and his mother answered, assuring the caller that it was fine; she understood. When she hung up she told Omar that Father Gannon couldn't go to Burlington this weekend. The Monsignor had been invited to stay at the Cushing family's summer home at Lake George, which left Father Gannon on duty in the rectory. He'd take Alice to see her father in another week or two.

The glass of water trembled in Omar's hand. "This is a setback, a devastating setback," he sighed.

"But even if Sam could give her anything, it probably wouldn't be for a couple of weeks anyway," his mother said.

Mouth drawn, eyes heavy, Omar nodded wearily. "Yes, with a week or two on top of that." He gave a bitter snort. "Roy Gold won't wait that long. And I don't blame him. Why should he? I mean, who am I when he's got people practically banging down his door to become a distributor."

"There must be some other way," she said.

There was a long pause. Now, Benjy thought, wishing him on with held breath and clenched fists. Now Omar would tell her about his own money. Not to worry, he would say. There's this little nest egg. . . .

"If there is, I don't know about it," Omar sighed.

"What about a bank loan?" she asked, and Omar laughed.

"I have about as much chance—"

"I mean me!" she interrupted, grinning. "I can get the loan."

Omar pulled her close and buried his face in her hair.

Benjy slipped outside. He was puzzled but relieved that Omar hadn't told her about the money. Somehow it was a test. And if his mother did all the right things, if she didn't fly off the handle, if she didn't cry, scream, swear, or break things, then her reward might be happiness, like Mrs. Klubock's, he thought, as the piano lurched into a honky-tonk song, as strangely sad as it was raucous.

The bushes shook as the dog crept out in an eager wiggle. "Hey, hey boy, hey, how ya doin'?" He kneaded the dog's wiry coat with both hands. "Boy, do you smell. Jesus, you stink!" He drew back his hands and smelled the gassy foulness.

Snagged on the bushes was the strip of cloth. He reached, knowing as his fingers passed through air toward the cloth of yellow and red diamonds that it was a pattern like no other, from a shirt he had seen only once before, the same bright shirt he had seen that first warm day, that day in the woods, the day that Omar came. He threw the foul cloth into the bushes and ran into the house.

The next morning, Marie called work to say she'd be late. Omar was driving her to the bank, but she didn't tell Mr. Briscoe that. He was upset enough because it was the first day of his swimwear sale and Astrid had called in sick. Not sick, Marie guessed, but probably hungover now that she was going dancing every night at the Lake Hotel.

While she waited for Omar she watched Benjy at the end of the driveway, slashing a long stick into the lilac bush. Whatever the game was, he played it alone, as usual. His knobby shoulders and round bony head reminded her of Sam. He turned now with a piece of bright cloth dangling from the stick and as he headed behind the house she saw the bandanna tied over his nose. It was all she could do to keep from running out there and ripping it off his face. Why did he do such weird things? Didn't he know people were just waiting for one of her kids to turn out bad: Sister Martin, Helen, Mr. Briscoe, and all the neighbors with their pitying looks and long sighs that meant a boy needs a father, and it was her fault he didn't have one. No, what Benjy needed was a good kick in the ass, which she could deliver as well as any man.

Just then Omar pulled into the driveway. "Good morning, sunshine," he called as she came out the back door.

They parked in front of the bank. Through the window she saw Mr. Hinds lean over a desk, wagging his finger at the woman peering up at him.

"Well!" said Omar, checking his watch. "Here we are, your future at hand."

She took a deep breath, one more, another.

"Don't be so nervous. You're white as a sheet."

"What if they turn me down?"

"Then they turn you down. It's not the only bank in town."

"But a thousand dollars! God, that's so much money."

"Not for a double franchise it isn't. Not for five hundred dollars' worth of product."

"But I can't tell them that."

"No!" Omar laughed, bringing his face close as if she were a child. "But I told you what to do."

She chewed her lip and stared at the ornate gold lettering on the bank's plate-glass windows. They'd turned her down for a mortgage when she first applied. It was only with Renie cosigning the note that she'd finally been approved. What she had to remember, Omar was saying, was simply to tell them the truth, that the loan was for a surefire business opportunity. "That, they'll listen to."

She wasn't so sure. "But what if I do get the loan and the money's all tied up in the franchise and then Alice can't get Sam to give her any money for school? I can't very well come back here and apply for another loan."

"I told you," Omar said. "Your investment will double in less than sixty days."

"How do you know? How can you be so sure?"

"Because I've seen the statistics!" he cried, throwing up his hands. "I've met the sales force!"

"But you've never even sold one of these before!" There. She'd said it. But it was true. His eyes widened. He didn't know what to say. With all his big talk he was just as scared as she was.

He looked at her. "You're right. I haven't."

"For all I know this could be some big swindle here, some . . . some flimflam." Her heart was racing, but it had to be said. Maybe he could afford to take chances, but she had three mouths to feed, three lives that mattered more than anything else.

"Well, if so, then we've both been taken," he sighed. "The two of us. But no matter what happens, at least you've got your job and your family." He reached for her hand. "Do you have any idea what emptiness feels like? To wake up every morning with nothing to look forward to? I've told you before, Marie, I can endure any privation, but not the loss of hope."

She closed her eyes. Hope: God, there was more of that in her veins than blood.

"That's what sets my feet on the floor in the morning and keeps me starting over, day after day after day. Even if everything I touch turns to ashes, hope still keeps me going. I'm a believer, Marie, first, last, and always. I need to have faith. Faith gives me hope. Hope gives me faith. You ask me how I know about these franchises. I can only believe in the people who tell me about them. If I don't, then what do I have? Where do I go?" He gripped her arm. "It's the same way I believe in *you*. That very first moment I saw you, I knew I'd found something." He tapped his breast and lowered his voice. "I knew I'd found someone so unusual, so unique, so genuine, and so rare that I knew if I left, if I kept going, that . . . that something terrible was going to happen to me. It felt like I'd been sent here. That everything I'd ever done in my life had all been geared toward that moment. And there you were. And for the first time in my life I had no choice, absolutely none." He tried to laugh, but his mouth trembled and he looked away. "You know when I said I had no money for a bus out of town? Well, I lied. I had just enough for a ticket."

"Oh no," she said, realizing how close she'd come to never seeing him again. "And then I gave you money and I even drove you there, but the bus had already left."

"No," he said, his head hanging. "I'm ashamed to say I lied about that, too. The bus was due any minute. I couldn't wait to get out of there."

"I remember you were so nervous."

"Nervous! I was shaking. I was dizzy. The whole ride back I had the strangest feeling." He looked at her. "The strangest desire."

Her face burned. She could barely keep her eyes open.

"I wanted to hide, to hide inside you. I had this feeling that I'd finally found something safe and good. Which I have. You are! And I'm not going to do anything to endanger that. This has to feel as right for you, Marie, as it does for me." He turned the key and started to back up.

"But what about the loan?" she called over the racing engine.

"To hell with the loan! I just want you to be happy, that's all." He drove down the street.

"I am! I'm happy!" she insisted as he turned the corner.

"But you're not ready for this. You don't trust it. And because of it, you don't trust me!"

He was driving fast, too fast for these streets. She held on to the door even though the cars both in front and behind were traveling at the same speed. It wasn't him. It wasn't the car.

"No! No, it's not that. It's me. I'm just scared, that's all. I'm so damn scared! And I'm so sick of being scared."

"Is that all?" he called. "Just fear? Puny fear?"

"Yes!"

"Well, now, that's something I can handle, lady. Fear's an old friend of mine. Fear and I have been on intimate terms for more years than I care to remember. You know what they say, don't you? Show me a fearless man and I'll show you a fool."

"I must be a genius, then," she said.

"Yes, because fear can be a good thing. It sharpens the instincts." The tires squealed around the corner. "It heightens the truth."

They were in front of the bank again now, sliding into the

empty space. Without another word, she jumped out and hurried inside.

The minute she left the bank, Omar started the car, and began inching from the space with her approach. "I feel like we just robbed the bank or something," she said, laughing, as he pulled into the traffic.

He looked over, grinning. "You mean you got it? You got the money?"

"No, but I did what you said. I put my fear to work. I went right to the president, Cleveland Hinds, and he said, 'Gosh, Marie, I'd like to help, but we're just not making very many business loans right now.' And all I could hear was this awful roar in my head, and I started to get up and go, and then I said, 'Well, you make loans for home improvements, don't you?' 'Well, yes,' he said. 'We're always doing that. Depending, of course, on the kind of improvements you're talking about.' 'Improvements that are investments in the future,' I said, staring him right in the eye, 'that's what I'm talking about.' 'Sounds good to me,' he said, staring right back, 'but we're going to need something more specific than that on the application, like a new roof, you know, or rewiring, or maybe you're thinking of paving your driveway or finishing the basement off into a rumpus room.' And just like that, I said, 'Rumpus room. And a whole lot of other small jobs, too, like new chimney flashing and some reroofing. And new floor tiles in the kitchen.' " She held up the application. "All I have to do is fill this out and the money's mine."

"What makes you so sure?" Omar asked, trying to sound skeptical through his wide grin.

"Because it was like you said. He does want to help. All he needed was for me to show him how."

"Aren't people wonderful if you just give them half a chance?" He took her hand and held it tightly while he drove her to work.

All the next week she would try to recapture even some of that exhilaration while she waited for the bank to process her application. But every time she thought about the loan, this rushing would start in her ears again. The trouble was that she needed a cosigner. No problem, Mr. Hinds had said, the obvious choice was Renie

LaChance. She'd start to dial Renie's number, then slam down the phone. The last thing she wanted was another favor from her ex–brother-in-law, oh God, with his wet mouth plunging hers, the naked turkey cold against her chest, a disgusting price to pay for kindness. When he'd cosigned the note on her mortgage he seemed to think he was buying himself a family, that he could just show up at midnight with a turkey and be welcomed with a kiss. She'd pushed him down the stairs and thrown his raffle turkey after him. But in the end she'd gotten her revenge when she reported him to the IRS.

So now a week had passed, and she still couldn't bring herself to ask Renie. Typical, she berated herself. Put things off, wait just long enough until she had a disaster on her hands. But then again, she reminded herself, she still didn't know if the bank had even approved her application.

In the meantime she wished Omar wouldn't keep asking about the loan. She didn't want the children to know. They wouldn't understand. They'd misinterpret it the way they did anything connected with Omar. Lately their superior attitudes were starting to wear her down. Astrid was right about one thing. The more she gave, the more they demanded. Because she had devoted her life to her children, they thought they owned her now, thought her every waking moment, every scrap of energy and attention should be theirs.

The back door flew open and Norm rushed in, pulling off his filthy T-shirt. He threw it on the washing machine, then opened the refrigerator. "Hi, Mom," he said, turning with a bottle of milk and loaf of bread. He kicked the door shut, then reached past her and took a glass from the cupboard. She looked up with the sudden realization that he was a head taller than she was. His chest was broad, his arms newly muscular.

"Guess what I just heard. Weeb says Father Gannon's mental."

"Your friend Weeb should talk—anyone who'd blow up a cat." She stared at the meatball she was rolling, at the grease coating her palms.

"Why do you always bring that up? Why do you always have to say things about people I like? Besides, he didn't actually blow up the cat. He was just tryna have some fun."

"Some fun?" She looked at him.

"Jeez, Mom, he was twelve years old!" he said, pouring his milk.

"Give the guy a break, will you? It's not like he was in some loony bin, some funny farm, like the priest there, Father Gannon!"

"Like your father," she said.

He glanced at her. "Why'd you say that?"

To take the wind out of your huge sails, she thought. *To cut you down to size.* To hurt him, she knew, and could not understand why.

A little while later Omar came through the door, asking the same question he asked every night. "Did you hear anything? Did the bank call?"

"Not yet," she said, turning up the burner. He was in a rush again. If she wanted them to eat together, she'd have to speed things up. The spaghetti sauce bubbled to a boil, so she stirred rapidly to keep it from burning.

"Maybe you should call and make sure nothing's wrong." Omar opened the bag of bread Norm had left on the counter.

"What could be wrong?" she asked. Hot sauce splattered her forearm.

He shrugged. "Maybe some of your verifications—I don't know." He folded a slice of bread, which he dipped into the sauce. He ate it dripping over the pot.

"No," she said. "You know how many times I went over everything."

He redipped the bread, so sodden now that a chunk broke off into the pot. She tried to skim it out with the spoon, but it disintegrated into the sauce. She never would have allowed her children to do that. "And you even checked it all," she reminded him.

His chin glistened with bright red dots. Now he took a crust from the bag. He seemed preoccupied, uneasy. ˙

"You said you went over all the figures." She kept stirring. "Were any of them wrong?"

He dunked the crust until it bloated with sauce. "Nothing major," he said. "Just a few things here and there." He bent over the pot and slurped at the dripping crust.

"What do you mean a few things here and there? You said everything looked fine!" she said, frightened by the shrillness, the familiar bitterness in her voice.

"Well, I didn't want to worry you."

"Didn't want to worry—"

"No. No. Now listen! I already took care of it. A few changes here and there, that's all, some adjustments. No big deal."

"Changes, what kind of changes?" Hands shaking, she turned off the burner and laid down the spoon. "I mean, all my expenses, my income, I had everything down. I couldn't have made a mistake. I know I couldn't."

"The income was too low. It just needed a little . . ." He smiled and leaned close. "Help," he whispered.

"What do you mean?" She spoke carefully because something sharp and hard and deadly like a bone or shard of glass lay across her throat. A single word might dislodge it.

"I colored in the background a little," he said.

She shook her head. Colored in the background? What did that mean?

He grinned. "I changed a few things here and there, that's all." With a flourish as if he were daubing paint on air, he said, "See, a little gray here, a little red here, a little green. I prettied it up."

"I can't believe you did that," she said, hugging her arms against the shudder of a chill. In the other room Norm was telling Benjy that Father Gannon had been in a mental hospital. She turned and saw that the table sagged in the middle. She tried to concentrate on what Omar was saying. She kept wondering why the table sagged like that. Was it the extra plate every night, the weight of his arms?

"Look, no harm done. It's the American way. Everybody's expected to shoot some bull—enough, anyway, to offset the other guy's." Now he was stirring the sauce, the spoon cutting through the oily red thickness. "You're doing them a favor, that's all. They want to make the loan, and you've just saved them some steps."

I did? she thought. Me?

He shook basil into the pot, then garlic powder, then black pepper. He stirred them a moment, then sipped from the edge of the spoon. "I don't know. It needs a lift, something." He glanced back. "Got any oregano?"

———

The bank called the next morning. Her home-improvement loan had been approved. The papers could be signed in three days. "And is that also a good time for Mr. LaChance?" asked the loan officer.

"Yes," she said, and the minute she hung up she dialed Renie's number before she could change her mind.

" 'Ello," he answered breathlessly on the first ring. "LaChance Appliance Company! Renie LaChance speaking!"

She closed her eyes, repelled by his eagerness, the hunger she remembered.

" 'Ello! 'Ello!" he kept calling. "Who is this? What do you want? This is Renie LaChance! Is that who you want? You want me? You want Renie LaChance?" he was shouting as she hung up.

The next morning she called from work, then hung up again, and as her ears rang with his desperate demand to know who was doing this, she made up her mind. She would ask Mr. Briscoe to cosign the note. If he'd said it once, he'd said it a hundred times: anytime he could help her, anything he could do, just let him know. She trusted Mr. Briscoe's judgment. She was even tempted to tell him about the soap franchises, except that, shrewd businessman that he was, he'd probably buy them all up himself. She waited until he'd finished his coffee before she went up to his office.

"I don't know," he said when she finished. "Seems like real poor timing to me, Marie. I mean a rumpus room with all you've got going right now, kids to raise and Alice going off to college, not to mention that old clunker you're driving." His chair squeaked as he swiveled away from the one-way glass. He had been watching Morton, the bicycle salesman, trail two boys through the store. He squinted up at her. "Speaking of which, you sell your car? Twice this week I could've sworn I saw that old Chevy, but there was this fellow driving it. Big guy, black hair."

"A friend of mine's been using it. His own car's not running right," she said, smiling, relieved to finally speak of him.

Mr. Briscoe adjusted his glasses. "Hmm, don't know him," he said upon hearing Omar's name.

"He's not from around here," she said.

He nodded. "Well, that explains it, then. You maybe oughta clue your friend in."

"About what? What do you mean?"

"About that . . . that, well, that Bernadette Mansaw I've seen him with."

"Oh! Well, that's just some business thing," she stammered, her face flushing.

"Monkey business if it's a Mansaw," Mr. Briscoe said with a sly grin.

"Mr. Duvall is a businessman like yourself, Mr. Briscoe! And just like you can't control who shops down there in your store, he can't stop people from investing in his company." Her mouth was so dry her lips kept sticking together.

"What's his company? The A&P?" Mr. Briscoe scoffed. "That's where I saw them, loading groceries in your car."

O mar Duvall felt drained. He had spent most of the day in pay phones trying to get through to Roy Gold, who finally came on the line after he told Gold's secretary that he had "spectacular, absolutely fabulous news."

"Wait, wait, wait, wait!" Gold interrupted. "This is fabulous news? That some woman's got an appointment at a bank?"

He tried to explain that at nine o'clock tomorrow morning Marie would be signing the note for money to buy two franchises.

There was a pause, then Gold sighed. "Don't you understand? That's just another promise, another maybe, Mr. Duvall. You see, right now, at this very moment, I have hundreds of men out in the field doing, I repeat, *doing* the very thing you only want to talk about. And that's selling, Mr. Duvall. Actually *selling* franchises. I'm a very busy man, Mr. Duvall. In fact right now, at this very moment, there are twenty different lines all lit up here, calls from all over the world. England, Germany, Europe, France. Montana! God almighty, now Montana's just come on! Miss Handy"—he yelled away from the phone—"take care of Montana, will you? No matter what, this country comes first!

"You see, Mr. Duvall, these are all my district distributors and franchisers trying to call in orders, real orders, while we're chit-chatting about maybes and promises. No! No, Mr. Duvall! This is for real! I've got a huge operation to run here. I thought you understood that. We may look small, but this isn't some two-bit, penny-ante front job I'm running here. This is global, Mr. Duvall, *global!*"

"I know that, sir!" he said quickly. "I just didn't want you to think I wasn't trying, that I'd given up and gone away or anything."

"Look, Mr. Duvall, I like you, and I have faith in you. A man like you could have a great future here, but God almighty, man, you've got to come cash in hand to prove it. Do you understand, Omar? Cash in hand!"

Yes sir, cash in hand, he thought as he drove, more determined than ever to prove himself to Roy Gold. As of tomorrow morning he'd finally have a future. With Marie's money he'd finally be in on the ground floor of something as big and as innovative as Presto Soap. Gold was right. The days of maybes and promises were over. He wasn't getting any younger. Lately there were too many days when every bone in his body ached, when he was almost too tired to talk or even think, which was the way he felt now as he pulled into Marie's driveway. He got out of the car with a groan and rubbed his back, then sniffed the air. He could smell onions frying and green peppers. Adjusting his tie, he hurried up the back steps. Marie stood in the doorway and held out her hand.

"Marie!" he said, reaching for her hand with a glance beyond into the redolent kitchen.

"Give me back my keys!" she demanded, batting away his hand. "And then I want you out of here!"

He was stunned, and yet it was all so familiar he could close his eyes and recite every line of her venomous charges. It would get ugly now. It always did, but in the end he would be relieved. Freedom had its price, but all it ever took was a few miles before the disappointment sloughed off like scaly old skin and hope infused his pores with the prickly tenderness of healing flesh. She had trusted him, and now she wanted him out of her life forever. Forever, forever, forever: the reverberation throbbed in his bones. But what about their business? There was no business, just talk, and talk was cheap. Talk was shit.

She had children to take care of, and she had no time for any more of his talk or his shit. But he could explain. She didn't want to hear it. She wanted him to go. She kept saying it. Go, just go. His chin trembled. His voice cracked. He had never felt so alone. She looked surprised; welcome to the club. But he had no one. Well, that was his fault, wasn't it? But where would he go; what would he do? She didn't care what he did or where he went, but she wanted him off her property right now, this minute. He didn't dare move. Even if he wanted to, he couldn't.

"I can't," he said in a voice. "I need you. You're my future. You're everything."

He was in the kitchen now, trying to convince her that his relationship with Bernadette Mansaw was purely business, which in a sense it was, he thought, because beyond the satisfaction of his more base needs, she meant nothing to him.

Arms folded, shoulders hunched, Marie stared over the table. "Purely business," she repeated. "Oh, so that's why you went to the A&P together! Well, that explains everything. Now I understand." She nodded. "Of course, business! After all, anytime Mr. Briscoe tries to sell someone an outboard motor or an archery set, the first place they go is the A&P."

He sighed. "What you have to understand is that going to the A&P was a desperate measure."

"Why?" she demanded. "Why desperate?"

"Well . . ." He sighed again and for a moment wasn't sure. He felt tired again, very, very tired, he thought, closing his eyes on this wounded woman hungering for persuasion in her dull kitchen that reeked of grease and more neglect than he could ever resolve.

"Tell me," she insisted. "Look at me and tell me!"

Opening his eyes, he saw how near the edge he was, flesh-bound and artless, his cuffs soiled and frayed, his damp limbs heavy against their French seams. Once, in such cornered moments, grace would have come, an infusion of spirituality he felt only then, when his soul soared and he knew and saw and heard what others could not. It was inconceivable that he had been delivered from every hardship and adversity to have it all end, not in beauty or love or fortune, but in a petty, mud-grunting struggle with Earlie. Had that futile wallow been the quest every day, every mile of his way? Had he been buffeted and tumbled through life for that?

"Why desperate?" she said through clenched teeth.

No, it was more than that, because he was more than just a speck in time, an idea, an amusement, a conceit of some vain and twisted higher consciousness. Yes, he thought, feeling the heaviness subside, it really was quite simple. "Desperate," he mused. "I had been desperate, I felt desperate because . . . because right on the verge of signing a franchise contract, Miss Mansaw went and got cold feet." He sat back with a look of disbelief. "She insisted on comparing the price of supermarket detergent with my product, Presto Soap." Yes! Yes, that was it, of course, he thought, buoyed by her relief as she sighed and ran her hand through her hair.

"And I suppose while you were there on business, she just happened to buy her groceries!" Marie sniffed.

"Yes!" he cried, awed by the facile logic of the tale and, once again, his skill, his power as its teller. Of course Bernadette might have, could have, so therefore had done, just such a thing. "She's precisely that kind of young woman, capricious"—Marie blinked, and he knew the minute he left she would be at the dictionary—"and coarse, and selfish, but of necessity," he added. "After all, she's got two kids to feed and there she was in a supermarket when she needed groceries."

"Which you carried out to *my* car!"

"Marie, oh Marie! What could I do? I'm a gentlemàn. I'm chronically polite. I'm incapable of hurting anyone."

"But you hurt me. Doesn't that matter?" She stared, her gaze so keen it seemed to pour into him.

It mattered. Of course it mattered. Looking at her, he felt his chest expand with a sense of abundance, of himself filling the night. "I need you," he said, almost crushing her in his arms. "I need you, Marie," he whispered, meaning more than she could understand, because what he needed was beyond flesh or love. What he needed, what he most craved, was her eager faith to continue providing his words with resolve and, ultimately, with truth.

———

Later, as he drove, the night cooled, sagging low with bright stars that flooded every street and yard. He drove past the boardinghouse.

The television was on in Bernadette's apartment. He crept by the couch where she lay curled, snoring with her mouth open. Her shiny slip sagged below one breast. He tiptoed into the bedroom and closed the door. He sat on the edge of the bed and removed his shoes, setting them down without a sound. He undressed, then crawled between the gritty sheets, wincing with each creaking spring. He closed his eyes and slept.

It was the middle of the night when she knelt over him.

"I thought something happened," she whispered, stroking his arms, his legs, his chest, and now his belly. "I told my mother I'd get the kids tomorrow." Her hair whisked his face as she kissed his throat, his chin, his mouth.

Clutching the cold bedpost while she nibbled his earlobes, he drifted in and out of sleep and the glow of Luther's and the Reverend's eyes through an old dream, dark and speechless.

"I went looking for you," she said with a slurp in his wet ear. "The lady at the boardinghouse said maybe you were outta town on business."

"Umm, lady at the boardinghouse," he muttered. His eyes opened wide.

"Yah, 'Or maybe at Marie Fermoyle's,' she said. Why there?"

"She's an investor," he said, pulling the sheet to his chest. "And please don't go tracking me down me again like that. I told you before, this is a small town and I have to be very, very circumspect."

She sat up and folded her arms. "What's that mean? Embarrassed? Ashamed?"

"Careful," he said, reaching to touch her face. "Extremely careful." Her cheek was cold.

She looked down at him. "Omar?" Her voice trembled. "Who's car's that you drive?"

"One of my investors. I already told you that."

"Yah, but the way you said it, I thought you meant some guy."

"Well, it's not," he sighed. "It's Mrs. Fermoyle, who as of tomorrow morning will be my very first franchisee."

"Jeez!" she squealed happily. "Well, let's celebrate, then! C'mon!" She tugged on the sheet.

"I'm really very tired," he said, anchoring it at his chin.

"Are you and her, you know, are you doing it?"

"What? For God's sake, child, the woman is an associate, a respected member of the business community, a vital link in my franchising network. Please!" He shuddered.

"So. You could still be doing it."

"Bernadette, listen to me. I swear to you. On my honor, Mrs. Fermoyle and I are not *doing it*. *You* and *you* alone are the only one I *do* it with."

"Yah? Well, anyway, I wish I could be your first franchisee," Bernadette said, pouting.

"Well, you can be my second, dear."

"Yah! With what, my good looks?"

He glanced up at the sound of a car slipping into the alley. The window swelled with light. The car idled a moment, then backed out. "Who's that?"

"I don't know." She yawned. "My X-ray vision's a little off tonight."

He grabbed her wrist. "Don't you be flip with me! Did you tell anyone I come here?"

"No! I swear! I said I wouldn't and I haven't! Honest!" she cried, pulling away from him. "It's probably just the cops. Sometimes they check the back door of the fruit store."

The cops. He jumped up and crept from window to window. He ran down the hallway and stood on the wooden landing. Except for Marie's car and a jumble of crates, the alley was empty. His heart was racing. The biggest mistake would be to start thinking everyone was after him. He assured himself that he hadn't made a false step in this town. Not a single law had been broken. This was his fresh start, the reason, the justification, for every other fiasco. The old ways were over. Now he would do it with honesty and hard work.

He came back to bed, apologizing and trying to explain what a bad day he'd had. "I finally get there with the papers and it's the night before the loan and Mrs. Fermoyle goes and gets cold feet. It took me hours! Hours! I thought I was going to jump right out of my skin. There weren't—"

"Omar?" she interrupted. "How could I be your second franchisee? What'd you mean by that?"

"Well, it would probably take a little juggling of the figures, but it looks like I'm going to make enough cash off Mrs. Fermoyle to maybe—just maybe, now—eke out a franchise for you. Provided," he said over her squeals, "provided you can come up with *some* money. Maybe, I don't know, fifty, seventy-five? Could you manage that?"

"Maybe!" she cried, collapsing next to him.

"But of course Mrs. Fermoyle can't know any of this. That, you see, is being circumspect."

"I don't even know Mrs. Fermoyle," she said. "But I know her kids."

"What do you mean, know them?" he gasped as she curled close, her face in the crook of his arm.

"I mean I know who they are. Alice and me were in the same grade. She was always real quiet, one of those goody-goodies." She slid her hand down the front of his shorts.

"Not like you," he muttered, spreading his legs.

"Yah, and her brother, he tried to put the make on me."

"What? He what?" He kept trying to sit up, but she had climbed on top of him.

"Yah, but that was before I knew you." She was licking his mouth. "So how would I come up with the money?"

"What about your diamond?" he said, feeling it graze his thigh.

"I couldn't do that," she gasped, pulling away. "That's my engagement ring from Kyle!"

Marie couldn't stop shivering in the bank's air-conditioned conference room with its marble walls and high paneled ceiling. Opposite her at the long oak table were Jim Hubbard, the senior loan officer, and Cleveland Hinds in their dark suits, white shirts, and striped ties. Grunting from line to line, Hubbard read another form, which he passed to Hinds for his elaborate signature.

Hubbard glanced up at her. "Will Renie be here soon?" He slid over another paper, and Hinds's pen scratched his name.

"Umm. No, he won't be," she said, trying to clear the nervous tickle in her throat.

Both men looked at her.

"You see, I'd really like to do this myself. You know, to keep my business to myself," she tried to explain, squirming under their gaze. "I mean, I have a good job and my own car and, you can check for yourself, I just finished off paying on the refrigerator, and right now the only money I owe is Dr. Yale and really, that's my son's—"

"It's out of the question," Hubbard sputtered, gathering up the papers. He held them against his chest. "I'm really rather surprised, Mrs. Fermoyle. I thought I'd made everything quite clear." He slid the papers into a folder, to which he gave a sharp tap for proper alignment before pushing back his chair.

He couldn't be leaving. No, this couldn't be it. "Wait!" she said, hitting the table as he stood up. "I need this loan!"

"You *need* a cosigner," snapped Hubbard.

"Why? I've never once been late with a mortgage payment, you know that! That house is all I've got. I'd never let anything endanger that," she said, her voice rising.

"Now, Marie." Hinds sighed. "What can I say? This is the way we do it. This is the way it's done. This is the way!" He threw up his hands. "We know you're a good person, a hard worker. But the only income you've got is your own. Someone in your circumstances needs a cosigner, someone who'll—"

"My circumstances? You mean because I don't have a husband?"

"Yes," said Hinds with a smile and a grateful nod.

"Because I'm divorced." She stared at him.

"Well, now, not just that you're divorced. It would be the same if you were a widow. It's because you're a woman alone. And a woman alone is a woman in tenuous circumstances and therefore needs a cosigner, someone who'll pay the bank if you should get sick or laid off or if you can't pay." He took a breath. "Nine times out of ten it doesn't matter. It's really just a name on the dotted line, you know, to satisfy the auditors and all the darn government regulations."

"So in other words, it's like a formality," she said slowly, taking care both to decode his message and show that she understood.

"A formality," he mused. "Well, I suppose, in a sense."

"So what you need is Renie's signature on those forms?" She watched his face, relieved when he smiled and nodded. "Can I take the forms over to Renie?" she asked him.

"I'm afraid not," Hubbard spoke up. "Bank regulations mandate these be signed in person."

"But that way," she tried to explain, "he won't have to close up the store, and I won't have to take time off work to come back, and you won't have to take up any more—"

"Hell, what's the harm?" Hinds interrupted, with a sour glance at the piqued Hubbard.

"Just drive around the block a minute," Marie told Omar. "Go slow now," she muttered as she signed "Renie LaChance," on both documents. "It's just a formality," she said, uneasy with his silence. "Besides, it's not as if he'd even care."

When she returned to the bank, Cleveland Hinds was alone in the conference room. With Hubbard gone, something had changed. Hinds seemed more subdued, distracted. Had it occurred to him that she might have forged Renie's name? Forgery! The word's reality stung her cheeks. Hubbard was probably calling Renie right now. Then he'd call the police. She held her breath as Hinds glanced at the forms. The check was being prepared, he said in a soft voice. If she had to get to work, she could pick it up later.

Later! He was obviously stalling for time. Oh God, she never should have done it. What had she been thinking of? If she could only get the forms back, she'd rip them up and never do anything like this again.

"I'll wait, if you don't mind," she said in a small voice.

"Mind! Heavens no! It'll give me a chance to find out how things've been going for you lately."

"Oh, pretty good."

"That's all? Just pretty good?" He smiled and slid the forms into the folder.

"Very good, actually," she said, relieved to see him push aside the folder. "Now with the refrigerator paid off. And the car's running okay." She knocked on the tabletop. "And the two oldest have jobs this summer, Norm and Alice. And Benjy's taking swimming lessons.

He's always been afraid of water. Mr. Briscoe wants to take him fishing. He's such a nice man. Such a good businessman." She was beginning to babble with his eyes boring into her like this. "I couldn't ask for a better boss."

"That's good to hear. But how're things with you? I mean with you personally, Marie."

"Everything's fine," she said stiffly.

"I know it must be difficult with three children, but do you ever go out?"

She froze. She had been right. This was a trap.

"You're a very interesting woman," Hinds said. He kept smiling at her, trying to give her time to confess, to stop this fraud before it went any further.

"You know, Renie didn't really read any of those papers," she blurted, gesturing at the folder. "Maybe I should take them back and tell him to read them. I really rushed him. I've had so much on my mind lately."

Hinds chuckled. "About the most the women I know ever have on their minds is a hat." He reached across the table and patted her hand. "The papers are fine," he whispered. "Don't worry about them."

"I just want everything to be done right," she said, not moving.

His hand covered hers. "And I just want to get to know you better, Marie. How do you feel about that?" He stared at her.

"Well, I'm awfully busy and . . ." Shocked, she pulled away her hand. "And you're married!" Not just married, but, my God, married to Nora Cushing, who'd been engaged to Sam.

His cool gaze warmed with amusement. "And I'm a very nice man, too. And a very good businessman." He grinned. "We'll have a lot to talk about."

Omar hadn't wanted to take her check from the bank, but she was glad she'd insisted. One thousand dollars had obviously snagged Roy Gold's attention. For the last three days Omar had been in Connecticut, where Gold was giving him a personal run-through of the whole operation from top to bottom. Marie was cooking dinner when Omar called to say he'd have to spend at least one more day there.

"He's showing me everything," Omar said, "the plant, executive offices, his suite, the distribution . . ."

"What's that?" she interrupted, straining to hear.

"What? I don't hear anything."

"Sounds like a little kid crying."

"Must be crossed lines again. You really ought to have your phone checked. For all you know, somebody's listening in on your calls."

"But all they keep hearing is me being stood up again." She laughed uneasily. He had promised to come to dinner tonight with the paperwork for her two franchises.

"I wish you could see this, Marie, the people here just hanging on my every word," Omar whispered into the phone.

"I should hope so, with all the money you're giving them." All your money, she expected him to say.

"Well, this is a different element now," he said with the hushed urgency of a reporter calling from the midst of some tumultuous event. "These are the men that make the world turn, and they don't do it with small talk."

"Are you coming back tomorrow?"

"I hope so. There's so much to learn. I can't keep all the different solvents straight, much less all the new business terms," he said. In the background there was a woman's sudden laugh.

"Where are you calling from?" she asked, hating the shrillness that betrayed her fear, her certainty that in the end no man could be trusted because she herself was so inadequate.

"Somebody's office, I'm not sure whose. I've met so many different people."

"What's the number there?"

"I'm not sure. Let me see here. . . ." In the pause came a rustling sound. "Well, I'll be . . . it doesn't say. That's strange."

"There must be a phone in another office," she said, her temples pulsing with the old dread. He seemed so far away. When Sam was drinking she never knew where he was.

"They're all locked, though."

"Where are you staying?"

"Tonight I'm not sure. I couldn't get my room back at the motel. Why, Marie? Did something happen? Is anything wrong? Is anyone looking for me? Do you want me to come back? I'll tell Gold some other—"

"No! Oh no, no, don't! Don't change anything. Just do what you have to."

"I miss you," he said.

Her eyes filled with tears. "I miss you, too," she said, looking up as Norm's bright whistle carried down the street. She quickly removed Omar's place setting from the table.

At dinner Norm had seconds of everything, but Benjy only picked at his food. He kept glancing at Omar's empty chair. Norm was telling them how every time Joey Seldon complained about his popcorn stand Jarden Greene made sure he accompanied the laborer who would be repairing it. Aside from these tales about Greene, Norm seldom complained about his job anymore. He liked his work crew, especially his foreman, Kenny Doyle. She could see how much he enjoyed not having Omar here. He had the floor to himself again. "When something breaks, like today it was the whole front counter, Greene says, 'Don't rip it out. Just nail a new board over it.' "

A car pulled into the driveway, and Benjy looked toward the door. Outside, Harvey Klubock was clapping his hands, calling the dog.

"What's the matter, Benjy?" she asked.

"Nothing." He shrugged.

"One of these days you'll go up and find the whole thing boarded up," Norm was saying. "Just this little hole for Joey to stick his hand through." He plopped more mashed potatoes onto his plate. Tanned and with his hair streaked blond from the sun, he was becoming a handsome young man, she thought. Now when he came into the office Astrid flirted with him. Compared to his brother, Benjy looked peaked, almost sickly. Last night he'd run downstairs after another one of his nightmares. She'd found him on the couch watching television with all the lights on. He pushed back his plate now. He had hardly eaten.

"Omar called," she said, watching Benjy. "He's coming back tomorrow!"

"He is?" Benjy grinned.

"He has to spend another day with the company president." Repeating everything he'd said made her so happy she felt light-headed. "They've got all these solvents and each one has its own ingredients. And Omar has to learn what's in each one. The chemical names." He hadn't actually said this, but she was sure it was true.

Norm had been looking at her. "Where is this soap place?"

"Connecticut," she said, pushing Benjy's plate back. "Come on, Benjy, finish up." She snapped her fingers, and Benjy picked up his fork.

"Didn't he say where in Connecticut?" Norm asked.

"Hartford," she lied, rather than admit she still didn't know.

"How'd he get there?" Norm asked.

"On the bus."

"The bus! Boy, that must really impress everyone." Norm laughed as he reached for the last slice of bread. " 'Course he probably said it's his own private Greyhound."

She folded her hands over her plate and took a deep breath.

"They took his car, Norm! It's not his fault," Benjy said quickly, looking between the two of them.

"Yah, that's *his* story," Norm said.

"No, it's true. They did. They were looking for him. There was this old Negro man with white, white hair and the other one, he was young, and they were driving Omar's station wagon. They were!"

"When?" she and Norm both asked.

"That day. When he came." Benjy's eyes darted between them.

"What do you mean, white, white hair, how do you know?" Norm asked the very thing she was wondering.

"I guess Omar told me." Benjy shrugged. "I don't know, maybe I just thought so because he said one of them was real old. Remember? He said that."

She looked away. She hated seeing him squirm like that, his shirt collar hanging off his bony shoulder, his eyes, cornered and miserable because Norm had caught him trying to defend Omar.

"I saw Uncle Renie today," Benjy said quickly. "He bought me a piece of cake."

"Uncle Renie!" Norm said. "Don't tell me you're hanging out with him now!"

"No, I went to see his cat, but his sign said he'd be back at two, and it was almost two, so I walked down to the luncheonette—"

"Two!" she snapped. "But don't your swimming lessons start at one forty-five?" She watched him shrink into the chair. "Did you have a swimming lesson today?"

He stared at the table.

"Did you?"

"No."

"How many lessons have you had so far?"

He shrugged.

She watched him. "You never signed up, did you? You lied to me! Benjy, come here," she said, gesturing.

"Shit," Norm muttered, pushing his plate away.

Wincing, Benjy stood in front of her.

She put her hands on his sweaty shoulders and could feel the same caged tension as in his father's bones. "What are you so afraid of?" she asked, struggling to stay calm. "I wouldn't let anything happen to you."

She blamed herself for their fears. They had seen her hope for too long for Sam's recovery. With each birth, each new job, the separation, the divorce, with her tears, with her love, and with every denial she had continued to plumb him, sinking deeper each time in the search for his decency, his strength, his love, drowning, pulling her children after her, instructing them not with words but with example and the tenacity of her hope that if they loved him enough, if they were patient enough, if *they* were good enough, and kind enough, and forgiving enough, then he would not drink again. He would mend his life and theirs.

But she was beyond that now, beyond believing in broken things. Her future extended past this narrow yard, this town, those mountains. Omar had brought her the world. He had been places, seen things. He knew people. He was making her feel young again and whole. Less and less this sexless man-woman, every day she grew more conscious of the weight of her breasts, her firm thighs and slim hips, along with this longing, this ache in her heart and her belly.

T he next day his mother picked him up on her lunch break and they rode in silence to the municipal pool, which stood higher than the road, a colossal bowl of blue water, deep, deep blue water. Benjy hadn't slept most of last night, dreading this very moment, his mother in her wrinkled skirt, her worn brown pumps skimming over the slimy concrete to Mr. Tuck, who sat behind the counter on a tall metal stool, purveyor of the hundreds of mesh baskets in the wall grid behind him. Each basket held a swimmer's clothes. Down here below the pool, the air reeked of mildew and rancid sneakers. His mother leaned over the counter and said she wanted to sign him up for lessons. That would be twenty-five cents a day, Mr. Tuck explained, fifteen cents for the lesson and ten cents basket rental.

She glanced at Benjy, who was wearing his bathing suit under his pants. "You don't need a basket, do you?"

"He needs one," sighed Mr. Tuck as he removed an empty basket and set it on the counter.

"But he's already got his suit on. I can take his clothes with me," she said.

Benjy looked at her. Didn't she care that he'd have to walk the three miles home in a wet bathing suit with no shirt on? No, she wouldn't. He could see that.

"His sneakers." Mr. Tuck smirked. "Or is he gonna go home barefoot?" He was a teacher. During the summer he ran the pool.

"I didn't even think of that," Marie said with a nervous laugh as she gave him a dime.

Three girls had just come in. They waited as Mr. Tuck handed Benjy his numbered metal disk that matched the number on his bas-

ket. The disk was clipped to a big safety pin that attached to his bathing suit. Mr. Tuck explained that if the disk fell off in the water, he'd
have to keep swimming around the bottom of the pool until he found
it, or else he wouldn't get his clothes back. Benjy fastened his pin and
then he couldn't stop checking it.

"Intermediate?" Mr. Tuck was flipping through the water-curled
pages of the lesson book.

"He can't swim at all," his mother said. "He's afraid of water,"
she added in a voice that echoed off the damp concrete walls, "Afraid
afraid of water water water."

"He's afraid of water," hissed the little girl behind him.

"Shh," said her older sister.

"Beginner, then." Mr. Tuck turned a page. "Fermoyle," he repeated when Marie gave the name. "You work at Briscoe's, don't
you?" he asked, extending his hand. "Dave Tuck. Ferd Briscoe's my
wife's uncle, her mother's brother."

Benjy's hair stood on end. Mr. Briscoe, who wanted to take him
out on the lake fishing, just happened to be related to Mr. Tuck. It
was some kind of weird water conspiracy, and his mother was part of
it. Mr. Tuck grinned at him, and he tried to smile back.

As he went through the showers on his way to the pool, he could
hear Mr. Tuck calling after his mother, "Don't worry. He's in good
hands. We'll take care of him ... have him swimming like a
fish. ..."

The water in the crowded pool churned with twisting, flipping,
glistening bodies. The announcement came over the loudspeaker that
the beginners' lessons were starting, but Benjy didn't move. He sat on
the lower pipe railing with his arms looped over the hot top rail so no
one could push him in like they'd done last year. He watched the lessons from his perch, and when they were over he ran all the way
home.

Omar didn't come for dinner that night, or the next. Marie's face
was drawn and her hands shook as she put milk on the table. When
Norm asked where Omar was, she turned back to the stove, whipping the potatoes to a gluey thickness.

"How did the swimming go?" she asked while they ate.

"Good," Benjy said.

She nodded and said no more except for sighs that ended in little cries that gouged so many pieces from his own heart that his chest began to ache.

Every time the phone rang he saw how still she sat, how she seemed to stop breathing. Omar hadn't called in days.

It was late and Benjy couldn't sleep. The moonlit night was ripe with the smell of skunk and from a nearby street a dog howled.

At midnight Norm came home with Alice. Downstairs, chairs scraped over the floor and the refrigerator opened and closed. Glasses and milk bottles rattled on the counter. In his bed Benjy sniffed hungrily at the hamburg and French fries that Alice was smuggling out nightly for Norm. They whispered and laughed softly together.

The toilet flushed. Water splashed. Again the toilet flushed. Pipes clanged in the walls. The lights went out. For a time there was quiet and then he heard muffled sobs from the next room. "Oh God," his mother wept. "What am I going to do? Help me. Please help me."

A week had passed with no word from Omar. Benjy went to the pool every day, paid his money, then twined himself around the hot railing, watching until the lesson was over. His mother had finally stopped asking about the lessons, so on Thursday he didn't go. Tonight when supper was over she said she wanted him to go for a walk with her. She walked quickly and hardly spoke to him. He was convinced that she'd found out about the lessons and was taking him up to the pool, where she'd probably push him into the deep end and make him swim back. As they came along Main Street she kept staring ahead toward the distant boardinghouse, where the old woman, May Mayo, was sitting on the porch. His mother stopped and asked if Mr. Duvall was home. She was smiling, but Benjy could see the cords tighten in her neck as May Mayo said she hadn't seen Mr. Duvall in almost two weeks now, but that she'd certainly tell him Mrs. Fermoyle was looking for him. Yes, just as soon as she heard from him. "Which better be soon," she whispered as she leaned over the rail. "He's only paid up three more days, and my sister doesn't much like him, you know. She says he's a fast-talking salesman, and Claire hates salesmen, you know."

They turned the corner and headed back home. "If he doesn't come back, I don't know what I'll do," she gasped, quickly covering her mouth. She began to walk so fast he had trouble keeping up with her.

Later, he heard cries from her room. "Oh my God, he's never coming back," she sobbed, and he lay in his bed crying, too. Something terrible had happened to Omar, and without him something terrible would happen to his mother.

His mother was late for work and the car keys were missing. Norm had already searched the house for them, and now he was outside on his hands and knees looking under the car. Alice had just come downstairs in her nightgown. She was positive she could remember Norm carrying the keys into the house last night. "We sat here and ate," she said, yawning as she sagged into a chair at the table.

Marie stood in the kitchen doorway in her slip while she brushed her teeth, telling them through the foamy toothpaste dribbling down the corners of her mouth that here she was, late for work again because of their carelessness. She spit into the sink, then threw down her toothbrush. How the hell would they like it if Mr. Briscoe fired her for being late all the time? What would they do then? She pounded the tabletop. How would they eat? How would they keep a roof over their heads?

"Mom," Alice said. "Please, Mom, don't. You're going to hurt yourself."

"And then I can't work, right? And that's all you care about, isn't it?"

"No, Mom!" Alice said.

"That's all any of you care about. I'm just a workhorse. That's all you think of me. That's all anyone in this whole goddamn world thinks of me, an ugly workhorse."

Norm came inside then and ran into his room. Benjy pushed the cushions back onto the couch. He didn't know where else to look.

"That's all I'm good for, isn't it?"

"Will you stop? Please!" Alice begged.

"I'll stop! I'll stop when I'm dead, that's when I'll stop."

"I can't stand this," Alice groaned, covering her face. "I can't stand living like this anymore!"

"Oh you can't?" his mother taunted in that voice that turned Benjy's stomach. "Poor thing! It's just too much for you, isn't it?"

Norm raced into the kitchen. He'd found the keys in his pants. "Here they are! C'mon, Mom, it's not her fault."

"Poor sensitive Alice!" she hissed, bending over Alice. "You're just too delicate for all this shit, aren't you?"

"Leave her alone! Will you just leave her alone!" Norm flipped the keys onto the table.

"I'll leave her alone. I'll leave you all the hell alone." She picked up the keys and threw them. As they hit the wall, the chain separated, scattering keys in both rooms. Norm turned without a word and ran upstairs.

In the kitchen his mother crawled from key to key. She strung them on the chain while Benjy picked up the ones that had landed in the living room. "That's right, Alice, don't help. Don't lift a finger," she panted. "Just sit there. It doesn't matter that I'm late for work."

"That's not what's wrong," Alice replied coldly from the table. "That's not what the real trouble is."

Benjy punched the sofa cushion. *Don't!* he wanted to shout. *Don't say his name. Don't say it.*

His mother grabbed the countertop and pulled herself to her feet. "What do you mean?" she asked. "What's the real trouble?"

"Nothing," Alice muttered.

"No, tell me. What do you mean, the real trouble? Go ahead, you said it, now finish it, you think you know so much."

Alice stared down at the table.

"You think you know so much about real trouble, do you? Well, let me tell you what real trouble is. Real trouble is killing myself day in, day out, all my goddamn life, and for what? So you can sit there with your snide remarks, so your lazy brother up there can fling the keys at me like I'm some piece of dirt, like I'm annoying him, so Benjy here can hide out in the house all day and night turning into a zombie when he's not with Klubocks' weird kid, who only comes over here because his mother wants to find out what's going on in this nuthouse I break my ass trying to make a home out of."

Throughout her tirade she had been sliding the rest of the keys back onto the chain, putting on her skirt, tucking in her limp blouse, and now jamming her callused feet into her shoes.

They hung their heads and said nothing.

She darted toward the door, then stopped. "I'm sorry," she whispered without looking back. "Oh God! Oh God, God, God," she moaned as she opened the door and ran outside.

The car's riddled muffler roared down the street.

"Goodbye, Mommy," Norm called down in a sweet falsetto from his bed. "I love you!"

Alice and Benjy ran into his room and jumped on top of him. He tried to push them off, but they had him pinned under the blanket. They laughed and wrestled one another, arms and legs ensnared with sheets as they concocted an escape plan for their father from the "booby hatch," as Norm called it. In the deep of the night, with blackened faces, they would cross mountains and swamps. They would scale walls. They would sling him across Norm's back and haul him out, beating off guards, nurses, and doctors. They would restore their father to power. "The king will reign again!" Norm promised.

"But what if Daddy doesn't want to come with us?" Alice asked.

"We'll promise him wine, whiskey, and beer!" Benjy shouted.

"And haircut money." Alice laughed. "All he has to do is get rid of Duvall for us!"

"Death to the peddler!" Norm cried, shaking his fist, and Alice shrieked as the bed collapsed and they fell onto the floor.

"Oh our papa," Norm began to sing as he lay on his back, waving his arms in the air. "To us he is intoxicating. To us he is so fine. Our mother says he's just a drunk. And we say we don't mind."

Alice and Norm couldn't stop laughing.

"But if Omar comes back, then everything'll be all right and Mom'll be happy again," Benjy said, and they both looked at him.

"Why do you always say such weird things?" Norm moved away from him.

"I don't always say weird things," he said, getting up.

"Yes, you do," Norm said as he and Alice lifted the springs back onto the warped bed rails. "Like all that shit about Negroes with white hair and Duvall's car. I mean what's that all about? How come you have to defend him? And what's this, going down to see Uncle Renie's cat? Jesus, Benjy, why do you have to act so creepy?"

The telephone rang and Alice ran to answer it. It was their mother calling for Benjy.

"Do you know what I'm looking at right now?" his mother asked him.

Benjy shook his head. He closed his eyes.

"Do you?" she demanded.

"No."

"A note from Mr. Tuck. It says you haven't been taking your swimming lessons. And to top it all off, you didn't even take the first one, did you?"

"No."

"Benjy, I'm only going to say this once, so you better hear it right the first time. I'm going to call Mr. Tuck and find out, so don't try and lie to me, because if you don't go to that pool today and take your lesson, when I get home you're not going to know what hit you. Do you understand?"

"Yes," he gasped, nodding.

"By Jesus, you'd better!" She slammed down her phone.

"What's wrong?" Alice asked when he hung up.

"What?" Norm asked, and Benjy shrugged. "You didn't go to swimming, did you?" Norm said, and Benjy shook his head. "Jesus, Benjy!" Norm cried with a backhand to his shoulder. "Will you stop being such a creep, always scared of everything? Jesus Christ, you're gonna be in eighth grade, and what? You're still not gonna know how to swim? C'mon, don't be such a faggot all the time. You drive me nuts!"

"Shut up!" Benjy yelled.

"You make me sick."

"Shut up!"

"I just wanna puke sometimes!"

"I said shut up!" Benjy tried to push him away, but Norm grabbed his arm.

"Leave him alone!" Alice shouted, trying to get between them. She shoved Norm back and stood in front of him.

"The fucking little faggot, you better get him away from me!"

Benjy was halfway out the front door when Norm shouted, "That's it, go ahead, run! Go find Duvall and maybe everything'll be all right again!"

Masses of cold white clouds teetered in the sky. Benjy made his way through the field with careful steps as the dog trotted alongside. The world felt cramped and still, and in its deadness there was nothing he loved, not a person, not a thing. Even the dog seemed heavy and menacing. Because of Mr. Briscoe he couldn't hang around the store anymore, and now Mr. Tuck was writing his mother notes, and Norm thought he was a fag. Every day just got worse and worse, and now he was convinced that something terrible had happened to Omar.

As they neared the woods the dog began to run. At the treeline it sat down and watched Benjy's hesitant approach. Its tail thrashed from side to side. Benjy stepped into the woods. The answer was in here. He knew it was. Something terrible had happened in here. There had been the strip of yellow-and-red cloth, the money clip, and now Omar was missing.

Branches snapped and battered his face. Mosquitoes hummed in his ears. He ran now to keep up with the galloping dog. The dog's fur glistened in the sunlight, then disappeared as its blackness passed into the thicketed shadows. He paused as the dog bounded down the rise and through the clearing below. A crow cawed and in the distance pigs squealed. The dog came running back and sat waiting, its panting black lips split in a wet grin.

He came slowly into the clearing. Even if he found Omar's body he would never tell her. Instead he would say, "He called when you were out." Or "I saw him down on Cottage Street." With hope he would keep her alive. He would bring her things, flowers, perfume, a gold pin, a book of poems, and with each, he would say, "Omar left this for you. He said it reminded him of you."

"What else did he say?" she would ask.

"That he loves you," he would answer tenderly, touching her cheek, the way Omar would, or his father would, the way a man should, especially the man who would love and care for his mother. All at once now, it came to him that it would not be Norm, but himself, who for the rest of his life would be making everything go right for her.

Suddenly, the dog sprang ahead and he followed it into the muck, toward the distant rooftops where dogs yipped, and cows mooed, and a red tractor rumbled down a bumpy road. Here the woods grew not with a forest's chance symmetry, but with an urgency and demand, thickened and enriched by denial, the ravenous wildness of encroaching trees that are continually sawed back, vines that are slashed and suckers lopped off, the dense cane hacked and beaten until it had all tangled and entwined to form this brambled green cave, skyless, and vastly, vastly still.

The dog snuffled through the undergrowth. The dog growled.

"C'mon, boy. C'mere," he whispered, wincing with every crackling step. For a moment, until his vision adjusted to the muzzy dimness, all he could discern were the dog's eyes shining back at him. Now the dog fell on its side and rolled against a long, dark log. With a laugh of relief he stepped closer, then cried out. It was not a log, no longer a man but a form, a mass of putrefaction, all the more inhuman because it was so human and so foul. A green vine grew across its chest. The red-and-yellow-diamond shirt was torn. A trouser leg was ripped. One dark arm had holes in the dusty distended flesh. And protruding from its chest that so strained against the shirt that it gapped at each button was the snakeskin hilt of a knife. This was the young man he had seen struggling that day in the woods with Omar. This was Earlie.

The dog stood then and nudged the body with his head, playfully, as if to amuse Benjy by prodding the corruption to life. "Stop it," he hissed. Staring down at this face, unable to look away, he felt himself caught by the same expression of surprise he had glimpsed through the willow leaves that day, the day that Omar came, which for this swollen mass, this creature, this man, this boy in the old man's worn photograph had been the very last. And so, from then to now, had only taken a moment. There had been the struggle, the chase, the fatal blow, and now they met again, but for Earlie there had been nothing in between.

Again the dog nudged the body. An arm moved and in that quick stirring, the air seethed with a corrosion so foul it sent him staggering back, breaking his way through the thick entanglement. With the dog panting at his heels, he ran all the way to the street. A high wind swept through the treetops, but the smell stayed with him, in his clothes, his hair, his pores. The man they called Earlie was dead. But hadn't he known that, known he'd been in here all along, known he'd find not only Earlie but the mystery of Omar Duvall? Of course he had, of course he had, his heart pounded with his running feet. It was over for them all. The worst had happened. Not theft or treachery, but murder. We have come to this, she would moan from her dark bed. Murder. Murder. Murderer! Without him there was no more hope, and now, even if he did return, it would never again be Omar Duvall sitting at their table or caressing their mother, but Death.

When he came into the house the phone was ringing. His mother sounded relieved and angry to hear his voice. She had been calling for an hour. What was he doing there now? Why wasn't he on his way up to the pool?

"I think it's going to rain," he said.

"I don't care if it snows, you get up there!" she said.

Mr. Tuck took the basket with his clothes and gave him the numbered disk to pin on his trunks. A crowd of kids pushed and jostled each other through the showers. Benjy waited until they were gone, then sped through, shivering and gasping as the icy jets of chlorinated water blasted down on him. He stepped into the warmer chlorine footbath and then he went upstairs. At least he felt cleaner now. That stink was gone. He was relieved to see so few people here today. To the east the cloudy sky was quickly darkening. The wind had stopped. The lifeguards kept glancing at the clock. Benjy hunched over the rail, praying for the rain to start before the lessons did. Now with only the smell of chlorine in his nose he did not have to think of Earlie. He kept his eyes wide open, knowing if he closed them even once he would see that dark bloated face. He had just spotted six of his classmates diving into the deep end. With only a few strong strokes they swam to the ladder, then climbed out for the next dive. Jack Flaherty was on the board now, hairy legs and chest, the long muscles flexing down his back as he jackknifed into the water.

One twenty-five. A cool wind snapped the flag. Two little girls in white bathing caps stood near Benjy under the flag that said LESSONS. The sky roiled to a menacing gray. The instructor was headed toward them, swinging her whistle by its red-and-white gimp chain. He jumped up and started to walk to the other end. Please, dear God, he prayed for the one lightning bolt that would close down the pool. The heavy air tingled with particles of energy before the faint rumble of thunder. The lifeguards were already scrambling down from their posts when the first lightning split the sky. The two little girls screamed and clutched one another. Mr. Tuck's voice boomed over the loudspeaker. "The pool will be closing. I repeat, the . . ."

"C'mon, Benjy," called Jack Flaherty, looping an arm through Benjy's.

"One last duck," Kenny Brown said, laughing, holding his other arm as they dragged him to the edge, pushing him, watching him fall through the twelve feet of bubbling blue silence. Arms out at his sides, he sank to the bottom. It wasn't the drowning, the dying, that was so terrible; it was having to do it in front of kids he knew. Earlie had died alone. He held his breath. His ears roared with pressure. He would sleep, deep in this watery place. He closed his eyes. It would be all right. It wouldn't hurt. He didn't want to hurt. After a while Earlie must have welcomed sleep to stop the pain of that steel shaft so embedded in flesh and bone that every twitch or breath must have burned like red-hot metal in his draining chest with Omar staring down at him. Omar must have seen the stricken eyes, pleading release, aid, comfort, in that moment before he ran away.

An explosion of thunder shook the pool and sent a shudder through his body that suddenly kicked and clawed at the water. A silver pole broke through the surface and sudden whirlpools surged around him, with blurred inquisitive faces emerging from the foam. He was rising straight up, straight up. As his head broke through the surface, the air seemed to slap his face with their voices. "Benjy! Benjy! Are you all right, Benjy?"

Up on the deck Kenny Brown sobbed and rubbed his eyes. It was pouring rain as Benjy clung to the ladder, gasping. There were lifeguards behind him in the pool as well as lifeguards reaching to him from above. They kept grabbing his arms and legs, trying to get him out of the water.

"No! No!" he grunted, struggling. He batted them away. He had not been drowning. He would climb out on his own.

B lue Mooney knew Alice Fermoyle's route by heart. At three-forty she would be in front of the church. From there it would take her five minutes to reach the park and twelve more to get to the A+X. In the last few days he had twice offered her a ride but she'd refused. Yesterday he'd even driven alongside, assuring her he was on his way up to the drive-in, anyway.

"No thanks. I like to walk," she'd said. But at least she'd looked at him and spoken pleasantly. It was a start. Today he planned to come walking around the corner just as she got to the gas station. Perry, the kid who was pumping gas, said he could wait in the office, but he had to leave his car down the street where Mrs. Bonifante wouldn't see it. He was sitting with his feet propped on the greasy desk when Perry came in from the pumps, wiping his hands on a stained towel. He leaned over the desk to see why Blue was staring out the window. "Somebody owe you some money or something?" Perry asked.

"That's a curious nature you got there, kid," he said, squinting with his first glimpse of her hurrying along Main Street.

"Yah, well, I can tell, Blue. You look mad."

"Is that right?" he murmured, getting up to stand by the dusty window. He patted his wave flat and hiked his sleeves higher on his biceps. She was almost running. He checked his watch, ten minutes late. Girls like her always always made him feel this way, nervous and unsure of himself. They were the kind of girl that needed to be cut down to size. But there was something different about Alice. She was pretty, but in a quiet way. That was it, he thought. It was the quiet, the softness of her.

Perry was counting the money from his last sale. He put it into the register. "When's your leave up?" Perry asked.

"Not for a while," he said.

"You been home—what, since April, right? Ain't that a pretty long leave?"

Mooney looked at him. "Commandos get long leaves before special assignments."

"What's the special assignment?" Perry asked.

He shook his head with a rueful snort. "Be serious, will you? You really think I'm gonna give some hick-town grease monkey that kind of high-clearance, top-secret, national-security information?"

"Yah, well, maybe I was just testing you." Perry grinned. "Maybe I'm a double agent. Maybe these are all Commies coming in here for gas."

"Hey!" he said, grabbing Perry's arm. "Don't even kid, okay? I mean this is a fine line we're walking here, if you know what I mean."

"Sorry! I didn't know you were gonna take it so personal. I'm sorry, all right?" Perry squealed.

He let him go. "Hey, it's the training, that's all, so let's just forget it," he said, rubbing his temples. He had to be careful. The simplest things seemed to be getting out of hand lately. It was this constant panic, this festering sense of his own fraudulence. Of all people, Blue Mooney, who loved freedom and hated fakery more than anyone, was now trapped in a lie he could not make right.

"What kinda training?" Perry asked. "In your head? You mean brainwashing?"

"Just forget it. Forget I said anything. Hey, so how do you like it here?" he said to change the subject. "Bonifante still a bitch?"

Eunice was okay, Perry said. But the pay was lousy. Some guy said the tire company was hiring, so he was thinking of trying there.

"J. C. Colter?" he asked, and Perry said yes. Mooney cracked his knuckles. He was desperate for money, but he couldn't very well go looking for steady work when everybody thought he was home on leave. He glanced out the window. She was only two blocks away. The service bell rang as a red Mustang convertible with its radio blasting pulled up to the high-test pump. Perry ran outside.

He looked at the register. He didn't have to move from the window, just reach over and hit the right key. Apron in hand, Alice crossed East Center Street, then stepped onto the curb and raced along. The register drawer popped out. Loaded with cash. Easy money, and the way Eunice Bonifante ran this place she wouldn't even know the difference. Alice was crossing Terrill Street. Her ponytail flipped up and down as she neared the station. His fingers closed over the bills. Perry was propping up the Mustang's hood when the driver called to him. Perry ran around to look at the map she'd been studying. Twenty-five, thirty, thirty-five dollars. Sweat trickled down the small of Mooney's back. Alice started past the station. Just then the corner light turned green and a pickup truck suddenly swung out of the traffic into the station. He couldn't believe what was happening. The truck was veering in Alice's direction. In a moment, a second more, she would be directly in its deadly path. There wasn't even enough time to get to the door. All he could do was bang on the plate glass with his fists. Perry and the women in the convertible looked at him. "Look out! Oh Jesus, please don't! Please don't!" he was bellowing as the truck turned, just barely missing her. It pulled up to the other side of the pump. He was shaking. His fingers were locked over the crumpled bills. Opening his hand, he let the money fall into the cash drawer. Images kept popping in his head with flashbulb intensity: the truck, her bouncing ponytail, Perry studying the map. She was safe. He closed the register, certain it had been a test, a sign that she was part of some mysterious transaction he did not yet understand. She was already a block away.

He hurried outside, chasing after her, careful not to call her name or say a word or make any sound loud enough to startle her, because she was running fast and he was so close now that even the sound of his boots on the pavement might terrify her, so he ran on the grass strip between the sidewalk and the street, calling softly, "Alice! Alice! Alice!" until she finally looked back.

"Are you all right?" he asked before she could say anything. "I saw what happened back there. I tried to tell you. I was inside, banging on the window. The truck was coming right at you," he said, taking a step closer.

She glanced warily back then, out at the street.

"I couldn't believe it was happening," he said. "I kept banging. Did you hear me banging and banging like that?"

She looked at him. Her eyes were a deep blue, the lashes dark and thick. "I don't know what you mean," she said.

"Back at the station, the truck, it was going to hit you. It was awful. I thought something was going to happen to you."

"Why are you doing this?" she said, her face reddening.

"What? Doing what?" The panic in his own voice stunned him. The last thing he wanted was to make her mad.

"Why are you following me?"

"I'm not. I was out, you know, walking. I'm always walking. I love walking," he said, trying to be careful that his wobbling boots did not stumble on the frost-heaved sidewalk as he hurried alongside. "Sometimes our platoon, we used to march twenty or thirty miles a day." He looked down at her. "You ever been in Texas?"

She didn't answer.

"Real wild country, lemme tell you. Tough men, real tough." He wasn't making sense, but all he had were words to tether what was slipping away. "My sergeant's from there, his name's John Henry Nickerson. He's almost seven feet tall, with a tattoo of a horse galloping across his back, most beautiful thing I've ever seen on a human being and that's the truth, more beautiful than some paintings, even. The horse has this long, streaming mane, and Nickerson can make the haunches ripple if he flexes a certain way."

Her eyes widened, and he could tell she was regarding him in a new light. He told her about his own tattoo, a full blue moon on his right shoulder blade.

Something in her quick glance made the tattoo prickle like sore flesh rubbing against his shirt.

"Yah, well, I wanted something original, you know. Not like hearts and roses and snakes. Especially snakes. Everybody's got snakes, you know, circling up poles or twisted around hearts."

The sharpness of her gaze saddened him. The truth was that it had been bad chemistry between him and Nickerson right from the start, which still mystified him, because Nickerson had seemed like such a badass regular guy that he'd really thought all he had to do the first time Nickerson barked that ridiculous name, Travis Mooney, was to step forward and explain how really his name was Blue, which was what he'd been called all his life. "I hear Travis and I start looking all around, wondering where's the idiot with a name like that," he had said, still rigid at attention.

"Is that a fact?" Nickerson had sighed through a hard smile.

"Yes sir, that's a fact. Sure is," he'd said, flashing his most eager grin.

"Well, I'll be damned. In fact, I'll be damned, hog-tied, and do-si-do'd now, Travis, but that's your name now, don't you see. That is your legal, U.S. government–issue, Marine Corps official and documented name. See? Right here, TRAVIS T. MOONEY. Travis T." His hooded eyes rose over the clipboard. "Travesty, kinda says so much now, don't it? For instance, it tells me that you are every bit a travesty of a man as you are of a soldier."

He'd had one week of soldiering, one week of Nickerson's constant harassment, one fist-clenching, tongue-biting week of insult and humiliation, until that moment with the fly-buzzing noonday sun on his back and the salty sweat stinging his eyes when he had Nickerson pinned under him as he pummeled the sergeant's face to raw flesh. For that he had served his nine months, and now here he was, not on leave at all, but dishonorably discharged and sent home in shame.

She walked even faster now, as they got closer to the A+X.

"Hey, what's the big rush? You'll be rid of me in a few minutes," he said, noticing how she turned her head every time a car went by. She didn't want to be seen with him.

"It's just that I hate it when he yells at me," she said. "The other night he even pushed one of the girls."

She seemed so small, so fragile. *If Coughlin touches her,* he kept thinking. *If he so much as brushes against her . . .* He stopped and stared at her. "Look, if that . . . that"—he caught himself—"friggin' creep ever so much as looks at you the wrong way, just let me know," he said, pointing at her. " 'Cause I'll break him in two, I mean it. You just let me know," he said, his voice cracking with the same wild surge of emotion he'd felt at the gas station.

"Oh, yah, well, I guess I'd better get in there," she said, looking confused. She hurried into the drive-in lot.

"Just tell me," he called, suddenly feeling foolish. It was a strange sensation to be standing here without his car or his bike, without anyone or anything to make him whole and solid, to keep him from stepping off the edge of the earth. As he headed back to the garage, he set each foot down heavily, as if to spike himself along the sidewalk.

It was a hot starry night and even at eleven the lot was still jammed with cars. There hadn't been any breaks, and now everyone was tired and irritable. Alice hadn't minded the constant rushing and running, because the night had flown by without once having to consider what her encounter with Blue Mooney meant. She hadn't understood half of what he said. He almost seemed to be warning her or threatening her. He gave her the creeps the way he stared and stood so close, and now all his talk about snakes and hearts was a lot more weird than she could stand.

At eleven-thirty she had just taken her last order when Mooney's car squealed into the lot and parked behind the office. She pushed her slip through the window at Carper. Mooney swaggered across the lot, nodding over that peculiar gun-fingered salute he made to people he knew.

"Need a ride?" he asked, standing off to the side of the window.

Thinking he was speaking to his cousin, she kept tallying her slip. One more order and she'd be done.

Carper's blocky head moved close to the glass. "Alice in Wonderland don't speak to trash," Carper said in his high thin voice. He laughed.

Mooney touched her arm, and she jumped. "I just thought I'd check and see," he said softly, hunching away from Carper. "You need a ride home?"

"My brother's coming," she said, grateful that he actually was, so she wouldn't have to be ducking behind trees and telephone poles again all the way home.

Mooney slid something from his hip pocket and held it below the food-streaked steel counter so Carper couldn't see it. "I got you this," he said, but she refused to look down. She felt panicky. She was conscious of people watching from their cars. Carper giggled.

"Here," Mooney said, nudging her with it. "In case you didn't get a chance to eat."

The Hershey bar with almonds was soft with the warmth of his pocket, of his body.

"She's gonna throw up!" Carper snickered.

"Thank you," she said, her eyes blurring with the heat of her red face.

"Some late-night energy," Mooney said, his square teeth flashing in a wide white grin.

"That's right," she said weakly, "some energy." She slipped the candy bar into her pocket and headed toward a car that was flashing its light for the bill.

"That's right, some energy," Carper mimicked.

"Shut up, blockhead," Mooney growled. "Just shut up!"

When her last car left, she ran in to use the bathroom before Norm came. She took the limp candy bar from her pocket and squeezed it, then dropped it into the trash. What was it about her that attracted such weird people? she wondered.

Mooney liked this time best, with the floodlights out and all the waitresses gone. While Carper cleaned up the kitchen and bathrooms, he and Coughlin had a beer in the office. The thin frazzled man's filthy mouth amused him.

"How about you?" Coughlin asked, handing him his latest batch of dirty pictures. "Been getting much lately?"

"Naw. Not really." He cleared his throat. He didn't like the way the pictures made him feel. He pretended to look through them, but he was thinking of Alice. Last night he had dreamed about her. They were in the back seat of his car, and his head was in her lap.

"So what's your problem?" Coughlin snickered.

"I'm just here on leave, so I don't have all that much time, you know."

"No!" Coughlin laughed with raised eyebrows. "I don't know! Not for that, I don't! Especially for that! Especially on leave. I mean if you can't get it now, soldier boy, Jesus, you're never gonna get it."

He tried to smile. He slid the pictures back into the envelope. "Hey, don't worry about it. I'm not."

Coughlin set down his bottle and wet his lips until they glistened like his eyes. "You're making a move on that Fermoyle chick, aren't you?"

"Who says?" His foot twisted back and forth on his boot heel. He pushed the pictures back to Coughlin, suddenly repulsed by them.

"I seen the way you look at her. The girls, too, they seen it."

"I guess you're all full of shit, then," he said, getting up quickly before Coughlin's tittery laugh made him lose his temper.

"I guess so," Coughlin snickered.

The door opened, and he was grateful to see his cousin waddle into the messy room. "Here," Anthology said, tossing a mangled Hershey bar onto the table. "Some sweets from your sweetie."

Howard Menka sat up in bed, blinking into the darkness. He had been dreaming the dream of the dead faces again. It was a warning, a sign of how much had changed. First the trips to see their cousin had ended. Now Jozia had stopped cooking his dinners. Instead, she brought him the pigman's leavings, mushy packets of carrots in waxed paper or cold gray slabs of ketchup-smeared meat loaf. They covered the refrigerator shelves, green beans speckled with congealed butter, a stiff pork chop, a shriveled baked potato. She didn't care if he ate any of it or not. It only mattered that she brought them home for him. He was losing weight. His belt fastened on the last hole now. He was losing his life, and his sister didn't care.

He got out of bed and tiptoed into their tiny parlor, which was little more than an alcove; its arched opening was just large enough for two easy chairs and the coffee table. On this narrow table was the statue of the pretty Infant of Prague in his yellow satin gown and high-necked white cape. The Infant's delicate features glowed above the flickering red votive light. It saddened Howard to see Baby Jesus still wearing last month's gown. Jozia used to change the Infant's clothes weekly, choosing special outfits for the holy days of obligation and their favorite feast days. The last new gown she had bought from the store downstairs had been bright green for Saint Patrick's Day. The white cape had been dotted with tiny green shamrocks and there had been gold piping down the front. It seemed that years had passed since March.

Howard listened at Jozia's door, but he couldn't hear anything. Each night she got home later than the night before. In the morning he'd have to call her ten or twenty times before she finally answered, and then she could barely open her eyes. She was always too tired for early Mass, so he'd go alone. He'd sit in the last pew and cover his face, begging God to bring his sister to her senses and release her from the pigman's spell.

He squinted through the keyhole now, and a stream of cool air hit his eyeball. The bed was empty. It was three-thirty in the morning and she wasn't home. "No!" he cried, hitting the door with his fist. His sister, the only human being he loved, had left him. "No! No! No!" Love had failed him. Prayers had failed. It was true, God did not listen to fools.

Behind him the apartment door opened and Jozia rushed through the darkness. "What are you doing?" she cried, shaking him. "What's wrong?" she demanded, one side of her hair straight up in the air, her puffy eyes wide and fearful.

He let her hold him. She smelled different. She smelled of fried fish and something else, something he knew but had no name for.

"It was a bad dream," he said, and as he lay down, tears seeped from his eyes. Now he understood. The dreams of dying were about her. He began to tremble. Soon there would be a night when she did not come home at all.

The next morning he didn't go to Mass. He made a pot of strong coffee and waited for her to wake up. When she finally dragged herself to the table, he tried to explain his nightmares.

"I tole you a million times, if I tole you once," she said. "You wanna drink coffee all night long, then you gotta pay the sequences."

"No, no, it ain't got nothing to do with coffee," he insisted. "I been having these dreams no matter what. And every time I been waking up, shaking and sweating, thinking it's me that's dying. But now I know. It ain't me. It's you, Jozia. You're the one. You're dying on me!"

She stood up and peered down at him. "Howard," she said with chilling finality. "I'm thinking about moving." For a moment she seemed about to cry. Instead she took a deep breath. "It's time for us to be on our own now." She blinked. "Don't you think?"

"No!"

Father Gannon would not be put off a moment longer. He would meet with the Bishop this Saturday. Saturday was best because it was the one day he had no hospital or nursing-home visits. He had arranged with Father Krystecki to have one of his visiting curates hear afternoon confessions.

The Monsignor poured more coffee into his cup. He picked up the paper and a faint smile parted his lips as he read the stock page. "Mrs. Arkaday!" he called. She poked her head out from the kitchen, and he asked for a pen and paper. "Eight and five-eighths, up a quarter," he murmured, scribbling on the pad the moment she set it down. "Times seventy-five . . ." His mouth hung open as his breathing quickened. "At three and a quarter . . ." Glancing up, he caught Father Gannon's anxious stare. "What is it, Father?" he asked, pointing with the pen. "Jelly? Coffee? More toast? You seem to be lingering."

"Please call me Joe," he said.

"Is that why you're still here? We have to go over that old ground again?" The Monsignor sighed.

"I just want to remind you that this is the Saturday I'm going up to see the Bishop."

The Monsignor leaned forward. "Why, Father Gannon? Why?"

"It's personal, Tom," Father Gannon said. There was no reason for two men living together to address each other by titles.

"Then I'm the one you should speak to," the Monsignor said with reddening cheeks. "I'm your spiritual counselor, not Bishop O'Rourke, who, as I hardly have to tell you, is an extremely busy man."

"This is something I have to talk to the Bishop about." He would be firm.

The Monsignor laid down his pen. "Then it's about me, isn't it."

"No!" Father Gannon insisted. "Not at all, Tom. It's me. It's something I need to get straight with him."

There was a difficult silence before the Monsignor finally spoke. "Does it occur to you that while you're devoting an entire day to yourself there are people here, people in this parish, who need you?"

"Well, actually, I'm doing some of that in the process." Pleased with his foresight, he smiled as he told of his arrangement with Mrs. Fermoyle to bring one of her children to see their father in the hospital.

The blotches on the Monsignor's cheeks deepened. "Why?" he asked in a guttural whisper that seemed to choke him. "What could possibly be the purpose?"

"I thought it would be good for the family."

"For your information, Father Gannon, Marie and Sam Fermoyle are divorced. They are *not* a family," the Monsignor said.

"Well, the children," Father Gannon said, groping. "And their mother, they need—"

"This parish has plenty of good Catholic families that need your attention every bit as much. If not more," the Monsignor added.

The afternoon grew cloudy, with sharp gusts of wind that kept snatching the water from the sprinkler and spraying it back at Howard as he weeded the flower beds. His wet shirt was plastered to his back. He knelt on the marble walk, weeding the snapdragons.

The Monsignor was in the rectory, meeting with the Sodality executive committee. Mrs. Squireman's deep voice droned through the open window above him. "And so next year the four bake sales will be held after all five Sunday Masses. . . ."

Across the street, Jozia had just hung bath mats and scatter rugs to dry on the Fermoyles' porch railing. When he thought of her leaving him, his chest ached with this swallowed sob. The pigman was painting and wallpapering the guest room for her. They had already ordered her new bedroom "sweet," she'd said at breakfast this morning and almost made him cry then. She would be a rent-paying tenant, she'd said, adding cryptically, "For now." Whatever objection he'd raised, his sister had quelled it.

"But it's a sin!" he'd said.

"Then everybody that rents a place ever'where is committing sins, is that what you're saying?"

"What about Mrs. LaChance?" he'd asked. "You even said you and her been like sisters."

"I'll still be working there!"

"But you can't walk all that way to work."

"I'll be coming in with Grondine ever' morning."

"But what about me?"

"You'll be fine. I tole you, we got our own lives to live now."

"Maybe you got one to live, but I don't," he'd said, angry with her for the first time. He felt cheated, by the pigman mostly, but also in a way by Jozia.

"Grondine says you can get a room a lot cheaper. He says three places he hauls from got rooms to let," she had said without so much as a glance back as she crossed the street to the Fermoyle house.

He looked up now, startled, as a shadow fell over him. It was Father Gannon, eating a large green apple. "Howard!" he called, gesturing with the apple. "You're soaking wet." Father Gannon ran over and turned off the sprinkler. "What's that, some new gardening technique?" He laughed. "You work better wet?" He stepped closer. "Howard? What's wrong? Why are you crying?" He held out his hand. "Come here, Howard. Get up. Come on, now," the priest said, helping him to his feet.

He would not look at him.

"What's wrong?" the priest kept asking as he led him to the side of the rectory and sat him down on the steps. "Tell me what's wrong. Maybe I can help. At least give me a chance. Tell me what's wrong. Come on, now!"

"I'm gonna be alone," he cried in a high stringy voice. "I'm gonna be all alone."

"Maybe you'll like it," the priest said after Howard explained Jozia's plan.

"No," he groaned. "I won't never like it. I won't!"

The priest stared down at him. "You probably won't," he sighed. "Do you think maybe your sister would take you with her?"

He shook his head. "She said we gotta have our own life."

Father Gannon slapped his knee. "Well, then, you're just gonna have to make the best of it, Howard. Look on the bright side, now. You've got a good job, people who like you. People who . . . who care about you."

He had been shaking his head. His nose was running. Few people had ever heard him speak, but no one had ever seen him cry before. Ashamed as he was, he couldn't control himself. "But nobody loves me," he sobbed. "Nobody. Not even Jozia now."

"Howard! Howard! People love you. Of course they do!" the priest kept insisting as his fingers dug into his wet shoulders. "I love you! Do you hear me? I love you! Do you understand?" he shouted. "I love you, Howard!"

"Oh dear," came a woman's sigh from behind. The Sodality executive committee had left the rectory and were following Monsignor Burke down the flagstone walk to the driveway.

Howard hung his head in shame.

"Monsignor Burke loves you!" the priest cried, pointing. He darted toward the women. "And all these ladies, they love you." He ran back and gripped Howard's shoulder again. "We all do, Howard! We all love you!"

"Father Gannon!" commanded the Monsignor. "Mrs. Arkaday needs you inside."

As if a spell had been broken, the young priest blinked, and his hand fell to his side. He started toward the rectory, then looked back at Howard with a trembling smile. "I'll be right back," he said.

"Howard's going home now," the Monsignor said. "He's done for the day. Aren't you, Howard?"

That night he threw the leftovers into the garbage. He would cook his own food. The macaroni boiled over and then the cheese slices burned in the fry pan, but he ate it anyway, feeling stronger with every mushy noodle. After that he tried to watch television by himself. But it was a scary murder show, so he turned it off and sat staring at the sweet plaster face looking back at him from the coffee table. Poor Baby Jesus, Jozia had lost interest in them both. That's when he got the idea of changing the Infant of Prague's clothes. Maybe if he did, God might start paying a little closer attention to how bad things were going in Howard Menka's life.

He looked through all the boxes in Jozia's closet but he couldn't decide which outfit to choose, so he worked up all his courage and went downstairs to the Holy Articles Shoppe to ask if there were any special holy days coming up. Miss Brastus, a shy woman with a faint mustache, whispered through the chained door. She and Howard weren't used to each other. It was Jozia she always dealt with. "It's ordinary time," she said, looking down the hallway.

"I mean now. This month," he tried to explain, glancing back to see what she was looking at.

"That's what this is. The whole summer, it's ordinary time. There aren't any special feasts then."

"Oh," he said, and with her closing door, everything felt flat and hopeless again. It was ordinary time, and there was nothing to look forward to and no one to love. There wasn't even a special outfit for the Infant to wear.

Howard's eyes shot open. It was the middle of the night. One by one through the darkness, familiar shapes drifted to the surface, a plaster horse lamp, his Fort Ticonderoga mug, the nude Infant of Prague. Waiting for Jozia, he had fallen asleep in the chair. He felt his way to her room, where the white emptiness of her bed was all he could see.

He went outside and sat on the narrow porch, which was crowded with Jozia's summering houseplants. He tried to think of happy times, people and places he liked, but not one good thought came to him. After a few minutes, he got up and walked to the corner, standing close by the streetlamp, looking first one way and then the other for his sister. Slowly he began to walk up the hill. He headed south on Main Street, turning left at the church, past the rectory, past the Fermoyles'. He kept looking back over both shoulders, sometimes stopping and completely turning. Now that he was on Stratton Road he could hear dogs barking. Gravel crunched underfoot and roadside weeds snagged his ankles. The distance between houses increased until he was passing long wooded stretches that hummed with the dark rush of water and the steady beat of crickets, and now, the ghostly hoot of an owl. A branch snapped. His eyes widened and his mouth puckered with the parchedness of dry cotton.

He began to blink as his brain pinged with hundreds, thousands, millions of random words, thoughts, sounds, flashes of memory distant as stars—images of her hair, thin and grayly dry against her face; of her lost slipper found after its mate had finally been thrown out, and how sad that made them both feel, how frustrated, how stupid; of the quick scared way she'd call out his name through the dark: Howard! Howard!

He rubbed his nose against this stench that signaled the hot humusy rot of the dump and, a little farther on, the sourness of the pig farm. He passed a high chain-link fence clotted with blown paper, the mounds beyond glinting with sand and glass shards; and now, ahead on the same side of the road, Grondine Carson's house loomed tall and stark in the bright moonlight. Three trucks were parked in the front yard; the big black garbage truck, a panel truck mounted on cinder blocks, and the green pickup that usually brought Jozia home. Behind the house, two wide barns were linked by a maze of low, slant-roofed sheds and outbuildings, some so dilapidated, their fallen doors lay long composted in the weed-patched earth, and their windows, where there were any, hung by dint of a rusted hinge or stubborn splinter.

He hurried on, drawn to one lit window at the rear of the house. He ducked under a tree and stared at the long aperture of bright glass that seemed to grow both in size and brilliance until, like a giant blazing star hurtling straight at him, it was all that he could see, indeed was all there was to see. Now, as he crept closer, his eyes glowed with the light that contained Carson with a can of beer in his hand, and, across the table, Jozia, her eyes soft with an expression Howard had seen only in movies. He stood there for a long time, watching sadly as they talked. It seemed such a serious and important conversation that he knew it had nothing to do with him.

Suddenly a dog barked. Carson cocked his head, listening. Howard ran in a crouch, then flattened himself against a tin-walled shed. A door creaked open. "Better get the hell outta here!" Carson warned. For a moment there was no sound. "Probably them raccoons again," Jozia said, with such familiarity that a piece of his heart hissed out like a quick weak match.

When the door creaked to a close, he darted past the first barn. He ran, jumped, hopped, sloshed through muck, stumbled, then with skidding feet reeled headlong through a wooded darkness and down an embankment, and by then he knew he was completely out of control, helpless and unstoppable. He was panting, and sweating, and crying to himself when finally he fell and just lay there on his side, caught by brambles, but grateful that the earth held him and would not give him up.

At first he thought he was in a cave, but then he saw stars glimmering through the tangled branches overhead. After the few seconds it took for him to adjust to this deeper-bellied night, he continued to peer at the moonlit eyes staring up from the dark clover. And then he knew by its foulness and the slick darkness of its bloated gleam that he had done a terrible thing, that he had come too far to ever find his way back to the way things used to be. And worse, there was no one he could tell.

Another week had passed, a week of such intense heat that the tar on busy roads softened to ruts and people stayed in their houses all day, their shades pulled and curtains drawn. Business was slow downtown, but the lakes and the town pool were always crowded, and every night cars waited in line to get into the A+X.

In the two weeks since Marie had signed the money from her bank loan over to Omar, she had heard from him twice. His most recent call had come last week to tell her he was still in Connecticut in Presto Soap's training program. They had him out in the field covering small towns in the western part of the state. He had sounded tired and flat.

"I'm a little too old for all this driving around," he had sighed into the phone. "Tell you the truth, this is work for a younger man."

"Driving?" she'd asked. "Whose car are you using?"

"Damn! That was supposed to be my big surprise, but I can't keep anything from you, can I?" He had paused. "Marie, I went and bought a new car!"

"New?" she had said, almost choking. "How could you afford a new car?"

"Well, it's a used car, but new for me. It's a 'fifty-six Caddy," he had whispered. "White. Not one bit of rust. I can't wait for you to see it. I can't wait for you to be in it—with me."

"Omar?" she had interrupted, softly, so the children wouldn't hear. "When's the soap coming?"

"Let's see." Papers rustled. "Here we go. From the looks of these back orders, well, a couple weeks, anyway."

"A couple weeks! I can't wait a couple weeks! Omar, the first payment on the loan's due in two weeks."

"And that's right about when the soap'll get there, so don't worry. Relax, Marie. Just—"

"Omar, I need time to sell the soap to get the money for the loan. I mean I can't just get the soap . . . I mean the bank won't . . . oh God, Omar, do you see what I'm saying?"

He had assured her there was nothing to worry about. If worse came to worst, he'd make the first payment himself. Soon she'd have her soap and in no time at all the money would be pouring in. He said he'd be back in Atkinson just as soon as his training ended, but then he'd hung up without telling her when that would be or where he was staying in Connecticut. The next day on her lunch break she had seen a white Cadillac coming along Merchants Row. Certain it was Omar, she had left work early, expecting to find him waiting for her at the house. That had been five days ago.

She looked up now as Mr. Briscoe rushed through the door with an invoice. He was angry because he had waited all last winter for Kruter skis and now all they had sent him were children's lengths. A note on the invoice said the adult skis would come later.

"Call Kruter," he fumed, flipping through her Rolodex for the number. "Because they're getting the whole mess back. They must think I'm some kind of fool, some jerk they can keep putting off. Well, I'm not that desperate that I'm taking this crap. No sir. No way. And you can tell them that!" he said, stabbing his finger at the card. "You tell them if they want to do business with Ferdinand T. Briscoe, then they're going to have to deliver more than promises!" Wiping his brow, he stormed out.

Promises. The word emptied her with the eviscerating deftness of a gutting blade. She had signed over a thousand-dollar check to a man she had known for only a few weeks. He had her money, and all she had was a promise. *I'm a fool*, she thought, beginning to whisper, "a pathetic ignorant fool, always thinking I'm so smart, just getting into one mess after another, always thinking I'm so strong, so tough, and then what do I do but fall for the first man who pays me the slightest bit of attention, the slightest shred . . . Oh God, what am I going to do?"

The office door burst open and Mr. Briscoe rushed back in from the warehouse, demanding to know what was wrong. What was that moaning? What happened? Who said what? What? What?

Sobbing into her hands, she couldn't speak, couldn't admit that she had risked everything she had ever worked for—her house, Alice's education, her own reputation. "I'm such a fool," she wept. "Such a goddamn fool."

Mr. Briscoe wanted her to call Norm to drive her home. Alice, then, he said when she shook her head, gasping that Norm was at work himself. No! She wasn't going home. She couldn't afford to lose a day's pay, especially now. Mr. Briscoe assured her it would be a day off with pay, but that was even more painful. No sir. She hadn't taken charity before and she wasn't about to start now. She'd stay right here at this desk and do her work, come hell or high water.

"Marie, you need—" Mr. Briscoe was saying when the telephone rang.

"Briscoe's Sporting Goods," she answered in a ragged voice, before transferring the call to Don in the repair shop.

Mr. Briscoe backed into the doorway. "Look, Marie . . ."

"I'm fine!" she insisted, tears running down her face as she began to type, fingers scurrying over the keys, her hand shooting up to bat back the carriage return with increasing vehemence. "I'm going to be just fine," she sobbed as the door closed.

After that, everything she did or said was tinged with a sadness so palpable, it hung from her shoulders like a leaden cloak, causing her to stoop, pitching her forward with her head down, swishing behind her in a chorus of baleful sighs. She had been tricked, betrayed, swindled. Twice when Lester had called for Alice she had almost asked to speak to his father. This was clearly a matter for the police. But she was too ashamed.

Benjy and Norm were eating supper with their mother's untouched plate on the table between them. Without a word she had jumped up a few minutes ago and run upstairs to her room. Norm scowled as he cut his chicken, but Benjy could tell he was determined to ignore what was happening.

Benjy glanced back at the darkening stairs. Every day the sun set a minute sooner. In a few more weeks summer would be over. What if Omar Duvall wasn't back by then and she was still this sad? What would she do if she found out? Again he tried to push from his thoughts the image of Earlie lying at the edge of the pig farm with the woods beginning to grow over him. The worst of it now was the double-pronged certainty not only of the corpse but of how quickly and completely its connection to Duvall would destroy his mother.

"You think Omar's ever coming back?" he asked.

"Nah," Norm said, spearing a chicken wing from his mother's plate. "You kidding? That asshole's long gone."

"How do you know?"

"I know. Don't worry."

"C'mon, Norm, tell me. How do you know? Did you do something? You did, didn't you?"

"Let's just say I looked into it."

"C'mon, Norm! Tell me!"

"All right, but don't say anything!" His voice lowered, Norm leaned close. "You know that Bernadette Mansaw, right? Well, Weeb got his father's work ID and we dressed Tommy up in one of his father's suits and he went up there to Mansaw's place and he says he's a government VD investigator and he's tracking down Duvall. And she goes nuts. 'VD!' she's screaming and we're out in the hall listening. 'VD! Jesus Christ!' So then she says, 'That bastard. I gave him a hundred bucks, and then next thing I know, he's calling me from Connecticut.' So then Tommy figures, what the hell, while he's there, you know, he might as well, so he says, 'Well, there's something else, ma'am. I have to know the names of all your sex partners in the last five years.' And she starts telling him. Jesus! Naming guys like Billy Tides and Cleary from the bowling alley. But then he went too far. He looks up and he says, 'Oh and by the way, were those blow jobs or normal.' And that's when she flipped out and told him to go fuck himself." Norm's head bobbed over the table as he tried to muffle his laughter.

"Yah," Benjy said, "but maybe Omar's coming back. You don't know."

"C'mon, jerk. Figure it out. He obviously ripped the slut off for a hundred bucks and then took off. And besides, even if he does come back, she'll probably kill him or something."

He didn't say anything. The house seemed vastly, precariously still, as if an exterior wall had just fallen and if anyone dared move or speak, the rest would follow.

Norm peered at him. "You don't want him back here, do you, Benj?"

"No." He glanced at her plate, her crooked chair wrenched from the table, all the emptiness here. "But Mom does."

"You know Mom, she's all screwed up. She doesn't know what the hell she wants."

"She wants to be happy, that's all." His eyes stung, and he could not swallow against the lump in his throat that was studded with lies and denial.

"Well, have I got news for you! Nothing's gonna make *her* happy. You got that? Nothing!"

He wouldn't argue, but he knew it wasn't true. He'd seen how she was with Duvall, the high color of her skin, the light in her eyes, the ease of her laughter. No matter what Duvall was, he was good for his mother, and right now that was more important than anything.

For the last mile along the winding country road, Roy Gold's estate was enclosed by a high brick wall that had been painted black. The brick of the huge ivy-covered house, however, had been left in its natural state, as had the moss-chinked veranda that overlooked a large pond flecked with lily pads. In the soft light of sunset the pond glowed a warm shimmering green.

Omar Duvall turned from the dining-room window and took his place at the table among the twelve executive candidates who had been invited to dinner this last night of training. On the walls above the raised white wainscoting had been painted a vivid fox-hunting scene that wended among delicate trees, past dark ponds and distant misty hills. The red-jacketed hunters hunched over their horses, most in full gallop around the room to a far corner, where a circle of agitated dogs strained toward a small fox. The fox crouched, ready to dart into a crevice beneath a large rock. As Omar's eyes raced around the mural, he fully expected to see a horse suddenly rear back whinnying as its rider raised a strident bugle to his lips. Howling, the dogs would pounce, and there, there in the snarling, snapping blur of pursuit his breath quickened as he imagined the fox slithering down the hole, bellying through the damp hollow darkness, the safety of the tunnel beyond.

"I know exactly what you're doing, Omar," said Roy Gold, startling him. "You can feel it, can't you?" He patted his chest. "That's a good sign," he said with a wink.

Now some of the other men made a point of staring up at the mural, their attention focused on the hunters rather than the quarry, the hunted.

The door to the kitchen swung open onto a young woman in a black dress and white lace apron. She pushed a wheeled brass tureen from which she began to serve consommé. Duvall sat between a retired mailman from Paducah, Kentucky, and a grocer from Albany, New York. The grocer leaned forward to confide in the mailman that in spite of company police he planned to retail Presto products on his own store shelves.

"I don't know, Cal," the mailman said out of the side of his mouth. "Like Roy Gold says, it's not that kind of product. Presto's a people product."

"Hell, I got people up the gootch," the grocer snorted.

Duvall sat back stiffly and cleared his throat, so that no one would think him party to such ignorant dinner conversation.

"It's a word-of-mouth product," the mailman continued, his arms on the table as he spoke past Omar. "Now you take your Fabs, your Tides, your Ivorys, your Joys. Those're all Madison Avenue products. But Presto's a different product. It's different marketing. It needs a hands-on sell. And that's just the way it is, Cal. No two ways about it!"

'Hey, all I know is I got shelf space and now I got product!" The grocer chuckled, with a sly nod at Omar. "And with a seventy-five-percent markup, it don't take no genius to appreciate my situation."

Voices dwindled and spoons clinked as one by one the men began to eat. The maid was still ladling out the broth. His hands folded on the edge of the table, Omar waited for everyone to be served. At the end of the long table, almost obscured by the ornate candelabra, Roy Gold also waited. He was a small man, with glowing sculpted cheeks and even features. His blond hair was closely trimmed, his hazel eyes clear, his gaze direct, his nails buffed, his navy blazer a perfect fit. In Gold's presence Omar always felt sloppy and sprawling. He would start tucking in his shirt and hitching up his pants and buffing the toes of his shoes on the back of his pant leg. Gold was in charge of every fiber of his being. Omar still couldn't believe his good fortune in linking up with Gold. The man was a marketing genius with more dynamism, more compassion than anyone he'd ever met before. Uniquely, Gold's goal wasn't just to make money, but to share that opportunity with men like himself, bright ambitious visionaries.

As the maid steered the tureen into the kitchen, Gold took up his spoon, and then so did Omar. He noted how erectly Gold sat, never hunching over his bowl or slurping like the others. He noted how Gold ate from the side of his spoon, always refilling it away from himself, and so he did the same. Imagine. There were even rules for eating soup. In this complicated universe it was the ordinary things he found most exciting. Conversations rose and fell around him. His breast swelled with joy, with exuberance. There was no task he could not master. Nothing seemed past his grasp. Beyond this moment, a finger's reach away, like jewels in a glass case, glimmered a life of privilege and honor. He had come this far. Yes, he had; alert even in the depths of fear and the pain of betrayal, he had not despaired, instead had chosen another path, breaking off a lilac branch as he fled, stooping to retrieve an empty matchbook cover from the dust. Yes. Yes, he had come this far, and most surely for a reason. All at once the voices surged, and he looked around to see Cal pick up his bowl and drink the rest of his broth. Poor, poor fellow, he thought, such a minor man.

When everyone was done, Gold stood. With a knife blade he tapped his water goblet, and it tinkled like a crystal bell. "Gentlemen," he called in a pleasant voice. "May I have your attention, please."

Omar saw how his smile radiated genuine affection.

"For just a few moments, I assure you."

"Hey it's your place, Roy, so you go take all the time you want!" called Johnny Biggs with a hearty laugh. Biggs was a carpet installer from Detroit whose bad knees had ordained a new line of work. His life's savings as well his mother's had been invested in Presto. "Hear that?" he'd asked Omar during the cocktail hour, raising each leg up and down. "That's cartilage crunching."

"Well, I appreciate your patience, Johnny," said Gold, "and your forthrightness, which is a trait every one of you men possess. And it's why you're here tonight, why you've come this far. Why you've been chosen over countless others to be executive trainees in what has become *the* fastest-growing company on the face of the earth." He looked up and down the table.

"Quite a statement to make, isn't it, about a company that's only four years old, but it's the truth, no matter what you'll hear to the contrary, no matter what the cynics say—and believe me, there are a lot of those. Oh my Lord, are there ever! A cynic on every corner. You'll meet them every day, everywhere you go. It doesn't work, they'll tell you. It can't work, they'll tell you. It defies logic, they'll tell you. It's an unbalanced system, they'll tell you. It's malarkey, they'll say. Out-and-out hokey."

Roy Gold paced the length of the table, stopping now at the other end. "Is this malarkey?" he asked, gesturing from the coffee service on the mahogany buffet to the dramatic mural, the sweep of his hand stirring the chandelier's crystal pendants to a tremble of fiery flashes. "Is it hokey? You see it. I earned it. Does it defy logic that a man who's willing to sell an excellent product at a fair price can have all this? Does it defy logic that a man can love success so much that he wants—no! I take that back, *needs*—*must* share it with others."

He came down the other side of the table now, trailing a fragrance that reminded Omar of Marie's freshly hung laundry, warm in the morning sun.

"Of course it doesn't!" Gold said, turning abruptly. "But it shocks people because they don't know how to take me. I speak a plain language, gentlemen. There's an easy way and a hard way, a right way and a wrong way, and shame on me, but I don't know any other way to play except fair.

"You see, I grew up real poor. It was just me and my father and my mother. But you see, being poor didn't bother me. Going to bed with my stomach growling some nights didn't bother me. Wearing a grown man's clothes cut down to boy's size didn't bother me. No, what really really bothered me was not having any brothers and sisters. What really hurt was that my father never spoke to me and my mother unless he had to. And then what nearly tore me apart was losing my mother when I was just fifteen years old. That, that was the worst improverishment! All my life the thing I've wanted more than anything else is a family. For me that's all there is." He gestured around the room, which was so still not a man blinked or seemed to breathe. Johnny Biggs still held the roll he had taken one bite from.

"That's what this is all about. I can't stand being alone. I have this yearning, not for power, not for money, but for the strength and the support of a family. For community. Comm—*Unity!* That's what this company is. That's what I'm all about. *That's* what the cynics can't understand. And gentlemen, that's the way it's got to be for you, too. You've got to develop this need, this unquenchable thirst for the interrelationship and love and trust and comfort of a family. Support one another. Reach out, bring others in. Share your knowledge, your expertise, your market. Build an executive network every bit as strong, as durable, as caring as a family. Because, let me tell you, gentlemen, that's where the future of this nation is. That's where my future is. In you, my family."

Roy Gold returned to his chair and sat down. He smoothed his napkin in his lap as every man leaped up, clapping and cheering. Johnny Biggs put down his roll and whistled.

Once again, Omar felt this expansion in his chest, in his throat, behind his eyes. And now for the first time he not only knew its source, but could give it a name, this hunger, this limitless hunger.

Omar Duvall's first stop was at Bernadette's. The day had been long and mean with heat and, he supposed, the constant whining of her rashy-faced shirtless children. They clung to her legs as she spoke over the chain of the lock. She wouldn't let him in. She refused to come down and see his new car.

"What's wrong, baby?" he pleaded. "Please, please tell me." He reached in to run his finger down her nose, but she jerked back with a hissed demand for her money. Little bitch. He gripped the tacky doorframe and clenched his teeth. All the way back from Connecticut he'd fantasized their lovemaking after almost two weeks apart. In his jacket pocket were the black lace garter belt and bra he'd bought her in Hartford. And here he stood, horny as hell, pockets bulging, and she wouldn't even let him in. He should have called first, he thought, realizing now that her bedroom door was closed. She had some other guy in there, probably some kid. Remembering what she'd said about Norm sent a chill up his spine, and he stepped back, gesturing to let her know he understood, that it was okay. It wasn't her fault. He had no right to be angry or possessive. After all, who understood human weakness and need better than he did? "When's a good time to come back?" he whispered.

"Never!" she snapped. "And I'm telling you if I don't get my money back I'm going straight to the cops."

"Why? What's wrong?"

She released the chain and stepped into the hallway, dragging the little girls attached to her, one on each leg. She closed the door quietly and told him about the U.S. government "syphilis guy" coming to warn her about him. Jabbing her finger in his face, she said she didn't want him near her or her kids ever again. "Do you understand? Do you?" she spat. That creep talking like that about her private life like she was just some piece of trash was the worst thing that had ever happened to her. "Do you understand, not just the worst, but the most humiliating, the most disgusting . . ."

"Listen to me!" He grabbed her arm to calm her down. "What are you talking about? What man? What did he look like? Was he a Negro?"

He was white, she said, pulling away. He was a big guy, young, with a purplish birthmark under his nose. He had a U.S. government badge and his ID said he was a VD investigator for the Department of Public Health.

"You lying little . . ." He grabbed her again, wrenching her close.

"Get your fucking hand off me!" Chin out, eyes narrowed, she held his stare. "Now!"

He let her go. Luther and the old man. He could feel them in this. His eyes darted up and down the corridor, which seemed darker with their nearness and the dull tenacity of their mission. An itchy sweat trickled down his neck.

Whining to go back inside, the little girls tugged at their mother.

"I want my money back, every penny of it," she demanded.

He touched her face and tried to smile. "That's impossible, little Miz Mansaw." He told her that he had already purchased her distributorship and her product line.

"You can go to hell, you and your goddamn soap," she said, batting away his hand.

"I imagine I will. Someday," he said, grinning. "But first I expect to be delivering your product to you in approximately two to three weeks, Miz Mansaw."

"I want my money!" she called down the hallway after him. "I don't want any of your fucking product, your fucking soap!"

His next stop was the boardinghouse, where he would go through the Judge's files and compile a list of potential customers. He would personally call on everyone he could find and sell them a franchise. It was amazing how quickly people could be disarmed with just a few vital facts: your cousin Lena in Detroit; the stone house at the lake that your aunt left you, and your brother took you to court for. People were just dying to find someone they could trust, an intimate, someone who not only understood, but knew things without having to be told. And he didn't regard it in any way as taking advantage or preying on their troubles, because the truth was, he cared about people. He really did. Even when they turned on him. It pained him to see anyone hurt. There were still nights when he could not close his eyes, but what images of Earlie came to mind, that most headstrong, stubborn, and selfish young man who in a very real sense had been the instrument of his own harm. And of this he had no doubt. None whatsoever. He patted his temples and neck dry, then knocked on the screen door.

May Mayo held her finger to her lips as she gestured him into the parlor away from her sister. In the kitchen Claire sat at the table, shelling peas as polka music blared from the radio.

"Sister doesn't want you here," May whispered. "She thinks all the things we've been missing are your fault."

"Things?"

"The shower hose and the bath mat and the white urn lamp and her Wedgwood plates."

"Well, why on earth would I take those?"

"I don't know," she said. "But then those women started calling."

"What women?" he asked, knowing it must have been Bernadette and Marie.

"They never give their names. They just say it's about business. I didn't tell them a thing," May assured him. "But Sister wants to call the police."

"The police?" He coughed against his prickly throat. "The police?"

"Yes," May Mayo whispered, glancing past him to make sure Claire was still in the kitchen. "She thinks you're a flimflam man."

"A what?" he whispered back.

"A flimflam man."

"What's a flimflam man?"

"A sharpie, a crook, like a Gypsy."

The noon news broadcast began to play loudly on the kitchen radio now, and the announcer's deep voice steadied him. There were higher powers here that would protect him. He had suffered enough failure and disappointment, so now must be the time of his good fortune and triumph. Surely it was due him. Surely he had earned it. He reminded himself that it was not happenstance that had delivered him here, but some magnetizing force.

"But now Sister says you can't stay. I feel just terrible, Mr. Duvall, what with your government connections and all, but there's nothing I can do."

"Well, there's one thing you can keep on doing, Miss Mayo, and that's don't tell people anything at all." He looked over both shoulders. "There are spies around, Miss Mayo."

Her hand flew to her mouth. "Oh I was afraid of something like that! Spies! A fine kettle of fish! Especially now! Ever since the Judge passed on, Sister's had me walking a very tight rope here." The delicate little woman gestured him down so she could whisper at his ear. "Nursing home! The least little thing and she starts dialing them. So I've got to be careful, Mr. Duvall. Very, very careful!"

"Of course," Omar said, heading for the front door with May at his heels in a tremulous flutter. In the front hall, he stopped suddenly and looked down at her. "Have you ever been in business for yourself, Miss Mayo?"

"Oh no!" She tittered at the thought. "I leave all that up to Claire. She's the one with the head for business, the practical one." She looked around before whispering, "I'm the flighty one, Mr. Duvall. The dreamer!"

"Well, maybe it's time to change, Miss Mayo. Maybe it's time to take charge of your life. I mean I find it quite appalling that a lovely woman like yourself has to live in fear of being railroaded into a nursing home. I mean that, Miss Mayo."

Her hairy chin quivered. "Well, thank you, Mr. Duvall. I appreciate your concern."

"I'm very fond of you, Miss Mayo, and I'd like to help you—if you'd let me."

She had been staring up at him. "Yes," she said. "I'd like you to help me. I really would."

"Well, it's a business proposition, an investment, an opportunity to be independent, Miss Mayo, and to make your own decisions about your own life."

Marie was hanging towels on the line when Omar came down the driveway. Her hair was a mess and she had clothespins in her mouth and the front of her blouse was wet from the two loads of bundled wash she'd just carried out here. As she turned back to the line, the sharp grass scratched her ankles. She hadn't shaved her legs or underarms in days. The wash was piled on a paper bag because the laundry basket was coated with green slime from sitting outside all week, and there the lawn mower lay, rusting in the tall weedy grass. This wasn't the way she wanted things to be. She wanted to seem strong and in control when he returned, or *if* he returned; that one word, ballast to every hopeful surge: *if*. If. And here he was. She was amazed; amazed, and now in her relief so confused she couldn't think straight, couldn't think at all, could just continue this task, this vital, centering chore.

"Marie!" He stood grinning at her. "You look wonderful," he said. "A sight for sore, sore eyes."

She grabbed another towel, squeezing it so hard her fingers hurt.

"Oh. Oh here," he said, patting one jacket pocket, then another. "I got this for you." He pulled out a small framed photograph. "It's me shaking hands with Roy Gold." He offered it uneasily. "I thought you'd like it."

Her hands trembled as she pinned together the corners of two towels.

He cleared his throat, then studied the picture with a frown, as if noticing certain details for the first time. "Oh yes. This was at the ceremony." He held it even closer. "In fact, that's your certificate of franchise he's handing me."

She bent down for another towel, but he snatched it from the pile and hung it on the line.

"I've missed you terribly," he said, shaking out another towel.

"You did?" she asked, her chest suddenly daggered by all the pain she had suppressed or denied, and here it was, here he was, tearing her apart. No. No. No matter what he said or did, no matter how he explained it, she could not live this way again, leashed to a man's promises, knowing his every word so much by heart as she fell asleep analyzing a sentence that she would wake up hours later stuck on the exact same word, wondering, had he said this while meaning that, had he forgotten, had he just been too busy, had she misunderstood, oh surely she had misunderstood because he would not lie, because there were times when he seemed to care for her so, because she had tried so hard in so many ways, because she wanted, wanted, wanted, needed to be loved, because she needed . . . because she . . . because, because.

"Oh, you have no idea!" he sighed. "Sometimes in the lectures it got so bad I could barely concentrate." He glanced back at her. "I just kept thinking about you and the children and this yard and the house, and I'd be wondering how Benjy's swimming was going and was Alice still coming home so exhausted every night and did Norm still hate my guts, well, not hate"—he chuckled—"maybe resent, which I don't think will last too too long once he sees my new car, which you are going to love, Marie! It drives like a dream. It just hums along. I can't wait to see you in it. Truly, it befits you. Oh Marie, I just want the best, the very best for you and the children."

Arms folded, she watched him hang the last few towels and washcloths. Every time he bent over, his jacket and shirt hiked up his back. He'd obviously gained weight, while she'd eaten so little this last week that now even the smell of food sickened her. She started toward the house.

"You forgot your picture," he said, following her to the door.

"No," she said when he reached for the knob.

"Can't I come in?" His eyes widened. "I need to see you. I . . . I need to talk to you."

"We'll have to talk out here," she said.

"What's wrong, Marie?"

"I want my money back." Saying it made her knees sag.

"Why?" He looked stunned. "Why?" he asked again.

"I trusted you in a way I've never trusted anyone in my whole life, and now I feel like such a fool!"

"Marie!" He put his hands on her shoulders. "What in God's name is going on here?" His head shot up and he looked past her. "Has someone been around here besmirching my good name? He has, hasn't he? And you believed it? How could you? How could you? I'm very disappointed!"

No one had been around. She had no idea what he was talking about, and yet, oddly enough, she found herself on the defensive. She explained how his two-week absence had made her lose trust in him, and now he grew even more upset, wringing his hands and pacing back and forth on the driveway.

"What could I do? I had no choice. It was business—every waking moment was nothing but seminars and charts and workshops. I don't know what to say, Marie. I mean you, of all people. You know what this opportunity means to me. To us!" He threw up his hands, and with his back to her, he groaned, "I don't know. I don't know what to say." He looked around. "I thought you had such faith in me. I guess that was my mistake. I just assumed you believed me. I've been alone so long I'm just not used to verifying every move. I'm sorry. I had no idea you were so unhappy and so afraid. I feel like such an ass."

"I didn't know where you were!"

"But I told you where I was!" He came back and stood by the steps. His eyes were bloodshot and weary.

"Not really. You never really said exactly where, and then you didn't call again and I got very nervous." Her voice broke.

"Well, I'm here now." He touched her arm. "You don't have to be nervous anymore."

She closed her eyes. She had accused him so many times in her thoughts that now in his presence there seemed nothing more to say.

"Look what I have." He was unrolling a piece of parchment. "Your certificate of franchise. See," he said, pointing as he presented it to her. "That's Roy Gold's signature."

She looked up, her heart pounding. "But it only says one franchise. I gave you money for two. That's what you said." He grabbed it back and his look of shock frightened her.

"Damn," he said, examining the document. "It's a good thing you caught that, it got right by me. It's just one of those clerical errors a phone call'll clear up in two seconds flat." He sighed. "You don't believe that, either, do you?"

"I want to believe you," she said.

He leaned so close that she thought he was going to kiss her right out here in full view of Jessie Klubock's kitchen window.

"Can I come in, then?" he asked.

So far Marie had managed to ignore Norm's sullenness as he hunched over his plate. Actually it was Benjy who was putting a strain on the conversation right now. She wasn't even sure what Omar had just said, just some light-hearted remark, but Benjy was doubled over, his high-pitched laughter nervous and throbbing with eagerness.

"Somebody better do something, I think he's choking," Norm mumbled, not even looking up.

Benjy's laughter ceased so abruptly that his mouth still twitched. He kept blinking, and his hands shook as he cut his hamburg patty into tiny pieces.

In the fork-clinking silence her eyes met Norm's.

Omar slapped the table with both hands. "Well, what do you say, boys? Who wants to drive my brand-new Cadillac?"

Norm's head shot up. "New?"

Omar chuckled. "Well, new for me's new enough."

"Go ahead, Norm," she urged. Omar was trying so hard. It was true, he wasn't used to the complexities of family life. "Just go for a quick spin, why don't you?"

"I can't." Norm sucked loudly on his cornless cob. "I'm going somewhere."

"I wish I could drive," Benjy said, looking between her and Omar with that forced smile.

"Yah, and that'll be another disaster just like swimming," Norm said, with a smirk for her benefit. After Benjy's fall into the pool, she hadn't made him go back. She knew she should have. She'd always made Alice and Norm face their fears, but with Omar gone she'd been too frightened herself, too drained.

"There's a time to reap and a time to sow," Omar was saying, "and this just may not be Benjy's time to swim." He smiled at Benjy. "But it'll come, mark my words. When the time's right, he'll be ready."

She looked at Benjy, wishing it was so, but he was too much his father's son.

Outside, Klubocks' dog had been barking. Now the barking intensified with a sudden knock on the back door.

"I never even heard them!" Norm said, jumping up.

Omar leaned back and opened the door. Weeb Miller and Tommy Mullins glanced in nervously at Norm, who started toward them.

"Well, hello, young men, come in! Come in. My name," he said, extending his hand, "is Omar Duvall."

"Nice to meet you," Weeb said, blushing as they shook hands. He introduced himself as Lawrence, a name Marie hadn't heard him use in years. The other boy, who was as tall as Omar, was a jiggle of soft flesh. Though she hadn't seen him in a long time, Marie recognized him by the purple birthmark on his upper lip.

"This is Tommy Mullins," Weeb said, introducing his friend, who nodded and rubbed his arm as he shuffled forward to shake Omar's hand. His parents had sent him away to prep school, but she could see it obviously hadn't had any maturing effect on Tommy, who stammered halting replies to Omar's pleasant questions. He kept glancing miserably at Norm.

"We better get going," Norm said. He flipped a cookie and Weeb caught it.

"You look like an athlete, young man," Omar said.

Weeb shrugged and shook his head in flattered denial. "Norm's the jock. I just kinda goof around."

"Well, be that as it may, you've got one of those frames that's all muscle and tendon," Omar said.

Mouth agape, Norm rolled his eyes. "We better get going," he said again.

But Omar was asking Weeb how he'd been spending his summer.

"Sleeping," Weeb said, laughing, then, with a glance at Marie, he added, "I got ten lawns I cut."

"That's why you're in such good shape," Omar said, and now he asked Tommy.

"I work for my father," Tommy said. "He has the bakery on Beecham Street."

"Yah, he's the head muffin man. Can't you tell?" Weeb laughed with a jab at Tommy's belly.

"Hey, somebody's gotta do quality control," Tommy sniffed, and they all laughed, all but Norm. "Muffins just happen to be my specialty."

"And specialization, as we all know, is the future, now, isn't it?" Omar said. "I myself am involved in cleaning products, the marketing of soap and other various cleansers and detergents, both commercial and domestic."

"That must be interesting," Weeb said, shuffling his feet. He and Tommy Mullins looked at Norm, who waited at the door.

"You know, it is," Omar mused. "It's not the product. It's the people you meet. Let me tell you, young men, you ever get a few dollars together and want to be your own boss, you just give me a call, now. I mean that. Seriously. Or your mothers and fathers. Maybe you could even give them these," he said, taking pamphlets from his breast pocket and handing them to the boys. "Tell me, Lawrence, what line of work's your dad in?"

"He's a federal VD inspector." Weeb laughed.

The boys exchanged glances.

"Well, isn't that interesting," Omar said. He was staring at Norm. "I wouldn't imagine you'd find too many of them around," he said to Norm.

Marie felt bad. Omar obviously thought the boys were putting one over on him.

"I don't know," Norm said, glancing past Omar, who continued to stare at him. "C'mon, we gotta go now," he said to Weeb and Tommy, who hurried after him.

The look of dread on Benjy's face startled her, and she realized he was afraid of losing Omar, afraid Norm would drive him away. "Steve Miller really is a VD inspector," she told Omar, and Benjy winced.

"Is he now," Omar mused as he watched them through the window.

"He's always kept it real low key, but the boys are right at that age. I think they have a lot of fun with it."

"Umm." He nodded, turning. "I'll bet they do." He mussed Benjy's hair. "I'll just bet they do, now."

Later, when Benjy had gone to bed, she and Omar sat on the couch watching television. With Omar's arms around her and her head on his shoulder, she closed her eyes, grateful for this rare time alone before Norm brought Alice home from work.

"You're a wonderful woman," Omar sighed.

As she leaned closer, her hand pressed down on a metal ring. Thinking something was caught in the cushions she gave it a tug. She had pulled a black lace garter belt from his pocket.

"Oh Lord," he groaned. "Now you've seen it."

"What is it?" There was a store tag attached.

"So now I have to give it to you. Here," he said, also removing a black bra from the same pocket. "I bought them, but then I was too embarrassed to give them to you. So here," he said, holding them out with his eyes closed.

"Oh. Oh no. Oh dear," she giggled, dangling the bra in front of her.

"Now don't make me feel any more foolish than I already do," he pleaded, his head turned.

"It's so big!" She burst out laughing. "It's huge!"

"Well, pardon my inadequate powers of estimation," he said, turning back. "But how would I know?" His mouth moved close to hers. "How on earth would I know, dear lady?"

Benjy was halfway down the stairs when he stopped, surprised to see Omar asleep on the couch, where he must have spent the night.

"Take him somewhere," he heard his mother saying as she stood at the counter wrapping sandwiches for herself and Norm to take to work.

"Where?" Norm asked from the table, his mouth full of cereal.

"I don't know. Anywhere. You're his brother and you never spend any time with him. He's alone too much."

"Then why are you letting him quit swimming lessons?" Norm shot back. "Just because *he* said so?"

Wincing, Benjy froze on the steps.

"Because he's a nervous wreck," his mother said. "He almost drowned."

"And next time he probably will if he doesn't learn how. He's got to—especially if he's afraid. Mom, you're the one that taught me *that*!"

"Look, Norm, right now I can only do so much, do you understand?"

"No! No, I don't. Not about something as important as that, anyway," Norm said, his voice rising.

In the pause, Benjy held his breath.

"Okay, I'll tell you what," his mother said. "After work today you take Benjy to the lake and *you* teach him how to swim!" Her car keys jingled, and she opened the door.

"The lake! But at night just couples go there, Mom! Dates!"

"Just do it!" she ordered, then rushed out to the car.

"Yah, so you can do it with the peddler," Norm muttered, hurrying after her so he wouldn't have to walk to work.

Benjy glanced down at Omar, embarrassed to see him awake. He must have heard what Norm had just said.

"C'mere, son," Omar said as he sat up. "You know there's other things to do at the lake besides swimming." He reached for his pants and took five dollar bills from his pocket. "Here," he said, winking. "Maybe with this you can call your own shots."

It was late afternoon. Alice had left for work and Benjy was in the backyard. There was still an hour left before he met Norm at his mother's office for their trip to the lake. Over in the Klubocks' yard Louie and a friend were on their knees pushing trucks through the grass. Klubocks' dog came toward him, limping the way he did when he first got up. "Good boy," Benjy said, rubbing his flanks. If it was his dog he'd let him live in the house and not outside all year long. He threw a stick and the dog dove into the deep grass, then raced back with it. He found a dingy tennis ball in the washing machine box, and he threw it high in the air. It hit the ground and bounced, and the dog leaped straight up and caught it. He took the slimy ball from the dog's mouth and threw it as far as he could toward the woods. The dog shot after it. *Look at that,* he thought, smiling. All he needed was some attention to make him think he was a young dog again. A few minutes passed; then the dog came trotting back with something flopping in his mouth. Stepping closer, he saw that it was a shoe, a stained leather shoe. Earlie's shoe, he knew from the smell. "Give it to me!" he cried, trying to pry it from the struggling dog's muzzle, but the dog wanted to play. "I said give it to me!" he repeated, and when the dog continued to pull away, he slapped the side of his head as hard as he could. The dog growled and he yanked away the shoe. The smell was so disgusting that he had to hold his breath to keep from passing out as he threw it into the garage and locked the door. When he turned around, the dog was gone.

"You hit my dog!" Louie was shouting from his yard. "I'm gonna tell my mother on you, and you're gonna be in big trouble!"

Convinced that the dog had returned to the woods for the dead man's other shoe, Benjy ran down the street. No, no, no, he panted, needing to outrun that dark mass of swelling flesh, the secret rooted in his brain. He didn't stop until he was downtown.

He turned the corner to the sporting goods store, grateful that Mr. Briscoe's car wasn't in the parking lot. He hurried through the dim warehouse to his mother's office. Astrid smiled as he stepped inside. In the spill of fluorescent light, she was a dazzle of red lips, glistening skin, and platinum hair. The top of her sundress was a weave of gold-threaded red straps. Her desk was a colorful litter of plastic flowers, statuettes, paperweights, and pictures. On Astrid's side of the filing cabinet there was a mosaic of movie magazine clippings of Bobby Darin, who had bought her a drink once in Las Vegas.

"So, Benjy, I heard the good news!" she said, punching numbers into her adding machine. The long strip of paper curled onto the floor. "School's opening a month early—next week, I think they said." Pausing, she glanced up. "Jeez, didn't anyone tell you?"

Stunned, he shook his head.

"Aw, they probably just didn't want to spoil your last few days of freedom." She pulled the strip of paper close and examined it, then jumped up and wiggled over to him on her high red heels. "Jeez, that went over like a lead balloon," she said, placing her hands on his shoulders. Even in heels she wasn't that much taller than he was. Her breath hit his face with the warmth of spicy flowers. "I was kidding. I was just kidding." She shook him and he tried to smile.

She opened the top drawer of her desk and slid out a box of pink peppermints. "Don't be so polite," she said when he only took one. "Here," she said, slipping four more into his pants pocket; then, hearing his mother come through the warehouse, she scurried into her chair. She winked and he could feel himself blushing.

Right after his mother came back into the office, Norm arrived, looking as hot and tired as his mother. Benjy could see her grow more irritated as Astrid kept interrupting her. Fearing a blowup, he fixed on his mother's every word, nodding intently, as if his concentration might shield Astrid. His mother was explaining that he and Norm were to eat at the hotdog stand on the beach and not at the hotel because that food was too expensive.

"What the hay, live it up!" Astrid laughed. "Don't listen to her. Have some fun!"

"The blanket's in the car," his mother continued, trying to ignore her. "Here's your money."

"Thanks," Norm said, looking down at the two dollars. "It'll be a big night."

"Don't look so miserable," Astrid said, throwing her arm over his shoulder. "Maybe you'll meet some cute girls. Do a little dancing, a little . . . stargazing?" She laughed.

"Remember, now, Norm, you're going to teach Benjy how to swim," his mother said.

"Well, I hope that's not all he's gonna teach him," she said with a wink at Norm and a tweak of Benjy's nose. "Want Auntie Astrid to come, too?" she asked, and Norm burst out laughing, his face reddening.

"Go ahead, now." His mother steered them to the door.

Astrid ran into the warehouse after them. "Hey, Marie! I just thought. My party tonight! You said you couldn't come cuz of the kids, but they're going out, so now you can! I got tons of food and you'd really like the wire plant people. I mean it. They're all just a heck of a nice bunch. And besides, you'll really bail me out if you come. Somehow I got more guys than girls coming and Bobby's just gonna shit—oh, excuse me, boys, your Auntie Astrid slipped. But he's gonna think I did it on purpose, I know he is. And really, I wasn't even thinking, you know, boy girl boy girl or anything like that. I just went around inviting people I liked, and I'll be darned, most of 'em turned out to be guys. So will you come? Please? Please? Pretty please, with sugar on top?" She clasped her hands under her chin, pouting like a child.

"Astrid, if you don't mind, I have to tell my sons something," his mother said with a cold stare.

"Oh! Oh, yah. Sure," she said, backing into the office. "I'll be in here." She gave a little wave, and Benjy waved back.

"Why don't you go to her party, Mom?" Norm asked when the door closed. "Maybe you'll meet some nice guy. Some nice people," he quickly added.

"I have to learn the business tonight," she said with an odd startled look. "Omar's going to teach me."

"I'd like to know what the hell this is all about," Norm said as they waited for the light to change. He drummed his fingers on the sideview mirror.

"I don't know," Benjy said with a shrug, trying to seem as peeved as Norm, when actually he couldn't have been happier. He liked being with his brother. His troubles seemed very distant right now.

"I'll tell you what it is," Norm said. The light turned green and he shifted from park to drive; if they idled too long in gear, the engine would stall. The car lurched forward, and Norm banged the wheel. "She wants you out of the house so she can be alone with that fucking peddler."

"To learn the business," Benjy said, letting his arm trail through the wind.

"Yah, she'll learn the business, all right, the slimy no-good bastard. Someday I'm gonna put my fist right down that no-good fucker's mouth."

He could feel Norm's eyes on him, but he kept staring over the dashboard.

"I can't believe this!" Norm said. "I could be at Weeb's right now. Instead I gotta chauffeur you around."

"We can go to Weeb's. I don't care," he said, and Norm groaned.

"Hey! You used to always get carsick, didn't you?" Norm asked.

"No, you did," he said. "And then when I saw you get sick, I'd get sick."

"But that's it!" Norm cried. "I can drop you off, and you can say you almost threw up, so you have to go lay down." He grinned. "Yah! What's she gonna do, make you go sit on the steps all night so she and the fucking peddler can be alone?"

"No. I don't want to."

"Why?" Norm's voice cracked.

"I don't know. I just don't." Actually there were three reasons. He didn't want to spend the night in bed. He wanted his mother to be alone with Omar. And he wanted to have fun with Norm.

"You know, Benjy, I think you're probably the most selfish little asshole I've ever known!" Norm's face curdled with disgust.

Forget number three, he thought, his head snapping back as Norm hit the gas and they peeled down Main Street.

At the lake Norm parked in the hotel lot. Leaning against the car, he took off his sneakers and stripped down to his bathing suit, which he had worn all day. Grimy from work, he couldn't wait to get into the water. As he came down the grassy slope to the beach with Benjy on his heels he was relieved to see that he didn't know anyone. Most everyone here was older. This was going to be some night. The little creep had deliberately forgotten his bathing suit, and all he kept talking about was food. Norm spread their blanket, then started down toward the water.

"Can we eat now?" Benjy asked, hurrying after him. "Please, Norm. I'm really hungry!" He kept stepping on blankets and tripping over people.

"Hey, kid! Jesus Christ! Watch it, will you!" Voices cascaded after them.

"Shit!" He turned and grabbed Benjy's arm. "Will you leave me alone?"

"Can't we go eat? I'm starved!" Benjy begged so desperately that Norm was ashamed.

"Soon as I'm done," he promised, then trotted off down to the pier and dove into the cool water. He swam out to the floating dock, then climbed up and sat on the edge and looked back at the peeling gabled hotel, the bustling beach, and his skinny brother just standing there in pants that were too short, his arms folded, head hunched forward, with the water lapping only inches from his feet. Norm groaned. He still had his sneakers on, the little creep.

Tonight would have been perfect. Weeb's parents and his sister, Janice, weren't going to be home, so they would have been able to drink Mr. Miller's beer and listen to records in the comfort of Weeb's bedroom. Instead he had Benjy on his hands and two lousy bucks for food. Benjy waved. He kept waving. Norm refused to wave at him. Finally he slipped into the water and swam back.

"Wait! Norm! Wait!" Benjy kept yelling as he lurched through the coarse sand to the hotdog stand on the nub of the beach. They stood in line, reading the paper sign that listed the thirty different garnishes. "Here!" Benjy shoved something into his hand.

"Where'd you get this?" he demanded, peeling apart the sweaty clutch of bills. He grabbed Benjy's arm. "Steal it?" he hissed through a smile for the benefit of the throngs of people around them.

"No!"

His fingers dug into Benjy's armpit. "From Duvall, right?" he snarled, and Benjy's blank stare was answer enough. He turned away in disgust. The peddler was trying to buy Benjy off, and the little creep was just stupid enough and weak enough to fall for it. Since his return Duvall had surged in confidence around them, openly, brazenly embracing their mother, bragging about his mysterious connections and the vague distant trips he would take her on soon, soon. "As soon as this latest deal breaks even . . . soon as I see my way clear . . . soon as the market straightens itself out . . . soon as the big call comes . . . Soon. Even his mother was beginning to sound like him. Everything was "soon," with her hand on the back of Duvall's chair, her gaze focused on the top of his head as if she'd discovered some dazzling truth in the oily morass of his hair, her voice unfolding like tremulous arms to his lies. And lies they were, all lies. There was no Roy Gold, no soap coming, and he'd probably fast-talked that shitty Cadillac off some other desperate woman.

"Two dogs with piccalilli and chili beans and a Coke," he told the man behind the counter. "What about you?" he asked Benjy.

"The same!" Benjy's grin turned his stomach. Didn't he get it? Didn't he see how he was being used by Duvall to get to their mother?

They sat on their blanket in front of a grove of blue-needled trees. Around them on the beach couples moved closer to one another as the red sun sank behind the dark mountains. Lifeguards moved along the beach, calling through their megaphones for everyone to come out of the water. Far across the lake, approaching the opposite shore, a small boat cut its motor and drifted silently in the fan-shaped breach between darkness and the last sliver of daylight. Suddenly the light was gone, leaving only a faint pink glow that silhouetted the black trees on the jagged mountaintop.

They were going to leave at sunset. Benjy had agreed to go to Weeb's, but he'd promised to wait in the car. For that favor, Norm said he'd tell their mother that Benjy had done well swimming in the lake.

They ate with a startling urgency. "I was so hungry!" Benjy cried. "Let's have some more!"

Norm paused. He was ready to go now, but one more hotdog sounded good. "I'll get it," he said. He started to get up, then sank back onto his knees. "How come Duvall gave you that money?"

"I don't know. To be nice, I guess." Benjy shrugged.

Norm leaned close now. "Why do you think he's so nice to you? Because he knows Alice and I are on to him, so he's after you. He needs you on his side. I see him, the way he looks at you. The way he's always trying to make you laugh or get you to do things with him. Like last night, saying it's okay to quit swimming lessons. Why do you think he did that? He doesn't care about you. Benjy, he doesn't even like you. Can't you tell? To him, you're just . . . just Mom's, you know, her weak spot. Don't you get it? Don't you see how he's using you to get to her? I mean, tonight, right now, this very moment he's probably fucking the—"

"Shut up, Norm! You just shut up!" Benjy cried with a shove that reeled him back on his heels.

Norm got up and stalked off toward the hotdog stand. It's a good thing there were so many people around or else he might have beaten the shit out of the goddamn little creep, pushing him like that in front of all these people, the goddamn little bastard, forget the fucking hotdogs, he'd go back and drag him into the woods and beat the fucking living shit out of the goddamn little prick and teach him once and for all what the fuck loyalty was all about, the little—

"Norman!" came a familiar voice, a sweet, sweet voice. "Norman Fermoyle! Oh am I glad to see you!" Weeb's sister, Janice Miller, ran toward him with a cigarette in her hand.

It didn't matter if Omar liked him or not. The important thing was that Omar loved his mother, Benjy thought as he watched a boy and a girl on the blanket in front of him. The girl had short black hair and a deep tan. She lay on her side, squirming against the boy's thigh. She drew her fingers down his bony chest and up again to his chin. The boy grabbed her arm then and rolled her onto her back. He lay across her chest and kissed her mouth. Benjy forced his gaze into the hole he had been digging in the sand. For one so much alone, so accustomed to hours without speaking and days untouched, this intimacy so near was alarming. Now the girl gave a little whoop and tried to wrestle free. The boy laughed and pinned her down. Closing his eyes, Benjy tensed, waiting for the moment to turn. The boy would hit her. She would scream. She would cry and then she would not be able to stop crying.

All at once he remembered being a small boy perched on his father's shoulders as he ran out of a thicket where dark vines had snagged his hair. A troubled voice had trailed them through the night. "Benjy . . . Benjy . . . Where is he taking you?" He remembered the whisk of the trees passing, passing between him and his mother's voice, until all he could hear was the deep groan in his father's labored breathing below him as he ran. He didn't know where they had gone that night or why his father had taken him. He only remembered waking the next morning in a car behind a gray building. There were open garbage barrels and trash-filled cartons piled high against the wall. He remembered being afraid to move or speak under the weight of his father's stale damp head on his stomach. He remembered his father snoring, and then how suddenly his stubbly face had loomed over him. He remembered his raw puffy eyes streaked with blood and confusion and then the terrible grinding of his teeth as he peered suspiciously at his son, as if Benjy had lured him there. He remembered being slapped hard and not knowing why. He remembered seeing his father weep and knowing then that it was all right, that it wasn't anything he had done, or that anyone had done, that sometimes it just had to be that way.

The boy and girl sat up now, facing the beach, with their arms around each other's waist. It was taking Norm a long time to get hotdogs. It would be even darker than this in the woods, he thought, deep in the woods where Earlie lay. Maybe Klubocks' dog thought Earlie was alive. Maybe he had ripped Earlie's shirt and pants in an effort to drag Earlie back to Benjy. He sat up and hugged his legs. Maybe one of these days he'd open the door to find Earlie's body on the back steps, staring up at him. And what would he do then? What would Omar do?

"My roommate's down there." Janice Miller pointed toward the bathhouse on the far corner of the beach. The woods behind the bathhouse were where everyone went to make out or drink. "She met some guy and she hasn't been back since," Janice said, then took a long, deep drag on her cigarette.

Norm cleared his throat, wishing he could do the same with his brain. Here he sat on the beach finally alone with Weeb's beautiful sister and there was nothing on this earth he could think of to say to her. Damn it . . . He smiled, praying it wasn't the fool's grin it felt like.

"So what am I supposed to do all night while she makes out down there? Some friend!" she huffed. "Some beach party!"

"Where's the beach party?" he asked, looking over the various couples, some playing catch, some just talking, some huddled nose to nose, their fingers sifting sand.

"All around you, stupid." She laughed. "See! That's Sandy and Fitzie and that's Billy . . . Hey, I'm sorry," she said, realizing that he didn't know any of them. "They're all from school. My roommate was supposed to bring a date for me, but her date and mine never showed up, so off she goes with the first thing in . . ."

"Your date?" His chest ached. "The guy you're engaged to? The guy from college?"

"Lavaliered, we're lavaliered! No, not him. He's working. He couldn't come up all this way just for a night." She stubbed out her cigarette, screwing it into the sand.

"Oh!" Norm said, with the faintest hope. She turned over on her stomach, facing him on the blanket. Her white bathing suit glowed in the night. Perspiration glistened between her breasts. She hunched up on her elbows and sighed, looking down at the water. He lifted his head, straining to see more. Nipple, he wanted to see nipple. She flipped over on her side, one arm under her head. He lay on his side now and refocused.

"Well," she sighed. "This is a lost cause. If I had a ride, I'd leave now."

There, there it was, one fat brown nippled breast slung heavily over the other. Oh God!

"Are you here alone?" she asked.

"What's that?"

"Are you here alone?"

"In a way," he said quickly.

"Not with my brother, I hope." She grimaced.

"No . . ."

"With a date?"

"Not tonight," he said lamely.

"Would you mind terribly giving me a ride home, Norman? I have a brutal headache." She pressed her fingertips against both temples.

"Sure." He shrugged, trying to appear calm. What would he do with Benjy? He could leave him here and come back for him later. No, his mother would kill him. Benjy could ride in the back seat and he'd drop him off at home first. No, too obvious. He'd think of something. Janice was kneeling, putting on her white beach jacket. She wrapped her yellow towel around her waist, and when she stood up, one long dark leg showed through the slit.

"Hey Jan! Jan!" a girl called out. "Where you going?" A stocky girl in a red bathing suit ran up to them, waving her arms. She was out of breath.

"I have a headache," Janice said coldly.

"Hey! Who is this?" the friend drawled, her grin verifying what he caught glimpses of in every mirror or storefront he passed. Tanned and muscular from his long days laboring in the sun, he now had the body of a man.

"Norman Fermoyle, a friend of—" Janice hesitated, then added, "Mine."

The friend giggled and rolled her eyes. "Some headache, Jan. I should be in such pain!" she laughed, gesturing limply toward a skinny boy in plaid shorts who was hurrying toward her. "Jan and Norman, this is Peter Slavin from someplace called Dartmouth. Peter—Janice Miller, my roommate with the terrible headache, and this is Norman, her very obvious symptom. And I'm Kit Neal," she laughed, eagerly grabbing his hand.

"Careful," he warned. "It might be catching!"

"You mean contagious," Janice said through a taut smile.

"God, I hope so!" Kit howled.

"Actually I'm the remedy nine out of ten doctors recommend." He leaned close to Kit with a sly wink. Smooth as smooth could be, this was the big time, and he was on a roll.

"Oh God!" Janice groaned, slapping his arm.

"A blatant case of muddled metaphors," Slavin said, thumping a fresh pack of Marlboros on his fist.

He glanced at Slavin. Meta-what? Whores? Spores? Well, the girls certainly didn't look offended, though it seemed they should be. Janice and Kit whispered a moment, then said they were going down to the bathhouse to dress. Kit told Norm to wait and then they could all go into the hotel together. Before he could say anything, Janice grabbed his arm and pressed it against her chest. "Norman doesn't have his ID," she said quickly.

"That's all right," Slavin said, lighting his cigarette and Norm's with an engraved lighter that he stabbed in the air now to punctuate his plan. "He waits out here. We get a pitcher. He comes in, orders ginger ale, chugs it, and voilà! the man's got himself a glass!"

N orm hurried back to the car to put on his pants and sneakers and then he ran down to the beach.

"Where's my hotdog?" Benjy demanded as Norm snatched his shirt from the blanket.

"Look, Benjy, just shut up and listen," he panted. "I gotta do something that's very important. And you wouldn't understand, so I'm not going to go into details here." Damn, he'd misbuttoned the shirt, so he started over. "I won't be gone that long. I'll be right back as soon as I figure this out. Don't talk—just listen. Here, here's some money. Go get the hotdog. But don't leave here! Wait for me! You hear me? Just wait!"

"Where you going?" Benjy tried to grab his arm, but Norm scrambled up the incline.

"Hotel!" he called back over his shoulder.

"What for?" Benjy shouted.

Robert Haddad hadn't left the couch all night. Thankfully, the party seemed to be fizzling. Corinne, one of Astrid's girlfriends from the wire plant, sank down heavily beside him and yawned into her cigarette smoke. She was a skinny woman, heavily made up, with an intricately coiled hairdo. Like the rest of them in their slutty clothes, she drank, smoked, talked too much, and sat too close. "So how's business?" she gulped at the end of her yawn, and poured more beer into her glass.

Haddad ignored her. He watched Astrid, who stood by the hutch, talking to her manager from the wire plant. "That's terrible!" she cried, with a poke in his ribs. He was a tall balding man whose wife was divorcing him. He put his hand on the wall over Astrid's head and leaned toward her. Haddad was sure he was drunk.

Haddad tugged his shirt cuffs down over the tufts of hair on his wrists. Astrid admired tall, slim, blond men, as well she might, being so fair, so beautiful herself. Before her he had never known happiness. Just the sight of her roused this ache, this pride that all that shimmering scented softness was his. His breath quickened with the dizzying rush of giddiness and fear that was more than sexual. It was mystical, a religious experience. She was the core of his being, the purity and goodness that once had been only words. Because of her he was becoming a moral man. Of course there had been a few missteps lately, aberrations so alien, so reproachful they only reinforced his yearning for decency in all things.

Someone turned off a light and lit the candle on the windowsill. Didn't they see how close to the curtains the flame was burning? Just a gust of wind would turn this place into an inferno. Were insurance men the only ones alert to such dangers? He started to get up, then changed his mind. She would berate him in front of her friends if he blew it out and turned the light back on. She would say he was trying to spoil everyone's fun, and she would be right. He was tired. They were getting louder and drunker, and he wanted them to leave. A woman shrieked, then stumbled past him toward the bathroom. Her boyfriend banged on the door. "I gotta pee pee, too," he whined. Couples danced in the flickering darkness. He leaned forward. Astrid and her manager were dancing. Their swaying shadow loomed across the ceiling.

He tried to swallow. Business was lousy and the main office continued to hound him, and tonight, dressing for the party, she had again mentioned getting a job as a hostess in a cocktail lounge. It wasn't the money, she had explained when he said he'd sell more policies. No, it was the glamour she missed, having a reason to dress up fancy like this every night. She needed something that forced her to be cheerful and funny. She wanted to hear people laugh. "I miss that, Bobby," she had said, looking at his reflection in the mirror as she smoothed her yellow brocade dress over her hips. "I need that. I'm a very outgoing person."

This morning he'd gotten a letter from Sam Fermoyle, who wanted his policy sent to him at Applegate Hospital. There was no policy. He'd never sent that premium or any others in the last six months into the main office. Thinking that Fermoyle had been too plowed to even remember signing the contracts, he'd given the money to Astrid. She had probably bought that dress with it, the very dress that was glued against the manager's body.

Corinne shook his arm. She wanted to dance, too, she said, pulling him to his feet. She told him to kiss her and they'd make Astrid jealous, but he just shuffled clumsily to the music. She was kissing his neck. She wanted to give him a hickey. Astrid would love that, she said.

"I can't stay late, I told Astrid," she murmured. "I gotta meet this guy first thing in the morning. He's something. Hey, you're in business, you know him? Omar Duvall? He's an antroopeneer. Hey . . . hey . . . what's the matter?"

Haddad lunged at the manager, who was kissing Astrid.

"Cut it out, Bobby!" Astrid screamed as his fist bit into the man's mouth. The man reeled back, dazed, squinting as he lurched clumsily at Haddad, who struck him in the stomach. The man sank to his knees, then lay on the floor. Astrid tore at his arms as he kicked the crumpled manager's back. Someone pulled him away. He just stood there with weighted arms at his sides and closed eyes while Astrid screamed at him.

"Come on, honey," Corinne kept saying.

"Big deal, isn't he? Big deal, kicking a man when he's down. I hate you! I hate this place! I hate everything about you!"

Haddad went into the bedroom and closed the door. He sat on the bed and whimpered into his palms.

A door opened and closed. Voices called somber goodbyes. Someone was picking up glasses and closing windows. When he came out, the room was empty. The rug was still rolled up against the wall. The light was on under the bathroom door. He stood by it a minute, then moaned against the doorjamb. "I'm sorry, baby. I'll make it up to you. I promise. Next week you can have another party, bigger even than—"

"She ain't in here," a woman said; then the toilet flushed and the door opened. Corinne came out, spraying her hair. "She went to the lake. Jeez, you look shitty. Why don't you sleep. Astrid'll cool off and then she'll come home dragging her tail behind her," she assured him, with a quick glance in the mirror and one last spurt of spray.

When the last couple left the beach, Benjy grabbed the blanket and ran to the car. He could wait in here. He opened the windows, reassured by the music and the voices from the hotel that Norm was close by. Soon he had to close the window because of all the mosquito bites he was getting. Now the glass kept fogging up. He doodled on the steamy windshield, then on the side windows and the ones in back. He wiped them clear with the blanket, then began to exhale rapidly. As soon as they steamed up again, he started over, this time writing swears in the tiniest letters he could make. *Fuck you, Norm. Norm is a asshole. Norm is a dink.* He paused, wondering what the difference was. Well, an asshole would be a real obnoxious jerk and a dink would be a creep who was scared of his own shadow and so afraid to do anything that he was always spoiling it for everyone else. He was a dink. And by that standard Norm was an asshole—well, sometimes. Norm had never been a dink, but then again, he himself had never been an asshole, which seemed like a good thing right now, like something to be proud of.

Every now and again cars would arrive and people would go into the hotel. A man and a woman were coming down the wide wooden stairway now. Benjy ducked as they got into the next car and then left. A few minutes later another car pulled into the lot with its radio blasting. Three women got out. They were laughing so hard, they had to lean against the car with their legs crossed as if they were trying not to wet their pants. The last woman emerging from the back seat was Astrid Haddad. "Help," she cried, halfway out. "I'm stuck."

"Here. You're not stuck, you're just drunk," her friend said, giggling, pulling her the rest of the way out.

"I am not!" Astrid protested as she teetered in a stiff little circle.

The women linked arms. An uneasy feeling came over him as they bumped into one another on their way up the stairs to the hotel. Men were the perilous ones, not women. It was women who kept him safe, who always knew the limits. He lay back down on the seat and stared up at the bright stars and the moon for as long as he could without blinking. The record so far was two minutes. The windshield steamed up again. His eyes closed. He was asleep.

Two hours had passed, but it seemed he had been sleeping for only a little while. He sat up and rolled down the window. The moon had risen over the lake, trailing a luminous path across the black water. The crickets were louder. There were only a few cars left in the lot. He opened the door, sighing as he urinated onto the gravel from inside the car. The car Astrid had come in was gone.

What if Norm had gone home with someone else and left him here? He ran up the steps to the hotel veranda, which was lined with rocking chairs. The floorboards creaked underfoot as he crept from window to window, trying to find Norm. These were the dining-room windows, but he could see only a few people inside. Somewhere a piano was playing. Voices swelled now as he rounded the far corner of the building. He peered through the parted curtains in the long windows. There was a dimly lit smoky lounge with a three-piece band playing. A couple was dancing, their arms around each other's neck. The mirror behind the bar was cracked down the middle. Fishing nets and mounted game fish hung from the walls. He moved to the last window. From here he could see most of the tables.

People in this end of the room were standing and clapping as they sang, "So drink, chug-a-lug, chug-a-lug, chug-a-lug. So drink, chug-a-lug," while a guy drank a mug of beer in what looked like one quick swallow. Finished, he banged down the empty mug. It was Norm! Norm, blinking and wiping foam from his mouth with the back of his hand. Norm standing now, with his hands over his head, to acknowledge the cheers; his brother, Norm, drunk and sinking heavily back into a chair. A girl with long blond hair kept poking his arm, but every time she said anything Norm just laughed. A guy with a dark bushy beard had strutted over to their table, and now he was draining his mug dry while everyone chanted and clapped. Now Benjy noticed the chubby girl who had been timing the guy with a stopwatch. Norm hoisted his mug, gesturing for a refill. The blond girl said something, then got up and left. Norm raised the dripping mug to his lips, and Benjy ran back to the car. He climbed into the back and curled up on the seat, enshrouding himself in the blanket.

He slept so soundly in the fuzzy darkness that it was not the sluggish voices that roused him as the front doors opened, but the sudden glare of the dome light filtering through the brown wool. The doors closed. He started to sit up, then lay back down. Astrid was behind the wheel, not Norm. He could hear Norm, but he couldn't see him.

"Oh you poor thing. Just put your head right there, you poor thing." She started the car.

Norm struggled to speak. ". . . get one . . . go gone . . . go . . ." Suddenly Norm sat up and opened the door. ". . . gotta go get . . ." He waved toward the beach.

"All your friends're gone," Astrid said. "They left, honey. They left you all alone in there, but don't worry, I'm gonna take good care of you, sweetie."

The wet prickly wool rubbing Benjy's chin was all the shame he felt. How could Norm have let this happen? Especially Norm, of all people, Norm who couldn't bear humiliation, reduced to this incoherent babble. He lay perfectly still. When they got home he would pretend he had been sleeping all this time. He only prayed that Astrid wouldn't turn Norm in to their mother. This could be a double cross. How many times had they appeased and coddled his father just to get him out of the house or off the streets? She pulled onto the lake road with the back of Norm's head bobbing against his window. "I'll get you home safe and sound. Now, don't you worry about a thing, sweetie," she murmured. She was so short she had to peer between the dashboard and the top of the wheel to see the road that wended in and out with the shoreline. The tires squealed on the curve and Norm groaned.

"You okay, sweetie? You look kinda peaked," she said, and Norm grunted. "How 'bout if I just pull in here a minute? Actually I'm feeling kinda loopy myself." She turned off the engine and rolled down her window, then fanned herself with her hand. "Phew! Hot in here. You okay? Here," she said, reaching past him. "Let me get your window down. The air'll perk you right up."

Now Norm's head hung back out the open window. He was gasping.

"What's a matter, sweetie?" She touched his face. "You okay? Don't scare me now. Just take it easy."

He moaned.

"You're what? You're gonna what?" she asked. "Here, then, let's loosen you up some." Norm said something and she giggled. His belt buckle clinked. "So you can breathe better," she murmured. There was a zipping sound. "There, how's that feel?" She kissed him. "Feels good, huh?" She held his face and began to kiss him again. "It's okay," she kept saying. "I'm gonna help you, sweetie . . . Don't you worry . . . It's okay."

He couldn't tell if Norm was trying to hug her or push her away, but his arms kept slipping off her shoulders. He was panting. Or maybe crying. Benjy raised his head to see.

Astrid sat back. "God I hate bringing you home like this," she sighed. "Your mother's gonna kill you, you poor thing."

Norm's agitation increased. ". . . this with the . . . the the the thing . . . with . . . Benjy!" he cried, pawing at the windshield as if to part curtains. "Where's Benjy?"

"Benjy's home, sweetie."

"Benjy's home?" He looked at her. "Huh?"

"Yup. Sound asleep in his nice warm bed."

"Okay. Good. Okay." He belched and laid his head back on the window well. "Benjy's home. Good."

Astrid raised her arms and pulled her shirt over her head. "Come here, sweet baby," she said, sliding next to Norm.

Benjy could see her white shoulders, her bent head over the squeaking seat. He couldn't see his brother, but he could hear the sounds he was making.

"There, baby, there," she moaned. "Go ahead. Oh. Oh. Okay, here. Try this one now."

The smacking, slurping sounds continued along with Astrid's moans.

His brain was on fire as he eased onto the floor, cocooned in the blanket. Flames, red and orange flames, in his brain, in his eyes.

Norm hiccupped loudly and Astrid sat up. Benjy stared up at her breasts, hanging big and white in the moonlight just inches from his brother's face. "I'm . . . gonna . . . gonna . . ." Norm groaned.

"Gonna what?" Astrid gasped, trying to get her shirt back on.

Not "gonna" any longer, he knew from the hot gagging spew of it; Norm already *had*. The car reeked of vomitous liquor.

"Shit!" she cried, hitting the wheel. "Shit, shit, shit. That's it! I'm done! I'm through! I never shoulda come here! Never, never, never!"

"I'm sorry," Norm muttered as his head fell back against the open window again.

"Wake up! Norm, don't do this, damn it, wake up!" she said, but he was so deeply asleep that he began to snore. She started the car and drove back to Atkinson, crying all the way. Curled on the floor, Benjy felt every bump jolt up his spine. The car slowed, then turned, and he knew by the passing trees and rooflines that he was almost home.

The minute she pulled into the driveway, she turned off the motor and the headlights and got out of the car. Nauseated, Benjy pushed the blanket off his face. He looked up to see Astrid at Norm's window. She kept whispering his name, trying to wake him up. "Shit!" she gasped as Klubocks' dog began to growl from the lilac bushes behind her. She froze and Benjy realized she was staring at him. Without a word she stepped out of sight. After a moment he sat up and looked around. She had delivered them to the wrong driveway. She was running down the street with her high heels in her hands.

"Norm! Norm!" he whispered, shaking his shoulder. "You gotta wake up! We're in Klubocks' driveway!" The white Cadillac was parked out front, which meant that Omar had spent another night on the couch.

Norm's eyes opened. "There's Benjy! Good. Tha's good. Good." He smiled, then, with a heavy sigh, closed his eyes again.

He begged Norm to wake up. He shook his arm, nudged his head, thumped the top of the seat, warning of the trouble they were going to be in. Bad enough he was drunk and had thrown up all over the front seat of their mother's car, but being in Klubocks' driveway, well, that was the far greater offense. "You're gonna get killed, Norm!" And now it hit him. So was he. He opened the door and ran toward the house, not realizing until he got to the steps that Klubocks' dog was chasing him. He grabbed the dog's collar and, running in a crouch, dragged him back to the bushes, ordering him back in there! *Stay! Stay! Stay,* he prayed as he raced back to the car and tried again to rouse Norm, whose stupor had deepened. He looked at the parallel driveways. All he had to do was back straight out of Klubocks' onto the street, turn slightly, then head into their own driveway. That might even wake Norm up enough to get him inside. He just prayed the damn dog stayed where he was and didn't start barking. He got behind the wheel and turned the key, wincing with the thundering engine. He shifted into reverse and the car jerked back. Panicking, he tried to get it into park again, but the car lurched forward. He jammed his foot onto the pedal—the wrong pedal. It was the gas pedal, he realized as the car surged forward, turning, turning right into the lilac bushes. Branches cracked. "No!" he cried with the sickening bump. He hit the brake, shifted, then turned off the engine and ran into the house. He climbed into bed and lay sobbing with the pillow over his head.

In the morning Alice's eyes shot open to the commotion downstairs. She threw back the sheets and sat up trembling. She had overslept. The priest would be here soon. Her mother was screaming. She ran around the room, trying to get ready.

Norm's voice, congested and quivering, rose from the kitchen. "I said I'm sorry! It wasn't my fault. I can't help it if I got food poisoning!"

"Food poisoning!" her mother cried. "You were drunk! You were so goddamn drunk you plowed into Klubocks' lilac bushes and killed their goddamn dog!"

"You think I killed it on purpose? I was sick, Mom! Honest to God. I got food poisoning."

"Food poisoning! You don't even remember what happened!"

"Because I must've passed out!"

"How could you do that? How could you do that to me? To yourself! Jesus Christ, Norm! After all you've seen. After all we've been through!"

"We had those lousy hotdogs. Ask Benjy. That's what it was."

"Benjy!" she scoffed. "According to him he slept all night. He barely remembers coming home!"

"See! He's probably got food poisoning, too!"

"I don't want to hear about food poisoning!"

"Well, you should at least check him! I mean, what if he's in a coma or something!"

"Don't say it again. Don't! You hear me, mister? Because now I want the truth!"

"That is the truth!"

"What a mess," Alice groaned as she clipped her stocking into her garter belt. Poor Benjy, he liked the dog even more than the Klubocks did.

She wondered if Omar was down there in the middle of all that yelling. What on earth did he want here? she wondered as she brushed her hair. Did he think this was the way families were supposed to be? Didn't he know that in normal homes the sofa and easy chairs matched and the lamps had shades and the windowsill plants grew in clay pots, not rusting coffee cans, and a family's only anxiety sitting down to dinner might be bones in the fish, the boiled heat of gravy, or a nick in the glass rim, and not the sting of their mother's gasp when the phone rang, fearing another bill collector's ultimatum, or worse, their weeping father's thin wet love, his slurred vows to return as lethal a blade as his sorrow.

God, this was all so humiliating, having to go up there with a priest to beg her father for money she knew he didn't have. But her mother was convinced he was hoarding some fortune from her—as if he'd ever had a penny of his own. She slipped on her dress, then groped in the dust under the bed for her white shoes. With every wobbly step the heels squeaked, a painful reprise of graduation night. She twisted her hair into a bun so tight it pulled her eyes into slits. She looked older now. Her father would be shocked to see how quickly time was passing, how much of her life he was missing.

"Say it!" her mother demanded downstairs. "Say it!"

"Leave me alone," Norm moaned. "Just leave me alone."

She wound a cord of plastic violets around the nub of hair, then yanked it out. Damn it! What would she and a priest ever talk about on the long ride up and back. She could have taken a bus. She should have said no to him and to her mother. But she never did, never said no. That was the trouble, always letting people get in between the Alice they saw and the real Alice. The real Alice slept nude, touching herself under the sheets, drawing her fingers up between her legs, always stopping short, afraid of what she would find in there, even though she knew the nuns told lies and she wouldn't go crazy or suddenly bald, but afraid that she might like it too much. Last night at the A+X Carla had insisted that was the way lesbians got started—first they did it to themselves all the time whenever they felt like it, and got so much of it that they had to have it all the time that way, and only from women.

Two nights ago, Carla had shown everyone the pictures Mr. Coughlin hid in his office. The pictures showed nude women kissing and fondling one another. The pictures. She shuddered, ashamed of this raw ache in her belly every time she thought of the grainy breasts pressed nipple to shriveled nipple. It frightened her to think that might be the strangeness, the unattainability, that had repelled every other boy before Lester, and now, oddly enough, attracted Blue Mooney. He had even started wearing his Marine uniform to the lot now when he picked up Anthology. Everyone said it was to impress her. Oh God. She ripped the bun out of her hair and pulled it into a ponytail. She put on bright pink lipstick, and sprayed perfume down the front of her dress and up under her skirt. There was no real Alice. There couldn't be.

Norm sagged over the table, his forehead braced against his fist. His shirt was wrinkled and grass-stained, and he smelled. Her mother came into the kitchen, staggering under the weight of the bulging laundry basket that she hauled onto the table. Norm winced at the thud.

"Oh I'm so sorry!" she said, leaning over him. "Forgive me, Prince Charming, I forgot!" She glanced at Alice. "His condition! He's feeling just a little . . . delicate this morning. Hotdogs. Too god-damn many hotdogs!" she said with a poke at his back.

"Mom!" Alice said, seeing his head tremble. "He's sick."

" 'Oh, he's sick,' says the princess in all her finery while the servants shuffle around her," her mother said. She was sorting the dirty clothes into piles on the floor.

"Mom, you know why I'm dressed like this!" she said, but knew from the grim flick of her mother's eyes to say no more. She made toast and sat down across from Norm.

From outside came the sounds of digging, a metal shovel scraping grit and stone, rocks hitting a pile.

"Do you know what happened last night?" her mother asked.

"I heard," she muttered, head low over the dish.

"Along with everyone else." Her mother was flinging clothes faster and faster now into white heaps, blue, red, and black heaps, and swirling pastel heaps that grew to table height. The smell of foot sweat and body musk burgeoned with the piles. Alice bit into the toast and chewed dryly.

Her mother paused, gesturing with a pair of Norm's undershorts. "Of course what they don't know is how thoughtful he is. How after he threw up all over my car and ruined the Klubocks' precious lilac bushes, crushing and killing their dog in the process, how he didn't want to disturb his mother, so he crawled into the garage, where Mr. Klubock found him with his pants half off." She smiled down at Norm, whose eyes were closed. His mouth twitched. "My dear thoughtful son passed out on the dirt floor." She threw the undershorts at him and they landed on his shoulder.

He whipped them onto the floor. He turned and stared up at her. "What can I do to make you shut up?"

Alice stopped chewing. She didn't dare swallow.

"Say you were drunk!" her mother said through clenched teeth. "Say it! Say you're a lousy, stinking, selfish drunk and you're only sixteen years old. Say it and I'll shut up!"

Norm hung his head.

"Say it!" She grabbed his arm and shook him. "Say it! Say it!"

"Mom, what are you trying to do?" he whispered, his bloodshot eyes bulging with tears. "I told you I'm sorry. I'm sorry."

"Say it!"

"I was drunk," he said softly.

She leaned over him. "I'm a lousy, stinking, selfish drunk, and I'm only sixteen years old," she commanded, her features so contorted she almost seemed to be smiling.

"Lousy, stinking, selfish drunk, and I'm only sixteen years old," he mumbled.

"And if I don't watch it, I'll end up like my father!" she hissed.

She is, Alice thought. She's smiling.

"And if I don't watch it, I'll end up like my father."

Alice could barely hear him. She did it, she thought. *She always does it. Grinds and grinds and grinds until there's nothing left.*

Norm stared at his coffee cup, his shoulders hunched in a strangulated sob.

"Jesus Christ," came her mother's muffled gasp. Her hands covered her face. "Jesus Jesus Christ."

The back door flew open and Omar entered, grinning, a greasy doughnut bag in his fist.

"Good morning, lovely people." He shook the bag. "Sweets to soothe our sour spirits."

Norm didn't look up. Alice watched her mother's head lift and shoulders straighten, as if she were reassembling herself for Omar.

"You left. I thought you wanted to help them clean up out there, and then I saw you leave," her mother said, with a sickening breathless urgency.

"Well, I offered, but Harvey wants to bury the dog before his little boy sees it. Messy, I guess. All them guts and goo balls," he said as he arranged the doughnuts on a plate, taking great care with the alignment of the second tier. He tapped a jelly doughnut into place. "So anyway I went and got bakery for them and some for us. Jessie offered us coffee, but I promised I would later when I help poor old Harve with that lilac bush—well, patch, I guess you'd call it now. Here you go," he said, sliding the doughnuts in front of Norm, who covered his nose and mouth and looked away. "They are very nice people," Omar said, going to stand by her mother at the sink, where she peered out the window from an angle so she wouldn't be seen.

"Hypocrites," she said under her breath.

"You should see that man's hands, the knuckles all swolled up big as butternuts. I don't know how he's out there digging. Matter of fact, I don't know how he can use a butcher knife to any degree of accuracy." He leaned over the sink. "Now there's a man, I bet, just looking for an investment opportunity. He's . . ."

"I can't have people right next door to me selling the exact same product I am!" Marie interrupted. "I mean, think of it! That's ridiculous."

"Whoa! Whoa there! That's what I call jumping the gun, little lady. I was speaking generally. Theoretically, of course. I was about to point out, before I was so summarily interrupted, that the world is filled with Harvey Klubocks, which means . . ." He lifted her chin and smiled. "Opportunity."

Her mother glanced back, her uneasy gesture drawing Omar's attention to the table. "Well, well, well, look at you, Alice! This is the way you should be dressed every minute of every day." He sat down and pulled the doughnut plate close, studying it intently. He was sweating. The cuffs on his sleeves were zigzagged with grime. He smelled stale and yeasty. He chose a doughnut, then examined it closely before taking a bite. He closed his eyes, sighing as his teeth shattered the sugary glaze. "You know," he said between bites, "Presto is looking for a model right now. They are looking for a symbol, some clean-cut, pure, wholesome, shining American face to put on their labels. A face that says"—he stared up at the ceiling and thrust out his arms—" 'Buy me, use me! I am pure!' " He looked at Alice. "And you know something, you've got that look, Alice. I mean it, now, don't laugh! I've been in marketing long enough to know what sells a product and what doesn't."

Her mother clutched a stiff red sock to her chest, her eyes darting between them like a bird's among a surfeit of crumbs.

"Just the other day, Jim Perrine down at the main office . . . I gotta tell you about him, Marie, remind me sometime, a real fine gentleman. Anyway, Jim had these photos all over his desk of girls they been considering, and I tell you this in all honesty, Alice, without an ounce of prejudice, that yours is the face they want!" He slapped his forehead with the heel of his hand. "And it never occurred to me until now. What an oversight! Like they say, you can go around the world searching for a thing of beauty, and nine times out of ten, you ain't going to find it in but one place. Right in your own backyard, in your own kitchen. Sitting here right at your own table. Marie, could I have paper and pen, please? I hope it's not too late. I'm going to have to write this down so it doesn't get lost among all the other memoranda swimming through my brain so fast lately that I sometimes think I am drowning in details. Thank you, Marie." He bent over the paper, holding the pen stubbily, tightly in his fist as a child might. "There! Consider it done!" He took another doughnut, then pushed the plate close to Norm. "Have a doughnut. Put some food in that poor stomach of yours."

Norm grunted and shook his head. There were goose bumps on his arms.

"He can't," Marie said. "He's too hungover."

Norm covered his eyes.

"The boy's suffered enough, Marie," Omar said softly. "He really should sleep some."

"He can sleep," she said, staring down at Norm. "After he cleans his mess out of my car."

Groaning, Omar smiled up at Marie. "Your mother's a hard taskmaster, son. But someday you'll be thanking her. Take my word for it."

Father Gannon was knocking on the front door. Marie rushed at

Alice, pantomiming instructions. *Go to the door. Quick. Go straight outside. Don't let him in. Don't! Goodbye. Hurry up!* "Nosy priest!" she hissed from the kitchen doorway.

Alice opened the door on the young priest's eager smile.

"All set?" he asked.

"All set!" she said, trying to slide out quickly, but the door was being pulled wide open from inside.

"Good morning, Father," Omar boomed, sticking his hand out so Father Gannon had to step inside to shake it. "I'm Omar Duvall, a friend of the family's, and it's a real pleasure meeting you, Father. Mrs. Fermoyle here tells me you've taken quite an interest in her little family."

"How do you do, Mr. Duvall, it's nice to meet you," Father Gannon said, looking confused as Omar closed the door.

"We should go," Alice said, but no one seemed to hear.

"Omar, please. Just Omar. Could we offer you some small repast before your mission of kindness? Some coffee? A doughnut?" he urged as he led the priest into the kitchen. Alice and her mother exchanged accusing glances.

Father Gannon thanked Omar, but explained that he had just eaten. He smiled when he saw Norm. "Hey there, how's it going?" he said, patting Norm's shoulder.

"Great, Father. Just great." Norm forced a smile and Alice cringed. There was congealed blood on his front teeth. There were yellow stains on his shirt, and he reeked of stale liquor. Her bra dangled from one of the piles in this foul sea of clothing. A big black ant labored up the front of the refrigerator, slowly, slowly, while outside, the sounds of digging went on, and on. She wanted to die, just die.

"Sure now, Father? I used to be something of a preacher myself, visiting the jailed, the sick, and the infirm in my younger, more spiritual days, so I know it sometimes takes more than faith to fuel the soldiers in God's army." Omar winked. "Go ahead. Have one," he crooned, holding out the plate.

Father Gannon waved his hand. "Really, I—"

"Oh go ahead. One's not gonna hurt," Omar said, laughing.

"He doesn't want one!" Alice blurted. She looked at her mother. What was he trying to prove? That he was host here, the master?

"Omar," her mother said. "I don't think Father Gannon wants a doughnut."

Omar winced. "Oh I'm being a pest, aren't I?"

"No, no," Father Gannon protested, blushing. "As a matter of fact, if you don't mind, I'd love to take one for later." He picked up a jelly doughnut and the powdered sugar sifted onto his sleeve.

Omar patted his belly. "I guess I just assume everyone's got my appetite." He followed them to the door. "You be sure and come again," he called as they went down the walk.

The Klubocks paused to watch Father Gannon turn the Monsignor's car in the driveway. In the far corner of his yard Harvey leaned on the shovel and wiped his glistening brow. Still in her frilly housecoat, Jessie was raking broken branches into a pile. Alice looked up, surprised by a face in her mother's bedroom window. It was Benjy looking down at the burlap-covered mound next to the garage.

"He seems like a real nice guy, that—what was his name, Homer?" Father Gannon said, as he drove down Main Street.

"Omar," she said, low in the seat so she couldn't be seen. The jelly doughnut slid down the dashboard. It had already rolled off once, leaving a trail of white powder on the plush burgundy floor mat.

"Homer," he said, and she didn't correct him. "What was the last name again?"

"Duvall."

"Duvall. Homer Duvall. I have the worst time with names. Drives the Monsignor crazy." He laughed. "In fact, first time I met your father I thought his name was Termoyle. Sam Termoyle."

Turmoil. Was he being sarcastic? She just looked at him. All this cheeriness and gusto seemed not only forced but oddly fragile. He was telling her everything he had done so far this morning. The six o'clock Mass, two nursing-home visits, forty push-ups, a bacon-and-egg breakfast; he had called the Chancellery to verify his appointment with the Bishop, and then with the time left over had decided to shine his shoes. While he was at it, he figured he might as well do the Monsignor's, but somehow polish had gotten on the soles. When he left, Mrs. Arkaday had been on her hands and knees trying to scrub the black streaks from the light gray carpeting. He told her to leave it, that he'd take care of it when he got back this afternoon, but she said by then it would be too late. The stain would set. He glanced at her. "You're awfully quiet! Or am I just being my usual garrulous self?"

"I don't function very well in the morning," she said, wondering if *garrulous* meant annoying.

"I was like that at your age." He chuckled. "But then you find out, moodiness can be a real drag in the real world."

Moodiness! Typical priest. Say three Hail Marys, the sin's gone. Smile and the pain's gone. The real world! As if he had the slightest idea what it was all about.

"Is it that obvious?"

"What?" she asked, thinking she had missed something he'd said.

"That I'm a jerk."

"I . . ."

"It's okay. I mean I know I am. I just usually do a better job of hiding it, that's all."

She smiled weakly, then looked out the side window. The winding road carried them past tidy farmhouses and weathered barns. Cows stood swishing their tails in scorched hummocky pastures. This might be the day it finally rained. The sky was low and gray.

Father Gannon lit a cigarette, then stepped down on the accelerator as the mountain's climb gave way now to a brief stretch of straight road. "You don't want to be here, do you?" he called over the motor.

"Not really."

"Your mother didn't seem too happy about the idea, either." He put his cigarette in the ashtray. Smoke drifted into her face. "I could tell she was upset."

"It wasn't about that." She fanned away the smoke.

"Well, that's good." He picked up his cigarette and smoked the rest in silence. A few minutes later he looked over at her. "So where's that what's-his-name, that Homer from? Sounds like the South."

"I guess so."

"What's he do for work?"

"I don't know, some kind of salesman or something."

"Does he live in town?"

"Yah." She stared at him. He wanted her to say: he lives with us now, sleeps on our divorced mother's couch, and uses our divorced mother's bathroom.

"What's he sell?"

"Soap."

"Seems like a nice enough guy." He flushed under her scrutiny.

"He's my mother's boyfriend." She wanted to shock him, but the word made her squirm. Her face was red.

"Does that bother you?"

"No, why should it?" She folded her arms and crossed her legs. She wiggled her foot up and down.

"It shouldn't, not if you like him. I guess your mother's entitled to a little companionship, right? She must get awfully lonely sometimes."

She kept her eyes straight ahead. The sun had broken through, miraging the asphalt with puddles of light.

At Applegate, Alice flipped through a magazine as she waited for her father in the solarium. It was twelve-thirty, and Father Gannon would be back at one. She was feeling more and more uneasy.

Why hadn't her father come down by now? What had he been doing for the last half hour? The head nurse said he was in his room. He had been called. He knew she was down here. She squirmed in her seat and put down the magazine. The nurse smiled quizzically from her glass cubicle. With her eyes on Alice, she pushed one of the buttons on her console and spoke into the microphone. She held up a finger, nodding to indicate that he would be right down.

The French doors from the stone patio were opened by a haggard woman in a violet robe. She leaned against the doorframe and removed her velvet slippers, then folded them carefully into her pocket before stepping inside. Her toenails were painted red. She patted her long gray hair and stole a look at the nurse, who hadn't yet seen her.

"Is it lunch now?" the woman asked, sitting in the chair next to her.

"I don't know," Alice said, picking up the magazine again and pretending to read.

The woman rocked silently. She curled her painted toes into the light carpet, then rubbed them together. "The president sends me this polish," the woman whispered, exposing teeth as gray as her hair.

"Really?" Alice locked her gaze on the elevator door.

"I saw him at a party once. He made the orchestra play, 'Ain't She Sweet.' "

"Oh!"

"I was seven then. I used to hide in his garden when we went to visit, and nobody could find me." She giggled into her hand. "It was a magic garden, and these little tiny men used to take my clothes off. They ever do that to you?" The woman cocked her head.

"No." She cleared her throat. A bell rang. A man was laughing in another room. Someone began to play "Chopsticks" on a tinny piano.

An attendant passed through the solarium and into the next room, where the piano was playing. The woman's shoulders hunched in gleeful anticipation. "It's Marlin," she whispered. Her eyes narrowed as the attendant led a blond man in a red-plaid shirt into the room. The attendant told Marlin to sit and wait for the lunch bell with the others. He meant her, Alice realized; she was one of "the others."

"What's for lunch today?" the woman called as the attendant went down the hall.

"Finnan haddie in cream sauce," he answered without looking back.

The woman clapped her hands and stamped her feet. "I love finnan haddie in cream sauce," she squealed.

"I hate finnan haddie in cream sauce," Marlin snapped in a reedy voice.

"Who asked you?" the woman spat. "You never like anything nice, anyway." She leaned close to Alice. "Want to know something Marlin really likes?"

"I don't like you, dirty old fart!" Marlin turned huffily away.

"Marlin likes little boys," she whispered in a girlish taunting voice. "Marlin likes little boys. Marlin likes little boys. And that's why Marlin's hee-yer!"

Marlin rolled his eyes and shrugged. "What's your name?" he

asked, peering at Alice. "My name is Dr. Leonard," he said when she told him hers.

"He's lying to you," the woman said.

Marlin laughed politely. "Actually my name is Leonard Doctor."

"Liar!" the woman said. "His name is Marlin Ray and he's been here almost as long as I have."

Marlin rolled his eyes and sighed. "Are you a Democrat or a Republican?" he asked, as if these were questions on a practiced list, just formalities. It was vital they be asked, though the answers seemed of little consequence or interest to him. He waited, blinking when she hesitated.

"Democrat, I guess," Alice said. "I'm not sure. I've never—"

"Where do you live?"

"What do you care?" the woman hissed at him. "Don't tell him!" she warned Alice.

"Where do you live?" he repeated, pursing his lips impatiently.

"In Vermont." She turned the pages, frowning, as if she were looking for something.

The elevator door whirred open. Her father came toward her, carrying a small flat box. He wore a gray suit she had never seen before, the jacket too wide on his thin frame, the pants short and boxy. His red tie was bright and shiny. His slicked-back hair was still wet. He squinted in the solarium's brightness. He bent to kiss the top of her head, and she could almost taste his cologne. "Welcome to my nuthouse," he said. "I see you've already met Marlin and Miss Getchell. "They're both longtime members of the staff here," he said, winking. Miss Getchell sat rigidly in her chair, head cocked, trying to hear their conversation.

He grinned as he handed Alice the box. "You don't have to open it now. Just a little something I made in crafts." He had her get up and sit in the corner, away from the two patients. "I do leatherwork. I signed up for it because I've gotten so good." He laughed nervously. "You know, after being up at Waterbury so many times." He laughed again. "After I get my master's in leatherwork, I've been accepted in their doctoral program here in beading." He paused, and she knew he could see how close to tears she was.

He sighed. "Pet, I'm sorry you had to wait so long. I was trying to get a tie off somebody, you know, one that'd go with the suit. Like it? A guy up on three choked to death last week, and one of the orderlies is a buddy of mine, so . . ."

"Is that what you've been doing all this time, Daddy? Trying to find a tie?" She felt numb.

"I wanted to look nice for you. Better than the last time you saw me, anyway." He hung his head. "I'm sorry about graduation night, pet. I can't get that out of my head." When he looked up his eyes were raw. "What can I say? How the heck can I make something like that up to you?" He squeezed her hand. "Forgive your old man? Huh? Because I am going to make it up to you, I promise. As soon as I get my walking papers outta here I'm getting a job and then I'm moving out of Helen's, believe it or not. Don't laugh. It's true. I'm coming off the bench and into the ball game! You should see my room. I've got all these lists of everything I have to do, all the people I have to make things up to. And top of the list, babe, is you. I mean that." He grinned. "I'm going to get a good job. Of course the work might not be quite as skilled as my last job, when I was a diamond cutter." He looked at her expectantly.

"When was that?" She couldn't believe he would spend the few minutes that were left telling old jokes.

"The summer I cut the grass at the ball field? Remember? I was a diamond cutter?"

She nodded and forced a smile. He seemed relieved.

"I gotta tell you this funny story. You're going to like this one. There were these two old guys and—"

"Daddy," she interrupted, "Mom wants me to remind you that I'm starting college pretty soon, and it's going to cost an awful lot, and I really need your help."

"I know, pet, but don't you see? First I've got to get out of here. I've got to get this job thing lined up. I've got to find a place to live. I've got all these things to do, and here I sit." He held up his hands in disgust. "Day after day doing nothing."

"Mom says there's a trust, that there's money Nana put aside."

"I know. She's got this idea in her head. All of a sudden she thinks there's all this money. So you've got to tell her, pet, tell her if there is any money it couldn't be much. Just about every penny's gone into Nana's care."

"Yes, but she said—"

"What about you, now, Alice?" he asked, in the stern fatherly tone she'd seldom ever heard. "Are you working as hard as you can and saving your money? You know, when you get to be a certain age you really can't keep coming to your parents all the time for help. Look," he said, pulling a slip of paper from his pocket. "Here, read this."

I will be a man among men; and no longer a dreamer among shadows. Henceforth be mine a life of action and reality! I will work in my own sphere, nor wish it other than it is. This alone is health and happiness.
                                      —Henry Wadsworth Longfellow

"That's nice." She handed it back, feeling empty and dazed.

"Would you like a copy? Wait, I'll get some paper and a pen, and I'll do it right now." Before she could say anything he was at the nurse's booth tapping on the glass. He sat back down, and while he copied the saying onto the Applegate Hospital memo sheet, she tried again to explain how badly she needed money for school.

"Here," he interrupted, giving her the copy. "Whenever you're feeling a little shaky, just read this. It helps," he said, squeezing her arm, his voice trembling as if he'd just passed on the solution to all her problems. "It really does."

A tall woman in Indian moccasins slipped past the nurse's station. She stood in the hallway, sniffing at the closed door. "That's the one who keeps imaginary cats in her room," her father whispered; his pleasure in telling the story to her now, here, in such detail was more devastating, more painful than if he'd been roaring drunk. Every day, he said, the woman pestered the orderlies to bring her cat food for her cats. Finally, after enough refusals, she figured out a way to convince them she wasn't hallucinating. She would urinate on the floor and blame it on the cats when the orderlies came in to clean it up. They ignored her. So then she began to defecate on the floor and blame that on the cats. The orderlies cleaned it up, and still they ignored her. So then one day in the garden she caught three mice and killed them. She put the dead mice in her room and told the orderlies that her cats had caught them. The orderlies decided to teach her a lesson. They left the dead mice in the room. When they went in the next morning, the mice were gone. " 'What happened to the three mice?' they asked her. 'The cats ate them,' she said. 'I told you they were hungry!' "

Her father chuckled and shook his head. "Can you believe it? She ate the mice! So now they've got a whole new problem on their hands. It's the darnedest thing, but they say she's quite a mouser." He laughed, looking anxiously for her to join in. She tried to smile. He sighed, with an uneasy glance at the people lining up behind the woman in Indian moccasins. The lunch bell rang, and as the doors opened into the dining room, the line surged forward. Miss Getchell put on her slippers and hurried into the dining room.

"All they think about around here is food," he said as the faint odor of smoked fish drifted in from the hallway. He kept glancing toward the dining room. All the way up here she'd told herself to expect nothing, that it was a just a visit, something she had to do, when in truth she had expected something: that he had finally seen the light, that for her, because of her love and devotion, because she had written, because she had cared enough to come, he would repent and see that this one constant child, this chaste forgiver of his lies, this thirsty tongue lapping at his spilled and reckless love, could save him. But he didn't care. He wanted her to go. He wanted to be released. He wanted her to leave.

"I'd better get in there. If I miss lunch," he said, squeezing her hand for emphasis, "then I won't be able to eat again until dinner."

She laughed; she couldn't help it. "That's all right." She got up. Her legs felt shaky.

He fidgeted with his tie. "You could wait. What if you wait here while I eat? I didn't realize you'd be here at lunchtime, and now it's too late to get a guest pass. Can you wait?"

"No, the priest is coming."

He couldn't hide his relief. "Here, don't forget this," he said, handing her the box as he walked her to the door. Marlin watched from his chair.

"When you get back, pet, go see Aunt Helen. She has to get me out of here. My thirty days are already up and I'm still here. This isn't the same as the state hospital. The only way I can leave here is if she tells them to let me out. Will you do that for me, pet?"

Nodding, she tried to smile.

"Will you?" her father pressed. She had to help him, he insisted. Of all the people he had written to, not one had lifted a finger to help him. She was his only hope.

"But what'll I tell Mom about the money for school?" she asked, the ravenous claws opening slowly, slowly in her chest. His only hope, this dutiful child. What would he promise? What would he give in return?

"Don't you understand? That's why I have to get out." He gripped her shoulders. "What can I do in here? I can't start putting my life together until I'm out. Will you help me? Will you go see your aunt Helen?"

Just then the intercom sputtered on, consuming her father's pleas in the staticky announcement of the afternoon's croquet tournament. You help *me,* screamed a voice in her head. I'm the child! I'm the child! Me!

"She had no right to send me here," he continued when the intercom clicked off. "But don't tell her I said that. No sense in aggravating her any more than she is." His fingers dug into her bones. "What is it? Why are you crying?" He was astonished.

"I don't know. I'm just tired, I guess." She turned her head, wiped her eyes. "I get home from work so late, and then this morning there was all this commotion. Norm got in trouble, and that dog Benjy likes is dead, and Mom was all upset, and the priest came and . . . and Omar Duvall was there." She looked at him. "He's always there!"

"Shh," he said, pressing his stained finger to her lips. She could smell the tobacco. He had even smoked a cigarette, probably two or three or four, while she had been waiting for him. "Look, you go see Aunt Helen. That's the first thing that has to be done." He glanced back. People were already leaving the dining room. He kissed her forehead. "I've got to run, pet, and grab whatever's left. You write now," he called, waving as he edged into the dining room. "Write and tell me what Aunt Helen says!"

She turned with a gasp at the light tapping on her shoulder. "Excuse me," Marlin said, batting short gray eyelashes. "Where in Vermont do you live?"

F ather Gannon found Alice walking down the road to the main gate. It had just begun to sprinkle. When he apologized for being late, she said she had left early. They rode silently in the car's heat. Even with the window down, the air barely stirred. He drove deliberately, studiously, leaning forward, turning, squinting to appraise every sign and intersection as if the success of their journey hinged on each passing landmark. He smoked with the same intensity, taking such long, deep drags that the cigarette was burning his lips. He asked about her visit. It was all right, she answered in a flat voice. Just all right? She was tired, she said, turning her head to the side window.

His sweaty hands grew slick on the wheel. Squirming, he sniffed, wondering with alarm if she could smell his body secreting the fluids he'd never been able to mask with scent or cleanse away. Twice daily he showered. He used the best deodorants and most expensive colognes.

The Bishop had opened the windows before sitting down at his desk. "It's not for you to decide," the Bishop had said, fanning himself with Father Gannon's request for transfer. "You write in here of needs, spiritual needs, moral needs. You go on and on and on, citing example after example. What makes you so certain these same needs don't exist in Atkinson as well?"

"They don't. It's not the same," was all he could answer.

"What's not the same?" The Bishop had sighed with a frown that wrinkled his deep tan. He was a handsome man, dazzling eyes, silver hair, square-jawed. Before becoming a priest he had been an actor. Some people said he still was. "Everywhere sin is the same, and greed is the same, and poverty and despair and death. These are the same. Only the places, young man, are different and the faces—no, not even the faces." The Bishop leaned over the inlaid desktop. "After you've been a priest for as many years as I have, you will notice that the faces begin to be the same ones hour after hour, year after year. And this will wear you down some days to the bone, to the very marrow of your being. But on other days you will understand that everywhere, for everyone, life is sorrowful. You must minister to all these needs in all these places." He sat back, smiling patiently, basking in his own eloquence as he stroked his cheek with his ringed hand. "Your ministry, Father Gannon, is wherever you are assigned. Accept that reality now while you're still young and pliable. Be patient!"

"But don't you see, your Excellency, it's because I'm young that I know I can help more where I was than at Saint Mary's. In New York there were people who had to come to me at the rectory for milk for their children, for their babies. Some of them had no decent shoes, no blankets. . . ."

"Blankets!" the Bishop cried, throwing up his elegant hands. "Blankets! It's blankets that I hear all the time about you, Father Gannon. Blankets and little boys' jackets! Will you forget all that and just get yourself back on track? Please, please, please!" Clasping his hands to his dimpled chin, he whispered, "And now I am tired of this whole sophomoric discussion. You will remain in your present assignment until the Provincial sees fit to transfer you."

"But you don't understand," he said, and at that, the Bishop stood up, his face curdling with annoyance. "A bit of advice, Father Gannon," he said sharply. "You have already strained my desire to be understanding. And now the Monsignor tells me you strain his daily. The Monsignor is a very valuable man to me. And I won't have him upset just because you don't think you can set the world on fire in Atkinson, Vermont. To be priestly, Father, is first to learn obedience. And, I might remind you, humility!"

The Bishop stalked out, his cassock swishing through the closing door.

Humility. If he was nothing else, he was at least humble—the proof: this very trip, this sullen schoolgirl, too immersed in her adolescent gloom to even speak to him, much less show any gratitude.

All at once sheets of rain draped the windshield. The wipers were useless. The car sluiced through puddles that sprayed the top of the roof. Alice sat forward. "It's really bad," she said, looking at him.

"It's coming heavier, too," he called. The torrent of rain beat on the roof. He leaned over the wheel. "I can hardly see. I think there's a restaurant up there." He braked and the car shimmied, its wet engine sputtering.

"No, it's just an old shack or something," she called, her face pressed to the side window. "Keep going."

"But I can't see anything. I have to stop here," he shouted, pulling off the road. A buckled Coca-Cola sign dangled over the door of the boarded-up store. He ran his hands along the wheel. Rain poured down the windshield. "What a waste of time," he sighed. Hour after hour, the Bishop had said, year after year.

"I wish I'd never come," she said, twisting the handle on her purse.

"So do I," he said. He thought he heard her gasp, then saw that she was crying. "Oh I didn't mean that the way it sounded. I didn't mean you," he tried to explain. "Come on, don't cry." He raised his hand, then dropped it awkwardly on the seat between them. "It was the Bishop. I had a hard time, that's all. I meant that I shouldn't have gone up there to see him the way I did. That's all I meant."

"I know what you meant," she sniffed.

He looked at her a moment. "Was it your father? It wasn't a good visit, was it? It was a lousy visit. I'm sorry. Blame me. I shouldn't have interfered. Alice? Alice, please don't cry." He tried to make her laugh. "You can't do this to me, Miss Fermoyle. I never had this course at the seminary. I was flunking Latin, so they wouldn't let me take it." She hunched against the door, trying not to cry. He tapped her arm. "Want to know what the name of the course was? They called it Human Relations II, or What to Do When a Young Lady Cries in the Monsignor's Car on a Lonely Road in a Downpour in the Middle of Nowhere and You Don't Know What to Say. Please smile, please? Are you hungry?" he asked, opening the glove compartment. "I just happen to have this emergency doughnut here." He held it up, slimy and shriveled now that its sugar had melted. "Every good priest carries one."

"It looks so disgusting," she blurted with a teary laugh, then covered her face and began to cry again.

"Aw, you might as well. Go ahead. Just like the rain, when it's over, everything'll look new again," he said softly, then sat there with his arm over the back of the seat. But the more she cried the more helpless he began to feel. How many times had words failed; and yet it was all he had, words and prayers, his only tools from parish to parish. Words and prayers—when had they ever been enough? Jesus had beckoned the children to his side, then reached out and held them. The Bishop thought he wanted to set the world on fire, when all the time, every waking moment, it was himself that was on fire. His arm slid to her shoulder. "No," she said, as he pried her fingers from her face, then lifted her wet chin. She would not look at him. He could smell her mouth, her hair, the sweat on her neck.

"It's okay. It's okay," he whispered, pulling her closer. He was conscious of the shallow flutter of her breathing at his ribs. "There. There now," he said, touching her wet eyelids, her nose, her cheek-bones, her mouth, her soft mouth, her chin, her throat. The rain beat over the car. Careful. He would be so careful. See, she had stopped crying. That's all it took. He traced circles around her closed eyes, and then he kissed her.

She sat wedged between the door and the seat, saying noth-ing, arms at her sides, unresisting. Rigid, he realized with a start. "Alice?"

Her eyes opened wide with a shock that sickened him.

"Alice, I'm sorry. I'm sorry. I'm so sorry." It wasn't until he moved behind the wheel that she sat up and smoothed her skirt over her knees. "Alice, please look at me."

She did and he wished she hadn't, she looked so cold and angry.

"I mean it, I'm really sorry."

"I thought you'd be," she said, with a brusqueness that made him feel worse.

"You mean you saved me from myself, is that it?" he said, with a bitter laugh. She flushed and it was all he could do to keep from touching her soft warm cheek.

"I didn't want to embarrass you," she said stiffly.

"Embarrassed! I'm not embarrassed, Alice. I'm ashamed. You're the one that's been embarrassed. You are, aren't you?"

She shook her head yes as she toyed with her purse.

"Oh my God," he sighed with a bitter laugh, and her head shot up.

"I don't think this is very funny, Father. I don't know what I'm supposed to say now or what I'm supposed to do." She looked as if she were about to cry again.

"I don't, either." He hit the wheel and groaned. "God, what a fool I am, what a stupid, stupid fool."

"I think it's letting up a little," she said, staring at the windshield.

Her mother followed her into her room and sat on her bed while she dressed for work.

"How does he look?" her mother asked.

She turned her back as she stepped out of her dress. "He looks okay." She threw the damp wrinkled dress onto the bed, annoyed not to have even a few moments of privacy. She felt sweaty and soiled, as if there were handprints all over her body. Father Gannon had barely spoken on the trip back. By the time they got to Atkinson his eyes were heavy and hooded and he was hunched over the wheel, gripping it with both hands, his misery so pervasive that she had gotten out of the car feeling guilty, convinced that by letting the mask slip, by losing control, she had tempted him.

"Is he better?" her mother asked.

"I guess so."

"You guess so? Well, is he or isn't he? Was he shaky?"

"He's sober," she answered.

"Well, what did he say about the money?"

"Not much," she said, slipping her uniform pants up under her slip.

"What do you mean, not much?" Her mother's mouth was thin and white.

"He said he had to get out first, that he'd take care of all that when he got out."

"Damn it!" Her mother scowled up at her. "And you just let it go at that? Like it didn't even matter? What the hell's wrong with you? Where in God's name do you think that money's coming from? I ask you!" She pounded her fist into her palm.

"Don't blame me! I tried. I went up there with that . . . that weird priest. I didn't want to, but I went. And then I had to sit and wait for most of the hour with all these crazy people talking to me. And then when Daddy finally came, all he talked about was lunch and getting Aunt Helen to let him out of there, and he told a few jokes, and then he couldn't wait to get away from me. Here," she said, tossing the slip of paper and the box into her mother's lap. "That's all I got out of him, and now I'm tired and I'm hungry and I've got to get ready for work."

Her mother read the saying, then looked down at the wallet he had tooled, the edging he had laced. She closed her eyes. "That bastard. That no-good bastard."

Just as the first lights dimmed in the lot, a long, black Oldsmobile pulled into Alice's station. She was shocked to see Father Gannon, red-eyed, his pale face shadowed with stubble. He asked if they could talk for a few minutes. She explained that she had to help close up now, but he offered to wait and give her a ride home. She told him she already had a ride. What she did not say was that it would be Omar Duvall, because Norm had been grounded and her mother's car still smelled. Never again would there be a personal word between them.

"I really have to talk to you," he said. "I need to explain—" His voice broke off as Mr. Coughlin approached the car.

"Hey, come on, let's get a move on here!" Coughlin called with a jerky wave. It was said that by summer's end Coughlin was always in a state of nervous collapse. "Save the chitchat for later. On your own time," he bellowed, then raced into his office. Blue Mooney had just pulled in to pick up Anthology. Arms folded, he leaned against his car talking to Fawnie Anuta, a tiny black-haired girl with feline eyes. She was so obsessed with Mooney that she had taken to pumping Alice for information about herself that she could pass on to him. Looking at Alice, Mooney said something and Fawnie shrugged.

"I have to go," Alice said. This was so awkward. The priest kept rubbing some invisible spot on the door leather. She stepped back, and he looked up.

"I have to straighten this out."

"That's okay," she said.

"No, I need to explain it," he said. "I'm just so worried about the effect this could have."

"I'd never say anything. Honestly." That would be the last thing she'd ever do.

He closed his eyes and sighed. "I mean the effect on you, Alice. The effect of my poor judgment. Please, give me the opportunity to make this right. I beg you, please."

Coughlin opened his door and yelled for her to start cleaning up so everyone wouldn't be stuck here all night.

"Father, I have to go. I really do."

"Tomorrow, then," he said.

Tomorrow was her day off. Sometime next week, then. He'd come by at closing and give her a ride home, he called as she hurried into the kitchen. When he showed up she would say she'd forgotten, that her brother was on his way.

She was scrubbing trays when Blue Mooney strutted into the kitchen. He wore his uniform pants and a white T-shirt. He grabbed a towel and picked up a wet tray. She worked with her head down, determined to ignore him. She could feel him watching her over the tray he kept drying. He was a pervert like his cousin Anthology and Coughlin, just waiting for the carhops to leave so they could drink and look at their filthy pictures.

"You're real quiet tonight. You tired?"

"Yah."

"Long day, huh?"

"Yah."

"You look tired. Hey, I could finish this up so you can leave. I gotta wait, anyway."

"No, that's okay. But thanks." She held her breath. Would this, the longest, strangest day of her life, ever end?

"That guy out there, the one that just left, was he bothering you?"

"No."

"You didn't look too happy," he said. He rubbed the tray as he followed her between the sink and the dirty stack at the order window. "Something about him—I don't know. You know how you can tell about a person sometimes? You know what I mean?" he asked, right on her heels as she went back to the sink.

"Uh-huh," she said, scrubbing furiously, as if this dull brown plastic required all of her attention.

"Some people you just get certain feelings about," he said.

His toweled hand paused on the tray. He was staring at her. "So what're you gonna do in October, when this place closes?"

"I won't be here then," she said.

"Where you gonna be?" He stepped up beside her at the sink.

"College. I'm going to UVM." Just saying it was a release.

"Oh! College. UVM." In the moment's quiet she heard him swallow. "Yah, I know where that is. Burlington."

Burlington. And that was probably all he knew, she thought, feeling more confident than she had in weeks.

He took a deep breath. "So when're you going?"

"In a month." She turned on the hot water, grateful for the steam billowing up from the deep gritty sink.

"A month. Wow. That's not very long, is it?"

"I'm just counting the days. I can't wait!" she said with such forced exuberance that she was ashamed. She felt as if she'd just been bragging.

"Well, that's about when I'll be leaving, too. Probably right about that same time. In a month or so, right around then." He kept clearing his throat.

"You're not looking forward to it, I guess, huh?" she asked, confused by the unhappy eyes over his broad toothy smile.

"Oh no, I love the Marines. That's my whole life, the Corps," he said, his stance oddly rigid, his chin raised, gaze fixed. "There's nothing else I want to do. Nothing!" He looked down at her. "So I know what you mean about counting the days. Believe me, I know."

"Yah, well, won't be long now," she said, sighing.

"Sure won't," he agreed, with a hollow laugh.

She turned the water off and stacked the trays, banging them noisily together, then reached under the sink and dragged out the metal carton of disinfectant bottles. He began to wipe the stainless-steel hood above the grill, reaching high over his head, straining and grunting, while she bent close to the countertop she was scrubbing. It seemed that they were both trying to work their way back from some fragile precipice.

In winter the restaurant's knotty-pine walls, red tiled floor, and cavernous stone fireplace provided a cozy spot for skiers, but on this summer night the dining room was almost empty and the dusty hearth reeked of creosote and damp ashes. The Killington View was on the access road up the mountain, so no one from town would see them here. Omar had been hoping that dinner out might placate Bernadette, but at the moment she was threatening to call the police if he didn't give her back her hundred dollars. She had just found out that her fiancé's parole hearing would be at the end of the month, and she needed the money for her wedding.

"I don't give a shit how many fucking contracts you say I fucking signed."

"Shh. I don't, either, Bernie. I mean if it was just me, I'd rip them up and write it off to unforeseen circumstances." He stirred his drink. "But it's not just me. It's the whole GoldMine Enterprises empire you have contracted with."

"No! I keep trying to tell you, nothing counts. Nothing I sign. Nothing I say. Nothing I do."

"Come again?" he said, with a long, cool sip that choked him when she answered.

"I'm underage."

"Precisely my point," he wheezed, his mind racing as he cleared his throat. "You are so young, so inexperienced, so untested. You think it's all got to happen now. Slow down. Be patient so you can have the kind of life you really want and not the kind of life that's always being patched up and put back together. You are a top-of-the-line lady, so stop settling for secondhand all the time and second-best. It's time to show people in this town just how classy you can be!"

Time, that's all it took, he tried to explain; time, patience, and the determination to get her business started, and then she'd be able to have a dream wedding. Her eyes glowed brighter than the wagon wheel of amber lights above them.

He patted his breast pocket. "Sure, I could get you off my back and give this to you right now. But I'm not gonna be the one to dash those dreams. Not when I'm sitting here picturing you in one of them twenty-foot-long satin trains that Merry and Noelle each have ahold of, and this lacey kind of veil floating all around your pretty face," he said, swirling his hands around his own head as she began to smile. "Can you imagine those two little angels in their own sweet little flower-girl dresses, all poufy with crinolines, and rosebuds in their hair? I can! That's what I see for you. So don't you go settling for some mousy little suit and hangdog hat that says I made two mistakes and now I got to pay by slinking into some JP's ratty front parlor and hide my God-given moment of triumph, to do it in private like it's some kind of dirty thing. No sir! You be patient and you do it right and you do it big. Proud, like you should! Like you deserve!" he said, stabbing the tabletop so hard his finger would ache all the next day. "All you gotta do is wait a bit," he pleaded. "Just wait for the soap to come."

There was silence in the few moments before they both began to eat again. Well, maybe he was right, she said, chewing and gesturing with her fork as she spoke. She was so sick of being treated like dirt, people thinking they could say anything they wanted to her. . . . She looked at him, recalling the VD inspector at her door. He tried to explain how it had been a tasteless practical joke played on him by this horny fellow. . . .

"Played on you!" she gasped, beginning to choke on the chunk of beef she had been chewing. Her face reddened as she gagged. She squeezed her throat.

Should've ordered rare, he thought, already a leap ahead to the deposition, the testimony. Hadn't he told her? Hadn't he said, never order well in a two-bit place like that. Always order down from what you really want in degrees of doneness. Always. But the young never listen, do they?

"Of course on you, too," he said, leaning to peer into her stricken eyes. Just a momentary spasm here. That was all, but if something were to happen, if this was her time, then so be it, then the investment was meant to be his, free and clear. He patted her fists, gently harnessing them from banging the table again. "Especially on you, more than anyone, dear, who had to endure the vile and reprehensible questions. . . . Are you all right?"

Her lips were blue and her nose leaked. She pulled free and stuck her finger down her throat. She gagged and the gray plug of beef shot onto the table with a disappointing little thud. She held her head, gasping for breath.

Such a tiny piece, he thought, observing the few diners, who had no inkling what had nearly transpired. Imagine, cut just a wedge thicker and how different the mood would be. "My Lord, my Lord, my Lord," he sighed as he wet his napkin and patted her sweaty face. "Look at this," he murmured. "You're so tense every vein in your temple's just popping in and out."

"I was choking," she said in a raspy, accusing voice.

"Well, I thought things were getting a little strange. But you been so damn emotional all night long, I was confused." He looked at her closely. "You okay?"

She nodded.

"You sure? Can you talk?" He took her hand and squinted at the wink of light that was her engagement ring. "I've missed you." There was a stir in his belly.

"What about that lady, that Mrs. Fermoyle?" she asked, closing her fingers over his.

"That's something else. That's business. But this, this here's a powerful natural attraction," he said.

She pulled her hand away and looked at him. "So when's the soap coming?"

"Any day now," he said, probing his ear dreamily with a toothpick as Bernadette began to eat her cherry cheesecake. Her nose was still running.

GoldMine Enterprises had promised delivery sometime in the next two weeks. Nothing to worry about, they had assured him when he called. The soap would be a sure thing. Nothing like the lousy magazines, tramping all over New England with his sorry crew whining every second for hamburgs, cigarettes, hemorrhoid ointment, and rubbers. And then the kicker was the goddamn Bibles he thought he was getting such a deal on to use for a bonus if the pinch-faced little housewife would only buy three different subscriptions from the Negroes she let into her front hall and then didn't know how the hell to get rid of without hurting their feelings, or worse, having them think she was prejudiced and that it had anything to do with the color of their skin. Half the pages were blank inside the god-damn Bibles, all bound up in different-color fake leather covers with raised gold lettering, so he had to go spend even more money on clear plastic sheeting and tape to seal each one so he'd be long gone before they were opened. The damn Negroes loved it, two whole days spent in a motel room covering them while they watched TV, drinking beer and eating pretzels, with Montague at him every minute trying to fig-ure out what was going on, demanding to know why the others had to cover the Bibles. So they wouldn't get soiled, so they wouldn't get creased, to keep them like new, he explained over and over to the old man, who was almost totally blind, another of Fate's lousy pitches. In a million years he wouldn't have taken Montague Pease along had he known the old man was about blind as a bat. He had been eager to sign on Earlie, who was tall and well-spoken with a disarming boyish grin. But then Montague raised such a stink about the boy be-ing his only living relative and it was the night before they were to leave, and Luther alone was useless to him, and he just got too tired and worn down to argue anymore, careless actually, thinking maybe they'd just lose him along the way or maybe he'd die. But then the opposite started to happen; the old man just got stronger with all the traveling, happier and more determined to keep up and do his part, which was to be led onto those icy porches so he could tell the scared little lady of the house how the profit from each subscription sale went to build rest homes for blind and infirm old colored folks down in the terrible boiling South, where no such homes were now avail-able to them. Montague would start quoting from the Bible, his be-lief in the mission growing as real to him as his responsibility to it. The irony was that it came to be Montague who talked Earlie out of it every time he threatened to quit and head down home to Laydee Dwelley. The old man finally had a purpose. "One more week," he'd coax his lovesick grandson. "Just this next town."

Omar's mistake was, he started losing interest and then he kept getting more and more careless until it all turned on him, a blood-thirsty monster of his own creation. No, he told himself. What's done is done. Damned if he'd ever get involved in anything like that again. No sir, this was surefire, this soap deal, just cash passing hand over hand, dealerships piling up, multiplying in some sort of unstoppable geometric progression of investments pushing him up to the top of the heap, where he belonged, where he would have been years ago, except for crazy things, snags, flukes like Montague and blank Bibles always tripping him up, getting in his way, holding him back.

He'd always considered himself a religious man, a patriot, a man who believed in signs. Men were sent from their Creator to this scraggly earth with particular missions stamped indelibly upon their brains and souls. His he knew to be Success. Why else had the Lord sent him as a white man to America when He might just as well have dropped him down in India or Africa or Korea. Each time he stumbled the Lord picked him up and set him on a new road.

And so he figured it was the Lord who had caused the magazine deal to fall through. The Lord had sent Montague and then the lot of damaged Bibles. And when the police brought them in for questioning, missing Omar, who had just stepped into the woods to take a leak, he knew the Lord was stirring the waters again, jiggling him off the hook because his name was not on a single contract and not on any of the doctored checks carried always between porch and bank in old Montague's pocket. It was the Lord who had trawled him through the sudden spring heat onto that dead-end street into the voracious arms of Marie Fermoyle, who needed love and soft-ening, solace and attention like no woman he had ever met. Yes sir, it was the Lord. The Lord had led him home.

"You want to come back and see how I fixed up the place?" Bernadette asked as she wiggled out of the booth. She smoothed her skirt over her belly.

"Let me make a call," he said. "An appointment I can reschedule."

And it was the Lord that had given him this mighty appetite.

amuel Fermoyle woke up with the drone of air-conditioning throbbing in his temples. The clammy sheets trussed his ankles as he tried to curl into a ball. He couldn't stop shivering. He hadn't left this room since Alice's visit, which had depressed the hell out of him. The crumpled papers on the nightstand were all his attempted apologies. *Dear Alice, I'm sorry you had to wait so long . . . Dear Alice, I'm sorry I kept you waiting so long . . . Dear Alice, I'm sorry . . . Dear Alice, As you must now realize, I don't belong here . . . Dear Alice, Every day I get sicker and sicker . . .*

"Not sick now, Mr. Fermoyle," the nurse had corrected him this morning, with a wag of her finger. "You're just not well." The difference being, according to Dr. Litchfield, an insidious fixity of negative attitude that overtakes and impairs a life. Therefore Sam Fermoyle was no alcoholic, but a man who needed to control his drinking. Not a shiftless, chronically unemployed parasite, just someone in need of a job. And this was not a fucking blinding migraine, but a mass of soft tissue that needed to redirect its energy surges. Pain gripped his skull like a spiked helmet. He groped for the buzzer.

"Help," he groaned when the nurse opened the door.

"What seems to be the problem?" she asked, towering over him, arms bolted across her starched pleated chest.

"No problem. I'm just having a little stroke here, that's all. Just an exploding artery."

"I'll get Dr. Litchfield. He's on the floor." She hurried off, and Sam waited, cringing.

"Uh-huh—up . . . now down. . . . Look right . . . look left . . ." The light shining in his eyes had to be probing the roaring depths of hell. Sighing, Litchfield clipped the penlight into his jacket pocket. "Headache," he said. The nurse left, then returned with tepid water in a paper cup.

"I have to get out of here, Doc," he said as the nurse handed him two pills. "Before I get really sick."

"You had a visitor the other day, Sam. Your first, right?" Litchfield toyed with his wedding band.

"Right."

"Your daughter," Litchfield said, nodding. "And how did it go?"

"Just great, Doc." He lay back and closed his eyes. "We laughed. We danced. We ran through the fields in slow motion. We even sang some hymns together."

"Why did it take you almost an hour to get downstairs to her?" Litchfield asked.

"I was dressing."

"You were procrastinating. You didn't really want to see her, did you?"

"Maybe I didn't want her to see me looking like one of the screwballs." He knew where this was headed.

"She made you nervous, didn't she? She made you feel guilty and anxious."

"Whatever you say, Doc," Sam sighed. "Look, I'm beat. I want to go to sleep. Like you said, it's a headache, that's all, not a fucking breakdown."

Litchfield smiled. "That's why you're not ready for release yet, Sam. That's what I've been trying to get across to you. You're treating this like a sentence, the way a prisoner would. You think if you just do your time, your thirty or sixty days, then it goes without saying that you're automatically going to be released." As Litchfield began to walk around the room, Sam forced himself to sit up a little. He lit a cigarette he didn't want and tried to keep his squinting eyes on Litchfield, who paused to examine the painting over the table, the thermostat setting. He wet his finger and rubbed at a nick on the nightstand. "It doesn't work that way, Sam. Rehabilitation, that's the only way out of here."

He blew smoke down the length of the bed. At least he had stopped shivering. "Suicide," he said, tapping the ash into his palm. "You forgot suicide."

"Dr. LaSalle tells me you've stopped going to group therapy," Litchfield said, obviously trying not to lose his temper.

"I couldn't take the shit, Doc. I told you before, I'll knock it around with a few drunks, but I'm not going to spend every afternoon with the crazies. It's humiliating as hell, Doc."

"Miss Lanette feels she's made quite an emotional investment in you, and now your absence is a personal affront to her, Sam."

"Miss Lanette is a personal affront, Doc. And Miss Lanette can take a flying shit for herself." He coughed hoarsely.

Litchfield's eyes narrowed. Miss Lanette, Sam knew, was a prize patient, a hospital pet, who had managed to turn instability into a calling. She knew all the jargon. She was a group leader. She was LaSalle's right-hand loony.

"Perhaps, Sam, these headaches are merely another manifestation of your frustration and hostility." Litchfield lowered his voice. "Miss Lanette says you spit on her in leatherwork."

Sam began to laugh. Raging through his cells was this hysteria that threatened to turn what was a battle with the bottle into a battle for his own sanity.

Litchfield's face reddened. He swallowed hard. "Miss Lanette is one of our best group-therapy people. She's been with our sessions for five years now and she's topnotch at spotting hostility and frustration in a patient. But today she refused to come to therapy, and when Dr. LaSalle went looking for her, he found her hiding in her closet. She said she couldn't stand being spit on by someone she was trying to help."

"I never spit at her," Sam groaned, closing his eyes.

"I've never known her to lie, Sam. At least not about another patient. She takes therapy very, very seriously."

"Then why the hell is she still here after five years of it?" he countered, disgusted with himself for continuing this bizarre debate. He knew why. It was all so seductive that here even conflict was safe.

"Some patients take longer than others. Even Miss Lanette has a few problems left to resolve," Litchfield conceded with a nod.

"A few problems! One of which is imagining that I like to spit on her. Come on, Litchfield, cut the shit!"

Litchfield stared at him. "Sam, what do you think Miss Lanette's problems are?" He came closer. "Really, now. In your own opinion."

"Uh-uh." He smiled wanly. "I can't come out and play with you, Doc. Sorry."

"Think about her a minute, Sam, how she picks the skin off her calluses, how she squeezes that wart on her neck until it bleeds, how she's always bumping into tables, knocking her elbows against the walls, tripping when there's nothing to trip over. What does that tell you?" Litchfield's eyes were dancing.

"I don't know. How the hell should I know." He sighed.

"Try, Sam. The first thing into your head, whatever it is."

"She hates herself because she knows what a beast she really is. Who cares?" he added hastily, seeing the eagerness flood Litchfield's eyes.

"Exactly, Sam. I knew it!" he cried. "At long last I've got a group member who can spot self-negation. You don't know how very valuable you're going to be to me from now on, Sam. You have no idea," he said through clenched teeth. He patted Sam's shoulder.

"Shit," he sighed.

"Tomorrow afternoon we begin," Litchfield cried. "You know I haven't had a good self-negation sleuth in . . . ooooh . . . let me see, six or eight months, anyway. And it's hurt the groups considerably." He grinned. "We need you in there pitching strong, Samuel, so you get some sleep now."

After Litchfield left, Sam pulled the pillow over his face. Helen was going to pay for this. He was getting out of here.

Alice rushed through her closing chores so she could leave work the minute Father Gannon drove into the lot. Tonight she'd finally get the ordeal of his apology over with. He'd called every morning this week offering her a ride home from work, until she had finally accepted.

They were driving down Main Street now. She could tell he was nervous, though he hadn't said a word yet about last Saturday. He was in the middle of some long, involved story about the Holy Name Society's barbecue at the lake. There had been the horseshoe competition in which he had been pitching a close second until the Monsignor pulled him aside and confided that Jim Quillan had been champion for the last five years.

"Which I take to mean Jim Quillan's the man to beat." He

chuckled. "So thinking the Monsignor really wants this one, I bear down and start tossing them meaner and cleaner, and everyone's clapping and cheering me on, and I win by six points. And all the way home I'm trying to figure out what's wrong with the Monsignor. How come he's not talking to me. How come every time I say anything he just grunts. And then right as we pull into the driveway, I happen to mention the rattle in the engine, and that's when he tells me. 'Better get used to it,' he says. 'Since it's Quillan who provides the rectory with a new car every two years.' Apparently the horseshoe event is the little man's big claim to fame." He looked over and grinned. "I seem to be the Monsignor's worst fears come true—a fool in priest's clothing." His bitter laughter made her squirm. She forced a smile. Why couldn't he just apologize and be done with it. Her neck ached with the long, strained silence.

Father Gannon sighed. "So!" he said, then sighed again. He turned down the next street and pulled in front of a house that belonged to a girl in her class. She wished he'd say what he had to and be done with it.

He turned off the motor. "So," he said, taking a deep breath in the sudden silence.

She tried to focus on the stars beyond the dark trees, because this was going to get really weird. There were millions of stars up there, and all the millions and millions of brilliant stars were dead and she didn't understand any of it, and her stomach was growling, and he kept clearing his throat. Oh God, this was going to be even worse than she'd thought. As he began to speak he ran his hands over the steering wheel. He recentered the magnetic crucifix on the dashboard. "Anyway, what I really have to say . . . I mean, what I want to say . . . well, actually, you see I can't stand the thought of you . . . that is, the possibility of you being in any way . . . damaged . . . no, that's not the right word. Disillusioned, that's it! Disillusioned by my poor judgment, and so I think it's important that I explain things . . . well, myself, that is . . . I mean, about being a priest. Well, of course, you know about that, generally, but I mean about myself and what being a priest has been like. Not the whole vocation, I don't mean that. I mean me."

"That's okay. You don't have to. Really." The story of his vocation was the last thing on earth she wanted to hear.

"No, you see I don't want you thinking badly of all priests or being confused about your faith or the Church because of me, because of what I did. You know what I mean?"

The more she assured him that none of this was necessary, the more determined he was to explain. He was telling her about his family. His father had been a janitor in their parish grammar school, working for little money all his life, drinking too much on weekends and holidays, shaming his mother and older sister, both devout churchgoers. All his life his mother had wanted him to be a priest.

"From the day I was born, according to my father," he said, making himself sound uniquely chosen, "she would tell me all she wanted in life was to see her son a priest. And I'll tell you the truth. For a long time it wasn't even near what I wanted. I loved sports and girls and hanging out and going to the movies and playing cards. But I wanted to go to college and I really wanted to help people, you know, with their problems, with their lives. It was this thing, this real need I had. Nothing made me feel as good as when I was helping someone. And so at that point in my life, it all kind of came together, college, my mother wanting me to be a priest, me wanting her to be proud as much as I needed to be a good person and help people." His head was back against the headrest, and she wondered if his eyes were closed. He was explaining that his desire to help people had always been a stronger motivation than any deep and mystical love of God. He sat up and looked at her. "Does that shock you?" he asked.

It bewildered her—not only what he was saying, but that he was telling *her*. She didn't know what to say. Like beating Mr. Quillan at horseshoes—this was a distant world. "Well, you could still be a good person and help people without being a priest," she said.

"I know. Of course you can. But I think a priest can do more. I mean, being a priest carries more weight. People listen to you." He laughed. "That's what I always thought, anyway. But you see, my point is, then something like the other day happens, which was wrong, which never should have happened, and that's the terrible dilemma of making mistakes as a priest. It makes it all that much more confusing and burdensome for you. I mean my . . . my actions." He shook his head with a futile sigh. "I'm afraid I'm not articulating this very well."

"No, I understand. I do," she said, afraid he'd start explaining it all over again.

He started to say something, then stopped with a rueful snort. "You're a good kid and I appreciate your patience and your understanding." He patted her shoulder and told her she was too fine a person and too vulnerable right now for anyone to mess up. "I'm sorry. I'm really sorry for what happened," he said.

"That's okay," she said. "Really."

"No," he said sadly. He kept looking at her. "No, it's not. Believe me." He turned suddenly and started the car. He drove slowly, the silence awkward between them. When he pulled into the driveway she fumbled for the door handle and thanked him for the ride.

"Alice," he said as the door opened; then he cleared his throat.

Looking back, she was repelled again by his intensity, a rawness pulsating like an exposed nerve.

He took her hand. "Thanks," he said, squeezing so hard her fingers hurt. "Thanks for listening to me."

"Oh God," she groaned, running up the driveway.

Norm was allowed out of the house to go to work, but he had to come straight home afterward. He still couldn't use the car or the phone or see his friends. He lay on his bed like this in the dark, night after night, his insides shriveled, a mass of pain in the cavity where his heart had been. Even swallowing hurt, with this constant lump in his throat. Every day a new crop of pimples erupted on his cheeks and the bridge of his nose. With his hands under his head he listened to the branch scraping back and forth across the screen. Hearing another sound, he sat up and listened. Was someone crying? He put his ear to the wall, but his mother's room was silent. Was it Benjy? Was it Mrs. Klubock?

His stomach turned every time he thought of driving the car over Klubocks' dog. He'd tried to get Benjy to tell him what had happened, but he wouldn't. Benjy could barely look at him. The poor kid had probably felt every crunch and crack under the tires. His last memory that night was Weeb's sister, Janice, pushing him away as she told him to stop slobbering over her. He didn't know why his pants were unzipped, and he couldn't even remember driving home. When he asked Benjy if there had been any close calls, all he'd said was "Nope."

He was worried about his brother, but if he said anything the whole mess would be thrown in his face again. Benjy was always in the house, either watching television or sleeping. And now that the couch had become Duvall's bed, Benjy spent most of the night in his room.

There it was again. He sat up. It sounded as if Benjy was crying. He got out of bed and tapped lightly on his door. Shadows flickered on the stairway wall. Omar was down there, laughing at something on television. Benjy didn't answer, so he opened the door. Benjy was sitting on his dark bed in this niche the previous family had used as a sewing room. There was just space enough for a bed and small chest of drawers. There was a doorless closet and one narrow window, directly over the bed.

"Jesus, Benjy, it must be a hundred degrees in here." He knelt on the bed and opened the window. He braced it with the split yardstick from the windowsill. This had been the last sash rope to fray and break. Getting off the bed, he told Benjy he still remembered how when they'd first moved in every window had stayed open by itself. He knew from Benjy's breathing he was trying not to cry. "I even remember there was a door on that closet, but it wouldn't open with the bed in the room, so me and Mom had to take it off." He didn't say it, but his most vivid memory of the day they had moved in had been their mother's elation at having their own home, and his sense of power and pride at being the man of the house carrying boxes and dragging rugs inside with his mother. Funny how these tiny rooms had seemed so enormous then.

Benjy knelt on the bed. He was trying to close the window.

"What're you doing?" he asked.

"It's that smell. I hate that smell."

Norm sniffed. "It's just the pig farm. It's not even that bad tonight."

"It makes me feel sick," Benjy said, letting the window fall shut.

He locked it, then sat back against the wall and slapped the broken yardstick against the mattress.

Norm turned on the light, and Benjy squinted in the glare. "You're scared. Why're you scared?"

"I'm not scared." Benjy stared down at the weathered stick.

"Then why're you up in your room all the time? Why're you acting so creepy lately?" His chest ached with anger. Why couldn't Benjy be as strong as he was? There was nothing and no one to fear. No one but their mother.

Benjy shrugged.

"Why won't you even look at me? What is it? What the fuck did I do?" he demanded.

Benjy kept flipping the yardstick, his features dulled by teary bloat.

"You think I ran over that dog on purpose? You do, don't you?" he cried, grabbing his brother's wrist and yanking him close, but Benjy stared past him. "I didn't do it on purpose. I didn't! I wouldn't have done that, you know that. I never would have. I know I wouldn't."

The tears running down his brother's face revealed the truth, the vast and horrible truth about himself: he had aimed the car and killed the dog coldly and deliberately, and Benjy knew it. He stood up and began to pound his head with his fist. "Fuck! Fuck! Fuck! Fuck!" he groaned as Benjy sobbed into his pillow.

He was going into his room when the television went off. Duvall was roaming around downstairs. It was all his fault, the peddler, Norm thought, crawling into bed; because the money he'd gotten drunk on the night he humiliated himself in front of Janice Miller, the night he killed Klubocks' dog, probably chasing him, crossing over the grass strip and Klubocks' driveway as the dog dove into the lilac bush, that money had come from Duvall in a twisted convolution of betrayal and setup. And ever since that night Duvall had been completely in charge here. Duvall was calling the shots, with everyone just where he wanted them. He closed his eyes. Duvall was pulling the strings, making them all dance faster and faster. His heart began to race. And now through the hollow wall between the rooms, there came that thin cry, that gasping again.

He rolled over and listened in astonishment. That's what he'd heard before. That's what he'd walked in on. Jesus Christ, his little brother hadn't been crying, but going at it full throttle. Imagine that. He pulled the pillow over his head, to muffle the last pathetic groan. That bastard Duvall. It was all his fault, everything.

On Friday morning when Alice got up, Benjy told her that Father Gannon had called earlier. He'd said not to wake her up, just give her a message. He was going to be in Proctor late tonight helping Father Krystecki stack firewood, and he'd stop by the A+X and give her a ride home from work. She was mad at Benjy for not waking her up and mad at Father Gannon for being so nervy, but then by the end of the long, hot night was too tired to care anymore.

Father Gannon arrived the minute the lights went out. He waited while she finished her closing chores. She saw Blue Mooney peer down into the Monsignor's car on his way into the kitchen. She began to hang the clean pots over the grill. Mooney was telling Fawnie Anuta about a fight he'd had earlier this evening with two creeps who thought he'd tried to cut them off the road. His voice rose and she realized the story was really for her benefit. Now he was bragging about some job he was trying to get. He'd be driving a truck. Far from here, she hoped.

Father Gannon grinned when she got into the car. As he drove he told her how Father Krystecki was clearing the lot behind the rectory himself so that a new parking lot could be paved. Whenever he could, Father Gannon went out there to help him split and stack the wood.

"What a workout," he sighed.

"Sounds like it," she said, both yawning and rubbing her nose against the sharp smell of sweat.

He slowed down as he approached her street. "You're tired, huh?"

"Yah I am. I really am." They'd been busy all night and she couldn't wait to go to bed.

"Here we are," he said, turning into the driveway. "Well, that didn't take long." Something in his voice made her think of that dark rectory, the only sound the Monsignor clearing his throat, grunting, and sneezing the way he did all through Mass. Before she could close the door he leaned across the seat to say he'd be coming back from Proctor this same time tomorrow if she needed a ride.

At eleven o'clock Saturday night it was still eighty degrees, with the temperature in the A+X kitchen at least a hundred degrees. They had been too busy all night for anyone to take breaks. Even Blue Mooney had been put to work on the grill with Anthology, who bullied him and laughed every time his cousin made a mistake. Mooney was rolling a trash barrel through the lot when Father Gannon pulled in. Alice saw him lean into the priest's window to tell him they were closed. Father Gannon gestured toward the building. Mooney pointed toward the street and said something. When Father Gannon started to back up, she ran outside. "He can wait here!" she said.

"Well, I just didn't want people thinking we're open," Mooney said, his face reddening.

"I can wait out there. That's no problem." Father Gannon started to shift again.

"No!" she insisted, surprised at how angry she felt. "You wait right here, Father. I'll be done in a few minutes. And no one's going to think we're open!" she said, glaring at Mooney.

"Father!" Mooney said, on her heels heading toward the kitchen. "What do you mean, father? Like someone's father father?"

"He's a priest," she said, even more annoyed by his relieved grin.

Instead of his collar Father Gannon wore a soiled dark-blue shirt. He apologized for his appearance, the bits of bark on his shoulder and even in his hair. He and Father Krystecki had been splitting word since suppertime. When they finished they'd collapsed on the back porch, both so thirsty that Father Gannon said they'd each downed three beers one after another.

Something went cold and tight inside. Three beers. She kept glancing at him, but he seemed perfectly normal. Definitely more relaxed, if not a little silly. He was laughing now because he had early Mass tomorrow and he still hadn't prepared his sermon.

"So what're you going to do?" she asked, yawning.

"Actually I was thinking I'd work on it now if you don't mind riding around awhile." He looked at her and smiled. "I've kind of got the gist of it."

"Oh. Okay. Sure," she said, trying not to show her exasperation. She was so exhausted she could barely keep her eyes open, and now she had to listen to a midnight homily.

He hunched over the wheel and cleared his throat loudly. He drove down Main Street. In the moonlight the marble church glowed a ghostly white. He passed her corner. "My sermon today is about value and redemption," he began. "Now I know not everyone collects the same kind of stamps, but you probably all have the same difficulties when it comes to redemption. . . ."

Her eyes closed. Her head bobbed as she dozed, lulled by the drone of his voice and the car's engine. She dreamed she was in a store filled with feathered hats, bright silk dresses, and soft leather shoes. Her arms ached from carrying all the beautiful clothes she wanted to buy if only she could find a cashier. She staggered up and down the aisles, but there was no one to help her. Finally she saw a tiny woman standing by a cash register at the front door. The woman, who was no bigger than a child, kept shaking her head as she piled the clothes onto the counter. "You're just wasting your time," the woman said.

"Alice!" Father Gannon was nudging her arm. "Alice, wake up! You're home."

She stared at him. Her eyes were burning. Her thoughts raced. She was home. The woman would only take green stamps. And Father Gannon had just been saying there weren't enough redemption centers.

"Are you awake?"

"Yes."

"Boy, that was record time. You were sound asleep two sentences into my sermon."

She tried to explain how tired she was and what a long day it had been, but that it had been a wonderful sermon, really. And now he was laughing so hard he could barely speak.

"I was only kidding," he finally managed to say. "I was talking about saving green stamps. It was a joke." He turned so instantly somber that she thought he might be angry. "I was trying to be funny," he said with a self-conscious laugh. He kept looking at her as if he needed to say something.

She could feel him watching her as she hurried down the driveway.

She lay in bed for a long time, unable to sleep. She kept thinking of him saying her name, "Alice? Wake up, Alice," over and over. Alice, Alice, with his hand on her arm.

By the end of the next night she kept glancing up at the clock. She was in the supply room when Mr. Coughlin limped out of Carla's car on crutches. Carla had driven him to the hospital, where they'd been for the last hour. Earlier in the evening one of Carla's customers had driven off with the tray attached to his car, an oversight that always enraged Mr. Coughlin. While he and Carla were screaming at each other, he reared back and kicked the side of the building. His big toe was broken.

Mooney came to the door. "That same guy's here, that priest," he said.

She looked out and waved. Father Gannon raised a hand to tell her to take her time. She could feel Mooney watching as she jammed the last dispenser with napkins and wedged it onto the full tray. Before she could pick it up, he had the heavy tray balanced on his fingertips. The muscle in his arm bulged his American flag tattoo in and out.

"He a relative or something?" he asked, holding the door open with his foot.

"No, he's just a . . . a friend," she said, surprising herself.

"That's weird," Mooney said under his breath. "That's really weird."

Father Gannon's clerical collar glowed under the passing streetlamps. He hadn't been able to help Father Krystecki with the wood because he'd been at the nursing home all night with an old woman who was dying. Her family, who lived in California, had asked the Monsignor to be there, but his gallbladder had kicked up.

"Did she die?" Alice asked uneasily.

"No." He sighed. "As a matter of fact, she was having some broth when I left."

Somehow, though, she didn't believe him. He seemed too nervous. He kept sighing and rubbing his chin. The woman had died and she, Alice, was the tail end of a death mission.

When he turned at her corner she was surprised at her disappointment. Lately it seemed she was always either working or getting ready for work.

"Tired, huh?" he asked.

"Not really. I had coffee right before I left, so I wouldn't fall asleep."

"You did?" He smiled at her. "How about a little ride, then?"

"Oh a ride's fine," she said and he headed back toward Main Street.

"I hope the coffee doesn't keep you up all night," he said.

"That's one good thing about this job. I can sleep late in the morning."

He groaned with envy and said he had the early Mass.

Feeling guilty, she pointed to the stop sign ahead and told him if he turned right, then he'd be back by her street.

"It's okay." He laughed and said he hadn't been sleeping too well lately. "This is good, getting out like this. Especially with someone under the age of forty. God," he added, "thirty."

"Twenty," she said in a small voice, and he laughed.

"That's even better," he said, and he laughed again.

They seemed to be following the moon as they drove into the hills. The pastures looked wet in the moonlight, the trees of the bordering woods dense with shadows. The houses they passed were dark and still. In all this way they had only seen a single car, the one that seemed to be aiming straight at them on this narrow winding road. Father Gannon jerked the wheel, pulling onto the soft shoulder to let it by.

In the last few minutes they had been matching mother stories: holes in socks, burned toast, and for some reason tears right before Sunday Mass.

He pulled back onto the road.

"Maybe all mothers do it," he said. "They just get so exhausted trying to get everything to go right."

"Well, I won't!" she said so sharply that he looked at her.

"Won't what?" he asked. "Go to church?"

"Not if it means getting everyone all upset." Actually she hadn't meant that until she'd seen the look on his face. This was the same thing she'd done to Lester. She'd enjoyed shocking him. But Lester's reaction had always been so pained and personal, while Father Gannon seemed amused. "I mean," she continued, "you go to Mass to be close to God, but when the whole time you're sitting there a nervous wreck and you can't concentrate on one single word the priest is saying, much less pray yourself, so what's the point? I mean, wouldn't it be better to just stay home and be quiet and calm and filled with good feelings instead of worrying what everyone around you is thinking!" Her voice had gone too high.

He glanced at her. "Is that a question?"

"Yes. Really, I mean it." She took a deep breath, uneasy with his silence.

"I don't know," he finally said. "I guess it's the good-feelings part. You can get good feelings from a lot of things, right? A big juicy steak? A funny movie? Being with someone you really like?" He shrugged. "I don't know. I don't think that's quite the commitment Christ had in mind."

She looked out the window.

"Do you?" he asked after a moment, when she still hadn't replied.

"I don't know." She felt young and stupid. She watched the fence along the road, its barbed wire glittering as they passed.

"No, tell me. Tell me what you think," he insisted.

She looked at him, shocked by what she was thinking and feeling right now.

"You meant what you were saying. Why won't you explain it? Why won't you tell me?"

"I don't know. I guess I was just sounding off or something, I don't know."

"You can't talk to me." He sighed. "I make you feel uncomfortable, don't I?"

"No, it's not that. I just, I don't know, I'm just starting to feel really tired, for one thing. I think my coffee's wearing off, and gosh, it's really getting late," she said, studying the moon as if it were the bright face of a clock. "You'll never get up in time for the six."

"I can turn here," he said, pulling onto the soft shoulder. He sat so still, staring over the wheel, that she thought something was wrong with the car. Or maybe with him. He spoke suddenly, in a faltering voice. "Alice, I've got this terrible feeling, this awful pain like an ache that goes from here," he said, gesturing at his throat, "right down into my stomach." And then for a moment he didn't say anything.

"Maybe you should see a doctor," she said hesitantly.

"That wouldn't do any good," he said with a long sigh. He turned and looked at her. "Besides, all the doctors I've seen don't want to hear what's really wrong."

In the uneasy silence she began to twist the apron string around her wrist, binding it tighter and tighter. "What's that?" she asked, though she already knew.

"I just want to touch you. That's all I want. That's all I think of every minute, all day long. And now here I am right next to you, and I can't, because I'm not supposed to. Because it's wrong. Because of who I am. Because you're young. Because . . . because you might not even want me to."

She unwound the apron string, pulling it up into the air. Her mouth was dry. She kept swallowing. She heard his breathing quicken.

"Alice! Do you know what I'm talking about? Do you?"

She looked up and nodded.

"Tell me what to do," he whispered. "Is it all right?"

She closed her eyes as he moved toward her.

"Oh you sweet girl," he kept whispering. "You sweet, sweet girl." His entire body was trembling. His hands shook as they touched her face.

She told her mother she was getting rides home with different girls from work. Night after night he was there. Always on time, freshly shaven, cheeks slapped pink with spicy cologne, glowing when she appeared, grinning at her so often that he was always swerving away from parked cars, from oncoming cars, jerking the wheel back into the lane. She rode gripping the door handle. He wore a white T-shirt, his black clerical pants, black shoes. His Roman collar and black shirt were in the glove compartment. The Monsignor was at Lake George with the Hinds family these last few days, and there was a visiting priest helping out, so he could come and go as he pleased. Mrs. Arkaday went to bed early, and he always left a note on his door telling when he'd return in case there were any sick calls.

Even if there had been anything open this late at night, they really couldn't be seen together in public, so they would drive around and talk; then, right before it was time to bring her home, he would stop on a back road and move across the long, deep seat to take her in his arms. He no longer trembled, but now his apprehension had taken the form of apology. Her back was against the door handle, he was sorry. She was rubbing her chin. Had he hurt her mouth? Was it too hot in here for her? Too cool? Too buggy? Was he too heavy? His hands too rough? His embrace too desperate? He was so afraid of hurting her, he said, afraid of forcing himself in any way on her.

"Just tell me to stop," he whispered at her wet ear. "And I will. That's all you have to do," he panted. The choice was hers. He was kissing her throat, her shoulder.

Eyes closed, she shook her head, panting herself. Don't talk, she wanted to say. His breathing was enough, his lungs, his heart against hers. The sound of his voice, his groaning, stirred her, blinded and deafened her. Words ruined it. Words turned them back into Alice Fermoyle and Father Gannon, both in uniform, in the Monsignor's car, on a dark road dense with brambles and guilt. "I'll do anything, anything you want," he pleaded at her breast.

She shook her head, her bra dangling loose.

"Tell me. Please tell me."

Her eyes opened. Where were they? Was that a car coming? She raised her head to see, and he writhed with the sudden motion. She slid across the seat, half onto the floor. He was pulling down her pants and then she helped him with his.

"My God," he groaned when she held him. "Oh my God, I'll do anything for you. Anything!" he cried with the anguished fervor of prayer.

She pushed away and got back up on the seat. "No," she whispered, pulling up her pants and reaching back awkwardly to hook her bra.

"I'm sorry. I hurt you, didn't I?" He reached to touch her, then drew back. "It's all too fast, isn't it? I'm sorry." He covered his eyes. "I don't know what I'm thinking of. You're so young. My God, I'm sorry. I'm so sorry, Alice."

It was all right, she kept trying to tell him. She had gotten scared, that was all, afraid that someone might drive by and see them. She couldn't explain it, but what she feared was this presence she felt, this sense of all that was between them. She said it again. "I guess I just panicked, that's all."

"Oh God, I've got to be careful," he said, buttoning her shirt-front as if she were a child. He straightened her collar and smoothed back her hair. "I won't let anything hurt you, I promise."

As much as she believed him, she was still afraid.

Norm sat up in bed when he heard Duvall's car pull in. For the last two hours his mother had been pacing from room to room and up and down the stairs. At one point she had gotten into her car and roared off down the street, only to peel into the driveway soon after, slamming the car door, the back door, cupboard doors, as if doors both fueled and exorcised her rage. He knew better than to offer to help or ask what the problem was. You, she would say. You are the problem. You are the cause of all my pain. Once my pride and my hope, you are now my greatest disappointment. He was through battling with her. She was too shrewd, too quick to attack, and she was inexhaustible. And yet with Duvall she continued to be so passive, so gullible that it was not only bewildering, but, lately, frightening.

It was one-thirty and Duvall was just getting back. Alice had arrived awhile before with some lame story about going to a girl's house after work. His mother might believe it, but he didn't. Whoever was driving Alice home was dropping her off at the corner. He'd look out the window and see his sister hurrying down the shadowy street, and he'd be filled with rage, wondering who the son of a bitch was who couldn't even see her safely home. She denied it, but he was certain it was Lester. The fag probably had some weird rule about driving down a dead-end street after midnight.

Duvall came in the back door. Norm tiptoed to the top of the stairs.

"You said you'd be here by eight," came his mother's clipped voice as the light went on down in the kitchen. Glasses clinked. The refrigerator door squealed open.

"I know," Duvall sighed. "I just got further and further behind with every appointment."

"You could have called."

"I should have." The refrigerator door opened again. "You're right, I should have." Footsteps. A drawer opened. The silverware drawer rattled open. "You look tired, Marie." Duvall was talking with food in his mouth. Probably eating cold spaghetti, leering at her while he chewed, red sauce on his lips: the pig, the disgusting pig.

"I feel as if everything's starting to cave in on me. The first payment's due. It's all going crazy with the kids. I can't think straight at work. Mr. Briscoe's always on my back. 'What's wrong, what's wrong,' he keeps saying, as if I knew. As if I could tell him."

"You're just tired," Duvall said over a clinking fork.

"No. No, I can feel it. Something's going to happen. It's like this big thing that keeps swelling up around me, and then you say you'll be here no later than eight, so I count on that. I . . . I need that, do you understand?"

"Yes, I do," Duvall sighed. "I most certainly do."

"There's something wrong, isn't there? I can tell," she said, her voice rising.

Duvall insisted there was nothing wrong. She insisted there was.

"Get him!" Norm said under his breath. He leaned over the railing. They were still in the kitchen. Their long shadows faced each other on the living-room wall at the bottom of the stairs.

"I am just not accustomed to accounting for every waking moment of my day," Duvall said.

He tensed with the abrupt silence. Okay, now, Duvall was finally going to get his ass kicked right through that front door. And if he said one word to her, one word . . .

"Of course you're not. I'm sorry, Omar. I'm so sorry."

He threw up his arms in disbelief. Jesus Christ, that was her chance!

Duvall sighed. "You see, it's hard, Marie, hard being around a woman you . . . I don't know how to put this . . . but it's being here all the time and never being able to . . . You see, aside from being a very busy man right now, Marie, I'm a loving man, a robust man with a healthy appetite, and you can't expect me to sit here night after night aching with desire. So I try to keep busy! Keep my mind off of . . . those kind of things, if you know what I mean."

"That asshole!" he groaned.

"You're a good Christian woman, Marie," Duvall continued in a pained voice, "and I know you've been hurt, but there has to be more between a man and a woman than a peck on the lips and laying side by side. Comes a time when it just ain't natural!" he said with a bawdy laugh that enraged Norm.

Her reply was indistinct and small with apology. Duvall was whispering.

He could hear a window being closed, the click of a light switch. Her flat shoes scuffed grittily along the floor toward the living room. He stiffened back. She wasn't going to bring him up here to her bed, was she? And she couldn't very well do it right out in the open down there on the couch. A chair scraped out from the table.

"Come here," Duvall coaxed through the darkened kitchen. "Come on, now. Oh," he sighed. "You are light as a feather. Just as soft as fluff."

He waited until he couldn't stand it another moment, then he came down the stairs. When he turned on the lamp in the living room they pulled apart. She started to get up from Duvall's lap, but he held her there.

"What do you want?" she said as Norm went to the refrigerator.

"I'm hungry," he said, taking ice cream from the freezer. Behind him he heard her trying to struggle free of Duvall. "Let her go, you asshole!" he said turning, wielding the quart box like a brick. "I said—"

"Norm!" she cried, then burst into tears. She ran into the bathroom.

"Now look what you've done," Duvall said, coming toward

him. "Your mother's a good woman and she deserves better than that."

"Come on! Come on!" He held up his fists, but Duvall just shook his head, chuckling as he went past him to the bathroom door, where he called in softly to tell Marie he thought it best to leave now. He'd call her tomorrow.

Norm hugged the pillow over his head so he wouldn't have to hear his mother crying.

Marie's day had started badly. Alice had come in late last night, her cheeks raw with whisker burns while she continued to insist she had been hanging out with a bunch of girls from work. Instead of being contrite for his behavior last night, Norm had announced at breakfast that he wasn't going to spend the rest of his summer grounded. He intended to go out that night. Actually, she'd been relieved. It would mean a little more privacy in the house for herself and Omar. But then, right before she'd left for work, Omar had come by to tell her his good news. Claire Mayo had agreed to give him his room back in the boardinghouse. "She thinks she's so shrewd, but I know," he said, laughing. "She figures by keeping track of me, she can keep track of her sister May's franchise investment."

She watched him take his razor and shaving cream from the back of the toilet. "But you can stay here. You know I want you to," she said.

"I know that, but it'll be better, Marie. Just for a time. Alice is staying away more and more. Norm and I could go to the mat any moment, you know that, and Benjy, my Lord, I worry about that boy. I think he needs his mother right now."

"No, what he needs is a man in his life." Her fierce stare held his bright eyes.

"Maybe, but not me, not right now. I seem to be the agitating factor in this whole situation, and so I'll remove myself. But just for a time." He took her chin and lowered his face to hers. "I'll still be coming down that driveway right about suppertime. I just won't be cluttering things up for a time, for the children, Marie."

For a time. She kept repeating the words. *For a time.* She had lost control these last few weeks. She would get it back. She would be just as strong, just as tough as she used to be, and she would get her life and her children back on track. So when Mr. Briscoe offered to take Benjy fishing the following Sunday, she accepted gratefully.

All week long, whenever she reminded Benjy of his fishing date, he'd mutter, "I'm not going," and she'd growl back, "Oh yes, you are!"

Mr. Briscoe arrived early Sunday morning, laden with poles, tackle boxes, and bait. He was wearing a wide-brimmed canvas hat with feathery lures tucked into the leather band. Benjy would be right out, she said through a hard smile. He offered to wait in the car, and she could tell he was disappointed when she agreed.

Benjy was in the bathroom. "I'm not going," he said at the other side of the locked door.

"You have to. He's out there. He's waiting."

"Tell him I'm sick."

"You're not sick!"

"I'm going to throw up." He gagged.

"Goddamn you, Benjy, open this door!"

"I can't," he moaned. "I'm throwing up."

The retching intensified.

"You're not sick! You're afraid. You can't do this. You've got to go!"

"I'm sick."

"Open this goddamn door or I'll smash it open!" she cried, beating it with her fists and kicking it. The hollow door banged against the frame. Benjy's gagging grew louder. Mr. Briscoe's car idled in the driveway. "Benjy, how can you do this to me? That's my boss out there! Don't you understand? He's out there, waiting!" The bones in her hands throbbed.

"Mom! Stop it! Stop it!" Alice cried, pulling her away as Norm hurtled down the stairs in his underwear. "Jesus Christ!" he said, then raced to the door and told Benjy to come out.

"Make him go," she groaned.

"I'll tell him Benjy's sick," he said, starting for the front door.

"No," she said. That wasn't what she meant. She couldn't lift her head. Here it was, all over again, the never-ending chain of weakness and failure. "You make Benjy go with him."

"He's sick, Mom."

She looked up now. "Don't you understand? He needs to go. He has to!"

"No, Mom, not like this, you can't make him. You can't!"

"Yes, I can and I will!" she said, pushing past their reaching hands. "Benjy, you open this door!"

It opened, and on the floor Benjy sagged against the spattered toilet bowl. The smell of sickness spewed out of the damp little bathroom. His skin was white and there were circles under his eyes.

She burst into tears. "Now what do I do?" she sobbed. "I don't know what to do."

"I'll go," Norm was saying. He ran upstairs to put on his pants, then ran back down, carrying his sneakers. "Me and Mr. Briscoe'll have a good time. Everything's going to be all right, Mom. You'll see," he said at the door.

Here, in the middle of the lake, soft breezes undulated their drifting lines. Waves stirred by distant boats slapped the sides of Mr. Briscoe's dinghy. Mr. Briscoe had packed ham-and-cheese sandwiches. There were crunchy dill pickles and hard-boiled eggs, peanuts, potato chips, cupcakes, and ice-cold sodas. Out here everything was different. The food tasted great, and Mr. Briscoe wasn't half the creep Norm had always thought he was. "This is the life, isn't it, Norm?" Mr. Briscoe sighed again. He stretched back in the boat, arms under his head, his hat brim covering his eyes, his white legs crossed at the ankles.

"Sure is," Norm sighed, squinting back at the crowded green haze of the shore.

"Keeps me sane," Mr. Briscoe said.

"Fishing?" he asked, the conversational shorthand more natural as the day wore on.

"Not even. The daydreaming."

"Yah?"

"Sometimes things get too much, I put my head down on the desk and see myself out here just floating along, not a care in the world, not a one."

"Yah," he said, eyes closed, his face and bare chest baking in the sun.

"Too bad about Benjy," Mr. Briscoe said.

"He'll get over it."

"I know how it is."

"Probably the grippe or something."

"I mean his, uh, his problems."

Norm opened one eye into the searing sun. He clenched the oarlock. The asshole was still an asshole. "What problems?"

"Well, you see, Norm, I caught Benjy taking something from the store. I told him it would be our little secret. I promised him."

He sat up, shielding his eyes. "Then how come you're telling me?"

"Because I know how it is for a boy, how hard it can get and how much it can hurt. A boy needs a man in his life." He reached out to touch Norm's knee. "Do you know what I'm talking about?"

"No," he said, moving so that Briscoe's hand fell away. He felt drained by the ease of Mr. Briscoe's familiarity.

"Just try to be the man in your brother's life, Norm. He needs that. And don't say anything to your mother about the glove. I've been really worried about her lately. Really worried."

Suddenly the air glittered with sunlit spray as they heaved back and forth in the wake of a speedboat skimming past. Norm gripped the seat, feeling puny and naked. He had been the man in his brother's and his mother's life. Until Duvall.

Benjy sat stiffly in Mr. Tuck's living room. A cat jumped onto his lap and rubbed her back against him. Mr. Tuck's little girls peered through the glass door. The taller child with the long sausage curls was making faces at him. Her younger sister giggled and held herself as if she had to go to the bathroom.

Mr. Tuck had taken the afternoon off. He was all dressed up in his best suit, his only suit, the one he wore during the school year. He didn't own a summer suit. All he needed at the swimming pool was a T-shirt and bathing suit. He came down the stairs, annoyed to see his daughters giggling at his first patient. Two quick whacks on their bottoms sent them howling through the house. He lifted the cat by the scruff of its neck and threw it out the door. He sat down across from the boy and tried to appear thoughtful, as if preoccupied with an earlier patient. This took the form of a scowl. He was grateful to his wife's uncle Ferdinand Briscoe for this opportunity. It might be the beginning of everything, he'd told Grace in bed last night. Sending away for college catalogs for seniors and setting up class schedules for terrified freshmen was not enough. Who knows, he'd sighed to his wife, after the Fermoyle kid there just might be an avalanche of parents bringing their troubled offspring to his door for counseling. Exhausted, he steadied his frown on Benjy. He'd been up half the night figuring out how much of the house expenses, including the mortgage, would be tax-deductible if he used the living room as his office. One sixth of everything would amount to quite a savings.

Benjy kept swallowing and trying hard not to blink. "Look him right in the eye," his mother had said, "and answer his questions, except if you think he's just being nosy about my private life or something like that, because, after all, don't forget, he is Mr. Briscoe's nephew." With so many secrets, this was going to be tricky.

Mr. Tuck was trying to light a pipe. He sucked at the stem, frowning when he couldn't get it lit. Mrs. Tuck came to the door and glared through the glass. Her daughters were still screaming. Mr. Tuck smiled sheepishly as his wife opened the door. The cat ran inside and jumped into Benjy's lap.

"That wasn't necessary," Mrs. Tuck hissed.

"This is a private session, Grace!" he snapped.

She wiped her hands on her apron. "It's a fine turn of events, David Tuck, when your own children have to be beaten so that you can help some stranger's child." She slammed the door.

Mr. Tuck's stomach burned. He hadn't even begun and it was falling apart. He looked back at the boy stroking the cat. It wasn't going to be easy. He would have to partition off that door from the rest of the house to keep his family life from interfering with his professional life.

"Well, Benjamin, where should we begin?" The boy's stare made him nervous. "At the beginning, I guess. Let's see, you don't have any friends, you're scared of water, and, let me think now, there was something about a dog. Give me a minute now, it'll come to me." His laugh was meant to relax the boy, but it came out high and cackly. The frown slipped back over his face. He felt himself blush. "I know! You saw a dog get hit by a car, am I right, Benny?"

"No sir, I didn't see the car hit him. I just felt it."

"Hm! Now, was this your dog? I think your mother said you and the dog were close."

"No, he was the Klubocks' dog from next door."

"I see," Tuck said, flipping through a notepad for a clean page. Damn, he should have been making notes from the beginning. This would go in the boy's record, in his file. He would need file cabinets. The girls' piano would have to be moved into the den. Another battle with Grace. He glanced up, pen poised. "Do you know what today's date is?"

"No."

"Well, anyway. You were in this car and the driver's intoxicated." He looked up from his notes. "Now it's your father that drinks, right?"

"Sometimes."

"So it's late at night and you're in the car and you don't see the dog, but the car hits the dog. Have we got that right so far?"

"Well, the car ran over the dog. It didn't just hit him. You know the wheels, they went over him."

"The wheels, they went over him. Okay! Good! Now tell me what happened next."

"I don't remember. I'm not sure."

"Hm! You don't remember. You're not sure," he said, pen scratching as he recorded the boy's every word. "Well, what did you say?"

"I don't remember what I said."

"You must have said something. Try to remember. Maybe you said, 'Oh my God' or 'Shit.' I mean under the circumstances that would certainly be acceptable, don't you think?" He chuckled to loosen the boy up.

"Yah, I guess so."

"So what did you say?" he asked, pen poised.

"I don't know. Probably I didn't say anything. I was pretty upset."

"Is that what you do when you're upset, Benny, you go silent?"

"Yah." The boy shrugged. "I guess. Sometimes."

"What about your father? What did he say?"

"He didn't say anything. He wasn't there."

"You mean, in a manner of speaking, not there?"

"No, he's in a hospital."

"Oh I didn't realize he'd been injured. No wonder! Oh my heavens!"

"No, he's in a hospital for drinking. He wasn't in the car that night." He blinked. "My brother was."

"I see," Tuck said with a skeptical glance. Classic case of denial, he thought. He continued writing: "Benny and brother in car." He looked up. "Now, your mother says you're so upset, so haunted by this tragedy that you won't leave the house, that it's all you think about."

"It's not all I think about. I try and think of other things."

"Are you sublimating your grief, son?" he asked. He'd done some reading in his old textbooks last night.

"I don't know what that word means."

He tried to light the pipe again. "Of course you don't." He coughed. "This is your first encounter with psychiatry, isn't it?" He waved away the smoke between them.

"I guess so." The boy kept looking toward the door.

Tuck sensed that he was honing in on something here. Better not to seem too eager, though. Take it slow and easy. "What that means, Benny, do you mind if I call you Benny? Benjamin's such a mouthful."

"No sir, I don't mind, if you want to."

"What that word means is that you're hiding your true feelings, that you are pretending the accident never happened." He paused. "Is that what you're doing, Benny?" he asked softly.

"I know it happened." The boy shrugged. "I just try and make it seem different." The cat purred loudly as he stroked it.

"How do you do that, son?" Maybe the cat would be a good idea after all. An innovative technique to relax his patients. The cat food would definitely be deductible. Grace would have to start saving the grocery slips.

"I just think about it like it was a program I saw or a movie or something."

"That's sublimation, Benny," he said, checking his notes. There was still the fear of water to cover. And no friends.

There was a tap on the door. Tuck looked up to see his daughter crossing her eyes and sticking out her tongue at his patient. He threw open the door. "Don't you ever do this again!" he said, grabbing her arm and shaking her.

"Mommy says it's lunchtime and she's not gonna wait around all day, so he has to go now, because Mommy said so!" his daughter screamed.

Tuck released her, and seeing the print of his grip red on her flesh, felt dizzy. He tried to pull her close to soothe her, but she ran off shrieking to her mother.

He closed the door quickly. He didn't know what it was lately about his older child. Something about her was driving him to these frenzies. He felt the boy's eyes on him, and he was ashamed. Last winter she'd spilled milk in his lap. In his anger he'd dislocated her shoulder. They told Dr. Lawson that she'd fallen down the cellar stairs. For months afterward she had had such terrible nightmares that Grace had to sleep with her. It was only two weeks ago that Grace had moved back into their bedroom. Since then she'd let him make love to her once, the whole time hushing him while she listened for her daughter's cry.

He bent over the boy, speaking rapidly, to fit it all in before the explosion. "Now, remember, Benny, don't sublimate. What happened, happened. Talk about it to people."

The door opened. Her mouth twisted. "You make me sick, you hypocrite."

He hurried toward her with both hands raised in supplication. "Please, Grace, not now. Wait until he leaves. I beg you."

"Tell him to get out now!" she demanded, shaking her fist. "I want him out now!"

Benjy jumped up with the clinging cat's claws embedded in his chest as he headed for the door. Tuck wavered, glancing between his wife and his patient.

"Tell your mother that'll be a dollar, Benny, and I'll call her to set up the next session," he called.

"No," Mrs. Tuck was hollering. "There'll be no more of your little sessions, you hypocrite, you monster."

The door slammed and the cat leaped onto the porch, and then Benjy heard a sound like a woman crying, as if she was in pain, as if Mr. Tuck had punched her in the mouth or something. He ran down the steps and up the street.

The little room off the rectory parlor was a warm gray fizz of television static. Mrs. Arkaday dozed in the green leather chair, her feet on the hassock, arms crossed. Her head bobbed with a drooling smile as she dreamed of Howard waving at her through the glass.

"This is the end of our evening programming."

Her eyes shot open and for a moment she couldn't stop trembling as she stared at the sputtering test pattern on the screen. She was exhausted after supervising Howard Menka's window washing all day. Every time she tapped on the glass to point to a spot, he glared at her. One of these days he was going to haul off and hit someone. And what would the Monsignor do then? Whose responsibility would that be? Poor man, he certainly had his hands full, people always pestering him with their problems—now it was his cousins the Hindses and their dying son—when he had so much to run, rectory, church, school, and on top of it now, this strange new priest, prowling up and down the back stairway in his stocking feet all hours of the day and night on his way God knows where. He hadn't worn his shoes inside since the polish fiasco. There were still streaks in the carpeting, and now every room smelled of his feet. "Father Gannon," the Monsignor would shout, bearing down on her. "Where's Father Gannon?" As if she should know, as if she had any say at all about what went on here. Good thing, too, because if she did, the first thing she'd do would be to fire Howard Menka, and then, next, she'd show Father Gannon these two red barrettes snagged with long brown hair that she'd been carrying like red-hot embers in her apron for days since first discovering them in his pants pocket.

Hearing a sound now, she tiptoed to the door, a little woozy with the turbulence of sweet cologne in the dim hallway. "Father Gannon!" she called as the back door opened.

He smiled as she hustled into the kitchen. He was freshly shaved, his cheeks high with color. His dark eyes glistened. "Kate, I didn't want to disturb you, but would you make sure I'm up for the six?"

"Where are you going?" she snapped. Her chin quivered. In all her years here, not a single priest had ever called her Kathleen or Kathy, much less Kate. "If the Monsignor asks me, I don't know what to say. Especially at this hour."

"Oh, Kate, I'm sorry. That really puts you in the middle, doesn't it?" He glanced past her to the dark stairs. "I haven't wanted to say anything. You know how the Monsignor feels about politics. But I really like Jack Kennedy. They meet over in Woodstock—his committee, that is—and there's not much I can do to help during the day, so at night . . ."

"Of course," she whispered, a finger sealing her lips. Of course, that handsome young Senator and his beautiful Jackie. Waving, she shooed him out the door. He had to say no more. Naturally, an energetic young priest would want to do all he could to help elect the first Catholic President, even if it meant dragging around dog-tired all the next day. She had to admit, it gave her a little thrill, the thought of him defying the Monsignor. Father Gannon was every bit as courageous and rugged as Senator Kennedy himself. She opened the trash basket and tossed in the barrettes. My Lord, all these days of worry, and they probably belonged to some child, and him like a child himself in so many ways. She stood by the window, smiling as she watched him go down the moonlit path. Must've broken a few hearts when he got the call. Her own heart stirred. It was a fine and noble life, this selfless giving to God. "Now what the devil's he doing?" she muttered, startled to see him kneel by Howard's perennial bed and cut himself a bouquet of Shasta daisies and baby's breath.

Mooney finally had a job. He was driving a truck for J. C. Colter and Sons, which was the biggest tire distributor in the state. He was on the road four days out of five, hauling threadbares up to Burlington for retreading. It wasn't just any zombie steering job, either, since he had to load the truck himself here in town, unload up at the plant, then reload the return shipment of retreads; plus he was responsible for all the paperwork, every invoice and bill of lading, each of which had to be date-stamped and signed at both ends of the run. He carried all the forms in a green plastic folder attached to a clipboard he'd bought himself. Getting into his truck in the morning, he could almost hear the drumroll, the chorused voices heralding another successful mission.

He smiled a lot more often. The old swagger was back. He wore his soft green collar up, and now, with his hair all grown out, he was cultivating just the slightest swell at the base of his sideburns. He bought himself brand-new hand-tooled cowboy boots and cigarettes by the carton, which he kept locked in his trunk along with every other possession—not that he was afraid Anthology would steal from him, so much as that it continued to make staying with his cousin seem like a temporary arrangement, one that could change at a moment's notice. "Any calls?" was still his first question through the door. "No calls, no telegrams," Anthology always answered back. In some illogical way it began to seem that this job was the special assignment, the lie becoming not only a force but a possibility for redemption.

Colter didn't pay big money, but he'd assured Blue the job was his as long as he delivered on time and didn't get in trouble with the law, which included any kind of traffic violation as far as Colter was concerned. Like every other prospective employer, Colter had questioned his brief stay in the Marines, but he was the only one who'd accepted Mooney's explanation without question. All he asked was to be notified the minute Mooney received his assignment, its covert nature thrilling the old man, a former leatherneck himself.

"Yes sir!" Mooney had answered, as he did now to all of Colter's orders, which continued to mitigate Colter's initial misgivings. It was not kin or rumor that gauged a man's true worth, but performance, Colter had said, looking him straight in the eye.

BETTER DEAD THAN RED proclaimed the decal on every truck in Colter's fleet, and every uniform had an American flag sewn on the sleeve. Mooney was proud of his new uniform, with his name scrolled on the pocket flap in orange thread. BLUE, plain and simple, like the dark-green pants and shirt, securing him in the ranks of like-minded men. Tonight before he picked up Anthology at the A+X he stood his collar straight up, turned his shirt cuffs back just one fold, and set the wave in his hair one more time before going inside.

He followed Alice from the storeroom into the kitchen. "I saw your school today, your college, that is," he said.

"That's good," she said, hurrying back into the storeroom for straws. Wisps of hair had slipped from her ponytail and lay on her collar. He blew a quick puff of air, grinning as the little hairs riffled up and down. She glanced back at him.

"I go right by it," he said, returning quickly with her to the kitchen. "Hey! Maybe I'll stop in and see you when you're going there."

Her head shot up, and she opened her mouth, and her cheeks flared red, but she only took a deep breath.

"If I can, I mean. There's no telling how busy I'll be then. And you, too," he added quickly.

"Yah, I probably will be." She sounded relieved. "Especially at first."

"Yah, especially then." A month, he thought. He'd give her a month, then he'd stop by and see her. Maybe take her out in the truck to eat someplace. Someplace nice. By then he'd have plenty of money. He'd buy her a present, maybe a book or a megaphone or whatever it was college girls liked.

While she finished her chores, he sat on the counter, smoking a cigarette with Coughlin. A few minutes later a car pulled in at the back of the lot and doused its lights. Taking off her apron, Alice ran outside and climbed into the car. Mooney looked down as the car passed under the order window. It was him again, the priest. Alice's head was lowered to smell the flowers she was holding.

The priest's car was in the distance as they pulled out of the lot. "Guess where they're going!" Anthology called as he strained to see over the dashboard.

"Jesus, he's a priest!" Mooney said.

"Yah? And what's he picking her up this late for? To pray?"

Mooney shrugged. "They're friends. He's a priest."

"Oh they're friends. But the priest is plugging her, believe me. I can tell."

He held his breath. Anthology was baiting him. They'd really been getting on each other's nerves lately. His cousin liked it better when Mooney was completely dependent on him. "Need butts?" he asked, slowing as they came to the gas station, where Anthology usually got them from the machine.

"No, let's follow them. Come on!" Anthology said.

Saying he needed cigarettes himself, he pulled next to the air pump. But he already had a full deck in his pocket, Anthology protested. "Come on!" he squealed, pointing ahead. "Look! They went through the lights, right past the church."

"He's taking her home," he said as he got out of the car. "Down to Edgewood Street."

"Holy shit!" Anthology hooted out the window. "You even know her street!"

When he got back in, he closed the door hard, then backed up and shifted forward with a jerk to remind Anthology of his status here. "I get any calls today?" he growled as they peeled down Main Street. If Anthology said one more word about Alice and the priest, he was afraid what he might do to him.

"Like always, no calls, no telegrams." He laughed. "Hey, let's

stop for coffee!" he said as they came to the silver diner at the bottom of the hill. They hadn't stopped in since Blue had started work.
Anthology loved coming here on their way home.

"I can't. I'm tired." He gave it just enough gas to race them by
the diner.

His cousin looked back at the diner and then up at him. "You
know something, Blue, you're turning into a real prick. You don't
wanna do nothing anymore! Not with me, anyway!"

"Look, I been on the road all day, and tomorrow I gotta be up at
five." It felt so good saying it, he couldn't help smiling.

"Hey, I wanna ask you something. How come you got a job if
you're still in the Marines?"

"I told you. You're supposed to."

"You're supposed to what?"

"You're supposed to do that when your, your . . . cool-
down's up."

"Cool-down? What's a cool-down?"

"Come on, don't," he warned. "I told you so much I shouldn't've
already." Like Colter, Anthology enjoyed the intrigue of his secret
mission.

"So what, you tell me one more thing, big deal! What am I gonna
do, go tell another spy or something?"

Mooney laughed. "I'm not a spy! I'm a Marine that's waiting for
orders."

"Okay, okay, so what the hell's a cool-down?"

"That's when you . . . you cool down."

"Yah?" Anthology persisted.

"Three months, you cool down. I been out three months," he
said, exasperated that Anthology couldn't comprehend such an obvious concept.

"So you cool down and now you're what? Cool?"

"Yah, you know, as far as in civilian terms, that is. Cool. Not
all . . . what do I want to say, not always acting like a soldier all the
time." He glanced over, his smile fading with the amusement on Anthology's face.

"You're full of shit, and I hope you know I know that. Okay? I
do know. I do," Anthology said softly.

"Yah, what the hell do you know?"

Anthology grinned. "I know you're not waiting for any special assignment. This is it, isn't it? What'd they do, throw you out?" His laugh was high-pitched and grating. "Come on, Blue, it's me, Anthology. You can tell me!"

"They didn't throw me out!"

"What? You quit? You couldn't take it? What happened, pretty boy? Someone muss up your hair?"

"Shut up, you little freak!"

"Hey, I don't care. I'm just sick of your shit, that's all, thinking you're some fucking soldier of fortune all the time or something."

He jammed on the brakes, hurling Anthology against the dashboard. "Get out! Get outta my car!"

"I'll get out! I'll get outta your fucking car! And you get outta my fucking apartment!" His stubby arms and legs churning, Anthology scrambled onto the side of the road.

"I'm out! Consider it done!" He roared off.

This road led straight up into the Flatts. Mooney's radio played softly, the spill of its pale glow on the seat the car's only illumination. He thumped the steering wheel and tried to sing with the music. His voice cracked and the words trailed off as he thought of what Anthology had said about Alice and the priest. He remembered the little church in Cuttingsville his mother had taken him to once a long time ago for some uncle's funeral.

"Our Father who art in heaven, hollow be my way!" he yelled out the open window as he sped over the dark winding road past uncles and cousins and more distant kin, to the three narrow chicken coops he used to tend and now his mother let stand empty, rotting into the black loam, and a little farther on, here, her brown cottage and lush garden, vegetables, when it was flowers he wished for her. And there from its post by the road, the bug light's sickly glow puddled out from the yard onto the road, yellow as beer.

"No," he muttered, then said it again as he reached up and unscrewed the hot bulb. Just as he put it into his pocket, the porch door squealed open.

"Put that light back on," his mother called. "You hear me? I said put that light back on!" She charged down the steps holding her bathrobe closed.

"It's just me, Ma," he said. "Blue."

"What do you want? What're you doing out here?" she demanded.

"I told you, Ma, don't be doing this anymore. I'm making good money now."

"Well, you make your good money, and I'll make mine!" She held out her hand. "Now give me that bulb."

"Let me move back, Ma. Please!"

"I said give it!"

"I could be paying you room and—"

"Give me the bulb!"

"Ma, I haven't been in one bit of trouble since I've been home. You know I haven't. I wouldn't pick a penny up off the ground if I found it, I'm so careful. I drive careful. I walk careful," he said with almost painful longing. "All I want is good things now. That's all I want, Ma. Honest to God!" Good things, sweet air in his arms, this uniform ironed every day, pants creased and his own money in the pockets.

"Then how come you're here? How come you're not still in the Marines?"

"I am! I told you, I'm waiting for orders, that's all."

"Travis!" She laughed and shook her head. "You're just like Kyle. You're nothing but trouble, and I'm sick of trouble, so give me the bulb. Give me the goddamn bulb!"

"Here's your bulb! Here's your bulb! Here it is!" he bellowed, whipping it at the side of the house. The tiny glass pieces glittered as they drifted down through the night.

All day long Marie had been filled with dread, with this sense of catastrophe looming. On her way to work this morning she'd almost hit a boy on a bike. Then no sooner was she at her desk than Mr. Tuck called looking for his fee, which she promised to send right out. He asked if Benjy would be able to come tomorrow afternoon, because it seemed clear he needed to be seen more than just weekly. She said Benjy wouldn't be coming again.

"Oh! Oh dear," Mr. Tuck said with a catch in his voice.

Benjy wouldn't be coming. He was fine now. The session had obviously snapped him to, she lied. She had to keep reminding herself that this idiot's wife who'd thrown her son out of her house was Mr. Briscoe's niece.

"Well, remember, with the slightest relapse, you be sure and give a call."

And then at three o'clock Renie called. The minute she heard his voice she felt sick to her stomach. Had the bank discovered the discrepancy in signatures and contacted him? But he only asked if she'd heard from Sam. Sam? What did he mean, hear from Sam? All Renie knew was that Helen had just told him to call and ask after the hospital had called her. Why? What was wrong? Was Sam all right? Renie didn't know. "But I think so," he said. "Because Helen was mad. She was so mad."

When she got home she found the overdue notice on her first loan payment in the same day's mail as the bill for Alice's first semester at UVM. At the table now Omar was fanning himself with one of the torn envelopes. His collar rim was dark with sweat. "I can't understand the delay," he said. "They promised delivery two weeks ago. And I even covered the newest franchise orders out of my own pocket and paid the freight myself to make sure this wouldn't happen."

"But it has," she said, pacing between the sink and the table. "It has happened, Omar, so now what do I do?"

"Stay calm," he said.

"Stay calm!" she cried, slapping her sides. She wheeled in a little circle. How could he just sit there? "Stay calm? I could lose this house!"

"I'll take care of it," he insisted. "I told you I will and I will."

"Then here!" She held out the red-stamped bank notice.

"Believe me," he said, sliding it into his breast pocket, "this is the last time you'll ever see this."

"I can't have them contacting Renie. Oh God, I can't believe I did that. What was I thinking of? I mean, that's forgery, isn't it? That's against the law!" She couldn't recall thinking anything at the time, only feeling, for the first time in years, actually feeling something deeply.

"Marie, I'm going to say it one more time now, and I want you to listen carefully. As soon as the soap comes, you will be so busy selling your product that all these worries, all these fears, will seem like a bad dream."

A chill went through her, and with it, the image of Sam's clammy hand groping toward hers, to seal another oath, another promise, reaching from his bed, from a dark corner, promising never to have another drink ever in his whole life, assuring her that someday this would all seem like a bad dream. She folded her arms over the cluttered sink and stared out the window.

"Marie?" He got up and stood next to her. "What is it?"

She closed her eyes and bit her lip.

"Tell me what you're thinking right now."

"That I've gotten myself into a horrible mess." She looked at him. "I'm trapped. I'm stuck. I'm really, really stuck."

"No, you're not!" he cried. "You're not stuck. You're not trapped. You're rooted, Marie, wonderfully and, I know, sometimes painfully, rooted. But look at all you've got! A home. A family. A job. A town you've lived in all your life, everything I'd give my right arm to have."

Her eyes filled with tears. She shook her head, as struck by his passion as by his naiveté. The wonder was that he could continue to believe, to have so much faith, so much trust. Didn't he see what was happening here?

"You're a pioneer," he was saying, flinging his arms in the greasy supper air. She had fried ham steaks in this dented pan on the counter. Disks of the white fat floated in the soak water. "The first of a new age," he was saying, "a woman as strong and as fearless as a man—no, stronger even than a man, because you need neither man nor woman. You are a woman without guile or excuses." His eyes gleamed. He smiled, panting a little, not so much to catch his breath, she realized, as to fuel the dwindling flame.

"I'm a pioneer, all right," she muttered. She turned on the water. It had to run a good five minutes to get hot. Astrid had a brand-new dishwasher. Last week Astrid had left her husband, had gotten as far as Albany before he caught up with her, and now she pushed buttons to clean her dishes. "A pioneer," she sighed.

"Yes! And believe me, Marie, someday there'll be more of you, women who can stand on their own two feet."

"These are awful tired feet," she sighed.

"Here," he said, reaching toward the faucet. "Let me do them."

"No. I'd like you to do something else, Omar. I'd like you to call Roy Gold. Right now. In front of me," she said, looking at him.

Apparently he knew Gold's number by heart. He was halfway through dialing when he abruptly hung up. "I've got to admit something," he said. "I've been calling all week and I keep missing him. So don't be disappointed. He's a very busy man." He started to dial again. Frowning, with his eyes closed, he asked for Mr. Gold. He looked at her. "Mr. Gold, this is Omar Duvall!" he said, grinning and pointing at the receiver. "Roy, yes. Yes, of course. Well it's my orders, sir. I've got all kinds of anxious distributors here waiting for their soap. Well, I know. Yes sir, I can appreciate that . . . You're just so busy, just out straight, business is so good." He winked at her. "Just fantastic, you say. . . . Well, I'd certainly appreciate your doing that for me, sir. . . . You see, there's this one very special distributor that's . . . Yes," he said, nodding. "Yes, she is. She's right here, as a matter of fact, sir. Here," he said, holding out the phone. "He wants to tell you himself."

The voice on the line was reassuring and pleasant. Gold apologized for the company's two-week backup on deliveries, and he promised to do everything in his power to get Omar's orders out immediately. "These things happen when it's a product everyone wants, and not only that, but a merchandising concept that's just all of a sudden now catching fire. Believe me," he said, "you'll be glad you waited, because you are getting in on the ground floor of the fastest-growing company in America!"

"Thank you," she said. "Thank you so much." She handed the phone to Omar.

"Yes sir." Omar was glowing. "She feels much better now, and so do I, sir. So do I."

A few minutes later she was sitting at the table watching him wash the dishes when the phone rang. It was Sam. Right after lunch he'd walked out of the dining room, out the front door, he said, out of Applegate, and onto the highway. He'd hitchhiked most of the day to get here.

"Here?"

"Home. I'm back home, pet. And this time everything's going to go right. You'll see."

Sleeves rolled up, Omar was humming. He winked as she sat back down at the table.

I t was Alice's day off and she and Joe were driving toward Albany, looking for some out-of-the-way restaurant where no one would know them. This was the first time since the trip to Applegate that they had been together during the day. In the early-afternoon light he looked much older than he did at night. His face was already dark with stubble and, like his mood, grim.

The Monsignor had caught Joe sneaking into the rectory Monday at one a.m. His excuse had been a Kennedy for President rally in Bennington. There wasn't much the Monsignor could say after last week's letter from the Bishop urging clerical support of those candidates whose positions would be in the best interest of the Church. But for the next two nights Joe played it safe and stayed home.

This morning when he told the Monsignor that he'd be working all day in Albany on a telephone poll for Kennedy, the Monsignor complained about his mileage. He said if it kept adding up the way it was, he would have to bring the car in again for a tune-up to that crook Archetti, who felt he could charge top dollar just because Archetti footed the bill for the altar lilies every Easter.

Alice had missed Joe these last two days, and now all he could talk about was the Monsignor. She yawned and smoothed her skirt over her knees. She hated these tirades. It didn't take much to stir him up. He could go on and on over nothing.

"And then just as I'm leaving this morning, you know what he said? He said, 'No stickers, Father! The heat just glues them on the car forever. And don't forget,' he said, 'we have some very important Republicans in this parish.' And then you know what he said? He looked at me in that judgmental, that critical, that . . . that sarcastic way he does, and he said, 'And I should think that you of all people, you more than anyone, would have learned by now, Father Gannon, that a good priest is apolitical.' "

It confused her to see him so agitated over something that wasn't even true. Kennedy was just an excuse for them to be together. And here they were, together. She moved closer and smiled.

"Every time I think of it, I see red! I can't believe he said that to me!" He banged the steering wheel.

Said what? Had she missed something? She tried to listen more closely.

"He's had it in for me since the day I came!" There was a catch to his breathing, like a pant or a ragged little cry. "A good priest is apolitical, is he? No, a good priest keeps his mouth shut. A good priest doesn't think! A good priest doesn't feel! That's what he really means!" He kept glancing at her. "That's what he wants, ears and a mouth. That's what they all want, you know. Maybe he figured I'd been lobotomized or something." He laughed so suddenly that she laughed, too, then squirmed in the mirthless silence.

For the next few miles neither one spoke. She twisted her purse strap miserably as he brooded over the road's curving glare. He was so emotional, so volatile. This intensity she'd first sensed in him made her as uneasy now as it had then. There was too much power here, too much energy for one so used to fleeing it. She felt as if she were being crimped smaller and smaller, like a scrap of paper the air might at any moment seize through the open window. She wished she hadn't come. Maybe it was better at night, when they were tired, when all they could do was hold each other.

"There's one!" she said, pointing to the little white restaurant ahead. Even the crushed stone in the parking lot was white. She read the sign, "The White Cottage," relieved when he said he was starving. Maybe he'd be in a better mood now with all that off his chest. She waited while he locked the car. He put his arm around her, and she leaned against him as they came through the parking lot. It must be awful, she thought, having to listen to people's problems all day long and never being able to share his own with anyone.

Inside the bustling dining room his gloom returned, so she tried to do most of the talking. UVM had sent her information about her dorm, her academic adviser, her courses. She even knew her roommate's name. She still hadn't decided whether to get the linen service or not, and she had to let them know soon. "But whenever I bring anything up my mother says, 'Not now. Wait until the soap comes.' That's all she talks about now: 'when the soap comes, when the soap comes.' God, she thinks her whole life's going to change when the soap comes."

"Don't be so hard on her. Maybe it will," he said, making her feel childish and petty.

Bristling, she carved off a small piece of steak. She hadn't been criticizing her mother, just trying to keep the conversation light. There was so much she wouldn't burden him with, her father's escape from Applegate, her mother's crying herself to sleep every night because Omar hadn't been around in days, and her own terrible guilt. Last night she'd dreamed that she was kneeling at the rail waiting for Communion. When the priest came to her she closed her eyes and held out her tongue, but instead he gave the Host to the person next to her. "Wait," she called softly. "You skipped me." He looked back in disgust, and she saw that it was Joe.

"That's just the way my mother was about my going into the seminary," he was telling her as he began to cut up his entire steak.

For a moment she wasn't sure what Presto Soap and UVM had to do with his going into the seminary. Suddenly she wanted to tell him that she hadn't gone to Mass in weeks. She wondered if he would tell her it was a mortal sin.

"You know I don't think she ever had one single moment, or accomplishment, or person in her whole life to be proud of until I went into the seminary. Right away I knew it was different for me than for the others, but I kept fooling myself. I kept thinking somewhere along the line I'm going to change, I'm going to find exactly what God wants me to do. I thought it would come like wisdom, you know, this enlightenment like a tongue of fire over my head. I waited for it. I actually did." He laughed and she felt a little better. He chewed and talked and gestured with his fork, all at the same time. He really had terrible manners, but at least his mood was improving. Maybe he just needed a chance to talk about himself.

"My first parish was in this little mill town in upstate New York. I said Mass, I did the novenas, the evening catechism classes, I visited the hospital and the nursing homes, I went by the parish school once a week. And still I had all this free time, all this energy, so I asked the principal for a group of troubled kids maybe I could help. I took them on hikes and picnics and played ball with them. They were always at my door. Winter came and there was this one kid, this runt named Radlette, who was wearing sweaters because he didn't have a jacket. So I bought him one, fleece-lined with a hood and buckles all over the place. No other kid had a better jacket, let me tell you, than Radlette had. The other kids picked on him for it. Radlette's mother told me to mind my own business, that she could get her kid a jacket, which I guess caused trouble with her and her husband, because one night he got drunk and said he'd punch me out if I ever laid another queer hand on his kid. Pretty soon Radlette wouldn't even look at me, his life had become so miserable. Next thing I know, my pastor's accusing me of buying the jacket with the priests' birthday party money. It was gone from the jar, twenty-five dollars. I was transferred. I couldn't figure out how one kind act could brand me a pervert and a thief. This must be it, I told myself. God's testing you, that's all. He's getting you ready for that tongue of fire. Later, that pastor wrote and said they'd found the birthday money, after all. I was exonerated. At least I wasn't a thief."

Again his laughter rang with bitterness. Each piece of steak seemed to take longer to chew.

"My next assignment was the Bronx, in a crummy, beat-up, lousy neighborhood like the one I grew up in. Only worse. All the kids were Radlettes. Most of the young priests in that parish hated it. Not me. I was so happy I thought I was going to cry that first day. It felt like I was trembling all over. I thought, This is why the crazy Radlette thing happened. This is what God wants.

"I got right to work. I got stores to donate their day-old bread and bruised fruit to the needy, and I delivered a lot of it myself. I wrote to some seminary buddies in rich parishes and had their parishioners send their old clothes and shoes to our parish. The rectory basement started looking like Macy's, people going through the bundles and trying things on. But that's where the trouble started. They said it was in direct competition with the Bishop's relief fund, that I had no business running my own clothing drive without going through the proper channels. I was told to submit my requests in writing on the proper forms directly to the Chancellery officials. So I did, but all I got back were these polite notes saying how the needs of our parish would be met as soon as other parishes ahead of us on the list had gotten their share. I tried to accept that. I'll be patient, I told myself. Then a letter comes saying there'd been an earthquake in South America somewhere and all the clothes had to be shipped there. My parish would be on next year's list. And would we, by the way, take up a special collection that Sunday for the suffering disaster victims in Bolivia. Okay, I said to myself. I even read the letter at one of the Masses."

He had stopped eating.

"Then winter came. An awful winter. People were heating their tenements with their oven doors opened twenty-four hours a day, because the landlords kept the building thermostats locked at sixty degrees." He leaned over the table and looked at her. She swallowed hard.

"There was this one woman," he said, his voice falling to a whisper. "She wasn't much older than you, with two babies. She came to me crying. She showed me her gas bill. Sixty dollars for one month! I told her I'd get the money for her somehow. While I was begging around from people I knew, the gas company shut her off. Her three-month-old baby got pneumonia and died. Sure, she should have gone to Welfare. Sure, she should have taken the baby to the hospital whether she had the money or not. But she was one of those that just didn't know how to make things happen. She went crazy and she tried to drown the other baby, so they put her away and sent the baby to a foster home." He rubbed his face in his hands.

There seemed to be silence at every booth and table.

"That's awful. At least there's nothing like that here," she said, but he didn't seem to hear her.

"That's when I took my first real look at the polite and pious and obedient Father Joseph Gannon. I started visiting every apartment in the neighborhood. Catholics, Protestants, Jews, it didn't matter. It took me two weeks. And what I saw made up my mind for me. I knew if I did nothing but pray for these people and go through the charade of proper channels, then I was no better than their landlords.

"I mimeographed leaflets, calling for a rent strike until the thermostats were turned up, until the broken windows were replaced, until the holes in the roof and the walls were patched. A lot of the landlords, the big ones, the ones who had five or six or ten of these hovels, reacted by turning the thermostats down even lower. So I went out and got blankets. I asked for blankets everywhere, from stores, the Salvation Army, Goodwill, hospitals, my fellow seminarians again. Even my own rectory. I took every extra blanket and tablecloth I could get my hands on, even old drapes from the attic. Word got around and three other priests joined me and a nun. We set up a kind of relief station in the parish hall. We passed out I don't know how many blankets. We had soup and coffee for them when they came, and cookies for the kids. We wrote letters to the papers. It looked like a couple of the smaller landlords were coming around. But then three of the biggest landlords, and two of them were Catholics, went to my Bishop with checks in hand. They convinced him I was disturbed, the nun was a Communist, and the other priests were drunks.

"I was put in a hospital in New Mexico for a month." He looked at her. "I wasn't there a month, Alice, but a whole year. They said I had a nervous breakdown. I don't remember much of it besides crying a lot." He sighed. "I certainly did cry. I stayed in one little room and wouldn't go outside for months. I never saw the sun or the rain. I didn't want to know anything."

She moved the peas around on her plate, remembering Marlin and his breathy questions and her father pressing the flat white box into her hand and her mother's bitter laughter at such a gift for their only daughter, their firstborn child, whose conception had seeded a marriage and disaster.

"I wanted to tell you," he said. "I thought you should know."

She nodded.

"Can't you say anything?"

"I'm sorry," she whispered. Why was he doing this? Why here, with all these people around?

"I don't want you to be sorry," he said irritably. "I want you to understand."

"I understand," she said, as cautiously as if she were extricating the very bottom piece from a jumble of pickup sticks, because, as always, to blink or take a breath might bring her father lurching through that door, might fill this quiet place with her mother's prayerful entreaties that were as bitter as curses, "Sweet Jesus, help me. I beg you, please, please help me!" Didn't he know how fragile it all was, how precarious the balance?

"You see, it wasn't Radlette or rent strikes or blankets I needed, Alice, it was you! I love you!" he said fiercely.

"Shh." She stiffened and did not dare look away from his rough face that glowed with sweat.

"This is what God wanted for me. I know that now. Love!"

The waitress was coming.

"Aren't you going to finish?" Alice tried to ask, but he kept on talking.

"All this time I thought I'd lost my faith. . . ."

"Excuse me," the waitress said with a toothy grin. She reached for Alice's plate and asked if they were done.

"No!" Joe said so sharply that the woman's hand jerked back.

Alice's face reddened, and she stared miserably at her plate as the waitress moved to the next booth. She could feel them all turning, looking, listening.

"But now, now I realize that my faith has become a wholeness. It's a unity of mind and soul. And flesh," he said, taking her hand in both of his. "I finally feel like a real priest!"

On their way down to Hankham, Mississippi, a hose blew in the old green station wagon. They taped it up, but they had to keep putting water into the radiator every couple of hours. A nice white lady gave them two one-gallon mayonnaise jars from back of her hotdog stand. Luther kept them filled with water, their sloshing almost unbearable for Montague, whose own plumbing was so bad Luther had to stop about every half hour so the old man could pee. Like all their troubles past and to come, this, too, settled into the flux, fueling the rhythm, so that the minute the car pulled over, the old man would open the door, turn a ways and relieve himself into the dusty road weeds. The old man said he wished there was some kind of internal replenishment between his output and the leaky radiator, and Luther said maybe he could fix it so the old man could piss straight into the radiator hose from the front seat. *Replenishment*—that was one of Montague's favorite words: to put back what had been taken out. *Replenishment.* It played through his thoughts night and day like the fragment of an ancient hymn. *Replenishment.* It was a hunger beyond flesh. *Replenishment.* He had not eaten a meal or slept a moment since they'd lost Earlie. Not once. Oh, his eyes might close, but he was painfully, doggedly awake.

The little money they had came from the few Bibles they managed to sell along the way. Luther would wait in the car while Montague shuffled house to house, his soiled satchel bulging with the plastic-sealed Bibles and in his palm Earlie's worn photograph fondled now to the softness of cloth. "My only living relative," he would cry before they could shut the door. "I'm a tired and sick old man and ready to die, but I can't do it alone. I need to be mourned and prayed into heaven, and this is the only one I got to do it, this here handsome young man."

Luther said the first thing he was going to do when they found Earlie was beat him to a pulp. Every day the old man had to endure this idiotic reverie, although the closer they got now, the less he minded it. He liked to recall the good times along the way with Luther and Earlie sparring just for the hell of it. He remembered how it made him laugh and how it got on Duvall's nerves.

"Gonna twist his arm up tight behind his back," Luther was muttering. "Gonna say, 'Why'd you do that? Why'd you dump us like that, Earlie? Tell me now, why?' "

Montague knew. He knew why, but Luther would scoff, insisting, no, that wasn't it, if anything a woman's swelling belly would be enough to keep Earlie from ever going back. But the hunger had grown so strong with the deepening heat that Montague knew, knew that in Hankham they'd find Earlie and Laydee with their newborn child. She'd already missed a month when they left, which was why Earlie had been so quick to jump at Duvall's offer: all expenses paid and a chance to see the country while he parlayed a small investment (his Army savings, which he'd just handed over to Duvall, not a paper or a note signed) into a sizable nest egg. Montague had begged the boy not to do it, but Earlie was determined. His child wasn't going to grow up poor as him. This was his big chance and he wasn't about to turn his back on it, especially when a man of Duvall's caliber had such faith in him.

"Why'd you run out on us with Duvall's money, Earlie! Come on, Earlie!" Luther's head bobbed over the wheel away from the imagined jabs. "Unh! Unh! Unh! Tell me! Tell me, Earlie!" he grunted, grinning with his vision of revenge.

Well, well, well, here they finally were, mayonnaise jars sloshing and the hunger boring a hole in Montague's gut all the way down Hankham's main street. But Laydee and her family were gone, having moved three times just in the last six months, the problem mostly being work for Laydee's father and that slew of children wrecking every place they got.

It took awhile longer, more driving, tracking down relatives, last jobs, with so much sodden tape on the hose Luther had to strip it off and start all over again, and then had come the day at last when here she was, Laydee Dwelley herself, grinning through the rusted screen, with the prettiest baby in her arms, the cream-colored image of its daddy.

A tiny girl, Laydee had clear skin, big bright eyes, and a soft little nose that squished against Montague's chest. He hugged her so tight for so long the baby started to cry between them. He let go and she gave a squeal as she looked past him to the young man springing up the steps, and he was grinning, too, as he turned so fast he wobbled dizzily, then grabbed her shoulder to steady himself, but it was Luther. Only Luther. Luther eager for his revenge, if not on Earlie, then on someone. Clearly it was not going to matter. Luther was swearing, and the three of them knew, and it was right then that Montague's heart started breaking off into chunks that floated through his bloodstream. Even now, weeks later, he could still feel them throbbing throughout his body.

"He ain't here," she said.

"But he's coming. He's coming," he insisted with the urgency of the wheels that still seemed to be rolling under him. "He started back such a long time ago. Be a month by now. Maybe two." It was hurt rising, pure hurt like a wall around his brain.

"End of May," said Luther. "Beginning of June."

"He ain't been here," she said, her whole face twitching. "I can tell you that."

"But the boy said, he said Earlie told him. He knew your name and he knew Hankham, Mississippi," Montague insisted.

"The boy lied," Luther said and kept saying all the long way back, every time he brought it up, puzzling over the particulars of the boy's tale that day, for instance Earlie's generosity, especially when it came to kids, and Duvall's money clip, silver with a fancy *D* engraved on it. "Now how'd he know, a boy like that, just coming along the street?" Montague would muse in his need to hone it all to a simple and unobscured gleam of light he could keep in the distance. The reply was inevitable, its voice dark and tired. "Duvall told him. He lied for Duvall."

"I don't know, that just don't add up."

"Don't make me say it, old man. Don't."

Well, it was a long way back. A long way still to go. Always low on money and gas, they were burning oil in a long black tail. Luther scowled over the wheel. Weeping, the old man had collapsed at Laydee's feet. Certain he was dying, Luther had carried him like a baby into the car. The old man started begging and gasping and then his eyes rolled back to whites, and Luther couldn't stand it any longer. Yes, yes, he had finally relented. They'd find Earlie.

"Something must've happened, I know that." Montague sighed. It was as much as he'd admit. He was still not eating or sleeping and now barely taking liquids to cut down on the stops.

"Yah, something happen, old man. Something evil. Something name Omar Duvall's what happen."

I t was that hour late in a summer afternoon when the stillness rose from the tree-lined streets like quiet from a well. It was the time when the calls often came. Her fingertips stained a fragrant

green, Jessie Klubock knelt on the thick warm lawn dead-heading orange marigolds. She tossed the faded blossoms into the forsythia,
where Harvey wouldn't see them. The compost pile was in the corner of the yard, and way back there she might not hear the phone
ring. The dog was buried next to the compost pile. That poor dumb
dog. She didn't miss him a bit. Of course she'd never admit it to Harvey, but she enjoyed gardening so much more now without the dog
slobbering all over her and charging down the driveway, barking
whenever anyone came up the street. And it was such a relief not
having to endure Marie Fermoyle's abuse every time she caught him
in her yard. Yard! Jessie had sometimes felt like shouting back; you
call that weed-filled, junk-strewn eyesore a yard? The house was a
mess with its peeling paint and missing shingles. The garage roof was
so sway-backed with rot that Harvey had long ago forbidden Louis
to ever go in there. The neighbors were disgusted, and a few had even
threatened to speak to Marie Fermoyle. Someone really should, she
thought, or, better yet, maybe they could all get together for a community fix-up, like in the old barn-raising days. Harvey had been
horrified when she told him this. Marie Fermoyle didn't want anyone's help, he said. People should just mind their own business.

"Well, we could at least offer," she persisted, aglow with the images of men on ladders scraping and hammering away in the hot sun
while the ladies scrubbed windows and planted flowers from their
own lovely gardens. "What would be the harm in that?"

"I couldn't begin to tell you," he sighed.

"That's what I mean, Harvey! You, of all people! You know what
that kind of life is like. How can you *not* help?"

"You don't understand, Jessie. Sometimes the best you can do is
to not make things worse," he said.

She didn't understand, but she knew enough to drop it. With
him, anyway. That was the difference between them. Life was too
short to be passive. She started by calling Cynthia Branch, across the
street. The Branches and Marie Fermoyle had not spoken since the
night Cyrus fired his rifle into the air to scare off drunken Sam
Fermoyle, who was beating on Marie's front door. When the police
came, Marie told them Cyrus had been shooting at her house, and he
was charged with discharging a firearm within town limits.

Jessie had explained to Cynthia what a boost this would give Marie. She said she couldn't imagine having to do all that Marie did on her own. And it could happen to any one of them. Who knew what the future held? They had to help one another; wasn't that what life was all about? Especially the women . . . Then Cynthia interrupted and, choosing her words carefully, said she and Cyrus would be glad to do anything that would improve the bleak view through their picture window.

Next she called the Wilburs, who were always complaining about Marie's unraked leaves blowing into their yard. Without a second's hesitation, Sandy Wilbur said she and Jim would be there.

Judy Fossi said she'd plan all the food. And beer, they laughed. Plenty of beer to keep the hubbies happy. Dick Fossi, with braces on his legs from polio, would be clerk of the works. It was up to Jessie now to pick a day when Marie would be away. It would have to be a surprise.

Something like this was bound to make a difference. Not just for poor Marie, but for everyone. The screaming that went on over there was so depressing. It was toughest on Harvey, who'd grown up in a house like that, the trauma of which had kept him single until he was forty.

Jessie thought it symbolic that she'd met Harvey in a waiting room. She'd been waiting for her mother to come out of the doctor's office and Harvey'd been waiting to go in. After years of painful joints his knuckles had begun to swell so much there were some days he couldn't close his hand around his butcher knife or pull the trigger on his rifle.

Before they met, Harvey's whole life had been long days at the Meatarama, with just about every weekend spent up at his camp. Now, with a wife and child, he only got to the camp a few times a year. Last spring he'd taken Louis, but they had to come home a day early. Everything had frightened him, snakes and spiders, moonlight shadows, and raccoons prowling on the tin roof. "Skittish," Harvey had said, lip curled, disappointed, as if his son had somehow failed him, when the poor little boy just wasn't used to sleeping out in the woods like that. It was the closest she'd ever come to disliking her husband.

Their worst arguments had been in June, when Louis began

crawling into their bed every night, convinced that bad men with knives were trying to climb through his windows. Harvey wouldn't let Louis go over to the Fermoyles' after that. Not only was Benjy too old for Louis, but something about the boy had always made Harvey uneasy. He said sometimes when he was working outside he'd look up and find Benjy watching him, which Jessie understood completely. Benjy was a lonely child without any men in his life, and he enjoyed watching Harvey work; it was probably some kind of novelty for him. But Harvey had been adamant; whatever the kid's problems, he wasn't going to have his son traumatized by them.

She had to admit Louis was happier now that he was playing around the block with children his own age, but she felt terrible seeing Benjy alone so much. The poor kid had lost Louis's companionship and then the dog's. Well, at least she and Harvey were getting along better now.

Lately their most sensitive topic was deciding how to invest the money Jessie's mother had left her when she died last year. In the last six months Harvey's worsening arthritis had engendered a score of panicky schemes: They'd move to Arizona and buy land. They'd stay here and breed cocker spaniels. He'd build a greenhouse onto the back of the house and they'd raise orchids for florists. She knew their wisest investment would be to buy the Meatarama from Mr. Guilder and hire a butcher to do the work Harvey had done for the last thirty years. But each mention of it only mired him in days of gloom. She hadn't brought it up since the morning he discovered the dog's crushed body in the lilac bushes. They'd heard doors slamming across the way and Marie Fermoyle yelling and then Norm's pitiful bellow, a wounded howl, as outraged as it was contrite.

Harvey had been at the table with his face in his hands.

"This isn't right! Someone has to do something," she'd said, heading for the door. "Things can't go on like this! It's just not right! It's not fair to anyone!"

"No," he'd pleaded, gesturing her back inside. "Don't! Don't," he'd whispered as if he feared being heard. "Because that's the worst thing. That's the worst thing of all!"

Later, when Harvey was filling the grave, Omar Duvall had hurried across the driveways offering to help. But by then there was little left to do. When Duvall had first come, she used to feel a little thrill seeing him go in and out of the Fermoyles'. She liked to think of Marie falling in love, softening, relenting. In the scenarios she played out, Marie wore clingy nylon dresses and bright red high heels. Jessie would do her dishes, gazing at the neglected little house, her knees trembling as she felt the intensity, the passion of Marie's submission after so many years of loneliness.

Jessie had done her best to make Duvall feel welcome in a neighborhood where he was so clearly out of place. People were always asking her about the stranger at the Fermoyles'; "the riverboat gambler," Cyrus Branch called him. At first she'd been intrigued by the white suit, the dark shirt, and the slicked-back hair. Now he gave her the creeps. In conversation he always stood with the close, unblinking scrutiny of someone examining a painting for the flaw only he knew existed.

That morning Harvey had leaned on the shovel talking to Duvall for a long time over the gouged lawn. Watching through the door glass, she had the strangest feeling that if she looked away something might happen. When Harvey finally came inside, he couldn't stop talking about the brilliance of Duvall's new merchandising operation. It just made so much sense, one of those ideas that's so simple, so obvious, people don't think of it. She kept washing the same countertop while he told her this was it, the opportunity he'd been looking for, but they had to be careful. Duvall said they weren't to breathe a word of it to another living soul. She felt a tightening in her chest. Harvey said he could finally be his own boss and set his own pace. What about buying the Meatarama? she asked. He'd be his own boss there.

He shook his head. Didn't she get it? Didn't she understand? He needed more out of life than a little butcher shop. All his life he'd been afraid, afraid of the unknown, afraid to take a chance, afraid what people would say, what they might think. Didn't she remember asking him once why he couldn't go out of his way a little to help Benjy Fermoyle? The truth was, he could barely look at that kid, because it was like seeing himself, not just then but now. Scared, always scared. Well, he was forty-nine years old, damn it, and he was sick and tired of being scared.

The phone was beginning to ring inside the house now. She wiped her hands on her apron. She got up slowly, taking her time, for if she rushed, if she appeared too eager, then she'd be disgusted with herself. She closed the door and took off her apron. She looked at the phone as it continued to ring. If she got it, she got it, whoever he was.

"Hello?"

"I been thinking about you." His husky whisper gave her goose bumps.

"What do you mean?" She looked around uneasily, even though she knew Louis was still down the street.

"I been thinking of kissing you. All day long I been thinking of that."

"Oh." She had to clear her throat. Her eyes closed. "I guess you haven't had a very busy day, then."

"I keep thinking of putting my mouth all these different places on you."

"What do you mean by that?"

"Well, first I start with your feet."

"My feet?"

"Yah. Your toes. I put my . . ."

Each part that he named tingled. His breathing was heavy in her ear. Through the window now came another man's voice: "Attaboy! Attaboy! Eye on the ball now, here it comes, nice and easy."

She sighed. It was the strangest feeling, this low voice churning waves of heat through her body while, blurred beyond the window screen, a priest kept throwing a ball to Benjy Fermoyle, who could not catch it. Finally the priest called out that this time the ball was going to hit him, so he'd better not miss. Benjy caught it. "That was great!" The priest whooped and clapped his hands. "That was really great!"

"And then," gasped the voice, "I carry you up the stairs and I put you down on the nice white sheets . . ."

It was almost closing time when a tap came at the office door. Marie Fermoyle looked up from her typewriter to see Cleveland Hinds peering in at her. He had just dropped Ferdinand Briscoe off after a Chamber executive meeting, and since he was passing by, he thought he'd just pop in and say hello.

She nodded. Omar had made her first loan payment, so that couldn't be why Hinds was here. Her throat went dry. Renie's signature. Oh God, that must be it.

"So how're things?"

"Fine," she gulped. "Things're fine."

"And the family?" He cleared his throat uneasily.

"They're fine, too." This was so humiliating. Oh God, she wanted to die.

He stepped all the way in now and closed the door. His silver hair shone above his deep tan.

"Where's your compadre?" he asked, gesturing at the empty desk.

"Astrid's part-time. She only comes in three days a week."

He smiled. "Well, that's nice. Makes things a little more private." He laughed. "She's certainly a tinselly kind of gal, isn't she? Not my type." She tensed as he picked up her stapler and clicked it a few times, catching the staples in his palm as they fell. "I've always admired you, Marie. I mean, *really* admired you. I hope you know that."

She held her breath, preparing for the accusation. Once an admirable woman, she was now a fraud.

He put his hand on her shoulder. "Do you know what I'm saying?"

"No," she lied into his elegant blue gaze. She would not blink or look away. His hand seemed to sink into her flesh, its weight deep inside her bones. *I will never do it again,* she wanted to say, but was afraid she would start crying.

"Tell me something, do you like to dance?"

"No. I don't."

"Would you ever consider having a drink, then, just the two of us?"

"I don't drink."

"Oh, you're much too virtuous, Marie." He laughed and slipped his hand away in a fragrant breeze past her face.

"I'm just busy, Mr. Hinds, that's all," she said, attempting to roll a fresh sheet of stationery into her typewriter. Her hands were shaking.

"Not so busy that you've forsaken all of life's pleasures, I hope." He smiled.

"Just the ones I don't need," she said, then began to type: date, address, salutation. She felt trapped.

"Well!" he said. "I'd best be on my way." He opened the door, then turned back. "By the way, how's the rumpus room coming? I saw Renie the other day, but I forgot to ask him. Are you pleased with it?"

She stared up at him, her fingers still striking the keys. At the mention of Renie's name, all color had drained from her flesh.

"Maybe I'll stop by and see it one of these days. Make sure you and the bank're getting our money's worth. Take care now," he said with a wink, then closed the door.

Rumpus room rumpus room rumpus room rumpus room rumpus room, she had typed across the line.

Robert Haddad turned over the envelope; another warning from the home office on all the unpaid premiums. If they didn't receive payment in ten days, the policies would be canceled. And he would be ruined. He dropped the envelope into the wastebasket, then stared out the window at the bar, rankled by the unfairness of all that cash just rotting away in Hammie's cellar. If he could only get back down there, his troubles would be over, but immediately after the break-in, Hammie had had thick iron bars welded across the cellar window.

Everything had gotten so complicated. Might as well just go home and tell Astrid the truth. Soon everyone would know the terrible mess he was in. At the sound of a car pulling up out front, he backed his chair into the shadow of the file cabinet. He could see the dented front end of Sherman Bloom's new Pontiac Bonneville. He'd promised Sherm his insurance check for the accident two weeks ago, but then he had to use the money for Astrid's new furniture, her red-and-silver dinette set and her Hollywood bedroom suite of blond ash.

"Goddamn you," Bloom called as he kicked the locked office door. "You no-good bastard! You lying son of a bitch!" Finally Bloom got into his car and drove off in a rattle of loose parts.

There had to be a way, he thought, watching the barroom door flash open and close across the street. First shift from the wire plant was getting out, and the men were stopping at Hammie's for a quick one before heading home with their empty lunchpails and grease-stained shirts. Not one of their wives had a glass-topped dressing table and a heart-shaped mirror framed with lights. Why couldn't Astrid be content with her life? She was going out with her girlfriends practically every night now, and it was tearing him apart. There was nothing he wouldn't do for her, nothing he wouldn't give her.

The phone began to ring. He stared at it for a long time, then picked it up, answering in a high feminine voice. "Haddad RIFCO! How may I help you?"

"Is Bob Haddad there? This is Sam Fermoyle calling."

He rolled his eyes. "Mr. Haddad is out right at the moment. Sorry."

"Okay, look, when he comes, you tell him I don't want any insurance. I just want the money back I paid him," Fermoyle said.

"That would require a notice of cancellation, sir," he said sweetly. The last thing he needed was Fermoyle barging in here.

"Well, then, that's what I want, a notice of cancellation, then."

"No sooner said than done," he piped, holding the phone close as he scrawled his pen across a sheet of dusty paper. "There! All I need now is, uh, let's see, fifty dollars for the notice of cancellation." He couldn't believe his own resourcefulness.

"Fifty dollars!" Fermoyle cried. "Look, miss, you don't understand. I just got out of the hospital and I don't even have fifty cents. That's why I want the money back I gave Haddad! I'm trying to get a job and I need money, you know, for decent clothes and things, so I can look presentable."

"I'm sorry, sir, but that's our normal procedure."

"Can't you take the fifty out of the money I'd be getting back?" Fermoyle pressed.

"Absolutely not, sir."

"So in other words I'm stuck with an insurance policy I don't even need."

"Not something you need, sir; something your children need," he said in his sweetest voice.

"What they need right now is money. Look, you tell Haddad, I'm coming—"

"I told you, sir, Mr. Haddad's not here!" he interrupted, lips pursed. "I'll certainly tell him you called, but as I said, unless you bring in fifty dollars for the notice of cancellation, your policy is absolutely ongoing and irreversible."

"Christ," Fermoyle sighed. "I can't get a break anywhere."

"Some days are like that, Mr. Fermoyle. Believe me, I know," he said softly.

"Well, thanks, anyway. You've been very helpful, and I appreciate that, miss. I really do."

"Well, thank you, sir. I'm just doing my job best I can," Haddad said, staring out at Hammie's with what, he realized, must be the same desperate longing this poor bastard felt for booze.

When Alice got up at noon, Benjy was eating a peanut-butter sandwich and drinking Kool-Aid in front of the television. "Father Gannon called," he said without looking away from the screen. "He said to tell you the time'll be the same." He glanced at her. "He's not coming over here again, is he?"

"No, it's about this what-do-you-call-it, this thing he's doing, this campaign, I think he said. He's working on it." She kept clearing her throat. Her face felt hot. Joe had popped in on her yesterday. When he saw how much that upset her, he tried to act as if he'd come to see how Benjy was doing, to throw the ball around in the backyard. Joe had to shoot down every one of Benjy's excuses before he had finally gone outside with him, and then Benjy had been miserable the whole time. He'd been embarrassed that he couldn't catch the ball. Joe had found Norm's glove hanging in the garage, but Benjy refused to put it on. It had been painful to watch. Last night after work she told Joe he was never to come here like that again.

A commercial came on, and Benjy hurried into the kitchen to put his dish and glass in the sink. Black ants were running over the countertop, their quarry a bowl of bloated cornflakes. He grabbed the insecticide and sprayed, then watched them curl up, dying in the glistening oily slick.

"That was bright," she said. "Now everything's covered with spray."

"I had to kill the ants! Mom said they're in the walls, they're all over the place."

"They probably are," she said with a bitter laugh.

"They were in the tub this morning and she started to cry."

"That's not why she was crying, not over ants. It's Duvall, that's what it is. God, I wish he'd just go. It almost seems like he's got some power over her or something." She shuddered. "I don't know, sometimes he scares me."

He was staring at her. "What do you mean?"

"I don't know, it's like he's just waiting."

"Waiting for what?" he whispered, his face white.

She tried to change the subject, but he persisted. What did she mean, waiting—waiting for what? She explained that it was just an expression, waiting, like trouble waiting to happen. She turned on the water and rinsed the dirty dishes. She was starting to feel that way about Joe, as if there were some pressure building in him, some imminent eruption.

"Alice?"

"What?" she asked, surprised to see him still there, biting his thumbnail. He kept opening his mouth, then sighing. "What is it? You can tell me. Come on, Benjy, tell me."

"Nothing," he said so miserably that she turned back to the sink. She was afraid it was about Joe, who was calling daily now. Sometimes it almost seemed as if he wanted people to find out about them. Last week with her in the car he'd dropped off a saw at Saint Dominick's for Father Krystecki, who walked Joe out to the car. "You remember Alice Fermoyle," he'd said, touching her arm, causing Father Krystecki to blush as much as she was.

Benjy's show was starting. He raced back to the couch. Last night Norm had told their mother Benjy should at least go to the pool. Even if he just stood there, Norm said, at least he'd be getting some fresh air. At least he'd be around other kids. There were only so many battles she could fight, her mother had answered. She barely had energy for anything lately. Haggard and heavy-eyed, she came home from work exhausted and often went to bed right after supper. Duvall hadn't been around in days. They didn't dare ask, but they were hoping he was gone for good.

Alice wrung out a wet rag and started to clean up the bug spray. The fumes turned her stomach, so she opened the window. Mrs. Klubock was hanging clothes on the line, gazing up with a little smile at the Fermoyle house. Mrs. Klubock had been her Girl Scout leader in the sixth grade. When all the other girls in the troop were given application forms for summer camp, Mrs. Klubock told Alice that she'd spoken to the director about letting her go free because of her family situation. After that, *klubock* became a family code word: you were being "klubocked" when someone acted as if he wanted to help, when all he really wanted was to nose around in your dirt.

After she washed the dishes she went in and sat next to Benjy. He glanced at her and smiled.

"Hey, Benj, you never told me what Mr. Tuck said."

He shrugged, his eyes never leaving the screen. "Just that I was similating about the accident, that's all."

"What's similating?"

"Making believe it didn't happen."

"What else did he say?"

"That's all. Then I had to go."

"Do you do that? Do you similate? Well, do you?" she asked, annoyed by his glassy stare.

He shrugged. A commercial came on. "I don't want to talk about it, okay?"

Thinking this might be the thing he'd been trying to say, she persisted.

"Benjy, you really liked that dog, didn't you?"

Eyes on the television, he nodded.

"You miss him, huh?"

"Sometimes."

"And you must be blaming Norm, but it's really not even his fault. I mean, he shouldn't have been drinking, but the thing is, he didn't know the dog was there. It was one of those things, like Fate, when everyone's in the wrong place at the wrong time. Benjy?" She gave his arm a little tug. "Come on, Benj, talk to me."

He shook his head.

"They say when bad things happen the best thing is to talk about them. Otherwise you have all these feelings, all this pain bottled up inside. Benjy? You know what I mean?"

He nodded and took a deep breath.

"So come on, talk to me. Tell me what you wanted to say in the kitchen. Come on," she said, playfully scratching the top of his head. She thought she heard him gasp. Eyes closed, he sank against her. The room seemed strangely full of the television; the pattern of flickering light and shadows it threw across the floor, the voices, the sputter, the laughter, the jangle—all gave her this prickly feeling of being on the outside looking in on all that was real.

They both looked up as someone began to knock on the door.

"Please open the door," Omar Duvall called. "My arms are full!"

"Omar's back!" Benjy said, grinning. He jumped up and ran to let him in.

A fter dinner Marie tried to sort through the bag of pamphlets and forms and promotional packets that Omar had brought. The first step was organizing all these materials before the soap came. When? Any day now. Could he be more specific? In a day or two. Tomorrow? The next day? When? Her second payment on the loan would be due soon. He was on the telephone now, explaining to one of his distributors that he'd just come from Connecticut, where he'd finally laid it on the line with Gold. There were to be no more delays. Too many people were counting on him. In Atkinson alone he had fifteen distributors clamoring for their product.

She looked up. Fifteen distributors in Atkinson alone? The table was covered with glossy green pamphlets and forms and order slips that had to be stapled together. When the soap did come they could be quickly attached to each box and bottle of detergent. It would take her hours, but she wanted to be ready. Nothing would be left to chance. Omar chuckled softly into the phone. As soon as he hung up she asked how was she supposed to sell all her soap if half the people in town had their own lifetime supply? Not to worry, he chided. It was the investment that counted. He had been over it and over it with her and she still couldn't get it straight. Why couldn't she trust him, he wanted to know. She did, she insisted, but she needed to understand how it worked, this pyramid that kept piling up riches, stuffing her pockets with money. It was like a chain letter, he tried to explain. She had never understood chain letters, either, had usually been the one to break them, had never been able to believe that anyone could get something for nothing. But it wasn't something for nothing, he insisted. She was forgetting her investment, her investment in a product she would sell, a product that would induce her customers to invest in their own franchises. So it always came back to the investment. Yes. Yes. Yes! For him it made absolute sense. The investment was the constantly growing base, pushing her higher and higher up the ladder. But it just didn't seem logical, not with everyone selling the same thing. But they're not, he said; it only seemed that way. It must be her, then; she couldn't get it straight; something was missing. Faith, he said, trust, those were the missing pieces. At some point she had to give herself up, she had to yield and let the process take over.

She began by separating the forms and order blanks and triplicated receipts that were all mixed up in these grocery bags. Some of the forms were soiled and dog-eared, and many were sticky from spilled soda. Mr. Briscoe had taught her that neat paperwork was the backbone of a business. Everything at your fingertips. Proof. Copies.

Norm came into the kitchen and watched sullenly while she

sorted the forms into piles. Earlier, when he'd asked to go out with
Weeb, she had told him no. He could stay home and give her a hand.

A few minutes later Benjy came in and stood looking over her
shoulder at all the papers. "Who's going to sell all the soap, Mom?"
he asked. "Are we going to do it like we did the Christmas cards?"

"Uh-uh," Norm said. "That's not what you're thinking, is it?" He
stared as she tried to explain it to him.

"And word just spreads that you've got the soap, that's all. People just find out you've got it and they come to buy it from you."

He looked at her incredulously.

She heard her voice weakening. "It sounds crazy, but Omar says
it's selling like wildfire in thirty-eight states already. It's a different
kind of soap. It's—"

"A detergent theory based on the principles of jet propulsion,
young man," Omar said, returning to the kitchen. "A product of the
future." He stood behind her, kneading her shoulders.

"How come nobody's ever heard of Presto Soap before?" Norm
asked with a peevish squint. "I never heard of it."

"And is to be ignorant to deny existence? I think what we have
here is a fine kettle of philosophical fish," he said, with a wink down
at Marie.

She tried to smile.

"All I know," Norm said, "is that in this whole country if something's going to sell, people have to know about it, and for people to
know about it, it has to be advertised. Who's going to advertise all
this stuff?" He pointed to the jumble of pamphlets and forms.

She turned in her chair and looked up. "He's got a point, Omar.
At the store—"

"At the store!" He grimaced. "Marie, Marie, you know that's an
entirely different operation. We've been all through this before."

"But I keep on wondering how people are going to come to me
to buy something they don't even know I have." The panic in her
voice registered on her sons' faces.

"And something they've never even heard of," Norm added.

Omar went to the sink. There were no clean glasses, so he filled
a coffee cup with water and drank slowly. Norm kept staring at him.
She was staring at him. Benjy was reading a pamphlet. Omar set the
cup on the counter and turned back to them.

"Right at this very moment," he said, "Presto Soap is being advertised all across the country."

"I've never seen any of their ads!" Norm interrupted.

"You are hardly the average American housewife, Norman," he said with a forced smile.

"Well, even if it is being advertised, how are people going to know it's here, that my mother's selling it?" Norm asked.

"Because she is going to tell them," he said, enunciating each syllable as if for a child's benefit. "And you are going to tell them! And you!" He pointed to Norm and Benjy.

"Oh yah, same as we did with the Christmas cards." Norm smirked at her. "You want to buy some?" he asked Omar. "We still have most of them."

She shivered. In spite of the night's heaviness, she felt a draft at her back. "I don't think that's enough," she said in a faltering voice, "just telling people."

Omar moved in to reassure her. "Of course, not just that alone, my dear. There are other modus operandi."

She saw Norm thrust out his chest and her own hand fell limply across the folders—green, the color of money, with white bubbles spelling out PRESTO. Presto, as if her luck could change with the wave of a wand.

"And where do we get any of those?" Norm asked sourly, then gave her a confident nod.

Omar regarded him with a pitying indulgent smile. "Forgive me for using such technical terms, but accustomed as I am to the fraternity of businessmen, I often forget myself when I'm dealing with laymen and children. Modus operandi, Norman, are methods, ways of operating. And one that comes instantly to mind, probably the most effective, are demonstrations."

"Demonstrations?" she asked.

"Yes, Marie. You give these soap parties. You send out invitations, people come, you demonstrate your product, offer door prizes, serve refreshments. There's even little games you can play," he said, shuffling eagerly through the leaflets. "One of these tells exactly how to plan a party. Here we go, Presto Parties, they're called," he said, reading the leaflet. "They're very popular. They have all these magic tricks you can do." He turned a page. "And demonstrations; ways to get out spots and stains; ink, grease, blood. You actually do it right in front of them. See!" he said, holding it out to her.

"I couldn't do that," she said weakly.

"Of course you can," he crooned, as he patted her arm. "You can do anything you set your mind to, Marie Fermoyle."

"No, I couldn't do that," she said again.

She got up from the table then and stood in front of the window. The moonlight lay in narrow strips across the Klubocks' lawn. Jessie Klubock had a husband who worked and a life that worked. Always baking cookies, planting bulbs in October before the ground froze, at Christmas sending over her own fruitcake soaked in rum, all done up in a red tin, then standing out there with the neighbors singing carols into the cold lonely night, the worst night of the year, rubbing it in, trapping them all inside here, as she hissed at her children not to go near the windows, they'll see us. All they want is to sing us Christmas carols. No, what they want is to get in here and have a good look around. Not a neighbor on this street had ever stepped foot inside this house in her ten years here, and now all of a sudden she was going to invite them in to witness the holes in the walls, the threadbare couch shored up with a can, the chipped red plaster lamps she and Norm had won at Bingo at the fair years ago, while she performed magic tricks—what? Juggling detergent bottles? My God, what had she been thinking of? What kind of mess had she gotten herself into here? For all his assurances, he did not know her at all, did he? All his promises, and what had he actually done? He had taken her money, that's what he'd done.

"I'll help you," he said. "There's more than one way to do this, you know."

She turned. She was very tired. She could see how much they needed her; him perhaps even more than her children. She was tired of being needed. She was so very, very tired. All this, she thought, biting her lip, all this because once, a long time ago, she had made a fatal mistake. She had fallen in love too young with the wrong man. Imagine, it was as simple as that and now she would never catch up. She would never be happy.

"Come on," Omar said, pulling out a chair. "Sit down and let me tell you another way to do it."

She looked at him. Because she couldn't speak, she just kept shaking her head. Mom? Mom? Her sons, her two boys were calling someone who was very, very tired.

"Marie?"

"She's not interested," Norm said. "She's not gonna sell soap! She's not gonna have stupid parties, so just get your crap out of here." He was sweeping the pamphlets back into the bags. Benjy glanced back and forth between Omar and his brother.

"Here!" Norm cried, thrusting the bag at Omar's chest. "Take it and get the hell outta here."

Fascinated, she watched her male image mirrored in her son's rage, the strong twin soul whose freer heart, willful and blunt, needed no man's approval or permission.

"You watch your mouth, boy," Omar warned, his sweat-slicked face at Norm's. "You hear me?"

Norm shoved Omar away from him. "Go ahead, do something about it," he snarled, yet almost seemed to smile, to take pleasure in this. "Come on!"

"Norm!" Benjy yelled as he grabbed his brother's arm. He kept trying to pull him back. "Stop it! Don't do that!" he begged. "Don't! Please, Norm! Please, don't!"

Her younger son's terror struck her from this daze. "Norm!" They looked, waiting for the rest of it. "Please don't," she finally said.

Norm stayed between her and Duvall, so that however she turned or stepped away, he moved with her, swaying, it almost seemed, his desperate fluidity demanding all of her attention. "Mom. Listen. Please. Just listen." She worked hard enough. They'd always managed before. They didn't need Duvall or any of his wacky schemes. There were jobs he could get after school. Benjy could get a paper route. One thing was for sure, she would never peddle soap door-to-door or do any goddamn magic tricks. No! Absolutely not.

"But I have to," she said with an eerie calm that coated every sharp edge and glaring plane with its dull veneer. "I've already paid for it, and I can't get my money back."

enjy hunched low in the seat. They were speeding down the narrow road from the house in the Flatts, where Norm had just bought four bottles of beer from the fabled Mrs. Carper, who turned out to be just a skinny lady in pin curls and red slipper socks. Norm guzzled the first bottle as he drove, then belched loudly. He slowed down as they approached a small country cemetery. Its dozen or so ancient gravestones huddled around a tall blackened stone cross that probably bore the family name. This Benjy knew from rides with their mother when they'd been younger. They didn't go anywhere together anymore. He wondered if they would be buried together in a family plot someday. His eyes widened with the thought of the dead man, Earlie, exposed and completely alone now that the dog no longer came to roll against its foulness.

Norm held the bottle by its neck, then hurled it through the window. It shattered on one of the markers. Norm's laugh chilled him.

"You shouldn't have done that," he said, goose bumps mottling his arms.

"Oh yah?" Norm said, glancing over. "Well, let me tell you something you shouldn't have done. You shouldn't have stuck up for that asshole Duvall."

"I wasn't sticking up for *him*. I just didn't want Mom all upset." What he wanted to say was that he had been sticking up for Norm.

"You know you've got this thing, this, this weird idea that Duvall's some knight in shining armor or something. I don't think you know what's going on."

Norm had opened the second bottle, which he kept between his legs now as they came through town. Benjy was afraid Norm was getting drunk. They stopped at a red light on Merchants Row and Norm finished the bottle. As they drove around, Norm kept looking for Weeb, who had found himself a girlfriend during Norm's house arrest. The beastly Donna Creller, Norm howled. Jesus Christ, how could he sink so low. Benjy didn't say anything about the time he'd seen Donna Creller with Norm in this very car.

They cruised up and down Merchants Row, deserted except for a few wandering dogs. Parked in front of the empty bus depot was a police car. Inside, Victor the cop was licking an ice cream cone. He scowled as they went by, and Norm groaned. "Tough duty!" Norm pretended to yell. "Hey creep, you got nothing to do, go pick up Omar Duvall before there's a murder!"

"What do you mean, murder?" Benjy asked.

"Just what I said. That fucking Duvall'd just as soon kill me as look at me." He glanced at Benjy. "Can't you tell? He wouldn't think twice about it."

Benjy held his breath with the vivid image of the two hands grappling for the glinting blade.

Now they were on a road Benjy did not recognize. They flew past still fields of young corn and hilly pastures, then dark stretches of woods. He begged Norm to slow down. The road was too winding. The car skidded around a curve. Now he was as mad as he was scared. Norm didn't care what happened to either of them. He opened another bottle and Benjy pleaded with him not to drink any more. He'd get in trouble again like that night at the lake, only this time would be even worse because he was driving.

"I got you home safe and sound, didn't I?" Norm said with a bitter laugh as he turned off the headlights. "See, I can even do it in the dark!"

Branches slapped against the side of the car and the tires crunched over gravel. No, Benjy was screaming now as he told Norm that Mrs. Haddad had driven them home from the lake that night.

"What?" Norm squealed. "What the hell're you talking about?"

It was Mrs. Haddad who had driven them home, he yelled, with the night rushing through the open windows. Mrs. Haddad who had pulled into the wrong driveway.

"You're full of shit!"

"It's true," Benjy gasped. "And then she left and you were so drunk you couldn't wake up, and I kept trying to wake you up to move the car, but you wouldn't, Norm! You were too drunk!"

Norm turned on the headlights, but they continued to race along. "So who moved the car?"

Benjy didn't answer. Norm jammed on the brakes and they skidded to a stop. He grabbed Benjy's arms. "It was that fucking Duvall, wasn't it? He moved the car. He killed Klubocks' fucking dog and then he set me up, didn't he?" Norm was shaking him. "And you let

him, you little creep! How could you do that?" Norm was hitting
him now with the back of his hand on the side of his head, his shoulders, his chest. "What's wrong with you? Don't you have any balls?
Doesn't anything matter to you?" Norm's voice pitched higher, then
broke. "I'm your fucking brother, for Christ sake!"

Benjy was sobbing. "It was me, Norm. I'm the one that moved
the car. I'm the one that killed Klubocks' fucking dog!"

"Jesus Christ," Norm roared, staring at him, his raised fists trembling. "And you let me take all that shit, you little bastard. I'm gonna
kill you. I'm gonna . . . aw shit. Don't cry, please, Benjy."

"I'm so sorry, Norm," he sobbed. "I was just trying to move the
car so you wouldn't get in trouble."

"Oh Benj. Oh shit. I mean, you really liked that fucking dog,
didn't you?"

Benjy nodded and he realized that Norm was crying, too.

A few minutes later when they were driving back into town,
Norm wondered aloud why Mrs. Haddad had never said anything to
their mother about that night. She was drunk, too, Benjy explained.

"But how come you didn't tell her it was the wrong driveway?"

"I was down in back. I didn't want her to see me." He tried to
clear his throat.

Norm looked at him. "Why? What else happened that night?"

He shrugged. "She tried to go parking with you."

"What do mean, tried?"

Benjy related the little he'd seen and all that he'd heard.

"Are you serious?" Norm cried as they drove by the park, where
Joey Seldon sat on his stool in the corner of his stand. "Hey, Joey,"
Norm cried out the window, honking the horn joyously. "Mrs.
Haddad put the make on me! Can you believe it?"

Joey raised both hands, waving the way he did whenever any of
the kids called out to him.

The horn stuck and kept blaring up the street, but Norm didn't
seem to care. Though he wasn't sure exactly how or what it was,
Benjy could see that he had just given his brother something
wonderful.

In the next few days a carpet of soggy heat rolled over Atkinson. The trees were dismal in the stillness, their meager shade teeming with mosquitoes. Children stayed indoors. Women dreaded entering their kitchens, where everything seemed to turn rancid and greasy. Ponds and lakes seethed with swimmers and boats, and at night the only breezes came through the open windows of cruising cars.

An eighty-three-year-old record had been broken. The heat was the topic of every conversation, even eclipsing Atkinson's crime wave. Though only Celeste's Beauty Parlor and Spector's Hardware had reported any money missing, five downtown stores had been broken into, and yet the *Atkinson Crier* ran a front-page picture of Renie LaChance smiling proudly in front of his window-fan display. "Fan Man," said the picture caption, calling Renie LaChance "the valley's largest supplier of fans." The reporter had asked Renie why he had ordered seventy-five fans instead of his usual fifteen or twenty.

"I don't know. I just did," he had answered, with a small dull ache like a hole forming in his chest.

"What was it?" the reporter persisted, pen poised. "Some kind of intuition, maybe, like a sixth sense—you know, like some animals have before storms and things?"

"I don't know," Renie said shyly as the photographer pivoted to shoot from another angle. "More like wishful thinking, maybe."

The reporter asked what he meant. Renie thought a minute. "Well, some things you want so bad you just forget everything else that's going on and even good common sense, and then next thing I know, just like that, suddenly I got seventy-five fans being delivered."

The reporter wrote down every word. He asked more questions. At first Renie's answers were tentative and awkward-sounding, but then the more he talked, the better he seemed to get at it. Soon the reporter had him reminiscing about his early years in Canada. It was all printed in the paper, right there on the front page along with his tips on how people could create their own air-conditioning by placing a washtub of ice in front of a window fan. He recommended wearing white garments, drinking tepid beverages, as well as deep breathing through the nose, since mouth-breathing built up gassy poisons in the belly. In that next week he sold thirty-seven fans. Everywhere he went, people said hello. And best of all, the Golden Toastee salesman was coming Friday to see if his business merited his being an exclusive Golden Toastee retailer.

When the salesman arrived there were four customers shopping for fans. Renie got Hannaby's shoeshine boy to mind the place while he took the dapper young salesman to lunch at the luncheonette. Renie was proud to be seen with him. People smiled at Renie, and a few even called him by name. He felt like a successful man in the community, vital and respected. So exhilarated was he that when Eunice came to take their order, he knew what he wanted, but couldn't remember the name. "It's two pieces of toast, and inside there's cheese. Melted cheese." He spoke loudly with exaggerated gestures as if she were deaf.

"Sounds like grilled cheese to me," she called back just as loudly.

"Yah, that's right!" Renie cried.

"Jackpot!" She winked at the salesman. "Your turn now. I'm gonna concentrate real hard. Hope I get it."

Renie slapped the table as he gasped with laughter. What a sense of humor. That Eunice, she was one funny lady. That's why he liked her calls the best.

"Tuna on rye with tomatoes sliced thin," said the salesman, his quiet dignity a dash of icy water on Renie's mirth.

Renie folded his hands on the table. Golden Toastee was serious business. They wanted to be represented by a serious man. "I usually don't take lunchtime," he said, explaining the importance of keeping regular hours. "Customers rely on that. Good business means happy customers. Happy customers mean good business." He'd memorized that this morning off a Golden Toastee pamphlet.

The salesman said he was impressed by the way Renie handled his customers, but he had to keep in mind that Golden Toastee's first requirement was a premier location.

"Which I got," acknowledged Renie with a confident nod.

The salesman looked puzzled. "But you're on a back street."

"I know, right across from the parking lot to Cushing's and the back door."

"Cushing's?"

"It's the second-largest department store in the state," he boasted, a bit deflated until the salesman said that this was new territory for him. To fill him in, Renie explained that on the average day 121 people went through those doors. "I know. I been keeping count every day for years."

"You have? Why?" The salesman was obviously impressed.

"I just like to," he said with a modest shrug under the young man's constant gaze.

The salesman cleared his throat. "Do they sell toasters?"

"No!" he whispered, leaning forward. "You see, that's just it. They got a household department, towels and dishes and stuff, but no small appliances, if you can believe it! That's why I know this is gonna be a big hit."

"You know, an intrinsic component of a premier location is a store's appearance, how it looks inside," the salesman said, with the last bite of his sandwich. Renie hadn't even started on his.

"Yah, that's a good idea," Renie said, waving Eunice over to the booth. He tried to order another sandwich for the salesman, who kept insisting he was full. "Then just take it for later when you get hungry," Renie persisted, while Eunice sighed and tapped her pen on the order pad. Apologizing for his indecision, the salesman said he'd love some deep-dish apple pie à la mode and coffee. Smooth, Renie thought, a really smooth guy. He took out his wallet and from a photo slot removed the soiled paint chip. Just holding it gave him a good feeling. "I'm having the whole inside painted. And this here's the color. Buttercup yellow." He squinted, pretending to read the back of the paint chip, though he knew it by heart, for he had shown it to so many customers. He held it out to the salesman. "I'm doing everything the same, the ceiling, the walls, and maybe, I been thinking, even the floor." He stared at the salesman, hoping he got the connection: Golden Toastee—golden atmosphere.

The salesman kept looking at the paint chip. "How many toaster lines you carry now?" he asked.

"Four," Renie said, "but to tell you the troot . . . troot . . . trooth,

I'd drop 'em all just to get the Golden Toastee." Damn. He never could say that word right.

When the salesman had eaten his pie, he seemed eager to leave. He explained that he had to submit the location survey along with his recommendation to his supervisor. That process alone could take a few weeks.

Renie smiled. He'd know in just a few weeks whether or not he'd been approved.

The salesman had left his car parked in front of the store. He walked so quickly Renie had a hard time keeping up. As they hurried along through the sharp heat, Renie was dizzied by the contrast of the sun-bleached sidewalks and glaring storefronts and then the deep black shade of the alleys. He couldn't help noticing that he and the young man were the same height. The salesman's brown hair was as dark and thick as Renie's had once been. He asked him his age. Twenty-eight, the salesman said, and for a moment Renie couldn't tell if he was still breathing. Though he had stopped walking, the black-and-white images continued to flash in his brain. He asked the salesman his birthday. August 21, he answered. *Maybe she made a mistake,* Renie thought. *Or maybe the baby came early.* He asked where he'd been born, and the salesman said that, to be honest, he wasn't really sure, because he'd been adopted. But he'd been raised in Tarrytown, New York. Renie begged the young man to come into the store. He paid the shoeshine boy and as soon as he left, he hung the CLOSED sign on the door. The salesman fidgeted with his car keys as Renie pulled out his slender green ledgers and opened them on the counter. In here, he explained, were all his most important thoughts. He had to be careful. He didn't want to shock the young man. And of course he might be wrong. But what if he was right? What if this was that moment he'd been dreaming of and dreading all these years? The young man shuffled his feet. Renie tried to ease into it. This was the ledger that contained the daily count of all the people entering Cushing's by that back door over there. The salesman looked out at Cushing's lot. Renie found just the page he wanted and began to read: "April 3. 49 degrees. Sunny. No wind. Business medium. Noon count—29 people use back door of Cushing's." Here it was. "Very nice family here. Mother, father, and son. They love each other. Father kept tying son's shoes. Every time father starts looking at stoves again, the boy unties his shoes. Finally father says, 'How come it's unlaced again?' and the boy says, 'I don't know.' Father says, 'I know—you keep doing it.' He hugs the boy and they all three laugh. I was happy and I was sad. All day I keep thinking that could be me and him—if only I'd of done the right thing." He closed his eyes and for a moment could not open them.

"Mr. LaChance," the salesman said. "I don't mean to seem rude, but I have more calls to make."

"Oh sure, sure," Renie said, running his finger down the page as if trying to find something. "I just want to get to the next part, that thirty-one people used Cushing's back door in the afternoon." He cleared his throat and tried to smile.

"Well, that's certainly good to know," the salesman said, extending his hand to shake Renie's.

The long, thin fingers made Renie's heart swell with pride.

He watched him drive away. A few minutes later he saw the salesman drive into Cushing's lot, then push open the gold-banded doors into the store. Renie smiled. Of course he'd want to verify Renie's data. Of course. Any son of his would be one shrewd cookie.

D r. Litchfield had sent Helen LaChance a treatment summary of her brother's confinement. The letter ended with the "strong suggestion that Mr. Fermoyle seek more traditional therapy than that available to him at Applegate." Stapled to the letter was the final bill, $529: $490 for the last week's regular rate, and the extra $39 for monies a certain Miss Getchell claimed that Sam had "borrowed" from her the night of his escape.

Helen sent a money order off the next day. She said little to Sam, tolerating his presence in her home, in her life, as another of the inevitable conundrums with which God had burdened her. Two of her apartments were empty; "the" apartments, she corrected herself, bile seeping into her throat as she thought of Jozia Menka, who was threatening to quit if Sam said one more word to her. Besides, she'd whispered shyly to Helen, she and Grondine Carson were thinking of getting married. He wanted to sell his garbage truck and the pig farm and move into a retirement trailer park in Florida. And after thirty years with the Fermoyles she needed a change, according to Carson, who had hiked his collection fee twenty-five cents a barrel, knowing full well there wasn't a thing Helen could say or do about it. And now on top of everything else there was Renie suddenly, in this heat, an authority in all matters, expounding on the weather, religion, politics, the way his wife treated him. Particularly the way his wife treated him. He was threatening to move back into her bedroom. Let her try hanging her clothes in the pantry closet and see how she liked smelling all the time of vinegar and fish. Last night he had burst into the house weeping and carrying on like a crazy man about the son he claimed he had seeded in the belly of a whore in New York City almost thirty years ago. He had thrown himself across her body and tried to pry her legs apart. For once in his life, he moaned, he was going to act like a man. Something had snapped inside to make her laugh, and that was when he circled this thick hands around her neck, whispering that it was the only decent thing about her, this fine long neck he had admired when he first saw her years ago.

She sighed now, her fingers pausing on the cold black beads of her rosary. Across the room Sam's head hung over the columns of figures he'd been adding and subtracting for the past hour. She tried not to smile. Her mind, ever the swifter calculator, clicked over a longer column of figures, sums that bridged years and far outspanned his meager accounting of how every cent of their mother's ten-thousand-dollar trust had been spent. She knew, remembered every penny, every nickel and dime he'd ever begged, lied for, or pilfered from her.

He raked his fingers through his thinning hair. He bit his lip, scribbled out one whole row, began again.

The last bead slid between her thumb and forefinger . . . *as it was in the beginning, is now, and ever shall be, world without end. Amen.* She laid the rosary tenderly in its silver case. The rosary, blessed by the Pope, had been given to her by the Monsignor when she donated money for the new sacristy doors. A two-inch thickness of oak, they bore her name engraved on a small brass plate that even years from now would continue to bear pure and fleshless testimony, as no child could, to her sanctity.

Suddenly a horn sounded outside. Sam rushed to the window and looked out, still afraid that they'd come to take him back to the hospital. She smiled. His money was gone, the last of it in the money order to Dr. Litchfield, who would never see her brother again. Sam could have saved himself the trouble of running away. She had planned on telling Litchfield at the end of that same week to release her brother, because his money had run out. She owed Sam nothing, not a penny. God would be good to her. She had kept her mother alive well beyond her time. And for the past ten years she had kept her brother off the streets. Hadn't the Monsignor himself pronounced her a living saint, declaring her path to heavenly reward well paved?

She got up and went outside, eager to pluck weeds from her vegetables. The garden now took up most of the yard. Every spring she dug up another foot or two, for an additional row of carrots or beets. Because it was too much food for just the three of them, she sent most of it to the rectory. She stooped between the cabbage heads and for a moment felt dizzy. Bees blazed across her vision. The velvety beans trembled with heaviness. Renie lied. He had no child, no son of his own. It was all this attention from the newspaper. Late last night she'd heard him whispering into the phone, insisting "it couldn't be too late." Then he'd slumped over the kitchen table staring at his own blurry baby picture.

The tomatoes were dazzling, but ripening too soon. Already some had split their skin, engorged with her care and the relentless sun. The annual panic seized her. She was never ready for the tomatoes that were almost obscene in their abundance. She was never quite sure what to do with them all. She stood up and straightened her shoulders. She felt old. Her flesh shrank on her bones while her breasts hardened to stone, she thought, as she labored up through the trapped heat of the porch stairs to the kitchen.

Inside, Jozia sluiced the wet rag mop over the dull linoleum. At first Helen thought the ammonia fumes had reddened Jozia's eyes until she heard the phlegmy sob. She pushed open the door and started past the crib, where her mother dozed, propped against pillows, chin on her chest. Her mother's eyes opened wide. "Please wash the rags," she begged in a tremulous voice, thin as a net snagged on some vivid moment in dreams or memory. "Don' throw them out. Please wash them."

"Yes, Mother."

"Please! Oh please, please, please!"

"We're washing them!" she snapped, pushing open the door. She bore down on her brother, still hunched over his papers. "What did you say to Jozia?" she demanded. "She's in there crying"

"Nothing." He flicked his hand as if at some insect. "I turned off her radio so I can hear the phone. I'm expecting a call."

"You'd best keep one thing in mind, Sam. The day she leaves here, you leave, too." She banged her fist on the table.

He stretched back with a lazy smile. "Actually I'm thinking of firing her pretty soon, anyway." He picked up his papers.

Her eyes narrowed. It sickened her to see him so amused and relaxed after his seven-week sojourn; the picture of health, better (she hated to admit) than he'd looked in years, and why not: his every whim having been catered to, with an entire staff wringing their hands over his selfish miseries while she was the one up night after night with their mother, changing diapers and kneading baby oil into her tissue-thin flesh that had never suffered bedsores or chafing.

She stood there, trembling. Who did he think he was, sitting at her dining-room table (yes, hers in spite of any documents, hers for the price, the duty paid in dark hours, long silent days, months, in years, a lifetime, her life), dismissing her with such smug confidence when one call to the police could send him back there. She told him this. He shrugged and said she was standing in his light. His light! Who were these people, Jozia, Renie, her brother, all fending her off, reaching past her. She refused to move, but he would not look up. In the other room, her mother's voice skittered with girlish nonsense, her sunless white hand groping through the bars for painted eggs and grosgrain ribbons for her hair. It was with greater love and tenderness ever yielded anyone that she'd bathed and fed and changed the towel-sized diapers of that withered child. And when the girl's voice sank into the dark folds of her mother's churlish demands, she'd stalk out of the room, refusing to answer or come until the child's soft cries returned to fill the barren space behind the bars and her loneliness. It was the child she more easily loved, the child lost in time, not the senile woman, for that was mere duty to a memory, to a mother who called her by her brother's name and even now, after everything, after all his failure and cruelty, still wept for him.

She stared at the back of her brother's head, her eyes dim with tears. They were turning on her. She had held this house and the apartments and this mockery of a family together by the sheer force of her will. She had kept a roof over their heads. She had kept her mother alive, not only because with her death everything would be lost to Sam's children, but because they were all she had, these cold, ungrateful people. Demanding, devouring her strength, they had scraped and sucked her dry.

Her hand trembled when lifting so much as a cup from its saucer. Things fell from her grasp. She felt breathless now as she hurried to the back of the house. Her mother clapped her bony blue hands as she passed by the crib. She needed to tell Jozia something, something about Carson, a vile tale heard years ago. Jozia stared uncomprehendingly at her. "No. No," she finally said, thickly, her hand at her breast. "That ain't true, Miz LaChance. Grondine never fornicated a goat. He never kept goats. Just pigs, Miz LaChance."

"It was a pig, then," she insisted, heart racing. "I remember now. It was a pig!"

Jozia blinked, thought a minute. "He wouldn't do that. Probably something to do with his first wife. Grondine says she was messier'n any pig he ever kept." She tried to laugh, but tears spilled down her ruddy cheeks. "I can't believe you just said that to me, Miz LaChance. All this time I been staying on because of you, because I thought we were like sisters almost." She had been untying her apron. She put it on the counter and then she left.

Five-forty, almost dinnertime. Renie glanced at his watch as he climbed the steps to the Fermoyle house. After all these years it was still known as the Fermoyle house, not the LaChance house. He had always been Helen Fermoyle's husband, Renie, a wart on the back of her hand, a minor affliction.

Even here at the kitchen table his place was one of deference, in the chair on Helen's left. Sam nodded when he sat down. None of them spoke as they ate. As usual the food was pasty, murky. Renie had little appetite. She would not look at him. She hated him for his foul secret expelled like gas in her bedroom. He stirred his watery summer squash into his mashed potatoes and was ashamed. With the heat wave letting up, sales were slow again, and no one gave a damn what Renie LaChance thought about anything. There was a shopping center coming to town. At the Chamber meeting he'd tried to warn his fellow merchants that people wouldn't come downtown anymore, but their biggest concern had been Joey's popcorn stand's being an eyesore in the park.

Helen picked at her dinner. She got up and scraped her plate into the garbage. She filled the sink with water. Sam, seeing her wait for his half-eaten plate, sat back and lit a cigarette, daring her to take away his plate before he was finished. Renie ate quickly, stuffing his mouth and chewing so loudly that Helen glanced disgustedly at him. He swallowed in a gulp and then began to choke. Sam whacked him on the back and Helen removed his plate.

Renie stared into his coffee, wondering how he had endured this stifling family all these years. Helen squished her dishrag in the soapy sink water. She had sapped him of youth. He had been a sensitive young man, though few had ever guessed it. His short thick fingers had betrayed him, his stocky torso had betrayed him, his runty legs had betrayed him. He had been a tender young man trapped in this coarse body when he first met Helen. His eyes searched the shelf of cups above her head. They were so precariously stacked, one tilted into the other, that for a moment he was sure they would fall.

Perhaps that had been it. He could bear no calamity, yet calamity had pursued him from birth, and with blind singleness of purpose he'd tried to outdistance it. And when confronted, he'd masked it, re-named it with lies.

He remembered when he first saw Helen alone on the bus at night. Hours earlier he'd pushed past his father as he waved the accusing letter in his face, bellowing that he'd gotten a girl in trouble and now he'd pay. Riding alone, without money or destination, he'd finally introduced himself to the quiet woman, who went on nibbling her dry biscuit and would not look at him. Everything about the courtship seemed to surprise them both. When they were married he had been so proud of her tapered fingers, her long, lovely neck, and careful manners: she proved what his thick fingers and clumsy tongue could not, that he was somebody.

Sometimes he thought that was the reason he had stayed with her all these years, that in spite of her brother, she was still respected in town, which gave him status. But it was more than that, more and therefore less, diminishing him. It was because he feared calamity too much to leave her. And so he had endured her sterility and her disdain with the secret comfort that somewhere there existed a child, who would be grown now with thick fingers and little brown eyes, his child living among strangers and waiting to be found.

It had happened in New York City when he was selling can openers door to door. Afterward, the woman had written in care of his company, which forwarded the crudely printed letter to his father. She was pregnant, desperate, alone, she said. Would he please do something, send her money for the hospital. Even then, he more clearly remembered demonstrating the nickel-plated can opener with all its gadgets, the bottle-cap opener, the knife sharpener, the two screwdriver heads, the dazzling corkscrew, than he remembered her face or any conversation they might have had. She had been a large woman, her heavy bones lunging against him, her breath smothering him with sour intensity. It had been a dark room. They had been drinking. It had happened quickly, passionately, though he had come to think of it as violently, in a damp creaking bed. Beatrice was all he remembered of her name.

He looked up now as Helen berated Sam for stubbing out his cigarette in the bowl of mashed potatoes. She'd planned on reheating them for tomorrow night's dinner. Sam laughed and said that's exactly why he'd done it. They bickered like children while, from the other side of the door, Bridget's voice rose in the agitated chatter their arguments always aroused. Helen charged out of the kitchen. "God, Renie," Sam sighed as he put his plate in the sink. "You've really got to do something about your wife's disposition." Sam went out on the back steps to smoke another cigarette.

Renie closed his eyes. The Golden Toastee salesman could never be the son of Renie LaChance and nameless, faceless Beatrice who drank too much and welcomed strangers to her bed. No, that son surely hid his sausage fingers in his pockets when he met refined, delicate people. But what if the son had sprung from a fine, delicate gene? It was possible: genes, eggs, sperm, something in that dark thrust, that zigzagging randomness, endowing him with such a child. He wondered if the son was married, had children of his own, lived not far from here. He smiled, imagining himself walking into that neat little house and filling it with every manner of appliance, all new, all free, with lifetime guarantees.

The salesman had said he was adopted; then how would he know that Renie was his father; then again, maybe he didn't want to tip his hand too soon. But what if he hated his father, hated the coward who had sired a bastard and left him to cry alone, his only solace Beatrice on her musty bed in that lightless room. Perhaps the son had spent all these years plotting his revenge. Renie's hand trembled on the tabletop.

It was eleven o'clock and Joey Seldon was still in his popcorn stand. He paused in his cleaning and cocked his head. He thought he'd heard branches snapping where the forsythia grew, but the only sound now was crickets. With a sigh he hitched up his sagging pants, which were weighted down by all the coins in his pockets. Tonight's crowd had been the biggest so far this summer.

He bent over the cooler and fished out the last two sodas from the elbow-deep water. All the ice had melted. He felt down the side of the cooler and unscrewed the metal plug, then smiled as he wiped his arms dry. In spite of the ruckus at the end of the concert it had been a grand night, just like the old days. "Come on, Joey, close up. As it is, there's going to be hell to pay," Sonny had snapped, last time he passed by. None of the commotion had been Joey's fault, but the Chief's patience had obviously worn as thin as everyone else's.

In recent years whenever Joey had offered to retire rather than submit everyone to the bitter rigors of the annual license renewal, the Judge wouldn't hear of it. Joey wasn't just the Judge's old friend, he was also his last cause. In his final quavery oration before the alderman, the Judge had declared Joey's popcorn stand as much a landmark as the bronze statue of Ethan Allen, both symbols of the community's goodness and strength. Joey hadn't been surprised at the buzz that ran through the members. There were still people who thought he'd been up at Ark Towler's still that night collecting hush money, when in truth his only crime had been love.

He sank wearily onto his stool. Lately he thought of her more and more, Winnie Towler, so young then with her tongue in his mouth. Sweet Winnie. She thought he'd planned the explosion to get rid of Ark so he could have her all to himself. But by God's all-witnessing eye it had been Ark who turned the flame a notch higher, then lurched at him with a drunken vengeance that for an instant had seemed just another crude and blundering misstep in a friendship that went way far back before Winnie, sweaty and jumping from his arms, from the bed, at the first creak of her husband's loaded-down truck chugging up the road. Her long, high-boned face was the last image, the last vision he remembered having, even though he'd gone straight down to the still at the back of the barn when she jumped from the bed, so Ark would think it was him he'd come to see and not her, sweet Winnie with her heat-frazzled hair caught in his mouth, and her eyes on his through the moonlight, frightened to hear Ark back. *He tricked me,* she hissed. *I don't know why he's doing this.*

Shh Shh Shh—I'll go down the barn and head him off.

I do what he says, but he don't even know what he wants anymore.

Probably just forgot something.

He'll beat me, she said, covering her ears as if she were hearing his heavy boots on the stairs. *That's all he wants. That's all he really wants.*

She was young, and Ark was his age, so once he started with her, love convinced him all she was to her husband was a drawing card, his bait. Pretty young thing, three babies in three years, not a sag or flab anywhere, the only blemishes the violet menacing blooms of Ark's legendary temper on her soft sweet flesh. But when he was thinking straight, he knew Ark Towler didn't need any other attraction than his whiskey, the best in that part of the state. Times were mean and, fortuitously, Ark's best friend had been Chief Joey Seldon.

Or was he? Ark had demanded that night, as he turned so suddenly from the bright jet at the end of the copper coil that he hadn't seen Ark's club until it cracked against his chest, knocking the wind out of him. It wasn't his whiskey, was it? Ark panted, whizzing the club past his head. It wasn't his booze and his friendship that kept the Chief from shutting him down. Because all that time Seldon'd been fucking his wife, leaving his smell in her to mock him when he crawled into his own bed dog-tired night after night, until he couldn't take it anymore, no more, no sir, he was going out of his mind because it was way past duty now, that was clear, more than a chore, so he'd circled back because Jesus Jesus Christ, it was just too steep a price to pay anymore.

The two men had wrestled and grappled, staggering in one's drunken, the other's guilty, embrace as they toppled stools and barrels and crates of empty bottles stacked for the new batch. Suddenly there was a poof, a flare of light, then flash after flash after flash as the spilled alcohol erupted in fiery hissing puddles across the wide-planked floor, and Joey dove for the door, heat-borne through the orange blast and the concussive roar. She knelt over him, shrieking that he'd killed Ark, hadn't he? God, she never meant that, never meant any harm to come to the father of her three baby girls. So that was that and no one ever knew the truth, maybe not even her, sweet Winnie, who went a little crazy afterward, or maybe always was, and he'd been as blind then as now, only then it had been love, the last he would ever know of it. Besides, to be fair, what young widow wouldn't be frantic, having lost not only the support of her husband (as well as any hope of it with a blind lover), but also all of Ark's money, burned under a floorboard where he'd hidden it from the thieving revenue agents and the pretty young wife he'd known from the start he couldn't trust, and so had put her to the test.

Sweet, sweet Winnie's face, still luminous as a shimmering moon in this lifetime of nights. So after all he'd been through, all he'd lost, tonight's trouble was nothing. He laughed. Damn boys, they'd done it again right when Jarden Greene started playing "Good Night, Irene" on his violin. Once again they'd managed to slip his radio out from between the broken boards and set it up on his roof, where he couldn't get at it. Right before they took off, they turned the volume up full blast on The Platters singing "The Great Pretender."

After the concert Greene banged his fist on the counter and told him to start counting the days; his time was up; the free ride was over. On Sonny's last trip by, he'd begged Joey not to give Greene and his cohorts any more ammunition. He'd assured Sonny he'd be closing soon. Sonny said he'd wait and give him a ride home, but then the cruiser radio sputtered with the report of an accident up on the access road: car on its roof, teenagers inside. The cruiser door slammed and Sonny raced off, siren screaming.

After Joey wiped down the inside of the cooler, he propped up the lid with a stick to air it out. He checked the outlets one last time to make sure all his plugs were disconnected. Smiling, he wound the cord around the radio and put it under the counter. Poor Greene. What a fool. Now there was a man who had not lived enough. Joey sat on his stool and began to count his money before he put it into the cigar box. He continued to take his time. This was all he needed anymore, the clear night air, the soft rustle of the leaves, the black sky he imagined pierced with stars.

Dressed in black, Robert Haddad peered out from the tangled forsythia. Sweat stung his eyes as he watched Joey Seldon. His hands shook. It was the waiting.

At eleven-ten the telephone jangled through the dark rectory. Sound asleep for the last hour, Monsignor Burke put the pillow over his head and waited for someone to answer it. When the ringing finally stopped, he rolled onto his side and fell asleep. Again the phone began to ring, this time louder, louder. Louder.

Monsignor picked up the phone, his gruff answer causing Sister Mary Patrick, the nursing-home supervisor, to stammer in apology, especially since poor Mrs. Ahearne had been through this twice before, but now there could be no doubt. The old woman was drifting in and out of consciousness. With her kidneys failing, this was surely the end. "Finally, the poor dear," the nun whispered, as if the call were being made from the old woman's bedside. "I tried to wait, with the late hour and all, but she's going fast, Monsignor. And besides, it's Father Gannon she's asking for."

He was relieved, if not a little hurt. A silly woman, given to nervous giggling in the confessional, Mrs. Ahearne had been his parishioner for years.

"Father Gannon's been with her the last two times," the nun explained. "Such a kind young man, holding her hand and all, but surely I don't think that'll be enough this time."

He assured her Father Gannon would be right up.

"Sorry to wake you," Sister said. "I know what you've been through lately, Monsignor, with the poor Hinds family."

"They've had more than their share lately," he sighed. Most of his free time these past few weeks had been spent at the lake with his cousin Nora and her husband, Cleve, though it seemed Cleve was having to be in town most nights these last few weeks. Nora said it was just all too painful for him, although the boy was in remission now.

"The poor thing, and him being their only son. Bernard, isn't it?"

"Yes. Bernard Thomas, actually."

"Sure and that's right, after you, Monsignor. I'd forgotten. Tell me now, is it . . . is it *that*?"

"Yes, Sister, it is." Cancer. Leukemia, actually.

Father Gannon's bed was empty, and the Monsignor was not surprised. Out all hours of the night, the young man could barely get up on time for morning Mass. When he complained, the Bishop suggested he should be grateful the young priest had found such a suitable outlet for his idealistic energies as the Kennedy campaign. "Sometimes," the Bishop reminded him, "to keep this new breed happy we have to let them roam just a bit farther afield than we might like." And besides, the Bishop added, he and the Senator's dad went way back.

He padded barefoot down the hallway, relieved when he came to the rim of light under the bathroom door. He tapped once, then turned the knob, bewildered to see Father Gannon at the sink, barechested, in his clerical pants, a razor poised at his lathered cheek.

"But I can't," Father Gannon said upon hearing that Mrs. Ahearne needed the last rites. "I've got a meeting."

His stricken expression troubled the Monsignor. "You have a sacrament to administer, Father Gannon, and that is far, far more important than any meeting." He looked at him, hard, adding, "With anyone." No. No, he thought, seeing Father Gannon wince. It couldn't be. Not right under his nose. No. He was a better pastor than that. In matters of celibacy the Bishop held his older clergy responsible for guiding the young men.

"But I'm expected. And I can't call now." He swallowed with widening eyes. "Could you do it for me, please, Tom? Please?"

His insolence was shocking. "She asked specifically for you, Father. Not me," he said.

Head bowed, the young priest shuffled miserably. "You could tell her I'm away. This sounds terrible, I know, but you see, this has happened before, and then nothing ever comes of it."

Something hardened in the Monsignor's throat. It hurt to speak. "I think you have a choice to make here, Father Gannon. I pray your decision is the right one." He returned to his room, where he sat in the dark on the edge of his rumpled bed, feet fast on the prickly wool carpet, eyes hard on the shaded window, until he finally heard the garage door rumble open and then the tires of his car turning over the pavement. There had been distant sirens wailing, and now their growing urgency seemed to justify his firmness with the troubled young priest. All this talk of nerves and needs and complexes was ridiculous. Father Gannon had been coddled, plain and simple. What he needed now was discipline before he ended up another of the insipid dilettantes who only dabbled in God's work when the mood hit them. The seminaries were sending them out in droves lately: me, me, me, and the needs of the Church be damned. Gone were the days when a young priest cared enough about advancement to do all he could to lighten his superior's load. It was time now for a dose of reality, time to teach Father Gannon responsibility to his vocation and his parishioners. He would call his cousin Nora in the morning. If

her invitation to the lake was still open, he'd accept and leave Father
Gannon completely in charge here.

S he didn't know what to do. She couldn't stand out here by the
road any longer. Joe had never been this late before. All the
lights in the lot were out. Mr. Coughlin had already left and the office
was locked, so she couldn't even call home for a ride. And she certainly couldn't call the rectory and ask for Joe. Two of the girls had
offered her a ride, and so had Blue Mooney, with Carper grinning
and echoing everything his cousin said, until Blue had snapped at
him to shut up. God, it was like living in a freak show, she thought
as she started to walk down Main Street. It was worse at home, with
Duvall in and out all the time, proclaiming that the soap was coming,
yes, the soap was definitely on its way. He'd just heard, the soap was
coming; the warehouse was working round the clock to fill all the orders. And now her mother was saying it, too: *When the soap comes.*
What, you need school activity fees in two weeks? Well, maybe the
soap will be here then. Whatever the problem, she'd take care of it after the soap came.

Her father had been home for two weeks now and hadn't called
them once. Benjy was a nervous wreck, and the open animosity between Norm and Omar was almost frightening. And on top of it all,
last night as she was putting her clothes back on in the Monsignor's
car, Joe had said that making love to her was all he ever thought or
cared about now. Even during Mass. Twice during the Consecration
that morning he'd lost his place and had to start over. When he
talked like that, she never knew what to say. Upset by her silence,
he'd beg her to tell him what was wrong, what was bothering her.
But how could she explain this violent commingling of guilt and
longing that left her feeling bruised and sore, without it sounding like
confession, an admission of the worst sin, desire but not love. What
if Lester was right? What if she was so tainted by base needs that
there would never be love, only corruption? When pressed, she
would tell Joe that it was the same with her, that she loved him, too,

thought of him every bit as much, all day long. And as the evening wore on, the desire would feel like another organ, as hot and throbbing as if it were about to burst. She was afraid of what was happening. But she couldn't tell him the truth, couldn't admit when he held her close, whispering that he couldn't bear the thought of her leaving, that she was counting the days until school started. It was the only way it could possibly end without the shame and damnation destroying them both.

She was walking past the municipal swimming pool now, when a car slowed behind her. Joe. She walked a little faster, smiling.

"Hey, hop in," Blue Mooney called as he drove alongside. "I'll give you a ride home."

She didn't need a ride; in fact, she was enjoying the walk.

"But it's late," he protested, cruising so close she could feel the car's heat on her legs. "Come on," he coaxed. "Please. You never been in my car. I'd really like you to see it. Look," he said with a sweep of his arm. "I got all velvet on the dash and same with the seats." He looked up, his pale eyes shining under the streetlamp. "I'll bring you straight home, if that's what you're thinking. Honest to God."

"No." She stopped and shook her head. "I really, really want to walk."

At that he turned off the lights and parked the car. He got out and came toward her. "Then I'll walk with you," he announced, tugging his jeans down over his hips and rolling and flexing his shoulders.

Stupid creep, she thought, hugging her arms and growing more annoyed as she hurried along to the clop of his thick-heeled boots through the midnight quiet.

"God, you're going to wake up the whole town," she snapped, irritated then to see him scurry onto the grass, where he kept stumbling in the ruts. He'd been telling her about his job and now he was advising her to avoid retreads. "Granted they're half the price, but when they blow, I mean, you have no idea what that's like, being so out of control. I mean, they lay down rubber in this, this whole long strip." He held out his arms to show her. "A person could get killed!" he said, his earnestness a poultice to her venom.

"Then how come you sell them then?" God, did he really think that driving tires back and forth to Burlington was such a big deal?

"Well, I mean, it's my job," he stammered. "You know. Besides, I don't sell them. I just haul them."

"Doesn't that bother you?"

"No, why should it?"

"Well, what if one of the tires you've hauled blows out and somebody gets really hurt or something. I mean, wouldn't you feel responsible?"

"No." He looked at her. "Not at all. I mean, why should I, you know?"

"Well, I would," she said, stepping off the curb to cross the street. They were near the park. Joey's popcorn stand was empty. The dark grass was dotted with cans and papers. Norm would be busy tomorrow with his pick.

"That's because you been hanging around that priest too much," Mooney said, and for a moment she stopped breathing. They came past the diner, the boardinghouse. "What's he, a friend or something?"

"Yah," she said with a weak shrug.

"Well, just make sure he doesn't pile all that Church stuff on you about sin and guilt. I mean, the way I figure it is, I'm just gonna do the best I can, and if it don't work out, hey! I'm not gonna go around feeling guilty all the time." He laughed self-consciously when she didn't say anything. "Jeez, listen to me with all the good advice tonight. Hey!" He stopped and put his hand on her arm. "Listen!" He cocked his head. "Can you hear that?"

All she heard were crickets and the stale rasp of his smoky breath by her face. He kept urging her to listen, listen close.

"What is it?" she asked, pretending to hear it as she eased from his grip.

"Must be an owl," he whispered, his eyes scanning the black treetops over the park. "There! Hoo, hoo," he called softly, cupping his hands to his mouth. "Hoo! Hoo!"

Now she did hear it, faint as an echo. Mooney hurried beside her. He said it sounded like a great horned owl. "We used to go down the pond at night and shine flashlights on them. It was weird the way they'd freeze for a minute. They'd stare back like they were ticked off, and then they'd raise these big wings and the weird thing was, they'd take off without a sound. That always got me, the way they seemed like part of the night, and then the light catches them, and they're, you know, what's the word I want, exposed, I guess, and then they're gone. Right back into the dark. That's what they know, you see. That's where they belong."

Goose bumps rose on her arms and then the back of her neck, as if a winter door had suddenly blasted open. *I don't know anything,* she thought, feeling big and clumsy beside him, though she was half his size.

He paused, listening, then cupped his mouth and hooted softly again.

"I can't believe you heard that. It was so, so faint." She hadn't heard anything that time, but she wanted to say something nice.

He smiled. "It's like, you know how some people have great night vision, well, I'm that way with sounds."

"Must be that same thing animals have, a real keen sense of hearing."

"I don't know. I hear things in this weird way. I don't know how to put it, but sometimes I hear things before they're even sounds. That's kinda weird, huh?" He seemed embarrassed.

"Well, it's probably like with dogs," she said. "They hear things we can't hear. It's this whole other range they've got and we don't. It's probably something like that."

"Yah, well, maybe," he said, growing quiet as they neared her corner. When they turned, he spoke suddenly, calling her by name for the first time. "Alice!" He looked surprised. "You're not still going out with Lester Stoner, are you?" he asked in a torrent of words and nervous gestures. "I mean, I never see him around or anything, that's why I was wondering."

Sensing what he had in mind, she said that she and Lester had broken up and that she wasn't interested in dating because there was so little time left before she started school.

He smiled. "Oh well, yah! I mean, I can see that. I mean, not having, you know, a steady boyfriend or anything—but how about just going out for a drive maybe or even a movie with somebody." He looked at her. "With me, I mean."

Oh God. "I can't," she said. "I'm sorry."

His mouth twitched as he struggled to hold the smile. "Hey! Don't be sorry! Like I said, you been hanging around that priest too much."

"There's my house. You don't have to go all the way down there." She assured him she'd be fine. He said he'd gone this far, and he just wanted to make sure she got the rest of the way home safely. There was nothing to worry about, she said, then hurried on ahead. When she was almost at the house the sound of sirens tore up Main Street. She looked back as she turned into the driveway, and sure enough, he was still watching her. He waved. Groaning, she waved back. She opened the door, then looked again before stepping inside. He was still there, watching.

In the park Sonny Stoner squatted by Joey's side, holding his hand until the ambulance came. His patrolmen's flashlights passed slowly over the litter-covered grass for clues. Whatever the weapon, it had split open the back of Joey's head but hadn't killed him. His cigar box with the night's receipts was missing. He had closed the stand and was coming along the path when he heard footsteps behind him. He had felt a tug as someone tried to yank the cigar box out from under his arm. He had held on to it, wrestling with his assailant, who kept begging him not to. "Don't," the man had pleaded. "Please don't. I beg you, please." And then the blow had been struck, and Joey lay at the edge of the rhododendrons "for so long," he told Sonny, his flat eyes rolling with pain. He had lain through green heat and wind and brilliant falling leaves and frost and drifting snow and chilly mud, then heat again, while to all his cries for help had come the answering hoot of an owl with fiery glowing eyes.

"I saw it, Sonny. Right there in the bush, watching me." He groped for Sonny's hand and held it against his face. "I never took money from Towler. Never." Tears ran from the corners of his eyes down his blood-smeared temples.

"I know that, Joey. I've always known that," he whispered, leaning close. "You're a good man, Joey, a good honest man." He squeezed Joey's hand. "You never took a damn thing that wasn't yours."

"No, listen. Listen!" he said, his voice breaking. "It was her I took, his wife. Winnie."

"Shh. Just relax, Joey. Don't say any more now. Just breathe deep, in and out. I hear them coming."

"He was my friend. He knew money wouldn't work. I'd go up and I'd say, Ark, Ark, I gotta do something. People're talking. You're forcing my hand, Ark. So what he did was, he let me have *her*. I'd come. He'd leave. I thought she loved me, but you see, I was just one more of her chores, only I was the one she hated doing most of all, and I was so stupid," he said, both laughing and crying, "that I never knew it. Took me years, all these years. Ain't that something, huh?" he asked with wonder.

"Don't, Joey. That's all—"

"No, no, I know, but you see, all these years I've been sending her money. The Judge took care of it. Sonny, if I die, send her what I got, please?"

"Sure, Joey, sure." He patted the old man's hand as he looked past the bandstand right at the spot where she'd stood all those years before, hugging her children to her skirt, with that peculiar look of bitter triumph on her angular face.

The arc of a patrolman's flashlight guided the ambulance down the path. The attendants jumped out and dropped to their knees beside Joey.

So that's why, Sonny thought, as they prepared him for the stretcher. All these years that's why he endured the town council's annual humbling. For her. For a woman he kept hoping might still love him.

"Jesus Christ," the ambulance driver called when the back door closed. "What a night!"

Sonny watched the ambulance speed up Main Street, its lights flashing and sirens screaming.

The accident up on the mountain earlier tonight had put two kids in the hospital, Donna Creller and Weeb Miller. There had been beer in the car. Young Miller wouldn't say where he had gotten it, but Sonny Stoner knew it had to be from Hildie Carper. Tomorrow, between Al Creller and Jarden Greene, and God knew who else, all hell would break loose. And where had their illustrious Chief been through it all? Getting laid, that's where, in Eunice's perfumed satin sheets while his wife shriveled to bones and the circles under his depressed son's eyes darkened.

"Chief!" Officer Harrison called.

His two patrolmen were leading Blue Mooney toward him.

"Look what we got here. Says he just happens to be passing by," Bernie Clapman scoffed.

"Yah, out for a little midnight stroll," Vince Needer sneered.

"Go fuck yourself!" Mooney growled, jerking free of their grasp, feeling safer now, Sonny knew, in his presence. "Chief, I—" Mooney was starting to protest just as Sonny grabbed his shirt and yanked him close.

"I'm gonna ask you one time and one time only. Did you touch Joey Seldon tonight?"

"No! Of course not! Jesus! I already told them. I never even saw him."

They drove Mooney back to his car. Harrison was going through the trunk, which was filled with cigarette cartons and bags of clothes. He emptied the bags onto the ground. "Look at this!" Harrison called, coming around the side of the car, carrying a cowboy hat. "Here," he said, holding it out. "Put it on."

"What for?" Mooney asked.

"Cause I said so," Harrison said, jamming the hat on Mooney's head, pulling it down over his ears. "Leave it on!" Harrison barked as Mooney reached to take it off.

"So tell us again, now," said Harrison as Needer took his place rifling through the mess in the trunk. "You're driving along, and all of a sudden, for no reason, you stop. You leave the car here, two blocks from the park. It's a nice night, right? So what the hell, you figure you'll take a little stroll through the park, and what do you see but old Joey gimping along with a box of dough under his arm, and you're broke, right? So you figure, what the hell, this is one easy—"

"Chief!" Mooney pleaded.

This time Sonny wouldn't interfere. This time he'd let them do their job. Besides, he was almost enjoying the punk's humiliation with the hat flapping his ears forward.

"I don't need to go mugging a blind man. I got a job, a good job! I'm working for J. C. Colter."

"A job?" Harrison said. "I thought you were on leave."

"He's on leave, all right. Permanent leave," Vince Needer said, swaggering around the side of he car. He handed Sonny the document stamped with the Marine Corps seal that attested to the Dishonorable Discharge of Travis T. Mooney.

Sonny squinted over the rim of his glasses. His officers, Mooney, the car—all glowed in the light from the streetlamp. He had tried to save men whose redemption was easier than his own, and now this was the end of the fouled trail. He was no better than any of them, only worse in his hypocrisy. Simpler, better men than he was saw the truth in life. Because Joey had looked the other way, the gods had demanded his sight. There was always a price to pay. As talesmen he'd offered Mooney and Joey, even, he realized now with disgust, his wife's suffering, to prove his goodness. He stepped closer and his shadow obscured Mooney's face. His voice was cold and steady. "I should've let them put you away when I had the chance."

"Yah, and how come you didn't?" Mooney leered at him.

He drew back his hand. "You're trash, Mooney," he said, slapping him again and again. "Just like your brother, nothing but trash."

Mooney lunged for him, but Harrison and Needer were on each arm now, pinning him in place. When it was over, Sonny walked back to his cruiser holding his heaving stomach. It was the first time he had ever beaten a man.

The oldest cells were in the basement under the police station in town hall. Bootsteps scraped along the dark granite passageway. His head ached with the approaching echo. One eye was still swollen, his cheek bruised a reddish purple. He lay curled on the damp cot, pretending to sleep. Needer had been the last one down. It was Sunday, and for two days they'd taken turns at this, but his story hadn't changed. He'd given his cousin a ride home from work, then had driven back to town, parked his car, and gone for a walk, alone. He wouldn't involve her. He wouldn't even think of her while he was here. The cell door creaked open.

"Wake up!" Stoner ordered with a jab at his back.

He lowered his feet to the floor, then sat up and pressed his temples.

"I can't keep you anymore, Mooney, but just so you'll know"— Stoner stood so close he had to lean back to see him—"We're going to be watching you." Stoner smiled. "And one of these days you're finally going to get what you've been looking for."

"You think so?" he said, only now that he was on his feet allowing himself thoughts of her, and these dizzied him more than the pain in his skull.

Sonny's eyes moved wearily over him. "You make me sick. You haven't even asked one time how poor old Joey's doing."

"Oh yah." He held on to the bars and looked back. "How's he doing? Better than me, I hope." He had to take deep breaths to keep from passing out.

Sonny just shook his head and stalked out into the corridor.

It was early Sunday morning. The kitchen smelled of bleach as the washing machine gurgled and vibrated from cycle to cycle. The table was covered with red-inked bills and the dreaded budget book, each fold-out pocket labeled *mortgage, gas, electricity, food, clothes, entertainment, medical.* Every week two dollars went into the electricity slot, ten into food, two into gas, twenty-five into mortgage. Clothes, entertainment, and medical were always empty. Anytime they dared complain about not having something, Marie would unpleat the budget book to show how close to the bone they lived.

Right now she was looking at Alice's bankbook. Benjy sat across the table from Alice. They were both in their pajamas. Norm was still in bed. There had been an argument late last night between Marie and Omar. It was the first time Benjy had heard Omar angry at his mother.

According to her calculations, Alice's earnings from the A+X, even counting these next few weeks, would pay only part of her first semester's bill.

"I told you," Alice said, her uncombed hair sticking out from her head. She'd gotten in late again last night, long after the argument, long after Norm told Benjy if Omar said one more word to her he was going down there and throw him out. She had gotten home long after Omar slammed the front door and drove off, long after their mother cried herself to sleep. "I could've made ten times that much at the lake, but you wouldn't let me."

"Norm!" his mother called again toward the stairs. "Get down here right now."

He came into the kitchen, squinting and scratching his chest. She didn't want any argument, she said, pacing back and forth, but she was going to have to use some of his money for Alice's first semester bill.

"That's okay," Norm said with a shrug. "Long as I have enough for my car," he muttered, and Benjy was relieved his mother hadn't heard. Ever since Weeb's accident Norm had been very quiet. In these last few days he seemed older, certainly more considerate. Both of Weeb's legs were in casts. Donna Creller had a mangled foot and a ruptured spleen, and the police had declared war on underage drinking.

Alice shook her head with a long sigh, which his mother pounced on. What? Didn't Alice approve? Well, maybe if she hadn't waited until the last minute she could have gotten a better-paying job in town. The nerve, sitting there sighing and giving one another looks,

the three of them. Well, what else could she do? If they knew of a better way, please tell her. Please! Because she was at the end of her rope.
This was it, the end of the line. "It only goes just so many ways, and
then that's it!" she cried, grabbing the budget book and with a flick
of her wrist snapping it so that like a card trick the manila pockets
cascaded open.

"It's okay, Mom," Norm said. "Whatever you have to do is fine.
I can probably even get some overtime these next few weeks."

She bit her lip and took a sharp breath. She'd done her best, she
said, but as always it just wasn't good enough.

"Mom, that's not true," Alice said. "Besides, we can get a loan.
Other people do."

"No." She shook her head and her eyes shimmered with tears.

"It's not like you're asking for charity or anything," Alice said
softly.

"I can't. I've already got a loan." She laughed bitterly. "And I
can't even come up with the next payment, so they're sure as hell not
going to give me another one."

"A loan for what?" Norm asked, but she didn't answer. Eyes
closed, she kept shaking her head and swallowing hard. "The car?"
he asked. "Something in the house? What?" He pointed. "The roof?
Mom? What is it?"

"Was it for Dad, Mom?" Alice asked. She touched her mother's
hand. "It was, wasn't it?" she said with a rueful sigh. In this painful
way they were all still a family. "You tried to help him, and he just
messed everything up again, didn't he?"

"Oh God, no!" She gasped as if that would have been the ultimate folly. She explained that it had been an investment in Omar's
new business, which she continued to have faith in, but her timing
had been all wrong. Instead of being so impulsive she should have
recognized Omar's promise of such a quick return on her money for
what it was, his unrestrainable enthusiasm and optimism. She had no
doubt that the soap was coming, and she knew she'd be making
money as soon as she got out there and started selling such a surefire,
wonderful product as Presto Soap was. But in the meantime, there
were all these regular bills as well as Alice's first-semester bill, forget
about back-to-school clothes, and now on top of all that, there was

the loan. And if she didn't come up with the money, they could lose the house. No one said anything.

"What're we going to do?" Alice said.

"I don't know. That's what I'm trying to figure out."

"I could postpone—"

"No!" she cried, staring Alice down, as if she were just trying to find a way out of going to school. "What I'm going to do is call your father and tell him he has to do something, that we're desperate."

"I'll say," Norm said. "That's pretty desperate, all right."

"Oh! And do you have a better idea?"

Benjy and Alice exchanged looks as once again their mother and brother geared up for battle, each drawing strength from the other's challenge.

"Yah I do, as a matter of fact." His eyes didn't waver from hers. "Why don't you get your money back from Duvall?"

Because, she explained, it had already been invested in her franchise.

"Yah, and in his Caddy and his mysterious trips and his—" Realizing she was crying, Norm jumped up. "I'll get your money, Mom. I swear I will!"

"No!" she said, ordering him back down, but he remained standing. She had faith in Duvall, she said, faith in the company. No, the trouble had been her poor timing.

Benjy had been folding an envelope smaller and smaller.

"That's not the trouble, Mom!" Norm cried, leaning over her. "When are you going to face the facts? When are you going to see what Duvall really is?"

She didn't answer, and in the silence Benjy folded the tiny wad again, now bit the edges to make it hold.

"I must have known in the back of my mind she'd arranged something," Sam was saying of his mother as Marie drove. "But if I did, well . . . I never knew what it was, exactly. And you know the Judge. He wouldn't give me the time of day without Helen's permission." He chuckled, then looked at her with a bitter sigh. "But I swear to you, Marie, I never knew there was a trust. I mean, ten thousand dollars! Don't you think if I had, I would've made sure you and the kids got part of it?"

No, she thought, he wouldn't have. If he had known he probably would have drunk himself to death with it. But she didn't say this; she didn't dare make him mad. She wanted to appear both firm and sympathetic. He said he'd spent these past two weeks at home getting himself ready. For what? came the old sour voice in her head. He'd spent a lifetime getting ready, getting geared up, trying to get back on track—God, she knew all the lines.

He had gotten a haircut. His nails were trimmed, his old shoes shined, the cracks in the leather dark with polish. His faded shirt and shiny pants were pressed. The jacket he wore was a loud green-and-yellow plaid, the sleeves too short, the cut too wide. He'd probably taken it from Renie's closet without even asking. In the old days he wouldn't have left the house in clothes like that. Now he obviously thought he looked quite natty. He was telling her how he'd made a list of every suitable want ad. She tried not to wince: suitable—she'd heard that before. Eighteen years later and he was still trying to get started. Such a waste. He smelled of Old Spice. His face was fuller, his eyes healthily bright, his grin as quick and boyish as ever. His hair was just turning gray, though not as much as hers, and she was twelve years younger.

"So how're the kids?" he finally asked, mouth twitching either with nerves or guilt, probably both, she thought now as she told him. Alice had gotten really friendly with that new young priest, Father Gannon, so in a way she was glad Alice would be leaving for school soon, because sometimes she was afraid Alice might choose the religious life (she'd almost said the easy way out).

Wouldn't that be something, Sam said, smiling. Especially under the circumstances. She looked at him. Circumstances. Surely he didn't mean that the way it sounded. Imagine, he said, their little girl, a nun. No, that would be terrible, she told him. That wasn't at all the life she wanted for Alice.

"Don't you think that's up to Alice?" he said, and again she bit her tongue: such wisdom from a grown man still bound to his mother. Had it been a life he had chosen? Yes. Yes, she had no doubt of it. Chosen, whether through decision or indecision, but still a choice: to do or to let happen. Just as all these years he'd known there was something his mother had done to take care of him, to protect him as well from the world as from his sister's whim and anger. But by not asking he had chosen the blameless realm of ignorance in which he could dwell powerless as a child.

The late-afternoon sun glared on the windshield as she turned onto West Street. When she'd called to say she needed to talk to him, he'd wanted to come to the house, but she never knew when Omar might pop in, and going to Helen's was out of the question, so she'd suggested they ride around town. She took a left turn at the fruit market, amused to see his foot tense for a brake. He had taught her to drive. There had only been her father's truck, so Sam used to take her far out into the country in the brand-new Chrysler his mother had bought for him when he and Nora Cushing got engaged. She began by sitting close and steering while he worked the pedals. She glanced over at him now, remembering the good times in those few months between their first meeting and their wedding. No, not their wedding. That would have been Nora Cushing's event. Hers—theirs—had been a formality, a dour priest and the two witnesses, one a friend of Sam's, a red-eyed man in a rumpled suit who kept calling her Nora. One drinking buddy doing another a favor, she'd come to realize. Her witness had been her younger cousin, who burst into tears when Sam told her to stop giggling.

Without planning to come this way, she was driving past Bridget's three run-down tenements. Built eighty years ago for quarry workers, they were home now to some of the town's poorest people. Knotted curtains dangled from open unscreened windows. The roof on one of the front porches sagged in the middle. While news of the trust had not seemed to surprise Sam, hearing that his mother had willed his children these hovels gave him obvious pleasure. He leaned forward to peer up at the curled roof shingles. "All these years Helen's been sucking money out of these dumps and never putting a penny back. And now I know why. God, the thought of it must kill her. No wonder she hates me. Once Mother dies she's got nothing. Nothing!" He shook his head in bewilderment. "Not even the house!" Chuckling, he rubbed his chin. "Let me see, now. I wonder how much rent I should charge Helen and Renie."

Even though she knew he was trying to amuse her, the thought of Renie, Helen, and Sam living together for the rest of their lives was as depressing as it was likely.

"I'm sure Bridget's taken care of Helen in ways that don't need a will. Her bank accounts are probably all in Helen's name. I'll bet they've been that way for years." She thought of the bankbook being slipped under her door. Ten thousand dollars her mother-in-law had offered if she'd only take Sam back.

He was pinching the frayed crease on his knee. He said he hadn't called the kids yet because this time he wanted things to be different. No false hope. No big burst and then the fizzle. This time he had to start with himself. "I have to do it for me first. Do you know what I mean, pet?"

Pet. The old ache. No matter how long ago or far away, he was the first and only man she had ever loved until—no, she dared not even think it. Omar was starting to scare her. All his promises and disappearances, and the other night, his cold refusal when she demanded her money back. Was it Sam in another form? Was she one of those women who needed to be hurt in order to feel loved? She pulled up to the curb. She would get this over with.

"I can't keep letting them down," he was saying. "You know, after Alice came to see me in the hospital I was so depressed I couldn't get out of bed for three days."

Her head whipped around. "She said she was in the waiting room most of the time." How did he do this? How did he always manage to make it their fault?

He sighed. "You want to know the truth? I almost didn't go down. I couldn't face her. I mean, ruining her graduation was bad enough, but here she is a beautiful young woman, and she has to come to a place like that to see her father." His voice broke. "She looks just like you. You weren't much older than that when we met." He put his hand on her shoulder, squeezing until it hurt. They both stared straight ahead. There were no words for that kind of loss, she thought. It never went away. The thing it had been, whatever was left, was as much a presence, as molecular, as organic as the children they had created. Yes, time helped, and yet even a word, a smell, the creak of the darkened bed in the night, could still bring it all back. Time helped in the bearing, the enduring, the hauling of it from crisis to crisis.

"Jesus!" he said, rubbing his eyes. "I don't know how you've hung in there all this time, pet."

"The kids," she said against the lump in her throat. "They keep me going. They're good kids. They really are." She took a deep breath to keep from crying.

"I've certainly screwed things up to a fare-thee-well, haven't I?" He sighed bitterly. "But I swear, pet, I'm going to make it all up to you and the kids." He groaned. "All the shit I've given you. Oh God, I can't even think of it. I can't believe it. I wake up sometimes in the middle of the night, and I lie there with my eyes wide open, thinking, So where's my life? What'd I do with it? How'd it all get this bad?"

"Well, that's a start, isn't it, Sam?"

"I don't know. I don't know how many more starts I have left in me, to tell the truth. I'm really scraping the bottom of the barrel, pet."

"You're feeling sorry for yourself, Sam. I'm sorry, but that's what you're doing." She tried to fight this surging anger.

"No, you're right. It's always this way. After all the promises and all the best intentions and fighting it off minute by minute, day after day, the same thing happens. It starts feeling like I'm banging my head against the wall. No matter how hard I try, I just can't put anything together. I get just so far, and this voice starts in my head. 'S-O-S. S-O-S. Same old shit. Same old shit.' It's this twisted cynicism. Me that can't believe me. I get up early. I shave and get dressed, and I say, Okay, this is the day. Today you're going to find a job. You're going to call your wife and kids. You're going to get things straight for once. And then the voice starts. 'Oh yah, yah, yah. Same old shit.' And that's about as fucking far as it gets." He gave a bitter laugh. "Me standing in front of the door, all dressed up and shaved, trying to work up enough courage to turn the knob." He looked at her. "Just to turn the knob, pet," he whispered, eyes wide with disbelief. "I can't even do that!"

"Yes, you can. Of course you can. Oh Sam, you're just so used to hiding out you don't know where to begin. Damn it! Damn it! Sam, sometimes I look at the kids, especially Benjy, and I get so scared. I'm afraid if I let up for even a minute they'll quit, they'll give up, they'll spend the rest of their lives taking the easy way out."

"Yah, just like dear old Dad!"

"That's not what I meant," she lied. "I'm talking about pushing yourself. I'm talking about putting your hand on the doorknob and turning it, Sam. What I mean is, I make sure the kids do that. No one ever made you do that, Sam."

He looked out at the street and smiled. "Being married to you, pet, was the happiest time in my life."

My God. All she remembered of it was tears and overturned chairs, broken windows, broken promises.

"The one thing that keeps me going, and damn it, I vowed I wasn't going to say this, but I want you to know, pet, I'm going to put this all back together. I swear, I am! I'm going to make you love me again, Marie. I am."

Poor Sam. Was that all he had to cling to? She sat with her eyes closed. She didn't want to feel anything right now, not for him or any man.

"You know, I may be a dumb son of a bitch, but I'm a lucky one. In what was probably the biggest foul-up of my life, I ended up with you! And the kids! I was telling the hospital shrink how I was supposed to marry Nora Cushing and how it was probably the smartest move I'd ever made. And then I told him what happened. How I started sneaking around after you, even though I knew it was crazy. You were so young, and there I was, thirty years old, with the biggest wedding in town planned to the richest girl in town. And you know what he told me? He said I couldn't stand the certainty and the deliberateness of success. He said I didn't think I was good enough, and so instead of facing what I didn't think I deserved, I found a way to foul myself, to ruin everything. In Nora's eyes and in my mother's eyes." Tears ran down his cheeks now. He shook out his handkerchief and blew his nose. "Oh pet," he sobbed.

"You bastard," she said, starting the car and shifting into gear. "You no-good bastard," she said over the roar of the engine as they lurched around the corner.

"Pet!" he called, reaching toward her. "Pet!"

"Well, the dirt you stepped in eighteen years ago is still here, like it or not. You've never done anything for those kids, but this time you're going to, damn it. Alice may be nothing more to you than a disgusting shameful mistake that ruined your whole life, but now you're finally going to have to pay for that. I want half that trust, do you hear me, Sam? I want five thousand dollars, and I want it right now. Those shitty tenements aren't doing my kids any good right now. And right now, right now, damn it, is when we need the help."

All the way back to Bridget's, his voice rose over hers, trying to explain. She'd misunderstood. What he'd meant was that she and the kids were the best, the finest part of his life. They were everything to him. Everything!

"Then you tell Helen that," she said. "And then tell her this for me—tell her I'm taking you both to court. And when I'm done those kids will have everything they deserve. This house and every penny you and your miserly sister have ever hidden away."

"You've got to listen, pet, please," he begged when she stopped the car.

"No. No, I don't. Do you know how many times I've heard that when you were roaring drunk? But for you to sit there, cold sober and say that to me—oh! Who the hell do you think you are?"

"A piece of shit," he said in a low voice. "A no-good piece of shit."

"Well, you're right there, Sam. Now get out!"

As she drove off, she refused to look in the rearview mirror and see his stooped figure in the pathetic jacket dragging up the stairs of that miserable house. When would she learn? He deserved no pity. None. He had spoken the truth. Skinny arms and legs with her baby belly bulging against her cheap cotton dress, she had been his masterstroke, the cruelest blow he could wield against those determined to love him, determined to save him.

"Is your dear mother home?" trumpeted Omar Duvall as he hurried into the house. For the past three days he hadn't come or called.

Benjy waited for Norm to answer, because that was who Omar was staring at.

"I said, is your mother home?"

"Nope," Norm grunted without looking up from the newspaper. He had been reading aloud the latest report on Joey Seldon, who was still in the hospital with a fractured skull.

"Do you know when she'll be back?" Omar asked with a hopeful glance at the cold potless stove.

"Nope," said Norm.

"Do you know where she went?" His tone grew strained.

"Yah." Norm glanced over the paper. "She's with my father. I'll tell her you were here."

Omar smiled, obviously pleased to hear this. "Save you the trouble, son, I'll wait." He pulled out a chair and settled down in a sigh of sweaty cloth and flesh.

His face flushed, Norm turned the pages.

"So what's new, Benjy?" Omar asked. He removed a toothpick from his breast pocket and began to clean his teeth in a delicate whittling motion, sucking the toothpick clean after every couple of teeth.

"Not much." Benjy shrugged, trying to hide his relief from Norm. With Omar here, their mother would be in a good mood again. Things would be better tonight, he thought, then shuddered, remembering his dream of that bloated body swelling in the damp heat until it finally exploded, its volcanic spew raining entrails and blobs of flesh over all the streets and houses. He'd knelt on his bed watching the bloody mess slide down the window glass. They said he'd been screaming. He only remembered crying.

"Well, it's certainly been a busy week for me, if not a profitable one," Omar was saying. He'd been on the road most of the time, trying to establish franchises in some of the more rural parts of the state. His target group had been farm families. The party-marketing concept had great appeal for such isolated women.

"Speaking of which," Norm interrupted, "where've you been staying?"

Omar looked right at him. "What do you mean, speaking of which? What exactly are you asking me, Norman?"

"I asked you where you've been staying." The corners of Norm's mouth flicked. "That's all."

"Kind of here and there, I've been on the road so damn much," he said with such a derisive snort his nose leaked. He groped in his pockets for a handkerchief.

Benjy's eyes widened. He thought Norm would surely laugh, but every feature was rigid as stone.

"I see your car down in back of the fruit store a lot," Norm said.

Omar made a face. "The fruit store?" he asked incredulously.

"Yah. I drive my foreman there to get his paper. I see your car out back."

"My car?" Omar frowned and shook his head.

"Four-two-six-nine-five. That's your plate number, right?"

Omar glanced at Benjy and laughed. "Tell the truth, I don't even know what my name is half the time."

"Yah, I'll bet you don't," Norm muttered.

"Come again?" Omar leaned across the table. "What'd you say?"

Benjy's eyes darted between them. *Stop it. Stop it. Stop it,* he wanted to shout. Why did Norm always have to stir things up?

"You heard me," Norm said each time Omar insisted he repeat what he'd said.

"You are pushing me, you hear me, boy? You are trying my patience, and I am sick and tired of it," Omar snarled, the undulating cadence so swiftly perilous that Benjy gripped the chair seat.

"Does my mother know you're living with Bernadette Mansaw?" Norm asked.

Omar's chest rose and fell with panting. "Your mother knows Miss Mansaw's one of my investors. But what she doesn't know is about you and your friends terrifying that young woman. And in the process, daring to bandy about my good name, slandering me— that's what your mother doesn't know. But maybe she should. Maybe I shouldn't protect you anymore, boy. Seems to me you're on

a downhill slide, anyway, drinking and brawling and killing an innocent creature in the process."

"You asshole!" Norm cried, running at Omar, who only had time
to raise his hands.

"Norm!" Benjy shouted.

Omar ducked as Norm swung. He grabbed Norm's arm and
yanked him off balance.

"Please, Norm!" Benjy yelled as Norm rushed at Omar again.
Omar was on his feet now. He raised his hands, palms inward, like
a priest's silent prayer during Mass. He stared in Norm with a rap-
ture that might have been pleasure but for the quivering bloodless
mouth.

"Come on!" Norm said.

"Norm!" Benjy grabbed his brother's shirt and tried to pull him
back, a futile gesture against Norm's straining chest and arms. But
not strong enough, Benjy knew, remembering Earlie's wide back and
thick arms. "Please don't, Norm, please!" he cried, unable to contain
the horror.

The kitchen shook with the familiar rumble of their mother's car
pulling into the driveway. Their hands fell to their sides.

She raced inside, too agitated to notice the breathless strain between them. She tossed her purse onto the table. "Oh!" she said with
a glance at Omar. "How good to see you back."

"I know. It's been one hell of week," he said, ignoring her sarcasm. "But harder on you than me, I'm sure," he added quickly,
reaching to touch her arm, but she darted away. He watched her
rummage loudly through the cupboard for a pan. "So how'd it go
with Sam?"

She stood at the sink filling the pan with water. "He knew about
it," she said in a high thin voice. "Of course he says he didn't really
know, that he wasn't sure just how much it was. But he knew. I could
tell. All this time when I never knew where our next dime was coming from, he's been sitting on his nest egg." She put the pan on the
burner and looked back at Norm posted in the doorway, watching
Omar. "You could've at least set the table," she said to Norm. "Is
that too much to expect?"

"No sooner said than done," Omar said, sliding the plates from
the shelf. "The boy's had a long day."

"Oh really?" Her voice trembled. "You want to hear what a long day is, I'll tell you." She was grabbing bowls of sauce, lettuce, and a cucumber from the refrigerator and banging them down on the table. "I've had it! I'm not fooling around anymore. I told him. He's got a week. One week and then I'll sue them all. Him!" she vowed, tearing the lettuce into chunks. "His mother! His sister! Renie! The whole goddamn warped bunch of them!"

Norm had gone to his room. Benjy turned on the television. Omar stayed in the kitchen, helping her cook and set the table, soothing her, finally making her laugh, softening her voice, whispering that he loved her. That he needed her so badly he was on fire inside.

After lying awake for hours, Benjy had made up his mind. To continue this way was too dangerous. He waited in the heat in his narrow room until the rest of the house lay dark and soundless.

He opened the door, listened, then tiptoed down the stairs to the couch, where Omar slept on his side, his naked back exposed, the rolls of flesh at his waist pale in the streetlight that shone through the open window. His shoes were on the floor, his suit and shirt draped over the chair. He did not snore, but wheezed, the high end of it like a whimper. Benjy stood by the couch, certain of his decision, but still not sure just how to handle it.

He'd never go to the police. He couldn't confide in Alice or Norm because they'd tell their mother, and she was the one person who could not know. He'd do anything to ensure her happiness, because only then could they be safe. Each clash between Norm and Omar stripped away another layer. He was afraid that soon there'd be nothing left. This would be his only chance. Days might go by before he saw Omar again or could be alone with him.

He touched Omar's shoulder. It felt warm and damp and bonelessly soft. Omar turned with a grunt, then sat up suddenly, feet flat on the floor, his head jerking back and forth as he struggled to focus through the darkness. "What is it?" he demanded in a frightened voice.

"It's me, Omar. Benjy. I have to tell you something," he whispered.

"What? What do you have to tell me?" he sighed, leaning his

head back on the couch. "What did you have, a bad dream or something?" he asked, yawning when Benjy did not immediately answer. "Your mother said you had another bad dream last night. Everything's okay, so why don't you just go back up to bed now."

He'd been trying to speak, but it wasn't words he needed to express as much as the wrenching force of this skirmish between his heart and his head.

"I'm beat, Benjy. Really, really beat." He started to lie down.

"Omar! I was there that day," he whispered, stepping closer now. "I saw you. I saw you and that Earlie fighting. He chased you, and then you were, I think, wrestling, and then there was this sharp thing, shiny like a knife, in both your hands. And he looked up, and I think he saw me, because he kind of stopped a minute. And you took off then. He ran after you. And I ran home."

There was a long moment of silence.

"My Lord," Omar sighed, stretching his arms back behind his head. "So someone does know the truth I speak. This comes as a great relief to me, Benjy, a great, great relief. That young man you saw didn't just rob me of my money. He took away my goodwill, and my trust in my fellowman, and my self-confidence. I'll tell you, if it weren't for your mother, I don't know, I hate to think where I'd be right now." He slapped his knee. "Well, be that as it may, you need your sleep more'n you need any more of my moaning and groaning. I just hope to God Earlie doesn't harm anyone else like he did me."

"Omar! He's dead. His body's right out there in those woods. I saw it. Klubocks' dog kept bringing back pieces of his clothes. He's all swollen up, and there's a knife in his chest. A knife with a snakeskin handle."

Omar buried his face in his hands. "Oh my God," he groaned. "This can't be. That poor, misguided creature. I wonder what happened?"

"You killed him," Benjy said, as if the question needed answering.

Omar's head shot up. "Tell me you're pranking me, Benjy. Please tell me."

"You did. I know you did, but—"

"You know what? Oh my God, your mother's right to be worried about your state of mind. Now you listen to me." He was stepping into his pants, his shoes, reaching for his shirt. "We have to talk, and we can't be waking everyone up, so you come outside with me."

"No."

Dressed, Omar filled the room, the night with whiteness. "What? You're not afraid of me now, are you?"

"No." And he knew he wasn't. He was afraid that one of these times Omar might do to Norm what he had done to Earlie. And he was afraid that if Omar left them, it would be the end for his mother. But he wasn't afraid that Omar would hurt him. Whatever had happened that day had been done in panic, in fear, in anger. Of that he had no doubt.

"Come with me. We have to talk." Omar opened the door. "We'll stay on the street."

As they headed toward Main Street he kept hobbling with the little stones underfoot. Omar was quiet. Benjy was amazed to hear himself talk so much. The words had been lodged in him for too long. All he really wanted, he tried to explain, was his mother's happiness. Nothing else was as important as that.

"I couldn't agree more," Omar said.

"She likes you," he said before Omar could say more. "Sometimes she cries when you don't come."

Omar sighed. "It hurts to hear that. And it's far more devotion than I deserve. Tell me, Benjy." He stopped walking. They were almost at the corner. "Who else knows this about poor Earlie?"

"Nobody."

"Not Norm or Alice?"

Benjy shook his head.

"And not your mother?"

"No."

"Why? Why not tell someone? That's a terrible burden to bear alone."

He tried to explain that the more terrible burden was his mother's pain. Earlie was dead, and nothing and no one could change that now. He couldn't adequately express what he felt, but he tried. Somehow in the midst of all this chaos there had to be room for love. Yes, Earlie was dead, but he couldn't let that death destroy his mother as well. Evil might be a force here, but then so was love, because without it, nothing made sense or would survive. Just as he couldn't hate his father for his affliction and the pain it caused, so was he incapable of condemning Omar for Earlie's death.

"But I didn't kill him! He must've fallen on his knife."

"They said it was your knife." He reminded Omar that he had sent him to talk to the two men.

"Liars, the two of them, armed to the teeth with knives and pistols every minute I knew them. What else did they say?"

"I can't remember," he said as they started back. He would not mention the silver money clip thick with bills. There seemed no point to it. Not now, anyway. Omar was right. It had been a terrible burden, and now with it shifted to Omar, he felt relieved. If Omar chose to, he could call the police and tell his side of it. What mattered most was that everything work out between his mother and Omar. And now he knew Norm would be safe with the line—the secret of Earlie's body—too broadly and plainly drawn for Omar to breach.

"But you see we can't believe everything we're told," Omar said as they walked along. "Nothing's the way it seems anymore. The world's too full of cruelty. People lie! They say terrible things! Sometimes the only truth we can know is what we feel in here," he said, touching his chest. "Benjy, you have to believe me," Omar whispered, pausing in front of the house. "I did not kill Earlie!"

When he didn't respond, Omar clamped his hand over his shoulder. "If that's what you think, then I can't go back in there. I'll just leave. I'll go now, tonight. And in the morning you can tell your mother." Omar stared at him for a long expectant moment, and then he turned.

Benjy watched him grow shapeless and blurred in the distant streetlight before he ran after him, calling softly, "Wait, wait! I'm not going to tell my mother. I don't want her to know!"

"Then you have to believe me!" Omar cried. "You have to! It's the only way I can stay, don't you see?"

Benjy nodded, confused by the sudden parry, the shifting ground, the trembling underfoot. He was just a boy. He was only twelve. There was so much he did not know.

"I'll tell you what killed Earlie Jones. It was avarice and lust!

Selfishness and dishonesty! Treachery! That's what killed Earlie
Jones, not me! Do you understand? Don't you know what must've
happened? He took my money, and he started to run. He was trying
to get back to the other two, who were waiting for him with my car,
my clothes, my goods, all my possessions, and so he's running and
huffing and puffing when all of a sudden his foot gets snagged in
something. Who knows, maybe a vine or a tree root, or maybe he just
trips, but down he goes, flat on his face, and the knife, the blade he
still carried against me, jams up into his heart." Omar sighed. Eyes
closed, he shook his head. "I just hope he went quickly, that's all."

"Yah," Benjy said, as oddly breathless as if he'd just been
sprinting through those spring woods. "I hope so, too."

They went inside, quickly, quietly, feeling their way through the
dark, each bound by the other's vision.

A rainstorm broke over the mountains, the sudden downpour
swelling rivulets into foamy gushing brooks. Gusts of wind
lashed spindly trees back and forth, bending them to the ground.

On the third floor of Atkinson Hospital, Nurse Annmarie Simros
moved quickly through the sleeping ward. There were eight patients,
all men, and most of these were elderly. She had three more meds to
administer before her break. The windows flashed with the brilliance
of the lightning. The thunderclaps seemed to come every few seconds
now. It was amazing how soundly everyone slept through the storm,
especially the older men, who usually tossed and turned all night
with insomnia. This was a phenomenon she'd noticed before.

"Mr. Seldon," she whispered, bending over the old popcorn ven-
dor, whose head was still bandaged. Tomorrow his sutures would be
removed. The blow had fractured his skull and for three days he'd
lain in a coma. Sonny Stoner had visited every day. A distant cousin
had driven down from Burlington to find a nursing home that would
care for him when (and *if*, his doctor interjected) he was released. But
Joey Seldon had come out of the coma. He insisted he was going
home and, as soon as he could, back to his stand. "Mr. Seldon,"

Nurse Simros whispered, the graze of her fingertips on his shoulder surely icy, she thought, as his eyes opened with alarm. "I have your pills here," she said, lifting him and bringing the cup to his lips. He swallowed, his sightless eyes locked on hers, even now as she eased him back onto the pillow. "Good night," she whispered, then turned to go. She glanced back. A bolt of lightning filled the ward with light and Joey Seldon's eyes flew from window to window. It was the brightness, she told herself. That was all, just the sudden intensity.

Almost a mile away in his apartment over the Holy Articles Shoppe, Howard Menka was wide awake. Usually, storms like this frightened him, but he was so excited over tomorrow's trip that he could think of little else. First thing in the morning he and his landlady, Lucille, were leaving on the bus to see Cousin Perda. He'd packed their lunch, four liverwurst-and-tomato sandwiches, two hard-boiled eggs, two Devil Dogs, and a thermos of cherry Kool-Aid. He turned on the light next to his bed once again to admire the gifts he had bought for Perda and the other patients. There were two red-and-black Japanese fans, a magnifying glass, a box of gold stars, six tiny plastic infants swaddled in bits of pink and blue flannel, and his favorite, the tumbling man in the squeeze bars. He squeezed the bright green sticks, smiling as the little figure spun and turned up and over the sticks, then down again. He couldn't wait to show Lucille how to work it. Maybe it would make her laugh. It was hard to make Lucille laugh.

Lucille was bringing holy cards. She'd wanted to give each patient a patron saint card, but the only name he could remember was his cousin's, and Lucille said there was no such saint as Perda, so she decided on the Sacred Heart of Jesus. Good idea, he said, but the truth was that the image of Jesus holding his bleeding heart always made him sick to his stomach and dizzy because of the way he couldn't stop thinking about that soft warm heart still beating as it bled in the palm of your hand, and the whole time, like now that he'd let it into his thoughts, he'd be trying to click it off, think of something else, come on now, he'd tell himself, anything but that, even though Jozia said it wasn't like a human heart, of course: a human heart would die outside the body, but Jesus' heart was eternal, didn't need a cord or any connecting thing to keep him alive, just love, she said, that was it, love, think of love, just love, love, love, and Lucille, whom he loved, loved, loved, but dared not tell because of the man who came sometimes. He was older, short and plump, with gray sideburns. He always brought her apples and pears. The last time, after he left, Howard heard Lucille singing through the heat register on the floor, where he'd been lying and listening the whole time. Tomorrow, after the trip to see Perda, he was going to tell her, maybe even on the way home in the dark bus, when they'd both be tired and feeling good about themselves and lucky the way he and Jozia used to feel in their realization not only of all they had, but that they had each other. Of course now that his sister was under the spell of Grondine Carson she considered the trip to see Perda "nothing but a waste of time and money," but not Lucille. She had said yes the minute he asked her.

All through the storm Chief Stoner had been dozing in the chair by his wife's bed. He woke up now, startled by the sudden quiet, the wet stillness, and the close scent of flowers in the room. He listened. When he heard her breathing, he gripped the arms of the chair and started to get up.

"Sonny?" Carol said. "Where you going?"

"Nowhere," he lied. The flowers on the dresser were from Eunice. She sent dinner over every night, and on Sundays when the nurse was off, she bathed Carol and spent the day with her. Sonny made it a point to be away from here on Sundays. On the night of Joey Seldon's attack he'd vowed to stop seeing Eunice. He'd called his sister in Rhode Island and asked if Lester could spend a few weeks with her. She had six kids, all athletes, but Lester had refused to go, preferring to spend his nights down in the kitchen monitoring police calls. He'd given up suggesting he call Alice Fermoyle. Lester said the world was becoming an evil place.

"Lay down with me," Carol said. "Please?"

"But I don't want to hurt you," he said.

"Nothing hurts anymore," she sighed through the swoon of her medication.

Buckles, badges, and key chains clinking, he lay on his side facing her, cringing to keep every pore, every bone, hair, and muscle from touching her. They hadn't been this close in months. "How's that?" he whispered, and when she didn't answer he asked again. He hardly knew what to say anymore.

"I'm sorry this is taking so long," she said.

"You sleep so much during the day, it's hard at night," he said.

"I didn't mean that," she said, and he realized she was crying.

"Oh, Carol, don't. Oh please don't."

"No, listen. This is important, Sonny."

As she spoke, he tried to let his mind wander. He had three patrolmen assigned downtown tonight. Two on foot and one in the car. If that didn't work . . . Her sadness tore him apart.

"You see, I know everything," she was saying. "That's what happens. Part of me's way up there, the good part . . ."

"No, the good part's here," he whispered, taking her small hard hand in both of his.

"Now, you just listen. I know how sad you are. You don't think you're a good man anymore, do you? But you are. You are! I know you are."

"No, I'm not," he said as he moved closer, holding her hand to his mouth, and now it all came out, his carelessness at work, his men's disappointment in him. Another store had been broken into since Joey Seldon's mugging, Hardy's Records, and though he was certain that punk Mooney was involved, he couldn't seem to prove it. There was some malevolence in the air, a heaviness he could smell and taste. He woke up dreading it and fell asleep dreading it.

"But it's not your fault, Sonny."

"Yes it is," he said. "Things just stopped being important anymore."

"What things?" she whispered across the pillow.

"I don't know." He thought a minute. "Rules, I guess. Seemed like being careful didn't matter anymore. All that time and always trying to keep one step ahead, you know, and what the hell, look what happens."

She didn't say anything. He heard the catch in her breathing.

"You don't mean me, do you, Sonny?"

"'Course I mean you! What do you think I mean?"

"Eunice. That's what you mean."

They lay in silence. He stared at the ceiling. He needed to tell how Eunice had pursued and seduced him, how by taking advantage of his grief she had betrayed her sister-in-law, her closest friend. For the first time now, he realized how much he hated her. Women like that left their poison everywhere.

"She always made sure she was right there, right ready and available," he began, but she stopped him. She didn't have the energy for it. What she meant by part of her already being up there was that she saw things differently now. "At first, it hurt real, real bad. But then I tried to stop caring, because I couldn't do both. I couldn't hate the two of you and still die. The hate was keeping me alive." She touched his cheek. "And besides now, in a way, I'm relieved. I don't have to worry so much about you and Les being alone. I can just concentrate on this."

"This?" But he knew what she meant.

"I just want to go now. I could, you know, honey. I could do it tonight if I wanted."

"What do you mean?" he cried. He jumped up and turned on the light. She cringed away from its glare. He pulled open the nightstand drawer, then all the dresser drawers. He was looking for bottles. She had pills hidden somewhere, pills or poison. That's what she meant. He picked up the bottle of Lysol from the windowsill and peered at the label. He searched through her closet, repelled by the stale odor of her unworn clothes in the airless heat.

"Don't, Sonny, please don't," she kept saying as he rummaged through the shoe boxes on the top shelf. Letters, photos, dried corsages whose brittle rusty petals crumbled when he touched them.

"You can't do that," he said, fumbling in her bureau drawers, through lace panties, silk slips, garter belts, and stockings she would never wear again. He kicked aside the scatter rug and ran his hand under the dresser. This was a familiar role. He took the chintz cushion from the rocker, unzipped it, and felt inside. He knew exactly what to do here. Many's the time he had conducted similar searches, looking for money, a gun, some evidence of malfeasance, in this case the damning proof of his own sins. In failing his family and his community he had failed himself.

"Sonny, please stop. You think you can control everything, but you can't!"

He stood in the middle of the room, looking around. It was in here somewhere, mocking him. Here under his own roof it had spread, tainting them. But he would not be that easily defeated this time. He would fight back and he would keep on fighting, protecting what was his. She held up her hand as he stepped closer. The lamp lit her face with a penetrating luminosity, the bones glowing through her flat white pallor.

"Don't, please don't," she whispered as he stuck his hand under the mattress. He pulled out three waxed-paper sandwich bags filled with capsules and tablets.

She begged him to put them back. They were all she had. Didn't he understand? Just knowing they were there was often comfort, strength enough. This was wrong. He had no right to take this from her. If he really loved her he would at least allow her this one last choice she could make for herself. Didn't he understand how much she needed this final freedom?

No, he protested, not freedom, but despair. To do this would make a mockery of her life.

"Of your life, you mean," she sobbed as he went across the hall. He emptied the bags into the toilet and pressed the lever, watching the swirl of colored pills gurgle safely away down and out through the sewer pipes under the wide rain-soaked front lawn to the road, deep below the street, all the streets, safely, safely away.

The rain had turned to drizzle, the lightning sporadic and distant. The faint rumble of thunder came like the weary aftermath to a wild party, chairs pushed into place, a couch dragged back, rugs rolled out. Smiling, Astrid Haddad lay in bed with her hands clasped behind her head. Beside her, Bob slept soundly. He'd just invested a lot of money in a business tailor-made for her show-business background. The minute Bob said the name Omar she recognized it as that mysterious guy Marie Fermoyle knew but would never talk about. He'd come into Bob's office and sold him a franchise in a business Bob said would more than double the money she made now. When she thought of poor Marie struggling to make ends meet, she realized how lucky she was to have sweet Bobby Haddad.

He'd stood behind her last night smiling as she removed her makeup; then he'd tossed the certificate of franchise onto her dressing table and told her to quit both jobs in the morning. Don't even worry about giving notice. This was a once-in-a-lifetime opportunity, the merchandising wave of the future.

Imagine getting paid for giving parties. It would be like Vegas in a way. Balloons, she thought, picturing the ceiling a mass of white balloons floating like soapsuds. Her color scheme would be pink, silver, and white. She saw herself on a little platform in one of her shimmering cocktail dresses. She'd open every party with a song. "Bobby, wake up," she whispered, nudging him. His eyes opened heavily and he curled his bandaged hands to his chest. "Listen to what I just made up." She'd forgotten about his hands, but she wanted him to hear this before she forgot. She leaned over him, singing in a husky whisper. "Don't you ladies just sit and mope. Sparkle up your lives with Presto Soap." He fell back to sleep, smiling.

There was so much to do, and she couldn't tell anyone. Omar Duvall had told Bob they should keep it to themselves for a while. First, she'd call Mr. Briscoe in the morning and tell him she was through. She sighed, relieved that she wouldn't have to spend every day afraid of seeing Norm Fermoyle.

She looked over at Bobby, ashamed now of all her fooling around. The poor guy had worked his hump off to do this for her. Out every night lately, and coming in so tired sometimes he trembled and cried out in his sleep. Tonight he'd come home not only soaking wet but with bleeding hands. He'd cut them on the old metal desk that he'd been moving to make room for her Presto Soap material. With her first profits from the soap business she'd surprise Bobby with a brand-new executive mahogany desk like her boss at the casino had.

It was almost three in the morning. Omar dozed on the couch until the front door creaked open and Alice tiptoed inside. He watched her shadow pass over him. No doubt of what she'd been up to, he thought, grinning, as her door closed upstairs. He waited until the only sound in the house was the drip of the kitchen faucet; then he crept up the stairs and opened Marie's door. She reached up to stroke his arm as he unbuckled his pants and let them drop to the floor. She lifted the sheet. The minute he crawled in, her legs scissored around him.

"Oh you woman," he moaned.

"Shh," she panted in his ear as he rolled on top of her. "Shh, shh, shh," she kept imploring him.

The certainty of Earlie's death had spawned this amazing passion. At first he'd thought it was fear, which in his younger years had always been a galvanizing force. But now with all that blind energy turned inward, his course was no longer set by that frenetic voice in his head telling him to run, but by desire, and all that he desired was here.

He understood now that this had been the mission. All his life he had been headed here, to success and the love of a strong woman. Benjy wanted his mother's happiness more than anything else, so Omar knew the boy would not betray him, if *betray* was even the proper word, because truly he could not even now recall the actual moment, the blow, the thrust—if there had been one. For how could so pure a heart have taken a life? Impossible. He could not comprehend such an act in the face of this desire. No, no, no, came the rhythmic pounding of his heart over hers. Because he would have this, have this, have this, this, this, this!

"What?" she gasped in his ear as she pulled him down to her.

"All of this," he whispered.

"I love you," she whispered.

The knife, he thought, turning his head for air. Other than the boy, it was the one connection to him.

When she was asleep and the sky beginning to lighten, he crept from the house, hurrying to the end of the puddled street where the woods began. He carried a bag and rags to clean the blade.

Blue Mooney initialed the sign-out sheet for the seventy-five re-treads he'd just loaded on his truck. Waiting on his dashboard was a cup of steaming-hot coffee and a jelly doughnut.

"Hey, Mooney," Colter called as he headed out of the office. "See if they got any extra snows up there, and if so, grab 'em."

"Yes sir!" Mooney answered with a brisk nod.

Colter's weather-beaten face softened with a grin. Both for his boss's benefit and for the ritual it had become, Mooney walked around his truck and gave the two chains securing the tires one last yank. He flipped his keys in the air with a quick glance back at the platform, where Colter was talking to one of his salesmen. That might not be a bad life, he thought, noting the salesman's shirt and tie, the shoeshine, yes, and a girl like Alice Fermoyle waving goodbye every morning.

"Blue?" a familiar voice inquired. He spun around to see Sonny Stoner getting out of his cruiser with one of his cops, Jimmy Heinze.

"What do you want? What're you doing here?" he asked. Colter had to be watching.

"Roll up your sleeves," Sonny said. "Okay, now let me see your hands. Hold 'em up."

"Why? What do you want?" he kept asking as Sonny examined his hands and arms.

"Where'd you get those cuts?"

"What cuts? I don't know. I always got cuts." He looked at his hands, just old nicks and scratches.

"Someone broke into Marco's Pharmacy last night." Sonny's blue eyes swam over him.

"Yah, so?" he said, pulling down his sleeves and trying to button the cuffs. His hands were shaking. No. No. Colter was heading down the ramp.

"They broke a cellar window to get in," Sonny said.

"And they must've cut themselves because we found blood," Heinze added.

"Well, it sure as hell wasn't me, Chief." He ignored Heinze. "Look, these are dirty old cuts. . . ."

"Where were you last night? You gonna tell me this time? 'Cause now I'm going to have to start looking beyond certain things. Now I gotta go on my instincts, Blue. And my instincts tell me you're heading out of control."

"I was at my mother's."

"Oh yah!" Jimmy Heinze snorted. "Sure!" He kept pacing back and forth behind Stoner.

"All night?"

"All night."

"Jimmy, go get Hildie Carper."

"She ain't there now."

"You said—"

"I stayed there last night. She said I could. Only she and my brothers went to Saratoga."

"Hey, Sonny, how you doing?" Colter said as they shook hands. "What's going on?" He looked at Blue.

"I just gotta talk to him for a minute, Jake, in private if you don't mind," Sonny said.

"Is there some kind of problem?" Colter asked.

Sonny gave Blue a quick look. "Nothing I can't handle, Jake."

"Well, that's good to hear," Colter said, smiling, though his flinty eyes shot from face to face. "Blue's a good worker. One of these days I'm gonna hate like hell losing him to the Corps."

Heinze rocked back on his heels and chuckled. "I wouldn't worry about it, Mr. Colter . . ."

"Jimmy!" warned the Chief, but the words had already met the air.

". . . seeing as how they drummed him out."

The three men stood there looking at one another.

"What's he talking about, Blue?" Colter asked.

But he couldn't answer. Arms at his sides, head up, gaze level, jaw clenched, he did not, could not, dared not move or speak.

As Howard Menka came down the street early in the morning with his landlady, Lucille, he saw the rectory door fly open. Unshaven and red-eyed, Father Gannon was fastening his clerical collar as he ran toward the church, late again for Mass. Howard felt bad. He usually tried to wake Father Gannon up in time, but he'd taken the day off. Today was a special day.

He and Lucille were on their way to the depot. He tried not to walk too fast. The first bus to Burlington left in twenty minutes. He and Jozia always got to the depot an hour early. Waiting was half the fun. They'd buy candy bars from the vending machines and eat them on the bench in front of the door where they sat watching the buses come and go with all their passengers. But Lucille said her nerves were in a bad way and she didn't want to sit in a depressing terminal any longer than she had to. He'd been both pleased and bewildered to find her so dressed up this morning. She wore a white dress, a big black picture hat, and white high heels that made her walk funny— like her pants were wet, he thought.

The excitement of planning a trip was one thing, but she could see that for Lucille, actually taking one was something else. At her worst Jozia had never been this snappish.

"I hope this cousin of yours isn't all stuck up," she huffed, trying to keep pace with him.

"No, she's not," he said.

"I hope we don't get there and she's too sick for company." She kept stopping to straighten her hat. She peered up at him. "I forgot her name again."

"Perda. Perda Menka." As they started walking, he glanced down at those wobbly high heels. He didn't dare tell her that when they got to Waterbury it was still a two-mile hike from the bus stop to the hospital, mostly uphill.

"And what's Perda's problem? You never really said." She made a face as if nothing could possibly warrant all this effort.

"I don't know for sure. She's just always been that way."

"What way?"

"Sick."

"How sick?" She rolled her eyes.

"Well, lemme see. She can't get out of bed. And she don't talk, I know that." He turned back to see where she was. She had stopped dead in the middle of the sidewalk, her hands on her hips.

"What do you mean, she don't talk?"

He shrugged. "I don't know. She just don't."

"So what're we gonna do, just sit and watch her?"

"We talk to *her,* me and Jozia, that is. We tell her things. Things we been doing. Things we seen. And there's all the others," he tried to explain. "Some of *them* talk. And they like us!" He grinned.

She didn't say anything. She just looked at him, and all of a sudden he got this funny feeling as if his limbs had turned to stone. Everything—walking, carrying the lunch bag and the gift bag, even counting out the money for the two round-trip tickets—took such energy that by the time they were seated on the bus, he was so tired that he fell into a strange half-sleep. He was distantly aware of the wheels turning under them, the stench of exhaust through the dusty sliding windows, and beside him, the wet crunch of Lucille's pointy teeth into a pear. And all the while, both awake and asleep, he dreamed. He dreamed of walking across the ice pond with Jozia on their way home from school. In his dream Jozia took his hand and they began to glide, their big black boots suddenly smooth as skate blades. Then he dreamed of hammering, pounding nails into wood while the Monsignor kept calling him. The Monsignor needed repairs done, but first he had to finish this enormous crucifix. Now he dreamed of Perda, the dream so real he could smell the stale pee in the ward as he and Lucille squeezed through the narrow space between the beds. When they got to Perda's side, Lucille pinched her nose. He told her she'd get used to it. "Well, that's her," he said of the curled form under the sheet. Her kinky red hair, uncut since his last visit, spread over the pillow. Jozia usually trimmed it, but today he would do it.

"Perda," he whispered. "I brung somebody new. Turn over, Perda. Just for a minute."

She turned, and the long red hair fell back from the gleaming, bloated face, the deep-socketed dead eyes staring back at him.

"Stop it! Stop that yelling! You're embarrassing me," Lucille said, shaking his arm. "They're all looking at us."

From the front of the bus to the back, heads craned over the seats, and heads poked out into the aisles to see what all the hollering was about.

About six thousand dollars, that's what Sam figured his sister owed him from his mother's trust. He had deducted expenses for whatever Helen had given him through the years for haircuts, papers, things like that, a pair of shoes a few years back, some dental bills, odds and ends really. For good measure he subtracted another ten dollars now, before putting away his papers.

She was barely speaking to him, or to anyone else, for that matter. As always, when life turned on Helen, she turned on her brother. She didn't call him to meals. His clothes went unwashed. Everyone in the house was sullen and miserable, except his mother, who hummed in her crib from sunrise to bedtime. Jozia crept past him in silence, her hounded eyes burrowing into her mops and rags. Renie shuffled from room to room to avoid the inevitable confrontation between his brother-in-law and his wife. In retaliation Sam had begun to cook his own meals, running the water minutes longer than he needed it. He spread the butter so thickly on his bread he could barely eat it, then laid the greasy knife on the tablecloth. He opened the refrigerator door countless times, wanting nothing from it but the satisfaction of hearing its motor rumble needlessly on and off. He left dirty dishes on the table, lights burning in empty rooms. When he bathed he used three facecloths, three towels, then left the floating soap to melt in the stoppered tub. But nothing was working. Nothing he did could rouse her to the confrontation he needed so that he could throw down his calculations and demand his trust money.

She ignored him. No one seemed to care one way or another that he was back. The only reason Marie had come was to badger him for money. Not one of his children had come or even called.

At odd dragging moments he would find himself thinking of Applegate. He thought of Marlin playing the piano, the sun-washed walls, the lush warm flowers, the brilliant green lawns, the sturdy white backs of the attendants steering patients in wheelchairs along the bumpy stone paths, the mannered authority of the doctors' voices drifting from paneled offices down the scented hallways, and the linened tables set with blue-traced china and sparkling goblets.

Here in his stale room he began to miss the rising and bedtime chimes and the far-ringing call of the mealtime bells. He missed Applegate's precision, its barricade of rules and schedules that protected him from all responsibility and decision and failure. He'd forgotten what this deadening emptiness was like. He'd forgotten how freedom afflicted him with this peculiar paralysis. He could hear Jozia dragging the vacuum cleaner up the stairs. She turned it on in the hallway. His heart raced with its sucking blast. His palms were moist. Squinting, he stood at the window. The rain had lulled him through the night, but now the sun swelled through the grayness. He leaned over the sill to watch the children skipping rope down on the sidewalk.

He sat back on the edge of his bed and flicked hairs off his pillow. He needed a haircut. The vacuum moved farther down the hall.

"Yes," he said in a low voice. "It's eleven-thirty now. I'll put on a summer shirt. Let's see, here now, the blue one, and then I'll walk downtown to the barber. When he's not looking I'll grab the paper and go read in the park awhile. Maybe feed the pigeons some popcorn. On the way back I'll stop by the library and get three books, one for tonight and two for the weekend. Then maybe I'll get a half pint of clams for clam stew tonight."

He began to feel better. Plans. That was the trick. He needed plans, things to look forward to. No long journey, just one small step after another.

He tapped lightly on Helen's door.

"What is it?" she snapped.

"I need two dollars for a haircut. . . ."

"Haircut's seventy-five cents."

"I thought I'd get a paper and some clams for tonight," he said, grimacing with his cheek at the door.

"Tell the barber to put it on Renie's bill," she said. "We're having smelt tonight."

He closed his eyes. "Don't make me crawl, Helen."

"You crawled back here, didn't you?"

Now, now was the moment to throw open the door and demand what was rightfully his. But he wasn't ready. It wasn't the right time.

He came down the stairs. On the street the jumprope stilled as the little girls watched him pass. The world smelled of grass clippings. He squinted under the hazy sun at people he had known for years, some all his life. They nodded uneasily, hurried on. That's all right, he assured himself, lightheaded on the first leg of this shaky voyage into his new life. It was just a simple walk downtown. What was there to fear? After all, he was sober and he had plans, plans just like these people had. The trick was to stay focused, to keep himself small and so tightly bound that the dead space could not get bigger, because if it did, it would engulf him. A cold sweat rose on his back. Deep breaths now. In and out. There. There, that's the trick.

The closer he got to the bustle of the downtown streets the more unnerved he became. He had no money, nothing to do. Not even a dime for a cup of coffee. No. No, he'd make it work. He had to put himself together.

Once, in the middle of group therapy, Litchfield had asked if there was anything or anyone in his life for whose sake he'd be willing to die.

"A drink," he'd said as much to jab Litchfield as to make the other patients laugh.

"Then you, Sam Fermoyle," Litchfield had said disgustedly, "are your own meager invention."

Now, as he neared the flat-roofed stores at the bottom of the hill, he tried to remember when he had not been poor Sammy, the gutless but witty Sammy, that lazy no-good Sammy who had spent a lifetime seeking and fleeing the smothering breast of his mother's need and love, his father's morose attention, his sister's resentment, and somehow settling for a vantage point of weakened pity that not only served him well but satisfied their thirst for his thin blood. Even his wife and children had succumbed, finding refuge in his failure. If Alice did not go to college, it was his fault. If Benjy was afraid of his own shadow, it was his fault. If Norm was a brawler, it was his fault. "I am all things to all people," he murmured through a forced smile.

The record store was playing stringed music through a speaker over its doorway. A high-heeled woman rustled past him. Little boys huddled around the bench where their baseball cards were laid out in rows according to teams. He stopped to watch. They glanced up at him, then resumed their argument about Whitey Ford's earned run average. He dug his fingers into the lint in his pockets. He felt shabby and useless. People strode by, resolute in their missions, shopping bags in hand, keys and coins, the minutiae of their successes, jingling with every step. He followed them, matching their brisk gait, their frowning concentration. He walked behind a thin-shouldered man half his age and trailed him up Merchants Row, silently, addressing the back of his head. *I also have places to go and books to pick out, and people to visit. Even on these narrow streets I know hundreds of people who if they see me will call to me and beg me to come inside. In high school I wrote a paper on the Proctor Marble Company that the Atkinson Crier printed. My junior year I was a starting pitcher with a curveball no one could hit. They said I was going places. They did, believe it or not.*

The young man turned the corner at West Street, and Sam turned with him. *Right here, on this very corner, there was an accident. I was on my way home from school. The car burst into flames and I helped the firemen lay down their hoses. The hair on the back of my hands was singed. My mother said . . .*

The young man went into the paint store. Sam watched the closing door. "Pathetic, isn't it?" he murmured with a bitter chuckle. "High school! My mother!" It ended there. After that came failure and degradation. He continued walking until he came to Renie's store, where a pyramid of dusty fans was displayed in the front window. A faded newspaper clipping was taped to the glass. *The Fan Man,* said the headline over Renie's picture. He had started to read the article the day it came out, but then had been too embarrassed for Renie to continue.

Renie's face glowed hopefully with the opening door, then darkened as Sam approached the counter.

"Hey, Renie, you've really fixed this dump up nice. I like the walls yellow like that."

"Brightens it up," Renie murmured, then looked back down at his open ledger.

"I'll say."

"Hot day," Renie said without looking up.

"I'll say."

"Muggy," Renie said.

"You can say that again." Sam tugged at his collar. He watched Renie's fingers grip the pencil stub and draw a heavy line through a row of figures. "How's business?"

"Could be worse," Renie sighed.

"Could be better, huh?"

Renie looked up suspiciously. He closed the green book and laid his hand flat on its cover. He took a deep breath. "Look, Sam, if it's money you want . . ."

Sam raised his hand to silence him. "Nope. Just a friendly visit to my favorite brother-in-law." He bent to look at the pictures taped to Renie's cash register, annoyed to see they were his children.

Renie smiled. "You know these walls, this color, this yellow— Alice was the one that picked that out."

"Well"—he chuckled—"what can I say? She's got good taste, just like her old man."

Renie's pride over his kids had always irritated him.

"She's a nice girl," Renie said, grinning. "I got her that job, you know, up to the A+X. I know she didn't want it, but you know Marie, how strict she is with the kids. She called me and she said, 'I don't want her at the lake. I want her home,' so I called him—the guy up there, that Coughlin—and I said, 'You know that walk-in cooler repair, that job I did, that bill I been after, well you give my niece Alice a job and then we're even." Renie gave a sheepish shrug. " 'Course I never told Marie all of it. I learned that about her. She's a very proud woman."

"Is that so?" Sam said. His brother-in-law was still thick as a post.

"Oh yah. With her you gotta be so careful."

"Hmph, I'll remember that."

"Yah. Like Norm's job. I musta called Alderman Greene a hundred times, anyway. So then one day the town clerk comes in—you know, Bill Sheets—and he wants one of them meat grinders there. 'For you, Mr. Sheets,' I says, 'that's twenty percent off. Only catch is, I got a real fine nephew that needs a summer job.' And just like that, Sheets says, 'Send him down to Jarden Greene.' But of course I never tell Marie the part about the discount. She's funny about that stuff. It's her pride, I can tell."

Sam ground his teeth. Was the dumb bastard trying to rub his nose in it?

"You see Norm yet?" Renie asked.

"Uh, no, not yet."

"Wait'll you see him. You're gonna be so amazed. He's got these big muscles like this." Renie's fingertips formed a circle. "His neck, he's just really filled in, like a man—you know, the job, all the hard work and the heavy labor."

"Renie, that reminds me," he said, touching the back of his neck. "I was thinking of getting a haircut. You got a buck you can sport me?"

"No, Sam, I don't, as a matter of fact. I just made a deposit."

The ring-eyed little grunt was obviously lying. He didn't want it to be his buck that knocked Sam off the wagon.

A door creaked open at the back of the store, and Renie spun around. A large cat strutted toward them, then jumped onto the counter. Renie looked from the cat to Sam.

"That's Tom," he said with stricken eyes.

"Nice to meet you, Tom," Sam said, nodding at the purring cat.

"He's a nice cat." Renie stroked its neck.

"Well, that's good."

"Helen don't know Tom's here."

"Where does she think he is?" He was confused by Renie's obvious alarm.

"I mean she don't know anything about Tom. I didn't tell her." He stared at Sam.

"So you keep a little pussy on the side, big deal." He laughed, but Renie didn't get it.

"I just didn't want her to hear about it. I just didn't."

"Hear about what?" And the minute he said it, he knew Renie meant his old dog Riddles. Renie didn't want to endure her old complaints about Riddles, about his deceit. Renie had said the dog had just followed him home one night. She claimed he had lured the dog home with him. Riddles had lived in the shed off the back porch. Whenever Helen went shopping or to church Renie would carry the stocky red dog into his bedroom, where he'd spend the furtive hour laughing and talking to Riddles until she came home, breathing into the back of her gloved hand, insisting she could "smell dog" in the house. One day Riddles disappeared. Helen said the real owners probably took it back. Renie said Riddles ran away because he was a hunting dog and not a house dog. But when he said it, he had gotten this same sheepish look, because he must have known it was a lie.

Renie began to rearrange a display of juice makers. He had on the same dark plaid shirt and brown tie he always wore. Poor bastard, Sam thought. Let somebody else tell him that Helen had paid Howard Menka to poison the dog. He couldn't bring himself to.

The cat jumped down behind the counter and lapped milk from a blue soup bowl Sam recognized as part of his mother's china. The Fermoyle legacy had come to this. He thought of Marie. He cleared his throat and asked Renie what he knew about Omar Duvall. His first night home, in the middle of her tirade, Helen had told him that Marie was going out with a trashy-looking man by that name.

Renie said he'd only met Duvall one time. Duvall had tried to interest him in some soap-selling scheme. He suggested using the soap as a promotional tool: a free ten-pound box of detergent with every washing machine. When Renie said he couldn't afford to do that, Duvall had explained that the thing to do was to jack up the price of the washing machine enough to cover each box. Renie said he didn't think that would work, not with the big new Montgomery Ward's opening up on Route 4. Well, then, just sell the soap then, Duvall had suggested. He could even keep it out back, sell it on the side, no wasted shelf space, no advertising, just tell his customers what a great buy it was. And that way, Duvall had said, it could all be under the table, nothing on the books, no trouble like he'd had before with the IRS and the cash sales.

"So right then, when he said that, I don't know, I got suspicious."

Renie stepped close to Sam and looked around, though they were the only ones in the store. "I think he's really a tax agent, that's what I think. I could tell the way he was looking around. He just knew too much about what was going on here." Renie looked around again. "You maybe oughta warn Marie there's something fishy going on."

"Not much gets by you, does it, Renie? You've always got your finger right there on the pulse of things." He leaned on the counter. "Hey, I'll bet you know something about my mother's trust fund for me."

"Nothing! I don't know nothing." Renie shook his head and this time held the shrug with upturned hands.

"Don't give me that shit," he snapped. Renie did this to him.

"I got nothing to do with any of that," Renie said, the color in his face draining as he eyed a long, black Lincoln that was parking in front of the store. "Ask Helen."

"I'll ask Helen. I'll ask her, goddamn it!" He pounded the counter, and the cat darted toward the cellar door.

"There's a customer coming," Renie warned as a tall, slim woman emerged from the Lincoln.

"I don't give a shit who's coming."

"Sam!"

The bells on the opening door rang, and Sam moved to the back of the store. He opened a refrigerator and peered inside. The woman wore a red-and-white-polka-dot dress. She carried a toaster under her arm as she marched up to Renie. She banged the toaster down, dislodging crumbs and charred raisins onto the counter. "It's defective! This morning the toast never popped up and it burned so bad that now my ceiling's stained."

Renie was still staring at the crumbs when the woman flung down a receipt. Renie picked it up and read it closely.

"I want my money back, every penny!"

"The toaster's a year old," Renie said. "It only had a ninety-day warranty. I'm sorry."

"Sorry! You're sorry? My ceiling's ruined and that's all you can say is you're sorry?"

"I could give you a new one, Mrs. Hinds," Renie said with a weak gesture toward the shelf of toasters behind him.

Sam peered down the length of the store. Nora Cushing. He hadn't seen her in years.

"All I want is my money back," she insisted.

She hadn't changed a bit, Sam thought. The Cushing fortune, and still tight-fisted with every penny and just as bitchy as ever.

"Look at them," Renie pleaded. "Take any one you want, Mrs. Hinds. You got your pick."

"I don't think you understand. It's the principle here. It's not the toaster. I mean, my Lord, Dad's getting the Golden Toastee line in the store, so it's not as if I need one of these!" she said with a flip of her hand.

"*You what?*" Sam remembered her gasping eighteen years ago. "*You married her? You married Marie Luseau? My Lord, you can't be serious.*"

Renie was staring at her. "The Golden Toastee line? You mean the toasters? You're going to sell them?"

"Yes, so it's not the toaster, you see, it's the principle—"

"Are you sure about that?" Renie interrupted.

"What are you suggesting, that I'm trying to finagle something here?" she sputtered.

"I think you better check, Mrs. Hinds. I don't think Cushing's is getting the Golden Toastee line."

The laughter rose from deep in her throat. "Well, we are, but that's beside the point. . . ."

"Nora!" Sam called, coming toward her now. "Nora Cushing!"

"Oh! Oh, Sam!" She glanced at Renie, then back at Sam. "Oh, I'm so embarrassed."

"How've you been?" he asked, conscious of his frayed cuff as they shook hands.

"Well, I guess I'm a little worked up," she said, gesturing toward Renie, whose whole body seemed to have caved in on itself. "It was just such an awful morning. I was busy with Bernard—he's been very sick, you know."

Sam nodded. He had heard that Nora's son had some terrible illness.

"But then smoke from the burned toast got all through the house, and it just seemed like there wasn't anything I could do about anything anymore, except this! The toaster!" She grabbed it from the counter and held it. "Renie, what can I say? I'm sorry. I'm really embarrassed."

Renie stared at her with bright wet eyes. His mouth twitched.

"See, Renie understands," Sam had to say when Renie still did not speak. "You're going through a lot right now."

"Oh God," she sighed. "It's just been so awful." She sniffed and wiped her nose on the back of her wrist. Her perfume smelled of roses and wrinkled dollar bills. Her tanned skin and smooth black hair looked expensive. Even under the store's dim lights her necklace and bracelets and rings glittered. She had begged him to marry her. Marie Luseau could go to a home somewhere and have the baby. She'd even pay for it herself. It wasn't a real marriage, Nora had argued, because she was just a child who had set out to trap him. They could have it annulled. Between her father, who was a Knight of Malta, and her cousin, Father Burke, they had plenty of connections to the Vatican. "I *can't*," he'd said to every entreaty. Can't. Could not, would not. *Why? Why? Why?* she'd demanded. They had been engaged for over a year. Her mother's parlor had been filled with gifts. *Why? Because. Because.* Because he loved her, loved skinny little Marie Luseau more than he had ever loved anyone. Had that been it? he wondered now. Had it been that simple, when all these years he had regarded it as a symptom of his failed life, a coward's way out, one more heinous escape. How grateful Nora must be now. Eighteen years ago she had wept hysterically in her father's car as she stabbed her wrist with a nail file. *How could you do this to me? How could you? How could you? How could you humiliate me with someone like her?*

"It's leukemia," she whispered. "We've brought him everywhere." Her eyes shone with tears as she recounted the history of her son's illness. The easy bruising and painful joints she had blithely ascribed to growing pains, the shocking diagnosis, the bewilderment, the unfairness of it all. He was their only child, just fifteen years old, a brilliant student. A gifted pianist.

Renie blew his nose into his handkerchief. Sam ran his fingers through his hair, a sad smile fixed against this sudden urge to push her out of his way and run up the street. She touched his arm, then reached suddenly into her pocketbook, pawing through it with the same intensity with which she had searched that night for her nail file. She pulled out a photograph of her son and handed it to him. He said the boy looked like his father. Yes, she nodded. He did. She asked about his children, taking deep breaths, smelling rich again, her pinched brave smile attesting to the blind injustice that would rob her of her one and only stellar child while the ragtag kids of a loser like Sam Fermoyle were spared.

"Is it true about Alice being interested in the convent?" she asked, patting her smudged eyeliner with a pale blue tissue.

"No, I don't think so."

It was a painful moment. Her look said it all: she shouldn't have asked, because how the hell would he know. "Actually, she's going to college in just a few more weeks," he said.

She asked about his mother and Helen. He realized she hadn't asked him what he was doing now. People who knew him never did. She asked if he was still at his mother's.

"Temporarily," he said. For the last ten years.

After she left, Renie said he had to close for a while. He had a headache, and his stomach was upset. Renie followed him to the door, and Sam asked again if he could borrow a buck. Renie took out his wallet that was so worn it had been taped together on the fold. Even the dollar he gave him was thin and frayed.

"Hey, thanks, Renie," he said with a flick of the bill; then, seeing the misery in Renie's expression, he turned back and asked what was wrong.

"Nothing," Renie said.

"You think I'm gonna go get a drink with this, right?"

"No, I wasn't thinking that."

"Well, what are you thinking?"

"It's a business thing," Renie said. He shrugged and shook his head, and now Sam realized it was the cat. Renie was afraid he'd tell Helen about the cat. Well, if that was it, he wanted Renie to know the secret was safe with him.

Renie nodded, then looked up at him. "You know what you said once, about Riddles being buried under the tomatoes?"

Sam pointed to himself. "I said that? Me? No! I'm like you. I don't know what could have happened to him."

"You think he ran away?" Renie watched him closely.

"Maybe. I don't know. Maybe he got lost. You know, maybe he took a wrong turn or something, and he got confused. Like when you found him, right? He was lost then."

"He wasn't lost." Renie looked at him sheepishly. "I just said that. I got him off this lady that came in the store. Her husband died and she said the dog was always howling he was so lonesome. She was going to put him to sleep, so I said I'd take him." A little grin came over his face. "And right off the bat he liked me. Just like he did her husband. She told me that. So I know he didn't run away."

"I don't know. It's just one of those things, I guess."

"Maybe somebody stole him," Renie said hesitantly.

"Well, there you go! That's probably what happened."

"Yah. And sometimes I think I hear him, you know. I get up in the middle of the night and I go out on the porch to see if it's him."

"Yah, well, who knows, Renie. One of these nights he'll probably be scratching on the door and Helen'll start yelling, 'That dog's ripping my screen,' and then Bridget'll start barking back at him again, and it'll be just like it used to be."

"I hope so," Renie said.

In Joey's absence a rotted cornerpost of the popcorn stand had been yanked out, and the roof edge was sagging, lifting at times like a tent flap in the wind. One night all the stacked wooden cases for empty cans and bottles had been toppled by raccoons or vandals, and so they had been hauled away by a town crew. And now Joey had a competitor. He was a pleasant young man who sold popcorn, soda, foot-long hotdogs, and French fries out of the side of an old school bus that had been painted red, white, and blue. The beauty of this arrangement was that the bus would be there only during the band concerts. By day the park could be noncommercial—that is, as soon as the aldermen could get rid of the old man's ramshackle stand.

No one was more disappointed than Chief Stoner when Joey returned to his stand just two days after leaving the hospital. Retirement would have been a more gracious ending than the eviction that even some of Joey's oldest sympathizers were considering. In the way that inexplicable events are often diabolized, the mugging had come to be regarded as almost inevitable. Once again, Joey Seldon had crossed paths with violence. Oddly, the town's indignation was less over the old man's suffering than it was over the defiant swagger of Blue Mooney. Fired from J. C. Colter, he now spent his days racing his motorcycle up and down the winding mountain roads and his bitter nights roaring through Atkinson's sleeping streets. There had been three more burglaries in the last two weeks, and now Jerry Coughlin was convinced his restaurant was next on Mooney's list. He'd banned Mooney from the A+X, which came as a great relief to Alice Fermoyle.

The police, in an effort to monitor Mooney's activities, began to sit in a cruiser parked at the end of the road that led up to his mother's cottage. Her young customers had stopped coming. Just as she'd predicted, her son's presence was harming her family.

So with the old man back in the park selling popcorn, it was a bittersweet time for Sonny. For Carol's sake, he and Eunice had tried being friends, but it was impossible. Without love's flattering veil she'd become the same loud, brash, irresponsible Eunice Bonifante who'd always grated on his nerves.

He had begun to understand how connected people were. The old Judge had known it. His father had known it. It amazed him that he'd veered so drastically off course.

He went home every two and half hours to give Carol her medication and spend a few minutes visiting with her. He had reinstituted the weekly firearm inspection. He filled the jugs in the fallout shelter with fresh water. He took the police radio out of the house and returned it to the station. He hired two shifts of nurses and insisted that Lester get out and have some fun. Call Alice, he told him. Lester said she wouldn't talk to him. Then go meet another girl, he said, relieved, not that he'd thought she was a bad influence on Les, but she certainly couldn't have been a positive one, not with all her family's troubles.

One day Lester went to the rectory and asked to speak with Father Gannon. He said he finally understood his life's calling. He wanted to be a priest. Father Gannon advised him to wait until he was older, until he'd experienced life a little more. Shocked and disappointed, Lester made an appointment with the Monsignor, who put Lester in immediate contact with a pious young seminary counselor in Saint Albans. The Monsignor leaned across his desk and told Father Gannon that he was never, ever to give such twisted advice to a young man again. The office door slammed. The kitchen door slammed.

Howard looked up from the hedge he was trimming to see Father Gannon sit down on the steps and light a cigarette. Howard had never smoked. He liked the smell of cigarette smoke, but no one else did, especially not the Monsignor, who had banned the unpriestly habit from his rectory.

"So how was your trip to see Perda?" Father Gannon asked, rolling the perfect white ash off his cigarette.

"It was okay," Howard said, pleased that Father had remembered his cousin's name. Most people couldn't even remember Howard's name.

"How'd Miss Brastus like the trip? You two have fun together?"

"She didn't like it too much." Howard's voice quavered. He wished he'd never told Father Gannon about Lucille. He lowered his head to the angle of shrubbery he continued to clip. It hurt to talk about it. Actually Lucille had said it was the worst time of her life.

"How come?"

"Too depressing there, she said."

"Really? Well, where does Perda live?"

"Waterbury," Howard said.

"Waterbury?" He took a long drag on his cigarette, all the while peering down at Howard. "You mean the state mental hospital?"

"Yah. That's where Perda lives. She's got the mind of a baby."

"Howard! That's not where you go on a first date!"

He couldn't tell if Father Gannon was surprised or amused. "It wasn't a first date. Me and Jozia always used to go see Perda."

"I know, but with Miss Brastus it was a date."

"It was?"

"Of course. Now you have to make it up to her. You have to take her on a real date."

"I do?"

"Yes, Howard! To a movie or out dancing. Women like that. They want to be fussed over. They like to get all dressed up and go somewhere nice—not to a mental institution." Father Gannon got up and ground out his cigarette. "Ask her. You'll see."

The tender branch tips fluttered to the grass as Howard's clippers scissored along the hedge. He didn't think he could do that. Besides, she and him hadn't spoken a word since the bus back late that night, when he'd tried to give her the extra plastic paperweight he'd saved for her. It was the prettiest one. Inside was a yellow flower that sprayed red droplets through the water when it was shaken.

"No, thank you," she'd said. "I think Perda would enjoy it a lot more than me."

Late in the afternoon Mr. Briscoe came into Marie's office. He sat on the edge of Astrid's desk, his legs outstretched and rigid, his arms folded. He seemed so ill at ease that for a moment Marie thought he'd come in to fire her. But of course he couldn't very well do that now that Astrid had quit. This morning Marie had been a half hour late for work, and then in her haste to make up for it, she had messed up his biggest ski boot order, which was going to mean a six-week delay in delivery.

Omar had shown up at ten-thirty last night, his trunk and back seat a jumble of boxes and bottles of detergent that he'd managed to talk the Presto shipping clerk into letting him take early. Thinking it was her shipment, she told Benjy to help him carry it into the kitchen so she could get a head start on attaching the promotional pamphlets. But then Omar said she could only take six of each. "A good-faith delivery," he called it, just enough to give her the feel of the product. The rest had to be parceled out among his other distributors. She couldn't believe it. She had paid a thousand dollars for *that*? she asked, pointing. Six bottles and six boxes?

"Your sarcasm is falling on deaf ears, Marie. I'm too tired," Omar had sighed, fanning himself with one of the shiny brochures.

Sarcasm! Sarcasm! Try shock, she'd shouted, as he hurried out to his car, then drove off.

Mr. Briscoe was having a hard time getting to the point. His employees' financial matters were their own affair and he never interfered. But he was so stunned by what Cleveland Hinds had just told him on the phone that he felt obligated to speak to her. The gray lightless space pulled closer around them. Was it true, Mr. Briscoe was asking, that she had borrowed a substantial amount of money from the Atkinson Savings Bank and had not only missed the first payment, but had made no attempt to discuss the situation with Cleveland Hinds? What could she say, that she thought someone had paid it for her, that Omar had assured her he would take care of it, had promised he would? Her hands wouldn't stop shaking. The kids were right. Every word out of his mouth was a lie.

Renie was polishing stove tops with a special cream. It smelled of pine needles. He reached up and dabbed some across his throat, then rubbed it in. His clothes reeked of last night's dinner, vinegary tripe. Bending over his reflection in the gleaming enamel, he wet his fingers and pressed his bushy eyebrows smooth. But nothing was working. Nothing made him feel any better.

"Hello, my esteemed brother Elk," boomed a voice over the bells on the opening door. He turned to see Cleveland Hinds. "With all the publicity you've been getting I figured you'd be in Hollywood or something by now."

"How are you doing, Mr. Hinds?" Renie said as Hinds pumped his hand heartily. *Oh to be able to shake a man's hand like that,* he thought, *to have such exuberance, such confidence.*

"Busier than hell, Renie. Busier than hell," he sighed, removing his straw hat.

"That's good," Renie said.

Hinds ran his hand over the stove, streaking it. He turned a few buttons, opened the oven door and peered inside. Renie's heart fluttered. It was the deluxe model. "Automatic timer and shutoff," he said, growing short of breath. "Put in a roast, play eighteen holes, and it's ready when you're ready. And this plug here's for the automatic coffee." He plugged in the pot that came with the stove. He hoped he remembered all the features. He felt dizzy. "Put in your ground coffee, set it for a half hour before you want to wake up in the morning, and not only does it start itself and perk a wonderful pot of coffee, but it wakes you up to beautiful music." He twirled a dial, then smiled up at Hinds as the *William Tell* Overture jumped from the console.

Hinds took a monogrammed handkerchief from his pocket and wiped his brow. "Listen, Renie, I hate to bother you. I don't want to take up too much of your time," he said.

"No bother, Mr. Hinds. Actually this particular model sells itself," Renie said, straightening up. "Once people get over the first shock of the cost."

"The thing is, Renie, there's a matter that needs discussion. It's . . . it's rather delicate."

Renie took a deep breath and reached for his wallet. He'd just give him the money back for his wife's toaster.

"Toaster? What toaster?" Hinds said, looking around, and then Renie understood. The bank owned this building and they were probably mad about the paint job. He knew he should have asked them first. And now that it looked so good they were probably going to raise his rent. Maybe they'd found out about the cat. Well, he wasn't going to get rid of Tom. No sir. He scrubbed Mr. Hinds's fingermarks off the stove top. They'd have to kick him and Tom both out.

Hinds held the handkerchief to his temple. He spoke slowly, wincing as if the words hurt. "I shouldn't be telling you this, it's of such a confidential nature, but it's been bothering the hell out of me. It's Marie Fermoyle, your sister-in-law—well, former sister-in-law.

She came in awhile back for a loan. Now as you know, Renie, we're a conservative institution, and with her situation being what it is, I had to say no."

He nodded, though he had no idea what Hinds was getting at.

"But then because of you, Renie, because I wanted to do the right thing by a fellow brother Elk, I said okay." His eyes shot into Renie's. "Well, didn't she get mad as hell and right up on her high horse, something about a washing machine and how every time it broke down you charged her for repairs."

"I gave her the machine at cost," he said. "And I only ever charged for parts, what it cost me. I'd never try and make a dime off Marie and those kids! They're family!"

Hinds held up his hand. "I know that, Renie. You don't have to tell me. I'm just trying to give you the whole story here so you'll see what a mess we've got on our hands, you and me."

"Mess?"

"You cosigned that note, Renie. You didn't want Helen to know, remember?"

Renie shook his head. At the time Helen and Bridget had told Marie the only way they would ever help her was if she took Sam back and stopped the divorce proceedings. Cosigning Marie's note behind their backs had been the most daring deed of his life. Nothing before or since had ever made him feel so powerful and so good. But then he'd ruined it by acting like a fool the night with the turkey, and Marie had despised him ever since.

"To make a long story short, if she can't make the payments, then we have no choice but to sue and put an attachment on the house." Cleveland Hinds wet his lips. "And of course now with your name on the new loan, and she hasn't even made the first payment—well, that's why I'm here, Renie. To see what you intend to do about this."

"Me? I never signed for any new loan."

"Well, it's right here," Hinds said, unfolding a thick document on the stove top.

"That's not my name," Renie said.

Hinds looked at it. "Of course it's your name!"

"I mean how I write my signature," Renie cried. "Somebody else wrote my name on that. Not me!"

"Wait a minute now. Just wait a minute," Hinds puffed as he flipped back through the typewritten pages. "Oh my Lord," he groaned, laying two forms side by side to compare signatures. "You're right." He looked up. "She forged your name! She falsified a bank document, a legal instrument of commerce. She could go to jail for this. She *should* go to jail, that little—"

"But when she signed my name, how come you didn't say anything?" Renie asked, puzzled.

Hinds cleared his throat, explaining how he hadn't actually seen the signing because he'd trusted Marie and given her the note to bring here to Renie. "Of course, now I know I never should have let her take the instrument from the bank, but to be honest, in a small town, things like this happen all the time in banking. You bend rules, you go around corners. You try to help people. In the long run it's usually good business." Hinds was pacing back and forth. "And damn it, I should have known, the way she was so nervous and shaky when she signed." Hinds waved his hand in disgust. "I'm sorry, Renie. This is my fault. I'll just let the Chief take over now and let the chips fall where they may."

"How much is the loan for?" Renie asked.

"One thousand dollars." Hinds choked out the words.

"If you got a pen, I'll sign the loan."

Hinds looked at him. "Are you serious, Renie?"

"Yah, I don't want Marie going to jail, do you?"

"No! God, no!" Hinds had given him a pen.

He bent over the stove, startled by the cold metal against his belly as he signed his name

"Believe me, Renie, I won't forget this," Hinds said, folding the document. He sighed. " 'Course, we've still got the problem of the late payment."

Renie stared at him. We? He didn't know what to say.

"I'll tell you what," Hinds said with a wave of dismissal. "I'll call her. We'll see what she says." Hinds patted his shoulder. "I'm going way out on the limb here, but we'll work this out."

"I appreciate it," Renie said.

"Well, I know you do," Hinds said.

"You've always been good to me, Mr. Hinds. Like the loan for all the fans last year." He smiled, expecting praise for paying that loan off in half the time.

"And the tax money," Hinds reminded him.

"Most of all, that," Renie said, his stomach suddenly churning with the sense that it might all be connected. Cosigning the mortgage and the humiliating audit with the IRS had both happened the same year, the same year he won the turkey at the Elks' Christmas raffle and brought it to Marie's house. It was late and he'd been drinking. He remembered her standing in the doorway in her pajamas looking grateful and confused. She told him how her father had always brought the turkey home the night before Christmas. In the snowy darkness a wild joy had risen in him and he'd staggered closer, seizing her arms and pressing his mouth over hers. She had pushed him down the steps and sworn at him as he ran to his car. Could it have been her, he wondered, Marie Fermoyle, who had turned him in to the IRS? She'd probably collected some kind of a reward, blood money off the one person who cared for her.

"You're a good man, Renie," Hinds said, with an even more vigorous shake of his hand. "A real solid citizen."

No, I'm not, he thought as he watched Hinds head down the sidewalk, tipping his hat to the ladies and stopping to shake eager hands all along the bright busy street.

The next day, Marie stood at her kitchen counter, jaw clenched as she tenderized a chuck steak with a wooden mallet, the red fleshy *whack whack whack* grimly satisfying. Norm sat at the table telling her and Benjy about the trouble in the park today. It had started with a couple of kids leaning on Joey's stand and Joey warning them to get away before it collapsed. When a few more kids came and began to taunt him by deliberately shaking the stand, Joey started hurling soda bottles and cans at them. Some of the bottles smashed on the sidewalk, and then when the kids tried to sneak up behind him, he'd turned and thrown more bottles at them as they fled across West Street. Some of the bottles smashed in the road and one even dented the hood of a woman's car.

"What a mess," Norm said. "Greenie sent a crew up, and they had to stop traffic so we could broom all the broken glass. And then Chief Stoner came, and he was talking to Joey and trying to get him to go home in the cruiser, but Joey refused."

"That poor man," she said, flipping over the steak to pound the other side. "That's what happens. The minute you're down, the slightest crack they see, they're all over you." She knew by their silence they were probably exchanging glances. Let them. Someday they'd know; when the dogs were nipping at their heels, then they'd understand all she'd been through for them. Once again she thought of that goddamn Cleveland Hinds calling Mr. Briscoe about her loan. *And that goddamn Omar and goddamn Sam, all the no-good, goddamn bastards,* beat the rhythm of the pounding mallet. There wasn't any kindness in this life. None. None at all.

"Joey said they'd have to arrest him to make him leave, that he was only trying to protect his property," Norm said. "And then this lady that lives by the park starts screaming that it's not his property, that he's nothing but a charity case and she's sick of having to see that shack out her front window twelve months a year, and maybe everyone else was afraid to speak up, but she wasn't."

"Wow," Benjy said. "Sounds like a show or something."

"Bastards!" she said, pounding the meat, pounding it, and pounding it.

"Mom! Mom!" Norm said, tapping her shoulder. "Someone's here."

She spun around, shocked to see Cleveland Hinds in the back doorway. She hadn't heard him knocking.

"Hello, Marie," Hinds said with a smile.

"What do you want?" She almost hadn't gotten that out. The nerve of him, coming here after he'd called Mr. Briscoe.

"Well, I was on my way home and I was going by here . . ."

"It's a dead-end street!" she said.

"Well, in a manner of speaking, going by. In any event I thought I'd stop by and see how the repairs are coming along." He glanced up at the stained ceiling, then down at the cracked floor tiles.

"Norm," she said, conscious of her sons' rapt attention. "I need milk." She pressed the money into his hand and told him to take

Benjy with him. "Go," she ordered, as he stood there staring at her. "Now!"

They kept looking back as they headed out the door.

"Nice-looking boys," Hinds said, loosening his tie and undoing his collar button. He stood by the table, smiling at her. "I'm glad you sent them on an errand. This way we can talk," he said, sitting down at the table.

She remained standing. "How could you come here? How do you have the nerve after what you did?"

"What I did?" he asked.

"Calling my boss! Discussing my business with Mr. Briscoe! You had no right to do that! You could have called me!"

He closed his eyes with a sigh, then told her he had taken the liberty of speaking to Mr. Briscoe because he cared about what happened here, and he hoped he might save her any future embarrassment. He took out a cigarette and lit it.

"You care so much, then maybe I should take the liberty of speaking to Mrs. Hinds to save *her* any future embarrassment!" She banged the table, startled to see her hand and wrist speckled with bits of raw meat and blood.

"I'm shocked," he said, gulping on the smoke he'd just inhaled. His eyes watered. "Shocked that you'd say such a thing. Especially under the circumstances." He kept clearing his throat. "You may not think so, but what you did is a crime."

"What?" She sagged back against the counter. "What are you talking about?"

"I'm talking about signing Renie's name on the note. That's forgery, Marie," he said.

She opened her mouth, but for a moment couldn't speak. This wasn't happening. She hadn't done such a thing. Had she? Had she? She had tried too hard for too long to be strong, and now she would pay. Merciless, they would swoop down, one by one, pecking, nicking her battered hide until she bled, until she could only crawl, until there was nothing left.

"Marie? Marie, listen. I'm sure we can work this out." He got up and stood close to her. "There are ways and ways of meeting one's obligations. But the most important thing is that we don't stop communicating. Listen, Marie," he crooned as she stared up at him, "we've got to talk about this, so why don't we meet sometime next week, oh in some quiet, nonbusiness setting where the two of us can move this thing back and forth a little. And that way, I know what's going on in your life, and you'll feel more comfortable dealing with me. What say?" He flashed a grin. "Tuesday? Wednesday? Let's make it Thursday night! Sevenish. We can meet at the—"

"What do you want?" she demanded. "Tell me what you want me to do."

"It's what I don't want, Marie. I don't want to see you in trouble over this. Our connection goes too far back."

"What're you talking about? We have no connection!"

"Well, you know. Sam, Nora." He grinned. "You know what I mean."

"Get out!" Her hand moved to the mallet. "Get out before my sons come back."

It was the next morning, and Omar Duvall lay in Bernadette's bedroom. The thin plastic window shade sagged with heat. In the other room Bernadette and her daughters were singing "Itsy Bitsy Spider" as she dressed them in bathing suits. The paper sack by the front door contained sandwiches and Kool-Aid she'd made for their day at the lake. He didn't want to go, but it was a promise he'd already broken twice. At the screech of the little girls' laughter he shuddered. His legs ached, and his heart was sore, actually tender now as he touched his breast. Each time Roy Gold had promised delivery he'd come away not only believing but inflamed, inspired, convinced that it was only a matter of time before the soap came. It wasn't enough just to impress Gold; he wanted to dazzle him, and so he had invested most of his distributors' money and his own. He wanted to be the best franchise supervisor Gold had. He had sold thirty-four franchises, with just about every cent of it going to Gold, and now the man wouldn't see him, wouldn't take his calls. His last trip to Westport he had to sleep in his car and slip out on diner tabs, and all he'd come away with was a carful of battered bottles and dented soapboxes, which he had begged from a warehouse worker.

"Is it because you're so swamped with orders?" Omar had asked, blowing dust off a bottle.

"Nah," the worker had scoffed. "Just one of them cease-and-desist deals. They come shut everything down. A few weeks go by, and we start up again."

How had this happened? he wondered. A few weeks! Everywhere he went, people wanted their soap, none more desperate now than Marie. Last night when he tried to make her see how bad things were, when he needed to confide in someone, she'd thrown him out of her house. She was giving him twenty-four hours to either return her money or deliver her soap, or else she was going to go to the police.

He rose up on his elbows, clutching his chest. This pain wasn't fear of the police, but his dread of having to move on again, a life of running and hiding, curled up to sleep on the front seat. These last few days he had been racked with hungers that food and comfort could no longer assuage. The worst deprivation would be losing Marie.

Bernadette's and her daughters' giddy voices rose against the door. "We're ready!" she cried, throwing it open. They were dressed in bright bathing suits with bright beach towels over their arms, their smiles so eager, so voracious, that he felt sick to his stomach. He hurried into the bathroom, where he splashed water on his unshaven face. As he reached for a towel he noticed the sparkle of light from the toothpaste-smeared shelf over the sink. He slipped the ring onto his pinkie finger and stepped closer to the window to examine the tiny diamond in the light.

When he came out of the bathroom he told Bernadette that he didn't feel up to going.

"Tough shit," she growled. "You promised, and that's all there is to it."

"But I have this pain," he said, wincing as he probed the tenderness in his chest.

"I don't care if you're having a fucking heart attack, they think they're going swimming, and that's where they're going."

They waited by the door with their sand pails and plastic boats, watching as hard-eyed as their mother as he buttoned his shirt. He bent to tie his shoes and pain shot down his arms to his fingertips.

"You're going like that?" Bernadette asked, pointing as he put on his rumpled suit jacket.

"It's all I have," he said.

"I have to go to the bathroom," Noelle cried, legs crossed and squirming.

"Then go!" Bernadette said, and Noelle ran into the bathroom.

"I can't!" the child cried. "I'm tied."

"Help her," Bernadette ordered the older girl. "Untie her bathing suit."

Merry ran into the bathroom.

"What're you gonna do, sit on the beach in your suit all day?" she asked, setting down the bulging grocery bag. "There must be something of Kyle's that'd fit you," she said, hurrying into the bedroom.

In the bathroom the little girls' voices rose querulously. Bernadette returned with a pair of red plaid shorts. "Come on!" she called, opening the bathroom door to find Merry kicking towels through the yellow puddle on the floor. "Goddamn it," Bernadette cried, shaking Noelle, who was patting dry her wet bathing suit and dripping legs with a washcloth. Bernadette grabbed the washcloth and wet it in the sink, then knelt to scrub the sobbing child's plump legs. Her head shot up, and then she stood suddenly, gripping the grimy glass shelf. Her cry of loss had an oddly soothing effect on Omar. The pain was gone. He felt stronger, more confident. So here it was, another impulsive action now so imbued with plausibility that he understood, with perfect clarity and unshakable faith, its purpose.

"You bastard, you little bastard!" she cried, shaking one child and slapping the other. "What did you do with it? What did you do with my ring, my beautiful diamond ring?"

"Nothing! Honest, Mommy!"

"It's down here, isn't it?" She clutched the chipped rim with both hands, grunting and pulling as if to tear the sink from the wall. "You dropped it down the sink! My future, my whole life!"

"Now, Bernadette," he said softly. "They're children. They meant no harm."

It was early evening. Marie's car was gone and her house was locked. Omar cupped his hands to his eyes and peered through the dusty windows. The television was off and the table was set for three. He came around the back of the house, wading through the tall grass. On the clothesline, which had begun to sag again, the clothes were already dry. As he unpinned them, he began to worry that she might have done something as reckless as driving to Westport for a personal confrontation with Roy Gold. Yes. She was just that impetuous and headstrong. He paused with a stiff towel bunched at his chest as he pictured those big eyes boring into Gold as she demanded her thousand dollars back. He would be so stirred by her pluck that he would get her soap sent out that day. He would fill all of Omar's orders. One could never know good fortune's spur. How many other times had despair turned out to be the first step, the bottom rung of joy.

Oh God, yes. He could feel it in his chest, the familiar swelling, this profound and ennobling exuberance reminding him once again that he was no ordinary man.

"Mr. Duvall! Mr. Duvall, I'd like a word with you," Harvey Klubock called as he tried to hurry down his back steps. Harvey limped toward him.

Omar set the laundry on a broken lawn chair. Harvey wanted to know about his soap order, not that he was having any second thoughts, he added; it was Jessie. "You know how women are. They think everything's a risk."

Omar told of a warehouse so busy the trucks waited all day in long lines to be filled. He told of a company parking lot jam-packed with the expensive cars of loyal but exhausted employees. "It's just too much success, too much good fortune all at once," he said. Now as he was describing Roy Gold's estate with its serpentine brick walls and glowing ponds, he realized that Jessie stood in the doorway above them, listening, her soft mouth parted. "Is he married?" she asked with that hesitation he found so touching in women.

"No," he said with a rueful smile. "All that good fortune and no one to share it with."

"That's sad, isn't it?" she sighed.

"Not necessarily," Harvey said with a reproving glance.

"Well, I think it is!" she said. "Not that my opinion matters, of course."

"Looks like you got some sun today," Harvey said, turning his back on his wife.

Omar touched his neck, surprised to find the skin so prickly and hot. He'd spent the afternoon at the lake consoling Bernadette while he tried to keep an eye on Merry and Noelle. It just wasn't fair, she'd sobbed, explaining that the ring had been bought with proceeds from the very break-in Kyle had gone to prison for, an irony that for Omar only further justified his possession of it now. When they got back from the lake he'd tried to make her feel a little better by explaining how an item with any weight to it might end up in the sink trap, which someone with the right-size wrench could open for her. She had run barefoot down the alley to use the phone in the fruit store to call Kyle's brother Blue to come and fish her ring out of the trap. Poor thing; it pleased him to have given her that hope, even though her ring was now an insignificance so easily transportable by even the weakest stream that it was certainly gone forever.

Jessie and Harvey's son, Louis, opened the door and called to his mother for ice cream. His eyes fixed on Omar.

"Do you know where Marie might be?" Omar asked Jessie.

"I think they went for a ride, she and the boys," she said, adding brightly, "They should be right back."

"I noticed the table's still set. They haven't had supper yet." His stomach was growling.

"They—" Jessie began.

"They had a big fight," Louis interrupted his mother. "Norm ran out and then Benjy . . ."

"Louis!" she said.

"Louis!" his father echoed.

". . . and then Mrs. Fermoyle went speeding down the street in the car."

"Louis, you don't know that," Jessie scolded. She looked at Omar. "I'm sure they'll be right back."

"It's not easy raising children alone," Harvey said. "That woman's got her hands full."

"They're nice kids." Jessie looked at Omar. "They really are!" she said, as if to convince him.

"The older boy's been difficult lately," Omar conceded.

"Well, let me tell you, if they were mine, they'd be toeing the mark. I'd have 'em out there right now fixing that place up." Harvey waved his arms in disgust. "No excuse for that. None at all."

"Harvey! I can't believe you're saying this."

"Well, it's the truth. It's so bad every neighbor on this street's—"

"Harvey Klubock, shut your mouth!" Jessie cried. "Just shut it right now!"

Harvey stared at his wife in astonishment.

"Look! There they are!" Louis called over the deafening rumble turning into the driveway.

It was an old pea-green car that couldn't have had a muffler. A coil of rope held one side of the front bumper in place. What at first appeared to be mud splatters were actually rust pocks. Norm drove with Marie beside him and Benjy in the back seat.

It was almost midnight and Marie's hands were still shaking. Last week Norm had taken fifty dollars from his savings account to buy a car, a '49 Chevy, from a man he worked with. She hadn't known about it until tonight, when she told him she had to borrow money from him after all. She needed it for the late loan payment as well for this month's. Because he hadn't dared tell her, he'd been keeping the car at Weeb's house. Every night when she thought he was visiting Weeb, whose legs were in casts, he'd actually been driving his junk of a car around town. She'd told him that he couldn't keep the car. He had to get the money back. That was impossible, he'd said. The car was already registered in his name. Impossible, she'd cried, almost insane with rage and panic. Nothing, nothing in this world was impossible! She'd demanded that Norm call the man and tell him he wanted his money back. He refused. He couldn't.

"What's the man's name?" She'd picked up the phone.

"Mom! Please!"

"What's his name?"

"Bob Hersey, but you can't—"

"Bob Hersey!" She'd known him as a kid. "Well, that idiot has another thing coming if he thinks he's going to pawn that piece of junk off on my son!" she'd panted as she flipped frenziedly through the phone book, ripping half the pages. She'd get the money back, goddamn it! Why was she humiliating him like this? Norm had groaned as she dialed. After Hersey had gotten over his initial confusion, he said he was sorry, but he'd already spent Norm's money to buy another car. He'd still been talking when she slammed down the phone.

"Now you've done it with your selfishness! With your stupidity!" she'd screamed at Norm.

"Jesus, Mom! I have to work with him! I could lose my job!" Norm had said in a high shaky voice.

"Lose your job! Thanks to you we're going to lose our home!"

"Home!" he'd laughed, tears running down his work-grimed cheeks. "This isn't a home, it's a nuthouse, and I'm getting the hell out!"

"Go! And keep on going!" she'd yelled through the front door as he stalked down the street, his head hanging, his pant legs and sneakers green with grass clippings.

Benjy had run after Norm, begging him to come back. And then she was speeding down the street after the two of them, the car bucking as she took the corner on squealing tires, with all the neighbors at their windows watching Marie Fermoyle's life fall apart faster and faster, like some crazy spinning top that would not stop until it had disintegrated.

Her car had broken down on Main Street. She still had a year of payments on it. The transmission was gone and there was no money to fix it, she was explaining now to Omar. They sat on the couch, the television on, the volume barely audible for privacy. Benjy and Norm had gone to bed, and as usual Alice still wasn't home.

"Have faith, Marie," Omar whispered. "Please."

"Faith," she gasped, laughing. She couldn't help it. Faith? Faith in what? Everything she'd ever tried to believe in had failed—her marriage, her kids, her house, her car; she was even doing such a lousy job at work she wouldn't be surprised if Mr. Briscoe let her go, and now the franchise was a disaster. So what was left? Did he have any ideas?

He sighed, his face buried in his hands, the light from the television flickering over them. "I'm sorry, Marie. This is all my fault. If you hadn't believed in me, if you hadn't listened to me, then you wouldn't be in this dilemma."

"Dilemma!" she cried, throwing her head back on the couch. "No! Disaster, Omar! This is a full-fledged, out-and-out disaster."

He looked at her. "I'm sorry. I don't know what else to say."

She knew that wasn't fair. He'd tried to help when no one else even cared. But she was tired now, too drained for this. He was trying to explain it all again, how they'd bought into the business right at the boom, and now with such a massive glut of orders . . .

"I know," she said. "You told me. But I'm tired. I am so, so tired." She stood up, and he reached for her hand.

"Marie," he said in a choked voice.

Let them take the house, the car, she thought. Let Alice go hide in a convent if that's what she was up to. It had to be a hell of a lot simpler life than this one. Norm could have his shitbox of a car and his beer and his brawls. And Benjy . . . Oh God, she had to be strong, had to . . . Why was Omar rubbing her finger like that? He was trying to work a ring over her knuckle. The stone glittered in the dim light. She held it close to her face. Peering at it, she asked what it was, though there could be no doubt. It was a diamond.

"An engagement ring," he said.

She looked at him. "An engagement ring," she repeated numbly.

"Yes," he said, nodding and smiling up at her. "That's exactly what it is."

Later, as Omar sat on the edge of her bed, putting on his socks, her voice moved through the darkness, like the blades of the tillers he'd walked behind as a child, watching the sweat plaster his father's dun-colored undershirt to his puny back, and all the time, his father's voice dragging him along, shallow and dead like the earth he turned spring after spring, promising magnificent harvests that were in the end no more than enough bushels of beets and carrots and corn to get them through another gray winter. One morning when he was fourteen he just up and left. And all along the way, until now, he'd moved through what he felt was the fine clarity of his intuition, his imagination and great foresight. Throughout his passage he'd always emerged unscathed from misfortune. So great did he believe his promise and vision to be that after all these years he still hadn't reconciled the disorder and the poverty of his youth with that brilliance he believed life held out to him. He sat here now, shocked by what he'd just done; the ring he'd taken to sell had become a marriage proposal, a jail sentence.

In moments like this, futility doused his soul like a sudden powerful rain. He was getting old, his feet swelling in the heat, the strangle of phlegm rising to choke him as he slept. His eyes were rheumy and pink-lidded. He was tired. But maybe he could do this, could lie down on this thin bed night after night. He could mow the lawn and paint this house. Maybe sell soap out of the garage. After a while he might even rent space downtown and get into hardware. He'd always believed in hardware. All across this great country men were building porches, toolsheds, garages, and if not, they would soon be dreaming of building something as they picked up one of Duvall's Miracle Ratchet wrenches—oh, he could just picture it—to hang on their workshop pegboard.

Yes! He could do it. He could stay here and never leave.

She switched on the light, and his eyes stung.

"It's beautiful," she whispered. She held up her hand. "But I don't know how the kids are going to take it."

"Just you be patient now," he whispered, leaning back to pat her cheek. "Let's just make sure the time's right. Let's wait."

"Wait! Wait for what?" She started to sit up.

"Till the soap comes," he said. "Then maybe they'll have a little more faith in me." He stood up and looked down at her. "And I'll have a little more faith in me, too."

Renie had called someone who knew someone at the new paper goods plant, and Sam had been hired third shift. It hadn't taken him long to hate the job. He found it demeaning. Every night as he walked to work in these dingy green coveralls and rubber-soled boots, there was a knot in his stomach. Educated men did not wear coveralls and boots that squeaked with every step. He had read everything F. Scott Fitzgerald had ever written. Here he was, a toilet paper loader, and there was nothing about love and life and beauty he did not know, did not contemplate here on top of this yellow loader, its wide rubber track vibrating so that his teeth clattered as it rumbled back and forth between the steel ramp and the conveyor belt that carried the enormous cartons into the warehouse, where they would be loaded onto trucks in the morning.

He threw the loader into neutral, then paused, staring at the hundreds of cartons piled to the mesh ceiling. It would take all night. No. The way to look at it was in stages. Parts of things, fragments. The whole did not exist. There was only here, only this moment, the shifting gears, the first carton, the next carton. One wall cleared, then the other. One step at a time; one foot in front of the other. *You are your own meager invention, Sam Fermoyle.* He backed up, shifted, rumbled toward the nearest stack. He was thinking of Alice. Thin-faced now and resentful, when once she'd been such a sweet child. When he carried her she used to hold on by slipping her hand down the back of his shirt collar. His children would punish him now. They grew older, more powerful. They could destroy him now, could walk right out of his life when he needed them most, more than he had ever needed them before. He would have to make them understand. What? That it hadn't been his fault. That he had been afraid. That he could never face the wholeness, because it always seemed so grim, so pointless, when failure was the only certainty, the one true wholeness of which he was capable. No, no, no, no. That was the trouble with this job. Too quiet, too much time to think. Suddenly he was afraid. His hand felt instinctively for the ignition. Turn it off if he wanted. Walk right out of here. He could find a pint or a nip somewhere. Anytime day or night he could find some, if he wanted, whatever he wanted. That was the trouble, everyone laughing. A one-hundred-percent, one-hundred-proof riot, Sam Fermoyle. All his life trying to make people laugh. Couldn't stand sadness, even hated daylight because of the way it magnified sadness. Water splashing in the bathroom, bacon frying. The brilliant glare of noon, the harshness, the boredom. The dinner hour building, the holocaust of their scorn, their disappointment. Pass the butter, please. Eyes on the plate. The tension weakening him. And when he could not make them laugh or love him, settling for pity.

His teeth ached, rotted in his head. When he yawned or coughed he could even smell them. When he had talked to the plant manager about the job, he'd held his hand to his mouth. The manager came right out with it and asked if he'd tried AA. Tried everything, he'd said, grinning, briefly forgetting the teeth. Tried AA and God and Sterno and straitjackets, and I'm just going to try me. The manager had looked away, hadn't laughed. Why the hell should he?

His first break came at three a.m. The night watchman came into the storeroom and offered him a cigarette. A bandy-legged old fellow with bright eyes and the white fuzz of unshaven whiskers, he glanced slyly from Sam to the door he had just bolted.

"They don't allow smoking in here," he wheezed, "but I'm careful enough." He held out a tin can of swollen cigarette butts floating in brown water that served as an ashtray. Sam turned down the cigarette. He'd rather go outside and smoke alone.

"So you're the new loader," the old man said, taking a deep drag.

"I'm the new loader," he said, anxious to get back up onto the machine and start the engine. He didn't like the empty sounds of the factory, the creak of wood, the persistent clanging somewhere of a pipe, the hiss of steam.

"A quick one," the old man was saying, sucking his gums, holding out the half pint of blackberry brandy. "Go ahead."

He shook his head, climbing quickly back onto the loader, turned it on. The motor roared and shimmied, its rumble oddly comforting. The old man tilted the bottle back, closing his eyes as he drank. When he was done he wiped his mouth with the back of his hand and blinked, eyes glistening as if he were on fire inside. Dying and alive, Sam knew. He looked away, afraid. It fizzed in his brain like flashing bulbs, like anger, hunger, this thirst, this need, this painless death where the mourners round the bier offered total absolution: *He was drunk. What did he know?* Right. *He knows not what he does. He didn't mean it,* chorus to his mother's dying litany. He didn't mean it. I know he ripped apart your lawn and knocked down your brand-new fence and smashed up your son's car, impregnated your eighteen-year-old daughter, spit in your face, stole the rents, hurled a bottle through the movie screen, set your newspaper on fire while you were reading it, passed out and vomited at his own sister's desperate and pitiful wedding, has never lasted a full year at any job, has cheated and lied, hastened the death of his father, has struck his wife, resented not only his children's needs but their existence as well, their very being, each birth terrifying him, diminishing him, but he didn't mean it. You see, he was drunk. Such power he had when he was drunk. That was it, he thought, seeing the old man shuffle through the door. Like someone who's dying, his mother, or a sick child. *Read to me, play with me, sing to me, don't go. I'm afraid of the dark. If you leave me, something terrible will happen. At least leave the door open.* Marie was the only one left. One by one they had tired of him. All his life there had been no end of people anxious to rehabilitate him. Pick up the pieces. Sober him up. Forgive him. *You were drunk. You didn't mean it. I didn't mean it.*

He called Marie today to tell her about his job, but her reaction had been disappointing. Her voice was different. The edge was gone, the nervous little tremble in her words, the caring, the hope, the sorrow, had been replaced by boredom, annoyance. He had become a nuisance. He thought he heard her yawn.

"I'm a changed man," he'd whispered into the phone.

What else is new? she might as well have said. She told him she didn't have much time. She was in the middle of something. She hung up. She didn't need him anymore, weak or strong. She just didn't need him.

There would be only Helen left. Waiting, reeling him in, closer each time, the line fraying and thinning, her lure that money as she devoted her life to his doom. And it was funny, really; as a child he had adored her, been desperate for her love, had leaped from trees and the pitched roof of the shed screaming, "Look, Helen, look!" Actually he'd had two mothers, the crimp-souled, stiff-eyed older sister, plain and sharp-tongued without love or humor, determined that he would have the upbringing she had endured. And the mother, mellowed enough by time and frustration and recognizing in her spinster daughter the folly of prayers, parsimony, and manners, allowing her late-born son every whim in the name of love, celebrating him, always looking the other way, and when he was in trouble she would weep at the thought that he might have been offended or injured by his accuser.

The sun had scoured its way through the high sooty windows of the storeroom. It was six o'clock. Four empty walls. He was done, all of the hundreds of cartons moved onto the loading platform, ready for shipment.

It was over. He walked home, exhilarated by the sweetness of damp, curling grass and cool asphalt. Windows were open in the houses he passed. He could smell bacon frying. A baby cried. Ahead, the milk truck rattled from stop to stop. The milkman dashed up each front walk, the glass bottles jiggling in his metal carrier. At one house a woman stooped through the open door, reaching for her newspaper, clutching the front of her bathrobe, aluminum curlers bobbing from her head. She saw him, stepped quickly back and closed the door. He smiled, rounded the corner home.

From her window Helen watched uneasily, peering down at his jaunty gait, alert for any sign that he had been drinking again.

———

Renie put the cat in the basement. "I won't be gone too long," he called as he turned the dead bolt. The cat meowed against the door. "You be a good Tom now, and when I get back we'll have us a nice big lunch."

He'd seen Mr. Cushing's car pull into the lot across the street two hours ago, but it had taken all this time to work up his courage. This was the fourth morning in a row he'd locked Tom in the cellar, then stood by the front door with the ledger under his arm. All his years of faithful record keeping, all the times he'd rushed out to help another old woman who'd slipped and fallen on the ice in Cushing's lot, not to mention all the cars he'd jump-started over there, all the door locks he'd fished open with his specially fashioned coat hanger, and this was his reward, to have the Golden Toastee line stolen right out from under his nose. No sir, it just wasn't fair. He was past the depression and the brooding, and now he was just plain mad. He marched out the door, but the minute he was on the sidewalk he wanted to run back inside. He took a deep breath. He had to do this. He crossed the street.

"Floor, please?" inquired Arlo, Cushing's elevator boy, as he pulled the door shut. Arlo wasn't a boy, but an old man, a contemporary of Patrick Cushing's. Arlo had started as Cushing's delivery boy. Through the years he had served in almost every position Cushing's offered. Now, the same driver who brought Mr. Cushing to work also picked up Arlo.

"Mr. Cushing's office, whatever floor's that," answered Renie. Sweat ran down his temples.

"That would be four, sir," said Arlo, his back turned. "Fourth door on the right."

They stared up at the brass arrow inching its way from two to three to four.

Renie walked slowly down the narrow corridor, counting the doors. He knocked and was surprised when the old man opened the door himself. Muttering for Renie to close the door, he shuffled back to his paper-strewn desk. Renie sat in the stiff chair facing him. He was disappointed to find the office so small and ordinary. There was no massive credenza, no wet bar, just four tall filing cabinets. The only picture, indeed the only color in the room, was a small photograph of Mr. Cushing's daughter, Nora, and her son, both waving from the deck of a ship.

"Yes, yes, of course. Renie LaChance," the old man interrupted Renie's stammered introduction. "And I know exactly what you're here to tell me," he said, leaning over the desk, unmindful of the dried oatmeal on his tie.

"You do?" Renie said, hopeful for a moment. The Golden Toastee salesman must have told Mr. Cushing how important this was to him.

"I've been waiting all morning for someone to face me, and not one single man in this town has had the guts to. Not one. Until you came through that door, I've been sitting here, stewing away and mad as hell. But more than I'm mad, I'm ashamed. Some people moan and groan how if only old Judge Clay was here, he'd set people straight, he'd get it all back on track. But I tell you things're too far gone for that anymore. It's a good thing the Judge doesn't have to live through this. I tell you, it'd break his heart, all he did for this town, and look what they do, they vote to evict his best friend. A blind man."

He realized Mr. Cushing was talking about Joey Seldon, the old popcorn man.

"It's shameful, that's what it is," Cushing railed. "Everybody figures good luck to the other guy, because they've got their own ass to cover. Nobody can take anything on face value all of a sudden. It's all why, why, why? When I was a boy if I asked my father 'Why?' the answer was 'Because I said so.' But now the old orthodoxies aren't enough anymore. Authority doesn't mean a damn. Sometimes it's enough to do something just because it's right to do. Why? Because! Just simply because!" He banged his fist on the desk. "Do you know what I mean? Do you, Renie?"

Renie nodded. Though he didn't know what orthodoxies were, there was in his breast this stirring that rose with the force of the old man's passion. For once in his life, come hell or high water, he would speak his mind.

"Of course you do. That's why I'm not one bit surprised you're here." Mr. Cushing peered up at him. "You're not like the rest of them, are you? You're a man that walks alone and thinks his own thoughts, and believe me, Renie, there aren't many of us around anymore."

Renie's hand closed over the ledger's rough binding. "Mr. Cushing," he said. "You see, the reason I came is to tell you something. You see, for a long time I been trying to get this one line, well, maybe not trying for that whole time. I mean, that I did really in the last six months—try, I mean. You know, painting the whole place and sprucing things up. But way long before that I always had this idea, you know, of being a Golden Toastee dealer, and now I can't."

Mr. Cushing had been looking at him. "I would say not," he said. A hardness rose in his features. He listened as Renie recounted the thirty-three long-distance telephone calls he'd made to Golden Toastee in the last year and a half, the six letters, the ads he'd clipped from magazines and studied so closely he knew them by heart. He told of meeting the young salesman and how impressed he was with him, the tuna-fish sandwich, how keenly he'd sensed the admiration of the other diners in the booths, and how he'd probably put too much pressure on the young man, especially insisting on the extra sandwich, and then how he'd read to him from the ledger. He described the ledgers and the years of record keeping, the accumulation of statistics he'd always wanted to share with Mr. Cushing but had never known how until now, so here they were—one book, anyway. Renie opened the ledger. He took a deep breath, then began to read, "May 14, rainy. Noon. 59 degrees, 31 shoppers. 5:30 p.m.—46 shoppers." He turned the next few pages, reading random dates. Mr. Cushing was staring at him. He obviously didn't understand. Renie explained that he was the one who had informed the Golden Toastee salesman that Cushing's didn't sell small appliances, and how he had been able to tell him how many shoppers used Cushing's rear entrance on any given day.

"I told him probably double that many use the front," Renie added.

"Actually, it's the back that's busiest because of the parking I've got. But the rest of the stores aren't so lucky. But I told them. I warned them. You remember, don't you, Renie? I said, 'Go ahead and meter Merchants Row, you damn fools, and watch what happens.' " Cushing pulled the ledger close and began to read various entries aloud. " 'November 26. Light snow. 29 degrees. 236 shoppers from morning to night. Day after Thanksgiving. First day of Christmas shopping.' This is amazing. This is really something." He looked up and grinned. "This reminds me of the old days, Renie, when people really cared about business. Aaahhh!" He waved disgustedly. "Now all they care about is putting in their forty hours and demanding more benefits than the small businesses can afford to keep shelling out. I tell you, it's a losing game we're playing, Renie, a losing game."

"Mr. Cushing, you can't take the Golden Toastee line away from me! You just can't!" he gasped.

The room was so still he could hear Mr. Cushing's stomach gurgle.

"It's not that way at all," the old man tried to explain. The Golden Toastee man had approached him. It was the American way. Golden Toastee had been aggressive enough to go looking for new markets.

"Because of me!" he cried. "Because of them ledgers there! Because I'm the one that told him you don't sell small appliances!"

"Renie, what can I say? We're businessmen. It's competition. There's room for both of us."

"But you don't even have an appliance department!" Renie cried, his voice breaking.

"Well, yes, I do," Mr. Cushing said softly. "As a matter of fact, we're in the process of starting one up. It's the only way to fight the shopping-mall competition. We've got to be a full-service store."

Renie nodded. He didn't know what to say or do. Everything felt alien. Even the ledger book open between them was no longer his, every extrapolation of weather, commerce, and his feelings diminished now by his rashness, his foolishness in coming here. He stood up and reached for the ledger.

"I'll tell you what I need, Renie. I need a manager for the new department. A man who knows the different lines, someone that thinks like me. I'll tell you the truth, Renie, all these years ever since my daughter's humiliation, I couldn't stand that Fermoyle family, especially Bridget and all her airs. But I noticed how she never took to you, and there again that told me something. You're a man of principle, aren't you, Renie? You could be a real help to me, Renie. I'm just getting slower and slower. My daughter doesn't care about the business except for how it supports her. There's only the one grandson and he's dying," he said with a wave of dismissal. The old man opened his desk drawer and pulled out a crumpled handkerchief. He blew his nose, then wiped tears from his eyes. "Do you think you'd be interested, Renie?"

Renie couldn't stop grinning. It was a dream come true, working with other people, supervising other workers. Helen would be so proud. People everywhere would know him. He could get Marie's children any job they wanted in town. But then he remembered Tom. What would he do with him? There was no place for Tom to go.

"No," he said. "I can't."

"Why?" Mr. Cushing asked.

"Because, because," he stammered. "Because my cat has to live in the store, because my wife hates animals."

"And I hate cats, Renie," said Mr. Cushing. "It's the one animal I can't stand."

Renie was turning his CLOSED sign to OPEN when Robert Haddad came to the door. The insurance agent wanted to buy his wife an electric mixer, the fanciest model Renie had.

"This here's the best one. MixMaid," he said, sliding a heavy white mixing set from the shelf. He blew dust from the box as he carried it to the counter. "It's got your four different-sized bowls," he said, tearing it all from the box. His hands could not work fast enough. He had to make this sale before Haddad heard about Cushing's new appliance department. "Your three different-sized beaters. Your special dough thing here," he said, holding up the rectangular steel paddle. "Your wife make bread?" he asked doubtfully. Mrs. Haddad sure didn't look like a lady that made bread.

"Well, let's put it this way, she's gonna be making a lot of dough." He laughed.

"Then maybe she oughta have more the commercial mixer," Renie said, crestfallen. He didn't sell commercial mixers. "This here ain't gonna give her the volume for a lotta dough."

"No. No, Renie, it was a joke." Haddad rolled his eyes and sighed. His wife was going to sell soap at parties. The mixer was a surprise. He was hoping to get her interested in cooking and baking.

"Then this'll do it!" Renie cried with relief. "See, it's got your seven different speeds, all the way from High whip to Slow blend. Your automatic beater ejection." He pushed a button on the side.

"How much?" asked Haddad.

"Thirty-nine ninety-nine," he said.

Haddad whistled. "That's expensive! I can go up to Monkey Ward's and get one half that price, but the thing is, I'd rather keep my business downtown."

"But they're not gonna be selling MixMaid," Renie said. "That's the thing. This here's a quality machine. Listen. Listen to this," he said, turning on the mixer. The beaters spun to a silver blur in the clear glass bowl. Renie moved the dial from speed to speed, his spirits climbing.

He looked up to see Haddad standing by the cellar door. "What's down here, storage?" he asked, opening the door. "Jesus Christ!" He jumped back, startled to see Tom pass in front of him. Tom sprang onto the counter.

"I don't keep much inventory," Renie said, stroking the cat's rippling back as it curled against him. Haddad didn't like Tom and the cat could tell. "I sell off the floor," Renie explained.

"Keeps things simple that way, huh?" Haddad asking, peering down the dark stairs.

"Yah, so I don't get stuck with ten models of last year's washing machine," Renie boasted. Of course, he couldn't afford to buy ten models in the first place. But Cushing's would be able to. Soon when his customers didn't see the model they wanted, they'd only have to cross the street for it.

"Yah, I know what you mean," Haddad sighed, returning to the counter, where he stood back, away from the cat. "I'm at the point now, I don't even trust banks, everything's so controlled and regulated."

"Me neither," Renie agreed with a vigorous nod.

"The way I figure it, they're gonna spy on me, I'm just gonna have to play it a little closer to the vest, that's all." He winked and patted his back pocket. "You know what I'm saying, right?"

"Yah, yah!" Renie cried, grateful for the camaraderie.

"You have to!" Haddad said. "They don't give you any other choice." He looked around. "I got a place, a box right in the store for certain transactions. Cash," he muttered, clearing his throat behind his hand. "If you know what I mean."

"Me, too!" Renie laughed.

"Mine's under the rug. I just lift up a floorboard," confided Haddad.

"Mine's down—" He caught himself, his eyes on the cellar door. "I almost forgot. You want the MixMaid?"

Haddad said he did, but the problem was, it was just too expensive. Renie offered to knock five dollars off the price, them both being fellow downtown merchants. "Thirty-four ninety-nine," he said as the cat jumped off the counter, its thick paws meeting the floor in a soft thud.

"I'll tell you what," Haddad said, moving out of the cat's way. "Things're slow so far this week. Give me a few more days and I'll be in."

"Sure thing," Renie said. "I'll even put your name on it." He was still printing ROBERT HADDAD on the empty box when the door closed. "The trick is," Renie instructed the cat, who had jumped back onto the counter and sat watching him, "to be flexible, and not be afraid to give a little." Tom began to purr. Renie smiled and the purring grew louder and louder. It filled the store, the streets outside, like a great engine churning out such longing that he could barely walk. He locked the front door, then staggered into the bathroom, into the reek of glossy heat, his ears ringing, ring, ring, ringing, while just outside the door the cat purred, as he waited, yearning for a woman's voice to answer, to speak to him.

"Hello?"

"Oh hello." He closed his eyes. This one was new. She'd come into the store last week looking at stoves. "Hello, you beautiful thing, you."

"Oh Lord, listen to you." She laughed nervously.

"It's you I like to listen to. Your voice is so sweet. It's sweet, sweet as honey."

"Lord!" She sounded different.

"And you got beautiful skin. It looks like there's dew on it, you know, like on grass first thing in the morning." The pause came like a flutter in the silence.

"Do I know you?"

"No."

"Then why are you calling me?"

"Because I like to talk to you."

"But I've never talked to you before."

"Is this Mrs. Brewster?"

"No."

"Well, who are you, then?"

"I'm not going to tell you! What do you want to know for?"

"I just want to talk to you."

"Why? Don't you have anyone else to talk to, a wife, a girlfriend, somebody?"

"No."

"Well, I really can't talk. My baby's awake."

"Oh I'm sorry. You go take care of the baby."

"She's crying."

"Then you gotta go."

"Don't you have any friends?"

He paused to think. "Not really. I know people, but not like friends, you know?"

"Can you hold on a minute while I get the baby?"

"Yes. Oh yes, I can hold. You go get the baby."

When she came back she was out of breath. She said she was in the kitchen warming a bottle. He could hear the soft cooing. He pictured her jiggling the baby on her hip while she stood in front of the stove watching the water boil under the bottle.

"How old's the baby?"

"Seven and a half months."

"What's her name?"

"Kathi-jean. That's *K* with an *I,* dash, small *j.*"

Kathi-jean. He told her that was a beautiful name. She thanked him and said her husband's family didn't like it, but then they didn't like her, either, so she guessed it didn't really matter. When he asked her why they didn't like her, she said it was a long story. But basically it was because she had thrown him out last year, two months before the baby was born.

"Why'd you do that?" He could hear a wooden chair scraping over the floor.

"There. That's better," she sighed. "I'm sitting down now. Ooo, she can't wait, the little pig." She asked him if he could hear her sucking. He said no, and so she held the phone to the baby's mouth. "Did you hear it?" she asked, coming back on.

"Yes!" he laughed, overwhelmed with giddiness. "Yes! It was so loud, I . . . I . . . I . . ."

"She's such a little pig. I just hope she's skinny as her father. He's like a beanpole."

"Why'd you do that, make him leave?" he asked to avoid having to mispronounce *throw* as *trow* the way he usually did.

"Because he's a bum. The whole time we were together he never stopped seeing all his old girlfriends. So I just got sick of it."

"Why'd you marry him?"

" 'Cause I was PG."

"PG?"

"Pregnant! What, you never heard of that? Jeez, here I am with an obscene phone caller, and I'm doing all the talking."

"I'm not an obscene phone caller."

"Yes, you are. You said you call ladies you don't even know, and you say things, right?"

"Yah, but never . . . never bad things."

"Well, what kind of things, then?" There was a catch in her voice, an eagerness.

He shrugged and closed his eyes, ashamed of all the glistening breasts and parted thighs, the lush mounds of kinky hair.

"Well?"

"Just . . . just mostly things about them. Like what pretty eyes they got and things like that."

"I got hazel eyes and long eyelashes, dark like my hair. My hair's brunette, but some people say black it's so dark. Hello? You still there?"

"Yeah," he said, grinning. "I'm still here."

"Okay, so now you tell me something. Tell me something about you."

"I got brown eyes and brown hair," he said, touching the sparse strands on the back of his head.

She asked if he was tall. He said he wasn't tall, and he wasn't short, just kind of regular. He told her about Riddles and about Tom and all the animals he'd grown up with on his father's farm in Quebec. He told her about his father and the little he could recall of his mother, the warm cream she would pour over his oatmeal and the way she patted water up her throat and rosy cheeks on hot days. He told her things he hadn't thought of in years, the go-cart his father made him, then let him help paint red, the torture to speak English in school when his brain worked in French. He'd had a lucky charm, a rabbit's foot that his mother said would let the English words slide over his tongue.

"Do you still have it?"

"No. I gave it to a girl. Her name was Solie. She was the first girl I ever kissed."

"What a sap!" She laughed, and now he laughed with her.

There was so much he had forgotten. Once there had been another life than this, happier, hopeful. There had been a playful boy, a shy romantic young man. Once he had been loved. There had been friends, the two Brien boys up the road. They called him Bobo. He had worn black boots and a leather jacket with a sheepskin collar. One day a girl named Edith had ridden on his bike, her arms around his waist, her cheek against his back.

"Oh jeez. She just spit up all over the place. It's running down my arm even. Call me back in a few minutes, okay?"

"Yah," he said. "I will. I will!"

Her phone clicked. "Wait!" he shouted into the buzzing receiver. "I don't know your number! I don't know your name! I don't know who you are!" he cried.

After so many years of forcing thoughts of his children from his consciousness, Sam didn't know what to think about Alice's entering the convent. Helen had heard it from Mrs. Arkaday when she brought a bag of tomatoes over to the rectory for the Monsignor. Of course it wasn't official, but when the Monsignor had asked, Father Gannon had confided that he was helping Alice with her vocation. Mrs. Arkaday said she shouldn't say anything, but she knew Helen would be "thrilled with the news." If anyone deserved a mem-

ber of the religious in her life, it was Helen LaChance. Mrs. Arkaday
asked her to please pass on her congratulations to Sam. At first he'd
been depressed, embarrassed not to have known, then proud. And
now he was frightened. Somehow this was his fault. He had forced
his daughter into an austere and sterile existence. Just when he was
rebuilding his life she would leave and become a stranger to him. But
wasn't she already a stranger? He had pushed her away. He still remembered that day at Applegate and the stricken look on her face as
he hurried into the dining room.

He wanted to call Marie before he left for work. He started past
the crib, where his mother sat propped against pillows, her eyes
closed, as Helen tried to feed her. Every day her breathing worsened
with wheezing so torturously long and deep that her jaw would tremble and her teeth would rattle. He was sure she was dying, but Helen
insisted it was the same cold she herself had endured all week. Yesterday he had watched Helen trying to spoon-feed broth into that gaping
mouth. Her trembling chin and neck had glistened with the yellow liquid. She was in a coma, he had told his sister, who insisted their mother's deep sleep was the result of being awake at night when he was at
work. Then feed her at night when she's awake, he told Helen, but
don't submit her to such indignities. Helen insisted she had tried, but
when Bridget was awake she wouldn't open her mouth. Then at least
use an eyedropper or something, he had said, surprised now to find
his advice heeded as Helen squirted broth from an eyedropper down
the back of Bridget's throat. She kept gagging and choking.

"Hello?" answered Marie on the first ring.

"It's me," he said softly. He didn't want Helen to hear him. Just
a few feet away, light glowed around the door to Renie's room,
where a ball game sputtered from the radio.

"Omar? Omar, where are you?"

"It's Sam." For a moment he was confused; then he remembered
who Omar was.

"Oh," she said in a flat voice.

"You sound tired," he said, forestalling news of Alice, wanting at
least a few moments of pleasant conversation.

Not tired, she told him, but exhausted. Her car had broken down
and she was having to drive Norm's junk, and then Astrid had quit

last week, so now she had the bookkeeping to do as well as her own work.

Astrid? He couldn't put a face to the name. Entire months had been lost. He felt his confidence ebb. If he told her about Alice, she would blame him. He'd never been a father to them. What did he expect? He tried to tell her about his job. Now that he had established his own rhythm with the loader, the hours passed quickly. The night watchman continued to be a problem, but—

"Sam," she interrupted. "What about the money? Did you talk to Helen? Is that why you're calling?"

"Well, I've been working on the figures to show her." He thought he heard Marie groan. He cupped the mouthpiece with his hand. "Mother's very sick," he whispered. "Helen says no, but I think she's in a coma."

She didn't say anything.

"This may be it," he said, throwing the old hook, anything to keep her believing, anything but action.

"I don't know what to say. I'm sorry, Sam. And whatever happens you can't let it destroy you."

"It won't." He sighed, flushing with the old warmth of her attention. He couldn't remember when he'd last heard caring words from her. He closed his eyes.

"You've been doing so well."

"I know," he said, smiling.

"You've really been trying."

"I have," he said, grateful for her acknowledgment.

"She's lived a long life, and these last few years haven't been pleasant ones."

"No, they haven't."

"How's Helen handling it?'

"Oh typically. It's just a cold, she says, that's all."

"Maybe she's right. Of course, at her age even a cold could be . . . terrible."

"Marie, I called to find out about something. I heard something. It's about Alice. . . ."

"What?" she cut in. "What about her?"

He repeated what the Monsignor's housekeeper had told Helen.

"Oh my God," Marie groaned. "No, that's impossible. It can't be true."

"But that's what the priest said. That's what he told the Monsignor."

"I wondered why he was giving her rides and coming around so much. And here I was beginning to think he was, well . . . Oh God, what's wrong with her?"

"Well, she's always been a quiet kind of kid, a good girl, a—"

"A coward!" Marie spat, and his ear rang with the familiar sibilance. "Always trying to find the easy way out."

"Marie! She's not a bad person because she wants to become a nun."

"She doesn't want to become a nun!" she said with a bitter laugh he remembered only too well. "She just doesn't want to have to work. She just doesn't want to have to go to college. She just doesn't want to have to listen to me anymore!"

"No, Marie."

"It's true. She wants to hide, just like the rest of them. They haven't got a backbone between them, the three of them. Well, I'm sick of being the only one who cares, the only one who tries. Oh God . . ." There was a long, wet sob, and then she hung up.

"Top of the seventh, and the Yankees lead eight to three," Renie's radio announced in a sudden swell of clarity from his room.

Sam laid out four pieces of bread for tonight's sandwiches, the four thin slices of ham, two of Swiss cheese. He spread the thinnest skim of mustard on it all, then wrapped the sandwiches in waxed paper and put them in the same brown bag used every night to achieve the constancy, monotony enough to keep from feeling the grooves or seeing the strings. If Alice wanted to hide, the convent was one hell of a better choice than booze. He returned the ham to the refrigerator and wiped crumbs from the counter. He covered the butter dish and switched off the light over the sink. Now that Alice wouldn't be needing money for school, his campaign of annoyance was over. Imagine, Sam Fermoyle's daughter, a nun. He grinned. Now wouldn't that make people sit up and take notice.

On Sunday the church was only half filled for the eleven o'clock Mass. Because of the heat most people had gone to the early Masses and were now probably sitting on the beaches at the lakes and ponds.

The Consecration over, Father Gannon turned to face the congregants. Accompanied by the altar boy, he carried the Host-filled chalice down the wide crimson-carpeted steps to the marble Communion rail. As he placed the small white Host on each quivering tongue, he would glance up from time to time. When he came to the end of the rail, he turned back to begin again. Pausing, he smiled, relieved to see Alice in the last pew, her head bent over her folded hands. Last night he had talked her into at least attending Mass, even if she would not receive Communion. What they shared was not only beautiful but sacred, he had told her. He might think so, she had countered, but the Church said it was a sin. Some things transcend the Church's scope, he had said. What? he had wanted her to ask, what things, so that he could tell her. Love did. Love! Instead she had burrowed into that frustrating remoteness of hers.

"*Corpus Domini nostri Jesu Christi,*" he murmured over a kneeling child with long, dark pigtails. Seeing Alice look up, he paused, still holding the Host above the child's head.

The child stuck out her tongue.

He couldn't help but smile. Alice's pale face glowed from the shadowed depths below the choir loft like a keyhole of light from which he could not look away.

The child looked up.

Alice bent so far forward that her forehead met her clenched hands.

"Father!" the child whispered loudly.

All along the rail, the communicants stared up at him.

"Why won't you give me Communion?" the child asked.

The heat filled every room in the Stoner house but Carol's. Here the windows were closed, the shades and curtains drawn. On the cluttered bureau a silver fan oscillated in a gentle rattle between the closed door and the small mound in the bed. For the past hour she had been trying to wet her lips with her tongue, but she couldn't. The door opened. It was Sonny. He tiptoed in and leaned over the bed. His cool fingertips trickled down her cheeks. Her eyes moved from the glinting badge on his chest to the wide belt and holster at his hip, the black gun butt. *Kill me. Take it out, shoot me,* she was screaming.

"You're a good girl," he whispered in the maddening silence.

Do it! Do it! Like that deer that was hit up on the Post Road.

They had found it writhing in the stony gully, a bloody gash in its side, legs twitching, its mournful eyes following the quick wordless arc of Sonny's aim. *Don't look, don't look, don't look now, Carol.* Closing her eyes her head had jerked back with each blast. *Pow! Pow! Pow!*

The door closed after him with a whoosh of air and light.

I am a poor dumb creature too, she screamed. But in the quiet no one heard.

The hood was raised and Norm was cleaning the spark plugs with gasoline. He spent all his free time working on the engine. Now that this had become the family car he felt an enormous responsibility to keep it running. His mother might have to wait for Omar's soap, her investment that had impoverished them, but it was his car that got her back and forth to work every day.

He had been daydreaming about Astrid Haddad. He'd almost convinced himself that Benjy had misinterpreted everything. But then when Astrid quit her job, his mother said she couldn't help thinking it had something to do with her. She said Astrid couldn't seem to look her straight in the eye anymore. Norm knew what it was. She'd quit because of him.

Twice last night he'd parked down the street from her house, staring at the light streaming through her filmy curtains, trying to work up the courage to ring her doorbell. Never had he felt lonelier than in these past two weeks. Sometimes it seemed that there was a hole so big inside him nothing would ever fill it.

When he was done with the car, he ate supper, and then he drove slowly around the park to see if any of his friends were at the band concert. It was a cool starry night with enough of a breeze so that people stood shivering with their blankets around their shoulders. Many had begun to leave. As he came down West Street he was surprised to see Joey Seldon sitting on his stool. Victor the cop stood next to the stand with his arms folded. It had been a week since Joey had been ordered to vacate the stand. Each day another town official came to reason with him, but Joey would have no part of their hypocritical logic. He had an agreement, a contract with the town, and it was the town that had failed to meet its own stipulations, he explained to anyone who'd listen. Even Friday's editorial in the *Atkinson Crier* was calling for "a reexamination of this most sensitive issue."

Norm parked the car and was reading the editorial, which was tacked on one of the cornerposts. "See," Joey said, poking a hand out between the boards. He pointed to the last line. "See what it says here. 'The shameful condition of the stand in the park represents the town's dereliction of responsibility to one of its most colorful citizens.' "

"Hey, that's pretty good, Joey," he said, pitying the old man's proud grin, and for a minute he didn't know what to say.

"So how's the new car?" Joey asked.

"Great! 'Course I got some work to do on it. The timing's all off."

"As well as most of the paint," Joey said, laughing, and Norm didn't say anything. Their eyes met and Joey looked away. "Here," Joey said, handing him a bag of popcorn. "It's on the the house," he said with an unmistakable glance at the dime Norm held out.

Up in the bandstand Jarden Greene's arms were a blur as the musicians played "The Syncopated Clock" faster and faster. Greene kept glancing back at the steady stream of people leaving the park.

"He thinks if the band plays louder and faster, they'll all stay." Joey laughed.

Norm looked at him. How had he known? Just by all the car doors opening and shutting. Engines starting. Of course. After all these years Joey knew all the sounds. All you had to do was say hello and Joey'd know if you were happy or sad. "Want some help with the empties? They're all over the place," he said, picking up a bottle.

"That's not even mine," Joey said.

"What?" he asked slowly. "What's not yours?"

"That bottle you got."

"What is it?" he asked.

"Kelly's LimeAde."

"How do you know?"

"By the smell," Joey said with an exaggerated wink and a grin.

Norm looked away. Could it be that he wasn't blind? That it had been a scam all these years, an act? He probably *was* getting a kickback the night Towler's still blew up. Norm thought of all the times he'd crated Joey's empties, guided him across the busy West Street intersection, felt so trustworthy to be able to count his money at the end of the night, when the whole time Joey'd been watching him like a hawk. He remembered his anger at Jarden Greene's insistence that Joey's mugging had been staged. The old man probably tripped and fell and then said he'd been robbed so that people would feel so sorry for him they'd stop trying to close his stand. Nothing but a phony, a con man like Duvall, milking people's kindness.

"Well I gotta go now, Joey." He tossed the popcorn into the barrel, certain he saw old man wince.

"Wait, let me get you a Coke, then."

"No, thanks," he said, calling goodbye as he headed up the street.

"How about a 7-Up then?"

"I'm not thirsty!" he called, and when he got to the Hotdog Bus he stopped at the window and ordered a raspberry freeze. He turned with the tall frosted cup and, sure enough, Joey watched sadly. He looked right at the old man, forced a quick cold smile before turning away.

Renie stared at the ceiling. In the kitchen Sam and Helen argued right outside his door. Water was running into a pan. Helen had just called Dr. Reynolds about her mother's congestion.

"Congestion!" Sam roared. "She can barely breathe. Will you face the facts, Helen. Mother's dying."

The linoleum made squeaky sticking sounds as Sam paced back and forth. Renie knew their footsteps, their sighs, and which closing door had been shut by whom. Surely now, Sam followed his sister from chore to chore. At their most agitated, each would be hard upon the other's tender heels.

"Sorry to disappoint you, dear brother, but Mother is not dying. She has a cold, a very bad cold, which Dr. Reynolds is treating." Helen's voice quavered.

"What's he going to do? Give her another shot?" Sam shouted.

"Yes, give her another shot! The penicillin's working."

"Come on, Helen!"

"Oh! And what's your solution? You're so involved, tell me what to do!" Helen said, and a cupboard door banged shut, all the cups tinkling on their hooks.

"Face the facts. . . ."

"The facts! Facts! I live with the facts every single minute of every single day and night. . . ."

The doorbell was ringing. Helen's heels hurried through the house.

"Jesus Christ," Sam muttered.

Renie jumped up and raced around his room, dressing quickly. He put his razor and rolled-up tie into his pocket so he could shave at work. He'd leave while Dr. Reynolds's presence kept them both at bay.

The driveway filled with a rumble that shook the walls. He

peeked out his window and saw the garbage truck idling below as Jozia kissed Grondine Carson goodbye.

"You're late," he heard Sam say when she came into the kitchen.

"Miz LaChance said I could," Jozia replied.

"Well, she's awful mad. She said she needs someone she can depend on."

"She said that? Miz LaChance said that? After all I've done for her. Well, that's it, I'm—"

"No, no, no. Calm down, Jozia," Sam said. "I was only kidding. Helen says you can do what you want. In fact, she was just in here saying how you need a day off, but it was probably too late to call you."

"Really?"

"Really."

"Grondine's still collecting. I can hear him."

"Well, if you hurry you can catch up with him."

"Will you tell Miz LaChance thanks?"

"Sure. I'll tell her. Bye, Jozia." The back door banged shut.

"Good morning, Renie," Sam said without looking up from his coffee as Renie came out of his room. Just then Helen looked in past the swinging door. "Where's Jozia? I need her."

Sam covered his mouth and shook his head. "The dear dim girl said it was her day off."

"Her what?" Helen gasped. Tears swelled in her eyes. Behind her Dr. Reynolds called and she stepped quickly back from the door.

Sam looked at Renie and shrugged.

"You shouldn'ta done that," Renie said.

"Tomorrow the ax may fall," Sam said with a grin, "but at least for today I can sleep without her goddamn vacuum banging my door." He winked. "But thanks for the warning," he said, opening the newspaper. He held it between them.

Renie stood, rubbing his forearm. He opened his mouth, then changed his mind. It was between them two. There wasn't much here that involved him. He started for the door.

"Hey, Reen, if you see any of my kids today, tell them their old man says hi."

"You tell 'em yourself," he muttered.

The newspaper lowered slowly. Sam tilted his head with amusement. "Sore spot? Sorry, Reen. Didn't mean to offend you. You can tape up all the pictures you want, but they are my kids."

Renie's lip trembled. He'd never felt more like hitting someone. "They're Marie's kids. She's the only one that deserves them," he said.

"You got that right, Renie," Sam called after him. "You sure as hell got that right."

As he drove down the hill he was thinking about the young woman on the phone last week. Since then he'd tried every conceivable combination of numbers, sometimes dialing and redialing in a breathless frenzy. He could barely recall her voice, but he remembered every word she had spoken.

The moment Renie turned the corner he saw the cruiser in front of the store. Officer Heinze stood on the top step talking to Mr. Fredette, the building manager. The front door was open. They hurried down to his car as he pulled up to the curb.

"Bad news, Renie," Mr. Fredette gasped. "You've been broken into. They came in through the cellar, and they left by the front door."

Renie raced into the store.

"They busted a window," Mr. Fredette said on his heels. "Jimmy called me at home."

"Doesn't seem to be too much missing," Heinze said.

"Tom!" Renie called as he ran down the cellar stairs. "Come on, Tom! Come on out! It's okay, Tom! I'm here now, Tom! Tom!" he bellowed, turning so suddenly he collided with Officer Heinze, who had followed him into the musty cellar. Tom's untouched food and milk dishes were still on the landing by the door. Maybe he was hiding up in the store. He opened every cupboard, looked behind every box and appliance, stretching his hand into the dirtiest crevices. Tom was gone. Heinze had spotted the front door ajar at five-thirty this morning. "He must've escaped, either out the busted cellar window or the front door," Heinze said.

Escaped. Renie cringed. That made it sound as if Tom stayed only because he was locked up. Escaped: as if, like Riddles, Tom just couldn't wait to get away.

Chief Stoner came through the door with Mr. Fredette and Heinze both talking to him at once. Renie looked out at the empty street. "So what's the story, Renie?" Stoner asked.

He shrugged. He couldn't talk now. Everything was too thin, his voice, his strength, the air. Mr. Fredette took it upon himself to explain that Renie felt bad because Tom had escaped.

Sonny interrupted to ask if anything else was missing besides the cat. Conscious of Sonny's stern gaze, Renie went down cellar and looked in the crevice under the stairs. It was gone. His secret cashbox was gone.

"No," he said, standing up. "Nothing I can see." He couldn't very well admit to three hundred dollars that wasn't even on the books, now, could he? He shuddered at the thought of the IRS examining all his records again, searching through his private life.

"What about inventory?" Sonny asked, picking up an electric razor. "Any of that missing?"

Renie glanced around. "Nothing's missing."

The Chief put the razor down so hard it banged on the counter. He looked terrible. He was unshaven and his eyes were bloodshot and puffy. "Why don't you look around, Renie, and be sure," he said, picking up the razor and setting it down again gently, then fiddling with it, moving it a hair to the left, as if to balance it with something.

Renie glanced over both shoulders. "I'm sure. Everything's here. Except Tom," he added, fidgeting under the Chief's steady gaze. He wished they'd leave so he could start searching. Maybe Tom was just hiding out in the alley. If he put the food dishes on the back steps, then Tom would know it was safe to return. He opened the cellar door. "Kitty!" he whispered, "Come on, kitty, kitty, kitty, kitty," he called softly as he bent to pick up the dishes. A hand grasped the back of his shirt and tugged him upright.

"Renie!" Chief Stoner barked, his tight jaw quivering. His forefinger stabbed the air for emphasis. "A crime has been committed here! And this is an investigation, and we need your help here now! And you damn well better give it! Do you understand?"

Renie took a deep breath. "I just want to find my cat, that's all," he whispered, the loss swamping his voice.

"You will, Renie. Tom'll come back. I know he will," Mr. Fredette piped.

Stoner closed his eyes and sighed. "I'm sorry about the cat. But you see, we have a pretty good idea who's breaking in all these places, but so far I got nothing concrete." He explained that if things were missing and if the suspect still had them, then they'd have the proof necessary to make an arrest.

Renie walked around the store and checked each display. He counted boxes on sheves, not because he knew exactly how many should be there, but to demonstrate his cooperation. Heinze had gone back down cellar with Mr. Fredette. Renie stopped and glanced back at the empty shelf next to the stoves. The MixMaid set was gone, and so was the box. The thief had even taken the box. "Chief!" he called, hurrying to the top of the cellar stairs. Behind him a door creaked. Oh God. Oh no. Sonny carried a telephone book as he emerged from the bathroom.

Renie explained that the MixMaid set was missing. "He must've packed it back in the box," he said as the Chief came toward him with a strange expression. "Probably because of all the parts. You know, beaters and whips. Not only that, but there's four different-size bowls. See," he cried, thrusting a MixMaid pamphlet at Stoner. "And covers, too." He cleared his throat while Sonny glanced at the glossy brochure, before slipping it into his breast pocket. The silence between them grew while downstairs the muffled voices seemed to scurry underfoot like the mice Tom hunted. "I almost could've sold it last week. Bob Haddad said he wanted to buy it."

"What's this all about, Renie?" Sonny asked.

Renie stared, shaking his head, teeth clenched.

Sonny put on his glasses. He wet his finger and turned the pages. "Eunice Bonifante," he said, looking over the rims. "You call her, don't you, Renie?"

He nodded, unable to look away.

"Sometimes at five, huh? But mostly at night. Around eleven. Sometimes Saint Mary's bells are ringing when you call." Sonny sighed. "You still call her, Renie?"

He shook his head. In the last few weeks Eunice had sworn and slammed down the phone the minute she heard his voice.

"Mrs. Tinsdale . . . Mrs. Block . . . Mrs. Cherno . . . Klubock . . . Heering. My God! You call all these women? Renie, do you know what could happen? Don't you know this is against the law?"

The voices rose and fell downstairs. Sonny talked and talked, and Renie absorbed every accusation and chastisement, though it wasn't necessary. Like an excised organ, some vital part of him was already beginning to shrivel up. It was gone, all of it, over, and with the loss, he was shrinking. He grew smaller and smaller, so small that he was surprised when Sonny continued to speak to him. Helen didn't care what he did or where he went. No one did. Strangely, the truth, instead of hurting, came as a relief, an unburdening. As a rule people did not like him, and no matter how hard he tried, nothing, nothing could ever change that basic fact. He felt so light now, so weightless that he gripped the counter edge to anchor himself. It was over, over, over, over. That's why Tom had run away.

"No more calls, Renie. You understand? Well, do you?"

He nodded. Eyes downcast, he kept nodding.

"Sometimes things happen, things a man wouldn't ever do if he was thinking straight," Sonny said. He glanced toward the cellar door. They were coming back up. Sonny grabbed his arm. "Believe me, I know! I know!" he insisted.

"Are you going to put me in jail?" Renie gasped, his tears distorting everything.

The two men came through the door with blurred features.

"'Course I'm not," Stoner said softly.

"Tom'll be back, Renie. You'll see," Mr. Fredette said, his voice shrill with indignation. "You were damn good to that cat, and he knows it." He patted Renie on the back.

"And me, I'm always around," Heinze said. "I'm bound to see him."

Sonny assured him the thief would be under arrest in a just a few more days. It was only a matter of time. From now on, he and his men were going to come down so hard on a certain individual he wasn't even going to be able to crap anymore without them knowing it. "Come on, Jimmy," Sonny said, patting the pamphlet in his pocket. "Let's go see what kinda cake his ma's making."

After they left, Renie poured fresh milk into Tom's bowl. He opened a can of tuna fish and emptied it into a dish. Some of the tuna chunks were blood-streaked. He had cut his finger on the jagged edge of the can. He squeezed the cut and let it bleed onto the tuna. Maybe the blood would be an even stronger lure, and then he would be a part of Tom and Tom would stay with him forever. He set both dishes outside the back door.

"Open the door, Mrs. Carper. This is Officer Jimmy Heinze speaking, and I got the Chief here with me, too. Chief Stoner."

"I know who you are, and I'm not opening the door," she hollered back.

"Okay, now it was his turn. "You have to, Hildie," Sonny said. "It's the law, and you just have to, that's all. Now open up. All we want to do is look around."

"Well, I'm not letting you. This is my home, and there's nothing here to see."

"Want me to?" Heinze hissed, gesturing his shoulder at the door.

Sonny shook his head no. "Blue in there?" he called.

"If you're looking for him, you came to the wrong place!" she said disgustedly.

"Well, actually, I'm looking for something. Something he brought here."

"What's that?"

He paused, considering how much to tell her. "A MixMaid," he read from the pamphlet. "That's an electric mixer, a kind of beater," he said, wincing at her sour laughter.

"There's no MixMaid here, I can tell you that much," she said with a derisive hoot.

Telling her he'd have to see for himself, he rattled the knob. When she didn't respond, he nodded at Heinze, who drew back eagerly. Just then the door opened and her angular freckled face stared up at them. A pretty woman, she looked a lot like Blue, but she was tiny, he realized as he stepped past her. With the shades drawn the house was dark, surprisingly neat. A lot cleaner than his own, he noted. Her two younger sons sat on the couch reading comic books. "How you doing, boys?" he said. "Could you maybe sit out on the porch a minute, till we call you back in."

But their mother insisted they stay put. "They got no use for their brother. He's a no-good, and they're better off knowing it."

The boys watched with sober impassive expressions.

She led Sonny and Heinze into the small kitchen, where she threw open every cupboard door, one after another, then went back and slammed them all shut. "See, I told you!" she said.

"Where's that go?" Sonny pointed to a door.

"The cellar," she said.

"That where you keep the booze?" he asked, and she darted to place herself between him and the door. He reached behind her and pulled it open. He counted ten cases of beer stacked at the foot of the stairs.

"That's my private property," she said from behind. "I can keep a hundred cases here if I want."

She had him there. For now, anyway. "What you're doing here is wrong, Hildie. Not only that," he said, pointing at her boys, "but what about them?"

"You get out of here," she growled, "and leave me the hell alone."

"I don't know," he sighed. "That's just getting harder and harder to do lately with people."

They were getting into the cruiser when Heinze told Sonny he'd be right back. He'd just thought of a way Mrs. Carper could help them and maybe herself as well.

The sun set a minute earlier every night. Here on the winding mountain roads it seemed dark already, even though it was only seven-thirty. Blue Mooney was on his way to his mother's house. He had spent the last few days looking for work in Burlington. At least up there, the minute he said his name doors didn't slam in his face. Two prospects looked good: one was for a moving company and the other on a demolition crew for a small company that specialized in large buildings. That was the job he wanted most. It not only paid twice what he'd gotten from Colter, but it contracted for projects all over the country. At first he thought the interviewer was a wise son of a bitch until he realized the guy was pushing him, testing his steadiness. He could tell the guy was impressed. He had given both places his mother's telephone number. If he did get a job in Burlington he planned to surprise Alice Fermoyle one night at her dorm. He'd be all dressed up like a college guy himself in a suit and a tie, and he'd hand her a dozen long-stemmed red roses and take her out to eat in the classiest restaurant in Burlington.

As he came up the last hill to his mother's house, two cars loaded with kids roared past. His hands tightened on the wheel. Both cars slowed as they approached the house. The bug light was off, so the cars drove on. Smiling, he pulled into the driveway.

His youngest brother, Carl, was playing cards. His other brother, Peter, lay on the floor watching television. They glanced up warily as he greeted them. "Where's Ma?" he asked, hearing her voice like a low tremble in the walls.

"In there," Carl said, pointing toward the kitchen.

"She's mad as hell," Peter said. "She's tryna get a job."

"No kidding," he said, grinning.

"Where you been?" Carl wanted to know.

"All over." He smiled, pleased that he'd been missed. The older they got, the better he liked them, though he was amazed the way she was dressing them up in chino pants and button-down shirts, trying to make them look like town boys. At least they didn't have crew cuts. He knelt down and gave Peter a playful jab in the shoulder.

"Ow!" Peter cried, shrinking back.

Outside, a car honked its horn, then drove off. Maybe someone he knew had seen his car. "Here, hit me back," he offered, hiking up his sleeve. "Go ahead. Hard as you can. Come on!" He laughed as Peter pummeled his arm. "See, I can take it. I'm not crying 'Ow, ow, ow, ow' like some faggot. Come on. I'll take the two of you." He hooked his arm around Carl's legs and pulled him onto the floor. He covered his head and giggled as they began to tickle him. It was an old game. In the entire world, only these two little boys knew he was ticklish. "Oh God," he squealed. "Oh God. Stop it! Stop it!"

They were laughing so hard they kept collapsing onto him. "You're the faggot," they gasped, scrabbling their fingers under his arms and down his sides.

"No, no, I'm not," he cried. "You are."

"You are!" they said.

Outside, a car had pulled in alongside the fence. A horn honked for the third time. He sat up so suddenly that the boys rolled onto the floor. But by the time he got to the door, the car had raced off, its tires spinning dirt and gravel back against the fence slats. "Hildie!" someone shouted from the car. He ran into the kitchen, where his mother was talking on the phone.

"Somebody's here," she said, holding his stare. "I gotta go." She hung up and lit a cigarette.

"Ma, what's going on? They're out there honking their horns and calling your name."

She picked a shred of tobacco from the tip of her tongue. She took a long-steadying drag. "What do you want?" she said, exhaling smoke through her mouth and nose.

He explained what had just happened. If they did it again, he said, he was going out there with the sledge hammer, and then, re-membering, he smiled and gestured behind him. "But the kids said you've been looking for a job. That's great, Ma."

"Yah? And did they tell you why? Did they tell you how the po-lice ride by here every five minutes, how one's probably parked up in the grove right now?" she growled as she stepped toward him now, jabbing her finger in his chest. "They tell you how the Chief and a cop went through the house looking for that electric mixer you stole?"

"What're you talking about? What electric mixer?"

"You're so damn worried about them in there, how do you think they felt seeing their whole house searched?"

"What mixer? What the hell're you talking about?" he bellowed in her face, enraged at the thought of cops humiliating his family.

She told him about the break-in at the appliance store and since then the steady stream of cruisers by here. He swore he hadn't broken into the appliance store, or anywhere else, for that matter. "Not since the gas station," he added quickly, before she could say it.

"Just like Kyle, you're nothing but trouble, Travis, and I can't have you around. It's that simple."

He laughed. "All you ever believe about me is what people tell you."

"I tried. But there's a limit, and I'm at it now."

"You tried! Yah, you tried real hard when you let them send me to reform school!"

"Let them! What the hell could I do? You and your brother were always stealing and breaking windows and—"

"Ma! I was eight years old! The same as them in there. You could've done something! You could've tried!"

"What? What could I have done?" she screamed.

"You know, all I ever wanted those five years was one thing." He looked at her. "Just one thing."

She stared up at him.

"You know what that was?" he asked, but she didn't even blink. "You don't want to know, do you?" he said with a bitter laugh. He was both relieved and embarrassed. He felt flat. There was a loaf of bread on the counter, so he took a slice, then opened the refrigerator for the butter. All but the top shelf was jammed with beer bottles. He spread the butter, determined to ignore the beer. The police couldn't be too much of a harassment, he thought. "How's Kenny?" he asked, trying to get things back on track. Kenny was Carl and Peter's father. She called him her husband, but he doubted there'd ever been a marriage. Summers, Kenny was a logger in Maine. Off-season, he collected unemployment and fixed cars on the side. But at least he was around some of the time for Carl and Peter. When Kenny was here, Blue stayed away. They'd never gotten along. His own father had died in a roofing fall soon after Blue's birth.

He sat at the table and told her how Sonny, like everybody else in town, had it in for him. It'd be a help, he said, if she'd just listen to his side of it for once. He tried to explain what had happened with his DI, but it was hard because she kept going to the window, and then she'd pace back and forth, smoking and sighing. He was losing his train of thought. He didn't want to get her mad again. So far she'd let him do all the talking, and it felt good. He was telling her things he'd put out of his thoughts for months, years even. He was hopping so from subject to subject that he was afraid she was getting confused. She looked distracted. A couple of times she went into the other room and yelled at the boys to turn down the television.

He smiled now as she passed him. In spite of her harsh way and the bad dye job, she was a good-looking lady. It pleased him that they had the same wide mouth and square chin. She stood by the window again. She leaned forward as if peering at something, then came quickly to the table and sat across from him. Maybe it would be the same with Alice Fermoyle. It would take persistence. He was just going to have to keep coming back and coming back, no matter the obstacles.

"I think I got a job in Burlington, Ma," he said. He told her about the demolition company, exaggerating their interest in him.

"You shouldn't have screwed up with Colter," she said. She sat way back in the chair and looked toward the window.

"Yah, well, listen, Ma, I gave them your number here to call."

She glanced back at him. "You're not moving in! I told you that!"

"No. I just want you to take a message, Ma. That's all." He smiled. "You know, just take a message."

She chewed her lip. A car was slowly passing the house. Its headlights shone on the wall behind her, and she looked up. "I just want you to know . . ." she began, then shook her head with frustration.

"What? What?" he kept asking, a knot in his throat.

She had been twisting her fingers, and now she stared at him, both defiantly and fearfully. "That electric mixer. I mean if it was for me I could understand. You could give it to me. Then, then I could understand. It would make sense." She kept wetting her lips. She tried to swallow, and her eyes widened. "Do you have it?" she asked, her voice so thin it seemed to seep out of her. "Or maybe you could go get it and bring it here."

He rubbed his eyes a minute. They hurt. Right now everything hurt, yet he couldn't help laughing. "You're a real sweet ma, you know that, don't you?"

"Well . . ." She shook her head, and sighed, and now couldn't look at him.

They both looked toward the window as a car braked to a squealing stop in front of the house. He stood up. "What would you do with the mixer, Ma? Make me something? A cake or a pie or something?" He chuckled. "Tell you the truth, I didn't even know you wanted a mixer. But now that I do, I'm gonna get you one." He went to the front door and flipped the switch. The bug bulb flooded the little porch and the yard and the road with warm yellow light.

"Hey!" he called down to the three couples in somebody's daddy's big new red sedan. "How much you need?"

"Three six-packs," called back the girl in the front seat. Her short blond hair was cut like a boy's.

"Be right out!" he said, aiming his finger like a gun. The girls in the car laughed. The boys watched warily.

"No!" his mother said, turning off the light and slamming the door shut. "You can't."

"Ma! There's customers out there."

She followed him into the kitchen, continuing to insist no, he couldn't, not tonight, the cops: they kept coming by looking for him.

He had filled his pockets and now he was loading more cold bottles into his arms. "They're not just looking for me, Ma," he said, opening the door. Carl and Peter watched from the couch. "They want me with an electric mixer, right? That's your deal with them, right? So why not do a little business? Don't let me stop you, Ma!" he called as he went down to the car and unloaded the bottles into the blonde's lap. "Whatever you got," he told the driver, who held out a five-dollar bill.

"Hey!" the driver called as he started back toward the house. "What about my change?"

"Oh yah!" He turned and fished the rest of the bottles from his pockets. "Here you go!" One after another he hurled the bottles, smashing them on the car. Inside, the girls screamed and covered their faces. Beery crystals of foamy glass ran down the side of somebody's daddy's brand-new car.

Headlights flared on from the nearby grove. And then came the red roof lights with sirens as three cruisers raced in to surround the red sedan.

"Sorry," he said with upturned palms to the approaching policemen. "No mixer. I just been too busy selling beer to these minors here." He looked back at his mother's cold face in the doorway. His brothers watched from the window. "Sorry, Ma. But maybe you can go back to business now." He saw Officer Heinze wince, and he laughed. "That was the deal, right? Sorry, beautiful," he called, bending to the blonde, who sobbed out her name to one of the policemen.

"Come on," Heinze said, nudging him toward his cruiser.

"Hey! Where's my hero?" he said, looking around. "Where's Sonny?"

Heinze looked at him and took a deep breath. "His wife just died," he said as he clamped handcuffs over his wrist.

"Aw, too bad! I'll bet that really broke old Sonny's heart, huh?" He chuckled with the image of Eunice Bonifante's fist plunged down the back of the good Chief's trousers.

"You bastard! You no-good son of a bitch!" Heinze cried, pummeling the side of his head, the blows so sudden and sharp that he sank to his knees, his eyes rolling as his head bobbed up and down. He toppled onto his side.

His mother stepped back, and with the click of a dead bolt, the door closed, and all the windows came down in the little gray house, and then all the shades, and the yellow bug light went out, and then it was dark, mercifully dark.

The morning paper had been thrown on the dewy grass and now the wet pages kept tearing as Robert Haddad looked for the obituaries. Here it was. Carol Stoner. The picture was of a younger, happier woman, whose smile seemed to mock him. Her policy was for twenty thousand dollars. Every time the phone rang he held his breath and looked toward the kitchen, where Astrid worked at the table. Sonny wouldn't call until after the funeral, so he had a few days, anyway. First off, he'd tell him the company needed a death certificate; then he'd explain how the submission and processing were often delayed by red tape. But the Chief couldn't be put off for too long. Haddad figured he might have a week, two weeks, a month at most, and then what? Where the hell was he going to get twenty thousand dollars? Of course, this whole thing was eventually going to blow up in his face. Hadn't he known that? Now he needed a big hit. What had he been thinking? Holy shit. He'd leave, that's what he'd do, just start driving; but she'd never come. No, this had been his big chance. It just wasn't fair. Here she was, happy with him for the first time since their wedding night, oblivious to the shame and ruin that lay ahead. Okay. Okay. He had to stay calm and try to think straight. There had to be a way to put this all back together. And once he had, everything would be on the up and up. Everything. He wouldn't put so much as a penny of petty cash into his pocket. The thing was . . . the difference here . . . the reason he deserved a chance to set this straight was that he wasn't a criminal. It had all been circumstance, lousy timing, one bad break after another. Same thing had happened to Jimmy Saultner at the Chevy dealership, plowing sales receipts into the big new house, the snooty wife, the kids' prep schools, the girlfriend's surgery, cover here, patch up there, until the bank's knocking on the front door while Jimmy's sucking a hose down in the garage. Well, not him, no sir. He'd use his head and wrench this runaway life back on track. What he needed here was a big hit. A very, very big hit. And from then on, no more. He'd take his lumps, get another job—selling used cars, mopping floors if he had to. Hell, he wasn't proud.

Astrid wandered in again from the table, where she had been making lists of people to invite to her soap parties. She planned to have one a week. Fifty a year. There'd be refreshments, door prizes, games, entertainment. What did he think? she mused, her rhinestone-studded glasses slipping down her nose as she studied the list for her first party. "I have so many names," she sighed, "but what if I don't really know them?" Looking up, she frowned. "Bobby, what's wrong?"

"Mrs. Stoner died," he said, gesturing at the paper. "The Chief's wife. They're policyholders."

She kissed the top of his head. "Well, aren't you something, caring so much for your customers." She pointed to the picture on the page opposite the death notices. "I met him," she said, reading the caption: " 'Mr. and Mrs. Cleveland Hinds, co-chairs of the hospital's annual Winter Ball.' He came in the store once."

"He's president of the Atkinson Savings Bank," Haddad told her, adding, as she scribbled the name onto her list, "It's the second-largest bank in the state."

"Might as well go for the big ones!" Astrid laughed, dotting the *i* with a flourish.

"That's right!" he said loudly, because suddenly the room seemed swollen with noise and turbulence.

Mount's Funeral Home was crowded with mourners. The lot was full, so cars had begun to park on adjacent streets, some of which were no-parking zones, but no one complained or called the police.

Alice waited in the long line that moved slowly into the old brick building. She wore her graduation dress and her squeaky heels. She chewed the edge of her thumbnail, then winced when it tore too close to the flesh. She hated this. She didn't want to be here, didn't want to see Mrs. Stoner's corpse, and dreaded seeing Lester again. She'd been the first person he called.

"My mother's dead," he'd announced in a cold voice. "It just happened five minutes ago."

"Oh Les," she'd said, trying not to cry. "I don't know what to say. I'm so sorry."

"Well. I just thought you should know," he'd said, his terse finality sickening her.

All day long she had tried to look forward to tonight. It was her first night off in three weeks, and Joe had planned something special. She couldn't imagine what it might be, since the Monsignor had been at the lake for two days with his cousin Nora Hinds. Her son, Bernard, was sick again. The Monsignor would be celebrating Mrs. Stoner's funeral Mass the day after tomorrow, but then he was headed straight back to the lake. The Monsignor had left Joe completely in charge, which meant he couldn't see her during the day or pick her up after work. He'd gone on every sick call and kept all the Monsignor's counseling appointments. Joe had been pressuring her so much lately with all his talk of their life together that not seeing him these last few days had been a relief. People at work were giving her funny looks, and last week her mother had demanded to know why she was spending so much time with a priest. The more she insisted they were friends, the more convinced her mother was that all the convent talk was true. Now she and her mother were barely speaking.

The line moved ahead. Once inside, she found it wasn't nearly as upsetting as she'd expected. The woman in the pale blue satin folds was so thin that all of her bones ridged up against her dress, and her skin was an eerie pearly white, and a few dry wisps of her own hair straggled out from under the wig, and yet this woman certainly looked more like Mrs. Stoner than Mrs. Stoner had in the last few months.

Chief Stoner stood by the casket. His eyes were red, but his voice was clear as he thanked everyone for coming and shook each hand.

"Alice!" he said as the man in front of her stepped away. "Oh Alice, how nice of you to come," he said, taking her hands in his.

"I'm awfully sorry," she whispered. "Mrs. Stoner was always very nice to me."

He shook his head and sniffed. "She was crazy about you, Alice. She thought you were the best thing that ever happened to Les." He wiped away tears. "She hoped . . . she wanted . . . she thought . . ." He took a deep breath. "Poor Carol, she didn't deserve any of this," he sobbed, and her face flamed as a hush fell over the room. "I'm sorry," she said again. "I'm awfully sorry." It felt as if she were apologizing for everything, for Mrs. Stoner's suffering, for leaving Les, for causing the Chief's worst grief. A man and a woman she recognized as Les's aunt and uncle from Providence came up then to stand with the distraught Chief. "I'm sorry," she said to the aunt, who put her arm around his waist. "I'm very sorry," she said to the uncle, who nodded. She moved gratefully along.

"Les is out back," the Chief called after her. "He needs to see you."

She found Lester in a tiny sitting room next to the office. He sat on the gold loveseat with a pile of wadded tissues on his lap. His eyes bloodshot, his nose red and swollen, he could breathe only through his mouth. "I had to leave," he gasped. "I just couldn't do it anymore."

"Oh Les, I'm so sorry." She hated seeing him like this. He was probably regretting all the times he'd been irritable with his mother. She sat down and tried to make him feel better by recalling the night they'd played cards with his mother and the times they'd had lemonade together, and the time his mother had showed them her high school yearbook and pretended to be so offended when they kept laughing at the weird clothes and hairstyles.

He covered his face. "I'm all alone," he sobbed. "And I can't stand it."

"You've got your father. He's such a nice man, and he needs you, Les. Especially now," she said.

His head shot up. "He doesn't need me. All he needs is me to forgive him, but I won't. I never will." His mouth was white and quivering.

"Les, I know. It's the same as my father. Only it's not even forgiveness he wants. It's understanding, and that's almost worse. At least forgiveness means it's over. My father just wants me to keep putting up with it."

"At least your father's not a hypocrite," he spat. "He is what he is. He doesn't go around preaching honor and responsibility like my father did the whole time he was screwing my aunt while my poor mother laid in her bed night after night, crying! But the worst thing is, he used me. He didn't have to feel so guilty if I was with her. And that way, it didn't look so bad. And that's the most important thing, what people think of good Chief Stoner. But no matter what he does or what he says, I know the truth about him. I know just how bad he is." Spittle foamed in the corners of his mouth. His eyes glittered. "And he can't stand that," he whispered, almost gloating.

"Les." It was an effort to look at him. The hair on her arms bristled. She had to get out of here. "Oh Les." She stood up. "Les, all of that's over now."

He put his head back and closed his eyes. The floorboards creaked outside as people passed through the corridor. "I'm leaving for the seminary in two weeks," he said.

"That's probably the best thing, then. Just get away from everything here."

He stood up as she moved to the door. His shoulders heaved up and down as he began to cry. "Alice. Alice, will you hold me? Just hold me, that's all."

"Oh poor Les," she said with a limp embrace where only cheeks touched, his queasily hot and damp against hers, and she was ashamed of the revulsion she felt.

Her face reddened as she came up the street toward the rectory. She stared at her aunt's house, praying no one was watching now as she turned onto the rectory walk. In the time it took to get to the side door she cringed with toes bunched, eyes almost closed, begging through clenched teeth, "Please hurry, please hurry, please, please hurry."

Joe grinned as she stepped into the warm kitchen. Lidded pans were on the stove, and she could smell onions and meat roasting in the oven. Joe wore a blue button-down shirt with his clerical pants and black shoes. The long lace-covered table in the dining room was set for two, with silver flatware, pale-blue-and-white china, gold-rimmed crystal, linen napkins, and a silver candelabrum that held five slender candles. In the middle of the table were gladioli and white carnations in a stuccoed basket she knew must have come from the church.

Mrs. Arkaday had the night off. Alice was relieved that this was the surprise. No matter where they went, even if they were just in the car late at night, there was always the fear of being recognized by a parishioner. The fear made her not only nervous but bitchy, she realized an hour later as she couldn't stop laughing at Joe's word, *feency,* on the Scrabble board.

"Sorry! No such word. I never heard of it."

"Feency," he said, getting up to check the roast beef again. His apron was a dish towel tucked into his pants. "That's what Howard Menka said his sister has now that she's engaged to Carson. A 'feency.' "

"It has to be in the dictionary," she said, laughing.

"Look it up if you insist," he called, and she smiled, watching him hurry down the hallway. He wanted everything to be perfect. She wasn't to lift a finger or to worry about a single thing. He had even made her feel better about seeing Lester at the funeral home. Joe said Lester was taking out his own guilt and resentment of his mother's illness on his father, and also, in a sense, on her. He wants to be rescued, that's what that was all about, Joe had said, and for some reason the words kept surfacing. *He wants to be rescued. Yes,* she thought, as he came back to the table. *We all do.*

They were midway through dinner when the phone rang. "Oh no, please, not a sick call," Joe groaned, hurrying into the kitchen to answer it.

She could hear him laughing.

"Just Mrs. Arkaday checking to make sure everything's all right," he said, returning to the table. He sat down and replaced his napkin in his lap with an irritating fussiness. "She hopes you like the roast beef. She ordered the cut special."

Alice gulped. "She knows I'm here? Mrs. Arkaday knows I'm here?"

He smiled. "She thinks I'm cooking dinner for Father Krystecki."

"But what happens when she sees Father Krystecki and asks him how he liked dinner?"

"Oh, he hardly ever comes here," he said with a wave of his fork.

"But when he does, she'll—"

"Don't worry about it," he interrupted. He leaned across the table and touched her cheek. "I'm not," he said, his wide grin startling her.

How could he not worry, when lately it was all she thought about? He confused her. Sometimes it seemed his priesthood was a miserable trap in which he felt hopelessly snared. And then there would be times like this, as he spoke of counseling Bernie Hinds, the Monsignor's young cousin, that his words ran together and his brow beaded with sweat, and his zeal and enthusiasm made her squirm.

Last week Bernie had refused to go to Albany for any more treatments, which he said only made him sicker. Nora Hinds had called in tears, begging the Monsignor to come at once to talk to him. Everyone had tried, but Bernie was adamant, Joe said, pouring more wine into their glasses.

"I don't know if I blame him after seeing what Mrs. Stoner went through," she said.

"Well, yah," he conceded with a wave of his fork. "But he's just a kid. He's got to keep trying."

"But why, if it just means more suffering and he'll never get better?" She'd already heard this story their last time together, and it had irritated her as much then as now.

"But that's not the point. You don't just give up. You fight. You fight back!" he said, eyes gleaming.

"But why?" she persisted. In moments like this there seemed a strange blankness in him.

"My God, Alice, you know why," he said with another wave of his fork, impatient to continue.

Yes. She knew why. Because Joe needed to be a hero, she thought, drinking more wine. That was his passion, to be a savior. And it was also the void.

"So when all else failed, I asked if I could try, and the Monsignor figured, well, why the hell not." He sipped his wine. "I'll never forget it, walking into that huge stone house, down that long hallway, opening the door into that dark room; and there he was, sitting on his bed, not only stark naked but so hairless with this terrible white skin. Like a radioactive ghost. That's all I could think of," he whispered, taking another sip. "A shining ghost. I kept thinking: He's already died. He's dead, and they don't even know it. But you see, I knew it. The minute I walked in there, I knew it. And I told him. I said, 'Bernie, your problem isn't your body. It's something in here, isn't it?' " he whispered, tapping his breast and staring as if she were the dying boy whose reply he now awaited, chin out, brow raised.

She drank her wine, drank more, filled her mouth with water, swishing to get rid of the bitter aftertaste now as he related the conversation that had left Bernie curled in his mother's arms, sobbing and begging for help. Joe had told him he was a spoiled rich brat who had never learned to fight back, who expected everything, including his recovery, handed to him on a silver tray.

"It's time for the hard fight, I told him. Time to find out not whether he can get better, *not* whether he's going to be cured, but whether or not he's got the guts to live."

She held her breath. The flickering candlelight deepened the cleft in his chin, the hollows round his piercing eyes, the tuft of black hair at his throat. His husky voice darkened with the wine and made her shiver. It's all right, she thought. He was a priest, and in spite of everything, always would be a priest, maybe even a better one for all of this. She felt not only safer with him when he seemed most priestly, but, oddly enough, in this moment, more womanly, more alive than she had ever felt.

She took another sip, this time savoring the lushness in her mouth. Every nerve tingled. Her eyelids were heavy. She smiled and pushed away her plate.

He was telling her how grateful the Monsignor had been. "He offered me a weekend off with my family, but I said not now. I thought I'd wait till you got up to school, and then maybe I'd take the time then, you know, stay someplace up there, the two of us."

She tried to smile, but now she was very tired. It was the wine. She had had alcohol only once before, a few sips of beer with Mary Agnes. She thought of her father, but not with the awful guilt she had experienced in Mary Agnes's cellar. She had often wondered how he could give up his family and all that mattered for the sake of some foul-tasting liquid. At least now, at this moment, anyway, it didn't seem quite the incomprehensibly selfish choice it usually did.

"Would you like dessert?" Joe asked. He had asked a previous question she had not answered, then had quickly forgotten. "I have chocolate cake."

"No, thank you," she said, making every effort to speak distinctly. Her tongue felt too big for her mouth. "I'm very full."

"You hardly ate," he said, looking at her.

"The meat . . . the meal was delicious." She smiled. "I mean it." She stretched back with a deep groan.

He suggested coffee, but she didn't want any. Just the smell of it was making her stomach feel funny. The phone rang. While he was gone, she braced her cheek on her fist and catnapped. He was back. She looked up, startled and trembling. He said it was someone from out of town wanting to know what time the early Mass was tomorrow. She watched him clear the table. He was telling her about a priest named Velecchi who had been in his first parish with him. Velecchi had called the other day to invite him up to his new parish, which was on a lake where they could go fishing. He paused and she was conscious of him looking at her, but she had been thinking of something else.

"So what'd that boy's father think you did? The one you gave the jacket to. You never said," she asked, peering at him.

"I don't know. I guess he—" Joe stammered. He was annoyed with her. The other night he had accused her of daydreaming while he was telling her about his most recent meeting with the Bishop. "I don't know what he thought."

"He thought you were queer." She giggled. "He did, didn't he? I know that's what it was, so you might as well admit it," she said smugly. She liked this honesty, this getting things out in the open, like a cool clear stream running straight through her, delivering her thoughts so smoothly she did not have to grope for or censor a word.

"I don't know what he thought," Joe said. He carried more dishes into the kitchen.

She blinked as the door swung in and out, its diminishing arc leaving her stranded and alone out here. "Joe?" she called, cringing with the thickness of her voice. "I'm sorry. I hurt your feelings, didn't I? Joe?"

"I'm right here," he said, backing through the door with a cup of milky coffee for her.

There was something she had to say, but he urged her to drink the coffee. It was something no one ever talked about. Like the boy and the jacket, there was always a part left out. "You know what it is, don't you?" she asked, bending low to sip from the edge of the dripping cup. "It's . . . it's . . . sex! That's what the problem is. That's what's so . . . so stupid!"

"Drink your coffee," he said, gesturing for her to lift the cup.

"Well, it is! It just makes everything so complicated and so dirty."

"No, Alice," he said patiently. "It's natural! It's part of living. Like eating and sleeping."

He didn't understand, and now she was losing her train of thought. She looked at him and started to cry. "But sometimes I feel like some animal that gives off this smell. It makes me sick, and every time I say the same thing. I vow I'll never ever do it again, it's so wrong. And then every night when I'm with you I can't help it. I can't stop myself. It feels like I'm out of control. And the harder I try not to, the better it feels. And then I'm so ashamed. Sometimes I even walk funny. I try to keep my legs close together."

"Alice . . ."

"No, no, listen. I know this is a weird thing to say, but I don't know who else to ask."

"What?" He looked frightened.

She rubbed her eyes, then scratched the back of her head. "Well . . . Oh God," she moaned, rolling he eyes. "I don't know how to say this."

"Then just say it. Whatever it is, say it." He kept swallowing and taking deep breaths.

"Is there a smell? Do I smell? Is that what happens? Is that how men can tell? How could you tell?"

"Alice! Alice, what have I done to you?" He came around the table and sat close to her. "Men can't tell anything. There's no, no odor. It's not like a dog in heat. It's not dirty. It's beautiful. You don't smell. You're the sweetest, purest, most wonderful person I know. Don't cry, please don't. There's nothing wrong with you, honey. Believe me. I love you, and love isn't dirty, Alice. It's not wrong."

She looked up and wailed with this soreness in her chest. She had to tell him: the thing was, the terrible, terrible thing was that she didn't love him. She didn't love anyone.

"Come here, baby. You're upset. You're tired, and you've had too much wine. Come here. Let me take care of you. Let me hold you," he whispered as they climbed the stairs to his quiet room, to his dark bed with its cool bleached linen. He eased down beside her. Curled against him, she drifted in and out of sleep as he kissed her ear, her eyes, her mouth, her throat. He stroked the length of her arms to the damp tender skin between each finger. He helped her unbutton her dress. She heard him move away and lay it neatly on the chair. He took off his own clothes, then pulled the sheet over them.

"I love you," he whispered with every new place he touched and kissed. "You taste like flowers."

A wall rose around her and in here nothing hurt. In here she was safe, as long as someone loved her and did not demand it back.

"Aaargh," the Monsignor groaned with every rut and bump in the road while his cousin Nora drove. He was doubled over with pain, his brow pressed against the dashboard. Nora kept insisting he go to the hospital.

"If I turn here, we could be there in five minutes," she said, slowing down. She wore a trench coat over her pajamas. He had come to her door at midnight.

"No! I just need to get in my own bed, and then I'll be all right." Damn, couldn't she ever take no for an answer? This was all her fault, anyway. She knew he had no willpower when it came to food, and yet her cupboards were stocked with all manner of things he couldn't eat. At least Mrs. Arkaday had some sense. At least she took care of him. His own cousin didn't seem to care.

"Maybe after a few days' rest you'll feel like coming back." She looked over with a hopeful smile. "This is the first time all summer Bernard's come down to eat with us. It was just so wonderful being able to have a normal conversation with him. In spite of all his suffering."

He groaned, and with this for assent, she continued to babble about her son. Bernard, Bernard, the hell with Bernard. His head reeled with this pain knifing through his gut. Bernard had never had to endure anything like this. No one had. My God, what was this test, this latest trial? *Release me from this misery, I implore you. Shrink the gallstone. Make it disappear. Take it away. You can do this, Jesus, my sweet, sweet Jesus. Damn it, I know you can! I know you can! So do it! Do it!*

"Tom?" she hit the brake, and he almost fainted with the car's sudden lurch. "What is it, Tom?"

"Praying," he grunted. "I'm praying."

"Almost there," she kept assuring him, jamming on the brake at every stop, then accelerating ahead as if to demonstrate her full awareness of his misery. "Almost there. Just a few more blocks." The car swerved around another corner.

Damn, why hadn't Cleve been there to drive him home? Nora said he was at the bank preparing for the annual audit, but the Monsignor knew what it was: the town's most powerful Catholic found him boring.

"Here we go," Nora said, pulling into the rectory driveway and braking so sharply he almost fainted. She hurried around the front of the car. She had to unfold him to get him out. Doubled over and listing to one side, he walked with his arms girding his belly. He grew dizzier with every step he climbed.

He was shocked when Nora switched on the kitchen light. A teetering pile of dirty dishes filled the sink. On the cutting board an empty wine bottle stood in a puddle of condensation that had puckered the familiar label: the precious Brechy-Cordell he'd been saving for the day he was named Bishop. Limp tomato slices shriveled on a plate: the season's first beefsteaks he'd been nurturing on the sunniest windowsill to full red ripeness. On the stove were a sludgy gravy pan and a pot of cold gray potato water clotted with white scum. A new pain rose in his chest.

"Something's happened to Mrs. Arkaday," he groaned, groping along the countertop to the door. They passed in wordless terror through the dining room. A long, brown slick of spilled coffee stained the crocheted cloth, the last his mother had made, the intricate pattern Donegal, home of his and Nora's good and decent ancestors. On the table were a dirty ashtray and a pack of Camels. A thin white plastic purse hanging on the back of a chair by its cracked and brittle strap swayed as he and his cousin passed by. Something was terribly wrong.

"Just go to bed, Tom," Nora whispered at the top of the stairs as he struggled toward Father Gannon's bedroom.

"Not until I find out what happened to Mrs. Arkaday," he said, turning the young priest's doorknob. "Father Gannon!" he barked into the musky heat that now, as the hall light bled into the darkness, was a sudden muddied swirl of naked limbs, an angry curse, and then a sobbing hunched whiteness over which a thrown sheet was settling.

"No, no, no, no, no, no, no," the woman bleated beneath the quivering sheet.

"Get out of here! Just get the hell out!" his bollocky curate roared, shoving him toward the hallway, where Nora stood staring, her hand over her mouth.

Staggering, the Monsignor clutched the doorframe. "No! In the name of Jesus, no, not now or ever!" he panted. "You! Out of here this minute, you terrible woman, you vile and disgusting . . ."

The two men struggled as Father Gannon pried his fingers from the wood, then pushed him away and shut the door.

"Tom!" Nora gasped as he tried to open it, and finding it locked, pounded on it with his fist, demanding to be let in.

"Stop it! Stop it," she insisted. "You're just going to hurt yourself." She held on to his hand. "Let them get dressed," she said at his ear in a low hard voice.

"This is more than a heinous sin," he cried. "This is a violation, the worst betrayal I could imagine." He looked at her, choking on his tears. His beefsteaks. His Brechy-Cordell. His mother's cloth, his legacy, tainted and consumed by lust. "My curate and . . . and my housekeeper!"

"No, Tom, that's a young girl. It's Alice Fermoyle."

He was relieved, then shocked and disgusted and angry all over again. "I want her out of here this minute!" he thundered.

Father Gannon said they'd come out as soon as the hallway was empty.

The Monsignor made his way downstairs, with Nora holding his arm. He went directly to the kitchen, where he removed the two sets of car keys from the brass hooks by the door. So now it all made sense, all the late nights, the odd stains on the upholstery, the greasy whorl on the door glass . . .

As Nora Hinds's Lincoln floated through the night, Alice kept her face to the window, but her eyes were closed. It had come full circle, the bastard conception that had driven Nora Hinds away was now being delivered by Nora Hinds to her mother without any underpants on.

It had been a terrible scene. When the Monsignor refused to let Joe drive her home, Joe had smashed a wineglass on the wall, bellowing that he couldn't take any more of it, that he was through, through, through, goddamn it, he was through. The Monsignor kept ordering him to his room while she sobbed in the foyer. The Monsignor staggered to the phone and said he'd call her mother to come and get her out of there. Joe grabbed his arm and warned him not to. That's when Nora Hinds, ashen-faced and trembling, said she'd drive Alice home.

Alice tried not to smile. Home. All the ugliness and discord, her breath stale with alcohol, her thighs sticky with lovemaking, and now they all knew. Well, good, it was about time. About time. About time.

"It's a little after one," Nora Hinds said.

Had she asked the time? Alice wondered. Nora Hinds sat so erectly behind the wheel that she towered over Alice. *Maybe I've shrunk. Maybe I can. Maybe I can. If I stop breathing and try real hard,* but now they turned down the street, and here came her pathetic little house, light glaring through the cracked globe over the front door, which opened the minute they pulled into the driveway. "No, no, no," she groaned, shaking her head as her grim-eyed mother waded around the front of the car through the shimmering headlights, with Norm at her heels, bending low a moment to see his fucked-up, dirty, crazy sister. She covered her face with her hands.

"It'll be all right," Nora Hinds said to Alice. "She's very upset," Nora Hinds told her mother, who was trying to pull her gently from the car, but with her arms and legs gone to stone, that was going to be impossible, because now she couldn't move, didn't know how anymore.

"I'll lift her out," Norm said, leaning in to get his arms under her, but for a grunting moment could not dislodge her.

"Alice!" her mother commanded.

"Poor thing's terribly upset," Nora Hinds said with her fingertips at her mouth as if she might cry.

"Come on, Alice," Norm grunted as he managed to get her legs out and his arms around her shoulders. "Let's just get in the house," he kept whispering as he guided her up the walk. "Just get inside and everything'll be okay."

"No, it won't," she said as they climbed the front steps. "It'll never be okay. Never, ever again."

Norm brought her to her room, where she lay in her dress with her eyes closed. Her mother came in and sat on the edge of the bed for a long time without saying anything.

I have come full circle. Full circle into the darkness.

"This is all my fault," her mother said. "I should have known. Oh baby, I haven't really seen you all summer. You were always such a good girl, I didn't think I had to worry much about you. But it's going to be all right. You'll see. I haven't told the boys yet, honey. At first I wanted to wait until the soap came, and then your father's been trying so hard with his new job, and I didn't want him all upset, but Omar and I are engaged, Alice! He gave me this beautiful diamond . . . would you like to see it? I'll turn on the light. Well, you can see it in the morning, then. You sleep now, and in the morning everything will start to look better, I promise."

The bed shook, and Alice covered her face with her hands. She couldn't stop laughing.

"Don't cry," her mother whispered, leaning close now. "Please, Alice, listen to me. We all make mistakes. Everyone does." She pulled her hands away. "Alice? Alice, stop that! I said stop it right now!" She grabbed her and dug her fingers into Alice's arms. "This *will* be over. Do you hear me? It's not going to change anything. Tomorrow morning you'll get up, just the way I've gotten up every morning, every day of my life, and you'll start all over again, do you hear me? Because this isn't going to stop you. Nothing's going to stop you. Nothing! Do you hear me? Do you? Do you? Goddamn it, answer me!"

The door burst open. It was Norm demanding that she leave her alone. She was too upset. Couldn't she see that?

"Upset? She's laughing! Look at her! Look at her, laying there laughing!"

"You know she's not laughing." His voice broke. "Jesus Christ, Mom, she's falling apart."

"No!" Marie cried. "No! No, that's too easy. You don't just fall apart and leave everyone else to pick up the pieces." She paced back and forth between Norm and Alice, who had pulled the pillow over her head.

"What you do is, you keep on going," she panted, chopping the side of her hand into her palm. "You keep on going and going and going and going and going and going, goddamn it, until you just can't do it anymore. Until you're dead, goddamn it! That's when you stop!" She leaned over the bed. "When you're dead! And not until then!"

The Monsignor hobbled from his bedroom to the bathroom, heaving sighs of pain and disgust that caused Mrs. Arkaday's rag to scrub faster and faster. The rectory smelled of pine oil. For days Mrs. Arkaday had been scrubbing floors, woodwork, and walls with an exculpatory zeal. The Monsignor was barely speaking to her. If she had been here that night, the incident never would have happened.

Father Gannon crept into the office. He needed to talk to Alice. Every time he called, one of her brothers answered and said she didn't want to talk to anyone. This time when he dialed, her mother answered. He closed his eyes, asking for her in a whisper.

"No," Mrs. Fermoyle said. "You can't."

"I have to speak to her, Mrs. Fermoyle, you don't understand," he said.

"Oh I understand all right," she said.

"No. No, you don't. You see, I love Alice."

"For God's sake, you're a priest!" she growled.

"But that doesn't matter. I—"

"It matters to me."

"What matters is Alice's happiness!" he said.

"Then leave her alone."

"I can't."

"Well, if you can't, then I'm calling the Monsignor. And if that doesn't work, I'll call the police!"

"Mrs. Fermoyle! Mrs. Fermoyle, please!" he begged, but she'd hung up.

The office door swung open and the Monsignor limped in, holding his side, his face pinched with pain and shock. "You're forcing my hand, Father Gannon. I swear to you, if you have anything more to do with that, that girl, then I'm going to call the Bishop!"

"Call the Bishop! Call the police! Call my mother! Call everyone! Who gives a shit!" He couldn't help laughing. They were trying to back him into a corner, that's what they were doing here, hoping he'd flip out again, so this time they could wash their hands of him, but it wasn't going to be so easy for them this time, because this time someone loved him and needed him. This time he'd *have* to fight back.

The Monsignor closed the door behind him and leaned on the desk facing the unshaven priest, whose hair was greasy and uncombed. His soiled clerical collar was limp and creased, and there was a disagreeable odor about him. Father Gannon was clearly out of control. For the past two nights the Monsignor had been sickened by the feeble sobbing from the curate's room. Mrs. Arkaday had confirmed his lack of bathing, and this morning she said he wasn't eating anything to speak of but coffee and sweets. When the phone rang he'd snatch it up on the first ring, then forget to pass on the messages to the Monsignor. And now he had violated the Monsignor's direct order. It enraged him to see Father Gannon's foolish grin as he twirled a pen between his fingers.

"How can you sit there? Don't you have anything to say? You've disgraced your vocation and humiliated me. You have caused a scandal, and worse, you chose as your partner in sin the niece of one of my dearest parishioners."

At this, Father Gannon's head bobbed with some brief amusement. The Monsignor gripped the back of the chair. What disturbed him most was this pharisaical air, as if he thought his priestliness of a higher, purer order than the Monsignor's, some divine aegis for which he was being so unjustly punished, so constantly tormented.

The Monsignor's stomach rumbled and his cheeks ballooned with a swallowed belch. In addition to gallstones he had an ulcer. The doctor had put him on such a restrictive diet that he couldn't sleep through the night, so violent were his hunger pangs. These last few evenings he found himself hurrying up to bed earlier and earlier, his cassock pockets sagging with the dinner biscuits and cold chicken Mrs. Arkaday left so providentially transportable in waxed-paper bags.

It occurred to him that these stomach problems had begun last spring about the time of Father Gannon's arrival. So it wasn't intemperate eating habits, after all, but the tension and anxiety this disturbed curate had brought into his life. From the start all Father Gannon had to do was walk into the room and the Monsignor would feel his temperature rising, his throat swelling in his collar. The man was always touching, grasping, picking up things that were not his, reading the Monsignor's mail, just because it was there, nervously sliding open drawers and cupboard doors while he spoke in that rush of words boiling over with some new cause or indignation. His most recent concern had been Howard, who would surely die of a broken heart if his sister married Grondine Carson. Father Gannon had proposed moving the dim-witted caretaker into the rectory guest room. It was for guests, visiting clergy, the Monsignor had countered. A room over the garage, then; they could build it themselves, he and Howard, Father Gannon had declared, slashing his pen back and forth across the bottom of the sermon he had been working on. See, a bedroom, parlor, small bath. He had drawn a floor plan. No need for a kitchen. Howard could take his meals with them. No, no, no. He almost had to shout before Father Gannon understood.

The Monsignor had done his best. And this time no one could accuse of him of not trying. He had been through this years ago with one of his first curates, but that had been more delicate. Not only had the curate fondled the nephew of the Holy Name Society president, but the curate himself had been the nephew of Father Mulcahy, treasurer of the diocese. At least this should be fairly easy. Father Gannon was a nobody with a history of spiritual and mental instability. And Alice Fermoyle, well, knowing her kind, she was probably the cause of this whole mess.

"I'm going to ask the Bishop to transfer you, Father, and in the meantime, you're not to have anything to do with anyone."

Father Gannon looked up and smiled.

"Especially with that Fermoyle girl," he added. All he needed now was Marie Fermoyle, that disagreeable woman, charging in here again.

The Bishop returned his call an hour later.

"Are you sure?" came the Bishop's equable response to every allegation.

"Am I sure? Am I sure?" the Monsignor finally exploded. "Don't you understand? There was a girl in his bed! And I was there! The three of us! Naked! So of course I'm sure!"

"Slow down now, Tom, you're confusing me. I'm just trying to get the picture here, that's all," said the Bishop.

"Well, it's not a very pretty picture, let me tell you!" the Monsignor said, his mouth against the sweaty receiver.

There was a pause. "The thing I don't understand, Tom, is why you were . . . undressed."

"No!" he groaned. "Not me!"

When he had finally explained everything, the Bishop said, "This is a shame, a terrible shame. I had some real hope for that young man. There was something about him, you know what I mean, Tom, that old-fashioned zeal you just don't get anymore. Aw, that's too bad to hear it's been so . . . so misdirected. I'm disappointed. I really, really am."

Misdirected. The Monsignor's jowls smarted as if he'd just been slapped. The Bishop not only didn't understand, but he thought it was the Monsignor's fault. Suddenly he found himself telling the Bishop how sick he'd been, how bloated and constipated he was, how he couldn't concentrate. It was all the pressure. The convent was leaking again, and Sister William Theresa was demanding a new roof. Demanding! And when he told her there were no funds for a new roof, she had the gall to ask him where the funds for next spring's trip to Rome were coming from. That was his silver-anniversary trip, which, by the way—he wanted the Bishop to be sure and know, just in case Sister should try and raise a stink over this—his cousin Nora was paying for. He still couldn't believe the way that nun had dared speak to him. The same with Father Gannon, who'd gone from calling him Tom to sleeping with women in his rectory. The old order was crumbling. He hoped the Bishop knew how short a path it was from impudence to anarchy.

"Chaos, your Excellency, that's what it's come to. You asked me to be patient, but this man needs help!"

"Um, what kind of help do you mean?" There was a rustle of pages turning as if the Bishop had been reading a newspaper.

"He needs to be locked up, that's what he needs!"

"Tom, he's already spent a year in the hospital. And he came out with a clean bill of health. Maybe he just got a little overburdened."

"A little overburdened!" His flesh burned with insult.

"You said you left him completely in charge. It was probably too much for him."

"Too much for him!"

"Look, Tom. I'll call his Provincial and get someone down there to talk to him. In the meantime maybe you could lighten the young fellow's load a little."

The Monsignor was stunned.

"And by the way, Tom," the Bishop added. "We're a little short of our goal statewide for the Bishop's relief fund. Maybe you could pick up part of the slack with a special collection this Sunday."

"But it's Saint Mary's first fuel collection this Sunday," he said in a cold voice.

"Try to fit it in sometime soon, then," the Bishop said airily, adding that he wished they could talk longer, but he was having a few people in for dinner and he really had to hurry.

The Monsignor slumped in the dark room's early twilight. What did the Bishop care, with his handsome face and silver-streaked hair that belonged up on a movie screen and not beneath the jeweled satin mitre that would never be the Monsignor's.

Overhead the floorboards creaked as Father Gannon paced back and forth in his room.

For two days now, the house had smelled of vinegary spices and steamed vegetables from his sister's canning. Samuel Fermoyle felt good, stronger, healthier than he could ever remember. It was midafternoon and he was on his way to see his daughter. When he had called earlier to see if Alice would be home, Benjy would only say, "Probably." The conversation had been so strained that he'd almost decided not to go. But it was time to see them. He was ready.

He braced his foot on the windowsill and tied his shoe. It was this easy, he thought, doubling the knot, leaving nothing to chance, not a moment untended. That had been the true lesson of Applegate. Not any of their psychological shit, but the order that had prevailed there.

As he headed out the door, he heard Helen's voice rise sharply in the kitchen and then Jozia's angry reply. They had been bickering for the past hour. Jozia wanted something, whether a raise or time off, he couldn't tell from her muttered demands, but Helen was growing angrier in her refusals. He felt himself borne by a great calm, an enlightenment, a contagion of wisdom and joy he would spread among his family, those doubters like his sister, who expected nothing more of him than the inevitable misstep, the lie, the omission.

He passed the rectory and smiled at Howard, who was dragging a garden hose down the church walkway. "Hello there!" he called, but Howard continued to tug at the hose and did not look up. It was then that he noticed the young curate sitting on the bottom rung of a ladder that leaned against the back of the Church. "Hello, Father. Lovely afternoon, isn't it?" he called. "Okay!" he muttered as Father Gannon looked quickly down into the bucket at his feet. Just keep going. Keep going, he told himself, determined to squelch the dread stirring in his brain. The Monsignor had probably warned the young priest not to get too friendly. A sudden image of himself shouting drunkenly at Father Gannon and careening through the polished rectory vestibule shot into his head. Jesus. Once again, he found himself adrift between the future's terrifying void and the past, an even stranger emptiness, festering with so many of these amnesiac violations and humiliations. It was like being stalked by his own maniacal twin.

He began to feel shaky. Maybe he wasn't ready to see the kids. Maybe they didn't want to see him. That's why Benjy had sounded so funny. After all, not one of them had bothered to see how he was doing. Not even a phone call. Didn't they care? Didn't they know how hard he was trying? At the corner, he turned toward the park. He was surprised to hear rock-and-roll music blasting. The bandstand was filled with musicians. Because they weren't in uniform he thought they were only practicing. But then he realized no one was playing an instrument. They stared glumly up at the podium, where Jarden Greene was waving his arms and shouting over the raucous din that they were a sorry group of musicians who had lost their passion.

"Play it big!" he cried, raising his baton. "Play it so big and so full of yourself that you will forget the fool is there! Drown him out! Obliterate him!"

As they took up their instruments a few of the musicians glanced toward Joey Seldon, who sat on a stool in his lopsided stand where speakers amplified his radio songs. Two trash barrels were overflowing onto the ground. Bottles and popcorn boxes were everywhere in the grass and on the sidewalk. Three sides of the stand were buttressed by stacked cases of empty bottles and cans.

"Gusto! Gusto! Gusto!" Greene shouted as the band played "When the Caissons Go Rolling Along."

"Joey!" Sam hollered, banging his fist on the counter, trying to be noticed through the concussion of music.

"What do you want?" Joey yelled.

"It's me, Joey! Sam Fermoyle," he hollered, leaning closer. The aluminum doors under the popcorn machine were ajar, and Sam was shocked to see a large black gun inside.

"Plain or buttered?" Joey got off the stool.

"Not today," he shouted, then tried to explain that he'd just stopped by to say hello and see how things were going.

"That's how they're going!" Joey said, pointing to the curled cardboard sign tacked overhead. It was an eviction order signed by Judge R. L. Begley.

Now that he had been ordered to shut down, the town claimed it was no longer responsible for picking up trash from an illegal business. As a result he had also been served with public health violations.

"It's all him," Joey shouted, pointing at Jarden Greene, whose body appeared to be vibrating on the podium.

Across the street the pharmacy door flew open and Marco, the druggist, stood on the top step in his starched white smock shouting into a bullhorn.

"Joey, turn off the radio! I repeat. Joey, turn off the radio! If you do not turn off the radio, then I am calling the police. I repeat. I am calling the police. And this time I'm swearing out a complaint!"

Turning, Joey reached under the counter, and for a chilling moment, Sam was certain he'd pull out the pistol and start firing away. Instead the radio went louder. Joey had turned it up.

"Joey! Joey!" he shouted. "What're you doing?"

"Same as they're doing to me! Harassment!" Joey shouted. "I'll stop when they stop."

Sam hurried down Main Street. When he got to Marie's, Benjy told him through the half-open door that Alice was sick in bed. Relieved, he took a step down. No. He was here. He'd only stay a minute. Maybe he could make her feel better.

"I don't think so," Benjy said, letting him in. "She's really not feeling good," he whispered, glancing toward the stairs.

"What does she have, a cold?"

Benjy's eyes flicked away, then back again. "I don't know. But she's really sick."

Alice lay on her side, curled under the blanket. With the window shade down, he couldn't see her face on the pillow, just tangled hair.

"Alice?" he whispered, touching the back of her head. "It's me, pet. It's Daddy."

Her breathing seemed to stop. He said he would have called sooner, but did she know he was still a fugitive from the loony bin? It was too bad there wasn't a reward out for him, because then at least she could make a few bucks off her old man. He laughed. She hadn't moved. He had a new job, did she know that? Well, it was a real cushy position. He chuckled. Toilet paper, he had always wanted a career in toilet paper—bet she didn't know that about her old man. It promised to be a real cleanup job—that is, if he didn't mind wiping someone else's . . . Oops, sorry for that rude slip. Well, anyway, it was a real sit-down job, if she knew what he meant.

"Hon, are you awake?" He cleared his throat. Okay, let's see. What other news was there? Renie and Helen were fine. Nana wasn't doing too well. Yesterday the doctor had given her two more shots. Helen said they were penicillin and B_{12}. But he was convinced it was some new embalming fluid. Nana just laid there. Well, sat up, really, to keep fluid from accumulating in her lungs. She never sang anymore. Every once in a while her eyes would open wide, but usually they were closed. Let's see . . . what else?

He told her he was reading a biography of F. Scott Fitzgerald. He was thinking of maybe getting all his teeth out and investing in some new choppers. *Jesus,* he thought, *she doesn't want to hear about that.* He cleared his throat and asked how Marie was doing. She didn't answer. He asked if she'd do him a favor: would she please tell her mother to stop throwing those pebbles up against his window every night? Thinking the bed jiggled with her faint laughter, he touched her shoulder and leaned closer.

"Hey, what's this I hear about you and the new priest?" He felt her hunch up. "Something about going into the convent? Is it true? Alice?"

She curled into a ball and moaned. He took his hand away and said he hoped he hadn't upset her. Well, whatever she wanted to do with her life was fine with her old man. There was a gasp. The bed shook.

"I mean that, pet. I know I haven't always been much of a . . . well, the kind of . . . kind of father you deserve, but I'm trying now, pet. I really am. I feel so good now. And it's more than the job and staying sober. The thing is, I want to make you kids proud of me." He took a deep breath. "Because I'm really proud of you three kids. Really, really proud, pet."

He realized she was crying into her pillow. He lifted back a strand of her hair. "You know, when you came to see me at Applegate and I made you wait? I wasn't getting ready all that time. Christ, I was so happy you were coming I'd been up since five a.m. getting ready. All that time you were down there, I was sitting on the edge of my bed, that's what I was doing. Just sitting on the bed and trying to work up enough courage to go down and face you cold sober. I almost didn't make it," he said, sniffing and wiping his runny nose on the back of his hand. "But then a nurse came and walked me out to the elevator and pushed the button." He closed his eyes as she sobbed. "I'm not trying to make you feel bad, pet. I'm just trying to explain something here. You see, when I'm sober, I'm usually walking around, you know, with my tail between my legs, and I'm feeling like such a loser all the time. Like I screwed up everything, you know, my whole life, you kids, your Mom's life. But then this day I was in Renie's shop and I saw those pictures he had of you kids on the register and I just got so damn mad. I kept thinking, Who the hell is he to put up pictures of *my* kids? What the hell's he trying to prove? And all that day it just kept bugging the hell out of me, and then that night in the middle of the night my eyes opened wide and it hit me. You're not even his kids and he's so proud of you, he wants everyone to know he's your uncle. And here I am, I'm your father, and the thing is, I'm such a shithead I don't know how to be proud of anything anymore, even my own kids. And I realize, you kids are a lot to be proud of." He grinned. "I mean that, baby. I really do."

"No," she groaned. "No, no, no, no, no, no."

He leaned over and tried to hold her, but she recoiled, her body rigid and convulsed with moans.

"Oh God, look what I've done. I didn't mean to upset you like this." He stood up and reached for the door. "I'll go!"

"No, no, no, no, no." Her moans tore through him.

"I'll call your mother. She'll—" He covered his ears. "Oh God, Alice, stop it. I don't know what to do!"

"No, no, no, no, no, no . . ."

Benjy met him on the stairs. He had to get out of here, away from the boy's torn sneakers, the fuzzy television picture, the caved-in couch, the lamp with its red-and-gold Gypsy, her chipped dirty arms ending in plaster stumps.

"What's wrong with her?" he asked.

Benjy shrugged and couldn't look at him.

"Did something happen? Is it school? Is she nervous about school?"

"I don't know," Benjy muttered.

"It's not because of money, is it?" The expression on his son's face said it all. "Oh shit, don't tell me that's what happened." He felt like such a fool with all his talk about getting on his feet and pride in his kids while she lay up there devastated because she had no money for college.

Renie was dreaming. He and a man had been following the steady heartbeat. They were walking down a narrow corridor. The man opened a door and the heartbeat stopped. Here, there was a sun-drenched laboratory. The white walls were lined with shelves. Glass jars glistened on the shelves. Suspended in the clear liquid that filled every jar was a gelatinous sac. The man said because he had not come the fetus had been aborted, expelled from Beatrice's coarse womb.

Let me see him, Renie said.

Christ, that was a million years ago, the man said.

Let me see him.

Him? Who? What, you think they give them names?

I want to see him.

You think it's some kinda weird nursery, man, with the bottles all lined up so the proud pops can come in and look? The man laughed.

Could she have done such a thing? No, it could not be. He struggled to wake up. His eyes closed heavily. He was floating in a jar of pickled cauliflower, and yet he lay here on his bed perfectly still, his arms folded over his chest, the dim room taking shape around him as he floated in the glassy brine. The lowering sun cast a blush from the window, an acrid stillness whose bilious sediment would stir at the slightest movement and rise to fill his nose and mouth, already puckered with the pinched sting of vinegar that seeped in from the kitchen. Over the bubbly clatter of boiling canning jars came the hollow *chopchopchopchop* of Helen's knife on the cutting block. It was canning time. She'd started early this year. He couldn't move. He hadn't been to the store in days. Losing Tom had drained him of all hope and energy. All he wanted to do was sleep, and yet it was never enough. He was exhausted, sometimes too weak to lift his head from the pillow. He hadn't eaten, but he wasn't hungry. He knew he had to get up and eat and wash and get back to work, but he was just too tired.

For the first time Sam detected a faint odor of urine from his mother's crib as he paused on his way to the kitchen. Between the canning and his mother's worsening condition, Helen had been on her feet for days. He dreaded going in there, where every surface was littered with peelings, pots, and spice cans. He hoped Helen's mood wasn't as foul as it had been yesterday, when Jozia had walked out in the middle of bathing their mother. Helen muttered something now as a cupboard door banged shut. Water began to run into a pan.

He reached between the bars and touched his mother's arm, shivering to find her skin so slackly thin and cold. Her eyes were closed and her mouth gaped open with wheezy breathing. At times she frowned and seemed to wince as if in pain.

"Here we go, Mum," he said with a sigh, then removed the thin notebook from his breast pocket. This at least would have pleased her. He was going to demand that Helen give him his money for Alice's college expenses.

The kitchen was a mess. Helen stood by the stove, her hands

bound in white towels. She almost looked like a child in Jozia's long, red apron that came to her ankles. Sam sat at the table, which was covered with cucumber peels, tomato skins, corncobs, seedy pepper cores, and scummy bowls. Helen lifted a rack of mason jars filled with red tomatoes then lowered it into the kettle on the stove. She set the lid on carefully, pausing a moment before she turned. She glanced from Renie's closed door to the yellow notebook in Sam's hand.

"Lunch is long gone," she said, unwinding the towels from her hand.

"I ate," he said.

"If it's supper you're after, get it yourself." She began slicing cucumber rounds with a long, sharp knife.

"Is that the knife Dad used in the store?" he asked.

"How would I know?"

He had forgotten. It had been Helen who had walked in on their father and the Sicilian tenant's daughter in the back room of the little grocery. After that neither Helen nor their mother ever again entered the store.

"You look tired," he said.

"*Look* tired!" she said with such an angry fling of the sweating white rounds into the bowl that the vinegar splattered in her face. She took off her glasses and wiped her eyes.

"Why do you bother with all this, Helen?"

"What should I do? Let it rot?" Her voice quivered as if under the weight of a question she had asked herself countless times.

"Send some over to Marie and the kids," he suggested with a twinge of pity now for his sister, whose garden grew because it had to, who had no friends to share her harvest.

"Hah!" she snorted. "That's good coming from you." She spooned sugar into the fizzing marinade, then carried the bowl to the sink. On the stove the pressure was rising in the dull steel cooker, hissing and vibrating loudly. Helen reached for the rattling lid and a jet of steam whooshed against her wrist. She jerked back her hand with an angry cry. He wet a towel and tried to hold it to the red splotch on her wrist. She knocked away his hand and the towel fell on the floor. "Leave me alone!" she cried as she bent to pick it up.

"Helen!"

"Get out," she said. "Just get out and leave me alone! Everyone, just leave me alone!"

"Helen, there are other people you can get to help. . . ."

"Hah! Misfits, nothing but misfits. The misfits I've wasted my life on! All these years I kept her on rather than see her used by such filth, such . . ."

She was crying, the tears and the kettle's harrumphing steam fogging her glasses when she looked back at him. "My father, my brother, my mother," she moaned. "And did I ever ask for anything? Did I?" she demanded. "For myself? No! All I've ever wanted was a little respect, that's all, some pride. That's all I've ever wanted!" she cried, striking the tabletop with the knife handle. "Just to be able to hold my head high. That's all! That's all I've ever, ever, ever wanted!"

"Helen, don't. Don't cry." He felt terrible.

"Don't cry! After what Jozia told me, that's all I can do!" She looked at him and shook her head. "She used it on me. Took that filth and used it on me. 'No,' I told her. 'That's impossible. It couldn't be. Not Alice.' "

"What? What are you talking about?"

"Well, don't worry. I called the Monsignor. I called him myself because I knew no one else in this family would have the decency to do it." She dabbed her eyes with her apron hem. "And he said I wasn't to take on any more burdens. He said it was their sin, their filth."

He sprang at her. "What the hell are you talking about?"

She drew back, almost daintily, her demeanor sweetened, calmed by his fury. "Alice and the new curate, the two of them! Naked in the rectory. That poor sick man, the Monsignor. I'll tell you just what I told him. Sin breeds sin, Samuel Fermoyle. Dirt breeds dirt!" Her head snapped back as his hand rose. "Go ahead!" she cried. "The last defilement," she hissed, glaring at his fist.

"Don't say another word about my daughter, do you hear me?" he growled, then stepped away.

"Oh I won't! Believe me, I won't," she said in a trembling voice.

Now he understood why Alice couldn't look at him. His temples throbbed, and yet he was able to remove himself, to do this. "I want my money, Helen. I need it." He opened his notebook and was steadied by the cool recitation of his figures. He had computed the sum after expenses, room and board, to be six thousand dollars. He glanced at her. "Six thousand dollars in trust . . ."

"Gone," she interrupted.

He looked up, confused by her smile. She must be kidding.

"On your haircuts and your shoes and food and laundry bills. On all the money you ever stole from me, the things you broke, the people you owed, Renie's car you smashed up."

"Six thousand dollars, Helen!"

She was in the closet now, feeling along the shelf over Renie's clothes. She pulled down a worn tablet and began to read.

"December 20, 1956, $2, Mrs. Camus, Christmas wreath stolen by Sam. December 29, 1956, $11.85, Atkinson Free Library, Five lost books. January 9, 1957, $102, Renew Upholsterers, Reupholster plum brocade sofa after Sam's cigarette burns. January 12, 1957, $55, ambulance to Waterbury. May 31, 1957, $13, Mrs. Camus's American flag slept in by Sam on her back porch, then vomited on. June 8, 1957, $18, Dr. Horace R. Reynolds, House call and medicine, Sam's tremors. June 9, 1957, $25 fine, District Court, for being a public nuisance. Same date, $45, legal fees to Abner Atkinson. September 1, 1957 . . ."

"Public nuisance." He chuckled.

"September 1, 1957," she repeated.

"Shut up, Helen."

"Let me finish," she said, flipping the pages. "The last entry is your total bill paid to the Applegate Corporation. And that was," she said glancing up, "as of August first, $3,469." She closed the tablet. "Bringing you to $10,500.34."

"Right over the top." He sighed, his head pounding. "Gotta hand it to you, Helen. I am not only a fucking public nuisance, but a fucking public idiot. You know, that's the one thing I couldn't figure out. Why Applegate, I kept wondering, and Doc Litchfield thaid, your thithter only wanth the betht for you, Thammy." He hung his head over his own meager figures. "Don't do this to me, Helen."

"You've done it. Not me," she said, stepping past him to return the tablet to its shelf in the closet. She began to snap string beans in two.

"Marie needs my help."

She looked at him over her glasses. "What does she need your help for now that she's finally got herself a boyfriend? Your wife and your daughter, they certainly make a good pair."

"Shut up, Helen." He leaned over the table. She was deliberately goading him. He had to be careful. To call the police and have him hauled out of here would give her great satisfaction right now. "There's one more thing. Something you and the good Judge neglected to tell me. This is my house. Mine."

"This is Mother's house!" she said, outraged.

"Yes, and when she dies it's mine. And the tenements go to . . ." He read from his notes what Marie had told him. " 'They go to Samuel's heirs, as well as any issue of my daughter, Helen.' "

There was no color in her face. Her huge breasts rose and fell.

"You shouldn't have exiled Renie in there, Helen," he said, pointing to the door with its arterial fissures of ancient paint. "You should have produced at least one issue, Helen. Messy, I know, but at least it would have been a good investment." He couldn't help laughing.

"Shut your filthy mouth. You make me sick." She tried to leave, but he blocked her way.

"Tell me, Helen, where will you and Renie be living when I throw you the fuck out of here? I know! Maybe the kids will rent you an apartment. In one of the tenements, Helen. Wouldn't that be great, you and Renie with all those low-class tenants. They love you so much, Helen."

"You're evil," she said, staring up at him.

"No. Not evil, Helen. I've never been evil, just stupid and weak."

"Your self-pity disgusts me. You've lived off pity all your life."

"You mean Mother, don't you?"

"Poor Mother. Do you have any idea how ashamed she'd be if she knew about Alice and that priest?" Her voice broke. "First it was you, and now it's your children disgracing this family."

He laughed. "Oh, oh, oh! What family? You and me and Mother? I know you don't mean you and Renie! Because he's just another tenant, isn't he? I'll bet he doesn't know he's out on his ass the minute Mother's gone. No. You didn't tell him, either, did you? Why? Were you afraid he'd want to move somewhere, just the two of you? Disgusting thought, isn't it? No, better to keep Mother here, keep her alive, so you could devote yourself to her, Helen. Being a saintly daughter's been a hell of a lot easier than being a wife, hasn't it?"

"Get out of my way!" She tried to get to the back door, but he blocked it.

He was almost enjoying this. "All the poor bastard ever wanted was for someone to be nice to him. You know how pathetic he is? He has a cat in the store and he has to hide it. He has to keep it a secret from you, from his own wife. The poor bastard. You couldn't even let him have his dog, you—"

"Stop it!" she cried, looking at Renie's door, but he knew Renie was at the store. "Please stop it!"

"You made Howard poison it. I mean, Jesus, Helen! Do you know what his life is like? People laugh at him. My kids can't stand him. He's a joke, he's a fool. Do you know who turned him in to the IRS? Marie! And you know why? Because he's so goddamn pathetic he tried to force himself on her. On my wife! On his own sister-in-law! So don't hold your nose for too long, sister. You'll suffocate. The stink is here! It's right here with you!"

Renie waited in his room on his narrow bed. He waited until Sam had gone to work. He waited until he heard the familiar squeal of Bridget's crib as Helen let down the slatted side to change the old woman's diaper. And then he slipped out of his room and out the kitchen door. He passed lightly down the back stairs. He passed the rectory and the church, head down, eyes averted, not with shame, but with this pangless numbing grief. Nothing was safe. There was no way to possess love. It would always flee from him.

The store was hot and airless. A thin veneer of dust claimed every surface. On the back steps the milk had curdled in the dish and the bloodstained tuna was swarming with flies. He went into the bathroom. He tore the pictures from the walls, and then he sat on the closed toilet lid with the telephone book in his lap. He stared at the telephone on the soiled linoleum. Marie had reported him to the IRS. Internal Revenue. The irony of her revenge cut like blades through his heart. Pathetic; Sam was right. It hadn't been the brandy that night at the Elks or joy at bringing them a turkey, but desire, this blind turbulence, this yearning. He was ashamed. Everything he had ever done for Marie and the children had been a tainted, venal transaction. It was true. No one wanted to waste their time on a fool like Renie LaChance. Even the cat had escaped through the first unguarded door. His business grew worse every year. What respect was there to be had when his own wife could barely tolerate his presence? He had lost the Golden Toastee line because he had wanted it too much. Better not to care, not to want, not to love, not to feel anything at all.

He came out of the bathroom and went directly to the gas display model, the one stove hooked up to the main. He opened the oven door, then turned all the knobs to HI. The steady hiss was almost amusing, like air seeping from a huge balloon. With the high ceilings and drafty windows and doors it would take a long time for the lethal fumes to work. Might as well keep busy, he thought, taking the roll of masking tape from under the counter. He began to seal the gaps around the doors and windows. He worked most methodically, butting each strip end to the next, pressing the tape smooth. There would be no doubt as to his intentions. He smiled, imagining everyone's shock to realize what a man of action he could be. This was the ultimate courage. All the women he called would regret their inability to save him. No, that was impossible, because none of them knew their loving caller's identity. If only he'd told someone his name, he thought as he began to seal the gap around the front door. He should have spoken up, should have demanded Helen's love. He glanced up. Across the street a pretty woman tugged her little girl along by the hand as they hurried through Cushing's parking lot. The little girl tripped and fell facedown. Her screams jolted through him. The tape crackled and peeled away as he forced open the door. The woman had picked up the screaming child and was carrying her into the store. He could not help himself. He hurried across the street. When he got inside the store, the woman was nowhere in sight. Confused, he watched the red lights over the elevator blink down from floor to floor. The doors swooped open and now he was inside.

"Fourth floor, Mr. LaChance? Mr. Cushing's office?" Arlo asked, cranking the latticed metal doors closed.

His heart was racing. He felt dizzy. He had gotten here too quickly. It was all so dreamlike. Maybe it was the gas. Yes, that was it. The gas, and this was the end, the last passage up, up, up. The elevator glided to a smooth stop and the doors opened.

Maybe it was a baby girl, he thought, a daughter, a sweet and lovely young woman, newly married and just setting up housekeeping. Odd that he had never considered a daughter before. His heart soared as he came down the corridor. It was a long walk. The door seemed so far away. Oh yes. This was so much easier. A daughter would be so much more understanding.

He opened the door and Mr. Cushing's wizened head bobbed up. He had been dozing. There were indentations on his cheek from the buttons on his sleeves. "Renie!" He smiled and held out a trembling hand. "I was just thinking about you."

Reverend Pease was out of the hospital now, and Luther was tired of working, but at least he'd been well fed. He'd spent the ten days in Asheville washing dishes in the KyDeeHo Family-Style Chicken Restaurant for gas money and a place to stay while the old man got his plumbing cleared. Food was plentiful: right off the plates through the dishwasher's steamy cubbyhole. Amazing how much came back, whole thighs and biscuits swamped in chicken gravy, congealed, but tasty all the same, he liked to tell the old man. Desserts were the best, though. Every kind of pudding, bread, grapenut, rice and raisin, lemon sponge, butterscotch, and his favorite, deep dark chocolate.

Every morning Luther went to the hospital expecting to collect the Reverend and be on their way north to find Earlie, and every morning the bald bug-eyed doctor said the old man still wasn't a hundred percent. Luther could tell the doctor was scared stiff of him, but he didn't show even a flash of temper until the tenth morning. Clutching Luther's arm with his cold bony fingers, the old man begged to be taken out of there so they could be on their way. It truly was time to go. Luther would miss the KyDeeHo's tender chicken, but just his luck, the tiny waitress who'd made room in her bed for him had turned out to be one of them crazy-when-drunk ladies that wanted to fight every breathing soul, including him. Night before last, when the police came banging on the trailer door, he was sure they were going to finally haul him back to prison in Baton Rouge, to the weed-clearing road crew he'd slipped away from one day—like a shadow into the night is what it had felt like. But they took one look at the ice-packed shiner she'd given him, who was three times her size, anyway, and they laughed, asking did he want to be taken into protective custody or did he just want to be on his way? Be on his way, of course. Out of town and long gone before anyone thought to check old wanted posters.

The doctor had tried being angry, but not too angry, which Luther took as admission he'd done as much for the old man as he could. They drove only a hundred and twenty miles the first day. The old man had to drink a glass of water and take two pills every hour, which was causing him to pee every twenty minutes. He was supposed to rest, which he could do well enough in the car, but he wasn't supposed to get overheated, which was near impossible in ninety-five-degree heat. He could barely eat. He said his stomach was too flooded. By night the old man was so weak and trembling that Luther was certain he was dying. He rented a cabin and sat up wringing out wet towels to pack on the old man's feverish head and chest. The old man kept begging for the cold sweet cherries he insisted Luther was hiding.

"You are a liar!" the old man cried, the few inches he raised his head off the pillow a remarkable feat after all his weakness. "Liar!" he cried as Luther hurried back with another dripping towel. As Luther bent over him he seized the wet towel and flung it, its heavy wetness slapping Luther's face. Eyes wide, he struggled to sit up. "Liar!" he cried again.

Holding him down, Luther told him to shut up and lay still or he'd leave. He'd walk out that door. And he would, knew he would, and knew he wouldn't think twice about it after. No kin of his, the old man was nothing but a terrible burden now, even a danger.

The old man's mouth trembled. The whites of his eyes were so yellow and blood-streaked they reminded Luther of the baby clots he was always sickened to find in eggs. It was a sign. Of what, Luther wasn't sure, but he could feel his blood run cold and the hair on his arms stand up. They were never going to find Earlie. Earlie was dead. The old man wasn't looking for Earlie. He was looking for someone to die with him. And it wasn't going to be Luther Corbett. He backed toward the door with the old man still staring at him. The chambermaid would come in a few hours and call an ambulance. He'd be better off dying in the hospital. Luther slipped into the dark and closed the door. Yes sir, he assured himself as he drove off, this was the right thing to do. Crazy old man like that needed a bed to lie in and kinder hands than his. Phew, he sighed, relieved that it wasn't his problem now.

The sharp sliver of moon hung like a scythe blade in the black sky. When he was back on the highway he got the old station wagon up to seventy, fast as it would go without shimmying. Duvall said he had bought this car brand new, but then when Earlie found a child's shoe wedged in the back seat, Duvall forgot and said it must belong to the man he'd bought it from in Tupelo. That child's shoe had been a sign. He'd forgotten how nervous it had made Duvall. Earlie had been too trusting. Even that last day he still thought he could reason with a snake like Duvall. All Earlie wanted then was to get back to Laydee Dwelley. *We got the car,* the old man kept saying. *We got the car and we're still all together. Tell him!* the old man had begged Luther, but Earlie kept insisting they get their money as well. Earlie and the old man were too easy. They hadn't lived among the evil. They didn't know, couldn't hear it and see it the way he did. He should have been the one to go after Duvall that day, but they knew if he did he'd kill him.

He kept thinking of the old man, how scared he'd be come morning. And where was he even going? He had no place to go. Alone, he was on the run, a fugitive again. He pulled onto the soft shoulder and turned back the way he'd just come.

The old man tried to lift his head as he came through the door.

"Here," Luther said, sitting down and paring away the soft fuzzy skin off one of the peaches he'd just picked. "You just close your eyes now and dream on cherries." He carved a juicy chunk from the warm peach and put it in the old man's mouth.

In the next two days they were able to get as far north as D.C.

The old man slept most of the time. When he did wake up it was only for brief snatches of confusion and wide-eyed dreams in which he thought Luther was his father, daughter, wife, and Earlie. Sometimes it was like having the whole Pease family right there in the car. At first he tried to set the old man straight, but he soon tired of shouting, "I'm Luther! It's Luther you're talking to," over the engine noise and the highway roar of the open windows and the old man's anxious chatter. So he gave in and got to know the family. Lornilda Pease had been a saint of a wife. All she lived for was to make her Reverend husband happy, except in one regard, thus forcing him into "the wilderness for relief," which is all it was, he kept insisting. "Just physical relief." Luther smiled and nodded as the old man scolded his daughter for planting bush beans when it was only pole beans he'd ever had. He looked at Luther now and asked if they were almost there.

"Almost," Luther assured him.

"Good," the old man said. "I haven't been to the grave, and I promised I would."

Luther shivered with a chill. Grave, what grave? Then the old man was asleep again, his head tilted back against the door, his slender fingers twined in his lap, the untrimmed yellow nails curled and bent. If they did find that Earlie was dead, he wouldn't let anyone tell the old man he'd lost his only living kin.

"Earlie! Help me, Earlie boy. I am in . . . oh . . . so . . . much . . . pain. . . ." The words bubbled from deep in the old man's chest.

He wrenched the wheel and changed lanes, pulling out so quickly that horns blared all around him. The old man stared at him as the car skidded into the breakdown lane.

"No!" Luther insisted, squeezing the unyielding bony arm. "Come on! Come on! Come on! We almost there!"

The eyes didn't blink or close. It didn't take but a few minutes to cover him with a blanket and arrange him, stretched out in the back of the station wagon. He continued north, not sure of anything now but this looming emptiness. Nothing to do and nowhere to go. With the magazine crew he'd been part of something. And even after that he'd had the old man.

A cruiser passed now and his foot lifted from the gas pedal. At the next rest area he pulled in and parked at the end of the strip. There were two other cars in here. As soon as they left he would get out, run through the woods, emerge farther down the highway, and start thumbing. The police would see that the old man got buried. Maybe a few people would say the kind of prayers and sing the kind of hymns a man of God deserved. The first car had left, but the woman in the second car was putting on lipstick and spraying her hair. She leaned close to the mirror and squeezed something on her chin. The police wouldn't know the old man was a preacher. No one would know and no one would care. He started the engine and drove onto the highway until he came to an exit.

He took the first route south he came to. He drove all that day, most of the night, then the next day into the night. He wasn't hardly tired. In fact he could feel himself growing more alert. He was bringing the old man to his only living relative, his great-grandson, the child of Earlie and Laydee Dwelley. He was doing a good thing, and he hoped the old man knew it.

Norm raised the hood and fiddled with the carburetor. It had finally happened. He had run out of tricks. The engine was dead. He was already late for work, and soon his mother would be, too. She was behind the wheel, frantically pumping the accelerator. She told him to go inside and get Duvall.

"My mother said to wake you up." He poked Duvall's arm, amazed at his energy just seconds after sleep. He jumped out of bed and followed him outside, zipping his pants and buttoning his shirt. He would give them a ride to work.

"It's the alternator, that's where the trouble is," Norm grumbled, climbing into the back seat of Duvall's car. He sat behind his mother.

"The trouble is, it's junk," she said, the lilt in her voice surprising him.

Duvall smiled at her as he turned the key and his own car started right up. "It's all in the maintenance," he said, lecturing Norm through the rearview mirror. "Oil, plugs, filters. Simple as that. Just a little extra time and attention now saves a whole lot of money later."

"Words to live by," Norm muttered as he stared out the side window. Duvall's lecture continued, with his mother smiling at him. With the soap shipment due next week she seemed impervious to every setback. The disaster with Alice had only made his mother more determined. She had called the bursar's office at UVM and they agreed to extend the first-semester payment until the end of the month. The bank was sending threatening letters, which she tore up and threw away. When his father called to say Helen had spent the money in his trust and there was nothing he could do about it, all she said was, "For God's sake, Sam, when the hell are you going to stand up on your own two feet?"

Hope was around the corner, bright as a new penny just waiting to be found. Every night this week she'd had Norm and Benjy combing the phone book for names of people to send letters to and pamphlets describing Presto Soap. She'd insisted that Alice come downstairs and help, but every time Alice heard a familiar name she'd start to cry. At first Marie tried to ignore it, but then she got mad. She said Alice had to snap out of it and get on with life. It was time to get back to her job and start getting her things ready for college. Alice just sat there shaking her head, crying, until Marie relented and let her go back to hide in her room.

His mother had been typing the letters for the soap promotion at work, using Mr. Briscoe's envelopes and stamps.

"Believe me," Duvall had assured her last night at the table as they licked the stamps and sealed the envelopes, "it's the way things are done in business."

She pointed now, and Omar stopped at the mailbox in front of Marco's Pharmacy. She was afraid if she took the letters to the post office Mr. Briscoe would somehow find out. She kept looking around now as she passed the bundled letters through the window to Norm. He dropped them into the mailbox a few at a time, as she instructed. When he started back she told him to check the mailbox to make sure none had gotten stuck. He checked. None had. Was he sure? Yes! Getting back in, he saw Duvall roll his eyes at him. Asshole, he thought; they would never be on the same side.

"One thing you can't ever do enough of and that's promotion," Duvall mused as they drove along.

"But it's starting to add up so," she said.

"Yah, Benjy counted a hundred and ten letters last night," he called from the back seat.

"And ninety-seven the day before." She sighed and shook her head. "Every time I look at Mr. Briscoe I feel so guilty."

"Well, don't," Duvall said.

"It's almost the same as stealing," she said.

"Yah," Norm called up to her. "I read that. It's called white-collar crime."

"No, no, no!" Duvall insisted. "It's all factored into the cost of doing business. The percentage of expectable loss, it's called. POEL." He kept glancing over at her. "In business you start with that, the poe-el is how you say it. It's a given. Mistakes, damage, shop-lifting . . ."

"Petty theft!" Norm interrupted, then scratched his head. "Or is that larceny?" His eyes scored Duvall's in the mirror. "What's grand larceny? Is that the same as embezzling? What's the difference?"

"I don't know, Norm," Duvall said.

"Really? I'm surprised."

His mother's head shot around. "And what's that supposed to mean? Why did you say that?"

"Ignore it, Marie. I intend to."

"No. I'm sick of his mouth! I'm sick of the way he talks to you!"

"Forget it, Marie, I got a very thick skin, 'case you haven't noticed."

She hit the top of the seat. "You can't stand seeing things get bet-ter, can you, Norm? Well, I'm sick of your sniping! I'm just sick of it!"

He'd gone too far, and now he was going to pay for the stalled car and all her guilt over Briscoe's stamps and envelopes. They were turning the corner onto Claxton Road toward the municipal garage. His crew was just climbing onto two trucks. They looked up as the car approached, and he was pleased that they'd been waiting for him.

"You apologize to Omar! Right now!"

Duvall parked in front of the truck. Kenny Doyle, his foreman, leaned over the wheel and peered down quizzically. Duvall turned to Norm with a patronizing smile.

"Apologize!" she demanded. The silence in the car crackled. The windows were open. She'd sit out here all day if she had to, and then all night, and on and on, until she got her way.

Kenny leaned out of the cab. "You coming, kid?" he hollered.

"Apologize!" she said, loudly enough to make every man on the truck look down.

"I gotta go." He jumped out and started toward the truck. "Sorry I'm late," he called up to Kenny, who looked past him. A car door slammed shut and from the corner of his eye he saw a tornadic blur.

"You get back here right now!" his mother called as she stormed toward him.

"Mom!" He couldn't believe she'd do this. Not with all the guys in the truck watching, guys he'd spent the whole summer getting to respect him.

"Don't you dare walk away from me! Ever!" She squeezed his arm, and for the first time he realized how small this woman was, skinny, almost fragile. "Do you hear me?" she demanded in the shadow of the big truck with the leathery-skinned, broad-shouldered men looming over them.

"Mom, please," he said in a low voice. "They're waiting for me."

"They can wait!"

"Mom, they can hear you."

"Good! And they're going to hear more if you don't get back there and apologize," she said even louder.

Not a sound came from either truck as he followed her back to the car and mumbled an apology to Duvall, who offered his hand. He hesitated.

"Norm," she warned.

He shook Duvall's hand.

"Apology accepted," Duvall said with a somber nod. He started the car and they drove off.

Norm's eyes burned as he walked back to the truck. A buzz of conversation began among the men, as if they hadn't heard or seen a thing. Both trucks started up. He had climbed halfway up the side when his foot skidded off the ridge and he slid back down. His right elbow was scraped. He braced his foot and started to pull himself up, and again his footing was off. This time he banged his knee. It would be a relief if the truck backed up right now and ran over him.

"Need a hand, kid?" Bob Hersey pulled him the rest of the way up into the gritty back of the rumbling truck. Hersey had barely spoken to him since his mother's angry call about the car. Shovels, rakes, and picks rattled in their clamps on the back of the cab. Hersey tapped his Camels on his fist and offered Norm one. He lit up with a long, painful drag, grateful for the burning in his chest that masked all the other pain, his elbow and knee, his pride.

"Your mother and me used to go to the same school," Hersey said, leaning over the side of the truck as they came through town. "Her father worked for the pigman, like mine did." He glanced over at Norm. "We come a long way since then." He paused. "And it ain't always been easy, lemme tell you," he said with a nudge and a wink. "I remember she used to come to school with wet socks. The tops'd be so wet and out of shape, you know, they'd hang down on her ankles." He looked at Norm. "That come from only having the one pair that never did get dry some nights."

In spite of the tattered eviction notice tacked to the post, Joey Seldon set up a hot plate to steam frankfurts. He'd beat the Hotdog Bus at their own game. The next day Chief Stoner pulled up to the stand. He spoke to Joey from the cruiser.

"I got a complaint here, Joey." The Chief looked wan.

"What is it now?" Joey sighed, and Sonny told him what he already knew. He had no license to cook. The owner of the Hotdog Bus had complained, as had residents around the park.

"You're not even supposed to be here, so don't push this thing, okay, Joey? I don't have the stomach for it right now." Sonny sat staring over the wheel.

At Mrs. Stoner's funeral, Joey had heard that Eunice had a new boyfriend, a young fellow from Tarrytown who sold toasters.

"Look, Chief, don't worry about a thing. I'm on my way down-town, so I'll go to town hall and see what I need."

"Joey! You're not listening to me, are you. I don't think you un-derstand how upset people are over this."

Oh, he understood all right, more than Sonny would ever know.

After Sonny left, Joey headed out with his cashbox in the crook of his arm. He had many errands—town hall, the bank, the First Na-tional for mustard and hotdog rolls. The Atkinson Savings was his first stop. There were only a few customers in the cavernous marble-floored bank, most of them women. As he came through the front door he saw Cleveland Hinds turn quickly and duck back into his of-fice. Had Hinds always and so obviously avoided him? He wondered how many others had as well. All these years he had thought himself fortunate to be so well regarded, and all the while people had prob-ably been leaping into bushes and doorways to get away from him.

He stood in line behind an old woman with white hair and a pro-nounced hump on her back. When she turned he recognized her as a girlhood friend of his younger sister's. Realizing how much he had aged since that night at Towler's had been more of a shock than any-thing else. His last image in a mirror had been that of a tall barrel-chested man with black hair and a square dimpled jaw. Now an old man had taken his place, white-haired, round-shouldered, and triple-chinned.

Ahead, on his left, a man in black pants and a black shirt hunched close to the teller's window. He wore a broad-brimmed fe-dora that concealed his face. The man slid a paper under the grate. As the teller read it, her hand flew to her mouth. He chuckled. She wouldn't be so impressed when she saw his life savings. The old woman counted her money, then put her bankbooks and cash into her purse. He was still trying to remember her name when she hur-ried past him. The most frustrating thing about his secret sightedness was not being able to greet people first. In a sense he'd been rendered even more invisible now that he was so keenly aware of being dis-missed, avoided, lied to.

"Good morning, Mr. Seldon," the teller said with a sweet smile.

"Good morning, dear." It was a great effort not to gaze at her round glowing face. He pushed the cashbox under the grate. She counted his rolls of coins and the few bills. "Seventeen dollars?" she asked as she rolled his passbook into her typewriter.

"Seventeen dollars," he repeated.

"Business is still good," she murmured as she typed.

He grunted. That seventeen dollars represented three nights' receipts, not one night like the old days.

"Now!" demanded the man on his left. The man leaned on the counter, his face at the grate. The teller was trying to slide something bulky under the grate. She pushed frantically with both hands, but it wouldn't fit through. The man snapped his fingers and reached over the grate for the brown canvas money bag.

Joey's teller glanced up and gasped. The man turned and Joey stared at his misshapen face with its flat squashed nose, distorted eyes, and smeared wet lips as he warned the tellers not to move or follow him because he had a gun. The man sprang from the counter. Joey's hand slid into his pocket. Head down, the man lunged past two empty desks.

Joey called out, "Stop or I'll shoot!" Squinting, he aimed, then pulled the trigger, but there was only a click. The man looked back. It couldn't be empty. He was sure he had three bullets in it. "I said stop!" Joey roared as the man leaped toward the radiance of the glass doors. The gun exploded. He fired again, and the man fell against the door. "Stand back," he ordered the tellers, who sobbed in one another's arms, and Cleveland Hinds, who peeked from his doorway. He stood over the man, relieved to hear him moaning. With the gun still aimed he reached down and peeled the nylon stocking from the creased and grimacing face.

"It's Mr. Haddad!" the tellers gasped.

In that instant some said was impulse and others called courage, the blind man's secret was exposed. And so, because he could see, the town felt it no longer owed him anything. There were even people who insisted he had never been blind, that he had hookwinked everyone for the past twenty years. All the old rumors surfaced, but Joey Seldon had caught the imagination of the town's young people. They came nightly to hear the story told and retold. They would ask the same questions. Had he aimed at Haddad's legs? Yes, Joey told them, the only time you aim at a man's heart is when he's aiming at yours. Had he been scared? Not until it was over, and then he couldn't stop shaking. Had it been a conscious decision to pull out the gun and shoot or had it just happened? Both, he said, with the realization that they were listening as he had for so many years, for more than words could convey. The eviction notice no longer fluttered from the cornerpost. One of the boys had torn it off and ripped it into tiny pieces.

Blue Mooney was released from jail. Sonny tried to apologize, but Mooney pushed past him and kicked open the door. As he stepped into the gray drizzle he glanced back and swore.

"What'd you say?" Officer Heinze called after him. The secretary and the other officers watched from their desks.

Mooney turned and walked back into the station. He stood in front of Heinze. "Fuck you. That's what I said. But what I meant was, fuck all of you. Every single one of you," he said, looking at each of them.

Heinze's hand shot out to grab him, but Sonny stopped him.

"Let him be," Sonny said. "That's all he's got right now."

He was right. Mooney only got madder. Everywhere he went he was turned away. Colter had hired somebody else and didn't need him. He went up to the A+X, hoping to see Alice, who was out sick. Carla told him there was some weird story going around about Alice and that priest. In the few minutes he was there, Heinze drove through twice in his cruiser, and then Jerry Coughlin told him to leave.

Haddad could confess all he wanted, but the shadow that had cauled Mooney from birth just grew thicker, the accusations only further proof of his badness. His mother wouldn't let him through the door. She had a boyfriend now, a well-respected gentleman who brought her flowers and perfume and candy bars for the boys. He was teaching them how to play golf by letting them caddy for him. He thought selling beer set a terrible example for them, so he was go-

SONGS IN ORDINARY TIME

ing to get her a waitressing job at the country club. She had met Cleveland Hinds when she went into the bank for a car loan. He had not only processed the loan in one day but had delivered the check himself that very night.

The only person glad to see Mooney was Bernadette, even though he hadn't been able to find her engagement ring in the sink trap. A friend of hers needed a truck and a driver to pick up a load of soap next week in Connecticut.

"I'm your man," he told her. He didn't have anything else to do.

It was early Saturday morning and the garage felt as close as if all the summer's heat were in storage here. Marie wanted to haul the junk inside to the dump, but without a car that was impossible. Norm's car was next to the garage with the hood up. He worked on it every day after work, but all he seemed to be doing was dismantling the engine. There were parts lined up on the fender and some had fallen into the grass.

She dragged a moldy braided rug into the driveway. Most of this junk had been here when she had moved in. If it weren't for the soap coming next week she wouldn't be doing this now, with the million and one other things she had to do. Damn. Where was everyone? She ran into the house and yelled up the stairs for the third time for them to get out there and help her this minute, no ifs, ands, or buts, goddamn it! Footsteps moved overhead. Doors opened.

She went back out and decided to move most of this stuff out of the way until they could get it to the dump. She began to slide boxes onto the back floor of Norm's car. She even jammed newspapers and a smelly old shoe under the front seat. In no time at all, she had filled the trunk and every inch of his car, with just enough space left for the driver. There. She shoved in five paint cans.

"What're you doing?" Norm said as she was forcing the door closed.

"This way when the car's fixed all you have to do is go to the dump," she said.

"I can't believe you put all that junk in my car, Mom." He threw up his hands and his voice cracked. "I can't believe some of the things you do!"

He'll be a good man when he grows up, she thought, as startled by the realization as by this surge of happiness. "I'm sorry," she said. "It just seemed like such a good idea. Once I got started I couldn't stop." Looking at the packed car now, she burst out laughing.

"Look what she did!" Norm said to his sister and brother, who had just come outside. "She turned me into the pigman. Grondine Carson!"

Now they were all laughing. Even Alice with her hollow eyes. She had lost weight and her hair was dull and stringy. She and Marie still hadn't really talked about what had happened. Alice spent most of her time in her room, which spared Marie the guilt of having to face her own failure.

"I know!" Benjy said. "You can just have it towed out of here, junk and all."

"What do you mean, towed? Look, I'm in the middle of fixing it! I got everything all laid out."

"Admit it, Norm. You have no idea what any of these parts do," Alice said, her gaunt smile catalyst enough for them to move around the front of the car, holding up parts for Norm to identify.

"That's a . . . I forget the name. . . ."

"Oh great, Norm!" Benjy said.

"But it has something to do with the—"

"Motor!" Marie laughed. "Very good, Norm!"

"No, no, no, it's part of the carburetor," he said.

"And where's that?" Alice asked.

Norm dropped to his knees. "Let's see. It's around here somewhere," he said, feeling through the tall grass and peering under the car while they laughed. Marie's eyes met Alice's. They would talk later, after the soap had come and she could think straight.

By the time Omar arrived they had almost emptied the garage. They had dragged the washing machine box behind Norm's car and they were filling it with old screens and the bug-infested firewood from the back wall of the garage. Omar was in the house making phone calls to set up deliveries. Marie had been shocked at the long list of numbers. They were all local calls, he assured her.

"You mean Atkinson? You mean all those people are going to be selling Presto here in Atkinson?" she asked.

"Just one or two are deliveries," he said. "The rest are potential customers for you. I thought I'd drop off samples."

Norm and Benjy were still carrying out firewood. Alice was attempting to make shelves with a few warped boards and old bricks. It wobbled, so she took it apart and restacked the bricks. Her determination pleased Marie. Work had always been her own best therapy. Tomorrow she'd tell her that there'd be no more hiding up there in her room. The hell with what anyone thought. She had to get back to work and earn as much as she could in these last two weeks before school.

She went into the house for rags so she could wash the garage windows. Omar covered the telephone mouthpiece. "Customer," he whispered, winking. She patted his cheek, and as he bent toward her, she thought she heard the dial tone.

"Well, you'll certainly get an invitation to one of the soap parties, then, Mr. Clyde," he said, and she knew she'd been mistaken. "I don't know of another cleansing agent like it," he was saying as she came outside.

"Mom!" Norm warned as she headed toward the garage.

She stopped at the doorway when she realized someone was in there with Alice.

"Please, Alice, please. I need to see you. We have to talk. Please just come in the car with me," Father Gannon pleaded. He hadn't shaved and his eyes were sunken in dark circles.

Alice stood before him, eyes closed, head down, her arms folded tightly across her chest. "No," she said in a small voice.

"Please! I can't stand this anymore!" he begged.

"And neither can she!" Marie said. "So leave her alone."

"Mrs. Fermoyle," he said, spinning around. "You don't understand." He held out his hand as if for hers.

"I understand! I understand plenty. You should be ashamed of yourself. A priest . . ."

"I am!" he cried. "I am ashamed! But not because I love Alice. I just can't stand it that she's been hurt like this."

"Then leave her alone! Walk out of here! Go! She doesn't want to see you!" She gestured to Alice, who was crying, her face buried in her hands.

"Alice?" He reached to touch her arm. "Let me help you."

"No," Alice whispered, shrinking away.

"Haven't you done enough harm?" Marie said.

"Alice! Look at me! I'm falling apart! I don't know what to do," he panted, pacing back and forth, running his hands through his hair. "Tell me what to do! Please, please, please tell me!"

Alice wouldn't look at him. Marie held her breath, afraid his inferno would consume the hesitant flicker of Alice's resolve. She looked back as Omar came through the doorway.

"I just want to be with you, is that so wrong? Tell me, is that so bad? I'll do anything. Whatever you say. What? What is it you want?" he cried, ripping off the stiff white collar and flinging it to the ground. He brought his foot down, stomping as if on some verminous creature he needed to obliterate. "There! There! Is that what you want?"

She stood between him and Alice.

"Father!" Omar said, placing his hand on the priest's heaving shoulder. "You are out of control! You are harassing this child. You are tormenting her, and I will not allow it for one more moment. You hear me now?"

"I love her."

"Then leave her alone."

"I'm sorry," he kept saying as Omar walked him to the car.

Marie went into the house, sick to her stomach and angry for what he had done to Alice, who was curled up in her bed again with the shades drawn and the sheet over her head. She picked up the phone and called the rectory. When she said her name, the Monsignor said, "Yes. What is it, Mrs. Fermoyle?"

"I'll tell you what it is," she growled into the phone so Alice couldn't hear, so that Alice could hear, wishing both to protect her and yet to emphasize the vile one-sidedness of sex with the humiliation and suffering it caused a woman. "It's not only a sin, what's happened here, Monsignor, but a crime. My daughter is only seventeen and your priest . . . your priest is an adult. I'm warning you, if he comes back here, I'll call the police."

"Oh God. Oh God. Oh God," Alice moaned in her room.

Norm went in to her, then Benjy, and now Marie. She sat on the edge of the bed and tried to hold her, but Alice stiffened away. It just wasn't fair. It wasn't right. Especially now when she was so close to finally being able to give them a better life, after so many years of scrimping by and being scared. She touched Alice's sweaty head. Alice curled forward until her hand fell away. *Is that it?* she wondered, her ears ringing with the old rage.

"You don't want things to change, do you? It's easier to hide, isn't it, and never face up to anything. Well, goddamn it, no matter how bad things got, I could never hide. No one ever took care of me while I whimpered in my bed! No sir! No one ever did!" She panted, trying to pull her up.

Alice's chest heaved up and down. She was gasping. Her eyes were bulging.

"What? Say it! What is it?" Marie demanded. "Tell me!"

She was conscious now of Omar behind her. "Let her be," he said softly.

"Say it!" she cried.

"What's wrong with me? What's wrong with me? Oh God, what's wrong with me?" Alice was moaning.

"Self-pity!" she hissed over the bed. "That's what's wrong. That's all that's wrong!"

"Oh God, God, God." Alice pummeled her own chest with blows that were sickeningly loud.

Omar grabbed Alice's wrists, and she froze so rigidly her back appeared to arch. Marie closed her eyes.

"No," said Omar, his voice soothing but emphatic. "There is no wrong here, child. I know. I know how it goes. I know how it went. There's only goodness in you, and love, and came a moment in your faith and trust when you were asked for more, more than you should have been, and you did not turn away. Because you are an innocent. You gave, and in the giving you were taken advantage of. Why, in the very asking you were taken advantage of! Nothing's going to change what happened. But that happened to a different person. You're someone else now, Alice Fermoyle. Don't you see, you're a brand-new person now."

In the hallway Marie covered her mouth so they wouldn't hear her cry. Thank God for Omar, she thought. She just couldn't do it alone anymore.

T hat night Alice dreamed that she was on television. Sitting at a table in front of thousands of people there were three of her. There was a glass of red wine in front of each contestant.

"Will the real Alice Fermoyle please stand up," the host called into the microphone.

The audience clapped. She looked down at the other two Alices. They looked at each other, then back at her.

"Will the real Alice Fermoyle please stand up," the host urged with an impatient gesture.

They each started to get up, then hesitated at seeing each other rising, then quickly sat back down again.

"I repeat, will the real Alice Fermoyle pu-leeese stand up!"

They rose in unison, standing while the audience hissed and booed.

The announcer snatched up their papers, wineglasses, and microphones. "I'm sorry," he said, turning back to the angry audience. "There's been a terrible, terrible mistake."

T he weekend was dragging by. Every time Norm looked out the window he saw his car filled with junk, all that crap piled to the roof for Duvall's sake. He was everywhere. The kitchen table was covered with Presto order forms and pamphlets. His razor was on the back of the sink, his black hairs clogging the drain.

On Saturday night Norm walked all the way to the Millers'.

Weeb's sister, Janice, left the room when he came in. It was the first time he'd seen her since that night at the lake. "Barf time," Weeb grunted, making it to the couch on his crutches. Norm asked if she was sick, and Weeb grumbled something about her always being sick.

"What do you mean, always sick?" Norm asked, and Weeb said it was nothing, never mind. "No," he insisted. "Tell me, tell me what you meant."

"I didn't mean anything!" Weeb said, looking at him.

"Yes, you did. You said she's sick all the time."

"What? What do you care? You getting weird or something, Norm?" Weeb said, his voice cracking. They watched television for a little while, and then Norm headed back home. Not having a car was humiliating. It was embarrassing to be seen walking all over town. He felt like Howard Menka. On his way home he passed by the industrial park. Curious, he went in and roamed around until he came to the Brace Paper Division building. He considered knocking on the door and saying hello to his father. If he was here, he'd be sober. He hadn't seen him since graduation night. Standing under the bright streetlight, he thought of the men he worked with and how proud they were of their kids. Kenny Doyle, who was the toughest man he'd ever known, stopped on his way home every Friday night to buy ice cream and root beer for his five kids. But Kenny was a good guy and his father was an asshole, so why waste time on a lost cause. Relieved that he'd talked himself out of it, he went home.

On Monday he got to work twenty minutes early. The town barn stank of grease and fertilizer. The men said that on one of these hot days the place was going to explode. The barn was actually an airplane hangar—government surplus the town had purchased right after the war to garage its Street Department trucks and heavy equipment.

Jarden Greene was in his office, berating Leo, a shy soft-spoken man who'd been the department's head gardener for twenty years.

"Don't tell me the fuck about elms!" Greene's voice rose, and the men looked up from their coffee.

"Yah, don't tell him the fuck about nothing," Kenny Doyle said in a low voice. " 'Cause that's what he knows best."

Their heads bobbed with swallowed laughter, and once again Norm felt proud that Kenny had chosen him for his crew. Kenny believed in fair play. He watched out for the little guy. He was tough and wise as hell and every man here respected him.

The office door opened, and Leo scurried out with his head down. Greene followed, clapping his hands for everyone to get up. "Let's get a move on, now. Come on, come on!" he ordered, going out to the trucks.

"Pompous little asshole," Kenny muttered as he walked to the back of the truck with his hand on Norm's shoulder.

That evening Kenny let Norm stay on for the weekly poker game in the foremen's cramped office. His job was to fetch beers and keep an eye out for surprise visitors, namely Greenie. He stood by the window behind Kenny, his heart sinking with every lousy hand. Talk about bad luck. At one point Kenny had lost fifty dollars. Now Norm was lighting one cigarette off the other as he peered down through the wafting blue haze of cigar and cigarette smoke. Sixty-five dollars. The pile of bills grew in front of Lonzo Thayer, who had stripped down to his undershirt. Lonzo Thayer didn't work here, but it was obvious he often played cards with the men. Norm didn't know how much Kenny made, but he was sure sixty-five dollars had to be a week's pay. On this hand Kenny lost eight more dollars. "Last hand," Lonzo announced.

Norm passed each man another beer, but he deliberately skipped Kenny.

"Hey, Norm, am I that much of a loser?" Kenny called, gesturing impatiently until Norm gave him a beer.

"Tonight you are." Lonzo laughed.

"Tough luck," Ed Jessing said.

"Hey," Kenny said, wiping his mouth after a long guzzle. "Cum see, cum saw, you know."

It's not right, Norm thought as Lonzo shuffled the cards. Wetting his fingers he began to deal, snapping each card onto the table. Kenny finished his beer. His hand was pathetic. His face was red, and he kept blowing out of his mouth as if he were trying to cool off. "Gimme a Bud, Norm." He held his hand back for the cold wet bottle. It was his tenth beer. Jesus Christ, the man was destroying himself. How many times had men handed his father another beer, another shot, another slug. Of course the difference was his father would be wiped out by the third round and all Kenny had was a red face. And no money. He'd just lost again.

Norm watched Lonzo's manicured nails tuck the bills into his thick black wallet, which he set on the table. This was nothing to him. He probably did this every night of the week. Norm thought of Kenny's five little kids and his pretty pregnant wife. Jesus Christ, didn't Lonzo or any of them care? They were talking about the pennant race. He couldn't believe what he was hearing. Lonzo was worried about the Yankees and Bobby Shantz's arm, and Kenny's kids were probably going to be hungry all week. Lonzo stood up, and as he reached for his shirt on the back of the chair, Norm was shocked to see the butt of a gun in his pocket. That explained everything. Thayer was a crook, a gangster. From outside now came a loud banging sound, then headlights filled the window.

"Jesus Christ! Shit! Turn out the light!"

The room went dark as the men crowded around the window. "It's a green Buick," someone hissed.

"Lemme see," Lonzo said, pushing to get near.

Norm's hands groped on the table for Lonzo's Thayer's wallet. No time for counting. He slipped a thickness of bills into his pocket, then refolded the wallet and stepped among the gaping men.

"Just parkers," said Charlie Puleo with a sigh of relief as the car pulled off the road and the headlights went out.

"Jesus Christ." Lonzo kept groaning even when the lights came back on. "When I heard green Buick I almost shit."

"Why, what's a green Buick, undercover?" asked Charlie Puleo, his eyes gleaming with admiration for slick Lonzo.

"No, worse. My wife," Lonzo said, and the men all laughed. He slipped the wallet into his back pocket, then buttoned the loop.

Norm felt dizzy. He could barely breathe, he was so nervous. He staggered a little when he stepped into the pure night air.

"You been drinking, kid?" Kenny eyed him suspiciously over the wheel as he started the car.

"No!"

"That's good."

They drove in silence. They were halfway across town when Kenny sighed and kept tapping the wheel with his fist. "Oh, Jesus Christ," he said under his breath. "I really took a beating tonight, didn't I?" He tried to laugh, instead had to keep clearing his wheezy throat. He pulled into Norm's driveway. "See you tomorrow, kid!" He gave him a jab in the shoulder.

"Here," Norm said, tossing the bills at him before he closed the door.

"Norm!" Kenny called him back. "Where the hell'd you get this?" He kept looking at the money and then at Norm.

"From that fucking Lonzo," Norm said, his heart finally beating.

"Norm, you shouldn't've done that. Jesus Christ! That was stupid! I can't believe you did that!"

"But it's your money. It was all you had, and that fucking Lonzo, he's a crook. He had a fucking gun!"

Kenny covered his eyes with the bills and groaned. "Lonzo's a trooper, Norm. He's a fucking state trooper!"

The next morning the crew was in high spirits. Jarden Greene had come down to the truck barn with coffee and doughnuts for everyone. Norm was relieved when Kenny sat next to him on the bench. He'd been awake most of the night, replaying in agonizing detail every stupid move of his life—getting thrown off the baseball team, beating up Billy Hendricks, getting slobbering drunk with Janice Miller, and then last night. Jesus, it was like having this crazy jack-in-the-box tucked in his brain. And right when it seemed things couldn't get any better, out he'd spring to screw everything all up.

"Here," Kenny said, offering him another doughnut.

Norm thanked him. He ate it in miserable silence, awaiting his bitter pill. And as sure as he knew Kenny he knew it was coming: Kenny would insist that the money be returned to Lonzo, which he'd already made up his mind to do, with or without Kenny, but in his most optimistic scenario it was the two of them meeting Lonzo somewhere by the side of the road, sitting in the trooper's cruiser, telling it straight, black and white, no excuses, just the facts, setting it right like a man. Jesus, it wasn't easy, learning this all on his own, not from any father or uncle, but from so much constant watching and listening that sometimes he felt like a goddamn spy out here in the world, an actor in constant rehearsal for the big performance.

Kenny and Whitey Martin were laughing at Jarden Greene's khaki shirt.

"How many fucking pockets he got in that shirt?" asked Martin under his breath.

"When's the fucking safari starting, that's what I want to know," Ed Jessing said as Greene headed out to the trucks.

The men hurried to finish their coffee. Kenny stood up. "Butt?" He held out his pack. Norm took one and Kenny lit it for him. He took a deep drag. Now, he told himself. Have some balls. Say it now.

"Hey, Kenny," he called, as Kenny started for the door. "You know last night, what I did with the money and everything, well, I want you to know—"

Kenny gripped his shoulder hard at Whitey Martin's approach. "Don't worry about it."

"No, but I—"

"Forgotten!"

"Yah, but—"

"Didn't happen." Kenny snapped his fingers. "A little amnesia goes a long way, kid." He winked. "A long, safe way."

They piled into two trucks, with Jarden Greene in the lead cab, his arm out the window, his smooth head gleaming through the dusty glass. The heat prickled Norm's face and it felt good. The men squinted into the early-morning sun as the old trucks lumbered through town. Horns tooted here and there and people waved from the sidewalks. When a worker spotted a buddy, he called out his name, "Hey Bopper," and everyone on the truck hollered the name after him. "Hey Bop . . . How's it going, Bopper!" Norm smiled. These were good men, and Kenny was the best of the bunch.

In the distance a man turned the corner. He was slightly built, but the familiar hunch of his tense shoulders was like seeing a reflection. He wore coveralls and he carried a black lunchpail. Norm was relieved at the steady stride. The trucks came alongside, and none of the men called out, though many had known Sam Fermoyle all their lives.

"Didn't you see him?" Kenny called over the creaking rumble.

"Huh?" Norm looked up, then back at Kenny.

"Your father. He was waving at you," Kenny said.

"Where? Oh, I didn't see him," Norm said, craning his neck now, peering back into the distance.

"I figured you didn't," Kenny said, watching him.

As they came up the hill toward the park, Joey was outside his stand stacking soda cases. When he saw them, he hurried inside, fumbling to padlock the door behind him. The lead truck drove over the curb onto the sidewalk and parked in front of the stand. Jarden Greene jumped out and stood talking to Joey. Both men's arms were folded, their expressions grim. In the trucks the crews leaned over the sides, watching.

"He's not doing what I think he's doing," Whitey Martin said as Greene held out a typed form that Joey refused to take.

"Sure looks like it," said Jessing.

Greene kept stabbing his finger at Joey's face as he tried to make his point.

"Little asshole better watch out," said Charlie Rideros. "Joey's liable to plug him."

"They already took his gun. Sonny's got it," said Whitey Martin. His nephew was Jimmy Heinze, the cop.

"That's too bad," said Jessing.

Joey's voice rose angrily as he kept insisting his dealings were with the town and not with Greene, who had no jurisdiction here and no power over him.

"You're in violation. You've been condemned!" Again Greene shook the paper. "And this permit allows me to raze this . . . this structure!" Greene cried, shaking a cornerpost so that the whole stand shook.

"Get the hell outta here, Greene, I'm warning you," Joey said, raising his fist.

"Holy shit," groaned Kenny as Greene reached up and pulled down the faded red-and-white sign with its popped kernels that the elements had muted to fluffy little clouds. The signboard swung on one nail, back and forth, as if timing the moment of shocked silence between the two men. Across the street the pharmacy door opened and Marco came onto the steps wiping his hands on a white towel.

Joey shouted that his lease wasn't up until next spring.

"Lease! You broke the lease!" Greene hooted. "And so now there is no lease!"

Norm looked at Kenny, who was lighting a cigarette. "How'd he break the lease?"

"By letting the place get like that," said Kenny with a nod.

"But that's not fair. Greenie wouldn't let us fix it!" Norm sputtered. "And Joey couldn't. Jesus, he was blind!"

"And now he can see," said Whitey with a shrug. "Amen."

"Well, he's still blind as far as I'm concerned," said Leo softly.

"Yah!" said Norm. "That's right!"

"I heard it ain't that much sight he's got back, anyway," said Charlie Rideros.

"Yah," said Norm. "That's what I heard, too!" He hadn't heard anything of the kind, but Joey needed all the help he could get.

"He's nothing but an asshole," Kenny said, turning his back on the argument below. Norm turned, too. Good. Let Greenie know how everyone felt.

"Uh-oh! Here we go!" warned Jessing.

Jarden Greene was ordering them down from the trucks.

"Where they going?" Norm asked Kenny as the men climbed out, one by one, slowly.

"C'mon!" Kenny snapped, then jumped onto the street.

The last man in the truck, Norm paused, then jumped out. "Hi, Joey," he said when he was next to the stand, but Joey stared fiercely past him, his chin trembling as Greene ordered the entire stand dismantled. The men stood in a half circle, their eyes on the ground.

Greene clapped his hands. "There's a job to be done, men, so let's get to it!"

Not a man moved. Norm chewed his lip to hide his glee. Forget it, Greenie.

"What? Was there some kind of vote or something?" asked Charlie Rideros.

"The aldermen's meeting last night. They want him out of here. That was the vote, so out he goes!" Greene swiped his hands together, as if wiping them of dust.

"But what'll he do?" asked Kenny. "You're asking us to tear down a man's livelihood."

"Yah!" said Jessing. "A man's livelihood. Yah!"

"Livelihood! Let me tell you something." Greene stepped closer. "That old buzzard has made more money off that stand than all of us put together. He's loaded and don't let anybody tell you different."

"Jesus," Kenny said, shaking his head. "I've known Joey all my life. We all have."

Greene was growing impatient. They had no choice. They were town employees, and the town fathers wanted this eyesore removed. Besides, he confided, again stepping closer, they'd be doing Joey a favor. The old man was out of control, carrying a gun and shooting people. Robert Haddad was still in the hospital.

A bank robber, Norm expected someone to point out, but no one did. They sighed and fumbled in their pockets and scratched heads and, muttering, dug their boot toes into the ground. Norm clenched his teeth. Never had he felt prouder. This was guts and he was privileged to be part of it.

"What?" asked Greene, looking each man in the eye. "You think you're going to tell me no, and then what? You're just gonna pile back on the truck and that's it? Uh-uh. You can tell me no, but then you're done. As long as you understand that, then you can do whatever the hell you want." He turned and rushed at the stand, yanking the stilled sign from its nail. He tossed it into the back of the truck, then raced back to face them. There was a crowbar in his hand. Again he ordered them to work, but no one moved. "It's not worth it!" he warned, so angry he was panting. "Take my word for it!" He raced toward the stand, and it sickened Norm the way Joey flinched, shoulder and arm raised as if to ward off a blow.

Greene rammed the crowbar into the counter, then pried up a board with a squeal of wrenched nails. Joey reached for the board, but Greene threw it down. Now he banged on the cornerpost, trying to loosen the crosshatch of braced boards. One by one he tossed them to the ground, and then the roof began to sag.

Norm couldn't believe they could just stand there watching this pathetic scene. "Somebody's got to do something!" he said to Kenny, who sighed.

"Jesus Christ," said Whitey Martin, stepping forward. "Come on, Joey. This has gone far enough now. Get the hell out of there now before you get hurt." He was kicking the locked door.

"Bastards!" Joey sobbed, his shoulder against the quaking door. "You're all no-good bastards!"

The sight of the old man, straining, pushing with all his might, was hideous. Greene was ripping out the rotted wood below the counter.

"Leave him alone!" Norm yelled, amazed to find himself trying to pull Whitey Martin away from the door, but the huge man just pushed him aside. "Don't make it worse," Whitey warned.

"He's an old man! He's not hurting anybody!" he was yelling when Greene grabbed his arm and spun him around.

"You're fired! You hear me, Fermoyle? You're done! Dead! Get outta here," Greene said with a shove that sent him skidding.

"You son of a bitch," he bellowed, with a lunge that knocked Greene to the ground. There were no blows thrown, just grunting and wrestling as Greene tried to free himself.

"Get off him, you stupid shit!" barked Kenny as he and Jessing yanked him to his feet.

"Call the police! Somebody call the police!" Greene screamed.

"What're you, nuts?" Kenny said, pushing him back as he strained to get to Greene again.

"He can't do that!" Norm panted.

"He's the boss, and he can do whatever the hell he wants, kid."

"He's an asshole!" he called over Kenny's shoulder. "A pompous little asshole!"

"Jesus Christ, you don't get it, do you?" Kenny growled, grabbing his arm. "Just get the hell outta here!"

He couldn't believe it. They were getting their tools out of the trucks. Whitey Martin had his arm on Greene's shoulder, placating him in a low anxious voice. Greene gestured toward Norm. "Aw, he's just a fuckup like his old man," Martin said. Charlie Rideros had climbed over the counter and was trying to get Joey out of the stand. Kenny picked up Greene's crowbar and began to tear the metal sheeting from the roof. None of the men would look at Norm. His eyes boiled with tears. As he hurried down the hill all he could hear was the wrenching of boards and the thud of impact as they were thrown faster and faster into the truck.

He kept kicking the same stone along the sidewalk. Just a fuckup like his old man, but at least he'd tried. He was sick of cowards, and looking the other way, and always turning the other fucking cheek. He ran, then kicked the stone so hard it flew from sight. He kept running. Everything had gotten so goddamn weird. He thought of his mother giggling at Duvall's jokes, then sobbing in the bathroom when he didn't come. Benjy and all his weird little secrets and Alice slipping from room to room, afraid to show her face. They were trapped and he would not be. He would not be trapped. Never again would he be called Sam Fermoyle's fuckup son. He looked up, startled to see the mountains. The goddamn mountains, he thought, suddenly overwhelmed by this need to rid himself of her, of all of them, to be as sisterless, and brotherless, and motherless as he had been, for the last ten of his sixteen years, fatherless.

He darted out between two cars, and horns tooted as he ran across the street. He paused at the post office, then turned and ran down the alley behind the fruit store. There it was, Duvall's Cadillac. He was up there again. Overhead the dismal curtained windows reflected the fire escape of the opposite asphalt-sided building. He kicked a large rock by the cellar door until it was dislodged. It was heavy, but as he reared back he was tall enough and strong enough to hurl it sailing, sailing right straight through the shattering glass of Bernadette's window.

He left the alley at a deliberate pace. He would not run or hesitate. From now on, this was how it would be. As people approached he hailed those he recognized in a sure voice whether they acknowledged him or not, and to all the rest he called, "Hello! Hi there! How're you doing! Beautiful day, isn't it?" even though the sky had thickened to a mass of white clouds so dense there was no sun.

It was the day her mother had been waiting for, the day the soap was coming. Even though it was Saturday her mother was dressed in her office clothes, skirt and blouse, her dark hair waved back from her face. She wore bright red lipstick and she couldn't stop smiling. Every time a car came up the street she ran to the window.

Alice had just set up the ironing board. This was her first night back at work. Her mother had talked Coughlin into taking her back. She told him Alice had been sick, "Which you have been," she said when she hung up. "You've been sick and now you're better." Just like that. Smile and it goes away. Smile and no one knows. Alice wet her finger and touched the iron. She heard the hiss but felt nothing, which was the only way she could do it, pass in the glare of their headlights with them calling out to her, hiding their trays, yanking her apron strings, so many ugly things and people reaching out to drag their fingers through her insides, mingling their foulness with hers. She ran the iron lightly over the black nylon pants. The steam smelled of Joe. No, not him, not soap or school or anything; better grayness without love or pain or shame, with only this dull tightness at the back of her brain like an old impacted tooth.

"What time is it?" Norm hollered into the kitchen again. They were supposed to help unload the truck.

"Three," Benjy told him. He went back into the living room.

"Three! When's it coming?" Norm called. "I've been sitting here all day waiting."

"You can keep on waiting," her mother called. "Because you're not going anywhere!"

He had been grounded ever since Jarden Greene's call to say Norm had assaulted him.

"Hey, Mom, what do you think happened?" Norm said, coming into the kitchen. "You think maybe he got lost or something?" He didn't even try to hide his pleasure.

"He's just held up somewhere. Business is like that. There's always a catch somewhere along the line."

"What if he doesn't come?" Norm asked.

"If he's held up much longer, I'm sure he'll call," her mother said.

"No, I mean, what if he takes off? What if he doesn't ever come?" He stared at her.

She tried to laugh. "Well, why would he do that? You know this isn't just my big opportunity, Norm, it's Omar's, too. I mean, the man has spent how many weeks, months now, on this, so he's not about to just let the whole thing fall apart."

"Why not? He's got your money! What else does he need?"

She looked startled. "It's not just the money, Norm." She got up and went to the window again. "Omar and I . . . we're . . . we're thinking about getting married."

"What?" Norm gasped.

"You heard me," her mother said.

Alice was folding up the ironing board. She could feel her brother's eyes on her, but he was there, and she was here. She could not be part of it. She unplugged the cord and bound it around the iron, tightly, every movement spare and controlled, breath, even thoughts, issuing in measured segments. *Don't yell, don't fight, not now with the veil so thin.*

There was rumbling out on the street. A large white panel truck was backing into the driveway.

"It's here!" her mother called over the window-rattling roar. "It's here!" Turning in a little circle, she ran her fingers through her hair, then daintily wiped the corners of her mouth. She tucked in her blouse, tugged her skirt straight.

"Yah, but they're in Klubocks' driveway," Benjy called from the back hall door.

"Klubocks' driveway?" her mother repeated, stupefied. She hurried to the window.

"Mr. Klubock's opening his garage doors. There's some guy with Omar." Benjy leaned farther out. "It's that hood Mooney."

"What's he doing?" her mother asked in a faint voice as she watched Omar and Mooney pass cartons down from the back of the truck to Harvey Klubock, who carried them into his garage. "He said he wouldn't sell it to them. I can't believe he's doing this."

Alice couldn't believe it, either. Not him, not Mooney, not now, on top of everything else. It was almost funny, really. Her life was turning into a crazy newsreel with everyone moving too fast and speaking in high-pitched scratchy voices. How had Mooney ended up with Omar? Any minute now Joe would show up with Nora Hinds and the Monsignor. Her father would stagger down the street with his arm around Anthology Carper. Mr. Coughlin and Lester would pull in on Mooney's motorcycle. Norm would be punching Harvey Klubock while Jessie screamed at Alice to do something, anything, but don't just stand there.

The truck had pulled out of Klubocks' driveway and was backing into theirs. Her mother told Norm and Benjy to go out and help unload the soap. At the door Norm paused and seemed to flex his entire body. Omar winked at Alice as he came into the kitchen. He carried three red roses wrapped in tinfoil. "The day has finally come," he said, holding them out to her mother.

"How could you do that?" she asked, ignoring the flowers. She couldn't believe he had sold a franchise to Harvey Klubock after assuring her he wouldn't. What was he thinking of, two franchisers living side by side selling the exact same products?

"A franchise?" He seemed bewildered; then his eyes widened. "Oh no. No, no, no. Harvey's just going to be a kind of warehouseman for me. This way I won't have to keep running to Connecticut every time a franchiser needs restocking. It's a favor."

She looked out the window. "I don't want any favors from those Klubocks. I know how that goes."

"Actually, it's not really a favor," he confided. "I'm paying Harve rent."

"Rent! How much?"

He touched her cheek. "Marie, what do I keep telling you? Some things you just have to leave up to me. Like the Klubocks, for instance." He looked over at Alice. "There's a young man out there's been asking me all about you," he said, grinning.

She turned and went upstairs to dress. When she came down her mother was outside with Omar. Alice looked out the window. Mooney worked from the back of the truck, sliding cartons along the ramp he had fashioned from two planks. Norm and Benjy ran back and forth carrying cartons into the garage. Mooney kept glancing at the house. She went to the front door. If she slipped out this way, he might not see her. She shut the door quickly when she saw so many of the neighbors out there. The busy Bartleys, the Branches from across the street, the Wilburs, and Mrs. Rose, the cheeriest woman in the neighborhood, were all standing in front of the house. Nervous little Mrs. Merton was being pulled along by her dachshund straining on its leash toward the Bartleys. Little Bobby Rose was pedaling his tricycle toward the gathering. Trapped, she went to the kitchen window.

Omar was giving some kind of a speech out there. Mr. Klubock had come to the edge of the driveway. The young couple who always played badminton on their front lawn stood beside him. All were careful to stay on the Klubocks' side. Up on her back porch Jessie Klubock was wiping a pot lid over and over with a red dish towel. Louis sat a step below her.

"Right now," Omar was saying, "I'll bet you're all wondering, Did Tide start this way? Did Rinso start this way? Did Cheer and Fab and Ivory Flakes? I know I always wondered. And guess what? The answer is yes. Yes, *yes!*"

Her mother's face was red. Her hands fluttered around her throat. Alice could tell by the way she stared at Omar that she was as proud as she was self-conscious. "All giants have small beginnings, humble commencements," he continued.

Mr. Klubock, Mrs. Rose, and the young couple were on the Fermoyles' side of the driveway now. Bobby Rose came pedaling into the backyard. Louis Klubock bounded across the yards to join him. Together they ran alongside Benjy as he worked.

"Of course they did!" Omar said with a clap of his hands. "And the product we offer is such as theirs, purity, cleanliness, spotlessness, neat and tidy lives, if you'll overlook my cheery pun, my fab-ulous play on word flakes."

Everyone chuckled. Ginny and stern Edgar Bartley, who had not spoken to Marie, nor she to them, for three years, were halfway down the driveway now. Mrs. Rose followed with Mrs. Merton. The dachshund kept circling her until the leash had wrapped around her legs. Omar grinned and with his sleeve blotted the sweat trickling into his eyes. He held out a plastic bottle of frothy pink liquid to them on the heel of his hand.

"Here it is, the magic liquid, the elixir of lustration. It will dry-clean!" His fingers snapped the bottle with each claim. "It will fumigate. It will disinfect. It will sanitize! It will be found in every toilet bowl, every shower stall, every sink and laundry room of America! Because . . ." He leaned forward and crooned hoarsely, so softly even Marie strained to hear. "Because this is more than just a bottle of soap. This is opportunity and freedom that's come to Edgewood Street."

If she waited much longer she'd be late for work. She opened the front door and hurried down the walk. None of the neighbors saw her because they were all facing Omar. She started down the road.

"Alice!" Omar called, gesturing as everyone turned.

She gave a little wave, but he kept calling her name and insisting she come back and speak with this young man. Bare-chested, Blue Mooney sauntered around from the back of the truck.

"Alice, come say hello to Mr. Blue Mooney here," he said as she came back to the head of the driveway. "A fine young man if ever there was one," he said, thumping Mooney's back.

With the notorious name, a hush fell over the neighbors.

"Hi, Alice." Mooney smiled. "How're you doing?"

Face red, all she could do was nod.

"Blue was hoping you'd be here," Omar said.

"I'm late. I have to go," she told Omar. She saw Mooney stiffen.

"Well, then, this just works out so fine," Omar said as Norm and Benjy emerged from the garage. "Blue'll give you a ride in his handsome white truck that now stands empty and idle."

"Sure!" said Mooney. He grabbed his shirt and ran to open the door for her.

The neighbors formed a little cluster around Mr. Klubock and Jessie, who had come down from the porch. She knew they were talking about her, trampy little Alice Fermoyle, look what she'd come to, my God, the town hood with a full moon tattooed on his back.

She tried to tell Omar that she wanted to walk. She needed to walk. She stepped closer to tell her mother she didn't want to go with *him*.

"Go!" Marie ordered through a clenched smile. "Just go now!" Her mother wanted the spectacle to end, wanted the neighbors to leave, wanted Omar to stop passing out bottles of Presto Soap to everyone.

"Mom!" Norm said, looking at Alice. "I'll give her a ride!"

"In what?" she snapped, the smile now trembling. "Go! Just go!"

As they drove off, Alice stared down at her folded hands. Her feet were close together on the mat. Her hair fell forward onto her face.

Mooney drove slowly. "That Duvall's something, huh?"

"Um." She nodded. The slower he went, the more nervous she became, and yet the closer she got to the A+X now, the more her heart began to pound. She was short of breath. She felt so light-headed that she was afraid she might faint. She was drifting and his deep voice was something to focus on.

"I just met him and you'd think we were best friends or some-thing." He kept looking over at her. "He knows so much about things. Everything you mention he's seen it or done it or been there."

"He's an entrepreneur," she said, swallowing hard.

"Huh?" said Mooney. "He told me was a salesman."

She pretended to look out the side window, but her eyes were closed.

"You're awful quiet." He cleared his throat. "I said, you're awful quiet."

"I'm late."

"You still got a few minutes."

She turned to see him biting his lip. "No, I don't. I should be there right now."

"Look, I just want to talk, okay?" he said, turning the wheel sharply. He pulled onto a narrow road through a wooded lot off Main Street. He parked, letting the engine idle. "You heard what happened, right? I know you did. You must have. Everyone else did. I got a real raw deal, but you want to know something funny? The whole time I was there it never really got to me, because then I would, I'd get bitter, you know, real piss—real mad. But then this other thing kept happening. All of a sudden I'd be thinking of . . . of things, nice things. Like seeing you up at work, and talking to you, and the night I walked you home. And that night at the lake. Grad-uation night."

Her eyes were closed and she covered her mouth to hold all these pieces together, to keep from laughing or crying, or both. The crazy film was playing again. The pieces were falling. Her head was made of wooden blocks that kept falling into her lap. How had she gotten here? How had any of this happened?

"And then the rest of it didn't seem so bad." He sighed. "Alice?" He sighed again, then cleared his throat. "I'm starting to feel like a real jerk here." He laughed nervously. "Oh boy, this is turning into a real mess, isn't it?"

"I have to go to work," she said.

"Will you talk to me, Alice?" he begged, almost groaning. "Please, please talk to me. Try. Just give me a chance. Please? You think I'm a loser, but I'm not. You don't know the first thing about me! Jesus!" He banged the wheel and the thud through the shaft seemed to vibrate in her head. "I don't get it! I just don't get it! You not only won't talk to me, but you don't even care how it makes me feel. Hey, what have I got, jackass written across my chest or something? You just sit there, you're like everybody else. You don't think I'm worth shit. I'm just here, right? This, this creep you don't even have to look at, much less speak to."

"I'm sorry," she whispered, but there wasn't a thing she could think of to say. She had too little energy and no desire to help him. He was staring so hard she tried to smile. Suddenly she was laughing. She covered her face to hide it.

"Hey, no problem!" he said with a bitter laugh. He backed down the road so fast he had to jam on the brakes to turn. "I get the point," he called as the truck rattled up Main Street. "I'm a whole other species from you—or so you think. But I got news for you, you stuck-up little bitch, I'm just as good as you, and I'm just as smart as you!" He tore into the A+X lot, which was already starting to get busy. He drummed his fingers on the wheel, then looked at her when she didn't move. "So go ahead. Get the hell outta here! That's what you want, isn't it?"

"I'm . . . I'm . . ." she tried to say, but she couldn't stop making this hideous sound.

"Get out! Just get out!" he roared.

A car pulled in and idled behind them. They were blocking the entrance. The car tooted once, then twice. Mooney jerked his arm out the window, gesturing for it to wait.

"What? You don't want to get out?" He watched her.

She wanted to die, that's what she wanted, to shrivel up and die. She closed her eyes.

"You want me to pull over?"

Now the driver behind them leaned on the horn, the close blaring like a drill on a nerve. She opened the door and was climbing down when Coughlin's office door flew open. Enraged, he tore across the lot, cursing and waving his arms for the truck to move and the car to kill the horn. "I don't need this!" he yelled. "Move it! Move it! Move it!" Seeing it was Alice, he grabbed her apron from her hand and held it up as if it were evidence of something. "First day back and you're late!"

"Shut up, Coughlin!" Mooney called from the loudly idling truck.

He peered at her. "You think it's funny? I don't need this! I'm not putting up with it! You hear me? I'm not putting up with it from you or anyone else."

"Don't be stupid, Coughlin. Leave her alone," Mooney warned.

Coughlin pointed up at him. "You! You get the fuck out of here, you hear me!"

Waitresses paused with their trays to watch. Drivers stared from their cars. The horn had stopped.

She started to walk away, but he yanked her back and whipped the apron at her. "You're here! You work!"

Mooney had jumped out of the truck. "You son of a bitch!" he yelled, grabbing Coughlin and spinning him around. "I said leave her alone!" He shoved Coughlin and the skinny man reeled backward, then tripped and went down on one knee. Whistling and cheering erupted from the cars, and now all the horns were honking. Alice tried to cover her face, but Mooney was hurrying her back to the truck.

"I'm sorry," she said as they pulled out of the lot. "I'm so sorry."

"You don't have anything to be sorry for, believe me. Not you, Alice."

It was Sunday. In the middle of the table was Marie's engagement ring. The big day had come and gone, and here she sat, trembling and alone. Because Omar had never paid her loan, she was two months behind and Alice was supposed to start school soon. She didn't have a car. Both of her children had been fired from their jobs, and she'd just found out that Harvey Klubock was a franchiser. This morning she'd seen three neighbors coming out of Klubocks' garage with king-size boxes of laundry detergent. Thinking it was *her* soap those nervy Klubocks were either selling or giving away, she'd called Jessie and demanded to know what the hell was going on. Jessie had been shocked to find out that Marie was also a franchiser. Omar had told them that he was using Marie's garage for storage space.

As the back door squealed open, she folded her arms to hide the trembling. Omar came in and sank into the chair across from her. He looked at the ring.

"Why did you lie to me about the Klubocks' soap?"

"I didn't lie," he insisted.

Of course he had; lied all along and right up to the very moment of delivery had lied, and if he would not admit it now, then he must be disturbed. There had to be something terribly wrong with a man who not only lied but had to have known when he told the lie that he would be found out.

He hung his head and tried to explain that he hadn't thought of it as lying. He had only wanted to help Harvey Klubock.

"But by helping him, you hurt me!"

"But that's not the way I was looking at it," he said.

"Oh really? Well, it seems pretty obvious to me that two people right next door to each other, selling the exact same product, are going to be competing for the same customers! It seems like a pretty basic concept, doesn't it? Doesn't it?" she demanded.

Eyes closed, he nodded.

He had deliberately misled her, she told him. He had used her, had taken her good faith and trust and made a fool out of her in front of her children. "And that, *that* is the worst thing you could have done to me!" she cried, hitting the table.

"You don't understand," he whispered.

But now she finally did. She pushed the ring across the table. He had gotten all the money from her he was ever going to get and now it was over. She didn't feel sad or even angry, just curiously quiet, still. She would find a way out of this mess even if it meant knocking on every door in town or setting up a roadside stand somewhere. She would get a second job if she had to. Nothing and no one, and certainly no man, would ever again threaten her children's future.

He had not meant to deceive her, had not intended it. "But you see," he tried to go on. "You see . . . you see . . ." He buried his face in his hands.

"If you have any of my money, I want it back," she said.

All he had after paying for the truck and the driver was this. He put the bills on the table. She counted twenty-one dollar bills.

"Thank you," she said with a bitter laugh. She stood up.

"Marie!" he cried. "Help me! Please help me!" There were tears running down his cheeks. He had only wanted to help Harvey, he sobbed, and she was right, of course; what he had done made no sense. In fact it was perfectly bizarre. But that was how he always got into trouble, by making promises and telling himself he would deal with it all later, by wanting so badly to please everyone that once again he had ended up ruining his own chance for happiness. It had been the same with his road crew. He had been so good, so generous to them that they ended up wanting all the money and all the inventory for themselves.

She was shocked at how frail he seemed, and for such a sophisticated man, how perilously innocent. She sat back down and tried to make him see how ruthless people could be. The more they were given the more they wanted.

"I know that. I know that," he said. "But knowing and doing have never been the same thing for me. It's a curse, a terrible, terrible curse."

"You promise too much. You give too much of yourself, Omar."

"I know, I know."

"Look at you, you're a wreck. Your clothes are all wrinkled and dirty. You've got dark circles under your eyes."

"It was that late run to Connecticut. Just like you said, it turned out to be a total waste of time. I don't know what's wrong with me. I have all these great ideas, all this energy and ambition, but I never seem to get anywhere."

"Because you bite off more than you can chew, Omar."

"But why? Why do I do that?" he asked, gripping the table edge.

"Because you don't have a family to consider before you make decisions."

"You're right. You are so very right," he said, and then for a few moments neither one of them spoke. "Don't send me away, Marie. Please don't." He reached for her hand and eased the ring back onto her finger. She would not have to sell soap door-to-door or set up a roadside stand. He would, he told her. He would! He would! He couldn't bear the thought of being alone, of going on without her. "Marry me tomorrow," he begged. "Tonight, right now, please."

Yes, but they would have to wait. There were the license and the blood test. And though she did not say it, she had to tell Sam.

For the last two mornings Omar had driven off with his trunk loaded with soap that he was selling door-to-door along every back road he could find. Again tonight, Marie had been amazed to see his empty trunk.

"They're selling like hotcakes," he said, over the armload of Presto laundry powder boxes he was packing into his trunk for to-morrow's route.

"Yah, I'll bet," Norm said to Benjy in the garage. "He's probably dumping them someplace." Norm picked up six of the boxes.

"Oh no!" Benjy said. "He is! He's selling them."

"Jesus, I can't believe you're still falling for his crap!" He shoved the boxes into Benjy's arms.

"He is, Norm. I saw all the money! He showed Mom!"

At that, Norm kicked one of the boxes, puncturing it. A stream of white granules gushed onto the floor. Benjy tried to hurry out-side, but Norm pulled him back. He brought his face close to his brother's.

"Am I the only one? Don't you see? Can't you feel it?" he hissed.

"What?" Benjy whispered.

"The disaster that's coming."

Benjy swallowed hard. "What do you mean?"

"Well, for one thing, them getting married," Norm said, annoyed by the relief on his brother's face. "Don't you see? It's going to be a total disaster!"

"Oh" was Benjy's only response.

They both looked toward the door as Marie called for them to bring more soap out.

"There's got to be something she'll listen to. Everything I say, she's got an answer for. I mean I could tell her he's wanted for murder and she'd say, 'Oh no, you don't understand. It wasn't really murder. It was just a little business thing, that's all!' "

Marie called in again. "What are you two doing in there, making the soap?" She and Omar laughed.

"What do you mean, wanted for murder?" Benjy asked.

He looked toward the driveway. "I mean she's getting just like him. Twisting the facts to fit the way she wants things to be. That's how desperate she is, because nothing fits together, nothing's real."

"What do you mean?"

"I mean him. Duvall, he's not real!"

Just then the garage darkened as Duvall stepped into the doorway, blocking the setting sun. "Don't tell me I've stumbled into some kind of brotherly conspiracy here," he said, laughing, and a chill went through Norm to see the cold fix of Duvall's eyes on Benjy before he hurried outside. Duvall picked up a carton of soap bottles and started for the door. "Come on, now. Your mother's waiting." He grinned, then added, "Son."

Norm watched the three of them pushing cartons into Duvall's trunk. Alice had gone to the lake to spend a few days with her girlfriend Mary Agnes. Without her he had the sensation of being the outsider, a stranger this family had to humor but found threatening. How long had it had been like this, the three of them standing so close, the quick hand on an arm, the wordless amusement of intimates. Seeing them this way through the garage door, framed by hazy shadows and the weathered beams, he felt the same compelling contradiction of tension and distance as if he were watching a movie. Nothing was real, and yet anything could happen, anything, at any moment, and there would be nothing he could do. *Let them believe his lies,* he thought, picking up the punctured soapbox and hurling it in a spray of white powder across the garage. *Let them be destroyed.*

But not me, he vowed, hurrying outside and realizing as he bore down on them that he enjoyed their fear and apprehension. He had become the spoiler, a force to be reckoned with.

Later that night, Weeb pulled up outside and honked the horn. It was Weeb's first night out since he'd had his casts removed. Norm was halfway out the door when Marie insisted he take his brother along. Benjy didn't want to go, but she was adamant, and he knew by the way she and Omar did not once look at each other, the reason for Benjy's eviction.

It was his first night out with Weeb in almost two months. It was a relief being able to burst into hysterical laughter at the sight of Myrna Merganzer in an orange dress arm-in-arm with her boyfriend, Freddie, their beefy hips and thighs grazing with every waddling step.

"Toodle!" Weeb cried, and Norm collapsed against the dashboard with tears running down his cheeks.

"What's *toodle* mean?" Benjy asked, leaning over the seat.

"It means . . . it means . . . oh shit, you tell him," Weeb gasped.

"I can't. Oh shit, I can't," Norm squealed. It was too complicated, too dirty and dumb, so long between them that it had come to mean just about anything.

A few minutes later, he asked Weeb the question that had been on his mind for days. "Has your sister gone back to college yet?"

"School," Weeb corrected him. "You don't say 'college.' That's taken for granted."

"Oh, okay, Weeb."

"Well, you don't want to sound like a jerk, do you?"

"So did she go?" he asked, rolling his eyes.

"She's not going back."

"She's not!" he cried so eagerly that Weeb looked at him. "How come?"

"Make him sit back," Weeb said with a glance in the rearview mirror.

"Benjy, sit back!"

Benjy sank low in the seat.

"How come?" he asked again.

As he spoke in a low voice, Weeb kept looking in the mirror.

"She's gonna have a baby, so she has to get married to her boyfriend from college."

School, Norm wanted to say, but didn't. Janice Miller, whom he had secretly worshiped since first grade, would soon be a bride, a wife, a mother.

They drove down Merchants Row. The stores were closed. They turned onto Center Street, where a line waited to get into the Paramount theater. Weeb honked the horn and a bunch of girls waved and gestured for them to come join them.

"Arf, arf," Weeb barked under his breath and drove on.

"What'd your mother and father say?"

"My father didn't say anything. He just punched out all the windows in the garage. My mother had to take him to the hospital for stitches."

He was shocked by Weeb's offhandedness. Of all the times his father had kicked in doors or been hauled off in a cruiser he had never spoken of it to Weeb. There had always been this fragile duality: the devastating fear that everyone knew and the desperate need to believe that no one did.

"He hasn't been to work all week. His hands are all bandaged. He just sits around playing his Glenn Miller records."

"That's weird, huh?"

"Yah, well, my mother's afraid he's having a nervous breakdown. Now he says he's going to quit his job. He says it was his work, that it was a bad influence, you know, sex and everything."

"Can I sit up now?" Benjy called. "I can't see."

"Shut up!" Norm said, waving his arm over the seat. He looked at Weeb. Something had just occurred to him, a nagging pinprick of doubt and fear.

Pain swelled in his chest as he recalled waking up in Klubocks' garage with his pants undone.

"Oh jeez," Weeb cried as a pickup truck slowed to a stop beside them at the red light. It was Jozia Menka snuggled so close to Grondine Carson that they both fit behind the steering wheel. "Let's go!" Weeb hollered, turning when the light changed. "It's egg-run time!"

They sped up the long dirt road to the untended pig farm, where their only concern would be the barking dogs. But Weeb knew exactly how to do it. He pulled in so close to the chicken coops that they only had to jump from the car to the coop door. Benjy had begged them not to come here, and now he refused to leave the car. He crouched low in the back seat, arms folded, eyes closed, lips moving as if he were praying. Inside the chicken coop it was hot and quiet until Weeb turned on the light, and then all the chickens started squawking. Hundreds of them, Norm thought, coming down the narrow walkway between the nesting birds. Their heads rose and their bright sideways eyes gleamed nervously. The reek of shit and ammonia stung his eyes. An old hand at egg runs, Weeb went straight to the end of the coop, where the egg boxes were stacked on shelves. They took ten boxes each, then ran back to the car, leaving the lights on in the coop and the door open.

"Hey, you wanna go to the wedding?" Weeb asked as they raced back to town.

"No!" he said too quickly. "I can't. I got something else that day."

"What do you mean? I didn't even tell you when it is yet." Weeb gave him a sour look.

"When is it?"

"September the sixteenth," Weeb said. "Come on, Norm. I'd do it for you."

Norm looked at him. Did he mean Alice? Had he heard about her and the priest? He was getting paranoid. "Janice won't want me there."

"I'll ask her," Weeb said, parking on Main Street across from the A+X. They didn't have long to wait. As soon as Coughlin's office door opened, they pulled into the lot. The minute he stepped outside, Norm rose up through the open window and pelted him with a flurry of eggs. He sprinted after them with yoke running down his face and chest, but they were already gone, on their way to Jarden Greene's house, then Kenny Doyle's, then Coach Graber's, Donna Creller's, the Monsignor's gleaming Oldsmobile. Benjy turned out to have the best in-flight arm. Splat, spat, splat. No questions asked. Back behind the fruit store. Splat, splat, splat, right up at the cardboard taped in Bernadette's broken window. They drove down to the baseball field and left the car running with the lights on the infield. Weeb stood on the mound, egg cartons at his feet. Norm's bat was a fence picket. Benjy sat on the hood, laughing and clapping every time Norm hit an egg. The impact sent shells and egg slime flying back at Weeb, but most of the mess covered Norm. It was disgusting, but strangely pleasurable, the sticky goo running down the bat between his fingers, down his wrists. It was dripping from his elbows. From his chin.

"Miller is on the mound," Weeb continued, broadcasting every pitch. "He gets the sign, sets, checks the runner, winds, and throws!"

Norm swung and hit another one. "Jesus, Weeb. You're gonna be great next year."

"You too, Norm. You haven't missed one yet!"

"I'll show that fuckin' Graber!" He crouched even lower over the plate.

Weeb fired it in, and he swung and missed. The egg flew into the dirt.

"Car!" Benjy yelled as headlights turned the corner. They jumped into the car and sped off.

They drove home, and Benjy went inside. Norm dragged the hose behind the garage. Weeb had gone first, and now it was Norm's turn. He stood against the back wall of the garage, his arms over his head, while Weeb blasted him with ice-cold water.

"Okay?" Weeb called, his wet clothes plastered to his body. "I'm freezing."

"No," Norm called softly. "Keep going."

"Shit," Weeb groaned, moving closer.

The full force of the water pelted his flesh like needles. His eyes smarted.

"Jesus Christ, Norm, are you through? You gotta be clean now," Weeb called, his teeth chattering.

"No."

"Are you through?"

"No!" he gasped, turning his head to answer. Each time the hose moved closer, and now Weeb was only a foot away. Norm was sobbing. Weeb dropped the hose and the water gushed through the tall grass around Norm's feet.

"That was weird," said Weeb, his wet pant legs slapping together as he started back to the car.

"What do you mean?" Norm said, catching up with him. Now he was shivering.

"I don't know." Weeb shrugged. "It was just weird, that's all." He got into the car.

"What the hell do you mean?" Norm grabbed his arm, afraid Weeb knew he'd been crying.

"Nothing, Norm." Weeb looked up at him. "I didn't mean anything."

It was hot and every seat at the eight o'clock Mass was filled. The dazzling stained-glass windows were alive with light and heat. Flames danced under Christ's thin white feet. The slender Virgin Mary smiled coyly at the muscular Angel Gabriel in his shimmering white gown. The Sacred Heart of Jesus pulsated with ruby blood, and saints trembled.

Every door in the church had been left open, which only drew in the exhaust of passing automobiles and the racket of barking dogs. The sound of fluttering paper grew as men and women fanned themselves with parish bulletins that were red this week. There was a large oscillating fan on the altar. Every time it turned toward the pulpit, Father Gannon's lacy surplice billowed and his voice rose, though he was as unaware of the brief respite as he was of the heat and his squirming flock's discomfort. There was coughing. Throats were cleared. Shoes shuffled and scraped on the dull oak floors. The sermon was now entering its twenty-sixth minute. At the rear of the church, ushers waited with their long-handled baskets poised. They kept looking at each other. If the parking lot wasn't cleared out by the nine o'clock, there'd be a traffic jam out there, the likes of which they couldn't imagine.

Father Gannon could see by the ushers' grave expressions that he had plumbed some deep well of concern in them. He smiled and held out his arms. There was so much to share with these good people. He was past bitterness, though his heart was sore with loss.

"No sparrow falls unseen," he said. "No cry goes unheard. It is when we feel most alone, when we feel most forsaken, that we are surrounded by angels, millions of angels, hordes of angels!"

Somewhere a baby began to cry. Their faces were a blur beyond the red flutter. He was telling them about the poor children he had tried to help. He told them about the rent strike, the hundreds of donated blankets, and now his voice broke as he shared the memory of the young woman and her dying infant, his tale all the more vivid with the baby's wails. They stared up at him over the red wings.

"It does not have to be that way," he told them. "We can stop that kind of suffering. Poverty is a man-made evil. God did not create some men rich and others poor. God does not allocate riches or misfortune. No, He creates all men equal. It is the choices we make that shape our destiny. This," he said a bit louder, "this is the key, the crucial element in life. Choice."

Hands on the pulpit rim, he drew a deep breath, and from the corner of his eye he was aware of an iridescent vapor shimmering in the sunlight through the open doorway at the side of the church. Howard was hosing down the Monsignor's egg-spattered car. And what were Howard's choices? he wondered. Had he been born with the same opportunity as everyone else? No, but God watched over such people. They were part of His greater design. But the injustice of this rose in his chest like sudden bile.

In the front row a woman coughed softly into the palm of her hand, and the sound seemed an explosion in the hush. Sweat rose on Father Gannon's back. He was stuck. There was no accounting for Howard. Because of him, nothing worked. Nothing was right or equitable. There had been Radlette. He tried now to explain the story of the sickly child and what it had meant, not so much for Radlette finally to have a warm jacket that was his own, brand new and not secondhand, but for him, a young curate, to have received so much by giving so little. He looked up. The two were connected, Radlette and Howard, but he could not find the key.

"You see," he tried to explain, sensing by the uneasy stir that he was losing them, not just their attention, but their faith. "There is giving of a higher order that the giving of things can only prepare us for. It is in the giving of one's self that we come closest to divine nature, to God's love."

Yes, this was the key element, for without love what were any of them? What was he? But still there was the problem of Howard, who had to be more than a testing ground for their values.

He began to tell them about love, all the kinds of love, and reasons for love, and how when he had nothing to give, he had given himself. And he would do it again and again, and in this giving he was sinless. This was the choice, he explained, truly the only one of importance, the choice to love or not to love. How simple. How pure.

"And so it comes in the end to that." He shaded his eyes and peered into the recesses of the church. The doorways were filling with people, so many latecomers just arriving. She would not be among them. She was afraid. She had not been ready to make the choice.

"Come in! Come join us!" he cried with an exultant wave. "Don't be shy. Let's make room for one another here. Push in closer to one another," he exhorted those seated as the new arrivals started hesitantly down the aisles. His altar boys whispered a moment; then one, Harry, a tall boy, burst out laughing and could not stop. Father Gannon winked and the boy covered his face with his hands. The sound of idling engines surrounded the church like buzzing around a hive. Patrick Muley, the head usher, made his way down the packed center aisle.

Watching him approach, Father Gannon waited with outstretched arms. He was sure it was about the problem of Howard.

"Excuse me, Father, but it's time for the nine o'clock. That's what all the people are here for."

Father Gannon pushed back his sleeve, but he must have forgotten to put on his watch this morning. He had stayed up late talking to the visiting priest sent from Boston to counsel him. All the counseling had consisted of was Father Norton's trying to convince him he should return to the hospital for a few weeks of treatment. After that he never did get to sleep, and now he realized he had not even bathed or shaved. He rubbed his whiskery chin, relieved that no one had noticed.

"Well, then, we'll just have to start over," he said, and a loud groan filled the church. "Come on, now, let's be good sports," he urged, tugging at his collar. Just then the visiting priest came out from behind the altar, accompanied by two new altar boys. The

Monsignor was entering through the side door, where in the background Howard stood by the gleaming car, his hands on his hips, watching. Patrick Muley whispered in the Monsignor's ear.

"Come down now," the Monsignor said, his voice soft.

"But I haven't finished," he replied.

"Father Norton will take care of it," the Monsignor assured him, and the visiting priest nodded gravely.

A woman in a pink dress dabbed her wet eyes with a tissue. A few people looked down at their folded hands, but most stared at the disheveled priest in the pulpit, running his hand through his unruly black hair as his breathing tore through the loudspeakers in staticky gasps.

"Well," he said with a little laugh. "I seem to have run over my time, as they say. I'm sorry. I'm very sorry," he muttered, as both the Monsignor and the visiting priest raised their hands to guide him down the carpeted steps.

It was noon when Sam woke up. He smiled to see his paycheck on the nightstand. He sat on the edge of the bed and charted another day in his notebook.

25 min.   BANK—cash and deposit 25% of check in savings
               acct.
20 min.   JELMAN'S—3 pr. socks + new handkerchiefs.
10 min.   TOLLIVAR'S—newspaper, get-well card—Nora's
               boy.
sympathy card—Sonny Stoner. birthday card—Helen.
10 min.   POSTOFFICE—2 stamps + mail cards.
10 min.   MARCO'S—box candy for Alice.
15 min.   A+P—oysters + ½ pt. cream for stew.

An hour and a half. If he left at two he'd be back at three-thirty, time enough to read the paper, have his stew, and then a nap before work tonight. He stood up and braced his foot on the windowsill to tie his shoe, and an odd sight caught his eyes. Sitting on the rectory's back steps was Howard, with his arm draped over two large black suitcases. In front of Howard, yanking the starting cord of the lawn mower, was Father Gannon. He knew he should be angry at the young priest, but so far the only feeling he'd dared allow himself was concern for Alice, and even that was more intellectual than emotional. Recovery was so tenuous, such a precarious hope, that most days he felt as if he were cascading down a raging river while he tried to balance himself on a tiny section of board, with his legs drawn up and his chin in his knees, holding his breath, afraid to look left or right or even blink.

Across the street the rectory door opened, and he saw the Monsignor call out to Father Gannon, who continued to pull at the lawnmower cord. The Monsignor checked his watch, then spoke to Howard, who came down the steps toward Father Gannon. At that moment the lawn mower started with a roar and surged forward with the priest lurching after it. Howard looked back, and the Monsignor gestured angrily as Father Gannon mowed a long, pale strip through the broad church lawn. Howard chased after Father Gannon, then tapped him on the shoulder. He pointed back at the Monsignor, but the priest did not even look up. Instead, he swung the mower at a right angle across the front of the church, coming down its farther side, then back past the steps, where the Monsignor leaned over the rail, shouting at the heedless curate, whose cassock was salted to the knees with green grass spray. The Monsignor slipped back into the rectory. Howard returned to the steps, where he nested himself between the two suitcases. The young priest hunched over the mower and went on carving great green squares around the church grounds.

A strange sight, he thought on his way to the kitchen, toward the vile smells of Helen's canning. He paused at his mother's crib. She lay against the stacked pillows, eyes and mouth open, her breathing shallow. "Hello, Mother," he whispered and reached through the bars to touch the cold bone of her arm. He started to leave; then, seeing her mouth tremble, he took her hand. Her head turned slightly, and he realized she was staring at him. She strained as if to raise herself, her eyes bulging with the effort. Her mouth opened and closed soundlessly.

"What's the matter, Mother? Everything's fine. Just lay back now and rest. Everything's fine. I'll be back. I'm just going to run some errands and I'll be back."

She grew agitated again. Her hand groped feebly, as if to part a curtain.

"You'll be pleased to know I have a very good job, Mother," he said, easing her back down on the pillows and talking to her, something he hadn't done in years. He described his job, and he told her how Renie was such a big deal at Cushing's now that he picked up old Mr. Cushing and Arlo every day and drove them to the store. He told her about Renie's new mustache and how tired Helen had been since Jozia finally quit. He told her that Alice would be leaving for college soon, and he lied and told her that he often saw his sons, who were fine boys. "Marie's done a good job with them. She really has."

Her eyes closed, and he tiptoed into the kitchen. Helen was at the stove stirring a steaming pot with a wooden paddle. Her hair stuck out in dry clumps from the back of her neck. Her apron had come untied, and there was a yellow stain down the side of her dress. The table was strewn with vegetable peelings and sticky bowls. Sam cleared a spot and sat down with his coffee and toast. He tried to start any number of conversations, but Helen only grunted in reply. They hadn't spoken in days. She was at the back door now, trying to drag a box of tomatoes over the threshold.

"I'll get that," he said, easily lifting the box. "Where do you want it?"

She pointed to the counter by the stove, and he set it down. "Thank you," he murmured, returning to his seat.

She turned now. "What is it? What do you want?" She peered over her glasses, which had slid to the tip of her nose.

"Nothing," he said, watching her turn back to the stove and pick through the tomatoes, removing the largest ones from the box.

"Actually," he said suddenly. "I was just thinking. Why don't you and Renie go out some night? Just the two of you. I could take care of Mother."

"Oh yes! You'd like that, wouldn't you?" She began to plunk the tomatoes one by one into the kettle.

"No, really, Helen. I can take care of Mother. I'd manage just fine. I'm doing okay. I really am."

She laughed bitterly into the kettle's mounting steam.

"Don't laugh, Helen," he said quickly. "I mean it. This time it's going to work."

"I've heard *that* before."

"But it was never like this before. You see, I have this calm inside, this feeling of . . . of goodness. Of peace."

"Well, that's typical," she snorted. "Thanks to you, everyone else's life is in shambles, and still you have the nerve to sit there with that smug look on your face because you've managed to stay sober two whole weeks." She waved her hand contemptuously. "Don't tell me about peace, or calm, or goodness."

"Eight weeks, Helen. I've been sober eight weeks!"

She glanced back at him. "My God, you're ridiculous, you know that?"

He stared at her a moment, fists clenched, then threw back his head and laughed. "You can't stand it, can you? It's driving you crazy, isn't it? But no matter what happens, no matter what you do or say, I am a calm, happy man."

He left the kitchen chuckling. It was true. Goddamn it, it was true. He could still hear the lawn mower across the street as he went into the bathroom and filled the sink with water. When the mower stopped, angry voices rose from the street. He ran into the bedroom and watched through the window. A long, black car was idling in the rectory driveway. Two priests, one on either side of Father Gannon, were walking him to the car while Howard followed with the suitcases. Father Gannon turned suddenly and embraced Howard, their faces as close as if they were about to kiss. The priests grabbed Father Gannon and hurried him toward the car. When they got him into the back seat, they took the suitcases from Howard and tossed them into the car. One priest slid behind the wheel, and the other climbed in back beside Father Gannon. Howard waved goodbye as the car pulled onto the street. Sam looked toward the rectory and in a second-floor window saw the Monsignor's haggard face. They both ducked back.

He returned to the bathroom and lathered his face with shaving cream. There was an uneasiness in his stomach. He could not raise his eyes to the mirror. Who was he kidding? Helen was right, he *was* ridiculous, a complete failure who had destroyed everything. The ruin and rubble were everywhere. Nothing ever changed. No matter how hard he tried. Nothing. He felt panicky. He'd call in sick, go back to bed, and sleep. No. No, goddamn it, not this time. Whatever had happened was not his concern. It was out there, and he was here, in this moment, his toes curling on the cool tile floor, his hand lifting the razor to shave, simply to shave. That was all he had to do right now, all he had to concentrate on, to shave, just to shave. He took a deep breath and began, staring at himself, leaning so close his breath fogged the mirror.

The phone was ringing. Helen came down the hallway, complaining how sick she was of "tenants and their leaky faucets and their plugged-up toilets and their broken windows . . ."

The phone would never ring, he thought, if it weren't for the tenants—and old Mr. Cushing, who called Renie every morning at six-thirty to say he was ready to be picked up. "Nothing but a glorified chauffeur," Helen had muttered the other day as Renie headed out the door in his new gray suit and tie.

"What?" Renie had asked, stepping back into the kitchen. "What was that?"

Helen had hurried in to change Bridget's diaper.

"Sam!" she called now, and the razor jerked, knicking his chin. He opened the door, pressing his finger to the cut.

"It's for you," she said holding out the phone. "It's her."

He grabbed a towel and dabbed his bleeding chin. "Marie!" he said happily before the phone was even at his ear. "How are you? It's so nice to get a call from you. I mean that," he said with a nervous laugh.

Helen lingered by the table. He motioned her away, and she reached up and snatched the stained towel from him.

"How's Alice doing?" he asked, and seeing Helen roll her eyes, he waved his arm again. "Talk about timing." He thought of the young priest, but said nothing. "I was just on my way out to buy her some candy. She still likes caramels, doesn't she, the ones with nuts and chocolate?"

"Oh for God's sake," Helen muttered at his elbow.

"She does," Marie said, "but she's not home."

Sam covered the mouthpiece. "Do you mind?" he said to his sister. "I'm talking to my wife."

"She's gone to the lake for a few days," Marie was saying. "She needs a change of—"

"Ex-wife," Helen spat.

"Her friends work there. Sam, there's—"

"Just a minute," he interrupted, covering the phone again. "Get the hell out of here. Now!" He waited until she was gone. "Marie, I'm back. I just had to get rid of Helen. She was hovering. She can't stand it that I'm doing so well. It kind of tarnishes her image, you know, losing one of her afflictions. But I am, I'm just feeling so good; so damn good, I can't even explain how good I feel. It's like I just woke up after a long sleep. It's like everything's finally falling into place. Finally making sense for me. Christ, in a way it's almost like being a kid again. I—"

"Sam, I'm at work. I can't—"

"No, I know, but just wait a minute. Just listen, Marie. I don't want to lose it, this feeling I have, it's like the whole world is singing, Marie, and I'm the only one who can hear. . . ."

"Sam, please, I don't have much more time before Mr. Briscoe comes back. He doesn't like personal calls. And at night you're at work."

"I'm sorry. I haven't let you get a word in edgewise, have I, pet?" He laughed and in the cold silence heard his own breathing. He heard the lather drying on his itchy cheeks. He heard her say she was going to marry Omar Duvall. His head jolted back and the ruby drool of blood trembled from his chin, seeping into his undershirt like a squashed bug. "Why? For money? Is that it?" he demanded.

"Of course not." She sounded insulted.

"Then why? Tell me why!"

"I don't want to hurt you, Sam," she said in a small voice.

"I said tell me why!" he groaned.

"Because. Because I need some security in my life."

"Security!" he scoffed.

"And because," she said, her voice rising. "Because we love each other."

"Don't tell me that. I don't believe that, Marie." He jabbed his fist into the air. "You've never stopped loving me, just like I've never stopped loving you." Tears streamed down his face, dissolving the lather. "I can take care of you! *Now* I can. I can take care of all of you. I just need a chance."

"A chance," she started to say, but he cut in.

"I know, I know, but this time's different. Listen to me, pet."

"I have to go, Sam. Mr. Briscoe's coming."

"Don't! Don't hang up! This will kill me. You understand? You're all that's kept me going. You, goddamn it!"

"No, Sam, that's a lie. That's a lie we both told ourselves. And now it's time to be honest. Omar's a good man, Sam. He's good to the kids, and he's helping me start a new business. In fact, he and the boys—"

"Jesus Christ, how can you do this to me? I'm trying so hard. I've never tried so hard!"

"Sam," she whispered. "Mr. Briscoe's out in the warehouse. I have to—"

"Fuck Briscoe! You listen to me! You listen!"

"He's—"

"I said fuck Briscoe . . . Marie? Marie! You bastard!" he screamed into the dead air. He hurled the phone at the table, knocking the small bisque lamp to the floor. "You bastard! You selfish bastard! You don't give a shit about *me*," he panted as he ran into his bedroom. "I know what this is all about, that bitch. I know what she's doing."

In the parking lot behind Briscoe's a large red truck was parked. The driver had just stacked cartons onto a dolly. Sam cut in front of him and hurried into the warehouse.

"What do you want?" Marie demanded as he burst into her office. She pushed herself back from the typewriter.

"Here!" He slapped his paycheck and bankbook down on her desk. "From now on, this is the way it's going to be. I'll drop it off every Saturday. I told you Helen says all the trust money's gone, and I can't prove otherwise, but when Mother's gone, you can sell the tenements. In the meantime you'll have this every week. I promise, Marie. And if it's not enough, if Alice needs more for school, then I can get work during the day. Hell, I've got so much energy lately I could probably work three jobs." He laughed. "Use the weekends to sleep. It's amazing what you can do once the brain dries out."

She picked up the check and looked at it. She was probably comparing it to Duvall's salary. "It just occurred to me. I could probably get overtime, time and a half, where I am now. In fact, my boss is such a rummy I'll probably be pushed up to his slot anyday now. Are the boys home? I've got a few errands to run; then I thought I'd maybe stop by the house and see how they're doing." She wanted to say something, but he had to show her, to make her believe. "Things can change, Marie, just like people change! I'm not the same person anymore. I'm better. I'm—"

"And I'm not the same person anymore," she said in a low voice.

"Of course you're not. How could you be?" He put his hand on her shoulder, and it was all he could do to keep from pulling her out of that seat and into his arms.

"Sam, listen to me. I'm marrying Omar Duvall. I am!"

"Don't," he warned. "Don't do this to me!"

She closed her eyes and sighed. "I'm not doing it to you, Sam." She looked up now. "I'm doing it for me. Not even for the kids. For once I'm doing something just for me."

He stood there, staring down at her.

"I'm sorry," she said, with such pitying finality that he was afraid to look away. If he even blinked, he would be lost forever.

"You'd better go. Mr. Briscoe's out there with a delivery." She got up and stood by the door. "Please, Sam."

His ears were ringing. He kept gesturing as if to snatch some elusive object from the air. "I can't," he stammered. "I can't do it alone. If I don't have you and the kids, I'll . . . I'll die."

"What are you talking about? You haven't had us or even wanted us for ten years, Sam."

"That's not true! I've always wanted to be with you and the kids. You know that! I've just never been strong enough, but now I am. I can do it now. I know I can!"

She left the door and stepped closer. "You really think it's all up to you, Sam, don't you? Well, *you* may finally be ready now, but it's too late, Sam. It's just too damn late!"

"No!" he cried. "It's not! It's not!"

The door swung open. "Is everything all right in here, Marie?" Ferdinand Briscoe asked, red-faced and glaring. "I thought I heard yelling."

"Sam's just leaving now, Mr. Briscoe," Marie said.

Briscoe held the door open. "Sam?"

"I'd like a minute alone with my wife, if you don't mind," he said.

Marie nodded and Briscoe looked at him, then stepped back and closed the door.

"I'll go, but first I want you to tell me one thing," he whispered. "Tell me you don't love me."

She looked up, lifting her chin as if for an expected blow. "I don't. Not anymore, Sam." She almost seemed surprised.

He made himself smile. "Well, I love you, pet. Always have and always will. And I'm going to prove it. You'll see."

It was almost dark when he found Duvall, who had just pulled into the driveway next to Mayos' boardinghouse. He called to him, and Duvall turned with a quizzical smile.

"Of course, of course," Duvall said upon hearing the name. He extended his hand over the car door in a brief grip. For a few moments the chatter was all Duvall's. They had met before, though under rather more difficult circumstances, the oily-faced man was saying as he patted his chin and fleshy neck with a wadded handkerchief. And of course, as in any small community, people's paths were bound to cross, and recross, their lives often converging at the strangest times, in the most unexpected and certainly most unplanned ways.

"If you marry my wife, I'll kill you," he said, pointing, his forefinger and cocked thumb like a quaking gun. "I mean that. I really will." His voice broke and he took a breath.

Now Duvall stepped out from the car door. He closed it slowly, then came toward Sam, once again extending his hand, the hand that now held a knife.

"No, you won't, Sam, 'cause you'd have to get past this first, and besides," he drawled, head tilted, his smile oddly attractive, almost affectionate, over the glinting blade, "you're just not the type. I would expect the only man you'll ever kill, Sam, is yourself, you been at it for so long now. And that said, you have to know I hold no ill feeling for you. None, none whatsoever. You see, all we're trying to do here in the little time we got left is find some happiness. That's all!

No ulterior motives! Nothing against you, and I have no intention of turning your children against you, sir. All we want is just a little happiness. And surely you can't begrudge Marie and those fine children that, so whyn't you go on back now to your sister and your dear old mother and leave the rest of us be."

He slipped into his car and closed the door. Turning, Sam watched him drive down the hill. The full pint banged against his thigh as he began to walk. The seal on the bottle was not even broken and yet the old intoxicant surged through him. He no longer needed to drink for courage and resolve. He now felt so, so intensely alive that the evening air was spangled with prisms of early starlight, and the chirping he heard was not a monotony of cricket sound, but thousands, millions and millions of bent-legged insects pulsating under every leaf and blade of grass.

Duvall had brandished a knife, a knife, he kept thinking with such giddy confidence that by the time he had run up the stairs and down the hall past the dark parlor where Helen dozed in her green velvet chair, he had begun to pant and had to concentrate on his breathing, on every breath, to slow it all down—the eddying fragments of voices, his own, his son's, in his brain, in his ear. Hello. Hello? Hello? And around the corner, his mother's lungs heaved and wheezed. "Benjy, let me talk to your mother," he demanded. "I have to talk to her." Have to, have to, have to tell her this, this, this. But she would not, could not, would not come to the phone, the boy said, said, said, said the boy, said his son.

But he had to talk to her, had to tell her something before it was too late; something she did not know; something terrible. It was about Duvall. "Tell her that!" he cried, one hand manacling his dry tight throat. But at least he knew by the muffled phone and the background rustle that she was nearby.

"She said for me to take a message," the boy said. "She's in the middle of something."

"Listen!" he said, panicky because he could not think of this youngest child's name, and then it came to him. "Benjy, listen, now. This is very, very important. Tell her that I just saw Omar Duvall and he threatened me with a knife. He had a knife, Benjy, and he threatened to kill me! Tell her that! Tell her right now!"

"I will," said the boy, and then he hung up.

Sam slumped into the chair at the foot of his mother's crib while he waited for Marie's call. He opened his bottle and took sips, small ones, the way Litchfield had taught him. From time to time his mother's eyes widened with sudden gasps of fear or pain. He wasn't sure which, for by now his bottle was almost empty and he kept drifting in and out of sleep. Marie still hadn't called. "Imagine that," he muttered. "She doesn't even care about a knife. Doesn't even care." A man had threatened her husband's life and she didn't even care. He put the bottle to his lips and sucked out the last drop, warm from his lap, warm like his gut, warm all the way down. His chin on his chest, he sank into a deep safe sleep.

"She cares. She cares very much," said the voice, the voice in his dream, in his head, the voice in the room, his mother's clear compelling voice.

"No, she doesn't, Mother. Not anymore. I messed it all up and now it's too late."

"It's never too late, Sam. There's always something you can do."

"No," he sobbed, heat and booze bleeding from his eyes. "No, it's too late, and that's all there is to it. Just too damn late; that's it and that's all. End of story."

"Be a man, Sam, and do something. For once in your life, do something!"

"What? Tell me what! I don't know what to do!"

"You know. You know exactly what to do."

Peering up, all he could see over the roll of sheets was her chest rising and falling. He pulled himself to his feet and staggered to the side of her crib. He reached up and slid back the bolts that locked the side in place. He let it down, then gently slid one of the pillows from under her head.

"I'll do us both a favor," he whispered as he covered her face with the damp pillow. But then he lifted it away and bent to kiss her cheek. Her mouth twitched and he listened, the only sound her gurgling lungs. "It'll finally be over," he wept as he covered her face. "First you, and then me." Her fingers opened and closed as he held the pillow fast against the brief and futile pressure of her rising head. "Don't," he sobbed. "Oh please, Mother, don't hurt me like this. Don't. Please, don't. This is my last chance."

She lay still; then suddenly he fell sideways under the body that lunged at him. He clung to the crib, confused and amazed at the strength and the ferocity of one so old and weak, until he realized it had been Helen. She lifted her mother's limp head, begging her to breathe, to stay with her. "Please, please, please," she cried as he pulled himself to his feet.

"You killed her," Helen screamed. 'I'm going to call the police!"

Just then, the tiny body twitched, then jerked up and down as if a jolt were passing through it. The chest rose, then fell against the thin bed jacket, and for a moment the only sound was her gagging.

"Sorry, Mother. I couldn't even do that right, could I?" he said with a wave of disgust.

"I'll have you arrested," Helen cried. "They'll put you in jail for this."

Her rage wearied him. He was tired, sick of it all, sick, sick to death. "Promises, promises, promises," he muttered, pushing through the swinging door into the kitchen. "Renie! Where are you?" He banged on his brother-in-law's locked door. "I know you're in there, Renie, come on out. You can't hide on me. I know you're in there, you little cockroach, you good-for-nothing frog, you—"

The door opened and he smiled to see Renie standing there in his brown-and-yellow-striped pajamas. "What do you want, Sam?"

"I want . . . I just want to die, Renie, that's what I want." He burst into tears, bawling, "I just want to fucking die."

"Then go do it, Sam," Renie said, starting to close the door.

"You little asshole, you," he cried, throwing himself at the door.

He was halfway into the room when Renie brought his fist back and hit him on the chin. His knees buckled with the blow. He drifted in and out of consciousness as Renie dragged him the length of the house to his own room, where he got him onto the bed. Renie was taking his shoes off.

"I'm sorry," Sam whispered as Renie covered him with a blanket.

"No, you're not," Renie said from the doorway.

"No, I am. I really am."

"Good night, Sam."

"Good night, Renie. Renie, wait! Renie, you never hit me before, and I feel really bad that you hit me."

"I'm sorry, Sam."

"No, you're not!"

"Yes, I am, Sam, I really am."

"Promise you won't do it again, Renie, okay?"

"Okay, but you gotta promise you won't keep getting drunk like this, Sam."

"I promise, Renie. Honest to God, I do. I really mean it, too."

"You gotta keep trying, Sam."

"I am, Renie. I'm gonna keep trying. I swear to God."

"Okay, Sam."

"Wait, Renie, wait. I just thought of something. I think Helen's trying to turn us against each other. I think she's trying to split us up, if you know what I mean. So be careful. Be real careful 'cause I love you, Renie. I love you like a brother. I mean that. I really do."

The door opened and Benjy froze under the sheet. It was his mother.

"What did your father want?" she called in softly from the doorway. She had just discovered the phone off the hook the way he had left it.

"I don't know. He didn't say." He lay on his sticky wet towel, arms folded on his still breathless chest.

She stepped into the tiny room and he drew up his legs and gripped the sheet with damp hands. "How did he sound?" she whispered so Omar wouldn't hear. "Was he drinking?"

"I think so," he said, closing his eyes against the lie.

"Oh God," she sighed, going to the door. "Get back to sleep. You and Norm have to be up early to help Omar."

He couldn't tell her what his father had said. He didn't want to believe that Omar had a knife and had threatened his father with it. He couldn't believe it. It couldn't be true. His father had lied before and now he was lying about this. But what if he wasn't? He had sounded upset on the phone, but not drunk. No, the only one who had lied was Benjy, telling her he was drunk when he was sober, telling the black men Earlie was alive when Earlie festered in the woods with Omar's knife in his chest. But wait, then that meant Omar didn't have a knife, couldn't have a knife. But he could have gotten a new one. But why would he?

He lay awake for the longest time, as he prayed and pleaded and bargained with God to make this right, to set it all straight, to just let her be happy with Omar. And if God would only do this most important thing, then he would never ever touch himself again. He would learn to swim. He would work hard in school. He would be the best son she ever had.

Soothed by the barter, he could finally sleep. When he woke to the smell of coffee from the kitchen and the warmth of Omar's hearty morning voice against his mother's bracing laughter, he was relieved. God had been listening. A deal had been struck.

Soon after he came downstairs the phone rang. He knew who it was by his mother's low muffled voice and the way her whole body hunched to the phone.

"It was Sam," she said when she finally hung up. "He's so drunk I could barely understand him."

"That's too bad," Omar said, carrying his cup to the sink.

"I was afraid of this," she sighed, and Benjy could tell she was fighting tears. "He thinks you want to kill him." She shook her head and tried to laugh. "Oh God!"

"He's upset." Omar put his arm around her. "But we can't let that get in our way, right, sweetheart?"

"No, I know. I know," she said, leaning her head against his chest.

Benjy smiled, watching them. So his father had been drunk and it hadn't been a lie, which meant there hadn't been a knife and everything was going to be all right.

Omar caught his eye. "Go get your brother," he said with a wink. "We got ourselves some soap to sell."

Benjy rode in back while Norm sat up front with Omar. It was three o'clock and they hadn't eaten lunch. Benjy's stomach rumbled, but at least he'd had breakfast. Norm had gotten up too late to eat anything. Omar had promised to stop somewhere as soon as they made a sale. Norm was complaining again about the heat and how it didn't make any sense to drive all this way to try to sell soap to total strangers, who kept closing the door in his face the minute he opened his mouth. At least at home they'd have a better chance with people they knew.

"Look, I didn't ask for you to come, boy. This was your mother's idea!" Omar finally snapped, his voice sharper than Benjy had ever heard it. "So we might as well try and make the best of it." He glanced at Norm with a forced smile. "Now that we're stuck with each other."

Nothing looked familiar. Benjy had no idea where they were, and with the tension so thick in the car right now, he didn't dare ask.

They pulled down the long, rutted driveway of the next farm, this one even more run-down than the last. The barn roof had caved in. Red and black hens sat clucking on the farmhouse porch railing.

"Oh this looks like a *real* possibility," Norm groaned as he reached in back for the samples, which they took turns carrying.

Benjy watched Omar wait for Norm to reach the porch before he knocked on the door. It was opened by a stout woman with long, gray hair. She shook her head and quickly closed the door on them. Norm stormed back to the car. "This is fucking ridiculous!" he said as he got inside.

"Watch your mouth!" Omar warned as he started the car.

"Forget about making a sale, let's just stop someplace! I gotta eat!" Norm said, slapping the dashboard, his voice high and panicky.

"I told you, we have to make a sale," Omar said. "I don't have any money."

"What?" Norm exploded.

"I always start out with an empty wallet," Omar said, turning down yet another back road, this one wooded and dense with shade. "There's no motivation like hunger!"

Benjy's and Norm's eyes met in the rearview mirror, Norm's smoldering with rage. Benjy was glad Norm hadn't heard Omar telling their mother not to bother making sandwiches because he wanted to treat them to lunch.

"Then let's go home! I want to go home!" Norm said, folding his arms and jerking himself back against the seat.

"Think of your mother now," Omar said. "We can't go back empty-handed. She'll be too upset."

Upset, Benjy thought. Upset wasn't the word for it. When Norm had finally gotten up the nerve to tell her he'd been fired, she told him to go live with his father. They deserved each other. Norm had slept in the garage for two nights while she pretended not to know he was out there. Yesterday the bank had sent a registered letter demanding the two late loan payments. Her car was finally repaired and waiting to be picked up at Hillman's garage, but she needed two hundred dollars. Mr. Hillman had called every single day this week. Last night he'd threatened to sell it.

The green-and-white sign at the top of the hill welcomed them to Kirkville. They drove down into a tiny village square surrounded by six white houses, the Kirkville General Store and Post Office, and a white wooden church with a cupola instead of a steeple. Benjy followed Omar from door to door. At the last house, the parsonage, just as the woman was about to close the door, Omar spoke up quickly, noting that she bit her nails; would she be interested in a dish detergent that contained a special ingredient so concentrated, so bitter, that she would never bite her nails again because of the terrible taste the powerful but subtle component would eventually, after a week or so of use, build up in her fingernails? The woman said she'd buy a bottle. Only one? Omar said, explaining that it might be months before they'd be by this way again. The woman said she'd like two bottles, and Omar said a check would be fine. No need to take all her pin money, and he could certainly trust the pastor's wife. Benjy couldn't believe Omar was refusing cash. How else would they eat? The woman returned with her checkbook. Omar talked her into buying four bottles and insisted she use his pen and not waste her own ink. Three dollars, the woman wrote on the check as Benjy's stomach growled.

After that they made no more sales. Omar was discouraged and Norm was disgusted. Benjy didn't dare tell him Omar had talked their only sale of the day into paying by check.

Omar and Norm hurried down the steps from a handsome brick house where a woman had threatened to call the police the minute Omar started his pitch. "What is she, nuts?" Norm said, getting into the car. When they were out of sight, Omar pulled to the side of the road. He said he was exhausted and asked Norm if he wanted to drive. No, Norm said, looking out the side window. He didn't want to drive.

"A whole day and just four bottles of soap. Your poor mother," Omar sighed. "I'm getting old, I guess. I'm losing my touch."

Now Norm looked at him. "What do you expect?" he said, with such disgust that Benjy was embarrassed for Omar, who stared glumly over the wheel. "I told you, nobody's ever heard of Presto Soap. What do they want *that* for?"

"But they're not even giving us a chance," Omar sighed.

"Us?" Norm muttered with a wide-eyed glance in the mirror. "Us?"

"You're right. We need some kind of gimmick here. You know, like the big companies do," Omar said.

Norm rolled his eyes. We? he mouthed incredulously.

"Have a big sale," Benjy said quickly. "Sell it for half price."

"We can't very well take those kinds of liberties with your mother's investment. She'd be losing money that way," Omar said through his dismal gaze.

"Tell them there's a prize in every box," Benjy said. He could feel Norm's eyes through the mirror.

"I wish we could," Omar sighed. "Oh do I ever."

"Tell them it's a contest," Benjy said. "Say the entry blank's in the box."

"Oh if only there was," Omar said. "If there's anything these ladies like better than a free juice glass, it's a contest."

"Then tell them we're running the contest. Make believe you're taking their names when they buy some soap," he said. There had to be a way to make this work.

"But that'd be, I don't know, promising something we can't give them." Omar winced. "That would be lying."

"Oh I know! I know!" Norm said, holding up his hand as if he were in class. "Why don't we just tell them the truth! That we can't go home until we sell the shitty stuff."

Benjy squirmed as Omar turned and stared hard at Norm. "You know something, Norm, you don't even realize it, but you—"

"Hey look!" Norm snapped, his chin out. "I don't want to be here and you don't want me—"

"No, no, no, no, no," Omar broke in. "Let me finish. You just came up with a brilliant idea, and you don't even know it." He spoke rapidly. His eyes gleamed. "You see what you're saying is we can't give them a prize, but we *can* give them an incentive to buy. Men go to college, they spend years and years trying to do what you just did"—he snapped his fingers three times—"right off the top of your head like that."

Omar pulled onto the road, trying as he drove to come up with some gimmick that would make people want to buy soap. Norm was talking about the Christmas cards they'd once tried to sell. Benjy chewed his lip, expecting another blowup, but Norm was explaining how it had worked. Every box sold earned them points, and with so many points they could order gifts from the card company's catalog. The problem had been that they never sold enough cards to order gifts, most of which cost hundreds of points.

Omar had been nodding. "Points," he murmured. "Points." He glanced over at Norm as he drove. "Points for a scholarship! You're trying to earn money for college, and for every box you sell the company gives you points toward a scholarship."

They pulled in front of a small gray ranch house that was almost hidden by the weeping willow in the front yard. "I'll let you do most of the talking," Omar told Norm as they got out of the car.

"I'm going to get this all flubbed up," Norm said.

"All the better. I'll let them think I'm checking on you from the company, and they'll want you to do well. One more thing," he said, with his hand on Norm's shoulder. "This is very important. Always encourage them to pay by check."

"But—" Norm was nervous. He kept looking toward the house.

"I know, I know. Cash seems best," Omar said. "But they trust you more with checks and they'll buy more if they're not paying cash."

Benjy prayed hard as they disappeared behind the silvery sweep of the willow branches. He reminded God of their pact: whatever it took for his mother's happiness would be all right.

A few minutes later Omar hurried back to the car for the two bottles of liquid soap and the box of laundry detergent Norm had just sold. The woman was writing the check out right now. "She said Norm reminds her of her brother at that age."

"A check?" Benjy asked, pleased but hungry.

"It's okay," Omar said, patting his breast pocket. "I just remembered my emergency gas money. I forgot I had it."

He hadn't forgotten, Benjy thought. He'd just wanted them to get good and hungry.

"Perk up!" Omar said, reaching in to tousle his hair. "Your brother's a natural. I knew he would be!"

Norm sold more soap at their next two stops. "What were you writing in the notebook for?" Norm asked as they pulled up to a roadhouse that advertised sandwiches and hamburgs. "It made me nervous. She kept looking at you and then I started looking at you."

"I know." Omar laughed. "That was the whole purpose. To make her feel bad for you."

"She should've felt bad," Norm said, walking inside with Omar. Benjy followed. "I couldn't even remember the name of the soap!"

"I know." Omar laughed. "It was perfect. That's why she ordered the extra cans of spray starch. To show me what a good job you were doing."

It was dark inside, cool and clammy. There were booths and a long bar, where Omar said they'd sit for faster service. Benjy looked around. They were the only customers here. Omar ordered hamburgs, a Coke for Benjy, and two beers.

The bartender, a short bald man with thick glasses, asked Norm's age.

"Eighteen and gainfully employed," Omar said. "I should know. I've been counting the days."

"Eighteen!" Norm whispered when the bartender pushed through the swinging door into the kitchen. "You gotta be twenty-one."

"Not in New York," Omar told him. "We're just over the line."

Benjy couldn't finish his hamburg. The meat tasted spoiled. The roll was mushy. His Coke was warm. The bar was sticky. The alcohol in the air turned his stomach. He couldn't look at himself in the opposite mirror. Every time Norm reached for his mug, Benjy's eyes darted to his hand. Beer suds glistened on Norm's upper lip and his eyes were too shiny. Benjy wanted to feel happy, but everything had taken on this peculiar flatness.

"Remember," Omar was saying. "People'll buy anything, if you sell it right."

"How come you kept calling me Charlie?" Norm asked Omar. They were still talking about their sales.

"Well," Omar said, leaning toward Norm. He looked both left and right. "You've got to protect yourself. There's a lot of lonely women out there, a lot of crazy ones, too. Best just to keep a very low profile. If you know what I mean."

Norm nodded. He had finished his beer, but Omar had taken only a few sips of his.

His mother had baked a ham for dinner. She flew around the kitchen waiting on them as they recounted each stop for her. Every now and again she would touch her flushed cheeks as if to check her temperature. She turned from the stove now to suggest that when Norm got his car running he could sell Presto on his own, on weekends and holidays.

"And school vacations!" Omar added. "The boy's a natural salesman."

"I got an idea," Norm said, smirking for Benjy's benefit. "Why don't I just quit school and do it full-time if I'm so damn good."

While Benjy was relieved to see Norm's sarcasm dissipating under the steady stream of Omar's praise, he was a little hurt that Omar had none for him. In fact Omar hadn't even mentioned the sale at the parsonage.

"Well, now, there's a thought," Omar said with a hoist of his milk glass.

"Don't even think about it!" his mother gasped, eyes wide with feigned irritation.

"I don't know, Marie. I've never seen anything like it. Some people just have the gift, and Norm's one of them. He's a born salesman."

"That doesn't surprise me," she said, and Norm looked up quickly, but she was grinning at him.

"Aw, people'll buy anything," he said with a shrug. "If you sell it right."

Benjy looked up, surprised that it would be Omar Duvall Norm would quote.

"The thing is, you've got to have a real feel for people," Omar said, cutting up his ham. "You have to listen to them. Some people are very, very lonely."

"And very, very gullible!" Norm laughed, cutting his meat.

Benjy noted his brother's protective hunch over the plate, with his elbows out and his darting eyes, like Omar's, already coveting leftovers.

"Don't say that," she said quickly. She kept watching him.

"Well, it's true," Norm snorted. "I tell you, these ladies, they'll buy anything. It's sad, really. It's like they're all just waiting for someone to come along and be nice to them."

"Well, in a way that's true," Omar said with a wave of his fork. "A lot of these women have been very disappointed in their lives. They feel stuck and trapped and helpless. So that's what you relate to. That's what you let them see in you. It's called empathy. But the trick is to let them think they're helping you, the whole time you're—"

"Setting them up for the kill!" Norm called out.

His mother put down her fork. She looked upset.

Omar laughed. "Priming them for the sale is a nicer way of putting it, don't you think?" He glanced at Marie. "Would there be any mustard? I don't know when I've had ham like this. It's out of this world."

She got the mustard from the refrigerator. The cap was stuck, so she began to tap it with the knife handle. When it still wouldn't open she held it under hot running water. "Damn," she muttered, trying it again. She banged the cap on the counter edge. "Damn it!"

"Sit down, Mom. I'll do it," Benjy said, getting up to take the jar. Her hands were shaking.

"Yes, it's quite a thing to see," Omar said as he scooped mustard onto his plate. "All he has to do is smile and he's got the ladies eating right out of his hand."

"I've warned him about that, thinking that's all it takes, just his good looks," she said, staring at Norm.

"Oh Jesus," Norm groaned, rolling his eyes.

"You know there's a lot of people in some real messes that they didn't do anything to deserve, and for you to sit there and belittle them like that—"

"Mom!" Norm threw up his hands. "I didn't say anything! I'm not belittling anyone! Who am I belittling?" He blinked. "You? You think I'm belittling you?" He tried to laugh. "I wouldn't even try to sell you soap!"

Benjy held his breath. She didn't say anything.

"You don't have to tell Norm these things," Omar chided with a look of surprise. Surely, he said, she knew better than anyone that her son was someone with substance, someone who had the eagerness, sincerity, and caring that are the traits of a great man. "Let's give credit where credit's due here, now, Mother," Omar coaxed, patting her hand. He leaned forward and tried to get her to look at him. He lowered his voice. "You don't always have to be so tough on him."

She kept staring at the table. At first Benjy thought she was angry; then he realized she was trying not to cry.

"She just thinks she's tough," Norm said with a nervous laugh.

"Oh yah, well, you just better watch it, mister," she said with the same nervous laugh, then blew her nose in her paper napkin.

Sales were better the next day, and even better the following day. Norm and Omar had such a routine worked out now that it was obvious to Benjy he wasn't needed. But he didn't dare change a single factor of the equation. Omar had started giving Norm a few dollars of his own that he didn't have to mention to his mother. At the end of every day, or route as Omar called it, they would stop for a beer. The fifth day was gray with showers. Norm had a cold and kept falling asleep in the car. By midafternoon, when they still hadn't sold very much, Omar headed back to Atkinson.

"Aren't we going to stop?" Norm asked, disappointed.

"Not with just five dollars in sales. We don't deserve it," Omar said.

"Hey look!" Benjy said as they drove past the park. "There's Joey!" Seldon sat on a bench surrounded by pigeons. They were eating the popcorn the old man threw at them from the grocery bags at his feet. "That's funny!" he said, reminding Norm of Jarden Greene's hatred of pigeons.

"Yah," Norm said, sighing. "That's funny, all right."

Norm went to bed the minute they got home. Benjy was watching television. Omar and his mother were in the kitchen. A pot lid clinked up and down with boiling steam. There was the crackling smoky sputter of chicken frying in hot grease.

"Fifteen dollars," Omar sighed.

"Well, that's not too bad," his mother assured him.

Benjy looked up. He moved to the end of the couch, trying to listen. They were laughing now.

"Stop that," she giggled. "Stop that!"

He knew by the sudden quiet that they were kissing. He tiptoed past the doorway and went upstairs to wake up Norm. His mother's bedroom door was open. Omar's clothes were mixed with hers in a pile on the chair. His new shoes were next to the bed. And hanging on the bedpost was his linen jacket damp from the rain. In the breast pocket there was Omar's pen and one check. Helena B. Olson, it said with today's date. It had been made out for fifty dollars. His mother was calling him to supper. "Wake up, wake up." He kept shaking Norm. He asked him how much money they'd made today.

"Five bucks," Norm groaned, pulling the pillow over his head. "Jesus Christ, will you let me sleep?"

"Was it a check?" Benjy whispered.

"Yes, it was a check," Norm snarled, looking out at him now.

"Was her name Olson?"

"Yah, Olson," Norm said. "Why?"

He told him that he'd just heard Omar tell their mother that they'd made fifteen dollars today.

"He probably doesn't want her to start panicking again, that's all," Norm said, and Benjy agreed with him. No sense in letting one slow day spoil her good mood. Yah, they both agreed. They'd just make it up tomorrow.

He didn't tell Norm that the check said fifty dollars. He couldn't. He didn't even want to think about it. But all through dinner and into the night, he heard Earlie's voice, accusing Omar of *changing them checks, changing them checks, changing them checks,* the words chugging in his head like wheels, turning round and round and round, going someplace, heading somewhere, if he didn't say something, say something, do something, do something, do something, but maybe not, maybe not. Maybe it was just that one bad day, that was all. Just that one bad day and he loved her so much he couldn't bear to see her disappointed. That was it. That must be it. That had to be it.

I t was two in the morning and Howard was wide awake. He crept from bed dressed except for his shoes, which he carried as he tiptoed to the door. He had already taken a walk earlier tonight, which was why he no longer bothered putting on pajamas. Now when he couldn't sleep he had to go out for long walks because Lucille complained about the creaking floorboards under his pacing feet. Yesterday she had told him he had to find another place to live. She didn't think it looked right to have a single man and a single lady living in the same house, especially in her kind of business.

The apartment was dark but for the weak flicker of the votive candle at the feet of the Infant of Prague, its yellow satin gown dim with dust. He had stopped going down to the Holy Articles Shoppe because of the way Lucille treated him there. "Don't touch that!" she'd snap, watching him from her tall stool behind the register. Father Gannon had been right. Taking her to see Perda had been a mistake. Hoping to set things straight, he had asked her to the Kong Chow, where he and Jozia used to share a pupu platter and pork chop suey with white rice, and then afterward a fizzy pineapple drink with an umbrella stirrer in it that always made them giggly by the time they were breaking open their fortune cookies. But Lucille hated Chinese food. That's easy, Father Gannon had said, just take her someplace else. But it wasn't easy. Nothing ever was. The Kong Chow was the only restaurant he had ever been in.

He missed Father Gannon terribly. In the days after his trouble over Alice Fermoyle, Father Gannon had spent a lot of time with him. Father Gannon had talked so much that Howard was having a hard time getting used to all this silence again. Father Gannon told him about his mother and his father. He told him about a boy named Radlette and some priests who said he stole the birthday money and all about the blankets he collected and the beautiful young woman asleep in bed with her dead baby and the Bishop with his pale-blue eyes and silver hair who said Father Gannon had to return to the hospital in the desert, only this time for a longer stay. But what Howard most liked hearing about was God and how kind He was. Father Gannon said God was not an angry old man in the heavens, who punished people for doing bad things. He said God was love, and so when we feel love inside us, what we were really feeling was God. Howard liked that idea and he thought about it all the time now. He had all this love for his sister and even for Lucille if she would only be nice. He loved God, and going to church, and praying with all the people. But no one ever loved him back. So what did that mean? Where was God? Why was He letting Jozia love the pigman more than her own brother? Soon all the old confusions between his head and his heart got so stirred up he had turned to Father Gannon and demanded to know why God let bad things happen. Father Gannon didn't say anything right away. Then he admitted he didn't know the answer to that. He said of all life's mysteries that was the biggest mystery of all. Maybe bad things happened so God could test not just our strength and bravery, but how much love we could keep on giving.

"That don't seem fair," he had blurted. "Not to the one that's always having the bad things happen to him."

"No, it doesn't, does it?" Father Gannon had said, and after that Howard felt bad that he'd made Father Gannon so sad and quiet for all the rest of the day.

The night before Father Gannon left, he had taken Howard to dinner at the Kong Chow. He had ordered two pupu platters and three other dishes with names Howard couldn't pronounce. Father Gannon had worn his collar, and all night long, people kept staring at them, and this pleased Howard. They were nibbling pineapple chunks off wooden toothpicks and sipping their fruity drinks when the waiter brought tea and fortune cookies. Howard broke open his and read his fortune: *A vision brings great wisdom.* He was disappointed. Jozia usually figured out the complicated ones. He felt bad remembering the times he'd accused her of acting like a know-it-all. He wished he could always just get simple ones, like Father Gannon's: *Good luck comes tonight.*

"How intriguing," Father Gannon said, reading Howard's fortune. He asked Howard if he'd ever had a vision, a strange experience, seen something he could not explain or understand. Only one time, Howard said, and he began to tell the secret, the terrible thing he had seen that night at the pig farm. It was a dead man, he whispered. Or like a dead man, but swelling with rot and overgrown with vines. He explained how when he finally told Jozia she said he was going off the deep end because he was so scared of finally having to live his own life.

"Well, that can happen," Father Gannon had said, pouring them both more bitter black tea. "You see Grondine Carson as this badness, this foul thing that's up there in the woods, waiting to consume you the way he's consuming your sister."

The tiny cup trembled and tea dribbled down Howard's chin. Consume, he kept thinking. Consume, such a scary word. *Consume.*

"But it's only your imagination, Howard. Don't you see? It's not real. It's all your own fears. We all do it. Our brains play tricks on us, and if we're not careful we see only what we want to see. And then we're in a terrible mess."

He was walking along Main Street now, through the moonlight-spattered shadows, down the hill past the empty fairgrounds. Every Labor Day he and Jozia spent ten dollars each at the fair. It was the one day in the year when he felt rich. This year Jozia would probably go with Carson.

As he walked he grew more lonely. The black sky was so awash with stars that they seemed to sway, sagging lower and lower overhead. He had not seen Jozia in days. Now that she had quit the Fermoyles' there was nothing to come to town for anymore, not even to bring him the pigman's leftovers. She loved the pigman more than him. Father Gannon had said Radlette's father tried to scare him away. Radlette's father told everyone the priest had kissed his son. A lie, said Father Gannon. But now Howard wasn't so sure. The morning they took Father Gannon away, he had thrown his arms around Howard.

"God loves us, Howard. No matter what happens, we have to remember that," he had whispered, then kissed him on the lips. That memory and the stars and Father Gannon's stories converged in his brain now like fireworks, the dazzling images bursting and receding one into the other, the dead baby's glowing face, Perda grinning up at him from her leafy tomb, the bloated dead body in Perda's hospital bed, and then Lucille asleep in his bed with the nude Infant of Prague suckling at her breast.

The air seemed thinner here, the road more narrow, steep and rutted. In the distance a dog howled. There were crickets and frogs, and now the splash of an unseen waterfall on rocks. Ahead lay the pig farm, its windows dark, all but one up on the second floor. Carson's two trucks were parked across the road in front of the barn. Here, the earth smelled of sweet warm rot. There was no dead body, but a vision, he assured himself, moving closer to the house. It was like Father Gannon said, our brains play tricks on us, and all at once now, he knew how to get Jozia back. Maybe if she thought there were ghosts around she'd be too afraid to live here. Maybe this was God's test to see how brave and strong he was, to see how much love he had. He picked up a stick and crept close, keeping his head below the windowsills. He reached up and tapped three times on the front windows. Then he went along the side, tapping on all those windows. He was at the back of the house now, but it was too dark out here. He scurried next to a narrow shed, its furrowed tin roof sparkling with starlight. He squatted down and raked his fingers back and forth in the dirt until he had a handful of stones. He darted into the yard and threw the stones against the side of the house. He ducked down next to the shed again and felt around for more stones. A light came on downstairs. A dog barked loudly from inside the house. The back door squeaked open with a glare of light that flooded the yard. Howard crept to the back of the shed.

"Who's out there?" Grondine Carson demanded. "I said who's out there?"

Now Howard was trembling. This was real. The stories had ended. The dream was over. This would end with Jozia even madder at him. He sprang blindly into the woods, branches batting his face and twigs cracking underfoot as he ran.

"Son of a bitch. You no-good son of a bitch." Carson panted in pursuit, and then a bullet whizzed past his head in a streak of heat.

He turned and scrambled up a brambly rise. Thorns gashed his neck and arms. He could hear a siren coming up the road. All that mattered now was that Jozia not find out. A dog growled nearby. The running footsteps were almost on top of him. He stumbled down the other side of the rise, his feet skidding along thick slippery pine needles.

"Hold it!" Carson cried as he started to run again. Carson fired.

And the night and all the stars and stories exploded, pinwheeling around him. As he fell the panting dog pounced on his chest, its thick paws pinning him there. His right leg was burning hot. He touched the sticky wet hole. The dog growled and snapped at his face.

"Oh Jesus!" Carson groaned above the beam of light in his eyes. "Howard! Why didn't you say it was you?"

His eyes closed and he thought sure he was dead, and then men were hollering, and lights spilled down the rise.

"It's Howard," Carson cried. "I shot him. Oh God, I shot Jozia's brother."

"Howard! Howard!" Jozia screamed, and his eyes opened as his sister ran past the policemen in her white bathrobe. She pushed Carson aside and dropped to her knees. "Oh poor baby Howard," she wept, cradling his head in her hands.

Two men carried him from the woods and slid him into the back seat of the cruiser. They sped him to the hospital, where Dr. Deitler cut the bullet from his thigh. The doctor held it up between tweezers to show him, then dropped it into a metal cup. As it clinked, Howard fainted.

It was the two remaining policemen who found the corpse, so decomposed they could not tell at first if it was a man or a woman. Man, they guessed looking down at the rank straw hat that had been underneath the body. The stained papers in the shredded pocket bore the name Earl Lapham Jones. Twenty years old, read Sonny Stoner. Probably been there all summer, Dr. Deitler guessed.

Probably had been, Sonny agreed just inside the mortuary door. Day after day, through rain and wind and heat. So that was it. There it lay, sealed in canvas. The corruption. The vile manifestation of his failure. He turned away, disgusted and weak with the realization that it was finally over. This morning he'd found out that there had never been a life insurance policy on Carol, and he'd been relieved. There would be no comfort from his loss, no profit from his sins. Some of his men wanted to pin this murder on Haddad, who had been transferred from the hospital to jail, but Grondine Carson was the only suspect. It didn't take any brilliant detective work to know what had happened to Earl Lapham Jones. The pigman had caught the young man trespassing on his property and had shot him. Carson continued to deny everything, even Sonny's carefully worded suggestion that Jones had threatened him, and Carson, after all the intrusions on his property, had been forced to shoot in self-defense.

"No sir," Carson repeated. "That never did happen."

Like a visitor in his own front parlor, Carson sat red-eyed and rigidly erect on the austere loveseat. He kept turning his cap in his big stained hands. Jozia was back in town tending her brother, and the taciturn pigman was alone again.

"Well, maybe it was the same thing as Howard, then," Stoner offered, noting the ruffled curtains in the bright rainy windows, the newly blacked woodstove, the waxed floors. He thought of his own neglected house. "Maybe you just heard a sound one night and you ran out and you fired off a few shots thinking to scare whoever it was away. And you hit him, but you never even knew it, and he ran in the grove to hide, and that's where he died. How about that?"

Carson shook his head. "No sir." He rubbed his eyes. "I told you, all those times, all the trouble I had here, I only once ever fired my gun and that was last night." His weary gaze sought Stoner's. "I thought they were trying to get in here. And Jozia was so scared again."

"Again? You mean it happened before?"

"No. Like I already said. Howard was always telling her bad

things, trying to scare her home. He told her there was a dead man in the woods." Carson shook his head. "Only I didn't pay no attention. Should have, but I didn't."

Sonny got up to go. He had already questioned Howard, who thought it had been six weeks ago, anyway, when he stumbled on the moonlit body. The only incongruity was Howard's insistence there had been a knife in the chest. But then again, even Jozia had said of her brother, "Half what he thinks he sees is all mixed up because he always puts the wrong parts of things in all the wrong places."

Howard Menka had definitely seen a body and was obviously confused about having seen a knife. Grondine Carson had shot and killed an intruder on his property. The only real mystery now was Earl Lapham Jones himself, a man no one knew and no one missed.

Sonny turned on the wipers and headed back to town. He would give Carson as much time as he could.

Norm honked the horn in front of Weeb's house. His eyes scanned all the windows, hoping for a glimpse of Janice. He wanted her to see him driving a Cadillac. This was the second night in a row Omar had let him drive it. Last night he had taken Benjy to the drive-in to see *A Summer Place*. It had rained and Benjy fell asleep and then the windows fogged up, so he had gone home early. "What's that?" Benjy had asked the minute they stepped inside. It had seemed in the dark with the creaking and banging that the whole house was shaking. It had been his mother's headboard hitting the wall as Omar moaned.

"Pipes," he had whispered, pulling Benjy toward the door. They had driven up to Seward's for ice cream.

He watched Weeb come down the walk to the car. "I'm impressed," Weeb said, leaning in the window. "What'd you do, finally catch him with the douche bag?" Weeb climbed in and turned the radio up as they drove off. "I saw her the other night," he yelled, drumming his fingers on the dashboard.

"Who?" Norm demanded, turning the radio down.

"Bernadette Mansaw," Weeb said. "I picked my father up down the bowling alley and she was there."

"Yah. So?"

"You know what she had on the counter? That soap, the same stuff as your mother. She was selling it."

"Oh yah? I guess a lot of people are doing that now." He nodded. "Going into business. Selling soap. That Presto Soap's pretty good stuff, I hear. It'll clean just about anything." He felt like stopping the car and shoving Weeb into the gutter for making him sound like such an idiot.

"I should tell my sister." Weeb shook his head. "She's always puking all over the place. Morning sickness, my mother calls it. Morning, noon, and night sickness," Weeb said with a shudder.

They drove around, but the streets were empty. There were only a few cars at the A+X. It was still summer, but there was a depressing chill in the night air. Hoping to see Janice, Norm kept suggesting they go back to the house, but Weeb didn't want to. He was sick of being in every night. But after a while his legs began to ache, and he said he'd better go home and put ice on them.

After Weeb filled the ice bags, they went downstairs to watch television in the rec room. Norm asked about all the boxes stacked in the corner. Weeb told him they contained Janice's belongings that were going to her future in-laws' house in Rhode Island, where she and her new husband would be living after they were married. He kept glancing at the boxes. So it was true. It was really happening. He asked if that meant Janice would be dropping out of school. Weeb shook his head. Russ wouldn't be going back to school, either, he said. He would be working for his uncle's construction company while he took night classes. Weeb said Russ's parents were barely speaking to Janice, they were so mad.

Norm and Weeb sat on the musty divan watching *Dragnet*. He could tell his questions were annoying Weeb, so he tried to pace them. They stared at the screen as Joe Friday jumped from his police car and ran into the lobby of an apartment building.

"So what are they mad about?" Norm asked when the commercial came on.

Weeb gave him a weird look. "Who?"

"That guy. Russ, his parents."

"I don't know. Everything. They're just mad." He looked at Norm. "What do you care?"

"I don't know. I just . . . I guess it's just interesting, that's all."

"Yah, well," Weeb began, then seemed to change his mind abruptly. "Well, maybe to you it's interesting, but I'm not used to all this commotion, all this trouble!"

Norm's cheeks stung. "What I meant was, well, you're going to be an uncle, for instance. Now, that's interesting." He knew exactly what Weeb had wanted to say. Every time there had been some new mess in Norm's life, Weeb had never once said anything, not even when Alice got caught with Father Gannon.

"Yah, that's right." Weeb grinned. "I am. I'm going to be an uncle, huh?"

Norm felt something in his chest jerk out of place. What if this Russ's family hated the kid? What if Russ hated this kid that might not even to be his? He told Weeb he'd be right back, he had to go to the bathroom.

Janice was in the kitchen. With one foot propped on a chair she was painting her toenails a bright pink. A cigarette burned in a cut-glass ashtray. Her wet blond hair was done up on enormous black mesh rollers that bobbed as she bent forward. Glancing up at him, she continued to stroke polish on the nail of her big toe. Cotton balls were wedged between each perfect toe. His heart ached. He had loved her for as long as he could remember.

"What do you want?"

"Oh, nothing. I just came upstairs." He gestured feebly at the basement door. "*Dragnet*'s on." He put his hands on his hips and exhaled through his mouth the way Omar would right before a sales pitch. "I don't know. It's kind of juvenile, if you ask me."

She took a puff of her cigarette, then blew the smoke straight up into the light over the table. "I didn't," she said.

"Didn't what?" he asked, smiling, then caught himself. "Oh well, no, I know, but I just thought I'd . . . come up and say . . . say . . ." His face burned and sweat rolled down his back. He couldn't get it out. She stared at him as he continued to stammer. "The thing is, you see . . . well, first off, I want you to know I never . . . Oh God," he moaned and shook his head.

"Norm, don't worry about it."

"But whatever happened . . . I mean, if it did, that is, I just want you to know I'm . . ."

"Forget about it," she said with a shrug. "No big deal. Really."

"But it is!" he said, pulling out a chair and sitting next to her. "For me it is. I'm not like that."

She couldn't look at him. "I know. And that's why I felt so guilty."

"Well, don't!" he pleaded. "Don't feel guilty! I don't."

"Well, I do. I mean, I was the one that started the whole thing."

"You did?" He could feel himself getting excited. If only he could remember it. "But I wanted to, too. I know I did!" He didn't want her feeling like a tramp when they were both responsible.

"Yah, because you were trying to impress everyone. They were all laughing and clapping."

"They were?" He was shocked. "You mean people were watching?" It had been an orgy. No wonder he'd blanked it out.

She gave him a funny look. "Well, yah, what do you think? They were even taking bets on how long you'd last."

His mouth hung open. He didn't know what to say or where to look as she continued speaking in a low voice. "I tried to get you to stop, but you wouldn't, and things were just out of control, and I didn't know what to do. Norm, promise me you'll never again let anyone talk you into another chug-a-lug."

A chug-a-lug. Oh Jesus, she'd been talking about a beer-drinking match, not sex.

She leaned toward him in a dizzying rush of smoke and scented soap. "I mean, God, Norm, you were so sick it was . . . it was pitiful. I mean everyone was blasted, but you . . . you barfed, and then you started to cry and say things, and then you passed out. God, you were laying in it. Your whole face was in it. We didn't know what to do. And this woman was there. She said she knew you, so we let her get you home."

His eyes widened with the humiliating image of himself with his hands over his face as she begged him to stop crying. "Well," he said. "I'm glad we finally . . ." He cleared his throat. He couldn't look at her. "You know, got this out in the open, then. Because that's what I wanted. I wanted to tell you I was sorry."

"That's what you kept saying then, how sorry you were."

"Well yah, for embarrassing you in front of your friends," he said, hoping to sound at least a little lighthearted.

"Don't worry about it. Besides, they all felt really bad for you."

Felt bad for him! Jesus Christ!

"You kept saying all these things about your father." She glanced away, adding softly. "I almost cried myself."

He turned to go. The bitch, he hoped he never saw her again. He was through with Weeb, through with this whole frigging town.

"Norm!" she called, following him to the door. "I probably shouldn't say this, but if I don't and then something happens, like, you know, years from now . . . you know, like, well, like your father . . . I mean, in a way you're like my little brother." She reached up and put her hand on his shoulder. "Just be real careful, will you?" She stood on her tiptoes and kissed his cheek.

He drove home, turning into the driveway so fast that the tires squealed. His mother and Omar were in the kitchen. "That boy's gotta go bad," Omar laughed as he stormed past them. He ran upstairs and slammed his door. A few minutes later there was a knock on the door. "What do you want?" he bellowed.

"I want to talk to you," his mother called back.

"Well, I don't feel like talking, all right?"

"Open the door, Norm."

"No, just leave me alone. Everyone just leave me the hell alone!"

The door opened and she stepped inside. "Omar was just telling me you're the best salesman he's ever seen. And I told him how proud I am of you, and he said I should be telling you that. And he's right." She came closer and scratched the back of his head. "I'm very proud of you, Norm," she whispered. "Very, very proud."

Today they had made so many sales that by midafternoon they were out of soap. Norm and Omar were a well-drilled team now, their every word and gesture significant, including his nervous stammer as he introduced Omar as his boss to each housewife. "I haven't been doing too well," he would confide, clearing his throat while the woman glanced uneasily at the tall man in the rumpled suit. Omar would merely nod, his sharp-eyed stare furrowing to disapproval the moment Norm patted his pockets, then began fumbling through sales folders for the missing product brochures. Shaking his head, Omar would watch him race back to the car. "It's a shame," Omar would confide to the concerned woman. "He's such an earnest young man. I was hoping to give him this one last chance to prove himself." And then he'd smile. "It's kind of you to be so patient."

"Oh I don't mind," they'd usually say, often adding that they thought the boy was doing a good job. He was just a little nervous, they'd tell Omar.

When Norm returned they would listen intently to the rest of his pitch, to show Omar what a good salesman the boy could be. They always ordered something, even if it was just one bottle of dish detergent. And Omar always urged them to pay by check. "Here," he'd insist, holding out his pen. "Use mine. No sense in wasting your own ink."

It was one of those personal touches customers like. Norm was grateful to be learning so much about business and life at the hands of a master. "Service in even the smallest details. That's what makes for success," Omar said, launching into yet another homily delivered in his hypnotic rhetoric as the big warm car cruised over the country roads. "People helping people, that's the bottom line. You see, I love people, Norm. I really do. I'm not ashamed to say it, and I'm not afraid to show it. No sir, never have been and never will be, because that's what being on this planet's all about."

He woke up every morning looking forward to another day on the road with Omar. They had already sold half his mother's stock, earning enough to get her car back from Hillman's garage and to make one of the delinquent loan payments. His mother treated him with a new respect, as if he were a peer. At this rate, she said, they would be able to start a savings account in a month or two. She looked younger. Her eyes glowed. Sometimes he would look up and find her smiling at him. Yesterday on their way home, after their sandwich and beer, Omar had taken him into a fancy dress shop on the outskirts of town. Omar kept holding dresses up and asking him how he thought they'd look on his mother. At first he'd been embarrassed. But the saleswoman was so charmed by the idea of the son helping his father pick out a dress for his mother that she began to model the ones they liked. They finally decided on a red dress with a black stand-up collar.

Marie was shocked when Omar handed her the box. It was too flashy, she said, not at all her type of thing. Norm could feel Omar's disappointment. "Well, try it on, Mom. At least give it a chance," he said.

When she came out of the bathroom, he and Omar were both grinning. With her dark hair and dark eyes, she looked beautiful.

"But when will I ever wear it?" she asked, glancing back at herself in the mirror.

"How about next week," Omar said. "When we apply for the marriage license."

It was late Friday afternoon when Alice came home, sunburned and irritable. She said she'd hated her week at the lake, but at least she seemed more like her old self, Norm thought.

"The wedding license!" she kept saying. "The wedding license!"

It was the first thing Benjy had told her.

"Oh God," she groaned, throwing her bag onto the floor. "I don't believe it! What is she, crazy? How could she do this?"

"But she's really happy," Benjy said. "You should see her. She doesn't even yell anymore. Nothing makes her mad."

She spun around to Norm. "What about Bernadette Mansaw? How could she forget about that?"

"That really was business," Norm said; then, seeing her shocked look, added, "I know for a fact."

"Norm's Omar's partner now," Benjy said. "They go out selling every morning."

"What?" Alice cried.

"Well, not his partner," Norm said. "I'm just kind of helping, I guess."

"But he said partner," Benjy insisted.

He wished Benjy wouldn't hit her with everything all at once like this. She'd end up back under the covers in her sealed room and all the recrimination and despair would start again. He followed her into the kitchen and tried to explain how well things had been going here. He told her about the bills finally being paid. He opened the cupboard and pulled out a plate from the new set of dishes Omar had bought. He pointed to the can of paint in the corner. Omar was going to paint the kitchen pale blue, Mom's favorite color. He told her how Marie and Omar had gone to the Klubocks' soap party and stayed on, visiting with the Klubocks, long after the other guests had gone home. Jessie Klubock had come to the back door the other night to ask Omar about ordering more soap. "She almost made it into the kitchen!" Norm laughed.

"Oh God, into this dump! How humiliating!" she groaned, looking around.

She didn't understand. Things had changed, he tried to explain. They hadn't really understood Omar or given him a fair chance. "He's really a sharp guy," he said.

"Yah, he can sell anybody anything," Benjy said from the doorway.

"Well, that's pretty obvious," Alice said, staring at Norm. "What'd he do, let you drive his big Cadillac all over the place?"

"Shut up! You don't know what the hell you're talking about!" he snapped.

"Oh, I know. He promised you something, didn't he? What? A hi-fi? A new glove! Or maybe your own little franchise! God, Norm, what a hypocrite you are! I didn't think you'd be this easy," she said, starting back into the living room.

"Not as easy as you!" he yelled after her.

She turned, her face white, lips trembling, and then she ran upstairs and slammed her door.

"Norm!" Benjy said. "Now she'll get all upset again."

"Let her! Who the hell cares! Miss Purity up there," he called loudly from the bottom of the stairs. "Looking down her nose all the time at everyone, when she's the hypocrite. She's the one!"

"Norm!" Benjy said, grabbing his arm.

Norm pushed him away and ran up to her room. He shouted against the door. "You kill me, you're so goddamn afraid of what people are going to think. You're embarrassed! Jesus Christ, how about us? Did you think about that? Did you give a fuck about that?" He kicked the door. "Goddamn you, Alice, why'd you do that?" he panted. He wasn't easy, goddamn it. He hadn't been gullible and he wasn't a hypocrite. All he wanted was to be part of something big, something bigger and better than himself or any one of them.

It was late afternoon and they were on their way home. As Norm drove, his tongue tingled with the thought of ice-cold beer. Exhausted, Omar had been asleep for the last fifteen minutes.

"What time is it?" Norm asked, but Omar's mumble ended in a gasping snore. He turned the radio on. They were almost at Bart's Bar and Grill, and he wanted Omar to wake up. Omar's head bobbed up and down.

It wasn't that he needed a beer. As a matter of fact, yesterday they'd finished the route too late to stop and that had been okay. He'd been disappointed, but it was no big deal. It wasn't even the beer he enjoyed as much as Omar's company, the camaraderie in the quiet darkness after a hard day. But right now, he had to admit, he was thirsty as hell. He turned the radio up louder, which only seemed to plunge Omar into deeper sleep. He called his name. Nothing. Finally he reached over and nudged him. "Omar, wake up, we're almost at Bart's."

Omar's head lifted and his eyes rolled as he tried to keep them open. "I'm just too . . ." he mumbled, then drifted off again.

Norm pulled into the parking lot and turned off the motor. "Omar!" he called sharply, then got out of the car. He came around to Omar's side and opened the door. "Omar, wake up! We're at Bart's! Omar, we're here!" His chin lay on his chest. Norm reached in and shook his arm. "Omar! Come on, wake up!"

Omar's eyes opened and he stared up at him.

"We're here," he said weakly. "We're at Bart's."

"So we are," Omar muttered, grunting as he got out of the car. It was obvious he didn't feel like stopping. Norm reached in back for Omar's jacket and handed it to him. A piece of paper fluttered onto the ground. It was a check from Minnie Hewlings, that nice old lady who had cut him a slice of hot apple pie. The sale had been for three dollars and thirty cents, but the check was made out for thirty-three dollars and thirty cents.

"Look!" he said, catching up to Omar.

"Well, I'll be," Omar said, then looked back at Norm. "A mistake or maybe a gift," he said with a wink as he slipped the check into his breast pocket.

"It's got to be a mistake," Norm said. "She was just a little old lady."

"I don't know, Norm. You said she liked you. Maybe it was her way of showing it, you know, slipping you a little something extra."

"Oh no, she didn't have any money, I could tell." He had seen the knife's brief hesitation between the thinness of her own rationed slices and then the wider one for him. *Certain things you just know.*

"Well, what'll we do?" Omar said, pausing in the vestibule. He checked his watch. "It'll take us a good hour to get back there. We'd have to leave now."

The door opened, and Norm stepped aside as two men in dust-streaked shirts emerged from the beery darkness.

"You tell me what to do. You decide." Omar smiled.

"Well, could we mail it to her?" he asked.

"If we had her address, we could."

"Well, how about if we just don't cash it?"

"Now, how can I do that to your mother? How in good conscience do I take money out of your mother's pocket to cover some old lady's carelessness?"

So there was only one thing left to do, he realized with a sinking heart. They'd have to head back there, when he'd been looking forward to this since last week. "I'll drive," he said on their way to the car. "That way you can sleep."

Omar thumped the hood of his car. "Wait, I just thought. What we can do here is cash the check, all right? We give your mother her rightful money. But what we'll do, you see, is take the difference and set it aside. Then next time we're out that way, we'll return Miss Hewlings's overdraft, which I guarantee you she will not have missed or even understand what it is we are talking about. How's that sound?"

"Sounds good!"

"Creative thinking!" Omar said as they headed into the bar. "Problem solving! Dexterity with the pieces, that's what it comes down to in the end, Norm, remember that."

Norm sat at a table while Omar placed their order at the bar. He didn't know why Omar preferred checks. He might be a shrewd businessman, but this just proved how easily mistakes could be made. With cash you knew what you had. From now on he'd scrutinize every check, read each line twice. A sharpness like pain made him blink as the old woman's shaky script scrawled across his vision.

Omar carried two mugs of beer to the table. "Here you go," he said, setting the mug in front of him. Foam slicked down the side onto the table. Omar sank into the chair with a sigh. "I'm so glad you didn't want to go back. I don't think I could stand two more hours in that hot car."

"You know, I was just thinking. I looked at that check. I could swear she wrote three dollars and thirty cents."

"What're you saying, Norm?" Omar asked in a low voice.

"I don't know." He shrugged. "It just seems weird, that's all. I know it doesn't make sense," he said, taking his first sip. He could see he was irritating Omar, who peered at him through the smoky haze. He took a long drink.

"Then what're you suggesting?" Omar asked.

"Nothing!" And he meant it. Obviously there had been two errors made, the old woman's and his. Omar was upset with him. Probably for being so careless in the first place. He downed the rest of his beer. He'd really messed everything up. Omar hadn't even wanted to stop. He was tired and wanted to go.

"That was fast," Omar said, and before Norm could say anything, he had gotten up and gone to the bar to order two more beers.

An hour had passed, and now three men had joined them. Two were plumbers and one was a salesman like Omar. They had been talking about bass fishing and lures, and now the salesman was doing a card trick called Chicago Hat, which Norm was having a hard time following. Now Omar was showing the men a trick. Norm was on his third beer. He had ordered it when Omar was in the bathroom.

"Now where's the ace of clubs?" Omar asked as the plumber searched through the cards he held. "You just had it."

"I'll be damned," the plumber said, laying the cards facedown. Omar spread his own hand on the table so the plumber could see them.

"You don't have it, either," the plumber said, and Omar pointed to one of the plumber's cards. The plumber turned it over. The ace of clubs. The men all laughed. Norm felt great. A baseball game played loudly over the radio. Eli Grba was pitching against the Senators. Omar was laughing. He shuffled the cards, then slapped down the deck for Norm to cut.

"Oh no, not your kid," the salesman cried. "I know how that one goes." He pushed the deck to one of the plumbers. "I'm not as stupid as your old man thinks I am," he said to Norm, who couldn't stop grinning. This was great. He felt great, really great. He wouldn't mind being Omar's kid, wouldn't mind having Omar for his old man. He just hoped his mother didn't go and screw it all up with her moods and her temper. Sometimes he wondered what Omar saw in her. The bartender was looking their way. Norm raised his hand and waved him over.

"Let's go!" Omar said, getting up so suddenly it took Norm a moment to disentangle himself from the chair rungs. He lurched through the door into the warm dusk of the parking lot. Omar unlocked the car then stood glaring at him.

"What's the matter?" His voice cracked. "Why're you mad at me?"

"I don't have time for losers, Norm. I don't drink with a man that can't stop."

"I thought you wanted—"

"You thought nothing, Norm," he growled in his face. "You weren't thinking anything. You were thirsting, that's all you were doing, boy!"

"I'm sorry."

"Yah, you're sorry," Omar said, shoving him back against the car. "I bring you home like this and who's your mother gonna blame? Me, damn you, and I don't want anything coming between me and her, you hear me? I don't want to see her upset. I don't want to hear her crying. She's too good a woman for this kind of shit. You hear me?"

Miserable with shame, Norm kept nodding. Omar was right.

"From now on, we stop for a beer, we stop for *a* beer or we don't stop at all."

"I'm sorry." He could barely utter the words. He felt like such a shithead.

"How'd you pay for that beer?" Omar's eyes narrowed. "You're not pilfering from me, are you, boy?"

"No! I had money! I wouldn't do that! I swear I wouldn't!"

"God, I hope not. If I can't trust you, Norm, I don't want anything to do with you," he said with such loathing that Norm felt his own stomach turn.

After all the time together on the road, after all the shared confidences, it was a shock to be so abruptly repudiated. He watched Omar walk around the front of the car. "You can trust me," he said when Omar got in. "I'd never take anything from you, honest to God I wouldn't."

Omar regarded him with a weariness that revealed a lifetime of disappointment at the hands of flawed men. "I hope not," he said, turning the key. "Because I like you, Norm." He glanced over at him. "I always wanted a son. I always did."

Three days had passed since the grisly discovery in the moonlit woods. And for as many nights in the dreams of children and Howard Menka, the hideous corpse, its clothes shredded in ghastly streamers, rose from swamp fog to stalk the streets and backyards on its way, its blind and ravenous way, to climb the stairs, on which each hollow treaded thud, each mounting wooden beat, was the nearing pulse, the implacable cadence of doom, deafening doom, down airless hallways to paper doors. Children ran screaming to their parents' beds, and in his, Howard Menka gasped, his fist at his swelling heart. Jozia lay in the next room, crying. The only man she had ever loved sat in a jail cell, refusing to talk to anyone, refusing to be helped. She blamed her brother. If only Howard had stayed away and made his own life, then he wouldn't have been shot. None of this would have happened. But the body, Howard had tried to tell her, the body had been there all summer. Remember? he said. Remember how he had tried to warn her? No, she said, looking right at him. He'd never said a word about a dead body to her.

People were surprised but certainly not outraged that Grondine Carson had killed a trespasser, because it wasn't just a man's right to protect home and property. It was his duty. What most found deeply troubling was that for two and a half months the body had lain undetected, only a few miles from town, opprobrious proof, many felt, of the carelessness and disorder that were in the air, not just in Atkinson, but in the whole state, all over the country. What the community found most chilling, most shocking, was that the victim could be so unmissed, that any man might be so unwanted, so unloved, that no one had tried to find him.

When his name was finally printed in the paper, no one came forward. Earl Lapham Jones was a mystery man, with even the cause of his death uncertain. No bullet had been found in or near the body. There were no weapons nearby. Grondine Carson would talk to no one, not the Chief, not his lawyer. He had told all he knew, and the rest was up to them.

Benjy watched the greasy haze waft over the kitchen table to the open window. The washing machine churned through its last cycles, spinning now with a steady click. After the long day's quiet he welcomed the noise and the clutter of pots and peelings on the stove and counter as they sat around the table. His mother had fried a steak, and the pan sizzled behind him on the burner.

There was a basket of wet clothes by the door. Alice had been told this morning to bring it down to the new dryer Omar had installed in the cellar. She said she would, but there it sat. Still in her bathrobe, she hunched over the table, working on the same crossword puzzle she had carried down from her room. Her eyes were puffy. Her skin had broken out and her hair was limp. She was always either reading a book or doing a crossword puzzle. Sometimes Benjy would hear her crying upstairs. She never went anywhere, not even out in the yard. Mary Agnes had called once from the lake, but

Alice made him say she wasn't home. She told him afterward that on her last day there she had overheard Mary Agnes and the girls in the cabin laughing and calling her "Alice, the patron saint of vocations." His mother said things would be better for her once she got away to school. Things would be better for everyone, he thought.

"Damn!" she muttered, erasing a word. No one said anything. "Damn!" she said again, then flung the puzzle and pencil onto the floor. She looked around the table, but they fixed their attention elsewhere. His mother continued cutting the steak into servings. Was there anything new in the paper about the dead man? she asked. They answered, their voices scuffling to fill the silence. No, no one had read it yet. No. Not yet. Benjy watched Omar mash butter into his potatoes. He shook salt into his palm, then sprinkled it over the potatoes. With his fork he patted the potatoes back up into a mound, then added more butter, which he watched melt.

"Mr. Briscoe said it was a stabbing," his mother said as she passed the steak platter. "He said they could tell by the internal organs." She shuddered. "Well, what was left of them, anyway."

"Mom!" Norm said as she slid the meat onto his plate.

"I cut them all the same size!" she said.

"No, I mean your . . . your choice of conversation when we're trying to eat here," he said, and she laughed as she came to Alice. Laughed gratefully, Benjy knew.

"No," Alice said, her hand over her plate.

"You love steak!" his mother said.

"Not anymore." She looked around the table. "I don't eat flesh."

Norm started to put down his fork. "Here," his mother said quickly, dividing the extra piece between Norm and Omar.

Benjy stared down at the rare meat, its red juice spreading over the plate, seeping into his potatoes. He watched Omar slice a ragged wedge, then stuff it into his mouth, his eyes closing with pleasure. A trace of meat juice welled on his lower lip, and he licked it away. Benjy forced himself to cut a small piece. He held his breath while he chewed, looking at Omar as he and Norm discussed the best way to move the washing machine down into the cellar next to the dryer. The cellar stairs were steep, and the narrow landing had a high railing. Eyes wide, Benjy swallowed and tried not to gag.

"Simple enough," Omar said. "We'll remove the railing."

Look at him, he kept thinking. Look at him, and everything will be all right.

His mother said she didn't care how they did it as long as it was soon. She couldn't wait to get it out of this tiny kitchen.

Omar glanced toward the vibrating machine. "It'll leave a good-size space in there," he said in a mushy voice, his cheeks bulging with food.

Alice half turned in her chair and shaded her eyes so she wouldn't have to see him eat. His mother glared at her.

"Mom," Benjy said to get her attention. "What'll you put there?"

She wasn't sure, she said, maybe one of those tall metal cupboards with all the shelves.

The Klubocks had one of those, he told her. Only it was out in the back hall. Mrs. Klubock didn't like the look of it. Mr. Klubock kept his house tools, and nails, and stuff like that in it.

"Well, maybe one of those utility carts," she said uneasily.

Omar was swabbing up his steak juice with his bread. Instead of eating the bread, he sucked the juice from it.

Alice groaned.

"Get one with a plug in it," Norm said. "Remember that old lady in Sutwell, Omar? She had one. She had everything on it, even her hot plate." Now Norm was soaking up the juice with his bread. Even in this he imitated Omar now. "She had this big house, but she only lived in two rooms. Remember her, Omar? The one that started to shiver." Norm laughed. He looked at his mother. "She said Omar made her cold. Her teeth were chattering," he said, making his chatter, too.

"Some people," Omar sighed, with a quizzical glance at Benjy's plate. Benjy gratefully passed the uneaten steak.

Alice rolled her eyes.

"What do you think?" his mother asked Alice, who only shrugged and kept eating. "You could at least say something," she said in a low voice.

"What?" said Alice. "What do you want me to say?"

His mother took a deep steadying breath, and Norm shook his head in disgust. Alice and Norm hadn't spoken in days.

"Now, Mother," Omar chided, wagging his head at Marie.

"Mother?" Alice said under her breath.

He reached for the last of the potatoes. "I think Alice has more important things on her mind than refurbishing this here kitchen."

"What do you mean by that?" Alice asked, staring at him.

"Alice!" His mother hit the table.

"Jesus," Norm groaned and threw up his hands.

"Well, what does he mean?" Alice said to Norm.

"He doesn't mean anything! Jesus, what're you . . . what're you doing?" Norm said.

She looked at Omar now. "You don't know what I have on my mind. Maybe you think you do, but you don't."

"No, I do not." Omar sat stiffly and looked directly at her. "As a matter of fact, I can't imagine."

"That's right, because if you did . . ." Alice began.

"Alice!" his mother warned. "You apologize right now."

"For what?" she asked.

"No, no," Omar protested, raising his finger. "Your point is well taken, Alice. No one can know the mind of another, and to suggest as much is nothing less than belittling. Actually, I find your candor quite refreshing."

"Thank you," she said with a bright smile. "Mother taught me that, to be honest no matter what. To hold my head up high and never quit, never give in. And most important of all, to never ever fall for anyone's bullshit."

The washing machine stopped. Into the silence came the clink of forks as they busied themselves with the food on their plates. From the corner of his eye, Benjy saw Alice still smiling. He saw his mother's hands shake as she put down her knife and fork and reach for her milk glass. Norm pushed back his plate. Omar kept clearing his throat. "Well," he sighed, patting his belly. "That was a fine meal."

They all shared Marie's vacillation between anger at Alice's foul moods and fear that the wrong word might send her over the edge again, Benjy more than any of them. Yesterday a letter had come for her from Father Gannon. Benjy had slipped it out of the mailbox and called his mother at work. She told him to hide it. When she got home she ripped it up, unopened, then flushed the pieces down the toilet. She made him promise not to say anything. "It's for her own good," she said, adding that someday he'd understand, but she needn't have; he knew about such things and had for a long, long time.

Alice got up and scraped her dish into the garbage. She had barely eaten anything. As she went upstairs they just sat there listening to her footsteps. The minute her door closed, Norm stood and put his arms around the washing machine. With a grunt he tilted it forward. He was sure the two of them could carry it down. Omar said he didn't doubt Norm's strength, certainly not with that physique. It was himself, his own back he didn't trust, he said, wincing as he massaged his neck. "Somewhere along the line, I managed to throw it all out of whack."

"Were you ever in a fight?" Norm asked with a hopeful smile.

"Only when I had to," Omar said. "When there was no other choice."

"How many?" Norm asked.

"Not as many as you, I'm sure," his mother snapped.

"They weren't really fights," Omar said in a grave tone. "They were more like standoffs. Tests of will in the field of moral combat." He winked at Norm.

The image of two men grappling in a bright clearing flashed into Benjy's thoughts, and he could not take his eyes from Omar.

"Which are the only fights worth fighting!" his mother said, her stern gaze on Norm.

"Exactly!" said Omar with a brisk salute that made her laugh.

Norm was outside cleaning Omar's car, as he did every night after supper. Benjy stayed at the table. His mother was reading the paper with her usual commentary between paragraphs. The thought of a corpse rotting all summer long out in those woods did something to her, she said, shuddering. Omar murmured agreement as he ate butterscotch pudding and tallied the day's sales.

Benjy had stopped going on the road with Norm and Omar. Omar said there was no sense in Benjy sitting in the back seat of the car all day, when he probably had better things to do. So he was back to watching television and answering the phone, with the fear it might be his father, or the police wanting to know about Earlie Jones. School started next week. Last night he had dreamed that his father pushed him into the pool. He kept his eyes closed as he sank to the bottom. A hand touched his, and he grabbed it, but it was the hand of a dead man, Earlie Jones, lying as he had in the woods, on his back, staring up at nothing. The shows and the dreams and the lies were all merging into one strange story. It was too close. There was the dead man's sodden leather shoe he had wrested from Klubocks' dog and thrown into the garage. There might still be strips of the red-and-yellow shirt in the damp mulch of the lilac shrub. There might be Luther and Reverend Pease returning to Atkinson, their quarry the boy who had sent them on a wild-goose chase, the boy who had not only spoken to Earlie Jones, but had seen a thick wad of bills in Earlie's hands. He imagined them telling the police, *Find the boy and you will find the killer.*

She looked up from the paper. "It's weird how it just throws everything off," she said. "I mean, it makes you think back. You say, 'August third, oh that was the day the car broke down, or July fourth, the night we went to the band concert.' But then you realize how much more there was to it. I mean, the car broke down, and I was so upset, it was just about the worst thing that could have happened, and the whole time something so much worse, something horrible was happening." Frowning, she shook her head. "Do you know what I mean?"

"Yes," Omar said, spoon clinking as he scraped the pudding bowl clean. "You mean it's all a matter of perspective."

"That's right! It's like you have this set picture and then all of a sudden," she said with a swirl of her hands, "all the parts in it change."

Spoon poised, Omar looked at her. "No. Nothing really changes. Life keeps on happening. Right?"

"I know. It just gives me a funny feeling, I guess," she sighed, taking up the paper again.

It wasn't until Benjy exhaled that he realized he had been holding his breath.

She read for a few minutes more, then looked up. "Well, I'll tell you one thing. Grondine Carson might be odd, but he's no killer."

"I'm sure he's not," Omar murmured, rising from the table.

Benjy watched him put his bowl in the sink. He rinsed his hands, then turned with a pensive look and stood wiping them on a dish towel. He chewed his lip. Was this it? Was he going to tell her? It would be a relief. He looked at his mother's troubled expression as she continued reading, and knew it would be the end of everything.

She slapped the paper closed. "I mean, I knew him when I was a little girl. And there's certain things children just know!" she said with a startling vehemence.

Omar chuckled. "And I'll bet you were just one darling child." He kissed the top of her head, then went to use the phone.

Benjy's chest hurt. At times Omar's equanimity seemed a force, a strength to emulate. If he wasn't worried or frightened, then everything must be all right, but how could it be when Benjy couldn't think straight, because nothing made sense, because he had seen the knife in the swollen flesh, and now the police said there had been no weapon near the body. Through it all, Omar continued to seem so unperturbed, so uninvolved, that in these last few days Benjy had begun to feel a new kind of terror. If only Omar would glance his way, break into a sweat, tremble, or stammer. If he would pull him aside once, just once, to say something, anything, whether in fear or reassurance, but he did not. Omar had known Earlie Jones, and yet it was as if the death had nothing at all to do with him. How could that be? Benjy wondered, hearing him dial the phone. Even if everything he had told Benjy was true, even if he was innocent, how could he be so unconcerned unless there was something wrong with him? Something terribly wrong.

"Lord, Lord, Lord," Omar sighed, turning from the phone. "He went and did it again. Roy Gold's got himself another unlisted number."

His mother spun around. "He can't do that! What about us? What about all his investors?"

"Don't worry," Omar said, bending to kiss the top of her head again. "It's just Gold's way of stepping out of the limelight a bit."

"But what'll we do?" she asked.

"Same as last time," Omar assured her. "I'll give him a few days; then I'll just hop in the car and drive down myself."

"But . . ." she began.

"Faith," he cut in. "Faith," he said, smiling down at her.

Faith. Yes, Benjy hoped, faith.

Like faith, there seemed no end to the money. There was the new electric dryer, the new vacuum cleaner, the new bedspread, thick and snowy-white, the flacon of French perfume, the white urn lamp, the freezer filled with real ice cream instead of the insipid store brand. Alice's tuition had been paid, and tonight Omar had given Marie the day's receipts so Alice could buy clothes for school. A hundred dollars. That was a lot of money for a day's worth of selling soap, Alice had said. It was still on the table.

When Benjy wondered about this, Norm confided that Omar must have been trying to impress their mother and Alice. They had made only twenty dollars today, so that was probably a few days' worth of sales.

"He does that. Sometimes he says it's more so she won't worry," Norm admitted, adding that Omar was a super salesman. He could sell anything to anyone.

"But you're doing all the selling," Benjy reminded him. "You said he stays in the car now."

"Well, yah," Norm said. "Now that I've learned all his techniques."

"So Omar just drives you around now?"

"Yah, basically," Norm said with a proud shrug.

"That's weird," Benjy said.

"You think everything's weird," Norm said. "That's because you're so weird."

That was certainly true, Benjy knew. Weird and getting weirder. All day long he had been thinking of Grondine Carson being strapped into the electric chair. Maybe the pigman *had* killed Earlie Jones. According to the paper, he still wouldn't talk to the police about it. But if he was innocent, wouldn't he want to talk to everyone, to anyone who would listen?

It was nine o'clock, and Omar and his mother had gone out for a ride. Alice was upstairs. Norm had fallen asleep on the couch watching television. Benjy dozed next to him.

The phone rang and Benjy sprang for it.

"Hello?" he said, then winced at the familiar sound of his father's ragged breathing. Yesterday he had come here banging on the doors and windows until Jessie Klubock told him to go away before she called the police.

"Marie?" his father cried. "Oh pet . . ."

"She's not here," he said.

"She's there," his father insisted. "I know she's there."

He held his breath as his father began to sob. It was true in every way. She wasn't here. The angry panicky woman she'd been was gone. That was Omar's power, he suddenly realized, the calm, the force that could pull them along with him. Bad things happened, and yet Omar was able to rise above it all.

Norm grabbed the phone away, but Benjy could still hear his father's voice. "You tell her over my dead body she'll marry that fucking—"

"I'll tell her, Dad!" Norm shouted over the drunken raging. "I'll gladly tell her!" He slammed down the phone, then stood there, hand poised, waiting. It rang again, and he jerked it to his ear so suddenly that Benjy heard it clunk against his head. "Don't call here again, you hear me? If you—" Norm's head shot up. "Oh. Umm, no, he's not. Can I take a message?" He gestured for Benjy to get him a pen and some paper. "Claire Mayo," he repeated, then nodded, listening. "Yah, yah, I'm getting it. I'm writing it all down. Basement filled with sister's soap nobody wants. . . . Better come get it out or you'll call the police. . . . Gee, Miss Mayo, have you tried selling it? Okay, okay, I'm listening. Yah, I'm writing it down. A what? A shower hookup? A turquoise bath mat and eight dove-gray plates?" He looked at Benjy now with disbelief. "Your white urn lamp and the month's rent he still owes you." They both stared at the lamp their mother was so proud of.

"What the fuck does this mean?" Norm said after he hung up. He threw down the list.

"May Mayo's crazy, so maybe they both are," Benjy said weakly.

The phone rang again. It was their father. Norm bellowed that if he called again he'd go over there and rip the goddamn phone out of the wall.

———

Norm waited until their mother had gone to bed before he showed Omar the list. Omar laughed and said May Mayo had sold him those things and now must be afraid to tell her sister. The month's rent had been part of the price of her franchise, which she was also probably afraid to admit to her sister.

"Oh well," Omar sighed. "The Good Samaritan gets it again, right between the eyes." He started up the stairs, sighing with every step.

"Didn't he say he bought the shower thing from some plumbing guy or something?" Norm asked after they heard the door close.

"I don't know," he said. But he knew, just as Norm did.

"Boy, they must really be weird, huh? Those Mayo sisters," Norm said.

"Yah," he said. "They must be."

They turned off the lights and had started up the stairs when the slow creaking began overhead. They whispered good night and tiptoed to their rooms. Benjy knelt on his bed and forced the window open. Cool air rushed into the room. He lay down and tried to hear only the crickets.

On Saturday, Benjy was helping Norm transfer the junk from Norm's dead car into their mother's trunk. They had just returned from the dump, with another trip to go. This morning Omar had told Norm that when he got the car cleaned out and had all his parts together he would give him a hand on the engine.

"Check under the seats," Norm ordered before Benjy could close the front door. Norm's back glistened with sweat as he stretched and grunted with a pleasure Benjy did not share. Didn't he know Omar wasn't going to help fix his car, that it was just another promise, as easily uttered as his compliments, and as empty? The washing machine was still in the kitchen, the paint can still in the corner. Last night's wind had bounced the last shutter off the house. The back door squeaked again, the kitchen chairs had begun to wobble, and the shower hose had slipped from the tile so often it always lay in the tub now, like a long green snake slick with soap slime.

"What the hell's this?" Norm said, pulling a stained leather shoe from under his seat. "Oh," he groaned, flinging it into the tall grass. "What a disgusting smell."

It was Earlie's shoe. In panic, Benjy kicked the grass to cover it.

"I'm waiting for you!" Norm yelled from the back of the car. "What are you doing?"

"Nothing."

"Nothing! I thought you said you'd help me!"

"I am!"

"Jesus, I never saw anyone get so distracted. That was Dad's problem, too, you know," Norm said with that worried look Benjy hated. "Mom said he could never finish anything."

"Dad's problem is drinking." He looked straight up at his brother. He knew what was going on with Norm's daily bar stops with Omar. "I don't drink, and I'm never going to drink. Never!"

"Yah, that's what I said, too. But you'll see," Norm said with a worldly chuckle as he started to drag a heavy old steam presser toward the driveway. Benjy followed its path through the flattened grass. "The trick is moderation. When you stop for a beer, you stop for *a* beer. Remember, Benjy," he said solemnly. "Know thyself. Every heart vibrates to that giant tune."

"I know myself," he said quickly. He was so sick of these comparisons to his father.

"You think you do, but Omar says you live in a dream world. He says people do that to protect themself. The problem is, the made-up stuff gets all mixed up with real life."

Benjy felt the hairs on his arms stand on end. Why would Omar have said that? He wished he could put the truth out of his thoughts the way Omar could. He wished he didn't know about Earlie. He wished it had never happened. No, the dream world was Omar's, but it was Benjy's fault that his mother and Norm had been seduced into it.

"Lift up that end," Norm said, and together they hoisted it into their mother's trunk. When they were in the car, Norm asked if Benjy remembered the time their mother had set up the presser in the kitchen, hoping to run an ironing service.

"No," Benjy muttered, staring out the window. As they drove, Norm recalled how she had put an ad in the paper and been flooded with work, only to fall as far behind with everyone else's ironing as she was with her own. More than once, while she was at Briscoe's, people had come to the house, looking for a certain blue skirt or the pink blouse they needed right away. They would search through the piles in the kitchen until they found their own, often mingling the contents of one family's ironing basket with another's.

"It was a disaster." Norm chuckled. "You can't believe what a fucking disaster it was!"

If that was a disaster, he wondered, the stench of the shoe still in his nose, then what was all of this?

"And you know Mom," Norm continued. "The minute they started bitching, that was it. She'd tell them to come get their goddamn ironing and do it themself then, if they were in such a rush. You know, like it was all their fault." He shook his head. "Like she didn't have anything to do with it. Jesus, she kills me."

This morning she had snapped at Norm for pestering Omar about his car. She said Omar had enough on his mind with the business.

"She forgets," Norm said. "She acts like I put all that crap in my car. The way she talks you'd think I just took the engine apart for no fucking good reason. Jesus, she always does that in front of Omar. I don't know why. It's like she's always trying to make me look like a jerk in front of him or something. Why does she do that?" Norm asked as they turned into the dump.

Because, Benjy realized with a sudden and utter helplessness, this was Omar's power, to be as irresistible to the son as to the mother, so that in vying for his affection each scrutinized the other, but never him. And this was his power, too, his easiest seduction, his beguilement of the younger son with their happiness.

It was later that same afternoon. Norm was in the house. Omar had promised to look at Norm's car after Omar and Benjy finished counting the boxes and bottles of soap in the garage. They were so low on stock Omar was afraid they might not have enough to sell this week. "Ninety-four," Benjy said, counting the last bottle. Glancing back, he saw that Omar hadn't even unstacked any of the cartons yet so he could count the boxes of laundry detergent.

"Well, that's a relief," Omar sighed. "I was dreading that trip to Connecticut, let me tell you. I don't know, all this commotion, it's taking its toll."

Commotion? Benjy froze. Did he mean the body finally being found? *Don't*, he thought. *Don't talk about it. You don't have to say anything.* "I thought you liked it there," he said nervously as he dragged the carton against the wall. The blue-sky holes in the roof were darkening. Thunder rumbled closer. There was no light in here. Omar loomed over him.

"I do," Omar said, looking down. "It's the traveling I'm tired of. I just don't want to do it anymore. A lot's changed in these last few months."

"It's like a mansion, you said, right?" Benjy asked, eager for any subject but the one he most needed to talk about and most dreaded hearing.

"Yes, it certainly is that." Omar sighed. He looked up as the rainburst began. Shafts of rain poured down through the holes in the roof. "I got an idea," he called over the downpour. "I'm going to take you with me next time I go. Just the two of us. What do you—"

"Quick!" Benjy cried, darting outside as if there had been some respite, when it was raining even harder now.

They were dripping wet when they came into the kitchen. Norm had been trying to close the window over the sink, but it wouldn't budge. Rainwater gushed from a hole in the drainpipe onto the windowsill. "Teamwork!" Omar declared, taking one side of the window, and together they forced it down. Norm wiped the sill with a dish towel, then threw it so hard into the sink that water splashed onto the countertop. Benjy knew he was angry because Omar had put the car repairs off for so long, and now it was raining.

"Omar!" his mother called, hurrying in from the living room with the newspaper. "Listen to this." She began to read. " 'Earl Lapham Jones is now believed to be the same man who posted bond last May in Woodstock for two Negro men arrested in a check-altering scheme.' "

Benjy saw Norm's eyes shoot to Omar.

" 'The two men,' " she continued to read, " 'had been selling magazine subscriptions in the Woodstock area and had allegedly changed the amounts written to them on a number of checks. Earl Lapham Jones was last seen leaving the Woodstock police station with the two men.' " She held the paper at her side and looked up. "Those wouldn't be the men you picked up, the ones that stole your car, would they?"

"Well, let me see now. What does it say? What'd they look like?" He took the paper, muttering as he read. "No. No, that's too bad. For a minute there I thought I might be getting my possessions back." He handed her the paper.

"But they were Negroes. Three of them; they were selling magazines," she said. She looked at the paper again.

"My cutthroats may have been blackhearted, but they were lily white on the outside," he said with a sad smile.

"Can I see that?" Norm asked his mother, who hesitated a moment, then gave him the paper.

Alice came into the kitchen then. She was in her bathrobe, but her hair had been curled and brushed. "Excuse me," she said to Norm, who stood by the sink reading the paper. She repeated it, and he looked up, startled, then stepped aside so she could turn on the faucet.

"But didn't you say the men you picked up were selling magazines?" his mother asked.

"I have no idea what those scoundrels were doing, other than waiting for me to let my guard down," Omar said with a sigh.

"I could have sworn you said they were Negroes," his mother said. "I remember thinking what a kind man you must be."

Alice turned from the sink, her glass filled with water. She looked right at Omar. "You did say they were Negroes."

"Oh my Lord. I'm afraid my florid diction has made murky the memories here." He kept smiling at her.

"No, I remember. I remember the exact conversation, word for word," Alice said, returning his smile.

Omar sighed and hung his head a moment. "I know you don't like me very much, Alice, and I'm not sure why that is, but all I can do is keep trying to be a good man in the hope maybe that'll prove how much I love your mother. I want to make her happy, just like I want to make you and your brothers happy."

"No, you don't," she said, the glass trembling in her hand. "You just use people, that's your idea of making them happy."

"Alice!" his mother said, glaring at her as she carried her glass of water past them, then up the stairs. "I'm sorry," she said to Omar.

"Well, don't be," he said, "I think our Alice just needs a whipping boy for a while." He held his arms out at his sides and, rolling his eyes, tilted his head to one shoulder. "And I am just the man for the job."

Each of them looked away uneasily. The only sounds were thunder and the heavy rain pelting the window. Benjy went upstairs to change into dry clothes. When he came down Omar was telling his mother that he and Benjy had determined that there was more than enough soap to last the week. When he made the trip to Connecticut he was going to take Benjy with him. Maybe next weekend. "After Norm's fine company, I can't imagine ever traveling alone again. I've been spoiled," Omar said.

Norm was reading the paper again.

"That's nice. Just the two of you," she said distractedly. She kept glancing at Omar as if she needed to say something but kept thinking better of it.

The outside door opened, and someone came into the back hall and knocked on the door.

"Hello," Blue Mooney said when Norm opened the door. "How're you folks all doing?" He grinned nervously, the umbrella at his side dripping onto his square-toed black leather boots.

"Well, Mr. Blue Mooney," said Omar. "What brings you out in such beastly weather? Your sister-in-law hasn't sold out of soap already, has she?"

"Bernadette's not my sister-in-law. She's my brother's . . . my brother's . . ."

"Fiancée," Omar offered, smiling.

"Yah, that's right! But I don't know how her soap's doing. I been out of town." Mooney glanced expectantly from face to face, but it was apparent that no one knew why he was there. He wore tight jeans and, under his black leather jacket, a white shirt and a red tie with black and white circles that Benjy saw were white-walled tires. Norm's hand stayed on the open door.

"I got a job up in Burlington." He smiled, then when no one spoke, added, "Yah, it's this big moving company up there." He cleared his throat.

"Well, glad to hear it, Blue," Omar said.

"I'm driving a cab, too," he said. "Nights and some weekends."

"Well, sounds like you're going to be one busy young man." Omar held out his hand and pumped Blue's. "Thanks for keeping me informed, Blue. I appreciate it." There was an awkward pause. "You be sure and stop by again sometime when we can talk," Omar said.

"Is Alice ready? I know I'm early. I told her six, but I made such good time down from Burlington I've been driving around trying to kill time, so I figured I'd—"

"Hi, Blue. I'm ready," Alice said, coming into the kitchen. She was wearing a skirt and blouse. She was smiling, but Benjy could see how nervous she was. Her mouth quivered. Her eyes glistened, and for a moment he thought she was going to cry. "I won't be late," she said, stepping past Norm, who was staring at her.

"I'll have her home early," Blue said with a dazed smile, which he fought to overcome, but couldn't. He tried to open the umbrella in the back hall and it got stuck in the doorway.

"Where are you going?" his mother called as they went outside.

"What the hell's that all about?" Norm asked, looking back in disbelief.

Outside, a car door slammed. Blue Mooney raced back to the kitchen door. "I heard you call, but I didn't want her to get wet," he said, holding the umbrella behind him. "We're going to go out to dinner. Is that all right?" he asked when no one said anything.

"That'll be fine," Omar said.

His mother went to the window and watched the car back out of the driveway.

"Is she nuts?" Norm said, then slapped the side of his head. "What am I saying? Of course she is!"

No, she isn't, Benjy thought. She was the only one who wasn't, the only one Omar hadn't gotten to yet.

Later that night the phone rang. "Benjy," his father gasped when he answered. "I'm so sick. I'm trying so hard to stop drinking. This time I really mean it. I'm gonna do everything for you kids, everything! I love you, Benjy. I love all you kids, you know I do. And I love your mother. I love her so much. I'd do anything for her. Anything she wants. Anything! You tell her that, Benjy, please! Promise me you'll tell her. Promise me!" he bawled.

"I promise," he whispered.

"Hang up!" Norm said, reaching past him to hold down the button. "Don't talk to that bastard when he's drunk!"

They were in Bart's Bar and Grill. It was the third day of heavy rain, and though Norm wanted to get home he dreaded the dreary ride back. "I feel like another one, how about you?" Omar asked, setting down his empty mug. With the second round Norm again followed Omar's lead and drank steadily, his somber gaze locked on the mirrored pyramid of bottles. They had sold a fair amount of soap today, but there had been little conversation between them, and Omar had grown increasingly morose.

Omar scooped peanuts from a bowl, jiggling them in his fist before tossing them into his mouth. Neither one spoke. Even the bartender had noticed the strain. He stayed at the end of the bar, his ear at a radio.

Alice had been right, and they all knew it. When Omar first came he had said he'd been traveling with three black men. Last night Norm had heard his mother and Omar talking into the early-morning hours. His mother kept insisting that he tell her. "There's nothing to tell," Omar kept saying. But in the end something had been told. This morning, she had been so pale that it seemed as if her hair had grayed overnight, as if all color had been leached from her mouth and eyes. When Norm said goodbye to her, she bit her lip and nodded. When Omar said goodbye, she squeezed his arm and whispered that everything would be all right. They would get through it.

Get through what? Norm wondered again. If Omar was connected to the dead man, then everything had been a lie, so how could anything be all right ever again? It made him sick to his stomach to think how easily Omar had won him over; flattery, beer, and promises—that's all it took. That's all it ever took, just a little attention and Norman Fermoyle would be running up your heels, his nose in your ass. With Duvall being such an obvious creep, it had just taken a little longer, that's all. He felt like an asshole. Big fucking cynic he was. A real sharp judge of character. Jesus Christ, he had to get out of here.

"Can we get going? It's getting late," he said, and Omar gestured to the little beer he had left. Norm swiveled around on the stool, waiting with his back to the bar. He folded his arms and watched different tables. Most of these men were losers like his father, he thought, suddenly despising them. He hated being here, hated the smell and the smoky drone, the contrived and fallow intimacy. Once he was through that door, there would be rain or sun. It might be harsh, but at least it would be real. At least there'd be a shadow. He glanced back. "You ready?"

"Not yet," Omar said, staring into his mug as if the dregs contained some dreadful message.

"Look, I'm sorry, but I just remembered, I gotta do something tonight." He slid off the stool.

"Norm! Sit down a minute. There's something I need to tell you," Omar said. He signaled the bartender for another round, then spoke in a rapid whisper. "It's about that newspaper article. The men that stole my car and all my possessions were the same men as in that story. Like I told your mother last night, after they robbed me of everything I had, I didn't go to the police because I was afraid they'd think I was part of their thievery. In fact, that's exactly what they told me they'd do if I said anything. I was just trying to get away and figure out what to do next, and then I met your mother."

Stunned, Norm sat back abruptly as his beer was placed in front of him. Omar waited until the bartender returned to the end of the bar before he continued, his face close to Norm's, his voice oddly melodic in its urgency.

"I had no idea one of them had died, and I have no idea what happened, though knowing the kind they were, nothing would surprise me now. Nothing, not even murder. I can only surmise what happened. They must've been still looking for me, whether to get rid of me, or drag me along—God only knows—but at some point Earl Lapham Jones ended up dead. I don't know if he died there in those woods, or died somewhere else and was dumped there, maybe, but he died. He's dead, they're gone, and I'm still here. Nothing I say is gonna bring that young man back. All it's gonna do is land me in a terrible mess, and humiliate your mother, and surely spell the end of our business. Those are the facts. I can't undo what's done. I wish I could, but I can't. All I can do now is ask your forgiveness for my lying the other day and your understanding as to why I had to. I love your mother. I love her more every single day I know her. She's a fascinating woman. She's strong and tender and honest, and she's the best thing that ever happened to me. There's a lot in my life I'm not proud of, Norm. I've known a lot of failure and I've been through a lot of bullshit, most of it of my own doing. But I'm proud of my life now, my life with your mother and with you three children. And I'm proud of what you and I have together, Norm. You're like your mother. You keep me balanced and focused. You keep me on the right track. I mean that, Norm. I'd sooner be Earl Lapham Jones, dead and buried, than have to go back into that old life again of wandering and self-delusion, thinking every morning I wake up, Maybe, just maybe this'll be the day I strike it rich, the day I make the right connection, the day I finally get to be the man I want to be. You see, I *am* the man I want to be. And I'm with the woman I want to be with. And that's all I want." His eyes were moist and bright.

Norm drank his beer and stared at the mirror. With his slightest movement, prisms of light glittered on the bottles. He wanted to feel something, but there was only this heaviness, this deadness. "Why don't you go, then?" he finally said. "Why don't you just leave? My mother's had enough trouble."

"I know she has, but she wants me to stay," Omar said, leaning closer. "I thought you would, too. I guess I misread you, Norm."

"Yah, you did." He thought a minute. "Actually no, you didn't. You had me all figured out, the jerk, the asshole, buy him a few beers, be his buddy, that's all he wants." Norm laughed. "And you were right! Absolutely right, buddy!" He poked Omar's arm and laughed. "Hey," he called down to the bartender. He held up two fingers. "For me and my good buddy here!"

"No, I do know you, Norm. You're right. You see, you remind me of me. I am the world's most gullible man, Norm. In order to fool you, I've got to fool myself first. In order to sell you, I've got to sell myself first. I stand now to lose everything I ever wanted, because I said yes when I should have said no to those three hustlers last spring. Poor judgment, it's the story of my life," he said with a bitter laugh. "I overextend myself. I make more promises than I can ever keep, because I hate to say no to people. I want everyone to like me, or better yet, love me. And for that, I am a fool. A fool." His voice broke.

The bartender came toward them with two dripping mugs. Norm drank his beer while Omar continued to talk. He'd been nice to Omar for his mother's sake, that was all, but now he'd do her a favor and tell the bastard to get the hell out of their lives tonight. And if he didn't, then Norm would call the cops himself. He'd get rid of the fucking peddler, he thought, chuckling to himself. Omar stood up abruptly then and said they'd better leave. He hadn't touched his beer, so Norm drank it while Omar watched. "I'll drive," he said as they walked out to the car.

"Fine!" Norm said, flipping him the keys. Let the asshole drive.

"On second thought, go ahead, Norm," Omar said, handing him back the keys. "I trust you."

To prove that he was sober and in complete control of the car, Norm drove under the limit all the way home. His eyes closed, Omar sat with his head back on the seat. But Norm knew he only pretended to doze, because from time to time with a sudden bump or lurch, his foot would flex toward an imaginary brake.

When they got to Atkinson, Omar opened his eyes and looked around.

"Norm, listen, I know you're not happy with me right now."

"Not happy!" Norm cried with disbelief.

"But you've got to believe me when I tell you I didn't do anything wrong." He reached over and gripped Norm's arm. His eyes were bright again and his voice trembled. "I swear to you, Norm. I am the victim of bizarre circumstances."

Norm knew he'd had more to drink than he should have. Not because he was drunk but because his perception was operating on such a high level that every nerve ending bristled.

He took the turn onto East Street a little too fast. The tires squealed and Omar's hands shot to the dashboard. Omar stayed silent as the car flew along. Norm bit his lip, trying not to smile as he savored Duvall's fear, the grim profile, the arm still outstretched, the long, white trousered leg stiff now.

"Slow down," Omar finally warned.

He touched the brake, but the car still squealed around the corner, shimmying a little as he straightened the wheel. As they came over the rise he saw the police car parked in front of the house.

"Shit," he said, recognizing Chief Stoner's cruiser.

Omar said nothing. Not a word. Not a sigh. In the second before Omar stepped through the doorway he paused and in an almost imperceptible convulsion seemed to realign his shoulders and stiffen his back. When they came in, Stoner was sitting at the kitchen table with a glass of ice water in front of him. Marie tried to explain why he was here, but Stoner quickly interrupted. Yes, besides the information from the Woodstock Police Department about the two Negro men with Earl Lapham Jones, there was a new lead that he was checking out. A lady right here in town had seen a white man in a straw hat in a station wagon with three Negro men.

Omar sat opposite the Chief, nodding somberly, his eyes fixed on Stoner's. "It's hard work, isn't it, going door-to-door like this. Believe me, I know."

Norm stood in the doorway to the living room. From here he could see Benjy's feet sticking out from the couch, and above him on the stairs he could hear Alice breathing.

"Well, actually, I'm not going door-to-door," Stoner said. "You see, I just remembered something Alice said once. Something about you being a peddler. That's such an old-fashioned expression, it just stuck in my head. Peddler. Peddler. You don't hear that much anymore."

"No, you don't," Omar agreed. "Now we all call ourselves traveling salesmen. Kind of gives us a little more respectability, I guess. *Peddler* sounds so kind of . . ." He paused. "Itinerant, temporary, like Gypsies bamboozling unsuspecting country—"

"So you are a salesman, then?" Stoner interrupted.

"Yes sir, I am."

"Do you work alone?"

Omar grinned. "Right over there, I'm proud to say, is my selling partner."

Stoner glanced back with a smile, which Norm was too slow to return. For some reason he waved instead. His mother kept looking at him.

"You work around here now?"

"Yes sir, we do," Duvall said.

Norm looked at him. Why lie about that? They never worked around this area. In fact Norm had finally given up asking why they had to drive an hour and a half each day to towns he'd never even heard of. Stoner was asking Duvall what he'd sold before he came to Atkinson. Household items, he said quickly. What kind of items, Stoner asked. Linen, Duvall said. All manner of fine linen, sheets, tablecloths, napkins. Norm remembered him at this very counter with the wire whisk in his hand, remembered it with a vivid clarity that returned butterscotch pudding to the bowls and the fragrance of lilacs to this close kitchen air. The window over the sink had been closed. His mother had been nagging him to see Jarden Greene for a job.

Stoner was asking if he always traveled alone.

"Most often," Duvall said. "Sometimes I'd take on an occasional hitchhiker for a few miles of company." He smiled.

"Did you see a young black man in your travels, maybe?" Stoner asked.

"From time to time," Duvall said, then quickly added, "Oh but not in this state. Mostly I'd see them down south. In fact, now that I think of it, I don't think I've seen a one here yet." He looked at Stoner. "Vermont even have any Negroes?" he asked in his most obvious drawl.

"You ever wear a straw hat?" Stoner asked, ignoring Duvall's question.

"No sir, never have."

"What kind of car you drive?" Stoner asked.

"Cadillac. It's all I've ever driven." Omar chuckled.

Norm watched his mother and knew the inferno behind her frozen smile.

"Where you from originally?" Stoner asked.

"Alabama," Duvall said. "Little place called Leestown. Town was founded by Duvalls but now, last I hear, there's not a one left. In fact, my granddaddy on my momma's side was sheriff of Leestown for some thirty-odd years. And what a man he was. I don't think there was a man, woman, or child he hadn't at one time or another helped or comforted."

Sonny had been sipping his water.

"Speaking of which, Chief Stoner," Duvall continued, "may I offer my condolences on the recent passing of your wife?"

"Thank you," Stoner said softly.

"Both Marie and Alice have spoken of her many kindnesses over the years," Duvall said.

"Well, thank you. Thank you, Marie. She was a good woman. And she was really very fond of Alice. In fact . . ." Here he hesitated, then swallowed hard. "In fact, she told me once she loved it when Alice came to the house, because it was almost like having a daughter."

Norm sensed Alice cringing in the silence at the top of the stairs. He was starting to feel drained, his own strength waning in the glow of Duvall's mastery. Stoner carried his glass to the sink. He was saying goodbye, shaking hands with Omar, and asking to be remembered to Alice. After he left, no one said anything. Only Duvall moved. He opened the refrigerator and took out a peach. From the window Norm watched the Chief crossing the driveways toward Harvey Klubock, who had been measuring a strip of broken lattice under his back porch. Louis sat on the top step. Harvey stood and the two men shook hands. Sonny reached up and tousled Louis's hair.

"Alice!" Norm's mother called, and Omar looked back quickly. He had been slicing the peach into the bowl.

"What is it?" Alice asked, coming into the kitchen. She was about to pay, to bear the blame of Stoner's visit, Norm knew.

"What did you mean calling Omar a peddler?" his mother asked, and Alice shrugged. "Why did you say that?" his mother persisted. "To the Stoners, of all people! What were you thinking of? Is that what you do? You go around behind my back belittling me?"

"I didn't belittle you," she said.

"Who do you think you are? What's wrong with you, calling Omar a peddler?" She was so angry she was shaking.

"Well, he is, isn't he?" Alice said, with that open gaze that had become so unnerving.

"He's a businessman!" his mother hissed.

"Oh, is that what we're supposed to tell people?" Alice said, smiling, and Marie grabbed Alice's wrist and pulled her to her. "What do you mean, 'tell people'? Tell people!" his mother said through clenched teeth, her face at Alice's. "You don't tell people anything!"

"What's there to tell? Are you kidding? Everyone knows everything!" Alice was laughing, but tears ran down her cheeks.

"Stop it!" his mother demanded when Alice kept laughing. "I said, stop it!"

"It's true." She laughed. "My God, there's a police car out there! Chief Stoner's grilling our neighbors!"

"Stop it! Do you hear me? I said stop it!" His mother ran to the window, then turned with her hand clamped to her mouth. "Oh God," she gasped, eyes wide with panic.

"Because of him!" Alice pointed. "Him," she said, walking right up to Duvall and pointing in his face. "Everything he says is a lie and you believe it." She looked at each of them. "What's wrong with you? You all know he's lying!"

Omar laid down the paring knife. "Alice, I am sorry that man died. I am sorry that my brief and ill-fated involvement with those people has come to this, but all I'm trying to do here is go about my business and be good to your mother."

"But it's all a lie," she said incredulously. "You know who those men were!"

Benjy had come into the kitchen. He looked from face to face.

"And the Chief knows, too! He knows as much as I do," Omar said, gesturing toward the window. "But all I'd be doing now is hurting your mother, dragging her through more dirt and humiliation. And I think she's had about enough, don't you?"

At that, Alice's head jerked back. "You mean me, don't you?"

"I don't point fingers like some people," Omar said, his voice dropping to a whisper. "I don't sit in judgment on any man or woman, particularly one that's been in such a . . . a fragile state, but I think it's about time you realized the toll it's taken on your mother."

"You son of a bitch!" she cried and then ran upstairs.

"Get back here!" his mother called as she started after her.

"Mom!" Norm said, catching her arm. That's how the bastard did it, hog-tying them with their own fears, hopes, and sins. "She's upset," he said.

"Well, I'm tired of it!" Marie cried. "You have no idea how tired I am of it."

"I know you are, Mom," he said, and seeing her move closer, thought she wanted to hug him. "Oh Mom, it's okay," he said, throwing his arms around her.

"You!" she said, sniffing, then cringed back in disgust. "You've been drinking! I can smell it! You reek of it!"

"No, Mom." He tried to explain. "We just stopped for a sandwich, and it was a bar, and I sat in some beer." He looked at Duvall, who was spooning sugar over his peaches.

"It was a very messy place," Duvall said, sitting down to eat, his eerie calm hypnotic in the midst of this nightmare. They were falling apart, coming undone, all but Duvall, who continued not only chewing his peaches, but relishing them. He swallowed. "Very messy," he said, wiping the corner of his mouth.

Norm couldn't believe it. That was the best he could do?

The back door squeaked open, and then a knock came at the kitchen door. Sonny Stoner returned, scratching the back of his head. He had just been talking to Harvey Klubock, when little Louis said the strangest thing. He looked down at Duvall. "He said the first time he ever saw you, you came running down the driveway, and you said you were scared, that 'Niggers' were chasing you—excuse me, but that's the word he said you used. You said they had knives and they were going to kill you."

"Oh my Lord," Duvall said, shaking his head. "What a tall tale from such a little child."

"Louis said Benjy was with him. He said they were sitting out back here, and you told them both the same thing."

Before Omar could say anything, Sonny turned to Benjy, and Norm knew by the tilt of his brother's head and his darting eyes that it was true. Sonny repeated everything, and Benjy looked at no one but Sonny as he told him that Louie must have made it all up, that it had never happened. Duvall was staring at Benjy. "He gets scared of things," Benjy said.

"Yah, that's pretty much what his dad said, too," Sonny agreed. "Well, it's tough on a little guy. Having to find out there's been a corpse out back of your house all summer long.'

"He's scared of his own shadow," Marie said so bitterly that both sons looked at her.

"And of course, there was his dog dying, too, don't forget," Omar added with a conspiratorial glance at Norm.

Norm wanted to get Benjy alone, but Omar wasn't letting him out of his sight. Norm asked Benjy to help him with something in the garage, and Omar followed. All night long, Omar sat between them on the couch pretending to watch television. At times his head bobbed forward, and he would awaken with a start. Finally Norm went to bed. He turned out his lights and pretended to sleep. When his mother's bedroom door closed, he waited for a while, then tiptoed to Benjy's room and opened the door slowly, just enough to squeeze through.

"Benjy!" he whispered to the curled form under the sheet. The cool night air flowed through the open window. He touched Benjy's back and he sat up suddenly.

"What? What is it? What do you want?" Benjy demanded until Norm put his hand over his mouth.

"Shh," he said as Benjy grunted and struggled. "Listen to me. I just want to ask you something."

"I thought you were Dad. I was dreaming of him. He wanted me to go somewhere with him, and I told him I couldn't." Groping for the light, Benjy turned it on.

Norm turned it off. "I don't want Duvall in here," he whispered. "Come on. I gotta talk to you. We'll go out this way." He started to remove the screen from the window. Benjy said no. Norm said not to worry, he'd go first and help him down. He'd even catch him. Benjy refused. It was too high, too dark, and besides they'd be in big trouble if they got caught.

"Jesus Christ, Benjy, will you have some balls for once! Why are you always so scared of everything?"

"I'm not scared. I just don't want to get hurt," Benjy whispered.

"All right, then we'll go out the door," he said as patiently as he could. "But be quiet. Don't make any noise." He eased up from the bed.

"Why can't we talk here?" Benjy whispered. "I don't want to go outside!"

He paused, sad at the thought that his brother's biggest fear might not be predators or the dark, but being alone with him.

"All right. We'll talk here." He sat back down and asked Benjy about that first day that Duvall had come. "Did he run down the driveway like Louie said?"

"No."

"Did he say anything about Negroes being after him?"

"No."

"Did you see him before he came to the house that night?"

"No," Benjy said softly.

"You're lying! I know you are. I can tell."

Benjy didn't say anything for a moment; then, "No, I'm not."

"Benjy, I don't get it. I can see lying to Stoner, but why to me? Duvall already told Mom he knew those men. He says he doesn't want to get her mixed up in it, but it's more than that, and we both know it, don't we? Don't we?" he said, squeezing his brother's arm, the bones sharp and alarmingly close to the skin. "Benjy, what if he killed that man? Doesn't that bother you? Doesn't it matter? Think of it, he might have killed a man, and he's in there right now next to Mom."

"He didn't! I know he didn't," Benjy said.

"How? How do you know? Because he said he didn't? Alice is right. He's nothing but a liar! Everything he says and does is a lie! His whole life is a lie. You can't pick and choose with someone like that. He's dangerous, Benjy. Can't you feel how evil he is? You saw how he turned on Alice. He uses people. He finds out what they're afraid of and the things they really want. I mean, I know! Jesus Christ, I went from despising the asshole to thinking he was the coolest guy I ever met. But it's all a game with him. He doesn't have real feelings for people. He's not normal."

"But he loves Mom, Norm! He does!" Benjy insisted, his need for this as desperate as her muffled cries when she thought they were asleep. Please God, help me, she would beg. Oh please help me. All at once Norm shivered, not with cold, but with the rawness of flesh being stripped away, exposing every bone and organ to the clear night breeze.

"Even if he does, that doesn't change anything," he said.

"Well, nothing's going to make Earlie Jones alive again," Benjy said.

And now Norm knew. "No, but there's a man in jail, and what if he dies for something he didn't do?"

"But maybe he did!"

"I don't think maybe's a good enough reason to die, do you?"

"But the police think he did it. Everyone thinks he did it."

"Do you think Grondine Carson did it?" He waited, the only reply Benjy's breathing, shallow through the dark. "No. You know he didn't do it. And you don't have the balls to do anything about it." Norm moved closer. "But I do, little brother. I do."

Benjy rode in back, his eyes darting between Omar and Norm in the front seat. It felt as if he'd been holding his breath for hours. His mother had made him come after Norm told her Chief Stoner would probably be back with more questions for him.

"Why'd you say that?" he had asked Norm on their way to the car.

"Because I'm going to prove something to you," Norm had said.

They were in dairy country now, a few miles past Albany. The farms they kept passing had their names posted on signs at the end of long roads that led to the gleaming main buildings. Large herds grazed behind the miles of neat fencing.

"I never saw such big farms," Benjy said, hoping to get a conversation going, but no one said anything.

Omar claimed he knew this area, but Benjy could tell he didn't. Omar and Norm were snapping at each other again. Norm said they were just driving in circles now. They hadn't stopped anywhere yet, though they had left so early this morning that Omar hadn't even shaved. Benjy had never seen Omar so nervous. And in spite of Norm's ominous talk last night of proving something, all he seemed intent on doing now was selling soap.

"How about here?" Norm asked, pointing to the farm ahead.

"No, it's like the others. It's really a business. It's too big," Omar said.

"Then they'll buy more soap," Norm said.

"No!" Omar snapped. "It's not the kind of business we want."

"Why?" Norm asked.

"Because I said so!" Omar stared over the wheel.

Norm glanced back at Benjy with raised eyebrows.

A moment later Omar smiled through the rearview mirror. "How you doing back there?"

"Okay," he answered warily, folding a Presto pamphlet down to a thick square.

"Good, we don't want our newest trainee getting bored." Omar's smile looked dry and forced.

Norm put his arms on the seat back and turned around. "You're not bored, are you, Benjy?"

"No," he said, shrugging. He'd never been so tense in his life.

"How about Stoner last night? Jesus, next thing you know he'll be coming to take everybody's fingerprints. I did a paper on that once, on fingerprints. Remember? Uncle Renie knew some guy down the police station. He showed me how they do it." He winked at Benjy. "You know those keys they found in the dead guy's pocket, I bet they get all kinds of prints off those." He looked over at Omar. "Hey! I hope those weren't your keys, Omar."

Benjy watched Omar. Norm was making that up. There hadn't been anything in the paper about keys.

"They weren't," Omar said.

Omar had finally gotten them on a road with homes on it, though they were often three and four miles apart. The road ran along a river that curved out of sight now behind the tall trees. They were parked in front of a gray house that had a small red windmill spinning on its roof. Norm had gone inside with his sample bag. It was their third stop, and Benjy was getting hungry. He could smell the Tootsie Roll Omar was chewing as he wrote on something in his lap. At least Omar's spirits were improving with each of Norm's sales.

"How come you don't like to use people's driveways?" Benjy asked, again to fill the silence. He sat forward, and Omar covered the paper in his lap. It was one of the checks Norm had given him.

"Because people don't like it," Omar said as he put the check into the glove compartment. He locked it, then slipped the key into a slot in the visor. "It oversteps the bounds," he continued, gearing up for another of his heartfelt speeches, whose rambling logic began to relax Benjy. "The driveway is for the family's use. It's for invited guests. Businessmen like ourselves show we know our place when we park on the street. Like everything else in life, Benjy, success starts with signs, the messages you send, which makes sense when you consider that half of life is illusion, anyway." He sighed. "All those things you hope you'll do, all your dreams and promises and aspirations." Omar turned, facing him. "I don't know. Sometimes I think things are getting just too complicated. But then I remember our promise, each to the other."

Benjy was conscious of the frantic horsefly hitting the glass in the trapped heat of the back window. Its buzzing came at him with the jagged urgency of Aunt Helen's doorbell. His father had called late last night after Norm had left his room. He had heard his mother whispering into the phone, "Sam, please, don't. Please don't, Sam." After that he had not slept. School started in a week. Eighth grade. His chest hurt at the thought of it. Yesterday he had seen Jack Flaherty come out of the drugstore and light a cigarette. He was as big as Norm now, with a silky growth over his upper lip. In another week he'd probably be shaving. All the boys would be. He pictured himself coming into the classroom, past rows of girls with their huge breasts in pointed brassieres and boys with menacing voices, shaving nicks, and jock itch, while he grew thinner and shorter, his voice a wisp of girlish softness. Alice would be gone, and Norm would have little time or use for his cowardly brother. Everything was changing, everything but him. A wave of sadness swept through him.

"I keep worrying about that Klubock child, Benjy. What exactly did you tell him?" Omar asked over the seat.

"Nothing," he said, recalling the day, the two of them sitting on the step in the dizzying bloom of sudden heat and blinding whiteness. This was the memory now, this flash, this image without details.

"You didn't tell him anything?"

"No. He was just there that day."

Omar's narrowing eyes seized his. "Where? Where was he?"

"On the back step. We were sitting there," he said, confused, until he realized Omar was afraid that Louie might have been in the woods with him.

Norm had come out of the house and was hurrying toward the car. "Four dollars," he said, presenting the check to Omar.

"Good job." Omar tucked it into his breast pocket.

"She didn't want to give me a check, but I said with cash I'd get in trouble. I told her my supervisor had light fingers." Norm laughed. "I don't know where these brilliant ideas come from!"

Omar had been staring at him. "Well, they're certainly coming fast and furious, aren't they, now?"

"Pop, pop, pop!" Norm said, tapping his head. "A million miles an hour! Faster than the speed of sound! It's a bird, it's a plane . . ."

"But it ain't Superman," Omar said, starting the car, and Benjy laughed. Norm gave him a disgusted look.

They drove around for a while looking for a place to eat. But there was nothing. They stopped at a gas station that consisted of one Tydol pump by a tiny cottage that had huge sunflowers growing to the roofline. When no one came, Omar honked his horn, and an old man in gray overalls and a golf cap rose sleepily from his rocking chair on the porch. Omar brought two dollars' worth of gas and asked to use the bathroom. The old man directed him to a shed behind the house. Omar got out of the car and removed his jacket, which he folded and laid over the seat.

"Asshole," Norm muttered, watching him, and the minute Omar was out of sight, he tried to open the glove compartment, but couldn't. He took the keys from the ignition, but none fit the lock.

From here Benjy could see the bulge of the key in the visor. The fly was buzzing inside his head now.

"You know what he does, don't you?" Norm said, searching through the pockets in Omar's jacket. "He changes the amounts on all the checks I give him." He felt under the seat. "Goddamn it. I know he's doing it. But I need proof. It's the same thing he was doing with those three guys. I know it is! He's using me the same way he did them. He stays in the car. Nobody ever sees him. Just me." Norm looked back at him. "Nice, huh? I probably got police looking for me all over the place. What do you think of that?"

Benjy had been watching the man clean the windshield with a clean white rag.

"Well?"

"He wouldn't do that. I know he wouldn't."

"He *is* doing it! I know he is! I already saw one check he did it on. Jesus, Benjy, you've gotta believe me," Norm said, turning to face him.

The old man had finished the windshield and was trying to get Norm's attention.

"You better smarten up before it's too late."

"Norm!" he said, pointing.

"You want to do the inside?" the old man asked, offering the rag. "I'll point to the spots."

"No, thanks," Norm said, and the old man started back to the porch. "Because we're probably not going to be in here for too much longer," he said in a mock whisper, then laughed. "I won't, anyway, now that I know what's going on."

"Nothing's going on, Norm," Benjy blurted. "He just doesn't want to get mixed up in that thing in the woods. He doesn't want Mom mixed up in it."

"What thing in the woods? You mean the murder?"

Benjy nodded.

"Well say it, then. Say the word. Because that's what it is. It was a murder, Benjy. A man died, and no matter what he says or how he tries to change it, he's involved. And that means Mom's involved, and I'm involved, and you're involved, and Alice, goddamn it, every one of us! And that's what he wants. That's how he'll keep everyone's mouth shut. But we can get rid of him!"

"Here he comes!" Benjy gasped as Omar came around the side of the house, buckling his belt. He stopped at the porch and paid the old man.

"Look at you. You're scared of him. You're scared shitless."

"No, I'm not."

"I thought he was your hero," Norm said, watching Omar.

"I never said that."

The old man was pointing up the road.

"Well, you like him, right?"

"Yah, I guess so."

"But you're scared of him, aren't you? You like him because you have to, don't you? If you stop liking him, you're afraid what he might do."

The buzzing was close behind his eyes now. He had protected Norm from Omar in the most fragile way, by bartering the truth for his mother's happiness. And now his mother was not here, and he could not stop Norm, and he did not even possess the truth because he did not know what had happened that day in the woods. All he knew, all he would ever know were the events as Omar had told them.

"Well, don't worry, I'm going to get this asshole right where I want him."

"Norm!"

"Just watch me."

"Hello, my good men," Omar said, opening the door. "I've just been told where we can get ourselves a lunch. But I'm afraid it's a half hour away."

Here the road was hilly and rose in steep curves. The recent rain had swirled gullies of sand into the soft shoulder. Below them to the right, the river was foamy and fast-moving. They had been on the road only a few minutes when at the crest of the hill they came to a drab green cinder-block building. The Schlitz sign over the front door said MOGLEY'S CAFÉ. There were two trucks and a motorcycle in the dusty parking lot.

"Talk about luck," Omar said, pulling in.

"I'll say," Norm agreed as they got out of the car.

Benjy dragged after them. He didn't want to be here, especially in a place like this, when all Norm wanted was trouble.

There was no one inside. "How about the bar?" Omar asked, pausing by the empty tables.

"Great idea!" Norm said. "Much faster service up here," he said, climbing onto a stool.

The door next to the beer cooler opened, and the bartender squinted out from the back room. Behind him four men were playing cards in a fog of cigarette smoke. "Yah?" the bartender asked.

"We'd like some lunch, please," Omar said, eagerly rubbing his hands.

"Lunch? What do you mean, lunch?" the bartender said with a scowl.

"Well, let's see." Omar squinted up at the curled cardboard sign. "Hamburg, hot dog, grilled cheese, that kind of lunch."

"The sign's old."

"Well, whatever you've got, then."

"I'm all out of the usual. All I got's pretzels, potato chips, pork rinds."

"Okay!" Omar said with a sporting nod. "Then that'll have to do for now. A bag of each," he said, laying his money on the counter. "Oh! And two beers and a Coke."

The bartender peered at Norm, then looked at Omar. "How old's the kid?"

"He's almost ni—" Omar started to say.

"Sixteen," Norm said. "I'm a little underage, sir."

The bartender let the door swing closed behind him. He put his hands on the bar and glared at Omar. They were the biggest hands Benjy had ever seen. "What do you want?" the bartender growled. "You trying to set me up or something?"

"Absolutely not," Omar said, and Norm snickered.

"What? You think I'm a shithead or something?" He glanced between Omar and Norm, and Benjy held his breath. Omar had asked the old man for directions to the nearest bar. Their arrival here was deliberate, and Norm knew it.

"Of course not," Omar said, sliding off the stool. "Obviously the misunderstanding's between me and the young man here."

"Obviously," Norm said. He leaned over the bar. "You see, it's me he thinks is a shithead. He thinks all it takes is a beer and I'll shut up and look the other way."

"C'mon, boy, let's get going now," Omar growled.

"Yah, I'll be right with you," Norm said, then turned back to the bartender.

"Norm!" Benjy warned.

"You see, he's got this thing going, this crooked check—"

"Get out of here!" Omar snarled, yanking him so forcibly from the stool that it started to fall.

Benjy caught it and hurried after them as Omar steered Norm outside by the back of his shirt. Any minute now, Norm was going to explode. *Don't,* he wanted to shout. *Don't. Don't. Don't.*

"You don't know what you're doing, boy. You have no idea," Omar panted. He opened the door and shoved Norm inside.

Benjy scrambled into the back seat. He sat there, shocked by the pleasure and exhilaration on Norm's face.

"The trouble with you is you're too damn cynical, boy." Omar glanced over his shoulder as he backed up, then pulled out of the parking lot, tires churning up a squall of dust and grit. "I like you! That's the only reason I wanted to buy you a beer. If I have any other reason it's your mother, and I don't hide that fact, and you know it. She wants us to be friends, and I'm trying the best way I know how."

Norm continued smiling as the car sped up the steep incline. His grin widened as Omar declared his love for their mother and his desire to make her happy at any cost. "Whatever it takes," he said so passionately that in the next moment's silence he seemed to be weeping. "Do you understand?" he whispered. "Do you?"

"No!" Norm chuckled. "Not really. Because when she finds out what you're really doing, she's not going to be happy. She's going to be bullshit!"

"See, you don't understand," Omar said, pulling the car to the side of the road. They were just over the rise. "You don't know what's going on. You don't know how it is between a man and a woman when they have complete faith and trust in one another."

"Okay!" Norm said, still smiling. "Then let's just drive back and tell her. Let's see what she says."

"Tell her what, Norm?" Omar asked, looking genuinely puzzled. "That in my campaign to make you like me, I maybe went a little overboard? Believe me, that's not going to be news to your mother." He put his arm over the seat and patted Norm's shoulder. "That woman knows me like a book. Like a well-worn, well-thumbed book." He sighed, squeezing the back of Norm's neck. Benjy could not take his eyes from the long, undulating fingers.

"Get your hand off me!" Norm snapped, jerking away.

"I'm sorry, Norm. I didn't mean to make you feel . . . Well, that is, I didn't mean to arouse any . . . any troubling feelings."

"You asshole!" Norm cried. "It's all over, Duvall. I know what you're doing with those fucking checks and I'm not going to be part of it anymore!"

"I think we need to talk, Norm," Omar said, opening his door, his tone, like his face, blank as stone. "And I think we need some air. And some space."

Norm shot out of the car, and Benjy's heart pounded as he started to follow.

"Stay there!" Omar pointed at him. "This is between your brother and me."

"No! He can come if he wants," Norm said. "Come on!"

"No, I said stay there! Your brother and I are going to get a few things straightened out once and for all."

"Come on, Benjy!" Norm insisted, then flipped his hand in disgust when Benjy closed his door.

He watched them walk along the side of the road. They stopped once, and it seemed that Norm yelled something, because Omar gestured as if to calm him down. They began to walk again. They grew smaller in the distance. Staring, he felt as if he were dreaming those receding figures as they made their way, passing in and out of shade and the dappled sunlight. There was a bend, a curve, and now they were gone. The road was empty, the only sound the rush of water from the river.

With the perfect stillness came the certainty they would be friends again. It would be all right. Omar would calm Norm down. He would explain everything. He was the only one who could, because Benjy did not know what he had seen or if he had even seen anything that day. Whenever he tried to recall the scene, what they looked like, their words, their movements, it was always himself he was most aware of, the boy watching the boy as he peered through the slender willow branches.

He got out of the car and climbed into the front seat. He slipped the key from the slit in the visor and unlocked the glove compartment. There were two checks, each with today's date. Each had been changed. One was for twenty-four dollars, and one for thirty-two. He put them back into the glove compartment and returned the key to the visor.

He stood by the side of the car, looking ahead. They must still be talking. He would let them work it out. His patience would be as inexhaustible as his hope. If his father's sins were forgivable because he was weak, then so were Omar's. He got back into the car and laid his head back on the warm seat and tried to sleep.

Later, when his eyes opened, he would sit perfectly still, struck by the sudden green depth around him. The river's rush would come at him in waves, in snatches of angry voices that terrified him, and he would close his eyes, listening as hard as he could. But then he would recognize the high leafy commotion of cawing crows as they chased off a soaring red-tailed hawk.

Norm and Omar had not gone far from the car, though it seemed so with all their stopping and starting and pacing back and forth. Nothing Omar said made sense or could satisfy Norm. Omar insisted he had not altered the checks. If this was so, Norm said, then why couldn't he see them. No, Omar said, because now it was a matter of principle, of trust.

"That's the way life has to work," Omar added, as if Norm had questioned this, too. As he spoke he snapped off the tip of a birch branch and tore off the small silvery leaves, one by one, without looking. "A man's word. It's his most precious currency. And believe me when I tell you I do not give mine cheaply."

Norm had just noticed a pale-blue piece of paper sticking out of Omar's shirt pocket.

"The choice is yours," he said, throwing down the stripped branch. "You either believe me or you don't."

"I don't," Norm said, staring at him.

"Then there's nothing more to say," Omar said glumly.

"I guess not," he agreed.

"Your mother's not going to like this, Norm."

"There's a lot she's not going to like," he said.

"There you go again," Omar said with a quick toss of his head, as if shaking himself dry. "Threatening me. Look, Norm, understand something here. Your mother knows everything about me, past, present, and future. She knows everything about this business, and she knows I'd sooner die than cheat someone out of their hard-earned—" Omar's mouth gaped open as Norm slipped the folded check from his pocket.

"Very good job, Omar." He couldn't help laughing. A four-dollar check was now a fourteen-dollar check. "Jesus, you can't even tell. I'm impressed. I really am. Same ink. Just like the old lady's handwriting."

A look of fatigue and sadness washed over Omar. His shoulders slumped with his deep sigh. "You shouldn't have done that. I wish you hadn't."

"So that's why we always had to sell so far from home," he said, looking at the check again. Margaret Winstead. How many others now hated the thought of him? How many times had they described him to the police? What did they say? *Such a clean-cut boy, I told him he reminded me of my son, my grandson, my nephew.* "And we never went back to the same place twice, did we?"

"You don't understand," Omar said.

"Yes, I do. Really." He turned and started to walk away.

"Norm!" Omar called. "You know I did this all for your mother. You know that. It was because of her. My God, why else would I do it?"

"Probably for the same reason you did it before with those Negroes. For the money!" he said, exaggerating each word.

"No! No, that's what gave me the idea, when I read that in the paper, I swear."

"Jesus, if that's the best you can do, I gotta go. I'm not that stupid. You can either give us a ride or we'll thumb." He walked on a few more feet.

"All right, Norm, all right." Omar ran up beside him. "I didn't want to have to tell you, but your mother's involved in this. She knows all about it."

"You liar, you no-good—" He spun around.

"She does! I swear! In fact, she was the one! She begged me to do it! You know how she got the money for the business? She was so desperate she forged your uncle Renie's name on the loan documents. I couldn't believe she'd done that, Norm. She came out of the bank and told me, and I was shocked. I said, 'Marie, you can go to jail for less than that.' But it was done. It was too late. All we can do now is get that loan paid off as fast as possible before anyone discovers the fraud she has perpetrated. You've got to help me, Norm. Please. All I'm trying to do here is help your mother. I love her. I'd do anything for her. Anything . . ."

The rest of what he said was lost in the squawking of the crows that circled overhead and the rasping surge of the river.

"You no-good son of a bitch," Norm cried, lunging so suddenly that Omar lost his footing and the two of them grappled and fell, skidding down the steep stony embankment until they were only a few feet from the fast-moving river. "Don't say another word about her, you hear me? Not another goddamn word, you no-good—"

Norm was on top of him now. Omar grunted and struggled, his eyes bulging with terror as Norm slapped his face so hard and relentlessly that it came as a great relief to see him bleed. He could stop this. He was strong. He did have power. He did! More power and guts than any of the rest of them—his mother, his sister, brother, father. The blood splattered from Omar's nose with every blow. Never again would he be made a fool of. Never again by anyone. Never again! Never again! Never!

"Norm! Norm! Norm!" came a high-pitched scream. Thinking it was her, his mother, he would not turn around. Good, let her see it. Let her see what she'd failed to do. Let her see what he had to do because he loved them all too damn much. Pebbles skittered down the hillside. It was Benjy trying to get down to him. Poor, scared Benjy. Well, there was nothing to be scared of anymore.

"Norm!" Benjy cried as Omar managed to push Norm far enough away so that he could get to his hands and knees; then, rising to his feet, he scrambled to stand up. Norm lurched forward just as Omar swung. The blow of his forearm hurtled Norm in a backward stagger down to the river's stony edge.

Omar kept walking toward Norm. Though Omar's back was to him, Benjy could see the sudden glint in Omar's right hand, the blade at that instant released.

"Norm! Norm! Norm!" he was screaming as he ran down the hill; falling twice, he continued to skid down on his bottom, advancing himself with digging heels and clawing fingertips. They were in the water now. Norm had lost his footing on the wet rocks and was down on one knee. Omar stood over him, gesturing as if unaware of the knife in his hand. Even as Benjy got closer, they still seemed to be a great distance away. Though he knew exactly who they were, he kept expecting to see the others, Earlie and the watching boy. He crept closer. He looked around for the boy, but there was no one to keep him safe now that he had come this close, close enough to see the streaks of mud on Omar's wet shirt, the darker wet cuffs of his pants, so close he could hear the hideous wheeze of his labored breathing.

Norm lunged again and this time grabbed Omar's arm, and the two of them locked arms in the same struggle, the same grunting struggle he had seen before. Omar was grappling with Earlie. Omar was choking Norm. Omar had killed Earlie, just as he would kill Norm. "My brother, my brother, my brother," he panted. They were knee-deep in the running water. Omar's face was red with smeared blood. There was blood on Norm's arm and chin. Omar was behind Norm with one arm around his neck while he held the knife edge at Norm's throat, backing him deeper into the river.

"No!" Benjy screamed. "Don't, Omar! Please don't hurt him! Stop! Wait, just wait!" The minute he stepped into the river the icy water stiffened his ankles. Omar continued to back away. "If you don't stop, I'll get the police! I'll get them right now!" he warned, turning as if to go, but Omar kept backing Norm in, deeper and deeper. The water was at their thighs. With Omar's forearm bracing his chin, Norm could not speak. He stared wildly back at Benjy, who had picked up a rock and was wading deeper into the water that was suddenly at his crotch. He thrashed toward them, slowed now by the strong current. When he reached them, the water was over his waist. Omar and Norm were both grunting. He got behind Omar and began to pound the rock into Omar's back, but he didn't seem to feel it. Stepping away, he hurled the rock at Omar's head, but it missed and sank into the water. Omar wrenched himself and Norm around. Omar was sobbing. Norm's eyes were huge with shock and fear. Seeing Benjy now, he stopped struggling.

"Help me, Benjy," Omar sobbed. "Help me. I just want your mother to be happy. You know that. That's all you want, too, right? I did what you wanted. I tried to keep this from happening. You asked me, and I promised I would. Right?"

"Let go of him!" Benjy said, his eye on a short thick branch that was bobbing toward them.

"I can't!" Omar said. "He'll ruin everything for us. You know he will."

"Let go of him!" Benjy panted, stepping into the path of the floating branch.

"I have this wonderful plan," Omar said. "Your mother would be the happiest woman in the world, but I need your help."

Benjy took another step. He tripped and water bubbled at his nose and mouth, choking him. He rose, gasping and flailing his arms.

"Be careful!" Omar was shouting. "Don't move, Benjy. It's deep here. It's over your head and you'll drown. You know you will."

The branch was coming. He reached out, but it was going to be too far wide of him. Omar must have thought he was trying to save himself with the branch, because just then he pushed it closer, and Benjy caught it with both hands. He kept stumbling and going under as he tried to get closer to them.

"Careful, Benjy," Omar pleaded. "Get back!"

"Let go of him!" Benjy screamed as he swung the clublike branch right into Omar's face. He staggered, and Norm pulled free, but now Omar jumped at him. They were fighting in the deeper water. Omar raised the knife and Benjy brought the club back again, this time smashing it into his elbow. The knife flew into the air and in its brief trajectory from hand to water he knew without doubt it was the same knife he had seen protruding from Earlie's bloated chest. The water churned with thrashing arms as Norm pummeled Omar, who was trying to get away. Benjy waded closer, and he swung the club at Omar's back. Omar had managed to get into the shallow water. With one last surge he pushed Norm away, then was out of the river and scrambling up the hill with both brothers after him.

"You bastard! You no-good son of a bitch! You better run, you no-good bastard," they screamed. "You asshole!"

When they got to the top of the embankment they saw him running down the road. They chased after him, but he had made it to the car. He got inside, and they picked up rocks and hurled them one after another, banging off the roof and the hood, and then the powerful engine roared on. As Omar sped past them they were still throwing rocks and cursing.

"Look at that!" Norm yelled. "The no-good bastard's laughing."

It wasn't laughter, Benjy saw, but Omar looking right at him and sobbing.

They trudged down the road dripping wet, their own breathlessness sounding at times like crying. Exhausted, they carried their heavy wet sneakers and their shirts, their raw red eyes stinging in the hot sun.

"The crazy bastard was going to kill us both," Norm said, hobbling over the sharp stones in the road.

Benjy limped alongside. "Yah," he said, though he did not yet mean it, because in such acuteness, such aliveness as this, there was no death or possibility of it.

There was not any pain in Howard Menka's leg as he carried the bucket across the church lawn. The only time he ever limped now was in Jozia's presence. He set the bucket in the grass at the base of the Virgin Mary. He squeezed his rag in the soapy water and began to scrub the pale marble, gently working the rag into the grimy crevices of her eyes and lips until they gleamed. Her chest was hardest to clean because of the gown's shirred folds. So accustomed was Howard to this chore that he gave her round breasts and hips little thought at all. In fact there was so much on his mind today that he as easily might have been scrubbing the mailbox as the Holy Mother of God.

Grondine Carson was out of jail. He wanted to sell the pig farm and move to Florida with Jozia, but she had told him last night that she couldn't go. Her brother needed her. When Carson offered to have Howard come, too, she said that would never work. Howard hated new things too much. Howard had been listening at his bedroom door when Carson came and knocked on it. At first he had pretended to be asleep when Carson called in and asked him to go for a ride in his pickup so they could talk man-to-man. But then he thought of all the bad things that might happen if he stayed in there. The worst would have been Jozia going for a ride with him and changing her mind. He could tell she was nervous when they left, but no matter what Carson said, he never weakened. Nothing, not a room in their trailer or the promise of his own, would change his mind. Actually, he would have lived anywhere to be with Jozia, but she was afraid of the pigman now. The police could search for Omar Duvall until the end of time, but she would never feel safe with a man who not only had been accused of murder but had shot her own brother. Besides, Helen LaChance had promised to double Jozia's pay if she'd come back, an offer Jozia was considering now that Sam Fermoyle was going away again.

"Good morning, Howard," called Father O'Riordan as he came softly along the path. The shy young curate was not having an easy time of it with the Monsignor, who wanted him to be more forceful and outgoing. Yesterday Howard had overheard the Monsignor talking on the phone to the Bishop about Father O'Riordan's whisper. "People are always asking, 'What did he say?' " the Monsignor complained. "I have to read his lips!"

"That's a fine job you're doing, Howard," the new priest said as Howard drew his rag up and down the marble bodice. Even with his back turned, Howard had no problem hearing him. "Splendid statue.

An exquisite work of art, isn't it?" The priest sighed. "The sculptor has certainly captured the essence of the Blessed Mother's spirit."

A pool of dirty water was forming around Mary's feet, leaving slivers of dirt between her toes. As the priest continued to talk, Howard scrubbed. It was time to rinse, but he was trapped here. "She is a beautiful, beautiful woman, don't you think?" Father O'Riordan said with a sigh.

As soon as he was gone Howard turned on the hose and began to rinse the statue. Water ran down her cheeks and gown. As he walked round the statue, spraying it from side to side, he realized just how beautiful she was, tall as Jozia, with the same long fingers and slender feet. He tried to imagine what Jozia might be doing right now. When he'd left this morning she was taking all of the Infant's clothes out to wash them. She was probably ironing them now, and then she would fold and wrap them in tissue paper before putting them back in their bureau.

From the corner of his eye, he saw the Fermoyles' front door open. Sam Fermoyle came out first. He looked away from the bright sun. At the bottom of the steps he raised his head and tugged at his shirt collar. Next came Renie LaChance. Both men wore suits and ties, but Sam's suit was baggy and the pants were short on him. They got into Renie's new car and drove away.

Howard and Jozia were going to see Perda next Saturday. He had already started planning their lunch and collecting presents for everyone in the ward, but he felt bad because Jozia never wanted to talk about the trip. He turned off the hose. There was still grime in the hem of Mary's gown. As he scrubbed, his fingers lingered on her cold wet toes and his eyes widened with happiness, because he knew once they were on that bus Jozia would get right into the swing of things again.

They had packed the car last night so the morning would be calm. Alice was still up in her room. She was nervous, and Marie was determined that nothing would go wrong on her first day of college. Marie had baked a loaf of banana bread last night and mended her skirt. She didn't know what mothers were supposed to wear when they took their child to college. "Whatever you want," Alice said every time she asked. So in the end she had settled on her brown work skirt and a new navy-blue sweater that didn't really go with the skirt, but it had been marked way down. Mr. Briscoe had given her the day off, but she was going to make up the time on Sunday. Losing a day's pay would be a disaster right now.

It would be good to get out of town for a few hours, away from all the stares and whispering that Marie Fermoyle had taken up with a con man and murderer. Chief Stoner had come every night for the past week, asking such asinine questions that last night she wouldn't let him inside.

"Please!" he had said, adding quickly, "I mean, if you don't mind. It won't take much time."

She did mind. She didn't want to talk about Omar Duvall anymore. She had told him as much as she could. She hoped they never found him, because she didn't want him back here. She didn't want the ordeal of a trial. She never wanted to see the man again as long as she lived.

"I can understand that," Sonny had said. "Especially when you've been so close to someone like that."

"We had a business arrangement," she had said, drawing herself up so stiffly that her neck still ached.

"Of course," he had said, too quickly, his face reddening in a way that confused her.

"Alice!" she called now from the bottom of the stairs. "Come down and eat." Marie didn't want her last breakfast here rushed. Everything in these last twenty-four hours had been too tinged with finality—the dry cough from Alice's bedroom in the middle of the night, the scent of shampoo and baby powder drifting by the door, the ratcheting squeak of the ironing board as she set it up in her bedroom. "Alice!" she called again, then suddenly buried her face in her hands, whispering, "Oh God, help me! Help me! Help me!" What was wrong? She had been looking forward to this day for months, for years, and suddenly she was terrified. "Alice! Can you hear me?" *It will be like this,* she thought, listening for footsteps or her voice and hearing nothing. Soon enough, there would be days and nights long after they had gone when she would do this—call out for one of them, then listen, knowing full well no one would come. But she would have the satisfaction of their strength and their success. That would make it all worthwhile. Yes, she vowed, that would be enough.

Klubocks' puppy began to bark. A car was pulling into the driveway. "Goddamn that Sonny," she muttered, hurrying into the kitchen. Well, this was it. From now on, if he wanted to talk, he could call.

"Hello, Marie," Sam said when she opened the door. "I just wanted to say goodbye to Alice." His face was a shocking red, his cheeks and the bridge of his nose mottled with blistery broken blood vessels. His thin yellow-tinged hand trembled as he held out a small white box tied with red ribbon. "This is for her."

From the next step down, Renie grinned up at the two of them.

"You should have called," she said. "We're running late as it is."

"Well, I . . . I was going to." He swallowed hard and shook his head, and, in the old way of knowing, she understood how for days he had wanted to, planned to, tried to, but then could not bring himself to even lift the phone, much less make the commitment.

"We just thought we'd stop," Renie explained. "On our way to Waterbury. I'm riding Sam up. He's going to stay awhile. The state hospital. He called and made himself all the arrangements," Renie said with a proud nod at Sam, whose modest grin saddened and wearied her.

"We can only stay a minute," Renie said. "Sam's got a nine-o'clock appointment."

She invited them in, and they sat at the table. Renie couldn't stop smiling.

"That there Bendix is quite a machine," she heard him telling Sam as she hurried up to get Alice. She'd be down when she was ready, she called from her room; and at her sovereign tone, Marie's hand shot to the doorknob. No. She would be patient. Today there would be no outbursts. She came down and sat at the table with them. Renie's eyes gleamed as he ate banana bread and bragged about the store. Mr. Cushing was turning the entire second floor over to Renie's housewares department. A lot of the old managers were jealous, but Mr. Cushing said they were all a bunch of crones and Renie wasn't to worry because it was time for new blood and new ideas. "And that's one good thing about me. I always have new ideas," Renie was saying.

Sam drank a glassful of water. He kept glancing up at the clock. There were sores on his mouth and his knuckles were scabbed. She tried not to look at the pulsing blue vein in his right temple. Cushing's was already planning their Christmas promotion. "A Winter Wonderland of Value," Renie said, eating the crumbs from his napkin. He helped himself to a third slice.

Sam was biting his lip. He kept taking deep breaths, then gulping when he tried to swallow.

"There's going to be a Santa Claus on every floor, and not only that, but out in the parking lot, real reindeer. Well, for the opening day, that is. That's going to be really something! You ever seen a real reindeer?" he asked Marie.

"Well, yes. Deer, they're all around in the woods." She didn't dare look at Sam.

"Oh!" Renie nodded. "Oh yah. That's right. Reindeer, they're like deer, the same, huh? I don't know, I was thinking they weren't really real, I guess, because of Rudolph and Santa Claus."

She and Sam looked at each other.

"Ain't he something?" Sam said, chuckling. "That's why I'm on my way to the nuthouse. Renie! He finally did it. He pushed me over the edge."

"No, now tell her the real reason, Sam." Renie smiled at her. "Sam's made up his mind. He doesn't ever want to drink again. And this time he means it."

"That's right," Sam said with his wry half-smile. "This time I mean it. Not like last time, or the time before that, or all those other times." He was still looking at her. "Believe me, this time I mean it." He closed his eyes and laughed. "Oh do I ever!"

She studied a jagged hangnail.

"I think that's great, just great." Renie patted Sam's shoulder. "Don't you?" he asked, but she had gotten up to see what was keeping Alice. She ran upstairs again and opened the door. Alice was sitting on her bed reading a book. She was dressed in her new

olive-green corduroy dress. "What are you doing?" And the minute
she said it, she knew the answer. "He has to leave. He only has a few
minutes."

"I'll be right down," Alice said, without looking up. "Tell him
I'm almost ready."

Sam and Renie had said goodbye and were on their way out the
door when Alice finally came downstairs.

"Oh don't you look beautiful," Renie said, holding out his arms
when he saw her, then quickly hugged himself.

"I wanted to say goodbye, pet, and wish you good luck," Sam
said. He handed her the box.

"She's gonna love them," Renie told Marie as Alice opened the
box.

"Thank you," Alice said with a nervous little laugh. "They're
beautiful."

"Look close," Renie said, reaching to take the fountain pen from
the box. "See on this hook thing here, it's got your initials. AMF in
that old English. Both pens got it. Real classy, huh?"

"Yes." Alice smiled at him. "Thank you, Uncle Renie."

"Oh don't thank me. Thank your dad here. He's the one giving
you such a nice present. Me, I'm only the driver here."

Alice smiled.

"That's the troot!" Renie said. "I mean, the troot. The truth."

"Aw she knows, Renie," Sam said with a sad chuckle. "My little
girl knows all about me, don't you, pet?" He pulled her close and
hugged her, looking over her head at Marie. "I just want you to
know how proud I am. I'm so proud of you," he said, looking at Marie, who stared back at him.

Marie had taken two wrong turns and had ended up ten miles
from campus.

"What time is it?" she asked again.

"Eleven-twenty," Alice said.

"Oh God." She drove so fast the car began to shimmy.

———

Alice's dorm was on Redstone campus, about a mile from the main campus. The circular road was backed up, so they waited in the long line of idling cars. Ahead, in front of the dorms, mothers and fathers were unloading their station wagons, carrying in suitcases and trunks. Boxes, pictures, and bulletin boards were stacked on the walkways. Alice's things were in grocery bags, which Marie thought would be easier to manage than boxes. She hadn't considered all these people seeing them carrying in paper bags.

"Two Gypsies, that's what we'll look like," she muttered, but Alice didn't say anything. The line was moving ahead. Alice had mentioned a trunk, but Marie had said no, and now she could see that everyone had trunks. Damn it, why did she always give in so easily? If she wanted a trunk, why not make sure she got one? If she couldn't pull something as simple as that off, how the hell was she going to make it on her own?

"There's no place to park," Alice said as they inched closer to the dorms.

"That's because we're late, damn it. You should have come right down when I told you your father was there."

"We're not late."

"Oh, okay! They why can't we find a parking spot?"

"Because they all got here early," Alice said, her eyes darting at everyone.

"Story of my life!" Marie sighed. "A day late and a dollar short." She drummed her fingers on the steering wheel.

Alice stared out the window. "I don't believe it. I'm the only one in a dress."

"Well, don't blame me. That was your decision."

"I know that, Mom. I'm not blaming you," Alice said, glancing at her.

The bottleneck was caused by a large panel truck parked in front of the second dorm. It blocked part of the narrow road.

"God," Marie said as a car ahead stopped and all four doors flew open. Four girls jumped out, and instead of waiting for a parking space they ran around to unload the trunk. Marie watched a group of women greeting one another on the sidewalk. "Look at all the mothers. They're all so dressed up." She felt drab and small and sweaty.

"No, they're not, they're just . . ." Alice's voice trailed off.

Just better dressed than you, Marie completed the thought. *In bright colors, soft and pretty swishy skirts, with husbands to do the hauling and lifting.*

The girls slammed the empty trunk shut and the car pulled out. The two cars directly ahead parked at either side, one on the left and one on the right, leaving just a narrow passage between them.

"Look, they're twins," Alice said pointing to two redheads. Each was unloading a car. "There's a spot!" Alice pointed to a blue car that was pulling out from behind the panel truck.

Marie eased ahead, trying to inch between the cars. Staring blindly ahead, she didn't dare look to either side, making her way on hope and the certainty that nothing could happen now. Not when she had come this far, gotten this close.

"Hey, lady!" someone called, and she hit the brake. They both jerked forward, and Alice groaned. "What do you think you're doing?" a burly young man called from one of the parked cars. "You're not gonna make it!"

"Then why don't you move? It's not fair to block everything just because you've got two cars."

"Mom!" Alice said.

"It's not my fault," the young man said. "It's that joker up there with the truck. He's taking up all the spaces."

"Mom! Why can't we just wait?" Alice hissed, her pinched white fearfulness the prod Marie needed.

No. Alice had better learn right here and now that waiting never got anyone anywhere. Besides, now all she wanted was to get out of here as soon as possible. There were too many people watching, and behind them the line of cars was growing longer. "I can make it!" The engine was idling so fast that just lifting her foot from the brake bucked the car forward.

"No, you can't!" the young man insisted, and she hit the brake, jerking them again. He angled his head to see. "One more inch and you'll hit my fender!"

Neither of the cars flanking her could be moved. The one on the left abutted a stone wall, and the one on the right was against the curb.

"Mom, please!" Alice groaned, eyes wide, fists clenched in her lap. "Everyone's looking. Why are you doing this to me? I feel like such a fool. I can't even breathe."

She couldn't back up, and she couldn't go forward. And she couldn't even open the door to get out. Somewhere in the long line behind them a car blared its horn. The young man hurried in a half trot toward the entrance to the circle, where he directed each car to back up.

Up ahead, the door of the truck opened. The driver jumped out and was walking toward them with a bouquet of roses.

"I don't believe it," Alice said in a low voice.

It was Blue Mooney in dark-green coveralls. He waited on the sidewalk while Marie backed up, and the car on the right pulled partially onto the sidewalk to let her by.

"This isn't happening," Alice said. "I know it isn't. Any minute now, I'm going to wake up."

When Marie parked behind the truck, Mooney opened Alice's door.

"Happy First Day of College," he said, handing her the roses. Their fragrance filled the car.

Alice seemed to bury her face in them.

"Movin'-in day, right? So I brought my crew," he said, with a wave toward an unshaven man in a soiled undershirt that did not cover his hairy belly and a tall skinny tattooed fellow with cigarettes behind both ears. They nodded and the tall fellow waved good-naturedly. "Hello, Mrs. Fermoyle," Blue called in. "You and Alice don't have to lift a finger. All we need's the room number." He squatted down with his hands over the door, grinning at her.

"That's awfully nice of you, but people don't do that," Alice said softly.

"I know, but I just thought you'd like it. You know, kind of classy having your own crew. Movin'-in day and you got your own crew," he said as if she weren't getting it. He gave a high uneasy laugh. With her silence, he winced. "But it's weird, huh?" He glanced back at the families hurrying in and out of the dorms. "Okay, I'll tell you what. Them two can go get a coffee, and I'll unload you myself like I'm your big brother or something. Without the monkey suit even," he said, unfastening his top button.

"That's a good i—" Marie started to say. With his help they'd have this over in no time and then she'd be on her way. Maybe she'd even get in a few hours at the store.

"No, that's okay, Blue. Really. It's one of those things, you know, you just do with your mother. What I mean is, I always looked forward to this. . . . I always pictured us doing this together. She even took the day off so we could do it," she said, gesturing back at Marie.

"Yah, I did," Marie said, pleased to hear Alice finally acknowledge her effort in getting the time off. "But I'm going to make it up tomorrow," she added, though no one was listening.

"Hey!" Blue said, cocking his finger at them. "I get it! It's a family thing, right?"

"Yah," Alice said, and then she thanked him for the roses. "They're beautiful," she said.

"You really like them? For a minute I didn't know if that was weird, too. I kept looking around, but nobody else has any bouquets."

Alice laughed. "No, just me. I'm the luckiest one here."

"Hey!" he said, taking a step back. "I'll tell you what. I'll come by one of these nights and we'll go for a ride." He laughed. "And I promise, no truck and no crew. I'll come dressed like a real college guy." He looked around. "Yah, and I'll get some of those what do you call them, those shorts."

"Bermudas," she said under her breath as he strutted toward the truck on his high-heeled boots. She laughed nervously as he drove off. They got out of the car and opened the trunk.

"He was just trying to be nice," Marie said.

"I know," Alice said, taking out two bags.

"Well, it wouldn't hurt to have someone like that around if you need help."

"If I need help," Alice said as they carried the bags up the front walk, "I'll just call you, Mom."

She had been to the freshman parents' meeting in the chapel while Alice registered at the Waterman Building.

"Tuition," she said, when Alice asked what the meeting had been about. She didn't tell her that moments after sitting down in the warm back pew with the dust-moted sunlight streaming through the tall leaded windows, she had fallen sound asleep, not waking until a man nudged her so he could get by.

Now there was a picnic on the green. Since they hadn't thought to bring a blanket, they stood under one of the graceful elms with their fruit punch and chicken salad sandwiches.

"We're the only ones standing," Alice said.

"No, we're not."

"Yes, we are! Come on, we can sit on the grass." Alice started to sit down.

"No! I don't feel like it. I want to stand." She had just realized that they were the only two women who were alone. What she wanted to do was leave. She hated things like this, hated all the false camaraderie and cheer.

"That doesn't make any sense," Alice said, getting up and leaning against the tree. "Why do we have to be the only ones standing?"

"Well, why don't you put your beanie on, then, like everyone else?"

"What's a beanie got to do with whether we stand up or sit down?" Alice asked.

"Well, you want to be so different. You don't want to be like everyone else. So we might as well just stand." There, she thought, relieved to have found some logic, some basis for this baffling rage.

Alice smiled with wide, apprehensive eyes. "I'm not trying to be different, Mom. I just think it's weird, that's all. But if you want me to wear one, then I will." She removed the beanie from her orientation packet and put it on. She smiled and tilted her head as if posing. "Now can we sit down?"

Seeing the green felt beanie perched on Alice's head made her feel worse. She had dreamed of this day, focused every effort toward this moment, and now all she felt was this terrible emptiness. Would anything ever be enough?

As soon as they sat down Marie noticed a white-haired couple and a thin girl with glasses who were sitting nearby on a red tartan blanket.

"What are they looking at?" she hissed.

"Shh," Alice said.

"They're obviously talking about us."

"Come on, Mom. Let's just eat."

Marie glanced down at her sweater. All her buttons were fastened. "What do they keep looking at?"

"Mom, please. You're so nervous and now you're making me nervous."

"I'm not nervous!"

The girl got up and came over to ask if Marie and Alice would like to join her and her family.

"Thank you!" Alice said, immediately getting up. "That's so nice."

Marie looked at her, then rose slowly. She was relieved to see what mousy little people they were. Grandparents, Marie thought, as they introduced themselves. Maybe the girl's parents were dead or divorced or maybe just plain lousy lowlife people and this cheery but plain couple were trying to fill the gap. As it turned out, Jean's parents were an Army family stationed in Germany, and the grandparents had driven up with her from their home in Virginia. Both girls seemed relieved to be in each other's company. Neither one had yet met her roommate. As it turned out they were both on Redstone campus, but in different dorms.

From there they walked together to the concert in the chapel. Jean and Alice strolled along in front while Marie bombarded the grandparents with a flurry of nervous questions so that they would have no time to ask any of her. When they got inside, she hung back to let them get ahead. But Alice hadn't noticed and ended up sitting with Jean and her grandparents. Marie slipped into the familiar back pew, pinching her wrist and jiggling her foot to stay awake as the university string quartet played *The Four Seasons*, which she thought was the saddest music she had ever heard. By the end her eyes stung with tears and she bit her lip and tasted blood. What was happening? Hadn't she looked forward to this day for years?

Yes, here they were. This was their start, their new beginning, the university president was telling them from the pulpit.

Then what was this overwhelming dread like a huge black wave that hung in the air ready to swamp her? Her thoughts began to race.

My God, Sam, Omar, what poor choices she had made in her life. There was a hole in her shoe and a small yellow bleach stain on the hem of her dreary skirt. Norm's last year of high school and then there would be two of them in college, and how would she ever pay for that? Benjy would be alone. She would be alone, alone, always alone, with a garage full of soap and an ancient car. One more major car repair would ruin her, but what did they know or care. No. Nobody cared. Not really. Not Sam, not her own children. In this whole world not one person cared what happened to her. She had tried too hard, worked too much, and now she had nothing. She didn't belong here, and everyone knew it. They could hear her pounding heart. They could feel her trembling limbs. She had to get out before something terrible happened. She excused herself along the row of angled knees and hurried outside.

A few minutes later everyone streamed through the doors, and Alice rushed down to her. "I didn't know where you were!" she cried, linking arms. "I never went to a concert before. Wasn't it beautiful? Jean said they have them every Friday night. She plays the violin. She's going to try out for the orchestra."

She stiffened, wanting, needing to pull away, but did not until they crossed the street; then she extricated herself, gently so that Alice might not notice.

"I'd love to play an instrument," Alice said as they walked toward Redstone campus. "That must be so wonderful."

"I'm sorry, but I couldn't afford the lessons," Marie said in a low clipped voice. There were parents and their children all around them.

"I know that, Mom. That's not what I meant. But anyway Jean said I could take lessons here."

It was too late, and this was her fault, too. There were certain things children had to be given early and if deprived they would never catch up. She knew this but did not say it.

The last event was the dorm reception, tea and cookies with Alice's housemother. She told Alice she had a headache and if she left now she could beat the traffic. Alice begged her to come, even if she only stayed five minutes.

"But I hate tea," she said, hesitating at the door Alice was holding open for her.

"Then don't drink it," Alice said. "I just want you to be with me."

The housemother's sitting room was packed with weary parents and their bright-eyed daughters. Alice led her straight to Miss Grady, the housemother, in pearls and a pale-blue suit, who stood next to the silver tea service.

"This is my mother," Alice said.

"I'm Rosemary Grady," she said as they shook hands. She paused expectantly. "It's so nice to meet you."

"Nice to meet you, too," Marie said, confused, but certain that something had been overlooked.

"I didn't get your name," Miss Grady said softly.

"Fermoyle," Marie said, stiffening. "We have the same last name." Did the housemother think because she was divorced their last names would be different?

"I meant your first name."

"Marie."

"Alice looks like you, Marie," she said.

"Well, I hope not now, but a younger version of me, maybe. Before all the wrinkles and bags set in," she said, in an attempt at modesty, graciousness, wit, anything but the inanity she saw reflected in Miss Grady's polite smile.

"You probably already know this," Miss Grady said, turning to Alice. "But for my money you have one of the best rooms in the whole dorm."

"Really? Actually it looked so small compared to the others," Alice said, and Marie glared at her.

"The thing is, it's right next to the kitchen and the lounge, so it always seems like a little apartment setup to the girls who live there."

"Rosemary!"

Miss Grady turned to greet a tall slim man and his blond wife, whose older daughter had lived in this dorm four years earlier.

"When you introduce me," Marie hissed, "you're supposed to say my name."

"I forgot."

"And don't be complaining about your room."

"I wasn't complaining," Alice whispered.

"You said it was too small."

"Mom, please."

"Well, you don't want to be like your aunt Helen, do you, always negative, always complaining."

"Mom! Please. Not now, not with all these people around."

"It's important to get off on the right foot with people."

"Mom, stop it! You're a nervous wreck. Your mouth is twitching." Alice touched her own mouth. "Please, Mom!"

"I want to go!" she hissed. "I have to!" There was no air in here. Everyone had someone to talk to. She had nothing in common with these people, who were probably all college graduates themselves.

"No, not yet. You can't. Come on over here," Alice said, leading her to a small wooden chair in the far corner of the room. "I'll get you some water."

Alice was on her way back with the water when her roommate, Laura Morgan, arrived with her parents, Marilyn and George. They were late because one of their cows had had a difficult delivery. Laura, who wanted to be veterinarian, had assisted in the early-morning birth.

"At one point I think George had both arms in up to his elbows," the mother said, and George nodded; miserably, Marie could tell, knowing just how out of place he felt. Clearly, this was the last place George wanted to be, perched on the edge of a fancy loveseat, his shiny dark suit pants hiked up over short white socks. Laura brought her father a plate of cookies, which he was devouring. "Poor thing hasn't eaten since last night," she said, patting his head. Full-busted and short, with muscular arms and and legs, Laura was built like her mother, who had just come back from the truck with three blackberry pies, one for Miss Grady and two for "the girls on First," as Marilyn now called the ten girls on Alice's wing. Marilyn had a faint mustache and she wore a handknit yellow sweater over her thin cotton housedress that snapped up the front. She wore wide black flats, no stockings, and she had a laugh like a roaring bonfire. Astonished that so many of these Vermont girls had never spent a day on a farm, Marilyn was making plans to drive down to campus in three weeks and fill the truck with anyone who wanted to come for the weekend.

"By that time," Marilyn promised, with her arm around Alice, who still held Marie's glass of water, "the girls on First'll be just dying for some home cooking."

"Me too! Me too!" Miss Grady called, waving her hand as the girls and their parents laughed. George was pouring tea from his saucer back into his china cup. Marie watched Alice's widening smile, and she realized that she was smiling, too.

Now that she was on her way home, she could think straight. Alone, she was starting to feel calm again. She envied Alice this new life, this opportunity to be anything and anyone she wanted to be. If she gave them nothing else, she could give them this. Their future was all that mattered. It was all she wanted. There would be no more misplaced hope. Never again would she wait for a man to save her. Omar was gone, leaving her with all that soap and a bank payment she would have to scrimp and scrape to cover from month to month for a long time to come. The worst of it was everyone knowing how weak and foolish and vulnerable she had been. Pathetic, really. So desperate for love that she had ignored the obvious signs. But then she hadn't been the only one, had she? Harvey Klubock and so many others had also fallen for his promises.

A few more miles and she'd be home. It was five-thirty. Right now Alice was probably eating her first meal in the cafeteria. Tonight there'd be a dance. Maybe she'd meet a nice boy, someone who would love her forever. She would have loved Sam forever, but now all she dared feel was pity. As long as she lived, she would never trust or have faith in him.

The sun was behind the trees. It would be an early winter. Each night came cooler than the night before, with the leaves on the trees already starting to turn. Now there were mostly yellows. Soon the hills and mountainsides would be aflame with red and gold. There would be the long nights, the long darkness, the first snow, all the dead earth. And when her children left she would be alone.

She drove along Main Street. It was a good feeling to be almost home. The closer she got, the stronger she felt. The air seemed clearer. She would tell Mr. Briscoe she could do Astrid's work as well as her own for whatever Astrid's salary had been. Maybe Sam was finally ready. Renie might be right. This was the first time he had ever hospitalized himself. Maybe now with the kids older he would feel less pressured by life. Maybe if he only worked part-time, there would be less stress. If Mr. Briscoe *did* pay her more, and if Sam could work part-time, and of course there would be the Fermoyle house and the three tenements when Bridget died, then maybe . . . What was she doing? No. She would not doom herself to such tenuous hope. She would do what she had always done. She would rely on the one person she could trust, herself.

She turned the corner, driving a little faster than usual. She couldn't wait to get home to her boys. Maybe they'd all go to a movie tonight. When was the last time they'd done that? She couldn't remember. This is how it would go, she thought with a burst of expectation and joy. She would move from moment to moment. She would make her way gradually. Because she was strong, they would succeed. It was all she wanted. By the force of her will she would keep them safe.

She peered over the wheel, bewildered by the activity at the end of the street. There were wheelbarrows in the road in front of her house. There was a woman kneeling on the corner of her lawn, a man pushing a roller out of her driveway. There were people everywhere. They were her neighbors. There were two ladders leaning against the front of her house, three on the driveway side. Harvey Klubock was on one of them, Norm on another, Bill Costello, Jim Wilbur, Cyrus Branch. They were all painting her house. Dick Fossi's married son knelt on her roof as he nailed shingles around the chimney. Her front lawn had been dug up, smoothed, and seeded. Straight lines of lime were disappearing as the sprinkler waved back and forth, settling dust and soaking the dirt. Jessie Klubock came around the back of the house with a trayful of paper cups.

They have no right, she thought. *Who said they could do this?* Benjy and Louis were dragging boards out of the garage. Nelson Hammond was on top of the garage, pushing a roll of tar paper over a new section of roof. She couldn't turn around and leave. She had no choice but to pull into the driveway. She sat in the car, trapped, stunned, as they turned, looked down, came from around corners, stood up to see her.

They have no right. Trembling, she opened the door.

"Mom!"

"Marie!"

"Surprise!"

"Surprise, Marie!"

Grinning, they came toward her, bearing hammers, saws, shovels, brushes, these strangers she had lived among for ten years and did not know, did not like, or want to know, or want to like, much less be now beholden to, as much the object of their pity as she had been of their scorn all these years, ten years of looking the other way, pretending not to see or care or hear. *Hypocrites. All of them. Sanctimonious hypocrites.*

"What do you think?"

"Hope you like it so far."

"What do you mean, so far? We're almost all done!"

Laughter! How dare they? Who did they think they were? What gave them the right to intrude in her life like this? She walked slowly. She would not pass out. Her ears were ringing, and she was dizzy, but she would not grant them this final satisfaction.

"We wanted to do this," Jessie said, hurrying alongside her to the back door. "We all got together. We just wanted to lend a hand."

But they had no right. Who gave them the right to turn her life into an occasion of public charity?

"Please go home," she said. "Just go home and leave me alone."

"Mom!" Norm said, touching her arm, his soiled face so close to hers she could smell his earthy sweat. "Everyone's been so nice. They just want to help, Mom, that's all."

"Thank you," she said in a small voice that could be heard now only because the yard, the valley, the universe had grown perfectly, dreadfully still. "But I don't need anyone's help. And I don't want anyone's help. So please just go." She stepped into the kitchen and closed the door, then stood there with her hands over her face.

"No!" Norm said outside. "She doesn't mean it. I know she doesn't. She's just not used to this. She doesn't know what to do."

The door opened, and Jessie Klubock came inside. "Marie," she said, touching her shoulder, then petting, stroking her as if she were some dumb creature. "It's okay, Marie. We just wanted to do this. We just wanted to do something."

But she had nothing to give back. Nothing.

"That's okay, honey," Jessie said, as if she could read her thoughts. "You just have a good hard cry now. I know just how you feel," she said, then tiptoed outside, closing the door softly behind her.

The kitchen wall rumbled as a ladder was being climbed. There was hammering on the far side of the house, the eastern side, where the woods began and ran for miles to the mountain that always brought the earliest light. The smell of fresh paint pervaded the house. Outside, the murmurous voices rose and fell.

Alone, she kept thinking, *alone, alone, alone, alone;* then suddenly she burst into teary laughter and could not stop.